THE HERITAGE *of* LANCASTER COUNTY TRILOGY

3-IN-1 EDITION INCLUDING
The Shunning,
The Confession
and *The Reckoning*

BEVERLY LEWIS

THE HERITAGE
of LANCASTER COUNTY
TRILOGY

3-IN-1 EDITION INCLUDING
The Shunning, The Confession and *The Reckoning*

BEVERLY LEWIS
THE
SHUNNING

BETHANY HOUSE PUBLISHERS
MINNEAPOLIS, MINNESOTA 55438

Published by Bethany House Publishers
A Ministry of Bethany Fellowship, Inc.
11300 Hampshire Avenue South
Minneapolis, Minnesota 55438

Printed in the United States of America.

ISBN 0-7394-3554-X

Dedication

To the memory of

Ada Ranck Buchwalter (1886–1954)
who left her Plain community and
married the man who would
become my grandfather.

ABOUT THE AUTHOR

❖   ❖   ❖

BEVERLY LEWIS is a former schoolteacher and the author of nearly forty books. She is a member of The National League of American Pen Women, Pikes Peak branch, and the Society of Children's Book Writers and Illustrators. Her books are among the C.S. Lewis Noteworthy List Books. Bev and her husband have three teenagers and make their home in Colorado.

I was *born* to other things.

Tennyson—*In Memoriam*

No living man can send me to the shades
Before my time; no man of woman born,
Coward or brave, can shun his destiny.

Homer—*Iliad*

PROLOGUE: KATIE

❖ ❖ ❖

If the truth be known, I was more conniving than all three of my brothers put together. Hardheaded, too.

All in all, *Dat* must've given me his "whatcha-do-today-you'll-sleep-with-tonight" lecture every other day while I was growing up. But I wasn't proud of it, and by the time I turned nineteen, I was ready to put my wicked ways behind me and walk the "straight and narrow." So with a heart filled with good intentions, I had my kneeling baptism right after the two-hour Preaching on a bright September Sunday.

The barn was filled with my Amish kinfolk and friends that day three years ago when five girls and six boys were baptized. One of the girls was Mary Stoltzfus—as close as any real sister could be. She was only seventeen then, younger than most Plain girls receiving the ordinance, but as honest and sweet as they come. She saw no need in putting off what she'd always intended to do.

After the third hymn, there was the sound of sniffling. I, being the youngest member of my family and the only daughter, shouldn't have been too surprised to find that it was Mamma.

When the deacon's wife untied my *kapp*, some pigeons flapped their wings in the barn rafters overhead. I wondered if it might be some sort of sign.

Then it came time for the bishop's familiar words: "Upon your faith, which you have confessed before God and these many witnesses, you are baptized in the name of the Father, the Son, and the Holy Spirit. Amen." He cupped his hands over my head as the deacon poured water from a tin cup. I remained motionless as the water ran down my hair and over my face.

After being greeted by the bishop, I was told to "rise up." A Holy Kiss was given me by the deacon's wife, and with renewed hope, I believed this public act of submission would turn me into an honest-to-goodness Amishwoman. Just like Mamma.

Dear *Mam*.

Her hazel eyes held all the light of heaven. Heavenly hazel, I always called them. And they were, especially when she was in the midst of one of her hilarious stories. We'd be out snapping peas or husking corn, and in a blink, her stories would come rolling off her tongue.

They were always the same—no stretching the truth with Mam, as far as I could tell. She was a stickler for honesty; fairness, too, right down to the way she never overcharged tourists for the mouth-watering jellies and jams she loved to make. Her stories, *ach*, how she loved to tell them—for the telling's sake. And the womenfolk—gathered for a quilting frolic or a canning bee—always hung on every word, no matter how often they were repeated.

There were stories from her childhood and after—how the horses ran off with her one day, how clumsy she was at needlework, and how it was raising three rambunctious boys, one after another. Soon her voice would grow soft as velvet and she'd say, "That was all back before little Katie came along"—as though my coming was a wondrous thing. And it seemed to me, listening to her weave her stories for all the rest of the women, that this must be how it'd be when the Lord God above welcomed you into His Kingdom. Mamma's love was heavenly, all right. It just seemed to pour right out of her and into me.

Then long after the women had hitched their horses to the family buggies and headed home, I'd trudge out to the barn and sit in the hayloft, thinking. Thinking long and hard about the way Mamma always put things. There was probably nothing to ponder, really, about the way she spoke of me—at least that's what Mary Stoltzfus always said. And she should know.

From my earliest memories, Mary was usually right. I was never one to lean hard on her opinion, though. Still, we did everything together. Even liked the same boys sometimes. She was very bright, got the highest marks through all eight grades at the one-room schoolhouse where all us Amish kids attended.

After eighth grade, Mary finished up with book learning and turned her attention toward becoming a wife and mother someday. Being older by two years, I had a head start on her. So we turned our backs on childhood, leaving it all behind—staying home with our mammas, making soap and cleaning house, tending charity gardens, and going to Singing every other Sunday night. Always together. That was how things had been with us, and I hoped always would be.

Mary and Katie.

Sometimes my brother Eli would tease us. "*Torment* is more like it," Mary would say, which was the honest truth. Eli would be out in the barn scrubbing down the cows, getting ready for milking. Hollering to get our attention, he'd run the words together as if we shared a single name. "Mary 'n Katie, get yourselves in here and help! Mary 'n Katie!"

We never complained about it; people knew we weren't just alike. *Jah*, we liked to wear our good purple dresses to suppers and Singing, but when it came right down to it, Mary and I were as different as a potato and a sugar pea.

Even Mamma said so. Thing is, she never put Mary in any of her storytelling. Guess you had to be family to hear your name mentioned in the stories Mam told, because family meant the world to her.

Still, no girl should have been made over the way Mamma carried on about me. Being Mam's favorite was both a blessing and a curse, I decided.

In their younger years, my brothers—Elam, Eli, and Benjamin—were more ornery than all the wicked kings in the Bible combined—a regular trio of tricksters. Especially Eli and Benjamin. Elam got himself straightened out some last year around Thanksgiving, about the time he married Annie Fisher down Hickory Lane. The responsibilities of farming and caring for a wife, and a baby here before long, would settle most any fellow down.

If ever I had to pick a favorite brother, though, most likely Benjamin would've been it. Which isn't saying much, except that he was the least of my troubles. He and that soft-hearted way he has about him sometimes.

Take last Sunday, for instance—the way he sat looking so forlorn at dinner after the Preaching, when Bishop Beiler and all five of his children came over to eat with us. The bishop had announced our upcoming wedding—his and mine—that day right after service. So now we were officially published. Our courting secret was out, and the People could start spreading the news in our church district, the way things had been done for three hundred years.

The rumors about all the celery Mamma and I had planted last May would stop. I'd be marrying John Beiler on Thursday, November twenty-first, and become stepmother to his five young children. And, jah, we'd have hundreds of celery sticks at my wedding feast—enough for two-hundred-some guests.

Days after the wedding was announced, Benjamin put on his softer face. Today, he'd even helped hoist me up to the attic to look for Mam's wedding dress, which I just had to see for myself before I finished stitching up my own. Ben stayed there, hovering over me like I was a little child, while I pulled the long dress out of the big black trunk. Deep blue, with a white apron and cape for purity, the dress was as pretty as an Amish wedding dress could be.

Without warning, Ben's words came at me—tumbled right out into the musty, cold air. "Didja ever think twice about marrying a widower with a ready-made family?"

I stared at him. "Well, Benjamin Lapp, that's the most ridiculous thing I've ever heard."

He nodded his head in short little jerks. "It's because of Daniel Fisher, ain't it?" His voice grew softer. "Because Daniel went and got himself drowned."

The way he said it—gentle-like—made me want to cry. Maybe he was right. Maybe I was marrying John because Dan Fisher was dead—because there could never be another love for me like Dan. Still, I was stunned that Ben had brought it up.

Here was the brother who'd sat behind me in school, yanking my hair every chance he got, making me clean out the barn more times than I could count . . . and siding against me the night Dat caught me playing Daniel's old guitar in the haymow.

But now Ben's eyes were full of questions. He was worrying out loud about my future happiness, of all things.

I reached up and touched his ruddy face. "You don't have to worry, brother," I whispered. "Not one little bit."

"Katie . . . for certain?" His voice echoed in the stillness.

I turned away and reached into the trunk, avoiding his gaze. "John's a *gut* man," I said firmly. "He'll make a right fine husband."

I felt Ben's eyes boring a hole into the back of my head, and for a long, awkward moment he was silent. Then he replied, "Jah, right fine he'll be."

15

The subject was dropped. My brother and everyone else would just have to keep their thoughts to themselves about me and the forty-year-old man I was soon to marry. I knew well and good that John Beiler had one important thing on his mind: He needed a mamma for his children. And I, having been blessed with lavish mother-love, was just the person to give it.

Respect for a husband, after all, was honorable. In time, perhaps something more would come of our union—John's and mine. Perhaps even . . . love.

I could only hope and pray that my Dan had gone to his eternal reward, and that someday I'd be found worthy to join him there.

❖   ❖   ❖

Thoughts of Dan and the streets of gold were still flitting through my mind long after Ben left. The attic was mighty cold now and I refolded Mamma's dress, trying to find the spot where it had been packed away, when I stumbled upon a tiny rose-colored dress. A satin baby dress. In the middle of our family treasures was the loveliest infant gown I'd ever seen, all tucked away in tissue paper.

I removed the covering and began to stroke the fabric. Amish babies wore plain dresses in pale hues. Never patterns or plaids. And never, never satin. Where in all the world had Mamma gotten such a fancy thing?

Carefully, I inspected the bodice, letting my fingers linger on its creamy smoothness. Suddenly I felt like dancing. And—unruly idea that it was—I succumbed to the impulse. Stood right up and began twirling around the attic, a whisper of satin pressed against my cheek.

I was lost in a world of my vivid imagination—colorful silk, gleaming jewels, golden mirrors. Turning and swirling,

I flew, light as a summer cloud, over the wooden floor-boards. But with my dancing came the old struggles, my personal tug-of-war between plain and fancy. How I longed for beautiful things! Here I was twenty-two years old, published to marry the bishop—and fighting the same old battles.

In my frustration, I started humming a sad song—a tune Dan Fisher and I had made up on his guitar, the one Dat had forbidden me to play. The one I'd hidden away from his stern eyes all these years.

Time and again, I'd offered up my music and my tendency toward fancy things on the altar of repentance. Long and hard I prayed, but in spite of everything, I'd find myself sneaking glances in a hand mirror, asking myself: *How would my hair look without the bun or the ever-widening middle part?*

Sometimes, as a child, I would pull off my white organdy kapp and let the auburn locks fall free, down past my shoulders. It was most tempting when I was supposed to be dusting or cleaning the upstairs. At least the Lord God had done me a favor and put a right nice color in my hair—reddish brown hues—and when the sun from my window shone on it just right, there were streaks like golden ribbons in it. At times like these, I hated having to wrap my hair back up in a bun, hiding it away under my head covering.

And there was the problem of music—my special tunes. Some fast, some slow; all forbidden. My church taught that music was meant to come from hymnbooks for the purpose of worshiping God. Anything else was sinful.

I'd tried to follow the *Ordnung*, the unwritten rules of our church district. With every ounce of me, I'd tried to be a submissive young woman. Yet finding the fancy dress had stirred it all up again—my stubborn streak and the conflict with Dat over the music. Did I dare marry Bishop John with these sins gnawing away at my soul?

I glanced at the trunk where Mamma's wedding dress

lay. Thoughtfully, I went to it, touching the heavy fabric with one hand and holding the satin dress in the other—comparing the two. I'd heard there were modern brides, outsiders in the non-Amish *English* world, who wore such things as satin and lace and gauzy veils.

Mamma's blue wedding dress was far from being truly beautiful, really. Except for its white cape and apron, it looked identical to her other church dresses. I held the dress up to me, tucking my chin over the high neckline, wondering what it would be like to try it on. But Mam had been much stockier than I when she married Dat. I knew I'd probably swim in it, so big it was.

Wear your mamma's clothing, get your mamma's life.

Dan Fisher had said that once, after I'd confessed my silly whim. "You know, it's just for fun," I'd insisted, surprised at what he'd said about my mamma's life—as if there were something wrong with it. I didn't ask him about it, though. Just let it be.

Dan must not have realized it, but what I'd meant to say was: What would it be like to wear "English" clothes—not Mamma's or another Plain woman's clothes, but fancy, modern clothes?

I put the wrinkled wedding dress away and reached for the satin baby garment. Glancing down, I saw a name hand stitched into the back facing.

Katherine Mayfield.

Instantly, I felt envy stir up in me toward this baby, this Katherine, whoever she was. What was *her* dress doing in *our* attic?

Thou shalt not covet.

I could hear the words from Dat's lips. He'd drilled them into me and many others like them from my childhood on. Words like, "If you don't kindle a little fire to begin with, you'll never have to worry about snuffin' out a big one."

My father was like that. Always chiding me about one

thing or another growing up. But now . . . now that I was a grown woman, my wicked ways were still very much alive. It seemed I'd never measure up, at least not for Dat. Probably not for God, either.

A half hour later, my brothers found me sobbing beside the attic trunk, still clutching the little rose-colored gown. And from that moment on, nothing was ever the same for me. Not for a single one of us here in Hickory Hollow.

CHAPTER ONE

❖ ❖ ❖

November days, being what they were in southeastern Pennsylvania, held an icy grip all their own. The wind, keen and cold, whipped at Rebecca Lapp's black wool shawl. Her long apron was heavy with logs for the cookstove as she headed up the snowy back steps of the stone farmhouse.

The sprawling house had been built in 1840 by her husband's ancestor, Joseph Lapp, and his stonemason friend. Now, over a century and a half later, the house was little changed. It stood—stately and tall—untouched by the outside world and its gadgets and gimmickry. Here, things went on as they always had—slow and tranquil—pacing out the days like an Amish *Grossmutter*, with serenity and grace.

Some time after, as was Amish custom, an addition called the *Grossdawdi Haus*—a grandfather house for aging relatives—had been built onto the east side.

The sky had deepened to purple as the sun prepared to slip down out of the sky, and Rebecca made her way into the warm kitchen to slide the chopped wood into the grate on top of her large black-metal stove. That done, she removed her full-length shawl and hung it over one of the wooden pegs in the utility room, just inside the back door.

Potatoes, now at a rolling boil, teased the sides of the

black kettle as she tested them with a fork—done to perfection. Turning, she noticed the table still unset and craned her neck toward the front room. "Katie, supper!" she called to her daughter.

Then with the expertise of one who had cooked and baked an array of farm produce for as long as she could remember, Rebecca reached for a potholder and leaned down to inspect the home-cured ham in the oven. "Jah, gut," she whispered, smiling in approval as she breathed in its sweet aroma.

Minutes later, as though on cue, Eli, Benjamin, and their father came inside, removed their wide-brimmed, black felt hats, heavy sack coats, and work boots, and headed for the polished black woodstove near the center of the enormous kitchen.

"Startin' to sleet out," Samuel said, rubbing his hands together. He pulled a chair up close to the old range and stuck out his stockinged feet, warming them.

"We're in for a cold snap, all right," Rebecca replied, glancing at the long sawbuck table adorned with a simple green-checkered oilcloth. "Katie-e-e!" she called again.

When there was still no answer, concern creased Rebecca's brow. Her worried expression must have baffled Samuel Lapp, for he spoke right up. "*Ach*, what's-a-matter? Do ya think daughter's ill?"

Rebecca gazed at the gas lamp hanging over the table and wondered what could be keeping Katie. It wasn't like her to be late.

From his spot near the warm stove, Samuel began to call, "Katie, supper! Come now, don't delay!"

When their daughter did not come bounding down the steps at his summons, he glowered. Rebecca felt her cheeks grow pale.

Apparently Eli noticed, too. "Mam?"

She stood there, stock still, as though waiting for an answer to drop from heaven. "Where could Katie be?" she managed at last, gripping the platter of steaming sliced ham with both hands.

Samuel shrugged, pulling on his bushy beard. "Wasn't she here in the house?"

Quickly Rebecca turned, fixing her sons with an inquiring stare. "You boys seen her?"

"Don't know that I seen her most the afternoon," Eli spoke up.

"Benjamin? When did *you* see your sister last?"

He ran his fingers through a shock of thick blond hair. "I don't—"

"Well, did you see her or not?" Rebecca demanded, almost immediately regretting the sharp tone she'd taken with her youngest son.

Samuel went to the sink and turned on the spigot, facing the window as the water rushed over his red, callused hands. "Eli and Benjamin were out shreddin' cornstalks with me," he explained over his shoulder. "No need to be pointing fingers just yet."

His words stung, but Rebecca clamped her jaw shut. A submissive wife was to fear the Lord and respect her husband, which meant letting Samuel have the last word. She turned slowly, placing the platter of meat on the stovetop.

Still in his stocking feet, Samuel strode into the living room and called up the steps. "Katie . . . supper!"

It was at that moment that Benjamin appeared to remember. "Oh, she might still be in the attic. I helped her up there a while back."

Rebecca's heart gave a great leap. *The attic?*

"What's she want up there?" Samuel mumbled, obviously annoyed at the delay, and marched back into the kitchen.

"To have a look at Mam's wedding dress, I guess."

Rebecca studied her son. "Well, go on up and fetch her

down, will you?" she asked, careful not to betray her growing desperation.

Following Eli, who steadied the oil lantern, Benjamin scrambled up the stairs, his hollow stomach growling as he went.

"Whatcha think's wrong?" Eli asked as they came to the landing.

Benjamin glanced up at his brother on the rung above him. "With Katie?"

"No." Eli snorted. "With Mamma."

Benjamin had a pretty good notion. "Katie's gettin' married next week—Mam's losin' her only daughter. That's all there is to it."

"Jah." It was pretty clear that Eli wasn't exactly certain what Ben meant. But they both knew one thing for sure: Getting married was a way of life in Hickory Hollow. You found a nice honest girl among the People and got yourself hitched up. Mam ought to be mighty happy about Bishop John; Katie, too—with the widower coming to her rescue, so to speak. At twenty-two, an Amish girl—no matter how headstrong and feisty—wouldn't be smart to be too picky. His sister had scared more than one boy away on that basis alone.

Eli continued his climb up the attic ladder but stopped halfway.

"Keep on going," Ben muttered, thinking about the tender, juicy ham downstairs. "Time's a-wastin'."

Eli put out his hand, shushing him. "Wait . . . listen."

"What is it?" Ben cocked his head.

"Hear that?"

Ben strained his ears, staring hard at the attic door above them. "Well, I'll be . . . sounds like Katie's cryin' up there."

Without warning, he charged past Eli—crawled right over the top of him and up the ladder—nearly knocking the lantern out of his brother's hand.

Downstairs, while Samuel read the public auction no-
tices in *Die Botschaft*, Rebecca pulled out the drawer nearest
the sink and gathered up five sets of utensils—one for each
of the Lapp family members who would be present around
her table this night.

Jah, this was a daughter's chore, but it didn't much matter who placed the dishes on the old table. Katie had been
busy, after all, caught up with wedding plans.

Of all things, her daughter—ending up with Bishop
Beiler and his young brood. The Lord God sure had a way
of looking out for His own. And after what happened to
Katie's first love—poor Daniel Fisher, who'd gotten himself
drowned in that sailing accident. Yes, Rebecca felt mighty
blessed the way things were turning out.

She sat down, recalling the first time Katie's pudgy little
hands had set this table. The memory was soothing—a
vision of days long past.

Katie's first table setting had been a surprise of sorts. At
only three and a half, the little girl was mighty pleased with
herself, knowing she'd be winning her mamma's approval.
Eventually, though, the years would show that when it came
down to it, what people thought of her had little to do with
what made Katie Lapp tick.

Rebecca's sweet reminiscence served to push back the
secret fear, push it deep into the inner sanctuary of her
mind. That place where she'd learned to carry it, seques-
tered from all conscious thought.

The secret.

She sighed, trying not to think of the consequences of
its discovery. Katie . . . in the attic? The thought sent a
shiver tingling down her spine. Rebecca rose and touched
her kapp, letting her hand trail along the narrow white ties

as she went to the back door and stood inside the utility room.

Lord God of heaven, forgive me. She'd prayed the words silently each and every day for the past twenty-two years, wondering if God had heard. Maybe, observing her dedication and contrite heart, He had forgiven her. But if so, what was God doing now? What was He allowing to happen?

Rebecca's gaze swept the wide yard and beyond, toward the barn. Layers of sleet covered the sloping bank of earth that led to the two-story haymow. The ice storm had brought fierce wind, its shrill voice whistling ominously in her ears. She felt it pound against the door like an intruder and was grateful for the reliable woodstove in the center of the kitchen, warming the spacious room.

Rebecca turned away from the cold window and glanced at the day clock, wishing Katie would hurry and come. Supper was getting cold.

Upstairs, a blast of arctic air greeted Benjamin as he shoved open the hatchlike attic door. With little effort, he pulled himself up the ladder and into the storage room. There he was met by a strange sight. Draped halfway over a rectangular trunk, his sister sat crumpled in a heap on the cold floor, her head buried in her arms.

The trunk lid was down now, and Benjamin saw no sign of his Mam's wedding dress. But there was an unusual-looking piece of fabric—he couldn't quite make out what—in his sister's hand. Was it a scrap for a quilt? No, from where he stood, it seemed almost shiny—too fussy for the bed coverings Katie often made with Mary Stoltzfus and their many girl cousins and friends down Hickory Lane.

Unsure as to what to do, he stood there watching as Katie whimpered within arms' reach. As far as he could remember, he'd never touched his sister except when they'd played together as youngsters. He wasn't sure he ought to now. Besides—all bent over that way—she wasn't looking at him, hadn't seen him come up. She'd probably jump right out of her skin if he touched her.

While Benjamin was still wondering what to do, Eli peeked over the opening in the floor, his blue eyes wide. "Psst, Ben," he whispered. "What's-a-matter with her?"

About that time, Katie began to stir. Wiping her tear-streaked face with her long apron, she seemed oblivious for a moment. Then she turned toward them, and in the lantern's glow, Ben could tell that she was trembling. "Mam's waitin' supper," he said, eyeing her carefully.

Katie leaned on the trunk, pushing herself to a standing position, and Ben put out a hand to help her. "It's freezin' cold up here," he said. "Why'dja stay so long?"

Katie ignored his outstretched hand along with his question and adjusted her kapp. Then slowly, she straightened until she stood tall and erect, her jawline rigid. "I'm coming down, so scram, both of you!"

Ben and Eli did as they were told and scuffled down the ladder—Ben, still thinking about Katie's tears. He'd heard about women getting all weepy-eyed before a wedding. His oldest brother, Elam, had said something like that just last year, several days before he and his bride tied the knot.

He scratched his head, puzzled. *Tears must mean Katie'll be missin' us come next week,* he decided. He broke into a grin. Wouldn't do to let on to Katie what he was thinking, though. The way she was acting, there was no telling what she'd say. Or do.

CHAPTER TWO

❖   ❖   ❖

Katie took her time leaving the attic room. She waited until her brothers were out of sight, then reopened the trunk and returned the baby garment to its original spot.

Downstairs, after washing her face and hands repeatedly, Katie took her usual place at the supper table—to the right of her mother. "Sorry, Dat . . . Mamma." Her face felt flushed, her eyes puffy.

Of course, she wouldn't lie. But she had no intention of explaining the *real* reason for her delay. No one must ever know of her dreadful obsession. Known sin required confession—she knew that. Good for the soul, maybe, but impossible under the circumstances. Confession would mean turning away, never again repeating the transgression. . . .

The fact that Katie hadn't looked either of them in the eye troubled Rebecca. Samuel didn't seem to notice, though. He bowed his head for the silent blessing without the slightest reference to Katie's tardiness.

After the "Amen," Samuel served himself first, then Eli and Benjamin wasted no time digging in to the heaping bowl of buttered potatoes. When the ham platter was passed, everyone took hearty portions. Next came lima beans, and

29

chow-chow—a sweet bean relish—cut creamed corn, and bread with apple butter. A fat slice of raisin spice cake topped off the meal.

An occasional belch from Eli and Samuel signaled that Rebecca's efforts had been a success. Aside from that, there was only the scrape of cutlery against plastic plates, the satisfied grunts of the men, the homey sound of a fire crackling in the woodstove.

From time to time, Rebecca risked a sidelong glance at Katie. The girl hadn't spoken a word since she sat down. *What's ailin' her?* Rebecca wondered, thoughts churning. But it was the fear gnawing at her stomach that brought on the indigestion.

Eventually, Samuel leaned back and folded his arms across his chest, his gesture indicating that he was finished eating. At first, Rebecca wasn't certain he was going to speak. Finally, in measured tones, he asked the question hanging heavy on all their minds. "Did you find your mamma's weddin' dress, then?"

Katie reached for her glass. Slowly, deliberately, she drank from it.

Silence draped itself like a shawl over the barren gray walls.

Seconds lagged.

Rebecca could take it no longer. "Katie, are you ill?" She slipped her arm around her daughter's trim waist, and Katie stiffened without speaking.

Samuel was not one to tolerate disrespect, and Rebecca knew what was coming. As sure as a brush fire in a windstorm. "Both your Mam and I have spoken to ya," he scolded without raising his voice.

Still no response from the girl with autumn brown eyes and reddish hair, wound tightly into a bun under the solemn white netting. Katie refused to look up until Eli kicked her under the table. A hefty, swift kick to the shinbone.

"Ach!" She glared across the table at the culprit.

Eli sneered, "Don't you have nothin' to say for yourself?"

"Eli!" his father cut in. "That'll do!"

Rebecca's grasp tightened on Katie's waist. Now the fire was sure to come. She braced herself for the heat.

"I . . . uh, Dat," Katie began at last, "there's something I have to say. . . ."

Rebecca felt the tension draining out of muscles coiled tight as a garden snake. Her daughter—only nine days before her wedding—had averted a near disaster. The kindling of her father's wrath.

"There is something I must tell you—both of you," Katie went on. She looked first at Samuel, then at Rebecca, who had folded her hands as if in prayer. "Ever since I was little, being Plain has been burdensome to me." She took a deep breath. "More burdensome for me than most, it seems."

"Bein' Amish is who you are through and through." Her father's voice was unemotional yet definitive. "Plain is how the Lord God meant you to be. You ought to be ashamed, saying things such as that after bein' baptized . . . taking the kneeling vow and all."

Rebecca clasped her hands tighter in a wordless plea.

"I best be speaking to Bishop John." Katie could feel her eyes filling with tears. "I have to speak to him . . . about . . ." She paused, drawing in another thready breath. "About the wedding."

"Now, Katie," her mother intervened. "Just wait a day or two, won't ya? This'll pass, you'll see."

Katie stared at her mother. "But I've sinned against Dat . . . and . . . the church."

Samuel's expression darkened. "Daughter?"

"It's the music—all those songs in my head. I can't make them go away," she blurted. "I've tried, but the music keeps tempting me." She bit her tongue and kept silent about the other temptings, the never-ending yearning for beautiful things.

Rebecca patted her hand. "Maybe a talk with Bishop Beiler would do us all some good."

"Alone, Mamma. I must see John alone."

Samuel's green shirt and tan suspenders accentuated the red flush creeping up his neck and into his face. "Maybe if you'd destroyed that instrument of evil when I first caught you at it, that guitar wouldn't be destroyin' you now."

He continued to restrain her with a piercing gaze. "You'll be confessing this before the next Preaching. If you're serious about turning away from sin and crucifying the flesh, you'll find a way."

"I've tried all these years, Dat. I wish I could shut off the music." But even as she spoke, a stubborn defiance surged in her, demanding its way. She did not *want* to stop the music—not her beloved music. Not the precious thing she and Daniel Fisher had so joyously shared.

Stubbornness gave way to guilt. She had just lied to her own father. One sin had given birth to another, and penance was long overdue. If she ever wanted to see Daniel in the courts of glory, Katie knew what was expected of her. A private confession in front of their elderly deacon and preacher Yoder. Her first ever.

Samuel adjusted his metal-rim glasses and scrutinized Katie across the table. "I forbade you to play music many years ago, and I forbid you now," he said. " 'Doth a fountain send forth at the same place sweet water and bitter?' "

He pushed his chair away from the table, causing it to screech against the linoleum floor. Significant in its absence was the silent table grace that always followed the meal. With a grunt, he shuffled into the living room. Eli and Benjamin disappeared into a far corner of the house, as if grateful to escape the shameful scene.

Under a ring of light, mother and daughter sat worlds apart. Rebecca willed her trembling to cease, relieved that her daughter's outburst had nothing whatever to do with the past—that dreadful secret that could swallow them up. Every last one of them.

Still, as she sat beside her only daughter—the child of her dreams—there was one consolation. *This* predicament could be remedied easily enough. A sigh escaped her lips, and with eyes closed, she breathed a prayer of thanks—for Katie's confession of sin. For having had twenty-two blessed years with this precious child.

She looked into Katie's eyes and wiped tears from her cheeks, resolving to pay a visit to the attic just as soon as the dishes were done.

Quietly, with Katie's help, Rebecca set to work clearing the table. She heated the water brought up by the battery-operated well pump and began rinsing the dishes. Then into the same hot water she added the dish detergent. Swishing it around, she lowered a fistful of silverware into the foamy suds, allowing the warmth to soothe her. *Things'll be fine*, she told herself, *once the wedding's behind us.*

The two women made quick work of the dishes, rinsing then drying each plate and cup, without their usual light-hearted conversation. Deliberately, Rebecca put away the few remaining leftovers before finding the courage to speak. "So you'll be thinking things over, then . . . about talking to the bishop?"

Katie swept the crumbs from the floor. "Don't you understand, Mamma?" She turned to face her. "I don't want to back out on the wedding. I'm just wondering if I'm the best choice for a bishop's wife."

Rebecca's eyes searched her daughter's. "The time for wondering is long past, Katie. Your wedding day's nearly here."

Katie's lip quivered uncontrollably.

"What's really bothering ya, child?" She reached for Katie and drew the slender form into her arms.

Long, deep sobs shook Katie's body as Rebecca tried to console her. "There, there," she whispered. "It's just the jitters. We womenfolk all get them, but as time passes, you'll get better at hiding them." She paused for a moment. Then, attempting to lighten the mood, she added, "Why, I 'spect you'll feel this way before the birth of your first little one, most likely."

Rebecca felt Katie pull away, a curious expression on her face replacing her tears. "What, Katie? What is it?"

Katie straightened, adjusting her long apron and dress. "I almost forgot to ask you something."

"Jah?"

"Mamma, who is Katherine Mayfield?"

Rebecca felt weak, as if her limbs might no longer support her. *This cannot be*, she thought.

"I saw the name stitched on a baby dress . . . up in the attic. Ach, it was so pretty. But where did you come by such a thing, Mam?"

Without warning, the strength left Rebecca's legs entirely. She stumbled across the kitchen toward the long table bench.

Katie reached out to steady her. "Mamma!"

Rebecca dropped onto the bench and tugged at her apron. Then she pulled out a white hankie and with short, jerky motions began to fan herself. Everything came home to her at that moment—the worry of the years, the long-kept secret. . . .

Katie ran to open the back door a crack. "There, Mamma," she called as frigid air pushed through the utility room and into the kitchen. "That's better, ain't?"

In spite of the draft, Rebecca felt heat rush to engulf her head. She tried to look up, to catch one more glimpse of the beloved face.

Only a deep sigh emerged. *Katie, my girl. My precious girl* . . .

Through blurred vision, she could see Katie closing the door, shoving back the wintry blast, then hurrying toward her, all concerned and flustered. But try as she might, Rebecca Lapp could not will away the peculiar, prickly sensation creeping up her neck and into her dizzy head.

She slumped forward, aware of nothing more. . . .

CHAPTER THREE

❖   ❖   ❖

Dat, come quick!"

At the sound of Katie's frantic voice, Samuel, along with Benjamin and Eli, rushed into the kitchen.

"I don't know what on earth happened!" Katie's heart was pounding. "We were just talking—Mam and me—and—" Her mother was as physically fit as any farmer's wife in Hickory Hollow, certainly plump and hearty enough to ward off a mere fainting spell. "I'll get some tea leaves."

Reluctant to leave her mother, Katie hurried downstairs to the cold cellar, where neat rows of cabinets stored canned fruits and vegetables. She found the dried mint leaves in a jar and quickly pinched some into her hand, still puzzled over what had caused her mamma to faint.

Katie had mentioned speaking to the bishop. Had the idea of not going through with the marriage troubled her mother enough to make her ill?

She returned the jar of mint to its spot on the shelf and closed the cabinet door, pondering the strange circumstances. "Katie, are ya coming?" Benjamin called out.

"On my way," she answered, running up the steep cellar steps.

In the kitchen, Katie brewed some mint tea, glancing re-

37

peatedly at her mother, who had come to and was leaning
her head on one hand, while Eli fanned her with the hankie.

Dat stood at Mam's side, pensive and silent. He seemed
shorter now, his wiry frame bent over his wife. Katie wondered if he was still vexed over her awkward yet truthful
admission at the table. Still, she was glad she'd told on herself. At least one aspect of her sinfulness would be dealt
with. And if she was to go through with the wedding, she'd
be offering her first private confession tomorrow or the next
day.

Katie stirred the hot water, hoping to hurry the tea-mak-
ing process. She stared at Rebecca apprehensively. Spouting
off those careless words—that she'd better have a talk with
Bishop John—had wreaked such havoc! She hadn't meant
to upset anyone unduly; now she wished she'd kept her
thoughts to herself.

"Hurry it up, Katie," Benjamin said, coming over to see
what was taking so long.

She moved quickly, spooning honey into the hot water.
But by the time the leaves had steeped long enough to embrace the soothing mint taste, Rebecca had gone upstairs to
lie down.

When Katie stepped into the room a bit later, she found
her mother still fully dressed but covered with the
warmest quilts from the handmade cedar chest at the foot
of the double bed. She held out the teacup on its matching
saucer, and her father took it from her with a curt nod of
his head.

"Is there anything else you need, Mamma?"

Dat answered for her. "That'll do."

Katie left without another word.

Rebecca settled back against the bed pillows with a
slight smile on her face as she accepted the cup from Samuel
and took a sip. "Des gut."

He reached for the kerosene lamp on the bedside table. "I'll go on down and stoke up the stove a bit. Can't let ya catch a chill, not with daughter's weddin' day a-comin'."

"No need to worry."

Samuel shook his head thoughtfully. "A body could get right sick in a cold snap like this."

Rebecca forced a chuckle. It caught in her throat, and she began to cough—as if in fulfillment of his prophecy.

Samuel Lapp was a dear and caring husband. A good provider of the basic needs—an abundance of food from their own land, a solid roof over their heads. . . . Gas furnaces, electricity, telephones, and such luxuries were for the English. Amish folk relied on horses and buggies for transportation, propane gas to run their camper-sized refrigerators, and a battery-operated well pump in the cellar for the household water. In fact, the Lapp family held tenaciously to all the Old Order traditions without complaint, just as generations before them.

"How can ya miss whatcha never had?" Samuel often asked his English friends at Central Market in downtown Lancaster.

Rebecca watched her husband, expecting him to slip out of the room without further comment. She was a bit surprised when he hesitated at the door, then returned to her bedside.

"Are you in poor health, then? Shall I be fetchin' a doctor?" His concern was genuine. "Wouldn't take but a minute to hitch up ol' Molasses and run him over to the Millers' place."

Peter and Lydia Miller—Mennonites who indulged in the "English" lifestyle—lived about a mile down Hickory Lane and had offered their telephone in case of emergency. On several occasions, Samuel had taken them up on it. After all, they were kin—second cousins on Rebecca's side—and modern as the day was long.

"Won't be needing any doctor. I'm wore out, that's all," she said softly, to put his mind at ease. "And it'd be a shame if Cousin Lydia had to worry over me for nothing."

"Jah, right ya be."

Shadows flickered on the wall opposite the simple wood-framed bed. Rebecca stared at the elongated silhouettes as she sipped her tea. She sighed, then whispered the thought that tormented her soul night and day. "Our Katie . . . she's been asking questions."

A muscle twitched in Samuel's jaw. "Jah? What questions?"

Rebecca pulled a pillow from behind her back and hugged it to her. "I have to get up to the attic. Tonight."

"You're not goin' up there tonight. Just put it out of your mind. Rest now, you hear?"

Rebecca shook her head. "You're forgetting about the little rose-colored dress," she said, her words barely audible. "A right fine baby dress . . . made of satin. Katie must've found it."

"Well, it'll just have to wait. Tomorrow's another day."

"We daresn't wait," Rebecca insisted, still speaking in hushed tones, reluctant to argue with her husband. "Our daughter mustn't know . . . she's better off *never* knowing."

Samuel leaned down and gave her a peck on her forehead. "Katie is and always will be our daughter. Now just you try 'n rest."

"But the dress . . ."

"The girl can't tell nothin' from one little dress," Samuel insisted. He took the pillow Rebecca had been clutching and placed it beside her, where he would lay his head later. "I best be seein' to the children."

He carried the lamp out into the hallway, then closed the door, leaving Rebecca in the thick darkness . . . to think and dream.

The children . . .

There had been a time when Rebecca had longed for more children. *Many* more. But after Benjamin was born, two miscarriages and a stillbirth had taken a toll on her body. Although her family was complete enough now, she wondered what life would've been like with more than three . . . or four children growing up here. All her relatives and nearly every family in the church district had at least eight children. Some had more—as many as fifteen.

It was a good thing to nurture young lives into the fold. Didn't the Good Book say, "Children are an heritage of the Lord; and the fruit of the womb is his reward"? Children brought joy and laughter into the home and helped turn work into play.

And there was plenty of work in an Amish household, she thought with a low chuckle. Cutting hay, planting potatoes, sowing alfalfa or clover. Families in Hickory Hollow always worked together. They *had* to. Without the convenience of tractors and other modern farm equipment, everything took longer. But it was the accepted way of parents, grandparents, and great-grandparents before them.

In the early 1700s, William Penn had made all this possible for Samuel and Rebecca Lapp's ancestors. Close-knit Amish communities were promised good land and began to form settlements in Pennsylvania. She thought again of Samuel's great-great-grandfather who had built the very house where Rebecca lay shivering in the dark, cold bedroom.

After a time, she felt the warmth rising through the floorboards, from the woodburning stove directly below. Samuel's doing, most likely. Ever kind and thoughtful Samuel. He'd been a good husband all these years. A bit outspoken at times, but solid and hardworking. A godly man, who held to the teachings of the Amish church, who loved his neighbor as himself . . . and who had long ago agreed to

41

keep her secret for the rest of his life.

"How's Mamma?" Katie asked as Samuel emerged from the bedroom, holding the oil lamp aloft. Evidently, she'd been hovering there at the landing, waiting for some word of her mother's condition.

"Go on about your duties." Samuel gave no hint of a smile, but his words were intended to reassure. "Nothin' to worry over. Nothin' at all."

He headed for his straight-backed rocking chair, pulled it up nearer the woodstove, and dropped into it with a mutter. Pretending to be scanning a column in the weekly Amish newspaper, Samuel allowed his thoughts to roam.

What had Rebecca said upstairs—something about Katie finding the infant dress? He'd always wanted to get rid of that fancy thing. No sense having the evidence in the house. 'Twasn't wise—too risky—especially with that English name sewed into it the way it was.

But he'd never been able to bring himself to force Rebecca to part with it—not with her feeling the way she did. As for himself, the grand memory of that day was enough, though he hadn't laid eyes on the infant gown even once since their daughter had worn it home from the Lancaster hospital.

Minutes ago, it had come to his attention that Katie had stumbled onto the tiny garment—had found it in the attic. How, on God's earth, after all these years? Had Rebecca ignored his bidding? She was a good and faithful wife, his Rebecca, but when it came to Katie, there was no reasoning with the woman. She had a soft place holed up in her heart for the girl. Surely Rebecca had obeyed him and at least done her best to hide the dress away. Surely she had.

Now that Katie had discovered the dress, though, he would remind Rebecca to find another hiding place. First thing tomorrow. Jah, that's what he'd do.

Eli and Benjamin weren't too worried over their mother, Katie observed as she wandered into the kitchen. They'd started a rousing game of checkers on the toasty floor near the woodstove and had barely glanced up at her approach.

She went to the cupboard where the German *Biewel* and other books were kept. Reverently, she carried the old, worn Bible to Dat and set it down in front of him, then seated herself on the wooden bench beside the table. She picked up her sewing needle and some dark thread.

Would Mam mind having company? Katie wondered as she threaded the needle. She'd feel better if she saw with her own eyes how her mamma was doing after the fainting spell a few minutes ago.

With threaded needle poised near the hemline of her wedding dress, Katie gazed at her brothers, unseeing. She'd always insisted on knowing things firsthand. And that stubborn streak in her had caused more grief than she dared admit.

For a good five minutes she sat there, sewing the fine stitches, hearing the steady purr of the gas lantern while a forbidden melody droned in her head. She suppressed the urge to hum.

Looking up from her work, she got up the courage to speak to Dat. "I want to go up and see Mamma, jah?"

Samuel lifted his eyes from his reading corner. "Not just now."

"Tomorrow, then?"

"Jah, tomorrow." With an audible sigh, he picked up the Bible for the evening Scripture reading and prayer.

Without having to be told, Eli and Benjamin put aside their game and faced their father as he leafed through the pages. He knew the Good Book like the back of his hand, and from the firm set of his jaw, Katie suspected he had something definite in mind for tonight's reading.

He read first in High German, then translated into English out of habit—and, probably, for emphasis. Katie put down her sewing needle and tried to concentrate on the verses being read. But with Mam upstairs recovering from who knows what, it was mighty difficult.

"Romans, chapter twelve, verses one and two." Dat's voice held the ring of authority they had all come to respect. He began reading: " 'I beseech you therefore, brethren, by the mercies of God, that ye present your bodies a living sacrifice, holy, acceptable unto God, which is your reasonable service.

" 'And be not conformed to this world: but be ye transformed by the renewing of your mind, that ye may prove what is that good, and acceptable, and perfect, will of God.' "

The perfect will of God. The words pricked Katie's conscience. How could God's good and perfect will be at work in her? She was harboring sin—continual sin—and with little regret at that, even dragging her feet about the required repenting.

After the incident in the attic, she knew without a doubt that she was spiritually unfit to nurture John Beiler's innocent children . . . or, for that matter, to bear him future offspring. What had she been thinking? How could she stand beside him on their wedding day and for all the years to come as a godly, submissive wife, an example of obedience to the People?

The questions vexed her, and when Dat finished his short prayer, Katie lit a second lamp, headed for her room, and undressed for the night. Before pulling down the bedcovers, she resolved to pay Mary Stoltzfus a visit instead of Bishop John. First thing tomorrow after the milking, she'd talk things over with her dearest and best friend. Mary would know what was right.

That settled, Katie congratulated herself on this decision as she slipped between the cold cotton sheets and blew out the lantern.

❖   ❖   ❖

Around midnight, muffled sounds were heard in the attic. At first, Katie thought she must be dreaming. But at five o'clock, when Dat's summons to get up and help with chores resounded through the hallway, she remembered the thumping noises overhead. Her heart leaped up at the prospect of investigating the attic—an unexpected opportunity to hold the beautiful satin fabric, the feel of it against her fingertips like forbidden candy. Perhaps one more delicious taste would satisfy her cravings.

Just once more, she thought while brushing her long, thick hair by lantern light. From sheer habit, she twisted the hair near her temples into a tight row on both sides, then drew the mass of it back into a smooth bun.

Dress modestly, with decency and propriety, not with braided hair or gold or pearls or expensive clothes. . . .

She set the white mesh kapp on top of her head, its ties dangling. Over thick woolen longjohns, she pulled on a solid brown choring dress and black apron.

Perhaps today she, Katie Lapp—soon to be the bishop's wife—might make a fresh start of things. Maybe today would be different. Maybe today she could be the right kind of woman in God's eyes. With all her heart, mind, and soul, she would try.

Katie heard the sound of Dat's voice downstairs; Mam's, too, as she leaned into the stairwell, listening. She was comforted by the thought that her mother was up, hopefully feeling well and preparing to cook a hearty breakfast.

If she did not delay, she might have time to visit the attic before morning prayer. She rushed back to her bedroom, reached for the oil lamp, and tiptoed to the ladder leading to the attic.

She climbed the rungs as quickly as she dared and, reaching the top, pushed the heavy attic door open. Then, scrambling up into the rectangular-shaped opening, she paused for breath before stepping over to the old trunk.

Silently, Katie set the lantern on the floor and opened the lid. With heart pounding and ears straining to hear her name in case Dat called, she searched the top layers of clothing in the trunk, exploring the area where she'd first discovered the satin baby dress. Finding no sign of the garment, she dug a bit deeper, careful not to muss things.

When she located Mam's wedding dress, she found that the spot next to it was vacant—obviously so. It was as though someone had deliberately removed the treasured item.

More determined than ever, Katie continued her search, pulling out lightweight blankets, solid white crocheted bedspreads and tablecloths, and faded cotton quilts, passed down from great-great-grandmothers.

There were the faceless cloth dolls Rebecca had made for her as a toddler, too, but not the satin baby dress. It simply was not there. The fancy infant gown was gone.

But where? And who had moved it?

She felt a deep sadness weighting her spirit. *Maybe it's as it should be*, she thought, reeling under the impact of the emotions warring within.

Attempting to shrug away her dark thoughts, Katie set to work reassembling the linens and things in the trunk before leaving the attic and joining the family in the living room. Her brothers and Dat—and Mam—were already on their knees, waiting for her.

"Thank you, O God, for all your help to us," Samuel prayed as soon as Katie's knees touched the hard floor. "Forgive us our sins and help us today with the land . . . *your* land. Amen."

Less than a two-minute ritual both at morning and at night, the prayers were an important pattern underlying the intricate stitchery of their family life.

When she stood up, Katie rejoiced at the light in her mamma's eyes; and her cheeks were no longer chalky white. But the splashes of rose in Mam's face reminded Katie of the frustrating attic search. Almost instantly, her happiness dissipated into thin air—like blowing out a match. She'd been deceitful by returning to the attic, hoping to indulge in one more moment of sinful pleasure. She had broken God's laws—the Ordnung, too.

"Mornin', Mamma." The greeting squeaked out. Katie kissed Rebecca on the cheek, and the two women headed for the kitchen. "I'm glad to see your color's back."

Rebecca smiled and nodded. "A good night's sleep was all I needed." She set a kettle to boil on the polished woodstove. She'd been up long before anyone else—an encouraging sign. And with her next remark, Katie was sure her mother was her old self again.

"You're mighty late coming down." She gave Katie a shrewd, sidelong look. "Are you feelin' all right?"

No doubt Mam was referring to the scene last night at supper. But Katie knew there was no use in bringing up the issue of the guitar and the tunes she loved to sing, nor her upcoming confession. And she dared not mention her wedding, which was only one week from tomorrow. Not after the fainting spell Mam had had last night.

Mary Stoltzfus was the one who would get an earful. Hashing things out with her would be much easier. Simpler, too. On both Mam and herself.

"Jah, I'm feeling fine." Katie took a deep breath. "I was up poking around in the attic this morning," she began. "That's why I was late for prayer."

She noticed her mother's eyebrows lifting in surprise. "Well, you better hurry now." She held out a plateful of jellied toast. "Dat's going to be wonderin' what's keeping you."

Katie carried the plate to the table and set it down. In the utility room, she sat on a stool and put on her work boots, then pulled an old choring coat from a peg. "Remember that little baby dress I was telling you about yesterday?" she called to her mother, barely able to restrain her eagerness to know more without divulging her sin. "I couldn't seem to find it just now."

"Baby dress?"

"Jah." Katie peered through the doorway to the kitchen, but Rebecca had turned to face the sink. "Don't you remember?"

"Things are a bit of a blur" came the tentative reply.

It was a good enough answer—enough to satisfy Katie that her mother hadn't been the one stumbling around in the attic last night.

"I'm sorry about coming down late," she blurted. "I won't be tardy again, Mamma."

Katie rushed outside with her piece of toast, feeling better for having confessed. Still, the thought of the satin dress haunted her. Where had it gone? And who would've taken it?

Rebecca waited for the sound of the door closing before going to the window to look out. Several sets of boot prints dented the hard snow covering the red sandstone steps. The steps led in a diagonal line through the side yard to the barnyard, where hay wagons and open market wagons ran to and from the barn during harvest season.

She watched as Katie hurried toward the barn door, coattails flapping in the cold. It seemed that here lately the girl was confessing every time she turned around. Last evening—about her music and not marrying the bishop because of it—and then again this morning, about being late to morning prayers. And once the deacon or the preacher was summoned, she'd be confessing again.

Rebecca sighed, not knowing what to make of it. She wondered if it was more than wedding jitters. A body could see that Katie wasn't herself. She'd even gone and changed her pony's name from Tobias to Satin Boy.

Rebecca thought about speaking with the bishop privately, but dismissed the idea and returned to the stove to begin frying up the cornmeal mush and some potatoes.

She looketh well to the ways of her household, and eateth not the bread of idleness. The words of a proverb ran through her head. No time to be idle around here.

Come breakfast time, there'd be eggs, liverwurst, and cooked cereal, too; bread, butter, and pineapple jelly, along with homemade apple butter—Katie's favorite.

Several times, before Katie and the men returned, Rebecca wandered to the kitchen door and stared out. Something was luring Katie to the attic. Hadn't she said she'd gone again this morning? Why?

Was it the baby dress? And if so, what interested her about it?

Rebecca pondered a bit, reassuring herself that the dress was safely hidden away, far from the attic trunk, never to be found again.

The family secret was safe.

She drew in a long breath and savored the tranquil scene through the window. The sun was still asleep over the eastern slope, where a Norway maple hung its stark branches over the stuccoed stone springhouse below. A weathered wooden bench near its wide trunk stood as a reminder of cheerful, sunny days dripping like golden honey.

Golden days. The thought brought a stab of sadness. *The*

best days. Days spent doting on her beautiful infant daughter. She'd given Katie two full years of total acceptance and adoration, as was their way. Then in the blink of an eye, it seemed, her baby was a toddler being molded and fashioned into an obedient Amish child.

It seemed no more than a whisper of time before a well-mannered, yet rambunctious, dimple-faced girl with braids wound around her head was skipping down the lane to the one-room schoolhouse. Then, before Rebecca could turn around, Katie was riding off to Singings with her brothers and returning late at night with one eligible young man or another—the "running-around years," they called them.

It was along about then that Daniel Fisher walked into her life—right up the back steps and into their kitchen. And if he hadn't gone sailing in Atlantic City the weekend he turned nineteen, Katie would be sewing the wedding dress she'd be wearing for *him*.

But eighteen months after Daniel's drowning, Katie had made her vow to God and the church—her baptismal oath—the promise to follow the orally transmitted rules that must be kept unto death.

Katie, her dear, headstrong girl. Surely she wouldn't be letting her foolish notion about music come between herself and a chance to marry. Another year and she'd be completely passed over. The *alt Maedel* stigma was nearly impossible to avoid among the People. Not going through with marriage to Bishop John would be downright foolish—if not irreverent. A transgression of the worst kind.

Rebecca stiffened her shoulders and purposefully turned from the door window. She would see to it that Katie kept her mind on the task at hand—preparing for her wedding. The satin baby dress must be buried—along with the memory of Daniel Fisher.

When the time was right, Rebecca would double-check the new hiding place under the cedar chest. Maybe the dress wasn't as safely hidden as she'd first thought. Even Samuel had spoken to her about it early this morning.

Tormented with fear, she resolved anew to conceal the secret. It would follow her and Samuel to their graves. Most certainly, it *must*.

CHAPTER FOUR

❖ ❖ ❖

When Katie arrived at the Stoltzfus farm, Mary was busy stewing chickens with her mother. Ten other women sat around the large kitchen table, chatting and sipping coffee. A quilting frolic! That's what it was, Katie decided. No doubt they'd be working on her wedding quilt.

Why else wouldn't I be invited? she thought. It was highly unusual for the bride not to attend her own quilting bee. But Katie suspected that since she was to become the bishop's wife, the People had planned something extra special out of respect for his position. Something in the nature of a surprise, which was more typical of the way Mennonites did things than their cousins, the Amish.

The quilting frames were set up in the large, sparsely furnished front room, where the women, ranging in age from eighteen to eighty, would sit on straight-backed chairs, sewing thousands of intricate stitches and chatting about vegetable gardens and flower gardens, new babies, and upcoming work frolics. Rebecca would tell her familiar tales, and some of the women might throw in the latest gossip. They would have contests over who could make the shortest stitches as they laughed and sang hymns and babbled endlessly. Later, there would be oodles of food, perhaps some of Abe and Rachel Stoltzfus's delicious pineapple ice cream—the crowning moment of such an event, especially for Katie, who often fought her craving for sweets.

"Something wrong?" Mary whispered, watching with a keen eye as Katie warmed herself near the black-metal stove. "You look all droopy."

Katie shrugged, glancing over her shoulder at her friend. "I'm all right." She wasn't in the mood for mentioning the strange commotion in the attic that had produced fitful rest. "I can't stay." The others would be wanting to get on with the quilting bee. "I best be going."

"But you just got here." There was a question in Mary's voice.

Her words went unheeded, though, and Katie turned to say good-bye to the group of women—women as fondly familiar to her as her own family. There was Rachel Stoltzfus, Mary's mother, and Ruth Stoltzfus, Mary's elderly grandmother on her father's side, as well as Katie's own great-aunt, Ella Mae Zook, also known as the Wise Woman, sitting beside her spunky daughter Mattie Beiler (married to the bishop's older brother), and Becky and Mary Zook, Ella Mae's daughters-in-law. Katie also spotted her first cousins—Nancy, Susie, and Rachel Zook; Naomi, Mary, and Esther Beiler—and more expected to arrive.

Each one greeted Katie warmly, eager to comment on her pending marriage. But none referred to the large piece of cloth and padding stretched over the frame, waiting for precut squares to be stitched into a colorful quilt. Or the fact that Rebecca, the mother of the bride, had not yet arrived.

Katie tried to be gracious, but at the first opportunity, she hurried outside and began to pick her way across the ice toward the family buggy.

She wasn't surprised when Mary Stoltzfus burst out of the back door, following close on her heels. "Katie, wait!"

But she kept going, watching her step as she crossed the side yard.

Mary was panting by the time she'd caught up, plump cheeks flushed from the cold and exertion. "You seem upset about something."

Katie stopped short and turned to face her friend. "We have to talk . . . and very soon."

"I'll come over after bit. Jah?"

Katie shook her head. "No. Not *my* house. We'll have to meet somewhere else—someplace private."

Mary slanted her a speculative glance. "Would've thought you'd be home sewing your wedding dress."

Katie forced a brief smile. "It's nearly done."

"Thought you'd have it *all* done by now."

"Jah, I know." Without explanation, Katie headed for the horse and buggy parked in the drive just west of the house.

Mary ran after her. "Maybe we could talk now"—she glanced apprehensively toward the house—"if ya hurry."

"There's no hurrying it. We'll chat later."

"Katie, something's awful wrong. I just know it."

At Mary's wide-eyed look of compassion, Katie felt the tears welling up, blurring her vision. "It's nothin', really." Her voice grew husky.

Mary reached for her with mittened hands, and Katie gave in to the heaviness inside. She buried her face in her friend's soft shoulder. "*Everything's* wrong," she cried. "Oh, Mary . . . everything."

Grabbing Katie's hand, she led her around behind the horse where they could not be seen from the house. "I knew it. Don't you see? Friends are for sharin'. The Lord puts people together for a reason, like how He put us—Mary 'n Katie—together."

At the sound of the familiar childhood connection, Katie's eyes grew even more cloudy.

"*Himmel*, it's not . . ." Mary paused, her expression grave. "This talk . . . it's not about the marriage, is it?"

Katie hesitated. But what she had to say was not for community ears. If there was even a slight chance that someone might overhear. . . . "Not now," she insisted.

"So, it *is* about your marryin' the bishop, ain't?" Mary prodded ever so gently.

Seeing the angelic, round face so concerned was a comfort. But Katie's heart sank as she looked into the all-knowing blue eyes. That look. It probed deep into her soul, reinforcing the sense that Mary always seemed to know what was good and right. "We'll talk tonight" was all Katie could say. "I'll ride over after supper."

Reluctantly, she climbed into the carriage and urged the aging horse toward Hickory Lane. She made the right-hand turn at the end of the Stoltzfus's dirt drive, now covered with deep, icy ridges from buggy wheels slicing into the encrusted snow.

Molasses pulled the buggy up the hill while a melody played in her head. For a time, she tried to put aside her doubts and ponderings, to allow the peaceful countryside to soothe her.

The smell of woodsmoke hung in the air as crows *caw-cawed* back and forth overhead. A bird sang out a low, throaty series of notes and flew away. Somewhere near the edge of the lightly forested area, on the opposite side of the deserted road, a lone deer—though she could neither see nor hear it—was probably watching her, heeding a primitive warning that it was not safe to cross this remote stretch of road buried deep in the Amish community. So isolated was the area that not even the smallest mark on the Lancaster map betrayed the existence of Hickory Hollow—home to two hundred and fifty-three souls.

One farm after another rolled into view—like a patchwork quilt of dusty browns and grays—as Katie trotted the horse over the two-mile stretch of the main road. On the way, she fought the notion that someone knew her as well as Mary seemed to. If Mary hadn't been the sweetest, kindest friend ever, Katie would have rejected outright the idea that a person could get inside your heart and know things almost before you did.

But back there just now, Mary had sized up the situation and guessed it was the wedding that was bothering her. Five years ago, she'd predicted that Katie would never love a man as much as she loved Daniel Fisher. She'd even had the nerve to say, when they were little girls, that Katie was her mother's favorite child. Yes, like it or not, Mary Stoltzfus was hardly ever wrong.

Quivering with cold, Katie tucked the lap robe tighter around her. Was it possible for someone to know you that well? Shouldn't a woman have her own sanctuary, that secret place in her heart and mind where no one else entered?

She slapped the reins and hurried Molasses along. *Maybe this time Mary is wrong*, she thought. *Maybe she's wrong about being right so awful much.*

◈   ◈   ◈

At home, Rebecca was running late. The quilting bee would be starting soon, but first things first. She had something important to do before she could leave the house. It was a convenient time, too, since Katie hadn't returned with the family buggy. And Samuel and the boys had gone to purchase walnuts and hickory nuts for the wedding.

Hurriedly, she opened the door leading downstairs to the cold cellar. Here, with the help of women from her church district, she'd put up and stored eight hundred quarts of produce. She, in turn, had assisted her neighbors with their canning, as well. Piles of potatoes, onions, turnips, and sweet potatoes were stored separately, more than enough until the next harvest. There were rows and rows of canning jars filled with pickled beets, chow-chow, tomato relish, bean salads, and Rebecca's luscious jams and jellies.

But it was not food for her table that brought Rebecca to the cold cellar. In fact, food was the last thing on her mind as she crept down the narrow steps. In her hand, she held a baby gown wrapped in tissue.

She had felt uneasy about its former hiding place—the underside of the blanket chest. Last night after Samuel had fallen asleep, she'd gone to the attic, found the dress, and taped the lovely thing—still nestled in its wrapping—to the bottom of the cedar chest. So worried was she about someone, anyone, discovering it, that when Katie unexpectedly left with the buggy after breakfast, Rebecca decided to take advantage of the empty house. She would find a better, more secure location for the dress this time.

Sadly, the thought of destroying the garment had tempted her, but upon approaching the woodstove, another thought kept her from tossing the tiny gown into the fire. A frightening flash of reason—and absurdity.

What if someday this is all you have left?

She tried to shake off the preposterous notion, but in its place came a lump in her throat, nearly choking her. Stunned, she dropped the dress. As she leaned over to retrieve it, a tightness gripped her chest, and she felt as though her heart might break.

Carefully, she removed the garment from its wrapping and began to pray silently, pressing the soft satin fabric to her face.

O Lord God, heavenly Father, keep this dress safe from eyes that would hinder and disrupt your manifold great grace and goodness over our lives through Jesus Christ. Amen.

The words were a mixture of Amish High German and down-home emotion. Rebecca never spoke her prayers the way she "thought" them. The Lord deserved respect and reverence, after all. Oh, she'd heard of other folk who felt that it was all right to approach the throne of grace the way you would chat with a good friend. But such ideas seemed nothing short of heresy to her way of thinking!

Deep in the dim cellar-pantry, beyond the cabinets of canned goods and crocks of pudding, Rebecca spied the beautiful corner cupboard and its matching sideboard. She found a kerosene lamp, lit it, and quickened her pace toward the lovely pieces handcrafted by Samuel five years before, about the time Katie and Daniel were seeing so much of each other. The solid pine furniture had been banished to the dark cellar—not a necessary gift for this marriage, although there had been some talk that the bishop wanted to auction off his deceased wife's furniture to make room for Katie's things. That idea had been discarded, however, when nine-year-old Nancy—sentimental about her mother's belongings—had pleaded to keep the furniture for her own bride's dowry someday. So Katie's corner cupboard would remain in storage for now.

Perhaps Eli's bride would enjoy it. Or Benjamin's. Both boys were secretly courting girls, Rebecca was almost certain. A double wedding might be in the air come November of next year.

This year, however, was Katie's. She would be moving into John's house, where she'd have the use of his furniture—everything a married couple would ever need. A typical bride's dowry such as a sideboard for the kitchen or a corner cupboard for the parlor would not be called for. Not even a drop-leaf table.

But there *would* be a dowry gift, and Rebecca had planned something very special. In addition to a Bridal Heart quilt and some crocheted doilies and linens, she would give her daughter eighteen hundred dollars.

Though she'd said nothing to Samuel, she was sure he'd

agree. In many ways, the money, which had accumulated interest over the past twenty-two years, was a befitting gift, and Rebecca found herself recalling the peculiar circumstances surrounding it. . . .

The morning sky had threatened rain the day she and Samuel climbed into the backseat of Peter and Lydia Miller's big, fancy car for the drive to downtown Lancaster. The trip seemed surprisingly fast—only twenty minutes—compared to the typical buggy ride of two hours or so, depending upon traffic.

Rebecca was grateful for the transportation at a time like this. Her contractions were much too close together, and she feared she might be going into premature labor. After two consecutive miscarriages and in her eighth month of pregnancy, she was weak with worry. She'd not felt life for at least a day now.

Married at eighteen, she was still quite young. Too young—at twenty-four—to be facing yet another loss. On some days, before this most recent pregnancy, she had found herself nearly frantic with longing and grief. Nearly two years had passed since Benjamin, her youngest, had come so easily that Mattie Beiler, the too-talkative midwife, was scarcely ready to catch him. But now there were problems. Serious ones.

Cousin Lydia had promised to pray for a safe delivery as her husband, Peter, stopped the car at the curb and let them out in front of the emergency entrance. But much to Lydia's dismay, Rebecca had insisted on going it alone. Not even Rebecca's closest kinfolk knew of her fears or the fact that the baby had stopped kicking. She needed only one person with her on this day. Samuel.

A tall, young orderly met them at the door with a wheelchair. Samuel answered the admittance clerk's questions while Rebecca sat very still, praying for life-giving movement in her womb instead of this dull and silent heaviness.

Forcing back tears, she thought of her little ones at home—happy little Benjamin, out of diapers now and a toddler of two; Eli, a busy, confident youngster even at three. Her eldest, Elam, a fine, strong five-year-old, was already helping Samuel with the milking and plowing.

Oh, but she desired more children—a little girl . . . maybe two or three of them. Samuel, after all, had gotten his sons first off—three in a row—and Rebecca loved them dearly. Still, something was missing. A daughter to learn the old ways at her Mam's hearth, to bear many grandsons and granddaughters for her and Samuel one day.

The baby had come quickly. Stillborn.

Rebecca would not stay overnight in the hospital after her delivery. Her body was physically strong, but her emotions were scarred. How could she face the People—her loved ones and close friends—with empty arms?

Be fruitful and multiply, the Good Book said. Barrenness was a near curse, and among the Plain community, infertility, an unspoken blight.

The doctor's words had been guarded, yet they cut to the quick. "Be very thankful for the children you already have, Mrs. Lapp."

The children you already have. . . . Meaning that their boys would be hers and Samuel's only offspring.

The nurses were kind, sympathetic even. Some, she noticed, darted inquisitive gazes away from her kapp, trying not to stare. Their curiosity she could bear. But not their pity. Enough pity came from within herself, enough for all of them.

Samuel had been ever so gentle, standing by her side after the worst was over, staying strong for her as she lay there under the white sheet, brokenhearted.

Yet "providentially speaking"—as Samuel would later come to say—the anguish of those dismal hours had turned into a day of rejoicing. Everything had seemed to fit, right down to the encounter with the teenage girl and her mother. *Everything.*

The timing itself had seemed somehow ordered—remarkably so. A divine appointment, she'd always thought. Who would've expected such an extraordinary thing to happen—within hours after losing their own flesh-and-blood daughter? But it had, and no one—*no one*—had ever known the difference.

The money—five hundred dollars cash—had come as a surprise later. But it had been there all the time, wrapped in the deep folds of the baby blanket. Rebecca had discovered it in the embossed, cream-colored envelope with the words "Please use the enclosed money for my baby's new life" written in a lovely, flowery hand and signed, "Laura Mayfield."

Wondering if they had gotten themselves caught up in some sort of trickery, Samuel hadn't wanted to keep the money at first. But the sum was soon forgotten, deposited in the bank to collect interest, awaiting an emergency or other needful thing. The tiny new baby—their precious Katie—immediately became the center of their lives. It was she, not the money, who'd soon won them over. As far as Rebecca was concerned, Katie was as much a part of her body as Elam, Eli, and Benjamin. She'd wet-nursed the infant until toddlerhood, coddled and loved her through sickness and health . . . just as she had her own sons. Katie was the same as her own flesh and blood. Just the same. Yet somehow—maybe because of the way the child had come to them—even more special.

The memories brought tears, and Rebecca turned, lifted the lantern, and beheld a pine baby cradle, perched high atop the corner cupboard. Eager to see it again, she placed the little dress on the bottom shelf, stepped on one of the old water buckets nearby, and reached for the cradle. When she'd recovered it, she noticed, quite unexpectedly, a milk white vase inside.

Rebecca smiled, remembering the flowers. Lydia Miller had come for a quick visit that June day after baby Katie's arrival in Hickory Hollow. She'd arrived bearing a gift of colorful blossoms from her own garden. Rebecca had been surprised, and if the truth be known, a bit startled to see the vibrant blooms plucked off their stems. She and her friends never picked garden flowers; it was believed that they were to be seen and admired right where God put them. Because of this, there was no use for a flower vase in the Lapp home.

Days later, when the cut flowers were dry and dead, Rebecca had stored the vase here in the cellar. And years later, she had placed it in Katie's infant cradle.

The tall vase, quite narrow and deep, would make an exceedingly safe hiding place. Carefully, Rebecca rolled up the baby dress and pushed it down into the empty vase, wondering what Cousin Lydia would think if she knew how her gift was being put to use.

Rebecca never once thought how she would go about getting the dress out again, or even if there would come a time when she would need—or want—to do so. It was enough that the deed was done.

CHAPTER FIVE

❖ ❖ ❖

Katie made her way slowly up Hickory Lane. The repetitious *clip-clop-clip* of the horse's hooves soothed her spirits and eased her mind somewhat. Out here on the open road, with only Molasses to hear her, she allowed herself the pleasure of humming. The tune was an old one. Familiar and cherished, it was the last song she and Dan had created together. Unlike the others, this melody had words. But Katie couldn't bring herself to sing them. Daniel—her love, her life—was gone. Drowned in the Atlantic Ocean, leaving her behind.

Too caught up in each other for trivial details, they'd not given the song a title back then. Their final sun-drenched days had been spent laughing and singing the hours away—as if time would stretch on forever.

On one such fine day, they had perched themselves on an enormous boulder, smack in the middle of Weaver's Creek, miles from Hickory Lane. There, with springtime shining all around them, the song had come easily, born of their love and their laughter, and the lazy, warm day.

Katie found herself humming much too loudly now, partly in defiance of the years. Years that had robbed her of Dan—someone to share her musical longings. Lonely years, in which she'd tried—and failed—to squash her stubborn need to sing, to give her heart a voice, accompanied by the joyful chords of Dan's guitar.

And now Dat was insisting she confess—before one of the deacons and Preacher Yoder—the sin that had kept her beloved's memory alive.

The idea seemed preposterous. To think of revealing the lovely thing that had connected her with Dan. Why, it would amount to betrayal, pure and simple.

She stopped humming, considering her options. If she refused to confess privately, then a *sitting* confession would be required. She must wait until after the next preaching service and remain seated in the midst of the members-only meeting. There, just before the shared meal, she would have to declare—in front of them all—that she had sinned.

Perhaps, she mused as Molasses picked up his pace nearing home, in order to come clean before God and the church, she should admit that she'd sinned repeatedly through the years—even after her father had caught her strumming the guitar in the haymow as a teenager and forbidden her to play. Still, she wasn't certain she'd tell the part about the repeated transgressions. It was bad enough—her humming forbidden songs on the way home from a quilting bee held in her honor, where the women were surely making hers and the bishop's wedding quilt.

Katie sighed, her breath hanging in the frosty air. Either way, she would be expected to say that she was turning her back on her sin, and mean it with all her heart. But she would keep Dan out of it. No need to place blame on someone whose body lay cold in a watery grave. Of that she was certain.

The confessing, private or otherwise, would be hers and hers alone. She would have to ask the deacon or Preacher Yoder to forgive her. Either that or go before the entire church membership. Because if she didn't confess on her own, surely Dat would go to Bishop John himself and report her disobedience.

On the day of her baptism years before, Katie had agreed to this process of correction by the church. A time-honored ritual, it was the way things were done. Repentance must be a public affair. If she delayed the confession, then in order to be reclaimed, the bishop would come to her with another witness—possibly Preacher or one of the deacons. Matthew's gospel made the procedure very clear: " 'Take with thee one or two more, that in the mouth of two or three witnesses every word may be established.' "

Thinking of John being told, her face grew warm with embarrassment. She didn't want her future husband, bishop or not, caught in the middle. A decision would have to be reached on her own. She must give up her musical inclination and abandon her guitar, now hidden deep in the hayloft. She must give it all up, forsake the love-link between herself and Dan. Forever.

The dull clumping sound of the horse's hooves on the snow-packed road lulled Katie into a feeling of serenity despite the turmoil within. She could trust the old ways. Repenting would make things right. Somehow—though it galled her to think of it—she would have to do it. For her future standing with the People; for Bishop John's sake and his dear children, if for no other reason.

She leaned back against the hard leather buggy seat and sighed. If she'd known what to say to God, she would've said it then—spoken it right out into the icy air the way her mother's Mennonite cousins often did at family get-togethers. Though the social times were few and far between, Peter and Lydia Miller were the friendliest, nicest people anywhere. And they seemed comfortable talking to the Lord, during the table blessing or anytime. On the way home from such a gathering, Dat was always quick to point out to Katie and the boys how glib the Millers' approach to the Almighty seemed to be. Mam agreed.

Another gray buggy was approaching in the left lane, heading in the opposite direction, and she saw that it was Mattie Beiler's oldest granddaughter. Sarah was probably on her way to the quilting. They exchanged a wave and a smile.

Katie rode in silence for a while, then away in the distance, she heard her name. "Katie! Katie Lapp . . . is that you?"

Little Jacob Beiler had been playing with a rope and wagon by the side of the road, pretending to be the horse, it appeared. His deep-set, innocent blue eyes, framed by wheat-colored bangs peeking out from under his black hat, looked up expectantly as he ran and stood in the middle of the road, waving her down.

Here comes my new mamma! Jacob thought with delight. *Can't hardly wait 'til she comes to stay all the time. Hope she cooks good.*

Katie Lapp always sat up tall and straight in the carriage, holding the reins almost the way his own *Daed* did, her bright eyes shining. But she was different from all the other Plain women, no getting around it. Maybe it was her hair. It was sorta red-like. . . .

Jacob thought about it for a moment. Katie's parents had no such hair. And her brothers were blond headed—*like me*.

She was real pretty, too, and full of fun. And she hummed songs. He knew she did, because he'd heard her humming as she came up the lane—something he'd never heard his own mamma do. But then, he'd been just a baby when she died. Still, he was sure his Mam had never, ever done any singing except at preaching service. None of the other women he knew hummed or sang tunes. Katie was the first. He couldn't wait for her to be his real, come-to-live-with-him mamma. . . .

Katie slowed Molasses to a full stop. "Well, hullo there, Jacob. Are you needing a ride home?"

The four-year-old hopped into the carriage, hoisting his long rope and little wagon onto the floor. "Jah. Pa'll wonder what's become of me." He clapped his muffled hands together snug inside his gray woolen mittens and hugged himself against his heavy sack coat.

Katie wondered if his mother had made the mittens before she died. Or if they were hand-me-downs. With four older siblings, the latter was probably the case.

She covered his legs with her heavy lap robe, picked up the reins and gave them a plucky snap. "It's mighty cold for someone your size to be out playing, ain't?"

"Nah. Daed says I'm tougher'n most boys my age." His eyes sparkled as he spoke.

"I think he's probably right." She glanced down at the bundle of wiggles seated next to her.

"Daed's 'sposed to be right." A touch of healthy pride rang in his voice. "God makes bishops that-a-way, ya know."

Katie smiled. She wondered how it would be to hear John's youngest child chatter every day over little-boy things. Gladly, she'd listen to his babbling. Gladly . . . except . . .

Giving her love to Jacob and his brothers and sisters would mean giving up something besides her music. Last week, when she and John had gone into Lancaster to apply for their marriage license, she had scarcely been able to restrain herself from gawking at the colorful clothes the "English" women were wearing. Could she give up her seemingly endless desire to wonder, to dream, to imagine "what if"?

What if one day she dared to wear a pink or yellow dress; let her hair hang down her back in curls or pulled into beautiful braids? How would it feel? Would it change who she was inside?

Several months ago she'd discussed the topic discreetly with Mary, and her friend had said that it wasn't only the wearing of plain clothes that made them Amish, it was who they were. "It's what we believe," she'd stated with conviction. "We've been taught to 'make every effort to keep the unity of the Spirit through the bond of peace.' You know without me telling you what that means."

Katie knew. Her best friend was, of course, referring to the Scripture in Ephesians that taught uniformity of dress, transportation, and dwellings.

"What about the Englishers—what about *them*?" Katie had persisted.

Mary had become exasperated with her. "They don't know beans, that's what. They—those worldly moderns—keep on changing and changing their clothes and themselves 'til they don't know which end's up. They don't know who they are or whatnot all!"

Katie had listened, wincing inwardly at Mary's stern reminder. "Besides, it's much too late now to be questioning. You already took the vow for life." She'd paused for breath, pinning Katie with an unrelenting gaze. "Better never to take the vow . . . than to take it and break it."

Disobedience to the Ordnung brought dire consequences, Katie was well aware. The Ban and *Meinding* were a frightful, fearful part of the way things were—*das Alt Gebrauch*, the Old Way.

Without warning, Jacob jumped up in the buggy. "Oh, look, there's Daed!" He pointed toward a large, two-story white clapboard house.

Katie jerked her thoughts from their ramblings. How much of Jacob's boyish jabber had she missed? In her preoccupation, she'd nearly ridden right past the Beiler house!

Her guilt made her almost shy as she returned John's exuberant greeting from the high porch that spanned the entire front of the house. "Gut morning to ya, Katie!"

Katie reined Molasses in to the barnyard, where he halted on the frozen ridges made by the bishop's buggy wheels. As was the Old Order custom, John earned an income for his family from the land and the smithy, while serving God and community as a bishop. From the tracks, she could see that he'd already made several deliveries to customers this morning.

Katie let the reins rest loosely on her lap as she took in the snowy landscape extending far out and away from the road—John's long-ago inheritance from his father, now deceased.

It was a peaceful, sweeping spread of land, with three stately mulberry trees gracing the front yard. She could almost imagine the purple impatients hugging the base of the trees on warm days, and the lush flower beds, well tended in the spring and summer by bright-eyed Nancy, the bishop's eldest daughter. Hanging from one of the low-lying branches, left over from the children's play, was a thick, long rope with an icy double knot tied in its tail.

Jacob turned to speak to Katie, short puffs of breath gusting in the cold air with each word. "Did I hear ya singin' back there just now . . . on the road?"

His innocent question took her by surprise. "Singing?"

"Jah, coming up the lane . . . I thought I heard a song."

Katie's pulse quickened. In a few long strides, John would be at her side. She certainly didn't want to be discussing her songs with Jacob when the bishop came to greet her.

"Oh, probably just a little humming is all you heard." Maybe the youngster wouldn't press her about it.

But he wasn't about to give up. "One of the hymns from the *Ausbund*?" Jacob asked. "I like singin' in church, too. I like 'The Hymn of Praise.' "

Katie smiled nervously. Here was a boy who loved music almost as much as she did. She only hoped that he hadn't noticed how different her song was from the ones in the sixteenth-century hymnbook.

With eyes shining up at her, Jacob pleaded, "Will ya come for supper tonight? We can sing some hymns then, maybe."

"Well . . ." She hesitated, uncertain how to answer, since his father had not yet declared himself.

"Oh, please, Katie? I'll even help ya cook."

John stepped up, tousled the tumbled curls, and drew the boy close just as the older children appeared at the window, waving and smiling, looking like a row of stairsteps.

"Then we'll invite not only Katie but her whole family, too." John's obvious delight was touching. Even in his heavy black work coat and felt hat—his full beard indicating his widowed status—the bishop made a right impressive sight. "And speaking of invitations, all my relatives and friends have been notified about the wedding. I finished up just this morning," he added with an air of satisfaction.

"Mamma and I are all through, too," Katie said, relieved that the first awkward moments had passed. "All except her Mennonite cousins, the Millers. We'll probably send them a postcard."

"Well, if you need to borrow any of our dishes for the wedding feast, just let me know." He reached into the buggy and touched her hand. "Will you come for supper, then?"

She fought back her fears and put a cheerful smile on her face. "Jah, we'll come. I'll tell Mamma when I get home."

"Gut, then. We'll be looking for all of you later." His blue-gray gaze held Katie's with an intensity and longing she'd not witnessed before, not in John Beiler's eyes. And he leaned close and kissed her cheek.

Despite the wintry temperature, her face grew warm and she looked down, staring at the reins in her lap. The desire in his eyes made her uncomfortable . . . aware of her own innocence and her femininity. She'd witnessed this look passing between other couples, long before she was old enough to comprehend its meaning. But there was no mistaking it now. Without further word, she inched Molasses down the slippery slope toward the main road.

"*Da Herr sei mit du*—the Lord be with you," John called after her.

"And with you," she replied, willing the sting out of her cheeks.

CHAPTER SIX

❖   ❖   ❖

Rebecca was in the kitchen pulling on her boots when Katie arrived. "I'm awful late," she sputtered in a flurry to put on her shawl and black winter bonnet. "What's been keepin' you, anyway?"

"Oh, I rode down to Mary Stoltzfus's for a bit."

Rebecca's lips twitched with the beginning of a smile. "Mary's?"

Katie grinned. "Everyone's there waiting for you, Mamma. Ella Mae, some of the cousins . . . and probably lots more by now. Better hurry."

"Jah, I 'spect they're waiting, all right."

She bustled out with a wave and a gentle reminder to Katie to finish sewing her wedding dress.

It seemed odd not to be attending the quilting bee today. Quiltings were popular in winter, Katie knew. When the land was resting, the women of the church district often got together to do their needlework, waiting for the first spring thaw that would wake the good earth again.

Katie could almost hear the chatter and laughter as she thought about the frolic and the quilt they'd be finishing by sometime around dark tonight. Some of the women would probably mention how lonely poor Bishop John had been

75

these past years since his first wife went to Glory, and how *wonderful-gut* it was that Katie had accepted his proposal. Most likely, they'd be passing on a bit of gossip, too, from time to time. And always there would be Mam's tales.

Katie wondered which story it might be today as she hurried to find her sewing basket. With the wedding only a few days away, she'd better listen to her mamma and finish up her wedding dress. She sank down into a rocker and was nearly halfway around the hem when she remembered Bishop John's invitation for supper. She'd forgotten to tell her mother.

And she'd forgotten something else. Mam would be happy to hear that she'd abandoned her doubts and decided to go ahead and marry John, music or no music. All around, it was the best thing. The *right* thing, as Mary would say.

Still, in spite of everything, Katie struggled with a restive feeling. She picked up her sewing and headed through the kitchen to the long, rectangular-shaped front room, where they gathered for Sunday preaching when it was their turn to host the meeting. Had she not been marrying a widower, her wedding night might have been spent here in this very house. As it was, her first night as John Beiler's wife would be spent at his place, a spacious farmhouse brimming with children. She would sleep next to him in the bed he had shared with his first wife.

Brushing tentative thoughts aside, Katie hurried to the doorway connecting the stone house with a smaller addition—the white clapboard house her ancestors had built many years ago. With both sets of grandparents now deceased, the *Dawdi Haus* remained vacant. But someday, when her father was too old to work the land, it would become her parents' home. Then Benjamin, the youngest son, would inherit the main house and forty-five acres of fertile farmland—passing the family homestead from one generation to the next.

Katie opened the door and surveyed the living room of the smaller house. Sparse furnishings had been left just as they were when her maternal grandparents lived here—matching hickory rockers with homemade padding on the seats, a drop-leaf pine table near the window, and a tall pine corner cupboard. Colorful rag rugs covered the floor, but the walls were void of pictures except for a lone, outdated scenic calendar hanging in the kitchen.

Katie closed the door behind her and entered the Dawdi Haus, wandering through the unheated rooms, wishing *Dawdi* David and *Mammi* Essie were alive to witness her marriage. She imagined them sharing in the joy and the preparation of the community ritual, knowing they would have delighted in becoming instant step-great-grandparents to five young children.

Katie sat down in Mammi's rocker, the unhemmed wedding dress still in her hands. She leaned back against the wooden slats and shivered. It was much too cold to sit here and sew, yet she remained seated, recalling a childhood memory involving her mamma's mother, Essie King—twin sister to Ella Mae Zook, the Wise Woman.

Mammi Essie had caught young Katie humming a tune, just as Jacob Beiler had earlier today. One of those fast, made-up tunes—way back when Katie was but a schoolgirl, around first or second grade. She couldn't remember which grade exactly, but it really didn't matter. The memory that stuck in Katie's mind was what Mammi Essie had said when she looked up from snapping peas.

"Lord have mercy—you're like no little girl I ever knowed! Like no other."

At the time, it seemed like a reproach—the way the words slipped off her wrinkled lips and stung the childish heart. Condemning words, they were, and Katie had blushed, feeling ashamed.

Yet, as she thought back to the incident in their backyard, where honeysuckle perfume hung in the air and bees buzzed messages back and forth, it seemed that Mammi Essie was making more than a verbal rebuke. Had her grandmother sensed a streak of stubborn individualism? Such a thing was strongly discouraged; Katie knew that. By the time you were three, the molding of an obedient Amish child was supposed to be evident. That is, if the parents had done a thorough job of teaching the ways of *Gelassenheit,* total submission to the community and its church leaders.

Katie had overheard her grandmother talking with some of the other womenfolk at a quilting frolic not long after. "Rebecca gives the girl a little too much leeway, if you ask me. But then little Katie's the only girl child—and the last 'un at that, it appears."

Leaning down, Katie placed her sewing basket on the floor beside the rocker. Silently, she crossed the room to inspect a deep purple and magenta afghan on the back of the davenport. She lifted the crocheted afghan and held it, feeling the rough texture in her hands.

"Mammi Essie knew I was different," Katie said aloud. "And she knew it had nothing to do with Mam's doting on me—nothing like that. Mammi knew there was something inside me . . . something longing for a way to let the music out."

There were no tears as Katie refolded Essie's afghan. Her Mammi had died suspecting the truth—that the music had been a divine gift within Katie. God, the Creator of all things, had created her to make music. It wasn't Katie's doing at all.

Still, no other living person truly understood. Not even Mary Stoltzfus. Only one had fully understood and had loved her anyway, and he was dead. Maybe it was because Daniel Fisher had shared the same secret struggle, the same eagerness to express the music within. While everyone around them seemed to be losing themselves—blending together like the hidden stitches of a quilt—Katie and Daniel had been trying to *find* themselves.

Looking back, Katie wondered why she hadn't been stronger in her stand, hadn't at least tried to follow the church rules. But, no, she'd gone right along with Dan's suggestion that they write out their songs. He'd shown her how to use the treble clef to sketch in the melody lines, notating the guitar chords with letter symbols.

Why hadn't she spoken up? Had she been too weak in spirit at seventeen to remind him of what the church required of them? Too much in love with the boy with blueberry eyes?

Trembling with cold, she heard a faint sound of voices through the wall. The men were back inside, no doubt warming themselves by the stove. They'd been out all morning—removing loose stones from the fields—and would most likely welcome some black coffee before taking the cab wagon down the road to a farm sale.

Katie hoped her father had not already summoned the preacher for a private confession. Reluctantly, she picked up her wedding dress and the basket with her needle, thread, and scissors, and opened the door leading from Mammi Essie's former home. Then she trudged into the front room, toward the toasty kitchen awaiting her on the other side of the stone house.

❖   ❖   ❖

"Ach, what a beautiful quilt this'll be," Rebecca said, hurrying to find her place at the large frame in the Stoltzfus house. She pulled out the only vacant chair remaining and sat down with a sigh. She waited a moment to catch her breath, then picked up the needle.

"A warm quilt'll come in mighty handy on such cold

nights, jah?" Ella Mae asked in a near whisper.

Rebecca glanced over at her petite aunt. Lately, the old woman's bouts with laryngitis seemed to linger longer and longer. But at her age, it was a wonder she continued to carry on as she did—attending quiltings and rug braidings, tending her herb garden, having the women in for pie occasionally, and even assisting her middle-aged daughter, Mattie Beiler, with her midwifery duties. Not all the young wives went to outspoken Mattie to have her "catch" their babies, but a good majority did.

"Ain't it lovely . . . our Katie getting married to Bishop Beiler?" Mary Stoltzfus remarked, speaking as only a best friend could. She tied off an intricate row of stitches and snipped the thread free.

"It's such a long time for the bishop to be without a wife—too long—raising all them little ones by himself," Mary's mother commented.

Rebecca agreed, thinking it would soon be time for her to entertain the quilters with one of her best stories. She'd told them all—the same tales over and over—so often that the women knew them by heart. But still they called for more. Did they believe the stories . . . that they were absolutely true?

She glanced again at dear Ella Mae, the Wise Woman. Through the years, the slight woman had been found to be trustworthy with shared confidences, as well as wise in counsel. Rebecca noticed that her wispy white hair nearly matched the kapp perched on her head till a body couldn't tell where one left off and the other began. The woman looked downright angelic—the way the light streamed in from the window. And today, for some reason, she looked more like Rebecca's own mother, Essie King, than she'd remembered. Being her mother's twin, Ella Mae had every right to look like Essie, of course, but Rebecca had forgotten how closely they resembled each other until now. Maybe it was the way the brightness shone through the curtainless windows, highlighting her aunt's pleasant, dimpled face and high forehead. Maybe it was the way Ella Mae sat with back erect, defying her eighty years.

Rebecca had always been interested in searching out the physical characteristics in families—especially the similarities between mothers and daughters, sisters and brothers. She hadn't meant to stare, but evidently she was staring now, because Ella Mae's wide hazel-gold eyes met hers.

"Something on your mind?" The hoarse voice penetrated Rebecca's thoughts.

"Oh, nothing . . . nothing a'tall. You just look . . . well, so lovely." Rebecca's words surprised even herself. She wasn't given to complimenting folk; it was not the way of the People.

Ella Mae was silent. To acknowledge such a remark would be to imitate the ways of the English.

"In fact, you're looking near like an angel today," Rebecca blurted out, blushing furiously.

Ten other heads jerked up at the mention of a heavenly messenger. Ella Mae chuckled demurely but said nothing.

If they could have read Rebecca's mind, they would know that she yearned for a resemblance between herself and her auburn-haired daughter—the same as others in this room. These family traits were like the very threads the women stitched into the fabric of Katie's quilt—joining, attaching . . . linking them one to another.

"The Samuel Lapp family is expanding by six more come next week," Mary Stoltzfus said, changing the subject.

"A gut thing, jah?" There was a twinge of doubt in Ella Mae's whispery voice, as though she suspected something amiss.

"Ach, we all know how ferhoodled Katie gets before time to do something awful important," Mattie Beiler cut in. "But my brother-in-law, the bishop, is a patient, kind

81

man—no question about it. He'll be gut for her."

Hearing Bishop John referred to as a patient man was not surprising to Rebecca. As long as she'd known him, she had felt at ease around him. He ran his farm well—working long hours every day—as well as handling much of the blacksmithing in and around Hickory Hollow. And he managed his children soundly, with help from young John—nicknamed "Hickory John" to distinguish him from his father—and Nancy, the oldest daughter, always admonishing the youngsters in the fear of the Lord.

But what had Rachel just said about Katie—that she got herself ferhoodled sometimes? "My daughter does no such a thing," Rebecca spoke up.

"But she does, and you know it," Mattie retorted.

Rebecca's eyes shot blazing darts across the quilt frame. "I'd be obliged if you'd not speak about my Katie that way."

A familiar look of disgust, accompanied by a snort, was Mattie's answer. The rift between the two women remained strong. Twenty-two years strong.

Rebecca was certain she knew what her cousin was thinking. Mattie figured she'd been deliberately snubbed on the day of Katie's birth. Instead of calling for the local midwife, Rebecca had gone to Lancaster General to have her premature baby. She'd let an *English* doctor catch her baby.

"Well, Katie and I'll be sisters-in-law very soon," Mattie managed to say. "I couldn't be saying nothing but gut things about her."

But in Rebecca's heart, she knew better. Here sat the very woman who'd made a big fuss over the plans for Daniel Fisher's graveside service, them having no body to bury and all. Even with Katie crying and pleading, Mattie and her husband, David, had gone to the Fishers and persuaded them to contact the bishop.

"Burying an empty coffin just ain't never done," David Beiler had insisted.

So Katie had visited the Fishers herself, begging them at least to have a simple burial service for their son—a quiet gathering of some kind, perhaps a prayer and a spoken hymn. And a wooden grave marker.

Sooner or later, Rebecca knew she'd have to forgive her cousin for the added grief Mattie had caused Katie. But not now. She pursed her lips and kept her eyes on her work—sewing her tiny running stitches into the wedding quilt.

It was a good thing Mary Stoltzfus spoke up about that time, asking Rebecca for a story . . . and the Telling began.

The women were soon responding with their usual lighthearted laughter. Everyone but Mattie.

And sensing hostility brewing, Rebecca was cautious today, avoiding any mention of her boys' childhood escapades . . . or of Katie's homecoming. It wouldn't be wise. Not wise at all. Not with Mattie Beiler acting up the way she was.

◈   ◈   ◈

Katie was grateful. Neither the deacon nor Preacher Yoder were waiting in the kitchen for her when she arrived from the Dawdi Haus.

Quickly, she made hot coffee and warmed up a fat, juicy jelly roll each for Dat and her brothers. But the minute he and the boys left for the farm sale, Katie headed for the barn. With her heart hammering and long skirt flying, she made her way through the barn and up the ladder to the hayloft.

The day was not as sharply cold as it had been for the past few weeks. Not a single cloud in sight and a powerful-good sun shining through the rafters. The perfect time to pull the guitar out of hiding. She found it under the old hay, back in the west corner near one of the hay bins.

Lovingly, she brushed the fine gray dust off the case with her wool shawl. She opened the case, lifted out the instrument, and cradled it under her right arm. Without hesitation, she found the frets and began to tune. Might be the last time for a long time—or maybe forever.

She sang several of Dan's songs first, then her own. She saved for last the love song they'd written together, knowing that it wouldn't matter really how many times she sinned by singing them between now and the confession she must give. Feeling the old rebellion rise up, she willfully disobeyed and played it again. And again.

While she played, she remembered. . . .

The sun glinted off the back of Daniel's sleek horse as the steed, groomed to perfection, pulled the brand-new open buggy down the road toward Weaver's Creek. His arm brushed against Katie's, sending tingling sensations up her spine. When he took the curve too fast, she leaned hard against him, making him chuckle. Then he put his left arm around her, holding the reins with his right hand and keeping his eyes on the road ahead.

"No matter what happens," he said, "remember I love you, Katie Lapp."

Her heart thrilled to his words, and she listened carefully to the echoes in her mind. She'd never felt so cherished, so safe.

They rode along in silence a bit farther. Then, quite unexpectedly, he reined in his horse and, in broad daylight, turned to look her in the face. She saw the longing in his shining blueberry eyes, the quiver in his lip.

"You love me, too, don't you?" he asked gently, holding her hands in both of his.

Katie glanced around. "Maybe we shouldn't be—"

"I want you with me, Katie, always," he whispered in her ear, and the worries about being seen like this skittered fast away.

She snuggled against his chest and whispered back, "I've

loved you since I was a little girl. Didn't you know?" She felt soft laughter ripple through him as she relaxed in his arms.

"You're *still* a girl."

She pulled away and looked him square in the face. "I'm old enough to go to Singing, and don't you forget!"

He leaped out of the buggy and ran around to stand on the left side, offering first his hand, then disbanding with chivalry and opening his arms wide to her. Not thinking—nor caring—what would happen if they were seen doing such a thing, Katie hopped down, letting him catch her and hold her.

He didn't let her go until he'd cupped her face in his hands and tilted it to meet his gaze. "You're the most beautiful creature on this wide earth, and I want us to get married tomorrow."

Katie sighed, understanding. "I'll grow up quick," she promised. "You'll see."

His face inched closer, and wistfully he gazed at her lips. "Oh, Katie, whatever happens . . ."

She didn't hear the rest. Dan's words were lost as he drew her close. His lips touched hers, lightly at first, then pressing ever so sweetly.

It seemed to her that he was never going to stop kissing her, and she wondered if she shouldn't be the one to do the stopping, because now her head was spinning and she'd never felt so wobbly in her knees before.

"Oh my," she finally said, pulling back and smiling up at him.

When Dan reached for her again, she purposely turned and looked at the old covered bridge up ahead. Some people called them "kissing bridges," but that wasn't why she wanted to go there. She needed some air—a bit of distance between herself and Dan. "Maybe a walk would do us good," she suggested.

"Jah, let's walk." He tied the horse to an old tree stump and held out his hand to her. "Did I offend you just now?" he asked as they made their way down the old dirt lane.

"No . . . no," she said softly.

At the old bridge, they turned away from the road and headed down the banks of Weaver's Creek. "Hold on now," he said. "I won't let you fall."

"I know you won't." She smiled, eager to trust this boy with the disturbing good looks, who stood out in the Amish community for his bright spirit.

"I've never been lip-kissed before," Katie admitted as they stepped barefoot across the creek, one stone at a time, finally reaching the huge boulder in the middle of the rushing water.

"Maybe it's time I caught you up . . . on kissing, that is." Daniel grinned.

"You been kissing for a while?" She had to know, even though she wondered if it was right to be asking.

"Not really, not like . . . back there."

"A peck then?"

"The smallest peck . . . and on the cheek."

Again, she listened to his words, studying his face. Mary Stoltzfus had always said that if you watched a fella's face when he talked, you could see if he was telling the truth.

So what did he mean—"a peck on the cheek"? Who, but his mother or sisters, would he kiss that way?

"You have to tell me who you kissed," Katie said, surprised at her own bold curiosity.

"I have to?" His eyes twinkled. "Well, ain't *you* the bossy one!"

She didn't mind the name-calling. Not with Daniel doing it. He could call her most anything he pleased, if he only told her the truth about whoever it was he'd pecked on the cheek.

She sat there with her long green dress draped over her

knees, hugging her legs as she balanced herself on the boulder next to him. "I'm waiting. . . ."

To that, he burst out laughing. "It was a little baby. I was
two years old and she . . . well, *you* were just this big." He
measured the space with his hands.

"Me? You kissed *me* when I was a baby?"

"Jah, when Mamma went to visit ya for the first time.
Your Mam's Mennonite cousin came, too. She brought flowers in a vase, from her garden."

Katie threw back her head, a ripple of laughter startling
a bird on a branch overhanging the creek. "People don't remember things like that so long ago. How could *you?*"

"Maybe it's because Mamma talked about it so much. It
was a big day—your coming into the world, Katie. Your
Mam was happy beyond words, finally getting her first
daughter." He paused, then took up again. "Might be I just
think I remember that day—hearing about it so many times
and all." He tossed a stick into the creek, and they watched
it float downstream and disappear under the bridge.

Dan slipped his arm around her waist, and the two of
them sat quietly, lost in their own world. "Just tiny . . .
brand-new, you were," he whispered. "So pretty—even back
then."

She turned to look at him, resplendent in the glow of
the sun's reflection, slanting off the creek.

"Your Mam had just come home from the hospital, and
there you were—all pink and pretty." A chuckle broke
through. "Guess I just couldn't help myself."

"The hospital?" Katie was puzzled. "Did you say the
hospital?"

"Jah."

"But I thought everyone around here had the midwife—
Mamma's first cousin, Mattie."

Dan shrugged. "Sometimes when there's a problem,
even the Amish use the English doctors."

"Oh." Katie pondered the thought. She'd never heard that explanation. She would be speaking to her mother about it later. But for now, it seemed Dan had other things on his mind, starting with the song he wanted to write. He pulled a sheet of staff paper out of his pocket.

"What's that?"

He pointed out the lines and spaces, and within twenty minutes or so, they'd written their love song. It seemed that even the birds joined in on the chorus, and the gurgling brook carried the melody all the way to the bridge . . . and beyond.

Katie couldn't recall now how many times they had sung the song that afternoon. But each time, Dan would gaze deep into her eyes and pledge his love—it was that kind of song.

She now remembered one thing, though, although the notion hadn't once crossed her mind that enchanted afternoon five years ago. She remembered his words. His strangely prophetic words. *No matter what happens . . .*

He'd said it at least twice that joyous day, the day he'd declared his love. What did it mean?

There'd been no apprehension in his face, no hint that he sensed what was coming. Yet, thinking back, Katie wondered. Had he known somehow that he would die . . . exactly one week later?

Some folks seemed to be able to predict such things with a kind of inner knowing. Ella Mae had told her so. She was chock-full of wisdom, that woman. Everyone knew it. Hickory Hollow was populated with Plain folk who'd gone to confide in Ella Mae Zook at one time or another.

After Dan's death, Katie, too, had gone to her great-aunt—not to share secrets, but out of desperation. At the time, she'd been surprised to hear such a thing. Yet looking back, it was comforting to know that just possibly her darling Daniel had not been completely startled by his own untimely death.

Her fingers having grown numb from the strumming and the cold, Katie placed the guitar back in its case. Slowly, she closed the lid. She'd never play again.

She would marry John Beiler come next Thursday. Hard as it would be, she must.

CHAPTER SEVEN

❖ ❖ ❖

Supper at John Beiler's house was served promptly at five-thirty. Katie knew that to be so. The bishop kept to a strict schedule, and his household hummed with the precision of a well-oiled machine.

The table was set for eleven people. Nancy and her younger sister, Susie, age six, carried the serving bowls to the table and set them in front of their father's plate.

When Katie offered to help, Jacob hopped off the bench and stopped her. "This is our doin's tonight," he said. And by that, she knew that the children—without the usual assistance from two helpful aunts—had fried up the chicken dinner, complete with homemade bread and jam, macaroni, green beans, corn, chow-chow, applesauce, and banana nut bread.

"Find anything useful up at Noah's sale today?" John asked Samuel after the silent prayer.

"Oh, not much, really. Nothing we needed."

"We saw some nice-looking hickory rockers, matchin' ones," Hickory John spoke up. "But we figured we wouldn't be needing 'em anytime soon." He cast Katie a sidelong glance through long lashes framing clear blue eyes.

Wondering if he were thinking of future Beiler babies,

91

she felt her cheeks grow warm. His mamma's rockers would have to do when that time came, she thought, half wishing she were bringing her own furnishings—along with her hope chest linens—to this house. Then she felt guilty for her ingratitude. Wasn't it enough that someone wanted to marry her?

Surely that was what Mam was thinking this very minute over there at the opposite end of the supper table—that Katie shouldn't be fussing about not bringing her own dowry to this marriage. That she shouldn't be fussing about anything at all. She sighed and took another bite of the delicious banana bread.

After the meal, Jacob startled her by asking, "Now will ya sing for us?"

For a breathless moment, Katie felt as if her heart would stop.

Nancy grinned, egging her on. "Jacob says you have a real nice singin' voice."

The others were waiting for her answer, while Dat glared. "Maybe we could all sing something together," she managed. "I could lead out on 'Sweet Hour of Prayer.'"

Dat frowned and shook his head. "Too fast."

She wasn't surprised to hear that opinion coming from her father. Samuel Lapp preferred the slow tunes in the *Ausbund*. But Katie hadn't expected to be setting the pitch and singing the first syllable of each line of those old, old hymns tonight the way the *Vorsinger*—song leader—did for the congregation at Sunday preaching.

The atmosphere was taut with tension. Katie prayed silently with unorthodox fervor, *Please, Lord, let Jacob keep still about what he heard today. Don't let Dat mention my sinning over the music. . . .* Above all, she was hoping that the others wouldn't notice her heart hammering wildly beneath the green serge of her dress.

Bishop John came to her defense. "Oh, I don't think

Katie has to lead out in singing just now." The slight reprimand in his tone sent Jacob's small shoulders drooping, but
the boy said nothing.

All five children, including mischievous Levi, age eight,
sat straight and still as fence posts on the bench across from
Katie—looking a little disappointed.

Katie thought the matter was at an end when Jacob
seemed to take on a burst of fresh enthusiasm. "But, Daed,"
he persisted, "couldn't she just sing the tune I heard her
hummin' today on the road?"

John's eyes widened, but before he could respond,
Samuel intervened. "No, Jacob, she won't be singin' tonight—and that's that."

Katie felt Dat's hard gaze on her.

When John shooed his children away from the table as
though they were a flock of chickens, Katie welcomed the
opportunity to escape and left the table to help with the
dishes. She was worried, though. What if Dat brought
up the subject of her music with the bishop, her willful
sinning?

So terrified was she that she did her best to eavesdrop
on their conversation, much to the dismay of Jacob and
Susie, who were trying to engage her in lively dialogue as
she stood in front of the sink, elbow deep in foamy suds.

"I can hardly wait for you to come be our Mam," the
little boy was saying.

"Me too." Susie's blue eyes were wide and bright.

Nancy stood near the sink, ready to dry the first cup. "*All*
of us can hardly wait," she added in her soft voice.

Katie gave a wry smile. "Well, you'll have to be patient
with me, jah? I've never been a mamma before."

Nancy giggled. "We'll be patient, all right. Just havin'
you here all the time will be wonderful-gut."

"And we can even teach ya—'bout being a mamma, I
mean," little Jacob prattled on.

93

The poor little things must be lonely, Katie decided. *They seem so eager for their father to remarry*. Well, no doubt they needed a mother. Someone to share their chatter after the school day. Someone to teach the girls how to can and preserve the bountiful harvests yielded by the land. Someone to be a role model, passing on the traditions of the People.

Nancy had six or seven more years before she'd come into her "running-around" years—*Rumspringa*—when Amish teenagers were allowed to see what life was like on the outside. During her Rumspringa, she'd also be meeting Plain boys at Singing every other Sunday night and ultimately having to decide between the world and the church.

Jacob, on the other hand, had many more years at home to be loved and nurtured and shaped. When Katie looked into those innocent blue eyes and heard his husky little-boy voice, she felt a strong tug. Already there was a soft spot in her heart for this child . . . for all the Beiler children.

Levi—a rascally glint in his eye—handed the dishes to Nancy without a word. He stared at Katie as she emptied the dishwater and dried off the counter. What thoughts were swirling around in his head? Levi had sat too still, too quiet throughout the entire meal, never once speaking. Now, it seemed as though there was something stirring inside him. Something he was itching to say.

Katie decided to make it easy for him. "You're a right tall boy, nearly as tall as your big brother," she said with a smile.

The smile was not returned.

While she was fumbling for another topic of conversation, Nancy stepped in to ease the strain. "Levi never says much," she volunteered.

"I say what I need to say."

There was a chorus of chuckles from the other children at their brother's abrupt announcement. Then Jacob began pulling on Katie's apron, tugging her over to the rocking chair near the woodstove. "Will ya play me a game?"

Nancy's eyes lit up. "Jah! Checkers it will be!"

The others—Hickory John, Susie, and Jacob—sat cross-legged on the linoleum floor with the identical checkered pattern as Rebecca Lapp's kitchen. Most of the kitchens around Hickory Hollow looked alike—same black wood-stove in the center, same gold-flecked countertops, same checkered linoleum. A gas lamp hung over the long table, and a tall corner cupboard stored books and odds and ends. On the far wall, near the steps leading to the cold cellar, was a picture calendar with farmland scenes. But no other ornaments decorated the walls.

Levi went to sit near the bishop, who was still talking with Katie's parents and brothers at the table. Twice Katie caught the boy glancing over at her playing with the other children. Should she invite him to join them?

Uncertain as to the approach she should take, Katie went on with the game. For a moment, she wished for Mary Stoltzfus. Mary would know just what to do to win over a boy like Levi Beiler.

"Crown my king!" Jacob ordered as his black playing piece made it through the maze of Katie's red ones.

"Already?" she said, suddenly aware that the child had been paying closer attention than she.

An hour later, when the time came for the Lapps' departure, each of the children gave Katie a hug. All but Levi, who stood aloof beside the bishop.

"I'll see you again soon," Katie called to Levi, deliberately singling him out.

The boy's cold-eyed stare met hers. There was something unsettling in his face. What was wrong?

On the ride home, Katie cringed when Samuel brought

up the music and the fact that little Jacob had heard her humming. "Were you singin' those songs of yours right out in the open for all the world to hear?" he demanded.

"Jah, Dat . . . I was." Katie's voice, from her buggy seat behind her parents, was subdued.

"That's no example to set for a young boy and his brothers and sisters, now is it?"

She had no answer. So this was how Levi Beiler must have felt tonight. As if he was cornered, with no way out.

She could hear Dat mumbling something to Mam, then his angry words burst out. "There's just not many left around these parts who live the way the Lord God intended from the beginning."

An uncomfortable silence followed, and Katie could feel the pull of the powerful undertow. She had precious little time to apologize.

When she did not reply, Samuel spoke again. "I have no choice, daughter. I'll be speakin' to Bishop John first thing tomorrow."

"But Dat, I—"

"Save your arguments. It's too late," he said with finality. In that dreadful monotone her father assumed for solemn occasions, he began to recite the Scripture about the bitter and sweet water. Eli and Benjamin sat soberly on either side of her, listening.

To say she was sorry would be a lie. Katie wished she could ask for forgiveness and mean it sincerely, but how could she? The songs she'd hummed and played today had marked the end of her singleness. She had celebrated her memories of Daniel Fisher. There on the road and later in the barn, she had reveled in the last bright days spent with her love. And when the song was done and the guitar put away, she had decided to turn her back on the music, once and for all. Yet, in all of it, she knew she had defied Dat, had knowingly and willfully partaken of one last forbidden expression.

"It would be displeasing to the Lord if I said nothin' to Preacher Yoder or Bishop John." Her father's righteous indignation seeped into the damp darkness. So heavy and oppressive was it that Katie felt it close in around her, suffocating her.

Rebecca was weeping now in the front seat as the horse pulled the carriage down Hickory Lane toward the sandstone farmhouse. Katie didn't have to see Dat's face to know what he must be feeling. Still, even as stern and devout as her father was, surely he was also torn between doing God's bidding and altering his only daughter's future.

❖ ❖ ❖

John Beiler read his children an evening prayer from the standard prayer book, *Christenpflicht*, before heading upstairs to his bedroom. It had been a long day, but an even longer night stretched ahead of him.

How fetching Katie is, he thought, settling down under the covers and quilts. *So kind and cheerful. . . . No wonder my children already love her.*

As for himself, he'd admired Katie Lapp from the day he'd become aware she'd grown into a young woman. From the day she'd knelt before him there in Preacher Yoder's barn in front of all the People. As the presiding elder, it had been his duty to administer the rites as the tin cup spilled baptismal water over her head and down her face. But he'd not been prepared for the silky feel of her auburn hair beneath his fingers.

Waiting for Katie to reach marrying age had not been easy for a man whose children needed a mother and whose own bed had been long empty. More than three years he had waited. And soon, very soon, she would belong to him.

He yawned and stretched, then let his tired body relax, eager for their first night of intimacy, when he would gather his new bride into his arms here in this very bed—hold her tenderly and demonstrate his love for her. Of course, a woman's beauty was not the main consideration when taking a mate, but when a woman was as pretty as Katie Lapp, the spark was stronger. Still, it was far more important that Katie create connections with the People as a married woman. Together, they would start their wedded life, taking on the added responsibilities of a bishop and his wife.

He yawned again and was dozing off to sleep when he heard the floor creak. In the inky darkness, he felt a presence. Which one of his children was out of bed?

"Daed," whispered his second son, "are you awake still?"

John sat up. "Come on in, Levi."

Levi, carrying an oil lamp, approached the bed.

John saw the look of hesitancy on the boy's face. "What is it? Can't you sleep?"

"I have to tell ya something, Daed," Levi said softly. "I can't put it out of my mind."

"Put what out of your mind?"

"Today after school, someone . . . a stranger . . . stopped by the house."

"Go on."

"A lady came up to the front porch—an Englisher. I went to the door . . . that's when I saw her face." His sleepy eyes were wide now with the telling. "She was askin' for directions 'cause she'd gotten lost or something."

"Well, I hope you helped her out."

Levi nodded. "I tried to tell her how to find her way back to the main road. She seemed ferhoodled some, said she'd looked and looked but couldn't find Hickory Hollow on the map, nohow."

John chuckled. "Hickory Hollow was never meant for outsiders. What was she doin' out here, anyway?"

Levi sobered. "Said she was tryin' to find someone's friend . . . a woman in her early twenties. Didn't know the exact name."

John was as puzzled as his son. "Mighty strange . . . an English woman away out here. And looking for the Hollow on her map, you say?" He squinted at the boy, who was breathing hard. "What's got you so worried?"

Levi shrugged. "Just curious, I guess."

"Why's that?"

"'Cause she had hair like I ain't never seen before . . .'cept for Katie's."

John suppressed a chuckle. Wouldn't do to be thought mocking his shy son. "Lots of folks have red hair."

"Not around here."

The boy was dead serious, and because Levi rarely spoke, John knew this information was more than a little troublesome. "Why don't you head on back to bed. We'll talk more tomorrow, jah?"

"Jah . . . good night, Daed."

"Good night, son."

When the boy was gone, John reached for the quilt and drew it up under his bushy beard. He reflected on Levi's words. 'Twas a curious thing. Why would an Englisher say she was searching for a Plain friend, yet be way off course? Seemed to be some kind of contradiction.

The more he thought on it, the more John realized that the woman might've been telling the truth. Maybe the stranger had simply lost her way on the winding paths off the main road. But even as he tossed about, trying to find a comfortable spot in his bed, John pondered the matter. He did not rest easy that night.

❂ ❂ ❂

In another Beiler home, Ella Mae sat quietly as Mattie's husband read from the German Bible. A familiar passage from Exodus, chapter twenty—the first of the Ten Commandments: " 'Thou shalt have no other gods before me,' " David Beiler read. " 'Thou shalt not make unto thee any graven image, or any likeness of anything that is in heaven above, or that is in the earth beneath, or that is in the water under the earth: Thou shalt not bow down thyself to them, nor serve them; for I the Lord thy God am a jealous God, visiting the iniquity of the fathers upon the children unto the third and fourth generation of them that hate me; And shewing mercy unto thousands of them that love me, and keep my commandments.' "

Ella Mae folded her arthritic hands for the German prayer, but long afterward, her thoughts were on Rebecca Lapp and the peculiar way she'd acted at the quilting. Rebecca had gawked at her, calling her "lovely" and "near like an angel," for goodness sake. What foolishness! And she'd kept staring with those clouded eyes. Worry-filled eyes.

Something about it didn't add up, not the way Ella Mae knew her niece inside out—almost as well as a woman knew her own child. After all, a twin sister's offspring had to be linked more closely to yourself, or so she'd always thought. And if that wasn't true, then why did Rebecca Lapp resemble Ella Mae herself almost as much as Mattie did?

The old woman sighed. What had gotten into Rebecca today, anyway? Her mind wandered. And why was it that Rebecca's daughter, young Katie, had not inherited a single one of their closely linked twin genes? At least, not so's a body could tell it. Where was the broomstick hair and the hazel eyes—their family mark? Or the high forehead and the deep dimples?

Ella Mae had never been one to worry her head over silly goings-on. She was the sensible one people brought their worries to—not the other way around. Still, she thought it mighty peculiar how Katie's reddish hair had shown up out of nowhere. Not even as far back as great-great-Grandmammi Yoder had there been a speck of red hair. Ella Mae knew that for a fact. Even though there were no photographs to prove it, the People of Hickory Hollow passed on the stories of their kin, knew what they'd looked like—right down to the last eyelash.

Not only that, she'd secretly traced the family line back several generations on Samuel's side—to the man who'd built one of the best-looking sandstone homes in all of Lancaster County. Samuel Lapp's ancestor, Joseph Lapp.

Later, after the family had gone to bed, Ella Mae closed the door between Mattie and David's big farmhouse and her smaller attached Dawdi Haus. She sat in her tiny front room, rocking and thinking about the events of the day, then snuffed out the only lantern in the room.

How long she sat there in the darkness, she did not know. But around the time the moon started its climb into the sky, through the wide branches of the old elm tree on the east side of her house—about then—she heard the distinct sound of a car motor out front. Turning, she peered out the curtainless window. The pane was a bit frosty, but clear enough to see a long black car creeping down Hickory Lane. The closer it came, the better she could make out its front bumper and chrome-trimmed doors.

Seconds later, the fancy car—a lim-ou-sine, she recollected—came to a gentle stop across the road from the house. The lone yard light cast an eerie glow over the streamlined chassis.

Ella Mae abandoned her rocking chair to stand in front of the living room windows, staring out at the unusual sight. Then, quite surprisingly, the window glided down on the passenger's side. A woman's face stared out into the semidarkness. Had it not been for the full moon, Ella Mae might have missed seeing the white fur hat slip back away from the woman's face, revealing a billowy cloud of hair. Such a splendid burnt red it was that instantly she thought of her grand-niece Katie.

"My, oh my," she whispered into the darkness. "Who is *this*?"

She inched closer to the window, knowing she could not be seen from the road. As she watched, a light came on inside the car. A man, dressed all in black and wearing an odd, beaked hat, unfolded a large paper. The woman and her driver bent over to study what must be some kind of map, best Ella Mae could make out.

"Strange," she said to herself. "Imagine bein' lost on a wintry night like this." If she hadn't been feeling her age tonight—what with the cold weather and all—she might've put on her warmest shawl and snow boots and tromped outside to help. Not wanting to risk a fall on the ice, though, she waited and watched from inside.

Soon, the English car rolled down the lane, and Ella Mae turned away from the window and headed for bed.

❖   ❖   ❖

There were two large flashlights in Benjamin Lapp's open buggy. Katie found them quickly and took one along with her. She stopped by Satin Boy's stall just long enough to whisper to him, "I won't be gone long," then quietly hitched up Molasses to the family carriage. Dat and Mam surely were asleep by now—Eli and Benjamin, too.

The wind was stiff and cold as she rode to Mary's house. Once there, she shone her brother's powerful flashlight up at Mary's bedroom window, grinning to herself. Her friend would probably think a young man was outside, wanting to propose marriage. That's how it was done in Hickory Hol-

low. The boy waited till he was sure—or hoped, at least—
that the girl's parents were soundly sleeping. Then he'd park
his open courting buggy out by the road, run to the house
on tiptoe, and shine the light up to his sweetheart's bedroom window until she opened it to tell him she'd meet him
downstairs.

When the window opened, Mary peeked out. "I gave up
on you ever coming over and went to bed," she began apol-
ogetically, "but come on up. The door's unlocked."

"Did you think this was your night?" Katie teased as
Mary closed her bedroom door behind them.

Mary was wearing a long white nightgown, her unbound
hair hanging down past her waist. "When I saw your flashlight, I sat right up and said to myself, 'O God bless me, he's
come!'" Mary confessed with a light laugh. "But someday
soon it'll be so."

Katie knew she was thinking of either Preacher Yoder's
middle son, Jake, or one of Mary's own second cousins,
Chicken Joe, who helped his father run a chicken farm. "Are
you sure your parents are sleeping?" Katie asked, removing
her coat and heavy black bonnet and perching on the edge
of Mary's bed.

"Jah . . . listen. You can hear Dat snoring!"

Katie leaned her ear to the wall. Abe Stoltzfus was saw-
ing more logs than one, and with that kind of racket going
on, Mary's mother couldn't possibly hear what Katie was
about to say. "When I was here this morning—before the
quilting—you thought I wasn't going through with marrying John Beiler, remember?" she began. "Well, since then,
things have gotten worse."

Mary frowned, leaning forward. "Worse?"

"Oh, I'll marry Bishop John all right, but Dat's making
things mighty hard for me."

"What do you mean?"

"Somebody heard me singing today." Katie took a deep

breath and dropped her gaze to her apron. "Little Jacob heard me . . . and told."

Mary gasped. "I thought you put your guitar away years ago!"

"It wasn't the guitar he heard. I was humming on the road home from your house this morning—and it wasn't a tune from the *Ausbund*. Dat says he's going to take the matter straight to the bishop."

"Over Preacher's head?" Mary asked, aghast.

Katie nodded, feeling the shame of it.

"So, then, are you guilty of sinning?"

"Guilty as ever," Katie replied. "But it's over and done with, the music is. And that's the truth."

"Then hurry and tell your Dat!" Mary was adamant. "Don't let him go to Bishop John—whatever it takes, ya have to confess!"

Katie stared at Mary in disbelief. "You're saying this only because you don't think anybody else'll have me if the bishop lets me go, ain't so?"

Mary shook her head. "You know that's not true. You're a good and kind woman, Katie, everybody knows that. And any man with eyes in his head can see you're just as pretty on the outside."

It was the first time Katie had ever heard her friend speak this way. She mulled it over before replying. "What good are looks when stubbornness gets in the way?" she muttered. "I just plain run the fellas off."

Mary was silent for a moment. "But there was someone who didn't run off. *He* knew about your humming and singing, didn't he? That's why he gave you the guitar."

She was right, of course, but Katie was determined not to let on about Dan. Not even to Mary. "Dan's long dead. Leave him be."

Mary scooted over and put her hand on Katie's. "You still

104

love Daniel Fisher, don't you? You're still clinging to him hard . . . but he's gone."

"Not his memory. *That* ain't gone!"

"No," Mary whispered. "Still, have you thought what you'll do when you're married to a man you don't love?"

Katie jerked her head around. "John's a gut man," she insisted. "He'll be a right fine husband, and I'll come to love him . . . in time."

"Maybe you will . . . and maybe you won't."

The two friends sat in silence, as still as their fathers' fields in winter. Katie wished the conversation hadn't taken this turn. Why was Mary asking these questions?

"I'm living the Plain life best as I can—" Katie stopped herself before adding "without Dan."

"You're angry, though." Again, Mary seemed able to read her heart. "You don't really like being Amish, but you're stuck."

"I never said such a thing!" Forgetting the lateness of the hour, Katie raised her voice, then clamped her hand over her mouth. Surely Rachel Stoltzfus would come running now, wondering what on earth was so important as to be discussing it in the middle of the night. Katie waited, listening. . . .

When no sounds of footsteps were heard in the hallway, she relaxed. "To be honest, it's no fun wearing these long, heavy dresses and dull colors," she admitted. "But that's nothing new—you always knew that about me."

"Jah, but you should be clean past that by now, Katie. You should be moving on to higher ground. How can you be a good Mam to the bishop's children if you can't control yourself—can't submit to the rules of the church?"

Mary had a point, but Katie didn't want to hear it. "Well, then, so you're saying I shouldn't marry the bishop—that it's not fitting or right?" The words tumbled out, echoing her own doubts.

"You're a baptized member of the church, Katie. That makes you eligible for a church wedding to any man—bishop, preacher, deacon, whoever."

Katie pressed harder, needing a straight answer from her best friend. "You'd say that—knowing what you know about me? Am I respected enough among the People, do you think?"

" 'The Lord God exalts those who humble themselves,' " she quoted. "It's not your doing, Katie. Things are ordered by Providence—ordained by God."

So that was that. Mary honestly thought Katie had been chosen by God to be the bishop's wife. Katie stood up and tied on her black bonnet, then pulled her shawl around her shoulders.

"Just remember," Mary said, looking solemn, "you can tell me anything. Isn't that what best friends are for?"

"Yes . . . and I'm real glad for that." Katie walked toward the bedroom door and turned to regard Mary with a helpless shrug. "So will you pray that I'll quit being so hardheaded? That I won't always be tempted so?"

"Temptation is not the sin. Yielding to it is." Mary jumped up to give her a hug. "Remember, 'Blessed are the peacemakers.' "

Katie smiled, agreeing with her friend. "I'll make peace with Dat first thing tomorrow. I'll catch him before milking and confess—make things right between us. I'll tell him I'm sorry about the music, and that I'll never sing or hum anything but the *Ausbund* for the rest of my born days."

"Des gut," Mary nodded briskly. "And after chores, Mamma and I and a bunch of the cousins will come over and help scrub down your walls and paint, too—for the wedding."

Katie left the Stoltzfus house with Mary's wise words

ringing in her ears: *He that humbleth himself shall be exalted.* She was deep in thought all the way up Hickory Lane—so deep that she scarcely noticed the long black limousine that slowed, then passed on the opposite side of the road.

CHAPTER EIGHT

❖   ❖   ❖

Eager to speak with her father, Katie rushed to the barn the next morning. Eli and Benjamin were prepping the herd for the morning milking, but Dat was nowhere to be seen.

"He's out runnin' an errand," Eli replied nonchalantly when she asked.

"This early?"

"He left about four-thirty," Benjamin volunteered. "I heard him out hitchin' up Daisy before we ever got up."

Katie went about her chores without saying more. She fed the chickens and pitched hay to the draft horses and her pony, Satin Boy, then to Zeke and Molasses—the older driving horses—and last, to the mules, wondering if her father was, even now, reporting her wayward behavior to Bishop John.

I should have talked with Dat last night—even if I'd had to wake him! she thought. Groaning inwardly, Katie headed for the milk house.

Ben was leaning over to get some fresh, raw milk from the Sputnick, a small stainless-steel mobile contraption used instead of milk cans to take milk from the cow to the large refrigerated bulk tank, its power supply coming from a unique twelve-volt motor attached to a battery. Ben had always liked the taste of raw milk. "Has a fresh, green taste about it," he'd often said, gulping down a dipperful.

Katie filled three large bowls for the barn cats, wishing she had the nerve to take the market wagon or sleigh and ride over to the bishop's place. As embarrassing as it seemed, there still might be time to prove her sorrow and repentance. The whole disturbing episode could then be dropped, and life could go on as planned. Wouldn't be the first time an errant soul had found forgiveness in the privacy of someone's barn.

"When did Dat say he was coming back?" she asked timidly, not wanting Ben to guess how worried she really was.

"He didn't say."

"So then you really don't know where he went?"

Ben stood up and narrowed his gaze. "If it's what you're thinking, jah, I do believe he went to talk to Bishop John. Dat sticks by his word, ya know."

Katie stiffened. Her brother was telling the truth. Not once had she known their father to back down on something he said he would do.

"If only I hadn't been so stubborn," she muttered to herself.

"Jah, awful stubborn ya were, Katie . . . *terrible* stubborn."

Deliberately, she turned away and clumped outside through the dirty snow toward the house.

◈　◈　◈

Down the main road, familiar road signs dotted the snowy landscape, directing visitors and tourists to the Hickory Hollow General Store. Levi, seeing that he was one of the first customers of the day, pulled on the reins, urging Dumplin', his tan pony, into the wide parking lot. Only seven or eight enclosed gray buggies were here ahead of him. But his sleigh was the only one of the kind in sight. He tied Dumplin' to the hitching post and hurried inside.

The faint smell of peppermint greeted his nose, and he spied the jar of green-and-white striped candy sticks near the cash register.

"Mornin' to ya, Levi," called Preacher Yoder, the silver-haired man who owned and operated the small Amish store. "Let me know if you need help finding anything, ya hear?"

Levi waved and nodded silently, his usual greeting. Grown folks used up way too many words, he'd always thought.

He wandered over to the glass display case where spools of white, black, and several colors of thread were stored under the old wood-paneled counter top. He stood there a moment surveying the sewing supplies, then pulled out a tightly folded list his older sister had written down.

"Don't forget to bring back everything—and I mean *everything*—on this list," Nancy had admonished him before sending her brother out into the cold. "And whatever you do, please don't dawdle . . . or we'll be late for school."

Nancy doesn't wanna be late, he thought. *But I wouldn't mind it one bit*. He chuckled under his breath.

Truth be told, he liked school well enough; he made good marks in penmanship and arithmetic. But today he had more important things on his mind—like that Englisher with red hair—the one who'd come to the front door yesterday, asking for directions. He secretly hoped the stranger-lady might still be riding around lost on some back road in her long black car with those shiny bumpers. That way, maybe somebody else in Hickory Hollow would lay eyes on her and that fancy car of hers. Then Daed would have to believe his story.

Levi unfolded the piece of paper, placed it on the counter, and smoothed out the wrinkles as best he could.

Without speaking, he made a mental note of each of the desired items—two spools of black thread, four of white, a silver thimble, and five yards of white Swiss organdy. Nancy was making new head coverings for herself and Susie. Brand-new capes and aprons, too.

All's because we're gettin' a new Mam, he thought to himself. He was mighty glad the Lord God hadn't made *him* a girl. Such fussy things as aprons and capes! And always that clean white color till a girl turned thirteen. Give him an old pair of "broadfall" trousers—broke in good—and he was happy.

When Preacher Yoder came over to help, Levi simply handed him the list and pointed. He wasn't one to speak much to people outside his own family. And Katie Lapp would be no different, he decided while the preacher filled his order.

"Shall I bill it to your Pop?" Preacher asked with a smile.

Levi nodded and accepted the sack of sewing supplies, careful to hold it out a ways—not too close. Now if that bag had held a fistful of peppermint sticks like the ones over on the counter, he'd have grabbed it right up next to him. Just so's he could snitch one or two of the delicious mints out of the sack on his way down the narrow grocery aisle.

He breathed in the soft, minty smell one last time before reaching for the knob on the jingle-jangle door.

From the corner of the store, someone with a raspy voice spoke to him. "Well, hullo there, little Levi."

He turned to see who was calling him "little." Because he was no such thing!

"Come on over here," Ella Mae Zook said, motioning to him as she sat at a square wooden table, having a cup of hot chocolate. "I could use some company." She smiled and her deep dimples danced for him.

Levi realized with a jolt that not only was the Wise Woman right here in the general store, but Mattie Beiler, his aunt, was with her—over at the sewing counter, picking out dress material. His mamma, before she died, had told him all about his aunt Mattie and how she'd helped bring him into the world. It hadn't been an easy birth, but he'd finally come, all blue and barely breathing. Mattie had saved his life eight years ago, and to Levi, who believed himself to be near half grown, that was a good long time past.

Ella Mae pulled out a chair for him, and he slid onto it. He couldn't honestly remember ever being this close to the woman whose daughter had saved his life. People said things about Ella Mae, called her "wise" and other such grand things. But now, looking up into her wrinkled face, Levi couldn't see anything too awful special about her. Except maybe for the way her kinda goldish eyes—like the barn cat's—seemed to look straight through somebody—deep into your heart somehow.

To his surprise, she ordered and paid for another cup of cocoa without even asking if he wanted any, then settled back to enjoy her warm drink. "Guess you ain't all that little now that I see ya up close," she said, squinting her eyes a bit.

Levi only smiled.

"Ah . . ." She put her hand on her heart. "That smile of yours reminds me of your dear mamma. And ya know something else?"

Levi shook his head.

"I think you got more than just her smile." The old woman took a sip of cocoa, not explaining herself, which made Levi a bit jumpy, wondering what on earth she was talking about.

Well, he had to know. "What do I got that's like my mamma?" He leaned forward, his elbows on the old table, his ears wide open.

Ella Mae straightened up, and her wrinkly face broke into a broad smile. "Curiosity . . . *that's* what. You're interested in people—think long and hard about 'em, now don'tcha?"

Levi blinked. Did she know, could she tell, that he'd been thinking about someone? Could she tell that he'd been thinking long and hard, so hard that his head felt stiff from the notions a-stirring around in his brain—about that stranger-lady with hair as red as Katie's?

"I . . . I guess so," he stammered. "Jah, I'm curious sometimes."

She nodded slowly, then picked up her cup and saucer, letting the steam rise to fog her spectacles. She was silent for such a long time that Levi began to think Ella Mae had forgotten all about him. He sat back in his chair and stared at the glass jar of unclaimed peppermints on the counter across the wooden floor. His mouth watered just thinking about them.

"It's mighty gut to be interested," Ella Mae spoke up out of the blue. "It shows you're thinkin' . . . just don't go and think too hard. Save your brain for schoolwork."

He thought she might tell him to drink his cocoa right down and run along. But when she didn't, he figured it was the same as asking him to tell her what was on his mind— that curious question he'd been pondering on. "Where do you think . . . I mean, uh, where do family looks come from—like hair and eyes, ya know?"

Ella Mae slid her cup and saucer away and studied him thoughtfully before she spoke. "Parents have physical traits that get passed down to their children—just like your blond hair came from your mamma and the point of your chin from your Daed."

He sat up straighter. "And I'm tall like him, jah?"

"That you are."

Levi glanced around because what he was about to say was for Ella Mae's ears only. "Can ya keep a secret?" he whispered.

"Do you trust me, Levi Beiler?" she replied, looking him square in the face.

Studying her for a moment, Levi remembered all the things he'd heard about the little old lady sitting across the table. Hickory John and Nancy had both looked her up several times after their mamma died. And Levi wasn't exactly sure, but he thought even his own Daed, the bishop, had come to see the Wise Woman secretly—when his heart was near breaking in two.

Once, Nancy had said right out loud at supper that Ella Mae Zook seemed to listen like she believed every last word you told her. Never handed out a bunch of *should*s and *shouldn't*s neither. Just let a body settle for himself what he ought to do.

So, Levi decided, if they—and most everyone else he knew in Hickory Hollow—had told Ella Mae their secrets at one time or another, why shouldn't he tell her just one of his own?

He drank his cocoa half down, then set the cup on the saucer with a clink. "I was just wonderin'," he said softly. "Who do ya think Katie Lapp gets her red hair from?"

Ella Mae didn't seem the least bit bothered by the question. "Oh, probably from a relative somewheres down the line."

Levi scratched his head, puzzled. "Wait now, *you're* related to Katie and she doesn't look nothin' like *you*."

Ella Mae smiled. "Every now and again, God gives us a wonderful-gut surprise."

"Like red hair?" He sighed, thinking about the stranger-lady. "Like shiny black cars stretched out longer'n three fence posts?"

Ella Mae jerked her head back a bit, her eyes wide with surprise. "Where on earth didja ever see a car that long?"

Levi felt his mouth go dry. Did he dare mention the English stranger and the flashy automobile parked and waiting on the road? "I . . . uh, I saw it yesterday after school . . . right in front of our house."

The whole secret was out now. What would the Wise Woman say? Levi stared at her, trying to read what was behind those know-everything eyes. Would she believe him—the way Nancy said she always did? Or would she brush him off like Daed had last night?

Her words came slowly at first. "About that car . . . was a man in a black uniform driving it?"

"Jah."

"And was there a woman all decked out in a white fur coat?"

Levi accidentally let go of his sack. Spools of thread flew all over the place, and he went running, chasing them across the floor. He stuffed Nancy's sewing supplies back into the sack and sat down at the table again, blinking his eyes to beat the band. "A white fur coat, ya said?" He leaned so close he could smell Ella Mae's chocolaty breath. "Then you musta seen the Englishers, too."

She nodded.

"Ya did? You seen 'em?"

Ella Mae frowned and opened her mouth to say something else. But Levi interrupted before she could get a word out.

"Didja get a good look at 'em?"

"I saw 'em. Both of 'em."

Levi kept his voice low, but he was about to bust wide open! "Didn't that lady have the reddest hair you ever seen?" He didn't wait for Ella Mae's reply but asked another question. "Where'd *you* see 'em?"

"Out front, parked in front of our house—like they was lost for sure."

"So then, they was still lost after sundown?" The thought excited him. "Do you think they're still 'round here somewheres?"

Ella Mae's worry lines deepened. Then, in the very next minute, a funny little smile played across her lips.

Levi couldn't help but grin. She'd seen right through him. "I just wanna have another look at that long black machine," he admitted before she could point it out, "that's all."

"Levi Beiler," she scolded softly. "I do believe ya best be runnin' along to school now."

He scooted his chair back. The Wise Woman of Hickory Hollow had witnessed the exact same thing he had yesterday. She'd just told him so. Now Daed would *have* to believe him—for sure and for certain.

❖   ❖   ❖

"Ach, I left my basket on the counter," Mattie told her mother outside the General Store as they were leaving close to thirty minutes later, and she handed her the reins.

"Now you hurry back, ya hear?" Ella Mae called from her warm nest of woolen lap robes in the front seat of the buggy.

Moments later, a shiny limousine pulled into the parking lot and came to a stop in front of Preacher Yoder's store.

Ella Mae gave the English couple a quick, astonished look; so as not to stare, she looked away. But it wasn't any time a'tall before she heard the sound of feet crunching in the snow and someone approaching the buggy.

"Please, excuse me."

Ella Mae looked up into the face of the woman she'd seen last night—the one with the burnt red hair.

"I am very sorry to intrude," the woman said, "but I've been trying to locate someone. Perhaps you can help?"

Ella Mae sniffed. She knew that scent. Lavender—sweet and delicate. "Who would you be looking for?" she asked, taking note of the woman's fur coat and leather gloves.

"I wonder . . . would you happen to know of an Amish woman named Rebecca living in this area?" the soft voice came again.

Ella Mae stifled a chuckle. "At least ten or more."

The woman sighed. "I'm sorry I can't give you the last name." Her shoulders sagged, and it was then that Ella Mae noticed something much heavier than disappointment weighing her down. The woman seemed downright desperate.

Tugging at her fur coat, the red-haired woman shivered. "Would there be a young woman in your community—about twenty-two years old—whose mother's name is Rebecca?"

Without much thought, Ella Mae calculated several daughters of her friends in the church district. "Sorry, but I can't be much help to ya if I don't know the last name."

"This Rebecca . . . I believe she would be in her mid- to late-forties. And her husband was somewhat older."

"Could be any number of folk, really," Ella Mae replied, wondering why the Englisher referred to the couple in the past tense.

The lady straightened a bit and continued to stand there, now leaning on the carriage. She took a deep breath before speaking again. "You've been very kind. I do thank you." She smiled a tiny, weak smile that faded like dew in the morning sun. Still her deep brown eyes twinkled with hope, matching the diamond choker at her throat. But it was the determined set of her jaw that caught Ella Mae off guard, and for the blink of an eyelash, the spiffed-up woman reminded her of someone.

Before she turned to leave, the lady reached deep into the pocket of her coat and pulled out a sealed envelope. "This may seem a bit presumptuous, but it would mean so very much—more than you could know—if you, or someone else could pass this letter on to some of the Rebeccas in your community—the ones with a twenty-two-year-old daughter. Oh yes, I forgot to tell you . . . the daughter's birthday is June fifth."

June fifth? There was only *one* woman who fit *that* description.

All of a sudden, the Wise Woman knew which Rebecca the fancy lady wanted, and why her face had seemed so startlingly familiar. As sure as she was Ella Mae Zook, she knew.

The lady handed her the sealed envelope. "With all my heart, I am forever grateful." And she was gone.

Mattie returned in time to see the tail end of the black limo pulling out of the parking area. "Some mighty fancy Englishers around today, jah?"

Ella Mae did not speak.

Mattie touched her arm. "Are you all right, Mamma?"

She nodded, then—"Are you going over to help Katie and Rebecca Lapp spruce up the house this mornin'?"

"Thought I would. How 'bout you? The company'll do ya good, Mamma."

"I'm all wore out, child," Ella Mae said, her thin voice sounding rough and hoarse again. "I best be gettin' off my feet and sit a spell."

Mattie trotted the horse up the lane toward their gray, wood-frame farmhouse. "I'll help you into the house, then, if you're sure you're not coming."

Ella Mae stepped down out of the buggy, holding on to her daughter to steady her footing. With her free hand buried in the folds of her long woolen shawl, she clutched the envelope. The envelope with a fine linen finish and the name *Laura Mayfield-Bennett* centered on the back.

❖ ❖ ❖

119

Mary Stoltzfus and her mother, Rachel, made their way down the narrow road toward the Lapps' house, a large basket of sticky buns fresh from the oven nestled between them on the buggy seat. Even by carriage, time passed quickly this morning—their conversation punctuated with speculation about the Englishers who'd been seen by both Levi Beiler and Ella Mae Zook only an hour earlier.

Before they knew it, they were turning into the Lapps' tree-lined lane and pulled up in the side yard, coming to a stop beside a row of identical, boxlike gray buggies. Mary helped her mother down, and they walked across the packed snow toward the farmhouse, waving at Eli Lapp, who'd come over from the chicken house to unhitch their horse and lead him to the barn for hay and water.

A four-sided birdhouse, accommodating as many as twenty purple martins in springtime, cast its tall shadow over the snowy walkway as the two women hurried up the back steps to the kitchen door.

At their first knock, Katie opened the door. "*Wilkom*, Rachel. *Wie geht's*, Mary." She hugged them both and helped Rachel off with her wrap.

"It's nice to see ya all smiles again," Mary whispered in Katie's ear.

"The smile's for hope, nothing more," Katie said under her breath.

Mary followed Katie into the bustling kitchen where cousins and friends had come to help the bride-to-be do a thorough housecleaning—a community effort. Everything must be thoroughly spotless for the wedding service next week.

So it was much later before she was able to have a moment alone with Katie. It was then Katie confided that her father had gone off on an early-morning errand. "And so far, he hasn't come back."

There was no mistaking the look of concern on her

friend's face. "Do you think he's over at the bishop's, then?"

"Ben thinks so."

"Oh, Katie, I'm sorry. It scrambles things up so."

"Jah." Katie's smile was forced, no doubt about it. "Now I'll have to be confessing to my future husband." Suddenly her mood shifted. "Come on to the kitchen. Maybe something sweet will take our minds off my problem."

She headed for the kitchen with Mary in tow. Together, they sampled the gooey pastries.

"Here, try one of mine." Mary reached down and tore a generous portion of sticky bun free from the rest.

Katie took a bite, finished it off, and licked her fingers. "*Du konst voll*—you do very well, Mary. You'll make a gut wife someday."

Then, glancing around for possible eavesdroppers, Katie dropped her voice to a whisper. "Will it be Chicken Joe or Jake Yoder?" she teased.

Mary felt her cheeks heat. "Don't worry. You'll be the first to know, most likely."

" 'Most likely?' " Katie slanted her an appraising look. "No, no . . . you have to *promise* me."

"We'll never be far apart, you and me . . . we're best friends, remember? Why on earth wouldn't you be one of the first to know?"

The look in those bright blue eyes told Katie that Mary would keep her word, as always. Mary could be trusted. It was one of the many reasons she had latched on to the jolly girl with the face of an angel. And a heart of pure gold.

"Then that's that." Noticing some of the women already at work, Katie jumped to her feet. "Can't let the others do all the chores for my wedding day."

The women had set about cleaning the house, beginning with the upstairs bedrooms and working their way down to the main level of the house—washing down walls and scrubbing windows till they sparkled. Every inch of the house would be needed for Katie's special day, so some touch-up painting was done in several rooms.

Before the noon meal was served, the men began to arrive, including Dat. It was the first time Katie had seen him all morning, and she was apprehensive. Since the men were served first, she helped with their light lunch—cold cuts, pickles, red beets, and a variety of cheeses—careful to avoid her father's end of the table. Instead, Mary served him and the others seated nearby.

Afterward, while the women sat down to their own meal, the husbands set about enclosing the large front porch to allow for more room for the many guests who would be coming for the wedding.

Bishop John stopped by shortly, bringing with him additional plywood and sheets of plastic, temporarily sealing off the porch. Katie felt his gaze on her, but pretended not to notice and managed to get lost in the crowd of women cleaning up the lunch dishes. Time enough to deal with him later.

"When will you be confessing?" Mary asked when she and Katie were alone once more upstairs.

Knees weak, Katie sank down on the edge of her double bed. "Not 'til everyone's gone," she said, then frowned. "But maybe John should know ahead of time, so he'll stay around after the other men leave."

"If you want, I'll tell your father, and he can tell Bishop John you need to speak to him," Mary offered, heaving a big sigh. "After that, things'll be right back on track where they ought to be, honest. You'll be forgiven and feeling gut again, jah?"

Katie nodded, unsure of herself. The confessing was to be her first ever.

Mary's smile was reassuring. "It'll all be over before you know it."

"Jah," Katie said, thinking the confessing was really only the beginning. *It'll be over, all right,* she agreed silently, then allowed her mind to wander. *If only Dan had lived. . . .*

With the thought of Dan Fisher came the realization that she'd gone for nearly twenty-four hours without humming or singing their love tunes. Not a single one.

CHAPTER NINE

Katie waited in the kitchen until the last few women had left the house before strolling into the front room as nonchalantly as she could manage.

"Come," Bishop John said, extending his hand to her as he stood to his feet. The blue in his dove gray eyes seemed to brighten as she made her way across the room.

"Dat told you about my songs?" she said in a near whisper, taking a chair across from him.

John nodded, and they sat facing each other. "It is a redemptive thing you're about to do, Katie. Unless a person backs up from takin' that first step away from the fold, the second and third steps will most likely follow. Those first steps can lead a person far, far away from the church. . . ." He paused, gazing at her tenderly. "Come, sister, find your peace where you lost it."

He continued on, now into his preaching mode, although it seemed to Katie that he was going about his admonition in a gentle way, in keeping with the Scriptures. "We must crucify our flesh, resist the things of the world. Do you agree to turn your back on songs not found in the *Ausbund*?"

125

"Jah," Katie responded, doing her best not to cry, not to think of Dan's love songs.

"And the guitar . . . will you destroy that instrument of evil?"

Katie caught her breath. Dat had told John Beiler everything! The request caught her off guard. What could she say? If she argued with the bishop, asking for an alternative to his demand, she raised the possibility of being banned—excommunicated from the church—for to talk back or argue with a church leader was definite grounds.

John had been chosen by lot, by divine decree. He'd prayed the baptismal prayer over her only a few years before. How dare she dispute with God's elect?

She lowered her head, staring at her folded hands. Her voice shook as she spoke. "I will destroy the instrument of evil."

John stood and turned his palms toward her. Hesitantly, she placed her small hands in his large callused ones and rose to stand before him. "This day, a sister has been restored to the faith," he declared.

Mary Stoltzfus was right, as usual. The confessing part was over quickly, made less painful by the obvious anticipation in John's eyes and the kind expression on his ruddy face. In fact, if Katie hadn't known better, she might have thought her soon-to-be husband had glossed over the issue of her singing, somewhat playing down the offense. Except for the startling request to destroy the guitar.

Little Jacob's words rang in her memory. *Daed's 'sposed to be right . . . God makes bishops that-a-way.*

Katie would have to follow through on her promise. A person just didn't go around making a vow to the bishop without meaning it. She didn't know how she would bring herself to it, but the Lord knew, and He would give her the strength when the time came.

She was greatly relieved, however, when their conversation—John's and hers—turned from sinning to the wedding. Still, she was wondering if John might mention her father's state of mind when he'd reported her transgression earlier that morning. But nothing was said.

With the confessing behind them, they headed for the kitchen, where Rebecca had set out apple pie and slices of cheese on the table.

"Have you decided who you want for *Newesitzers?*" John asked, referring to Katie's wedding attendants, who, as was customary, were not to be dating couples, but single young people.

Katie nodded. "I asked my brother Benjamin and my friend Mary Stoltzfus. Mary's already done sewing her dress and cape."

John smiled and reached for her hand as they sat down on the long bench at the table. "I asked my youngest brother, Noah, and . . ." He paused, casting a thoughtful glance at Katie. "Ach, I would've chosen my oldest daughter, but Nancy is still a bit young, I suppose."

Katie agreed. Surely he wouldn't have seriously considered asking a child to be an attendant. And in the next breath he was telling her that he'd chosen Sarah Beiler, Mattie's oldest granddaughter, John's grand-niece.

"How do you feel about Preacher Yoder being one of the ministers?" she wanted to know.

"Gut." John grinned at her, showing his gums like an exuberant young boy. "And I thought I'd ask Preacher Zook from over in SummerHill. He and I go way back to early days in Lancaster."

Katie wondered if Preacher Zook might be a relative of John's deceased wife. But she was silent, practicing the submissive role she had learned from Rebecca through the years.

It was settled. Two of their favorite preachers in the Lancaster area would preach the sermons right before the wedding ceremony. Other decisions had to be made as well, including the *Forgehers*—ushers—and the others who would assist at the all-day affair. Waiters, potato cooks, and "roast" cooks had to be chosen, and *Hostlers*—the boys who took care of the horses. Men to set up the tables and take down the benches were next on Bishop John's list, followed by a number of women who would launder and iron tablecloths for the enormous dinner crowd of around two hundred guests. The helpers were to be married couples, and occasionally a man would help out in the kitchen on the day of a relative's wedding—the one and only time such a thing would occur. Katie smiled, thinking of her older brothers Elam or Eli trying to cook up anything in their mother's kitchen.

Katie was grateful to John for allowing a large wedding with a feast to follow. Typically, out of respect for the loss of a widower's first wife, a second wedding was far less elaborate. But John, being the bishop, had waived the usual practice, much to the amazement of the People.

Before he left, John kissed her on the lips for the first time. She was glad no one was around to witness the kiss, for it was such a private thing and somewhat awkward, as well. Katie knew it might take some getting used to—this lip-kissing with the bishop.

Katie went upstairs to her room and contemplated the day. Things had turned out the way Mary had predicted, for which Katie was profoundly grateful. She felt more determined now to take on the task of daily crucifying her flesh— putting her wicked ways behind her. Confession *was* good for the soul, she decided.

❖   ❖   ❖

Long after John's visit, but before the afternoon milking,

Rebecca met up with Samuel in the barn. "I think we oughta go ahead and give Katie the money . . . that money from her birth mother, I mean," she blurted out when no one else was around, "as a dowry gift."

Samuel nodded. "A wonderful-gut idea for Katie and the bishop."

"I'll go and get it out of the bank on Monday, then." And without further discussion, Rebecca hurried out of the barn, glad that Samuel had agreed. Every wedding detail was settled now. Things had fallen into place nicely. Everything. Right down to Katie's confessing to the bishop about her music.

The wedding would be her only daughter's crowning day. Rebecca had never felt so good about anything in her life. Not since the day she'd gone to the Lancaster hospital and returned home with little Katherine Mayfield.

Rebecca was so elated that when a horse and buggy stopped in the side yard, bringing Ella Mae Zook, she bounded over to greet her like a young colt. "Wilkom!" she called, then helped the older woman out of the carriage and into the house.

"Have a cup of coffee with me," Rebecca said, pulling up the rocking chair close to the cookstove.

"Ach, I can't stay long," the Wise Woman muttered as she sat down. A look of concern deepened the frown lines in her forehead. "Are we alone?"

"Jah. Samuel is out in the barn. So's the boys and Katie."

Ella Mae sighed deeply and began to speak. "A young English woman stopped by Preacher's store this mornin'— and started askin' questions." She glanced down at her lap. "She gave me this envelope. I believe it's for you, Rebecca."

"For me?"

"Jah, and I feel it may be best if you was to read it in private."

A paralyzing dread numbed her limbs and brought an

involuntary gasp from Rebecca. "Wh-what do you mean?"

"I think . . . I have reason to believe it's only for your eyes," the Wise Woman advised. She handed over the envelope.

Rebecca trembled when she read the name penned in the flowing script—*Laura Mayfield-Bennett*—grateful that Ella Mae was kind enough not to ask questions.

"I best be going," the old woman said. "Mattie's expectin' me for supper."

Rebecca followed Ella Mae out to the carriage and helped her back inside. "Da Herr sei mit du—the Lord be with you," she said, her voice breaking.

"And with you, child." Ella Mae's tone—raspy as it was—had never sounded so sweet, so full of compassion, and Rebecca's eyes welled with tears.

Before picking up the reins, Ella Mae turned to Rebecca and spoke once more. "*Wann du mich mohl brauchst, dan komm ich*—When you need me, I will come."

Rebecca glanced down at the fine white linen envelope. "I know ya will," she whispered, shivering against the cold . . . against the unknown. "I know."

❖ ❖ ❖

Katie finished up her chores in the barn, trying to shake off the nagging thoughts. Her gaze wandered to the hayloft high overhead, where Dan's guitar lay hidden safely in its case. Forcing her eyes away, she headed toward the milk house, noticing her mamma waving to someone in a departing buggy. *Wonder who that could be?*

John's words tumbled over and over in her mind: "It is a redemptive thing," he'd said about her confession. And it was, of course. Her act of confession assured her a good standing in the church. So she must obey the rules. Her future depended upon it.

Yet why did she feel stifled? Trapped? Her heart imprisoned along with the forbidden songs?

Hours before, she'd come clean, but her heart felt wicked still. Not at all the way she thought she would feel after baring her soul. What was keeping her from the straight and narrow? What more could she do?

Dan Fisher had spoken of this very thing once during a buggy ride home from a Singing a few days before his drowning. Katie had listened in confusion as he rattled on and on about something he'd found in Galatians, where the apostle Paul spoke about not building your faith on church rules, but on Christ. Dan had even read aloud the verses from chapter 5, and she remembered being surprised that he was carrying a paraphrased version of the New Testament around in his pocket. An odd thing for a baptized Amishman!

"The Ordnung can't save us, Katie," he'd said with a serious look in his eyes. "Our forefathers weren't educated in the Scriptures . . . they didn't study the Bible so they could teach it to the People. They made rules for the Old Order to follow. Man-made rules."

Katie had heard about the four elderly bishops back in 1809, who'd issued a ruling about excommunicating members who failed to obey the Ordnung. But she was in love, and whatever Dan chose to believe about their Swiss ancestors was fine with her; she wasn't going to argue with him. Besides, he'd probably gotten himself invited to a Mennonite Bible study or prayer meeting somewhere. The Mennonites were known for seeking out the truths of God's Word, and many of them ended up becoming missionaries.

At the time, Katie figured Dan had encountered some Bible-thumpers, that was all. But she hoped he'd be careful about his affiliation with outsiders. Especially Mennonites.

He could get himself shunned for such things as that!

Katie cringed. Die Meinding, the shunning, was a frightful thing. The word itself stirred powerful emotions among the People. Feelings of rejection, abandonment . . . fear.

She could remember her Mammi Essie telling about a man who had been shunned for using tractor power. None of the People could so much as speak to him or eat with him, lest they be shunned, too.

"It's like a death in the family," Essie had told her. And Katie, only a youngster at the time, had been sorry for the outcast man and his family.

But it wasn't until she met his little daughter, Annie Mae, during a spelling bee at their one-room school, that Katie understood the depth of sadness involved. No one knew what to say to Annie Mae. They either said nothing at all or were extra nice, as if that could somehow make up for her father's pain.

Even though the children were pretty much sheltered from church affairs, they could all see that after the shunning, Annie Mae was no longer the same. It was as if she'd been stripped bare, robbed of something precious. Katie had even been fearful that, unless Annie Mae's father submitted to a kneeling confession and pleaded for forgiveness, his little girl might suffer for the rest of her life.

Along with all the other children in the Hickory Hollow church district, Katie had been taught never to deviate in the slightest from the Ordnung. Once you began to stray, you were on your way out the church door.

Well, nobody'll ever hafta worry about me, young Katie had thought after witnessing the plight of Annie Mae's father. Never would she willfully disobey and disgrace her family and her church. Never would she step so far from the fold as to be shunned. . . .

◈　◈　◈

Moments after Ella Mae Zook lifted the reins and drove her carriage toward the western horizon, now deepening to smoke gray, Rebecca stumbled into the house, her heart thumping hard against her rib cage. This letter in her hand, this stationery . . .

She clutched it to her, casting furtive glances about the kitchen to be sure she was alone. Alone, as Ella Mae had kindly suggested.

The room, strangely cold, fell silent. Rebecca reached for a butcher knife and sliced through the envelope, making a long, clean opening at the top. Fingers trembling, she reached inside to find a business-size letter folded in thirds. Slowly, she opened the page and read:

Dear Rebecca (the adoptive mother of my child),

I am sorry to say that neither my mother nor I took the time to learn your last name that day in the Lancaster hospital twenty-two years ago. Unfortunately, things were spinning out of my control that June fifth morning.

Perhaps I seemed too young to be presenting you with my newborn daughter. And yes, I was young. Irresponsible, as well, to have conceived the tiny life. The guilt is long since gone, but the grief for my lost child remains, forever imprinted on my heart.

It is with great apprehension that I contact you in this way. My prayer is that you may understand my motive, for I must be honest with you, Rebecca. The baby girl I gave to you has been living in my heart all these years. Yes, I must speak the truth and say that I am sorry I ever gave her away. Now more than ever, because, you see, I am dying.

A number of specialists have suggested that I "get my house in order" as I have only a few months to live. With this recent news, you will understand why I am desperately longing to see Katherine—if only once more—before I die.

Of course, it is very possible that you and your husband did not choose to keep the name I gave my baby, and perhaps, wisely so. However, I respectfully request your help in making a way for our initial meeting—my daughter's and mine. Since I am praying that you will respond favorably to my plea, I am enclosing my address.

Thank you, Rebecca, for all you have done for Katherine, for the years of love you and your husband have given her. Please be assured that I have no plans to interfere in her life or yours in any mean-spirited way. My search for my child is purely a love search.

May the Lord bless you always,
Laura Mayfield-Bennett

Halfway through the first paragraph, Rebecca had to sit down. "Oh my, no . . . no," she muttered to herself. "This can't be. It just can't."

She reread the letter several times, tears welling up when she came to the part about Laura's sadness over losing her baby. The loss of a child—any child—whether to adoption or to death was a searing, life-altering experience, she knew. She *knew*.

Yet everything in her resisted the notion of arranging for the meeting of this—this *woman* with her precious Katie! She—Rebecca Lapp, not Laura Mayfield-Bennett—was Katie's mother!

Still, hadn't the young woman said she was dying? Dying! What age would she be? Late thirties? Maybe even younger. Rebecca had no idea, for there had never been any information exchanged between the two families. The adoption had never been finalized. The infant girl had needed a home; she and Samuel had just lost their tiny newborn. Heartsick and barren, Rebecca had accepted the baby as a gift from the hands of the heavenly Father.

God, in His great Providence, had put her and Samuel in the path of the pitifully sad teenager with auburn hair.

And that teenager—Laura—had kissed her baby girl good-bye and placed her in Rebecca's open arms. Who was to question the rightness, the legitimacy of such an act?

But in her heart, Rebecca knew that the identity of the infant she'd named Katie—and raised on a Pennsylvania farm in a sandstone house passed down from one generation of Lapps to the next—had never truly existed. Not really. Such a flimsy arrangement would never hold up in a modern court of law. No, if truth be told, Katherine Mayfield, the daughter of a fancy woman . . . Katherine, with English blood coursing through her veins . . . Katherine, with a bent for forbidden melodies and guitars—*she* was the girl who had lived here and grown up Amish all these years.

"And now her real mother wants her back," Rebecca moaned, rocking back and forth. "She'll probably come right back to Hickory Hollow . . . and take Katie away from me."

She felt her heart skip a beat and the startling sensation caught her by surprise, taking her breath. With a great sigh, she stood up, crumpling the letter in her hand. "I won't be writing back, Laura Mayfield-Bennett. I won't!"

Without regard for Samuel's interest in the matter, or asking his advice—without thinking any of that—Rebecca got to her feet, walked directly to the old woodstove, and fed the letter—envelope and all—into its blazing belly.

As if from a great distance, she heard the back door swing open and Katie come rushing inside. She did not look up, but stared at the fire as it licked up the remains of the secret past.

"Mamma?"

She recognized Katie's voice and wondered how long she herself had been standing there, gazing into the red and orange flames.

"Mam, are ya all right?" Katie touched Rebecca's arm and she straightened, calling up all the strength left in her.

Slowly, she turned to face her daughter. "Where's Dat?"

"He's on his way in. He and the boys are coming for supper soon."

Rebecca went about fixing leftovers and forced a smile—a frozen mockery of a thing. Katie must not suspect that anything was wrong. She must never know that another woman, a complete stranger, had given birth to her. Or that this woman was even now dying of a terminal disease. Or that the letter—the one that might have opened the door to fancy dresses and mirrors and music—was shriveling in the heat of an Amish cookstove, only inches away.

CHAPTER TEN

❖   ❖   ❖

The third Sunday in November was an off Sunday. Every other Lord's Day, the Amish community had a day of rest. The time was to be spent quietly at home or, as was more often the case, visiting friends and relatives.

Katie and her family had planned a peaceful day together, tending only the necessary chores and, in general, enjoying one another's company—the last such Sunday before her wedding day.

After lunch, Mary Stoltzfus stopped by with the finished wedding quilt, eyes shining as she greeted each member of the Lapp family. Eli seemed to pay more attention than usual when Mary walked through the kitchen and into the front room. This did not come as a surprise to Katie, for her dearest friend was glowing today.

Mary's mother, Rachel, had often warned, "Perty is as perty does." If the old adage was true, then Mary was the model, for she was as pretty inside as out.

Eli followed them into the front room and sat down on a straight-backed cane chair across from them, looking up occasionally from his crossword puzzle as they made over the quilt. Then Benjamin came in and suggested to his brother that they "take to visitin'." But from the twinkle in

137

Ben's eyes, Katie suspected that they were on their way to see their girlfriends.

"So long," Mamma called from her wooden rocker across from Dat, who was snoring softly in his matching chair. The boys waved but continued on through the kitchen to the utility room, making plans in low tones and laughing softly.

"Will your *Beau* be comin' over after a bit?" Mary asked.

"Jah." Katie couldn't hide a blush. "John will be coming to take me with him to pay a visit to his preacher friend over in SummerHill. There's been some trouble with a few boys at the Singings."

"Really? What kind of trouble?"

"Oh, just boyish rowdiness, I guess. Some of them have been bringing fiddles and guitars—such like that."

At the mention of guitars, Mary frowned slightly, and Katie wondered if she was going to ask if she'd gotten rid of hers yet. To fill the awkward silence, she spoke up quickly. "I heard they even had a portable CD player over there one night. Can you imagine that?"

"CD player? What's that?"

"Oh, it's some sort of machine that plays music on tiny little records."

"Well, if that don't beat all."

"I tell you, Mary, things are changing mighty fast around here. I remember when we weren't even allowed harmonicas at Singing."

Mary nodded. "You're right, and they still don't use them much here in the Hollow. Not since John Beiler was ordained bishop a few years back. He's stricter than some, you know." She reached for Katie's hand. "But I'm glad we have a firm, *standhaft* bishop, really. And, just think, come Thursday, you're going to be his bride."

Katie smiled, gripping Mary's hand tightly. "And everything's all ready for the wedding." She looked around at the freshly painted walls and scrubbed floor. "Dat and the other men did a right fine job of closing off the porch, don't you think?"

She led Mary to the front door, where they looked out, inspecting the long porch area through the heavy, double-paned glass.

"Oh, Katie, I almost wish I was you," Mary whispered, her face close enough for her breath to cloud the window-pane.

"Really? Why?" Puzzled, Katie turned to regard her friend. "Did *you* want to marry the bishop?"

Mary's hands shot up to cover her flaming face. "Ach, no—I meant nothing of the kind!"

"What then? How could you be wishing you were *me*?"

Mary glanced at Dat, who was still napping, and dropped her voice to a hushed tone. "I just meant I wish I was getting married soon."

"Oh, Mary . . ." Katie reached for her friend and hugged her hard. "You'll have your day, you'll see. One of the fine fellas around here—one of them will be shining his flash-light at your window someday real soon now." She sincerely hoped she was speaking the truth—that it would happen just as she had predicted. "Come on now. There's apple strudel left from lunch!"

In the kitchen, Katie served hearty slices and filled two cups with her Mam's good coffee.

"Mm-m, des gut," Mary said after her first bite. "Is it your mamma's recipe?"

"Jah."

"Then I best be getting it."

"I've tasted your pastries, Mary Stoltzfus. You need no help there!"

They finished off their dessert, still chattering on about the wedding plans. "I couldn't be happier about you being my side sitter," Katie said, referring to her attendant for the preaching service, held during the first two hours of the wedding.

"Well, who else would you have picked?" Mary's eyes sparkled.

"Nobody. You're my one and only choice. I never had sisters to choose from, you know."

Mary brushed the crumbs toward the center of the table. "I'm glad . . . in a way. If you had, then maybe I wouldn't be getting to have a place of honor at your wedding. And maybe . . . we'd never have been such close, dear friends."

There was a moment of silence while they pondered the changes Katie's marriage would bring. "Oh, Mary, how will it be, me going off and getting married and leaving you behind, all single? Wouldn't it have been wonderful-gut if we could've had a double wedding?"

Then, thinking out loud, she added, "Maybe I should wait a bit longer, put the bishop off . . .'til Chicken Joe asks you to marry him . . . or Preacher's boy."

Mary's mouth dropped wide. "Don't you go saying such things! God's ways are best, Katie. Besides, poor Bishop John's been waitin' an awful long time for you as it is."

"A long time?" Katie was surprised to hear it. "How do you know?"

Mary frowned, and it appeared that maybe her friend feared she'd spoken out of turn. But Katie pushed for an answer. "Just what are you saying?"

Mary cocked her head and narrowed her gaze. "I know it's true. The bishop's had his eyes on you for a gut long time. I've seen the way he watches you. Ach, I wouldn't be surprised if he's been in love with you since before your baptism."

Katie groaned. "But Dan and I were in love back then, so how could it be that the bishop—"

"Oh, I'm not saying Bishop John was *jealous* of Dan,"

Mary quickly interrupted, eyes wide. "I didn't mean that at all."

Thinking back, Katie realized what Mary must be referring to. "Oh, *that*. John was just being extra kind and helpful after Dan drowned, that's all."

"Well . . . maybe so. John Beiler's a kind, God-fearing man, of course." Mary sighed. "It must be awful gut to have someone like that eager to be marrying you."

Katie cleared off the table, then came back over to sit across from Mary. "Before, when you were talking about John watching me . . . well, you didn't mean he had that serious, uh . . . that intense look in his eyes, did you?"

"Katie Lapp! I never meant to be putting such a notion in your head!" came the fiery retort. "John Beiler's an ordained bishop, for goodness' sake!"

Katie nodded, thinking, wondering. John Beiler was also a human being. She had seen clear evidence of longing in his eyes, but it wasn't something she felt she should share— even with her closest friend.

"Please, whatever you do, don't go telling anyone what I said just now, you hear?" Mary sounded almost desperate.

Katie nodded in agreement, but her mind went swirling off, thinking back to the way John had glossed over her confession. Was it because of his fondness for her? Because he didn't want to be harsh with his future wife?

"Whatcha thinking now?" Mary asked, straightening her apron as she stood and went to the cookstove to warm her hands.

"Nothing much." Katie remained seated, watching Mary, wishing things could stay the way they were between them.

"Well, that's gut, because I don't want you thinking at all 'til after the wedding. Then, in a couple of days, I'll come visit you over at the bishop's house and hear all about the names you've picked out for your first baby come spring."

Her broad grin revealed slightly crooked front teeth.

"Why, you . . ." Katie hustled over to her, jostling and poking at Mary's ribs. If it hadn't been the Lord's Day, she would have been tempted to hale her friend outside for a snowball fight. As it was, Katie's prayer kapp was knocked askew, and Rebecca had to shush them from the front room.

"We're still just like two kid goats, ain't?" Katie whispered, trying to squelch another giggle. "And here you are—talking about the little ones you think I'll be having soon."

Mary shrugged. "Maybe one of your children will have red hair. Wouldn't that be right nice?"

"My hair's not red!"

"Well, what do you call it, then?"

"It's auburn," Katie insisted. "But you're right about one thing. It's about time for someone else in the Hollow to have colorful hair, don't you think?"

Mary was thoughtful, unexpectedly so. "You know, I guess I never thought about it, but you're the only one around here with auburn hair."

Fearful of continuing on that conversational course, Katie rose and motioned Mary upstairs to the bedroom, where she dropped to her knees, opened her cedar chest, and showed her friend the many handmade linens and doilies she'd collected.

"Does it feel strange moving into a house that's already set up with furniture and whatnot?" Mary asked as they were refolding the dainty things.

"Oh, I can't say it feels strange, really. The bishop and I talked about it. We think it's best this way . . . for the children, that is. . . ." Her voice trailed away, and she sat back on her heels, staring off into space.

"But it bothers you, doesn't it?"

There she went again. Mary seemed to know instinctively what the real truth was. "Oh, it's bothered me a little off and on, I suppose, but I'll get used to it," Katie replied,

closing the lid of the chest and getting to her feet. "I'm sure
I will."

What she didn't say was that marrying *any* man other
than her first love would bother her somewhat, at least for
a time. Perhaps a good *long* time.

❖   ❖   ❖

Elam, Katie's eldest brother, and his petite, but expec-
tant, young wife of one year arrived a few minutes after
Mary left the house. Both Elam and Annie hugged Katie and
Rebecca as they came in.

"We have our dishes all ready to load up for the wedding
feast," Annie said, smiling as she removed her winter bonnet, revealing dark chestnut brown hair under her white
kapp. "Elam will bring them over tomorrow sometime . . .
whenever it suits."

Katie was pleased to be borrowing Annie's good dishes.
Her sister-in-law was probably the sweetest girl Elam could
have chosen to marry, even though he had to be the orner-
iest brother God ever made. Of their union, a new little
Lapp was soon to arrive—in mid-January. Eager for her first
niece or nephew, Katie wondered if the baby would look
anything like Annie's younger brother—her beloved Dan.

The first time Katie had mentioned the possibility, her
sister-in-law had nodded sadly, saying she truly hoped so.
"Dan had the dearest face in all the world, I do believe."

Katie had agreed wholeheartedly. She would have loved
to pursue the matter with Annie, but because her wedding
date had recently been published and was widely known
among the People, no more public talk of Dan Fisher was
appropriate.

"I think Mam's gonna ask you to be servers at my wedding," she whispered as Annie settled into the rocker near the woodstove.

Since his favorite chair was in use, Dat went to sit at the head of the table. He rested his arms on the green-and-white checkered tablecloth, looking as though he might be expecting a piece of *schnitz* pie, perhaps.

"Of course, Dat and Mam should do the asking," Katie spoke up, glancing at Rebecca across the kitchen as she pulled dessert dishes from the cupboard.

"Ach . . . ask away," Elam said, giving Mam a peck on the cheek. "We can always say no, now can't we?"

"Well?" Rebecca eyed her son. "Would you and Annie consider being servers for the wedding?"

Katie noticed Annie purposely glance at her tall, handsome husband, waiting submissively for Elam's reply. He would make the decision for the two of them.

"Jah, we'll serve," Elam replied cheerfully, without a trace of teasing on his ruddy face. "It'll be an honor, you know that." He grinned at Rebecca. "Who else will you be asking, Mam?"

"Oh, Aunt Nancy and Uncle Noah, and Dat's youngest brother and his wife. Close relatives, mostly."

"What about David and Mattie Beiler?" Elam taunted her. "Wouldn't you like to have them help, too?"

Before their mother could answer, Katie spoke up. "Mattie will probably be doing other things, but Abe and Rachel Stoltzfus will be helping out in the kitchen."

"Ah!" Elam threw up his big hands. "So . . . the best friend's parents are pushing Mattie out, jah?"

"Elam Lapp," Mam reprimanded softly, "hold your tongue."

Katie stifled a smirk. The scene was a little comical; interesting, too. She continued to observe the joshing between her brother and Mam, keenly aware of their striking resemblance—clearly visible, even to strangers. No one would ever doubt who had given birth to the robust twenty-seven-year-old man. She envied the bond between each of her brothers and her parents—especially the obvious physical link between the firstborn of the Lapp family and Rebecca herself. Even with a year's growth of whiskers, Elam's facial features matched hers closely—the high forehead, the dimples, the straw-colored hair. No doubt about it, he was her boy.

Elam had always seemed comfortable cutting up in front of Mam. Today was no exception. In spite of his sometimes obnoxious friskiness—Elam had a tendency to carry things a bit too far at times, Katie thought—he exuded a warmth of spirit, a connecting tie even now, as a married man living twenty minutes away from the old stone house. A married man come home for a Sunday afternoon visit, true, but one who loved his homeplace still. Katie sensed it, perhaps more strongly today than ever before.

"So . . . it's final, then—we won't be including Mattie?" Elam persisted, teasing his Mam.

"Jah, final" was Rebecca's firm answer.

"Are you sure, now? Don't you want mad Mattie over here taking charge of your kitchen, Mam?"

Dat let out a grunt of displeasure. After all, it was the Lord's Day.

Elam poked his finger into Katie's rib, carrying the frivolity one step further. She backed away, shaking her head. Mam would have to deal with her eldest son's never-ending shenanigans.

And deal with him, she did. Rebecca served up schnitz pie, a hefty slice of stink cheese, and black coffee to keep Elam's hands and mouth busy.

More relatives—Noah and Nancy Yoder, Rebecca's sister and husband, and six of Katie's first cousins—showed up in time to enjoy the dried apple dessert. And if it hadn't been a Sunday, the women would have made quick work of the walnuts and hickory nuts still waiting to be cracked for the wedding. Instead, Rebecca invited all of them back on Tuesday morning for a work frolic.

"Will you be telling your stories again?" one of the cousins asked.

"Oh, most likely." Rebecca grinned, and Katie realized that her mother had taken the question as a compliment.

Mam was beaming today—her extended family gathered around her like chicks around a hen. Warmth and goodwill seemed to permeate the house, and by the time Bishop John arrived on the scene, Katie was genuinely glad to see him.

John took the cup that was offered him and swigged down a few sips of Rebecca's delicious black coffee. Greetings were exchanged around the kitchen, with many relatives mentioning the upcoming wedding on Thursday.

When the good-byes were said, Katie bundled up in her warmest shawl and headed out to the buggy with John, wondering what it would be like to bring her new husband home for a Sunday afternoon visit.

CHAPTER ELEVEN

❖　　❖　　❖

The air was icy and sweet on Monday morning as Katie hung out the wash. She thought how much more pleasant it would be doing the same chore with Nancy Beiler, the bishop's eldest daughter, at her side. It was difficult to believe that three days from now, she would be saying her wedding vows. The hours seemed to be speeding by like wild horses, much too fast.

"Be sure and lock up the house when we go," Rebecca told Katie before leaving with Samuel to tend to some business at the bank.

Katie puzzled over her mother's strange request. Here in Hickory Hollow, folks had never felt the need to do such a thing. Nevertheless, she went around and locked the front and back doors, waiting until her parents were out of sight and Eli and Benjamin were off to a cattle sale before going to the hayloft. It was time to make good her confession promise to the bishop.

The smell of hay filled the drafty haymow, and although she was momentarily tempted to play the instrument of evil when she found it, Katie kept the guitar case securely closed and tucked it under her arm. Surefooted, she made her way down the long wooden ladder to the lower level, where the cows came in for milking and the horses and Satin Boy were stabled and fed. Her pony whinnied playfully, but she didn't take the time to go over and caress his beautiful long neck.

Nor did she allow her thoughts to wander from her original purpose. Resolutely, she headed for the house. Once inside, she opened the round grate on the top of the woodstove, almost succumbing to the reckless impulse to burn the guitar and get it over with—once and for all. But when she lay the case out on the table and unsnapped both sides, she hesitated. If she opened the lid and so much as *looked* at Dan's old guitar, her promise to the bishop might wither and turn to ash—much like the kindling consumed by these flames.

But what could she do to rid herself of this wickedness without forever reliving the heart-wrenching memory of the final, destructive act, carried out by her own hands?

There was always the cemetery. . . .

The notion startled her at first, but it was an option. A simple wooden grave marker designated the empty spot in the earth, making note of the fact that Daniel Fisher had drowned on his nineteenth birthday. Why not bury the guitar there?

But it was faulty reasoning, and she knew it. The ground was much too frozen now.

Katie snapped the guitar case securely shut and carried it downstairs to the cold cellar, uncertain of her next move. Had Bishop John meant for her to do away with the guitar completely? She tried to remember his exact words at her confessing. But the more she tried, the more difficult it was to believe that such a kindhearted man would have insisted on destroying a lovely, well-crafted instrument. Surely, it would be no problem to merely put it out of sight somewhere. The idea was appealing.

She knew she was grasping at straws, though, rationalizing away the bishop's actual words as she crept past the rows of canned goods in her mother's tall storage cupboards. Undaunted, she hurried through the narrow passageway to the darkest part of the cellar, where Dat had stored her former dowry furniture. Because it was dark, she backtracked, locating the flashlight Rebecca always stored in the bottom right-hand cupboard in front of several old tablecloths used for summer picnics.

She pressed the button, and the area ahead sprang to life. Katie aimed the beam toward the corner cupboard in the depths of the cellar and wondered what it would be like to flick a switch and bathe a room in light. The reckless thought was momentary, for her gaze fastened on the lovely piece her father had made for her. She forced down the lump that tried to form in her throat and clung to the guitar, staring at the dowry furniture that might have been hers. And all the wondrous, innocent love it represented.

With guitar in hand, she decided the tip-top of the corner cupboard was a good choice for the hiding place. She propped up the flashlight on the floor, shining it toward the cupboard, and pulled over an old water bucket to stand on, steadying herself as she hoisted the guitar case high overhead. When it was close enough to the edge of the cupboard top to slide it back and out of sight, she bumped into something.

"What's up there?" she said aloud, determined to accomplish the deed before anyone caught her in another act of disobedience. Carefully, she hefted the guitar case down and retrieved the flashlight, shining it high to reveal a wooden baby cradle. She thought it amusing that her mother had stored the baby bed in the exact spot—the same dark, out-of-the-way place—that she had planned to conceal her forbidden guitar.

Katie stood on the bucket again and reached for the cradle. When she did, something rolled out and fell to the floor, smashing into pieces around her.

"*Himmel!*" Annoyed, she got down and turned to investigate. There, in a beam of artificial light, lay an infant's dress covered with shards of white milk glass. Had the dress been stuffed into the vase somehow?

Startled by the thought, Katie leaned down and picked up the garment and gently shook away the splinters of glass from its satiny folds. Then she held the flashlight closer, completely amazed. This baby dress was strikingly similar to the one she had found in the attic.

Driven by an urgency to know the truth, to be absolutely sure, she checked the back facing. The name stitched there was "Katherine Mayfield."

It appeared that someone had purposely hidden the dress. But why? She fought back unanswered questions.

Quickly, she made her way through the dim cellar to the steep steps, climbed them, and snatched up a broom and dustpan from the utility room. She felt herself becoming frantic, her pulse racing as she surveyed the side yard for any signs of her brothers, who sometimes returned home to get something they'd forgotten. When she saw that no one was coming, she flew back down the steps to sweep up and discard the broken fragments of glass.

Moments later, she rushed over to the Dawdi Haus next door and deposited the guitar in a crawl space. The instrument would be safe there, far from the eyes of Bishop John. And Dat.

Back in the main house, she sat down in the front room unashamed. The deed was done—a deceitful act—yet she felt absolutely no remorse. Why should she . . . when someone in her family was being dishonest with her? Still, did another's sin justify her own? She dismissed the annoying thought.

The fact remained—Katherine Mayfield's infant gown had been moved on purpose. Sadly, Katie suspected her mother. She was so certain of her supposition that, if necessary, she was prepared to confront Rebecca with the evidence.

Rather than indulge herself in a mountain of misery, Katie set to work cleaning the oil lamps in the house, all of them. She struggled with her emotions, asking herself how her Mam could have possibly lied to her.

She thought about last Wednesday morning, when she had inquired about the baby dress after a second look in the attic had turned up no clues. What had Mam said? Something about everything being "a bit of a blur"? Was it that she truly could not remember? Or was she simply avoiding the issue entirely?

Katie had dismissed her mother's response as proof of her innocence. But now? Now everything seemed to be pointing to trickery. Why?

To keep her mind occupied, Katie set about making two green tomato pies and a pot of vegetable soup for lunch. But she found herself rushing to the kitchen door and peering out every time she heard a horse and buggy on the road. She continued to busy herself, hoping her parents might return in time to share the noon meal with her.

When they hadn't arrived by eleven-thirty, she went to the front room and sat in her mother's hickory rocker, twiddling her thumbs and staring at the lovely baby garment in her lap. The minutes seemed to creep by, taunting her. She examined the workmanship, the seams, the stitching—and came to the conclusion that the gown had not been purchased in a store but rather was homemade, with the aid of an electric sewing machine.

When Mam and Dat failed to appear, Katie went outside to check the clothes on the line. They were still a bit damp, so she left them hanging in the pale sunlight and went back inside.

Still restless, she carried the little dress with her each time she darted to the kitchen to look at the day clock—ten times in fifteen minutes—pacing back and forth between the two rooms. What was keeping them?

Things just didn't add up. But no matter how long it took or what measures she had to resort to, Katie planned to move heaven and earth to discover the truth. Beginning the minute her parents arrived home.

❖ ❖ ❖

The lobby of the bank was crowded; the line seemed longer than usual for a Monday morning, Rebecca thought. But she waited patiently with the other patrons, most of them Englishers, although there were a few Mennonites and other Plain folk. None, however, that she recognized.

When she finally reached the head of the line and the next available teller's number appeared in red dotted numerals on the counter screen, Rebecca hurried to booth five and set her wicker basket down in front of her. Hastily, she filled out the withdrawal form, while the woman in the open booth waited.

"I want to close out this account." Rebecca pushed the bank slip in the direction of polished red fingernails. "And I'd like the balance made out to Katie Lapp—in a money order, if ya don't mind."

The owner of the red nails nodded and promptly left to carry out the transaction.

Later, when Rebecca met up with Samuel at the designated street corner, she walked beside him in silence, ignoring the stares of the people whizzing by in their fast cars. The notion that one of those people might be Katie's natural mother was horrifying. Instinctively, Rebecca moved closer to Samuel's side, wondering if that woman—that Laura Mayfield-Bennett—was out there somewhere right now— observing her, watching her every move, in the hope that

Rebecca would lead her to the child she had loved for so long but had never known. . . .

Once she was safely bundled into the carriage, sitting to Samuel's left, Rebecca felt protected. Their familiar rig, pulled by old Molasses, stood as a shield against the modern English world.

"Did you get the dowry money for Katie, then?" Samuel asked, glancing at Rebecca.

"Jah, I have it."

"Wouldn't it be right nice to give it to her tonight at supper? That way Eli and Benjamin can be in on the celebrating."

Rebecca rallied somewhat at the prospect of a festive evening, sitting a bit straighter as they headed through the traffic toward the Old Philadelphia Pike. "Jah, a gut idea. Won't Katie be surprised, though?"

Samuel's face broke into a wide grin, and Rebecca knew she must tell him about the letter right away. But she would break the news as gently as possible. "It's a smart thing for Katie to be marrying the bishop this week."

"He's been waitin' for her long enough now."

"No, no, I didn't mean for the bishop's sake," Rebecca corrected. "I meant because . . . well, because something's come up."

"What do you mean?"

She took a breath for courage. "Our dear Katie . . . ach, how can I put this?" She sighed, then began again. "Our daughter's mother, her birth mother, is looking for her."

Samuel jerked his head around so fast his hat nearly flew off. Rebecca could see his struggle for composure as he pushed it down on his head and resumed his questioning. "This can't be. What're you saying to me?"

Dear Lord God, Rebecca prayed silently, *help me to speak the complete truth*. She eyed her husband tentatively, then began to explain. "Ella Mae brought over a letter last Friday, before supper. It was signed, 'Laura Mayfield-Bennett.' "

Samuel seemed thoroughly confused, and his brows bee-tled with an ominous frown. "Why on earth didn't you tell me before?"

Rebecca did her best to fill in the details, and by the time they made the turn onto Hickory Lane, Samuel had the whole story as best she could recall it.

"So you're saying that the young girl who gave Katie up is all growed up now and . . . she's dyin'?"

The pain in Samuel's voice ripped at Rebecca's heart, but she suspected that he was equally concerned about not having been told sooner. She could see now that burning the letter had been a grave mistake, and that it had created a thorny distance between herself and her husband.

She sucked in some fresh air and held the raw cold inside her lungs for a moment, then let it out slowly. "I never gave it a second thought, honest I didn't. I should've known how you'd be feelin', though. I'm sorry, Samuel, so awful sorry."

He nodded. "I see why you said what you did about get-tin' Katie married off. If she'd waited any longer, who knows what might have happened next?"

"Jah, who knows?" Rebecca was sick with worry that the stranger might just show up on their doorstep. Perhaps to-day, while she and Samuel were gone . . . too far away to protect their daughter.

Rebecca shivered and tried in vain to shake off the nag-ging fear.

◈　◈　◈

Katie forced herself to sit calmly in the front room when the carriage turned into the lane and Dat stopped to let Mam out. It was almost impossible to remain seated as though nothing were wrong. But *everything* was wrong, and when the back door opened and she heard the clunk of her mother's boots against the utility room floor, it was all she could do to keep from flying through the house.

"Katie?"

"I'm here, Mamma . . . coming." She gripped the baby dress and stood, steeling herself, and made her way toward the kitchen.

Rebecca rushed to greet her with a great smile on her face, arms outstretched. "Oh, Katie, wait'll Dat comes in. We have such a wonderful surprise for you."

Katie held the little dress behind her back. "Can I have a word with you first?"

Her mother's smile faded a little, and she touched Katie's face, letting her hand linger there. "Child, what is it?"

"Mamma, I'm *not* a child. I'm a grown woman—about to be married."

But her Mam seemed too preoccupied to hear and turned as Dat came huffing into the house. "Samuel, come," she called to him.

He tossed his heavy sack coat and hat onto a hook and hurried into the room.

"Let's give Katie her dowry now." Katie had never heard her mother's voice so full of eagerness, or seen her eyes more heavenly hazel than at this moment.

"I thought we agreed to wait 'til supper, so the boys can be in on it." His words, directed at her mother, were almost a reprimand.

"At supper, then."

What was this tension between them? But Katie didn't ponder long. Whatever her parents had agreed on presenting to her at supper was not half as important as the questions burning in her heart. So, without any warning, she flung the satin baby dress down on the kitchen table in front of them.

155

Her mother saw it first and gasped, backing away. But Dat reached for the tiny dress almost reverently, touching the hem as if recalling a fond memory.

"Dat?" Katie whispered. "Have you ever seen this before?"

Rebecca had now positioned herself in such a way that she was standing guard over the dress. She spun around, eyes glazed. "It's best you don't know!"

Katie grabbed the dress and clasped it to her. "What's there to know? It's an English baby dress, that's all—ain't?"

"Don't go asking about something that's nobody's business."

From the firm set of Mam's jaw, Katie sensed there was more—much more. "It seems . . . well, I think someone keeps hiding this dress. First in the attic . . . and now—"

"That's enough foolish talk."

"Foolish?" Katie studied Mam's face, knowing full well she was treading on thin ice. "Maybe you're hiding something from me, is that it?"

Dat glowered and moved in front of his wife protectively. "Your Mam deserves respect, daughter. Never, ever speak to her in such a way."

Seeing the quiver in her mother's lower lip, Katie left off the questioning, even though it was obvious that they knew far more than they were willing to tell. "Forgive me, Dat . . . Mam." She turned and left the room, her head in a whirl.

By now her stomach was churning, too, and she decided against eating lunch, despite the mouth-watering aroma wafting from the vegetable soup, now ready to be served.

Katie knew she couldn't remain silent forever, though. She would wait, possibly until evening. By then she might be able to approach her parents more discreetly. At least she'd try.

Still, the thought that her mother had been somehow deceitful was the most troublesome of all. Katie felt the old rebellion rise up in her. If her gentle, honest Mam—the soul of integrity—could be guilty of such a thing, then, "I ought to be able to have my own opinion sometimes," she spouted off to no one but herself and curled up on her cold, hard bed, remembering something she'd heard years ago.

Somewhere in Ohio, a group of New Order Amish had separated from the Old Order in the late sixties. There, the women not only wore brightly colored dresses, but weren't above having ideas of their own. In fact, at this moment, as Katie simmered and stewed, the idea seemed downright appealing. And if her memory served her correctly, little Annie Mae's father had moved his whole family out to Ohio several months after his shunning probation. The New Order had welcomed them with open arms. At least, that's how word had it here.

She dozed off, dreaming of life in such a place. . . .

❂   ❂   ❂

A welcome change in temperature—a foretaste of Indian Summer—lured Katie out of doors when she awoke. For old times' sake, more than anything else, she went out to the barn and hitched Satin Boy to the pony cart.

Without a word of explanation, she left the premises.

Most of the snow had already melted, clearing the way for two buggy-sized paths on either side of Hickory Lane. Numerous sets of buggy wheels had left their imprint—folks on their way to the cattle auction, most likely—which had served to turn the ice to slush. She rode on, enjoying the balmy weather, until she came to the turnoff to Mattie Beiler's house. And suddenly Katie knew what she must do.

There was not a sign of life at Mattie's place when Katie arrived, and she walked around back to the Dawdi Haus where Ella Mae lived. She tapped on the door, knowing it was unlocked, but waited for the Wise Woman to invite her in.

The sun shone steadily, warming her, and for a moment Katie amused herself with the thought that she might not have to bother with a shawl on her wedding day.

"Ach, come in, come in," Ella Mae said as she opened the door, panting a bit. "I was just cleanin' out from under my bed." She paused to give Katie her full attention. "It's so nice to see you again." And with that, she turned to the cookstove and set a teakettle on to boil.

Katie knew better than to decline Ella Mae's tea, for it was widely known that two sprigs of mint from the old woman's herb garden went into each visitor's cup. The brewing and the sipping went hand in hand with a visit to the Wise Woman.

"I always love it when the days get warmer along about now." Ella Mae stood near the stove, waiting for the water to boil. "Indian Summer makes for a right fine weddin' season."

"Jah, it does." Katie was eager to pull the satin baby dress from her basket right then and there, but the tea-brewing ritual mustn't be rushed.

"How's everybody at your house?" The quavery voice took on a little strength.

"Oh, the boys are down at the Kings' auction, and Mam and Dat just got home from tending to some business."

The old woman nodded. "Last-minute business for a daughter's weddin', most likely."

When the tea was ready, Ella Mae poured two cups, then settled down at the table across from Katie, sipping, then stirring in a second teaspoon of sugar.

In the momentary lull, Katie reached down into her basket and pulled out the baby dress. "Have you ever seen such a beautiful thing?" she asked, handing it across the table.

The old woman took the infant dress, fingering its

sleeves and the long, graceful folds. "It's awful perty, ain't?"

"It's satin . . . English, wouldn't you think?"

Ella Mae nodded thoughtfully, then glanced up at Katie with a curious glimmer in her eyes.

"I'm mighty sure it's English." Katie showed her the name sewn into the facing. "*Mayfield* sure isn't Plain." She took a deep breath, then launched into her story, including the suspicion that someone had been hiding the dress from her.

When she finished, Katie sat silently, hoping Ella Mae would offer some word of wisdom, tell her what to do.

Ella Mae took a long sip of tea, then set her cup down with a clink. "Talk to your Mam about it."

"Even if it means confronting her?"

The old woman's gaze was as tender as her words. "Talk to your mamma, child. Speak kindly to her."

"Mam won't like being accused."

" 'In quietness and in confidence shall be your strength,' " she quoted. "You can't be sure how she'll take it 'til you try. Go to her . . . in love."

Katie didn't feel altogether charitable toward her mother just now, but she would consider taking Ella Mae's advice. "If you don't mind, I'll have some more tea."

The Wise Woman beamed and rose to get the kettle.

During the next hour, Katie found herself pouring out her heart. This time, unwilling to reveal too much, she spoke in riddles. "Several days ago I agreed to something that I just can't bring myself to do, after all," she began hesitantly.

"Katie, our dear Lord was the only perfect Person who ever walked this earth. And if you're sorry and repent, you'll be following His teaching," replied Ella Mae. "Perhaps in due time, your promise will be kept."

Reassured by Ella Mae's quiet perception, Katie opened up a bit more, feeling her way through the maze of revelation. "Just today, I figured out another way to do this thing—a different way—from what I promised. And I'm not feeling sorry for it yet."

Katie doubted that the Wise Woman understood much of her vague explanation. But even in spite of that, she felt better for having told someone. It seemed to lift some of the load of guilt.

" 'In quietness and in confidence shall be your strength,' " Ella Mae quoted once more, this time her voice fading to a whisper.

But Katie wondered how she would manage to remain quiet if her mother spoke sharply to her again. Confidence was one thing, but the quiet part was something else.

She squared her shoulders. It was settled. She would bring up the matter of the satin dress at supper tonight . . . in love.

CHAPTER TWELVE

❖   ❖   ❖

Katie arrived home in time to help with the afternoon milking, feeling a bit weary and quite hungry now, having left in a huff and without her lunch.

Samuel and the boys did most of the heavy work—feeding the horses and hauling the milk to the milk house. It wouldn't be long before the three men would be doing all of the outdoor work. Katie would take her place in the world of married Plain women, attending work frolics—quiltings, cannings, and, once in a blue moon, a cornhusking, not to mention tending to the Beiler children and eventually her own babies.

Katie was thankful for her past experience with several English families outside Hickory Hollow—cleaning their houses and tending to their young children. The extra spending money had come in handy, and she'd enjoyed riding in a car occasionally. But all that had come to a halt a few months ago when Bishop John had asked her to become his wife.

"Will you be missing me when I get married?" she asked Satin Boy, stroking his glossy mane. The pony kept right on eating. "I'll come back and see you sometimes, I promise."

Eli hurried past her. "Don't be wastin' time talkin' to

that pony. Best go on in and help Mam with supper. She's feelin' *grenklich*."

Mam, ill again? It seemed to Katie that their mother was getting sick a lot these days. Strange, too, when she'd always been the picture of health—hearty and robust and working from sunup to sundown. In fact, now that she thought of it, before Katie found that baby dress, she didn't recollect Rebecca Lapp ever fainting—even once.

Concerned, she left Satin Boy to his supper and dashed toward the house. When she had hung up her work coat and winter bonnet, Katie found Mam standing near the wood-stove, staring hard at it.

"Mamma? Are you all right?"

She started, then straightened quickly. "Oh my, yes. I was just off in a daze somewhere, that's all. The wedding . . . and all."

"Eli said you were ill."

"I think it's just a touch of the flu, maybe. Not to worry." Then she brought up the question Katie had been dreading all afternoon. "You wanted to talk to me about something?"

"About the fancy baby dress, that's what it was."

Rebecca seemed relieved and went to test the potatoes with a fork. "Oh. I thought somebody might've stopped by while we were gone. You did lock all the doors, didn't you?"

What was Mam talking about? "Was Mary Stoltzfus supposed to drop by?" Katie thought for a second, then realized her friend had said nothing at all about visiting today.

"No, no, not Mary. I wasn't speaking about anybody in particular, really."

The evasive reply piqued Katie's curiosity. "Who, then?"

A worrisome look clouded the hazel eyes. "A young woman, maybe? A stranger?"

Katie went to stand beside her mother. "Forgive me, Mamma, but you're not making a bit of sense. Now start over. Tell me again."

Rebecca waved her hand in front of her face, a motion that usually signaled the end of a frustrating conversation. "Aw, just forget now, forget I ever said a word."

Katie leaned hard against her Mam and felt ample arms wrap around her. For a moment there, she almost gave in to the fear that her mother might be slipping—mentally, at least—and wondered if she should say something to Dat.

❖   ❖   ❖

The supper table was set with Rebecca's finest dishes and silverware when Katie came into the kitchen later. In the corner, near the utility room, her parents were talking together quietly, their expressions sober. Katie made her presence known with a light cough, and they broke off their conversation abruptly. Then both of them stood looking at her—heads tilted to one side, eyes slightly narrowed—as though calculating how she might receive what they were about to say.

Alarmed, Katie glanced from one to the other. "Is something wrong? Is Mamma really very ill?"

"No, nothing's wrong, nothing at all," Rebecca tossed off a casual reply and turned to dish up the food.

Still not convinced, Katie washed her hands and helped set the serving platters on the table. Eli and Benjamin slid onto the long bench, and the family bowed their heads for silent prayer.

Afterward, Katie observed Dat cueing Mam with a nod, and Rebecca promptly pulled out an envelope from her pocket. "Katie, here is your dowry gift from your Dat and me."

"Dowry?" Katie was speechless. "But I don't need—"

"We want you to have it," her father interrupted, sporting a rare smile. "Someday you and the bishop . . . well, you may have need of it—to expand the house, or who knows what all."

Katie caught her breath when she saw the amount. "*Wie viel*—how much *is* this, for goodness' sake!"

"Ach, just enjoy it." Dat helped himself to the potatoes and gravy, dismissing her exclamation of disbelief.

Mam seemed content to sit and watch as Katie slipped the envelope into her side pocket. "This is quite a surprise, really," Katie added, suddenly mortified at the thought of the fuss she'd made earlier over the baby garment. Now she knew why her parents had been so secretive—getting off to themselves and talking that way. She was relieved that they'd apparently given no further thought to her outburst.

Eli and Benjamin seemed more interested in feeding their faces than inquiring about the dowry money. It was not until Benjamin had satisfied his hunger that he spoke up at all. "Which of my white shirts should I be wearin' on Thursday?"

"One of the new ones I sewed for you last week," Katie put in, glancing at her mother's drawn face. "And wear black stockings, too, and don't forget to shine your good shoes."

When the conversation turned to preparations for moving her belongings to the Beiler home tomorrow, Katie was happy to see that her mother seemed as keen and alert as ever. "I know you'll be wanting your own things over there . . . and with the bishop's first wife's furnishings taking up so much space . . ." Rebecca waved her hand. "Ach, I do believe that house is big enough for both. Maybe even the corner cupboard Dat made you—"

"Mamma!" Katie interrupted, horrified. "Why would you say such a thing? You know Dat made it for—" She broke off before she embarrassed herself again.

"Well, I don't see why you shouldn't take it on over to John's place, after all." Instantly Mam took on that glazed, cloudy expression again that settled in her eyes as she spoke.

Dat must have noticed it, too. "Let's just be thinkin' about it for now," he soothed.

"Jah, *think*," Eli teased. "Just think about Katie bein' mighty holy—holy enough to be the bishop's wife."

"Eli Lapp!" Dat scolded. "You will say no such thing!"

His sharp rebuke snapped Rebecca out of her daze. "Well now, who's hungry for dessert?" She sprang to her feet and began to move back and forth between the kitchen counter and the table, serving apple cobbler and ice cream.

Katie observed her, wondering when she should bring up the topic of the satin baby dress. If at all.

The moment came later, while Samuel was having his coffee. Black. Not a speck of cream or sugar.

"If it wouldn't be too much bother," Katie began hesitantly, "I want to ask about that baby dress . . . the one I found in the attic." To the best of her ability, she did as Ella Mae had advised, approaching the subject gently. In a spirit of humility.

"I thought I told ya to leave it be." Dat stirred his coffee with a vigor.

"No, no." Mam touched his forearm lightly, letting her hand rest there. "We really ought to discuss it, Samuel. The time has come."

Dat shrugged.

"I have to make you an apology," her mother pressed on, looking now at Katie. "It was wrong of me to do what I did." Her voice grew velvety soft—the tone she usually used when telling of the day Katie was born. "You see, *I* was the one hiding the dress."

Eli and Benjamin looked up in surprise, lips still smacking over the tasty cobbler. And Dat . . . his eyes widened, then squinted into slits. "Maybe it'd be best if we did our talking to Katie . . . alone."

There was no mistaking the meaning in her father's look. Eli gave a bit of a grunt and gulped down another glass of milk before the final silent grace, then left the kitchen for the barn, lantern in hand. Benjamin bundled up and headed for parts unknown, leaving Katie alone with her parents in the warm kitchen.

Katie was aware of a portentious feeling, as though something she had always known deep down was about to be revealed—like the missing piece of a life-sized puzzle, maybe, or an explanation she'd waited her whole lifetime to hear.

Rebecca began, softly at first. "We—Dat and I—have to tell ya something, Katie. Do try and bear with us 'til we're all through, jah?" Her eyes were soft and misty. She took in a deep breath.

Then, before she could launch into whatever it was she had to say, Dat stopped her. "Wait, now. I'll be the one tellin' it." He got to his feet and lumbered over to the woodstove, turning to face them.

Mam leaned her elbows on the table, seemingly relieved that, for tonight at least, her husband would be the storyteller.

"When we first laid eyes on ya, Katie . . . well, there was no doubt in our minds that you came to us, straight from the Lord God in heaven himself."

Rebecca nodded. "We always considered you the same as our own flesh and blood."

"Wait!" Katie threw up her hands. "What are you both saying? I don't understand a word of this!"

"Aw, Katie, my dear, dear girl," Mam said, her chin beginning to quiver. "It's time you knew. It's time you heard how it was that you came to be ours." Her tears welled up and spilled over, leaving a watery trail down her flushed cheeks.

"You mean . . . I'm not your own . . . daughter?" The thought was too large, too shattering to bear, yet her mind was racing frantically. Somewhere from the misty past, something Dan Fisher had said drifted back from that summery day. Something about kissing her on the cheek "the day you came home from the Lancaster hospital." Some problem Mam had had giving birth. But Katie had been so deliriously happy that day, so giddy with Dan's nearness that she'd paid scant attention to anything but their love.

"It comes as a shock to ya, no doubt." Through the veil of tears, Katie could see the concern on her father's face. He paused for a moment, breathing hard.

"Dat and I, we love ya so—honest we do." Mam picked up the conversation. "Seems now it's our turn to be beggin' your forgiveness. You see, we never told you the truth, Katie—not all of it."

"What . . . truth?" Katie's heart was pounding, ringing in her ears until she could only hear as if from a great distance.

"The truth about who you are . . . really." Rebecca broke down, her tears giving way to sobs.

But Katie couldn't comfort her, couldn't move. She was rooted to the spot while the room spun crazily, tilting this way and that, like a windmill in the spring. "What do you mean . . . you never told me the truth? If I'm not Katie Lapp . . . then who am I?"

Her father came to hover over Mamma as she looked up, her eyes swollen and red. Her voice came out in a whisper, trembling with emotion. "You're Katherine Mayfield, Katie, that's who you are."

Katherine Mayfield. The name sewn into the satin dress.

It was Dat who attempted to explain. "You're English by birth and Plain by adoption."

The words came as a blow. "I'm . . . what? *Adopted?*"

"In so many words," he said, resting his big, work-roughened hands on Mam's shoulders. "We never made it legal . . . didn't see the need, really. We loved ya from the start, and love was enough."

"But I'm not *yours* . . . not your own *real* daughter?"

"Now, now, nothing's changed at all," he was quick to say. "Nothing's diff'rent because of your knowin' it. You're ours and ours forever, and in our hearts you'll always be our little Katie."

"But you never told me . . . not in all these years. No one ever told me." Katie could hear herself whimpering. Suddenly she felt cold and crisscrossed her arms in front of herself as if to create a shield against the complete and utter shock of it all.

"Not a soul knows of this," Samuel said. "Though a few may suspect it, I do believe."

Rebecca blew her nose and spoke at last. "You don't carry the family's traits in looks, you know."

"My hair's *red*, that's all." Katie was shocked at the words from her own lips. She'd never before used that term to describe her hair. *Auburn*, of course. But never red. Red was for worldly English barns and highway stop signs—not for the single most beautiful feature God had ever given a woman. But she didn't stop to correct herself; her thoughts were flying way ahead. "So no one in Hickory Hollow knows I'm not Amish?"

"But you *are* Amish, Katie, through and through," her Mam said gently. "In every way, 'cept blood."

Katie propped her head in her hands as the truth began to dawn. *I'm adopted. . . . I'm someone else. Someone else . . .*

Slowly, she looked up at them. "Do my brothers know?"

Dat shook his head.

"Shouldn't they be told, then? Shouldn't everyone know the truth?"

Mam gasped. "What business is it of anybody's? Life can go on just as it always has."

"No," Katie replied. "Things can *not* go on as they always have. Everything's changed, don't you see? *Everything!*"

She ran out of the kitchen, tears dripping off her cheeks.

Without a lantern to light the way, she stumbled up the stairs and fell across her bed, sobbing into the inky darkness. "Oh, dear Lord in heaven," she cried, "let this be some awful dream. Please . . . oh, please . . ."

It was only the second time in her life she had used such desperate, non-German words in addressing the Creator of the heavens and earth. She lay there weeping and trembling, remembering another dark and grievous time when her body had heaved with sorrow. And she could not be comforted.

❖   ❖   ❖

Rebecca's rest was fitful. Three or four times in the night, she got up to look in on her grown children as they slept, her heart breaking anew as she stood at the door of Katie's room and heard the intermittent hiccups that come from crying yourself to sleep.

Finally, past midnight, she gave herself permission to stretch out on the bed beside Samuel. She made herself lie there, trying, but not succeeding, to shut out the voices of the day. Wondering if she and Samuel had done the right thing. Hoping against hope that all of them could go on with their lives and prepare for Katie's wedding.

Despite the brightness of the moon, a cloud of gloom descended over her as she stared, teary eyed, at the ceiling. She knew full well that the whole wretched truth—that an English woman was searching for her birth child—had been withheld. That neither Samuel nor she herself had mustered the courage to tell Katie the complete story.

At last, she slept. And as she slept, she dreamed—a dream both distorted and hopeful. In her desperation, she reached into the belly of the cookstove and retrieved the charred English letter, burning her fingertips. But instead of hiding it from Katie's eyes, she handed the letter over to her.

Katie shrank back in horror, determined to have nothing to do with something so fancy—not the fine stationery nor the woman who had penned it. Instead, Katie fell into Rebecca's arms, declaring her love and loyalty, forever and ever.

Rebecca awoke with a start, not knowing whether it was outright fear or love that propelled her out of her warm bed and down the hall to check on Katie, asleep in her childhood room. On her way down the cold hallway, Rebecca wondered why she had not been able to part with the satin baby dress all these years.

Now, as she cracked the door to Katie's moonlit bedroom, she saw that her daughter, too, had been drawn to the small garment. For there on the feather pillow, clasped tightly in her hand, was the infant dress she'd worn home from the hospital.

The dress—was it a symbol of the wicked outside world? Had Rebecca herself been too attached to it, to the glorious memory of their day of days? Was this dress the cause of all their present heartache?

What had Katie said before flying off to her room? That everything had changed? That learning she wasn't their "real" daughter meant things could not go on as before?

Katie stirred in her sleep and murmured a name. "Dan . . ."

Was it Dan Fisher she was still dreaming of? Poor Katie, her darling child . . . losing Dan . . . and now *this*? Poor, dear girl.

Rebecca blamed the dress, and she blamed herself. *If only I'd told Katie the truth from the very start*, she groaned inwardly. *If only I hadn't been so proud.*

Pride. One of the deadly sins the People prayed against daily, lest it bring about their downfall.

Rebecca backed away from the bed, inching her way out

of the room. She could only hope that her past sins would not scar her daughter for life, that Katie wouldn't let her impulsive nature drive her to some reckless decision. That she would put the shock of her true identity behind her and get on with her new life. A glorious new life with Hickory Hollow's finest widower, the bishop John Beiler.

CHAPTER THIRTEEN

Katie doesn't think before she speaks . . . never has," Samuel grumbled to Rebecca at breakfast the next morning. "She leaps before she looks, ya know."

The milking and early-morning chores done, they sat at the table sipping hot coffee—just the two of them. Eli and Benjamin had excused themselves to go finish up some work in the fields, and Katie was still in bed.

"Where *is* that girl?" he went on, looking around with a frown on his face. "She ought to be up helpin' you."

"Aw, she's exhausted from crying," Rebecca told him, her heart in her throat. She wished he wouldn't go on being hard on the girl. It wasn't kindly of him, not when Katie was suffering so. "Our daughter's like a wheel with two spokes missing."

"Two?"

Rebecca didn't even attempt to explain. Matters of the heart made little sense to her husband, practical man that he was. Things such as losing your first sweetheart to the sea and then, on top of that, losing your own sense of who you were. Well, she couldn't fault him for not understanding. He was just like that.

"Our dear girl's lost right now, Samuel, swimming in an ocean of sorrow and—"

"You're not makin' sense yourself," he interrupted. "You can't be babyin' her along when she's got things to do to get this weddin' done up just right."

Among the People, weddings were a reflection on the father of the bride. Rebecca knew that her husband had high hopes that Katie's special day would come off without a hitch. Besides, no father had ever loved a daughter more, she thought, gazing fondly at his strong profile.

Rising briskly, Rebecca cleared the table. "I best run on up and see how she's doing. She's probably got herself a real bad headache."

"Jah, and I'll be havin' one, too, if we don't get her things moved over to the Beiler place 'fore sundown," he groused. "And don't you go lettin' her make you feel bad," Rebecca heard him say as she dried her hands on the kitchen towel. "Katie owes her life to us, ya know."

That's where you're wrong, Samuel Lapp, Rebecca thought. *Don't you know it was our Katie who gave me a reason to live twenty-two years ago?* It was Katie's coming that had filled Rebecca's empty heart, her empty arms.

She climbed the long, steep steps leading to the second floor, bracing herself for whatever hurtful words Katie might fling at her first thing. Her love was strong enough to endure it. Strong enough.

As it turned out, when Rebecca knocked on the sturdy bedroom door, Katie's voice was only a muffled, sleepy sound. "Come in, Mamma."

Putting a smile on her face, Rebecca tiptoed inside. At the foot of the bed, she looked down at the rumpled quilts and covers. "Were you able to rest at all?"

Katie yawned and stretched, then sat up and pushed up her pillow behind her back. "I don't remember sleeping much . . . but I must've. I dreamed some."

"Bad dreams?"

"Jah, bad ones, all right."

Rebecca sighed. "Well, a good breakfast will do ya some good." She hated to remind Katie that a group of cousins would be arriving soon to help crack nuts and polish the silver. "Elam came over yesterday with Annie's dishes while you were out somewhere with Tobias and the pony cart."

"Satin Boy. His name is Satin Boy now, remember? I renamed him."

"Ah, I keep forgetting. A new name does take some getting used to, I must say."

Their eyes locked and held, and for one chilling moment, Rebecca felt her daughter's incredible pain. She could see in Katie's eyes the reality of what growing up Amish had done to the girl. How it had changed her entire life—stripped her of her true origins. What it meant to be the birth child of a wealthy, worldly family, never having been told of your real roots, yet knowing it in your bones as sure as you were alive.

"It must take a lifetime of gettin' used to," whispered Rebecca. "But you're Katie now . . . Katie Lapp, soon to be Katie Beiler, the bishop's gut wife."

Neither spoke for a moment. Then Katie patted the spot beside her, and Rebecca moved silently to sit on the edge of the bed. "I don't blame you, Mam," came the gentle words. "I just don't understand why it had to be such a secret."

Nodding, Rebecca reached for her hand. "I was ashamed, you see. There was a baby . . . one that died before it ever got a chance to live. And after it was born dead . . . well, the doctor said I was barren, said I'd never have any more children." She stared down at the floor and caught her breath. "I felt cursed . . . wanting more babies . . . and knowin' I'd never have 'em."

Katie listened without interrupting, letting Mam pour out her own pain.

"Then when we saw you—your Dat and I—it was like the Lord God himself was saying to me, 'Here's your heart's desire, Rebecca. Rise up and wash your face . . . put a smile on your lips. The daughter you've been longin' for is here.' And that's what we did—brought you right home to be our little girl."

"Just like that?" Katie asked, full of wonder, not pressing to know how or when or what had happened to bring all this to pass.

"Exactly like that."

"And the People? They never suspected I wasn't your real baby?"

"Not for a single minute."

"And you never once thought I looked like a 'Katherine'?"

"Not after we undressed you and put away the satin dress. Once we renamed you, I guess . . . well, you always looked like a little girl named Katie to Dat and me." She thought for a second, glancing at the ceiling with her head tilted to one side. "Jah, I can say here and now, you looked just like a Katie . . . right from the start."

Katie stared dreamily into space. "Who named me Katherine? Was it my first Mam?"

The words were a hammer blow to Rebecca's heart. Oh, not today. Not with the wedding so near. Not with Laura Mayfield-Bennett driving around Hickory Hollow, searching.

"Jah, your biological mother named you, I think."

"Did you meet her?"

"Only for a little bit." Rebecca's encounter with Laura and her mother in the hospital corridor had been brief. In fact, she seemed to recollect Laura's mother more clearly than she remembered Laura Mayfield herself.

"Did you see her long enough to know what she looked like?"

Rebecca was thoughtful. "You have her brown eyes and auburn hair."

"Anything else?"

She shook her head. "I don't remember much now."

"Well, it doesn't really matter, I guess," Katie said. "I know who my *real* mamma is." She slid over on the bed and hugged Rebecca, giving her a warm kiss.

While Katie dressed and had a late breakfast, Rebecca jotted down a list of things to be done before tomorrow. In between the writing, though, she wondered at Katie's response. She marveled that the girl hadn't ranted and raved, hadn't caused a fuss. Hadn't threatened to tell the People the truth. But she'd done none of that.

Rebecca should have felt relieved. Instead, she felt curiously unsettled.

❖　❖　❖

Katie stood at the tall window in her bedroom, looking out. The best times of her life had been before she'd learned that she was the only adopted child in Samuel and Rebecca Lapp's household. Maybe the only adopted child in all of Hickory Hollow. The best times had been the carefree days of her childhood.

Blinding hot summer days . . .

She and Mary Stoltzfus—two little Plain girls—running barefoot through the backyard, Mamma's white sheets flapping on the clothesline, past the barnyard to the old wagon road connecting Dat's farm with a wide wooded area and a large pond that lay sparkling in the sunlight.

Two little Plain girls, telling secrets as they worked the oars of the rickety old rowboat, on their way out to the island in the middle of the pond.

Two little Plain girls—birds swooping overhead, oars

splashing, sending lazy ripples through the water—laughing and chattering away the sun-kissed summer hours. . . .

In those days Katie was simply . . . Katie. Not Katherine. Not someone sophisticated. Just Plain Katie, inside and out. At least, as Plain as she could be in spite of the constant inner tugging toward fancy things. Still, she did try to follow the rules—what was expected of the People, according to the Ordnung.

But things were changing. Had already changed—overnight, it seemed. And it appeared that they would keep on changing—just like the ripples on the pond, ever circling out and away into the distance. Far, far away.

She was not Katie inside or outside, neither one. The girl with autumn brown eyes and reddish hair had come to see herself as a different person. Someone she didn't know, didn't recognize. Someone with a mother who had given her an English name. A fancy, worldly name.

Katherine.

The name did not sit well. She fought the fog of numbness, attempting to sort out her feelings, to push resentment aside. The growing resentment she was feeling for her parents, the *adoptive* parents who had kept their secret locked up for more than twenty-two years.

For a moment, she allowed herself to wonder about her real parents, especially her birth mother. Who was she? *Where* was she? And why had she stayed away for so very long?

◈　◈　◈

The first thing Katie wanted to do when she saw Mary coming through the back door was to take her aside to a secluded corner of the old farmhouse and tell her the secret. Instead, she greeted her calmly and ushered her into the kitchen, along with about ten of her cousins. Then she rounded up extra chairs for the nut crackers as Mam put on a kettle of water to boil. There would be hot chocolate and marshmallows for everyone and slices of cheese, fresh bread, and melted butter. Apple butter, too, and pineapple preserves for those who preferred a tart topping on their warm bread.

Katie went through the motions, performing her duties like a sleepwalker, barely registering the chitchat and laughter swirling around her. She made it through—without a soul suspecting that anything was wrong—all the way to the end of the day, when Eli and Benjamin hauled her cedar chest off to the bishop's house along with several suitcases, the satin baby dress hidden inside one of them.

That evening, five men arrived to help Dat and the boys move furniture out to the barn for storage, to make room for the long wooden benches that would accommodate two hundred wedding guests indoors.

Early Wednesday morning, John Beiler and his son Hickory John arrived to help set up the benches when the two bench wagons arrived—one from the Hickory Hollow church district and one from a neighboring district. Several uncles and male cousins, as well as close neighbors, assisted in unloading the benches, unfolding the legs outdoors before taking them in the house and setting them up, following a traditional plan—the way it had always been done.

Since John Beiler, at his first wedding, had observed the customary ritual of chopping off the heads of thirty chickens needed for the wedding feast, he delegated the task to three of his brothers and other close relatives, out of respect for his deceased wife.

Rebecca, along with her two married sisters, Nancy Yoder and Naomi Zook, and their husbands, began to organize the workers, including those assigned to peeling potatoes, filling doughnuts, making cole slaw, roasting and shredding the chicken and adding the bread mixture, cleaning celery, baking pies and cakes, and frying potato chips.

Twenty-two cooks—eleven married couples—had been assigned their duties, as well as the four wedding attendants, including Katie's bridesmaid, Mary Stoltzfus, who arrived just after seven-thirty.

"You seem awful quiet again," Mary said as they escaped to Katie's bedroom for a reprieve.

Katie spread her wedding attire on the bed, leaving it out to be inspected one last time. She had starched her white apron and cape and ironed the wedding dress until there was not a wrinkle anywhere. From the sound of the hustle-bustle going on below, she knew there were only a few minutes left to tell her friend what she wanted to say. If anyone could understand, it would be Mary. "You might be surprised at what I'm going to say now," she confided.

Mary listened, her eyes darkening with concern.

"I'm thinking that I might not be able to love John as much as I should," Katie whispered. "Might not be enough to make a gut marriage, but I'll do my best. I'll do my very best." Having admitted this, she felt a weight lift from her heart.

Mary spoke tenderly. "I know ya will. And you might even surprise yourself and fall in love with the bishop. In fact, I'm sure of it. It'll happen, sooner or later."

"He's been awful kind, deciding to marry me." Katie touched the white cape, a symbol of purity. "I might've been passed over if he hadn't—"

"Now, listen," Mary interrupted. "That kind of talk won't get you anywhere. You got a lot to be thankful for, that's true, but when it all boils down, Katie, you are supposed to be marrying the bishop and don't ya ever forget it. He's a wonderful-gut man."

The way Mary said *wonderful-gut* made Katie wonder. Was her friend harboring some secret interest in the bishop?

"Just what are you thinking, Mary?"

"Well, I guess you haven't been paying much attention," Mary said, dumbfounded. "Don't you think John's nice-looking?"

"Well, I guess I never thought of him that way, really." *Not after staring into Dan's face the way I used to,* Katie thought, *wondering how on earth the Lord God could make such a handsome fellow. . . .*

"Well, you oughta be taking another look," Mary advised, slanting Katie a curious look. "You're lookin' through tainted glasses . . . and I know why. It's because of Dan, ain't? He's clouded everything up for you. But you're *supposed* to marry the bishop now."

Supposed to? If she only knew the truth. *I'm not even* supposed *to be living here in Hickory Hollow,* Katie thought, *let alone marrying a forty-year-old Amish bishop. I'm* supposed *to be Katherine Mayfield, whoever that is!*

But she didn't dare reveal Mam's secret—even to Mary. An unspoken pact had been made. Mam had suffered more than enough already. Now, faced with the opportunity to pour out her soul to her dearest friend, Katie had better sense than to add insult to injury.

She hid the numbness away, as deep inside as she could push it, just as Mam had pushed the baby dress deep into the white vase. If she did not suppress the pain, Katie feared it would surface to wound her mother yet again and tear savagely at her own future. And so she did what Mary would call "the right thing." She kept her secret safe—buried in her heart.

CHAPTER FOURTEEN

On her wedding day, Katie was up before four-thirty. It was so important for everything to go well that Dat had called a family meeting the night before to rehearse last-minute instructions. "A sloppy weddin' makes for a sloppy bride," he'd said.

Now, as Katie dressed in choring clothes by lantern light, she resisted the temptation to brush her hair down over her shoulders and play with it—arranging it this way and that—wondering how Katherine Mayfield might have looked on her wedding day.

Only in her mind, though, did she try on a satin wedding gown trimmed in lace . . . and discarded the kapp, replacing it with a shimmering white veil. So now she understood why she'd been drawn to lovely things her entire life. Understood—but didn't know what to do about it.

Katie's wedding would have none of the modern trappings such as flowers or wedding rings. The bride was to be content with her hand-sewn, homespun dress, apron, and cape. And since the day had turned out rather warm, she wouldn't have to fuss with a heavy shawl.

Won't Ella Mae be mighty glad about the weather? Katie thought, remembering how the Wise Woman had mentioned it on her most recent visit. And out of the blue came the thought that her great-aunt was probably one who suspected Katie's true origins—worldly Englishers, people outside the Amish community.

But the thought passed as quickly as it had presented itself, and Katie went about preparing for her wedding day, feeling neither pain nor joy. This numbing indifference to the shock of her mother's announcement carried her through the hours before she would answer "Jah" when Preacher Zook asked her if she would accept her brother in Christ, John Beiler, as her husband, and would not leave him until death separated them.

Delicious smells filled the house as each detail was checked off the list. At six-thirty, the assigned helpers began to arrive, and by seven o'clock, John, Katie, and their attendants were eating breakfast together in the summer kitchen, a long, sunny room off the main kitchen.

"What a heavenly day for a wedding," Mary Stoltzfus whispered in Katie's ear.

"You'll be the next one getting married . . . and soon," Katie predicted.

Overhearing the comment, John smiled. "It's a right fine day for our wedding," he said, stroking his beard. "May the Lord God bless His People."

Katie nodded, smiling back. For just an instant, a vision of Dan's face seemed to blot out John's, and she blinked in amazement. Then, rubbing her eyes, she glanced away. Would she never stop thinking of her first love?

"What's-a-matter?" John frowned, leaning toward her.

"Ach, it's nothing." She waved her hand the way her mother often did. "Nothing at all."

"Last-minute jitters often play tricks on people," John's brother Noah spoke up.

Katie opened her eyes wide, trying to erase the mirage. Mary had told her to forget about Dan Fisher, to put aside the past lest it poison the future. Mary was always right. But she'd failed to offer a suggestion as to how one did away with cherished memories.

Marrying John Beiler—putting him first—maybe that was the answer. Maybe that was why Mary had insisted that this marriage was *supposed* to be.

After breakfast, Katie went with John and the attendants through the kitchen, stopping to inspect dozens of pies that had been brought in. From the bounty harvested from their land, the good cooks of Hickory Hollow had baked up peach and apricot and cherry pies, apple and mincemeat and pumpkin.

Cakes, too. Five-pound fruitcakes and layer cakes of every variety. Later, after the wedding sermons and the actual ceremony, when Katie and John came back downstairs as husband and wife, they would see for the first time the two lovely wedding cakes decorated with nuts and candies. For Katie, who was known for her sweet tooth, there would be a wide array of other desserts to be sampled at her table—tapioca pudding, chocolate cornstarch pudding, and mouthwatering jellies, of course—Rebecca had seen to that.

In fact, the very best of all the foods was to be reserved for the *Eck*—the bride's table—a corner section placed so as to be most visible to the wedding guests. Ten twenty-foot-long tables, adequate for seating two hundred people, would be set with the best china in the house, including the dishes borrowed from Katie's sister-in-law, Annie, and others.

When it came time for members of the bridal party to change into their wedding clothes, the women—Katie, Mary, and Sarah Beiler, John's grand-niece—stepped into Katie's bedroom; the men, into Eli and Benjamin's room.

Outside, in the side yard, five teenage boys—cousins or nephews of the bride and groom—helped unhitch the horses as each carriage arrived and parked. It was an honor for a young man to be asked to be one of the Hostlers, who would care for the horses during the festivities.

Upstairs, Katie waited patiently as her mother fastened the white wedding apron and cape with straight pins at the waist, the bridesmaids looking on. When it appeared that Katie and Rebecca were ready to talk privately for the last time before the service began, Mary and Sarah discreetly left the room, waiting in the hallway as far from Benjamin's bedroom door as possible.

"I'll always love ya, Katie," Mam said, embracing her. "Always and forever."

"And I'll love you, too, Mamma."

"I wish we hadn't had to talk . . . things . . . over so close to your wedding day," Rebecca said as they drew apart, looking at each other fondly.

"Ach, it's over and done with." Katie brushed the painful thought aside.

"Over, jah."

"I'm just Plain Katie, ain't?" Even now, she was thinking of the satin baby dress, resisting the thought of its splendid feel beneath her fingers.

"Plain through and through" came the fervent response. Rebecca reached out and gripped Katie's wrists. "You do love John, now, don'tcha?"

"I love him . . . enough."

The words were hollow, and Rebecca pulled Katie to her. "You're not still thinkin' of someone else, are ya?"

Katie's voice sounded thin and desperate, even to her own ears, when she answered. "He was everything I ever wanted, Mam. Dan knew my heart. No one can ever take his place. No one."

Rebecca fluttered her lashes, and a deep worry line creased her forehead. "Himmel . . . you're in love with a memory!"

"I love Dan's memory, jah. I won't deny it. But there's more to it." She walked to the window, not wanting to hurt her mother by mentioning the music she and Dan had shared. Rebecca did not press the issue further, and Katie was relieved.

Below, gray-topped carriages were rolling down the long lane out front. Some of the young people were arriving in black open buggies. And there were a few cars—Mennonite relatives and friends, probably.

It was nearly seven-forty-five. At eight, the ushers would begin bringing guests indoors, seating them according to a prescribed order. First came the ministers, Preachers Yoder and Zook, followed by the parents of the bride and groom, and other close family and friends.

The haze that had carried Katie through the rituals of the past two days began to lift. She stared at Rebecca, not comprehending, and trembled. *Who am I, really?*

Planting a quick kiss on her mother's cheek, Katie hurried to meet Mary and Sarah in the hallway, in time for the bridal party to take their places downstairs on a long bench in the kitchen. The bench was set up near the stairway so that female guests could pass by and greet the bridal party on their way upstairs to deposit bonnets and shawls.

Bishop John sat between Katie's youngest brother, Benjamin, and John's own brother, Noah. He looked fit in his new *Multze*, a long frock coat with a split tail, and his black bow tie. He and his attendants wore high-topped shoes and wide black hats with a three-and-a-half-inch brim. His untrimmed beard was frosted with touches of gray, and although he needed reading glasses more often than not these days, he had come to his wedding without them.

Farther down the bench, Katie sat between Mary and Sarah, preparing to shake hands with the female guests. The men would assemble outside—in or around the barn—waiting until the ushers, Forgehers, brought them inside to be seated—men in one section, the women in another—same as Sunday Preaching.

Katie felt her stomach knot. She felt as though she were sitting on the middle plank of the rickety old boat, rowing toward the island—her secret childhood escape. In her mind she rowed faster and faster, energized by the sweeping pace of the oars in the water, yet feeling trapped between the shore and the longed-for hideaway. Trapped between two worlds—her place with the People, and her hunger for the modern outside world, forbidden as it was. The world of her biological parents had always beckoned to her, the world of the young woman who had sewn a satin baby gown for her infant daughter, lovingly dressed her in it, then given her away.

You got a lot to be thankful for. . . .

Katie stole a glance at John. Only two hours separated them from spiritual union. Man and wife . . . forever to live among the People, carrying on the Old Ways. She remembered her promise to him, the one she had made last Saturday—now broken. How many promises did one dare to break?

Like a sudden wind chasing wispy clouds, her thoughts trailed away and she could not recapture them. She began to greet the women, many of whom she had known since early childhood. She shook hands with Mattie Beiler when the time came, and watched as Mattie went back to help her aging mother, Ella Mae, move down the line. Katie thought of her deceased grandparents and wished Dawdi David and Mammi Essie had lived to see this day.

When Ella Mae stopped to offer Katie her thin, wrinkled hand, she felt an urge to hug the old woman. *People always do what they wanna do,* Ella Mae had told Katie once. *Even if a person sits back and does nothing, well, not doing somethin' is a decision in the end.*

Next came several of Katie's first cousins—Nancy, Rachel, and Susie Zook—followed by Naomi, Mary, and

Esther Beiler, and the girls' mothers, Becky and Mary—Ella Mae's married daughters.

Many more women came through the line. One of them was Lydia Miller—her mother's Mennonite cousin—the woman who talked to God as though He were really listening.

Lydia's handshake was warm. "May the Lord bless you today, dear," she said briefly, then went on to greet Mary Stoltzfus.

The Lord exalts those who humble themselves. . . .

If anyone was humble, it was Lydia Miller. She always dressed Plain—in long print dresses—and wore her hair tied back in a bun. Humility was written all over her round face. Love was there, too. You could see a singular compassion for the world in those eyes.

At that moment, Katie wished she knew more about Cousin Lydia, the woman targeted by the family as an example of how *not* to pray. Surely there was another side to this story.

In the short lull between guests, troublesome thoughts darted into her mind, stinging like nettles. *You looked just like a Katie . . . right from the start.*

Katie began to feel sorry for herself, though the sorrow was a mingling of anger and fear. Learning, on the eve of her wedding, that she was not truly a Lapp—a part of the fabric of the People—was like having finally learned how to sew the finest set of short, running quilt stitches and then, after criticism, deciding to rip them out.

She felt restless as the young people—the teenagers in the church district and surrounding areas—made their entrance into the house. Unmarried brothers and sisters of the bride and groom led the procession, followed by couples who were recently married or published.

I might've been passed over. . . .

A group of cousins, nephews, nieces, and friends came

in next, followed by the young boys, who quickly took their seats. All the men except Preachers Yoder, Zook, and Bishop John—because he was also a minister—removed their hats and put them under their benches. The formality represented the belief that Samuel Lapp's dwelling place was now—at this moment and for the rest of the service—a house of worship.

After the guests were seated, another old custom was carried out: The three ministers continued to wear their hats until the first hymn.

On the third stanza, Preachers Yoder and Zook stood up and made their way, followed by John and Katie, to the guest bedroom upstairs. There, Preacher Yoder began giving instruction, encouraging John and Katie, reminding them of their duties to one another as married partners in the Lord. Katie knew what was to come and wondered how embarrassing it would be not to be able to truthfully answer yes when asked if she had remained pure.

John's eyes shone with devotion as he reached for her hand and descended the stairs, entering the crowded room holding hands with Katie publicly for the first time. They made their way along the narrow aisle with their attendants.

When Katie spotted little Jacob Beiler in the crowd, he flashed an angelic grin at her as the People sang the third verse of the *Lob Lied*.

I can hardly wait for ya to come be our mamma. . . .

The bridal party found the six matching cane chairs reserved for them, and they sat down exactly in unison. Katie, Mary, and Sarah sat on one side facing John, Benjamin, and Noah.

Everywhere she looked, Katie saw the kind, honest faces of loved ones and friends—dear Nancy Beiler and her sister Susie, soon to be Katie's young charges. And there was Levi, their sullen brother, sitting with arms crossed, staring curiously at Katie. The boy would keep her on her toes; that was for certain. His brother, Hickory John, sat tall on the bench, reminding her of his father.

But there was not one soul in the house who had any idea that Katie Lapp was a disobedient church member—one who had willfully disobeyed her bishop, her beau. Who had chosen to hide her guitar instead of destroying it.

She was, therefore, guilty of unconfessed sin. And worse, she was a hypocrite—a wolf in sheep's clothing. Not having been born Amish made her quite different from anyone else present today, or so it seemed. She wondered if being adopted and never being told might not even nullify her baptismal vow.

You don't like being Amish, but you're stuck. . . . Mary's commentary echoed in her ears as the People sang the sixth and seventh verses of the next hymn.

No matter what happens, remember I love you. . . .

Would that beloved voice never stop speaking to her from the grave? Would she have to settle for an obliging relationship with John Beiler when her heart craved so much more?

The congregational singing ceased, and Bishop John's uncle stood up to give the *Anfang*, the opening, which included biblical accounts of married couples—from Adam and Eve to Ruth and Boaz. When the speaker was finished, each person turned and knelt for a period of silent prayer. While the others closed their eyes, Katie peeked at a familiar wall hanging. *One who wastes time, wastes life itself.* The old Amish saying caught her eye; the message spoke to her heart.

I've been wasting the People's time, she thought. *Dat's, Mam's, Mary's . . . Bishop John's. And my own life—have I wasted it away? Haven't I tried hard enough to follow the Ordnung?*

As quickly as the questions came, they were pushed away. She took a deep breath, remembering her life oath before God. She had made her baptismal vow before all the People, the same folk assembled here in her parents' house, soon to witness her marriage vows. *What's done is done*, she thought. And when the silent prayer was finished, she stood with all the others.

She waited respectfully as one of the deacons read the first twelve verses of Matthew, chapter nineteen, before the People sat down again. The Old Way, das Alt Gebrauch. Church order and rules—the way things were.

All of it bore down on Katie as she waited for the inevitable moment when Preacher Zook would speak first to John and then to her. He would ask her if she promised to be loyal to him and care for him in adversity, sickness, and weakness.

Preacher Yoder stood very slowly to begin the main sermon. His shoulders were slumped, and his voice so hushed that his words were almost inaudible. With each phrase, his voice grew louder, and soon he slipped into the familiar singsong manner of exhortation. Wiping the sweat off his forehead, he continued. After about an hour, he arrived at the account of Jacob and Rachel.

With eyes glistening, he reached for a German Bible and read, "For the husband is the head of the wife, even as Christ is the head of the church: and he is the savior of the body. Therefore as the church is subject unto Christ, so let the wives be to their own husbands in everything."

In everything . . .

Katie's heart sank. *Here I am, not even married yet, and I've already broken the rules of submission.* Sadly, she glanced at her father. Not even his rigid parental training had broken her will, causing her to submit to authority.

If I can't obey my own dear Dat, how can I obey a firm, standhaft man like the bishop? She wondered how long before her guilt would overtake her, before she would have to confess her refusal to destroy the guitar. Days? Weeks?

Ultimately, she would have to confess her sin to John. What a way to start a marriage!

You're like no girl I ever knowed. . . . Mammi Essie's strange words came back to Katie now like a specter, lurking in the corners of her mind.

Preacher Yoder sat down, and Preacher Zook took his place, speaking from the book of Tobit. He quoted long passages from the account of a couple named Tobit and Sara, then veered from his text and began to address the congregation: "We have before us a brother and a sister who have agreed to enter the bonds of holy matrimony, John Beiler and Katie Lapp."

Leaning slightly against her best friend and bridesmaid, Katie was tempted to reach for Mary's hand, but knew it would be inappropriate. She would simply have to get through this on her own. She must.

"If there is a brother or sister present today who can give cause why these two should not be joined in marriage, let him make it manifest at this time, for after this moment not one complaint shall be heard," the preacher stated.

Katie stiffened, and she unconsciously held her breath. Dat's words rang in her ears. *Doth a fountain send forth at the same place sweet water and bitter?*

Preacher Zook paused, giving ample time for someone to speak up, then continued, "If there be no objections, and if our sister and brother are in agreement, you may now step forward in the Name of the Lord."

Katie stood, but instead of taking John's extended hand, she walked past him, toward the preacher. Then, feeling faint, she turned to face the People. "I have something to say to all of you here." She took a deep breath, looking down at the floor for a moment.

Slowly, she allowed her gaze to drift up and out into the congregation. One by one, her family and dear friends came sharply into focus. Her parents, her brothers, Ella Mae Zook, the bishop's children, first cousins aplenty, and Mattie the midwife, who'd held a grudge for not being allowed to help bring her into the world. And there was Lydia Miller, one of the few Mennonites in attendance. Katie searched their familiar faces, wishing for a kinder way, one that would not bring anguish to her loved ones.

"I am so sorry to have to confess this," she began, "but I am not fit to marry your brother in Christ, Bishop John Beiler."

Purposely, she avoided John's eyes, knowing if she looked into them, she might break down, or worse—back away from what she knew she must do.

She made a single mistake, though. Her eyes lingered on her parents, and the pain in their faces wrenched at her heart. "I am so awful sorry," she heard herself whisper, "so sorry to hurt you like this, Dat . . . Mamma. . . ."

Rebecca gasped and stood up, her eyes bright with tears. She started to speak, but Katie didn't wait to hear her mother's pleas. She turned and fled down the narrow aisle, through the crowd of relatives and friends, to the kitchen, and past the startled cooks, her brother Elam, and Annie.

Katherine, called Katie, burst out the back door and ran from her childhood home—the temporary house of worship—away from the gaping mouths. Away from Rebecca's tear-stained face, far from the bishop she had shamed and disobeyed, from the People she had betrayed.

Far, far away.

CHAPTER FIFTEEN

❖ ❖ ❖

She's up and gone ferhoodled," Mattie Beiler whispered to one of her married daughters. "And my, oh my, ain't it odd? Why, I said this very thing at Katie's quilting just last week."

"Said what?"

"That when there's something important to do, Rebecca Lapp's daughter behaves poorly." Mattie shook her head, muttering. "Katie—running out on her own wedding. Well, if that don't beat all."

Several benches away, Rebecca whispered something to her husband, and while the baffled bishop stood at the front with Preacher Zook, she dashed toward the kitchen and proceeded to rush out the back door. "Katie! Katie, come back!"

John Beiler, eyes wide and hands shoved hard into his pockets—accompanied by his friend, Preacher Zook— headed for the now vacant chairs and sat with the rest of the bridal party, who appeared to be quite befuddled. He sat there for only a few awkward seconds, then stood up again and left the room, making his way into the enclosed front porch, which would have accommodated the guests during the wedding feast if Katie hadn't just run off.

"Well, what do ya make of it?" Preacher Zook asked.

John shook his head. "Something must be troubling her. She wasn't herself this morning."

"Well . . ." The Preacher paused, probably wondering how best to comfort his longtime friend. "Do you have any idea why she would have done such as this?" Before John could attempt a response, he continued, "It's not like the *Madel's* getting any younger. For all she knows, this might've been her last chance at marriage."

John nodded in agreement, but secretly suspected that Katie's rash act had something to do with the way he'd handled things at her confession last week. Had he failed to get over to her the seriousness of her offense? Treated the matter too lightly—seeing as how she was soon to be his bride? He scratched his beard and was mulling over the whole sorry mess when Samuel Lapp appeared in the doorway.

"What words can I offer ya?" Samuel inquired. "My daughter is gravely in the wrong." He bowed his head.

"Do not blame yourself for Katie's actions," Preacher Zook spoke up.

"I've done my best bringin' her up in the fear of the Lord, but this . . . this . . ."

Preacher Yoder came out of the front room to join them on the porch. " 'Tis a shameful thing witnessed here today."

"Jah, shameful," Samuel said, still hanging his head till his beard brushed his chest. "Our gut bishop . . . spurned by his own bride."

"Maybe she'll come to her senses . . . realize what she's done," Preacher Zook offered.

Samuel shook his head. "Ya don't know my Katie. The girl's headstrong, she is. Has been, since the day she was born. Only her Mam could ever do anything with her."

"Such a reproach to the church," Preacher Yoder put in. "She must come clean of it, repent."

John remembered Katie's penitent attitude last Saturday—the sweet, innocent way she had approached him, coming into the room toward him, allowing him to hold her hands a bit longer than necessary. He remembered . . . and longed for her, even now.

At last he spoke. "As for confessing, let the subject be dropped. That's all that need be said." The men ceased their speculating and went back into the house.

Inside, John heard the low buzz of conversation. Katie Lapp, running out of her own wedding . . . well now, nothing like *this* had ever happened in Hickory Hollow.

The bridal party—what was left of it—was still seated together, shifting nervously. With no precedent for such a thing, apparently they weren't sure what to do next. One by one and in pairs, the other guests began to move about but did not leave, waiting for a decision to be made as to what should be done.

As for John himself, all he could feel was a throbbing ache in the area of his heart—an emptiness that only Katie could fill.

"What could've caused her to do such a horrid thing?" Sarah Beiler asked Mary Stoltzfus.

Mary, noticing Bishop John the instant he came back into the room, colored slightly. "I can't say, really," she replied evasively. Feeling the bishop's gaze on her, she dipped her head in humility. Poor man. What he must be going through!

"You must know *something* about her getting cold feet," Mattie's granddaughter persisted. "You've known her all your life!"

"No, no, I have no idea what Katie was thinking." She couldn't always read the older girl's actions, although heaven knows she'd tried these many years. *What'll happen now?* she wondered, feeling a little guilty about the urge to sneak glances at her best friend's former beau.

Actually, truth be told, she hoped John Beiler was through with the likes of Katie Lapp. The girl had pushed her limits, after all. Hadn't listened to a thing Mary had been trying to tell her all along. Yet, in spite of her frustration, she couldn't help feeling compassion for her friend. "I best be looking for Katie," Mary told Sarah, excusing herself as she sailed past Benjamin Lapp, who was scowling fiercely.

Mary proceeded to search the house for Rebecca Lapp. Surely, if she could find Katie's mother, the two of them could talk some sense into the bishop's bride-to-be. What on earth had Katie meant by saying she was unfit to marry their brother in Christ? Didn't she consider John Beiler *her* Christian brother, too?

Ella Mae looked on as Katie's best friend scurried about the house, going from room to room. The Wise Woman knew that Mary would ultimately catch up with Rebecca— but no matter. Neither Mary Stoltzfus nor Rebecca Lapp would be able to talk Katie into returning to the house. Not now . . . maybe not for hours.

Ella Mae knew things about Katie. Intimate, sorrowful things. Over the years, she'd listened as the young girl had come to her, spilling out her woes—her fickle growing-up years, her heartache over Daniel Fisher . . . and here lately, something about an English baby dress and a promise she couldn't keep.

What the promise was, Ella Mae couldn't tell. But one thing was for sure and for certain: The broken promise— whatever it was—had some bearing on why Katie had left her groom so disgraced and alone.

She sighed, wondering what she might have said or done differently to change the way things were turning out for the poor, lost lamb.

"She was gonna be my mamma," little Jacob Beiler

wailed to his sister Nancy, sitting near the bridal party. "She was, honest she was. . . ."

"Now, now. Try not to cry." Putting a big-sisterly hand on his shoulder, Nancy patted him, ending with a firm shake. "You're a big boy now." She sure hoped her youngest brother wouldn't cause a spectacle—the way Katie had.

Ach—embarrassing her father like that! Nancy felt her face redden. It was a disgraceful thing. Surely God himself would rain down judgment.

Maybe it was just as well that Katie Lapp was not coming home to be their mother. Besides, no one could take their own Mam's place. . . .

Levi Beiler uncrossed his long arms and glanced about, his gaze falling on the old woman several rows behind him. Ella Mae Zook appeared to be as baffled as everyone else, although he thought he spotted a glimmer of hope in her eyes and wondered what it meant. He could almost taste the hot cocoa the Wise Woman had ordered up for him last Thursday, exactly one week ago.

Katie was making ready last week, he thought. *She was making ready to do this very thing today. Planning to leave Daed without marrying him.*

Usually timid and aloof, Levi suddenly felt bold. He was thinking of the lost English stranger with reddish hair and the long black car. Somehow or other, the fancy woman just might be connected to what happened here today. He stood up and sauntered back to say "Hullo" to the Wise Woman.

About that time, though, Samuel Lapp asked for everyone's attention. Levi listened carefully, hoping that the food for the wedding feast would be put to good use.

Samuel cleared his throat. "You're all welcome to stay on and eat the noon meal with us. We will break bread together in spite of what has just taken place."

Levi was sorely disappointed when Daed called his five

children to him and prepared to leave the house. He'd sure hoped they'd at least stay long enough to eat.

When all six of them passed the tables, laden with pies and cakes and all kinds of mouth-watering goodies, his stomach growled. And just when it seemed all hope was gone, Annie Lapp came to the rescue, calling on her husband to fill some baskets for "Bishop John's family."

In spite of Daed's forlorn look, Levi and the rest of them headed outdoors for the newly painted carriage—intended to carry home a new Mam—happy with their tasty treasures. He could hardly wait to get home and dig in.

In fact, he *didn't* wait. The preaching service had lasted over two and a half hours, and he was hungry. He pinched off a hunk of warm bread and stuffed it into his mouth.

His baby sister spied him. "Levi's snitchin'," Susie piped up.

Their father did not reply until the girl repeated herself. At last, John Beiler waved his hand distractedly. "Leave your brother be."

Levi grinned, and Susie pursed her lips at him. Simultaneously, Nancy and Hickory John each put a hand on Levi's shoulder. Daed was in no mood for their pranks, it was clear to see.

"Where's Katie, Daed?" little Jacob asked, looking a bit worried. "Ain't she comin' home with us?"

John shook his head. "Not today."

"Did she take sick, maybe?"

It took a long time for Daed to make up his mind, it seemed. "Can't say she's sick exactly. She didn't seem to be feeling poorly earlier today. But about now, I'd be guessin' she's feeling a bit sickly—same as I do."

Levi felt sorry for his father, and if they hadn't been out in broad open daylight, he'd have put his basket of food down and climbed up front to sit beside him. *Poor Daed. First, Mamma has to die . . . and now this. . . .*

❖   ❖   ❖

Rebecca made a beeline for the haymow, where Katie often escaped to be alone. She scrambled up the ladder leading to the soft bed of hay high above the lower level and called, "Katie? Are you up here?"

She checked behind several bales of hay, hoping to find Katie hiding there, sulking. She found only the barn cats and plenty of dust. When she was satisfied that the place was unoccupied, except for six or seven mouse-catchers, Rebecca turned to leave, heading outside again. This time she walked on the mule roads, choosing one that led toward the woods.

Discouraged, she trudged along the vacant clearing, willing away tears of regret and disappointment. If she expected to help her daughter through this crisis, she'd have to remain sober and dry-eyed. Yet she felt resentment growing in her. What had possessed Katie to abandon the bishop on her day of days? What on earth could have been more important than marrying such a fine Amishman?

A frightening notion struck her. Laura Mayfield-Bennett might even now be driving around the area, hoping for a glimpse of her long-lost child. She was dying, she'd written. That much Rebecca remembered, although there were times since she'd burned the letter that she wished she could remember more of its contents.

What would it be like to be dying . . . never knowing your only child? Rebecca sighed, pushing on. Much as she hated to admit it, she really couldn't blame the woman. Any mother would do the same.

The stillness was almost eerie. The sun seemed to have forgotten it was mid-November and shone as hard and hot as though summer had returned, beating against Rebecca's back. Her strides were short and swift as she made her way to the woods and beyond, then into the clearing and toward the pond with its secluded island.

She stood on the shoreline, searching the area with hungry eyes. The old boat was nowhere to be seen—Rebecca's first clue that her daughter may have chosen the childhood fortress as her refuge.

"Katie!" she called, cupping her hands around her lips. "Katie, it's Mamma!"

She waited, hearing nothing.

"Katie, are you all right?" she called again, studying the island where tall willow trees tangled with thick dry underbrush, creating a private cove unseen from this side.

Her heart beat faster, and she called again and again, feeling the sorrow and the rejection gouge as deep as the silence.

Would Katie answer if her flesh-and-blood mother were calling to her now? The thought left her weary.

"You don't have to tell me what's-a-matter, Katie, honest ya don't. Just let me be with you, girl."

She waited, longing for the voice she loved so dearly. But nothing could be heard except the sound of crows flitting back and forth across the placid water.

Then she knew what must be said—the one thing that might make things easier for Katie. She said it with great sincerity, her voice cracking as she aimed her plea again in the direction of the island. "You don't have to go back to the house just now. Don't even have to marry the bishop if ya don't want."

The waiting could have been likened to the travail of childbirth, so intense was it. Yet, just as her stillborn baby had never been given breath to voice its life cry, neither did Katie utter a sound.

Torn between the impulse to leap into the pond and swim to Katie, and her obligation to the People gathered in

her home, Rebecca sadly turned away and headed for the
wooded trail.

Under a willow tree nearest the center of the island,
Katie sat with knees pulled up tightly under her chin. She
had removed her devotional kapp and unpinned her bun,
allowing the long auburn tresses to flow down over the front
of her dress. Singing her favorite tunes, she ran her fingers
through the traditional middle hair part, separating the
strands, and swept it to one side, then plaited it into a thick
braid.

She played with her hair to her heart's content, wishing
for a small hand mirror to view the new look. The fancy new
woman.

She began to sing louder as she unraveled her hair and
rebraided it, weaving in dried wisps of willow leaves, wishing they were gold cords or silken hair ribbons.

"I'm Katherine now," she called to the sky. "My name is
Katherine Mayfield." She forced images of her parents' sad
faces from her mind.

Looking out toward the pond, she decided to have a
peek at herself and would have made it to the small pier,
except that she heard her mother's voice at that very moment. Quickly, she crouched in the shelter of the brownish
willow curtain. Despite the absence of lush greenery, she
was certain she was well hidden. Several times Mam called
out to her, probably hoping to lure her from her hiding
place. But Katie didn't budge. This was *her* day. A day to sort
out the questions and haunting fears. A day to let the fancy
side of her go unbridled, with no one to call her to account.

She waited until she saw her mother turn and, with
shoulders slouched, plod back to the wooded trail and home
to face their guests. Katie allowed herself just the tiniest
twinge of regret for placing her parents in this embarrassing
position. Still, they'd most likely go on with the feast as

planned, eating and visiting and wondering what had possessed her. There would be no lighthearted celebration under the circumstances, but the atmosphere would be sweet with the bond of peace and the kindred spirit of the People.

No matter. This was her time, and she planned to make the most of it. Katie crept toward the pier and flattened herself against it, staring into the pond water below.

Her hair. How different it looked. In place of the familiar center part, her shiny hair lifted at the top before dipping slightly over one eye, the silky cascade caught up in an intricate design. She pulled at the willow leaves twining through the thick strand and flicked pieces into the water, making ripples on the glassy surface. She watched the ripples widen until they washed up on the far shore. Somewhere deep within, she recognized the symbolism of her own life.

Who am I, really? she wondered. *If I'm Katherine Mayfield underneath my skin, then who is this Katie Lapp dressed in dull, homespun clothing?* She dangled her kapp over the pier, staring at its reflection.

She was on to something, but she didn't know exactly what. Pensive, she watched a leaf float lazily out of sight. A good Plain woman obeyed the Ordnung, was totally submissive. How could she have failed so miserably? In trying to be good, she had become weak. How had the teachings of the People turned her into someone she was not? Someone who could disobey the very bishop who had administered her life oath—her kneeling baptism? Someone who could hurt that same bishop beyond words, and in the presence of the entire church district, too?

But she must not dwell on that. Truth be told, she had been wounded the most.

Getting to her feet, she walked to the shore and pulled the old boat out from under the pier and turned it right side up. Then, stabbing the pond's surface with the oars, she rowed to the other side.

Within minutes, Mary Stoltzfus met up with her on the mule road leading back to the farm. "Where've you been? Your Mam's worried sick." Mary's eyebrows shot up as she took a closer look at Katie. "And what's happened to your hair?" She reached up and touched the wide braid, still adorned with the willow leaves. "Where's your kapp?"

Katie rumpled her head covering into a ball. "I'm not coming back to marry John, if that's what you're thinking. So don't be asking me what happened. Besides, I think you already know."

"But aren't you the least bit concerned about the bishop's feelings? And his children . . . what about them?"

Katie wished Mary hadn't mentioned John's family. Dear little Jacob's face would be forever emblazoned on her memory. She had let the lad down. She'd let all of them down.

"It was never meant to be—the bishop and I," she said. "And hard as I tried, I was not meant to be Amish, either."

Mary shook her head. "Ach, not this again. I thought you had all that business behind ya."

"Well, I don't."

"But the right thing to do is—"

"I'm not interested in doing the right thing anymore," she retorted. "I've been trying to do the right thing all my life, and it never worked."

Mary's blue eyes widened in horror. "But Katie, what on earth are you talkin' about?"

"Just what I said. It's not working out for me to be Amish. I wish it hadn't taken so long for me to see it, but I know now what's the matter with me . . . why I can't seem to measure up around here." Katie cast a woeful glance at the farmhouse just below the sloping grade. She would not reveal the truth of her so-called adoption—such things should be left to Dat and Mam to decide. For now, she was simply eager to play her new role as Katherine Mayfield.

"I'm going into town for a bit, so if you don't mind—"

"You're going . . . where?" Mary's eyes were becoming lighter and lighter, surprisingly luminous as though Katie's odd behavior were robbing them of their color. "What you *need* to do is go in there and apologize to everyone."

"No, I won't be doing any such thing."

Mary's voice came soft. "Aren't you sorry for what you did?"

"Sorry? I did the bishop a favor by running out of his wedding. Those sweet children, too." Katie felt a lump rise in her throat.

Mary frowned and bit her lip. "What did you mean when ya said John wasn't your brother in Christ?"

"You heard me right, Mary." The braid swung around as Katie headed for the barn. "Satin Boy and I are taking a ride."

"Satin Boy? When did you give him such a curious name?"

"A while back."

Before Mary could question her further, Katie hitched up her pony to the cart. "I'll be back 'fore dark. Tell Mam I'm all right."

"But you're *not*. I can see it clear as day, you're not all right, Katie Lapp!"

CHAPTER SIXTEEN

❖ ❖ ❖

The road was crowded with cars and trucks—buses, too—some honking their horns impatiently as they sped past, leaving Katie in their dust. But she persevered, riding in the pony cart, perched high for the whole English world to see.

At last she turned into a small strip mall, tied Satin Boy to a fireplug, and unhitched the cart. "I'll get you some water in a bit," she promised. "Be back soon."

Eager to see all she could, Katie glanced up and down the row of shops, her eyes coming to rest on an elegantly furnished display window. Squaring her shoulders, she marched toward the boutique, intent on trying on some fancy, worldly clothes.

"May I help you, miss?" The saleslady was obviously trying not to stare, Katie thought. Still, she must look a sight in her rumpled long dress and apron, her braid, woven with willow, tumbling over one shoulder.

"I'd like to try on the fanciest satin dress you have."

"Satin?"

"Jah. You do have it, don't you?"

"Well, no, we don't normally carry satin until later in the season." The woman picked up her glasses, which had been dangling from a chain around her neck, and placed them on the bridge of her nose. "Is the garment for yourself . . . or someone else?"

Katie chuckled under her breath. "Oh, it's for me, all right. It's time I get to see what I've been missing."

Blinking rapidly, the woman turned to the counter. "If you'd like, I can check with one of the other stores, say in York or Harrisburg. They carry a larger inventory."

"No, no," Katie interrupted, "it's important that I see something *today*." Spotting a rack of exquisite dresses with brocade bodices and lace detailing, she left the lady gaping at the counter and hurried over. "What about one of these?"

She lifted a soft chiffon gown off the rack and held it up to herself in front of a wide three-way mirror. Turning this way and that, she admired her reflection from several angles, humming one of the songs she loved the best. Dan's song.

"What size are you looking for, miss?"

"I don't know, really," Katie replied, thinking of all the sewing she had done for herself over the years. Still, it was a bit overwhelming—seeing all these garments in a dazzling variety of colors, styles, and fabrics, just waiting to be worn. "I've never been asked that question before, but I 'spose I ought to find out. Why don't I just try it on and see for myself?"

The clerk seemed at a loss for words. "Uh . . . yes. Of course. Right this way."

Without bothering to inspect the price tag, Katie followed her to a small dressing room at the back of the shop. At the touch of the saleslady's hand, a velvet pull curtain draped her in privacy, just Katie and the sheer golden dress—fragile as a butterfly's wing.

When she turned, she let out a little gasp, catching her reflection unexpectedly. The tiny space was covered with mirrors on all sides—from floor to ceiling. "Am I dreaming?" she whispered as she touched the glass with her finger.

Relishing every second, Katie removed her clothing.

First, her apron, then her Plain—very plain—wedding dress. With great care and near reverence, she lifted up the fanciest gown ever created. It slipped easily over her head and dropped lightly onto her shoulders, coming to rest at an astonishing mid-calf.

She loved the swishing song of the fabric, the silky feel of it against her skin. And, oh glory, the open neckline, free and unrestrictive!

Katie stepped back to admire herself, inching away from the mirror to grasp her full reflection. This was no Katie! This had to be Katherine. But even while reveling in the moment, she was feeling robbed, cheated of the years when she'd been deprived of her rightful heritage. Would she ever be able to wear the rich, vibrant colors of the English without having to do so in secret?

She wondered, too, about the woman who had named her Katherine. What kind of woman would allow herself to bring a child into the world without nurturing that life? Would give the baby a fancy name and then hand her off to some stranger? What kind of person did such things?

Her joy tainted, Katie stepped out of the filmy dress and retrieved her own clothes. "Someday I'll wear a dress like this out in public," she promised herself. "Someday I will." With tears filling her eyes, she slipped the hanger gently into each puffed sleeve and hung the dress on a two-pronged hook.

"Do come again," the salesclerk called to her.

Katie did not reply. She hurried outside to Satin Boy and the old wooden cart, never looking back.

❖ ❖ ❖

On the way home, Satin Boy began to labor under his load. "Aw, poor thing . . . can you keep going a bit longer?"

Katie coaxed him from her seat. "We'll stop by Elam's and Annie's and get some water for you. All right?"

Satin Boy struggled as Katie reined him toward the long dirt drive leading to her big brother's farmhouse, two miles east of the sandstone house on Hickory Lane.

"Look, Elam! Look who's come!" Annie called to her husband from the front porch of their white clapboard house. Annie waved at Katie as though she hadn't just seen her that morning.

"I didn't think my pony was going to make it here," Katie called to them, forgetting how peculiar she must look with her hair in the forbidden braid—and without her kapp. "My pony's dry to the bone. Can I water and feed him?"

Elam marched down the steps and promptly removed the harness from the tired animal. Her brother eyed Katie sternly. His look of reproach reminded her of Dat, but Elam didn't voice a single word of rebuke. Katie stood there watching as he led Satin Boy around to the barn behind the house.

He's put out with me, Katie thought. *And rightly so. I've caused everyone so much trouble.* She knew the pressure was bound to build up sooner or later, until her brother spouted off about the wedding.

Reluctantly, she headed up the steps where Annie stood waiting, her hands folded over her protruding stomach. "You should have seen the way Satin Boy was acting up on the road," Katie told her.

"I thought his name was Tobias." Annie eyed Katie's hairstyle and quickly looked away.

"Things change."

"Oh." Annie opened the screen door and went inside. "Come in and have something to drink for yourself," she called over her shoulder.

It wasn't until Annie had offered her a tall glass of iced tea and she'd sat down at her brother's table that Katie realized how thirsty and tired she was. "It was a pretty foolish thing to go so far with just a pony," she mused aloud.

Annie lowered herself carefully onto the bench beside the table. "Where'd you end up going?"

"Out to Bird-in-Hand." Katie would have gladly said more but feared she would be letting herself in for all kinds of questions. Besides, Annie Lapp knew nothing about ladies' dress shops and boutiques. She was a good, upstanding Amishwoman. Women like Annie were never tempted to peek into worldly English shops.

Annie's eyes seemed fixed on her now, Katie thought, probably because she was trying to figure out why she wasn't wearing her kapp. "Well, my goodness, what were you doing way over there?" Annie blurted.

Katie flinched. Should she tell? Should she divulge the secret pleasure of a few hours away from home, trying on the fanciest chiffon party dress in all of Lancaster County?

She took a good look at Annie—Daniel's beloved sister. She looked so like the boy with blueberry eyes! And oh, dear Lord, her baby would probably look like him, too. Katie shuddered to think of being haunted by Dan's expression on the faces of her own nephews and nieces. Of course, Elam's offspring would carry some of his traits, as well. But as spirited and attractive as Daniel Fisher had always been, Katie suspected that her big brother's children would bear a strong resemblance to her one true love. *Just as I must look something like my real mamma. . . .*

The notion startled her and she shrugged it off, trying to remember what it was that Annie had asked her. She was relieved when her sister-in-law brought it up again.

"Were you distraught today, Katie? Is that why you left the wedding ceremony?" Annie asked softly. "Because if ya need to talk, well . . . I'm here for you. Anytime."

Touched by the offer, Katie reached across the table to squeeze her sister-in-law's hand. "I just might be taking you up on that," she whispered as the guilt crept back, threatening to spoil her moment of freedom. She stiffened her back, determined to make every minute count.

Elam came in noisily, bumping around in the utility room and shutting the door with a resounding bang before making his way into the kitchen. One glance at Katie, and he began to shake his head. "You need to be findin' your kapp and wearin' it, don'tcha think?"

Katie tilted her head and surveyed her oldest brother. "I don't have to *find* it," she stated. "I know exactly where it is."

"Then why isn't it on your head where it belongs? And what're those knots all the way down your hair?"

Annie's eyes caught her husband's in a meaningful stare, much the way Mam and Dat often exchanged glances. Katie almost expected to hear Annie speaking up on her behalf, but when she didn't, Katie knew she was on her own. Rebecca Lapp was the one and only woman who had ever taken her side against a man.

Elam was close to scolding her now. Katie could see the telltale signs—his twitching eyes, the flaring nostrils. She didn't want to risk humiliation, not in front of Annie.

"I got a bit ferhoodled, maybe."

"Ferhoodled? Jah! And when Dat gets ahold of ya, you'll be wishin' you'd walked up to the preacher with John Beiler at your side and gone through with your weddin' vows!"

"Don't speak to me that way, Elam Lapp!"

"It's about time *someone* did," he said, barely able to check his anger. "Dat never could, that's for sure."

"Leave him out of this!" Katie demanded. "Dat's done just fine raising me and you know it."

"I'm tellin' ya right now," Elam went on, "if you go home with your hair lookin' like that, you'll be regretting it long before mornin'."

Her brother was right. Tonight there would be a tongue-lashing from Dat, and first thing tomorrow, either Elam or Dat would report her multiple transgressions to Preacher Yoder or Bishop John.

"I'm ashamed of ya, Katie. You must try and stay in Jesus," he said. "You must try."

Katie stood and headed for the back door. "I'll be going now. And don't call me Katie anymore. My name is Katherine."

"Since when?" Elam sneered.

"Since the day I was born," she said over her shoulder as she reached for the doorknob. Suddenly she felt uneasy, fearful that she had stepped into forbidden territory, a place that could only lead to betrayal.

"You're talkin' nonsense. Better get your hair done up in a bun. And don't say ya weren't warned," Elam called after her. "Sinning against the church is no laughing matter . . . it's sinning against God." Elam sat beside his wife at the table, his head bowed now.

"Good-bye, Annie," said Katie, completely ignoring her brother.

Annie's farewell was a whispered "Da Herr sei mit du."

❖   ❖   ❖

The afternoon was still hot, and the sun shone heavy on the round, full hills south of the road.

You must try and stay in Jesus. Elam's words echoed in her mind. But the logical side of her brain argued back: Did staying in Jesus require her to wear the kapp at all times? Must she wear her hair long and forever parted down the middle—squeezed into a bun? Was this the only way?

Daniel Fisher had not thought so. Salvation came, he'd often told her, through faith in Jesus Christ—not by works, not by following man-made rules.

213

She sighed, letting Satin Boy plod along at his own pace. If need be, she would get out and walk the rest of the way home.

Why hadn't she paid more attention to Daniel back then? Why had she gone along with the teachings of her parents' Meinding church without question, ruling out the other Christian churches outside of Hickory Hollow?

Katie knew why, of course. She was young, too unsure of herself to leave the Old Ways and embrace the New. Too ignorant of the Scriptures to debate them. Dan, on the other hand, had secretly joined a Bible study group somewhere. Not only had he memorized several chapters of the Bible, but he was learning what they meant and how their truths could change a life committed to Christ. Wisely, he'd kept his activities hidden from the rest of the People. Only Katie had been aware of his secret. Of this she was fairly certain.

If Dan had lived, she knew he could help her now. He could lead her to the truth—wherever it was to be found.

An ominous feeling settled over her as the red sandstone house came into view. The truth, she was almost assured, was not found in wearing a head covering or denying oneself an occasional braid now and then.

In defiance of it all, she sang—a vigorous rendition of "What a Friend We Have in Jesus." Satin Boy, apparently inspired by the rhythm of the melody, began to pick up speed.

"Gut boy!" Katie called to him and promised a long brushing and some fresh hay and water when they got to the barn. They passed the wide front yard and turned into the dirt lane leading to the barnyard.

She put off going into the house as long as possible. Finally, when she heard Mam call to the men, she slipped out of the pony stall and headed for the kitchen door.

Tiptoeing into the utility room, she remembered the festive atmosphere of the house just hours before—the multitude of wedding guests, the greeting lines, the sermons, and the cooks preparing for a feast. Its present somber appearance convicted her.

Quickly, she began to wind her hair around her hand, ready to put it up into the usual bun, but changed her mind and let the tresses fall down her back. It was too late now to make amends. What was done was done.

"Katie, you're back!" Mam cried, spotting her. She hurried over and wrapped her arms around the prodigal, appearing not to notice Katie's unruly hair springing free of the confining kapp. "I came looking for you after ya ran out of the house," she babbled. "I went out to the pond and called and called. Where on earth did you go?"

Katie shook her head. This wasn't the time. "Maybe you won't understand this, Mamma," she said, looking at the woman who had cared for her from infancy, "but I can't talk about it just yet."

"Well . . . it'll keep 'til after supper, then."

Katie held her breath as she entered the kitchen with Mam at her side. Even with Elam's warning, she was not prepared for Dat's display of righteous indignation. "Where's your head covering, daughter? Don't you have any respect at all for God's laws—not to mention the poor bishop's feelin's tonight—without a wife to warm his bed or a Mam for his children!" He ranted on for minutes that seemed like hours while, at her side, tiny gasps of emotion escaped Rebecca's lips.

"I know for a fact that Preacher Yoder'll be comin' to talk to you in a couple of days," Dat went on as the Lapp family sat down around the supper table.

"I'll speak to him," Katie agreed quietly.

"Gut, I'm glad you're coming to your senses."

Katie breathed deeply. "I don't mean that I'll be confessing, though, if that's what you're thinking. It's just that I want to ask him some questions—about the Scriptures."

There was no audible response. But when Dat bowed his head for the silent prayer over the meal, the ritual lasted at least twice as long as usual.

Eli gave her a long, cold glare and would not accept any of the serving plates she passed him.

He's treating me like I'm a shunned woman, Katie thought.

Benjamin, however, was kinder, passing the bowls of buttered potatoes, carrots, and onions, and the ham platter to his brother on behalf of Katie.

Halfway through the meal, Dat exploded. "I will not eat another bite until ya go put up your hair the right and holy way!"

Startled at this outburst, Katie got up from the table and ran upstairs to her room. With trembling hands, she brushed her hair and wound it into a bun, without even checking the straightness of the part in her hand mirror. Then, finding a clean, pressed kapp, she placed it on her head and scurried back downstairs like a frightened mouse.

Meanwhile, Dat had pushed his chair away from the table, still muttering about the disgrace she'd brought on the Lapp family.

Katie said nothing. She was wounded to the depths of her spirit. But she would not allow her father the satisfaction of witnessing the pain he had caused. In fact, his reaction—though not unexpected—only fueled her resolve to speak to the preacher when the time came.

Later that night, after the kitchen was cleaned up, but before evening prayers, Benjamin whispered to Katie that she must come outside with him. Katie, unwilling that Dat be aware of some vague conspiracy, agreed. They waited for the best time to slip out—during one of his longer snoozing sessions in front of the woodstove.

Once outside, Benjamin headed for the milk house at a brisk stride.

"What's so important?" Katie wanted to know, doing her best to keep up.

"I have to tell ya—Dat's not just encouraging you to confess," he said, his breath pluming in the frosty air. "He's madder'n a hornet at whatcha did today."

"Well . . . he's got every right."

"Jah, and he's not the only one who's plenty angry." Benjamin opened the heavy door and held it for his sister. It was warmer there in the milk house. "You spurned the *bishop* in front of all the People, for goodness' sake! Such a shameful, awful thing ya did."

Katie nodded but resisted the guilt that inched nearer. "I didn't expect John to be angry, really," she thought aloud. "Hurt or disappointed, maybe . . . but not angry."

"Jah, and here's what I wanted to tell ya before tomorrow. If you don't go ahead and promise to confess in front of the whole church come Sunday, you'll be in danger of the Ban, Katie. *The Ban!*"

She felt a sliver of fear—like an icicle—cold and tingly. Still, she shouldn't have been surprised to hear it. After all, she'd as much as announced publicly that John Beiler was not her brother in Christ.

In the eyes of the People, she was a sinner. She deserved to be excommunicated.

"Better be thinkin' things over, Katie. I'd hate to see ya put through die Meinding, really I would."

Die Meinding—the shunning. The mere thought of it sent another tremor rippling down her spine.

"There's been talk already. . . ." Ben paused and scratched his head, as if wondering if he should have kept his mouth shut.

"What're you tellin' me, Ben?"

"Well"—he glanced around, looking toward the house—"Mam asked Eli and me to go over to the bishop's and get your cedar chest and suitcases and things and bring 'em back home."

"Jah?" She felt her throat constrict.

"While we was there, Eli heard Bishop John talkin' things over with his friend, Preacher Zook." He paused, his eyes growing soft. "I'm tellin' ya, Katie, things could get real bad for ya. And awful quick, too."

"I can't confess. I just can't."

Benjamin stared at her in disbelief. "You can't *not* confess."

"But it would be a lie." She reached up and plucked off the kapp again, pulling out the hairpins that held her bun in place. "Look at me! I'm not the person you think I am, Ben. I'm not Amish."

He frowned, shaking his head.

"I ain't Plain. The kneeling baptism never happened to me—not the me you see standing before you here."

Ben was obviously puzzled. "You're talkin' in riddles."

"Jah, I am. But my whole life has been a riddle." She shook her head sadly. "I wish I could, but I honestly can't say any more about this now. Someday I'll be able to tell you, promise I will."

"Someday will never come if you're shunned, Katie. And ya don't want to wait and see, I guarantee!"

Ben's prophecy bore deep, plunging a shaft of terror into the very recesses of her soul.

CHAPTER SEVENTEEN

The next day the weather turned chilly again with needle-like pellets of rain pounding the frozen ground. Plumes of vapor from the horses' warm breath hung in the air, mingling with thready fog, as the People made their way to quiltings or weddings and an occasional farm sale around Hickory Hollow.

Katie still had no answers to the questions that plagued her like a swarm of mosquitoes on a summer day. Preacher Yoder would surely be able to set her mind at ease over the biggest question of all—the one she was hoping might solve all her problems and put an end to the talk of the Ban and shunning. But in order to inquire about it, she would have to tell Preacher Yoder her parents' secret.

Would Dat consent to it? After the blowup last night, would he allow her to reveal such a thing?

She decided to approach her mother instead. And while the two of them were working together, unpacking Katie's suitcase and rearranging her linens in the cedar chest, she brought up the idea.

"No, no, no!" Rebecca was adamant. "There'll be no telling it around that you're adopted!"

"But I have to tell Preacher Yoder."

"You'll do no such thing." The look in the hazel eyes was almost fierce.

"But don't you see?" Katie went on. "If Preacher knew the truth—that I'm not Amish by birth—then everything else would make sense to him."

Mam shot her a curious glance. "*What* would make sense?"

"My troubles with being Plain," Katie mumbled under her breath, so softly she wasn't certain she'd been heard.

The silence hovered between them for the longest time, and Katie wondered if she should repeat herself. She touched her braid, feeling the series of ripples up and down the length of it, and wondered if her father would force her to put her hair up again today.

Finally, Mam spoke up. "Your troubles don't come from being adopted, Katie," she admonished. "Your troubles come from a disobedient spirit."

Katie shrugged. "Still, I should be telling the truth about my birth mother, don't you think? My English background?"

The next outburst was such a shock that Katie could only gape in amazement. Was this the sweet-tempered mamma who'd never raised her voice in anger in her life? "No! You can't tell, Katie"—she was actually shouting now—"because I forbid it!"

Turning away, Katie hid her face in her hands and tried to calm herself. When she looked up, Rebecca was gone.

Katie tossed the remaining items of clothing into the only dresser in the room, and eyes filling with angry tears, she located the rose baby dress in a compartment of the suitcase. Then, stuffing the dress into a pocket of her apron, she hurried downstairs and out of the house, letting the storm door slap hard against the frame.

She would not wait around for Preacher Yoder to come to her; she'd go to him. What she was about to do would bring hurt to her mother, she knew. But her own agony was so raw, so deep, she simply could not bring herself to care.

❈   ❈   ❈

The preacher was helping a customer when Katie arrived at the General Store. "I'll be right with ya," he called, glancing over to see who had come in, jangling the bell above the door. His friendly smile vanished when he spotted her hair—done up fancy in a long braid—and the missing head covering.

Stepping away from the counter, Katie waited for him to finish making his sale, wondering how she should begin the conversation with the elderly man now that she was here.

The making of change and the final ding of the cash register signaled the end of business. It was her turn. "Preacher," she began, a bit sheepish now that the sting of Rebecca's words had abated somewhat, "I heard you wanted to speak to me."

Preacher Yoder, wearing a purple shirt and heavy homespun trousers, cut wide and full in the legs, scanned the store for prospective customers, then pointed Katie in the direction of a small back room behind the counter.

The place was sparsely furnished, except for rows of shelving that occupied one entire side of the room. The wide shelves stored odd bolts of fabric, arranged in an orderly fashion.

Preacher Yoder's countenance registered concern as he pulled out a chair for Katie, and the two of them sat facing each other. "Well now, I must say I'm glad to see ya comin' forward to confess. Will it be this Sunday?"

"No, no, I'm not here about confessing."

He frowned, creating deep furrows in his already wrin-kled forehead.

"I have something to tell you in confidence," she added softly. "It's something that nobody else must ever know."

He waited to hear her out, his expression unchanging.

Katie held herself erect. "Will you promise before God that you'll never tell a soul what I'm about to say?" The re-quest was a mighty bold one, she realized, coming from a young woman who just yesterday had humiliated the bishop in front of all the People.

Preacher Yoder rested both hands on his knees. "Well, I guess I'll have to be hearin' what you have to say before I can make any promises."

She drew in a deep breath. As far as she could tell, this was her one and only chance to clear herself without actu-ally confessing sin. She began to spill everything: how she had been told of her non-Amish heritage just days before her wedding; how her parents had kept the secret from her these many years.

"Now that certainly *does* explain some things." He shook his head in amazement, pulling on his gray beard. "You say you're not Amish by birth, then?"

"My real name is Katherine Mayfield. I have proof right here." She pulled out the satin gown. "This was my first baby dress, and you're the only person in Hickory Hollow besides Ella Mae and my parents to lay eyes on it."

"Ella Mae?" He leaned back in his chair. "Does she know your secret?"

"Ach, no. I never told her anything about the dress or where it came from."

"But she has seen it?"

"Jah."

"And why would you be tellin' *me* all this?"

She took in another deep breath and held it a moment. "Because . . . well, because I was wondering if it might change things in some way . . . cancel out my baptism. Me being adopted and all, wouldn't it do away with my vow to the church?" She paused, waiting, but her questions were followed only by silence.

She spoke again. "Don't you see? I was tricked, Preacher . . . I wasn't who I thought I was back then."

The old man pushed up his glasses and peered through them critically as though he'd never heard such strange talk. "The promise you made to God and the church will stand forever, whether ya call yourself Katherine or something else altogether." His eyes tunneled into hers. "Forever and always, you'll be held accountable to the church for the way ya walk—for the life ya lead before God. And if you choose not to confess come Sunday, you'll be in danger of the Ban at the meeting of the membership."

She knew better than to argue. To talk back meant instant shunning. The man of God had spoken. There was no recourse, no hope. English or not, she was bound to her baptismal oath for the rest of her life.

As for promising to keep her family secret, the preacher had vowed he would do so, but mentioned before she left that he truly hoped his brother and sister in the Lord, Samuel and Rebecca Lapp, would come to him voluntarily to confess their years of deceit.

Before Katie left, he gave her one more chance to confess her faults and ask the forgiveness of the church, "lest ya fall into Satan's snare."

Once again, she declined. So the decision to be shunned had been made. The probationary restriction hinged on her refusal to repent, and since she was determined not to confess, not to marry the bishop, and not to behave in keeping with the Ordnung, the wheels of the Meinding had already been set in motion.

On the way home, she thought of stopping by for a quick visit with Ella Mae but decided against it. Why prolong the inevitable? She knew she was in for a tongue-lashing from her parents just as sure as she knew she was the daughter of an English family somewhere out in the modern world.

❖ ❖ ❖

Katie was late getting up on Sunday.

Frustrated and sorrowful over the girl's deplorable conduct during the past week, Rebecca knocked on her daughter's door. "Mustn't be late for Preaching today," she sang out.

"I won't be going" came the terse reply.

"Not going? Katie, don't be this way," Rebecca scolded. Even though she was reluctant to incite another exchange of words with her rebellious offspring—in spite of that—she hurried downstairs to find Samuel and the boys.

Within minutes, the three men were standing outside Katie's room. Samuel was the first to speak. "Katie, don't be letting stubbornness hinder ya from going to church on the Lord's Day."

No answer.

"Come on, sister," Benjamin implored. "They'll be talking about shunning you for sure if ya don't go. At least come and act like you're sorry—a little humility would help a lot."

Katie groaned. "I told you already. I can't be confessing. Now leave me be."

"Then you'll burn in hell," Eli offered, since all else had failed. "You'll—"

"Eli, hush." His father pointed to the stairs. Samuel leaned forward, his beard touching the door. "If you choose to stay home, daughter, the bishop will have no recourse but the shunning!"

"I know," Katie replied. "But I won't go to church and

pretend to confess—not after the way I've been lied to all these years."

Rebecca breathed in quickly, her heart pumping hard at the accusation. Still, she had to speak her piece. "Don't go blaming *us*, Katie," she said, her voice breaking. "We did the best we could."

Why wouldn't the girl listen to reason? Why wouldn't she heed her family's advice? If only there was something else she or Samuel or the boys could say or do to prevent what was coming. . . .

Sorrowful, Rebecca turned away and descended the stairs. She couldn't bear it. Dared not ponder what Preacher Yoder would be thinking of them—her and Samuel—now that Katie had gone and told him everything. Katie said he'd promised not to breathe a word to a soul. But the truth was . . . now Rebecca herself and Samuel were in need of confessing. Most probably, they'd have to meet the preacher out in the barnyard behind David and Mattie Beiler's house after church service. Best they do it soon, too, before he had to approach *them*.

One thing was for sure and for certain. They'd be doing their confessing in private—before the situation spread out of control, like a cancer that could not be cured.

❖　❖　❖

Katie ate the noon meal alone. She thought of the People and what was going on over at the Beiler house—Bishop John's relatives; hers, too—Mattie being her mother's first cousin.

She could see it now—Mattie flapping her tongue every which way long before Preaching ever got started. She would be all ears, too, especially when the preacher began his discussion before the membership after the church service. He would mention Katie's unwillingness to come to Preaching on this the Lord's Day to humble herself before God and these many witnesses. He would say that she had been properly warned but would not refrain from her transgression and rebellion.

Each church member would be allowed to voice opinions about the wayward one in question. Ella Mae might speak up, remind the People of the hardships that had already befallen the poor lamb. Rebecca, too, might even put in a few good words on her daughter's behalf. At least, she'd think about it. But in the end, she wouldn't go through with it, because she was in need of repentance herself, and the preacher knew it!

Mary Stoltzfus might be brave enough to say something nice about her best friend—that is, if she'd been able to forgive Katie for the harsh words she'd spoken to her on the mule road the last time they'd seen each other.

At some point, the bishop would be called to the front. John's place was to decide what to do about the situation, and knowing how things were usually carried out, Katie was pretty sure the People would be warned not to eat at the same table with her, do business with her, and so on, for the probationary period of six weeks. After that, if she did not come to church and offer a kneeling confession, she—Katie Lapp—would be shunned "even unto death."

CHAPTER EIGHTEEN

❖ ❖ ❖

Mary Stoltzfus was not at preaching, either. A few minutes before the service started, Rachel told Rebecca that her daughter was suffering from a severe headache. But Rebecca's mind was not on such a small botheration; it was on the membership meeting to come.

Rachel, however, wanted to discuss Mary's problem, whispering behind her hand that one of Mary's beaus—Chicken Joe—had taken Sarah, Mattie Beiler's granddaughter, home from a supper with their buddy group last night. "Mary's terrible upset about it—and awful worried, too."

"Why's that?" Rebecca asked, hardly able to pay attention when her heart was breaking for Katie.

"Mary's . . . afraid she'll never get married."

"Ach, she will, she will," Rebecca said, waving her hand.

"Too bad Katie won't be able to help Mary with her disappointment," said Rachel, glancing at the preacher and the bishop already conferring. "The girls have been so close for so long. They seem to know how to comfort one another."

"Jah. But things are about to change, I fear," Rebecca said. "Unless the bishop's heart is softened somehow, there will be a Meinding amongst the People."

227

❖   ❖   ❖

The verdict was harsh.

Rebecca sat stiff and straight on the hard wooden bench, wishing with all her strength that something might happen to turn the tide. Her Katie—poor, dear, stubborn Katie—being the topic of all this awful shunning talk, well, it was more than she could endure. To keep from crying out, she clamped a hankie over her lips.

Mattie must have heard the muffled sob, because she glanced cockeyed at Rebecca from a few benches away. Rebecca felt anew the familiar twinge of conflict between them. Her cousin's look spoke volumes: *You didn't call on me to help deliver your daughter long ago, but look at me . . . my grown children are better than yours. My children never would think of goin' and gettin' themselves shunned.*

Rebecca closed her eyes, blocking out Mattie's haughty gaze and the distressing scene on all sides.

Preacher Yoder and Bishop John were both presiding over the membership meeting now. Rebecca heard the voices but kept her eyes shut.

The room was filled with confusing talk. "Love the wayward one back to the fold," someone suggested. "Impose severe restrictions so she'll know what's comin' if she don't repent," said another.

Then Bishop John spoke up. "The bride of Christ must not tolerate arrogance. Katie Lapp has shown rebellion and insolence repeatedly."

The Scriptures and theology behind the practice of shunning were familiar enough to Rebecca, but today the Meinding took on a heartbreaking new dimension. Today it had struck at her very heart—her beloved Katie. And with everything in her, Rebecca wished there was another way.

❖   ❖   ❖

Katie heard the news first from John Beiler himself. It came just before her parents and brothers arrived home in time for afternoon milking. She saw the bishop step out of his carriage and walk, rather awkwardly, toward the back door.

The thought of stealing away to the Dawdi Haus presented itself, but she knew, sooner or later, she must hear the truth from John Beiler's own lips.

He gave a firm knock. Then, standing tall as though braced for battle, he stepped into the house when Katie opened the door. He came only as far as the utility room, took off his felt hat, and faced her with a stern expression in his steel gray eyes.

Katie said nothing, did not even greet him or bid him welcome in her father's home.

When he spoke, it was with icy control. "I urge ya to attend church during the next six weeks. Come as a non-member and meet with the ministers"—by this, she gathered he meant himself—"but you'll have to leave before the fellowship of members and the common meal each Sunday. Not one of us in the Hollow will be speaking to you now. You may not eat at the same table as church members or do business with any of us until such time as ya return and offer a kneeling confession."

Katie listened, limp with disbelief. The swiftness with which the discipline had been issued left her reeling.

"The punishment is suitable for all those who have surrendered themselves to the Lord," he explained, then quoted Ezekiel, chapter thirty-three, verse nine. " 'Nevertheless, if thou warn the wicked of his way to turn from it; if he does not turn from his way, he shall die in his iniquity.' "

Die in iniquity. . . .

She kept quiet, eager for him to leave. *I nearly married this cruel man,* she thought with disdain. *How could I have considered such a thing?*

"Do you understand that this chastening is so that the weeds will not continue to grow while you wait for the judgment of Christ?" John asked solemnly. "To bring you back to the loving heavenly Father?"

She felt the fury welling up inside her. She began to shake her head. "No, no . . . I *don't* understand anything about my life here with the People. Not one little bit of it."

A frown, mingled with concern, flashed across his face, and for a moment, Katie feared that he might be thinking of addressing her in a more personal manner. But his jawline hardened, and he turned and let himself out the back door without another word.

❖   ❖   ❖

When Dat arrived, he came directly inside and set to work, putting up a small, square folding table across the kitchen a good distance from where the rest of the family ate their meals. He did not speak to Katie as he worked, not even to offer a smidgen of sympathy, and she knew the Meinding had officially begun.

Mamma came in not long after, her eyes swollen and red. The sight stirred Katie's compassion, and she wanted to run to her mother and comfort her. But she forced herself to sit stone still as Rebecca shuffled past her and went upstairs.

Eli and Benjamin appeared in the doorway and steered clear of Katie, moving almost mechanically as they headed toward the woodstove to warm themselves before the afternoon milking. Their faces were sullen, eyes cast down, as though they might be contaminated if they made any contact with their wayward sister.

Already, the rejection was unbearable. Unable to put up with it any longer, Katie went next door to the Dawdi Haus. The place was bitter cold, so she hurried outdoors and filled her apron with chopped wood to start a fire.

Inside, with teeth chattering and fingers shaking, she struck a match, ignited the kindling, and blew on the feeble flame. She had never felt so cold in all her life.

❖ ❖ ❖

Rebecca stood at the top of the second-floor landing, glancing at the bedroom she and Samuel shared, the numbness creeping through every fiber, every tissue of her being. This wasn't like her. Not at all. Not being sure of her next move. Not knowing what to do. . . .

With great hesitancy, she turned and forced her legs to carry her down the hallway to Katie's room.

The door was open. Dazed, Rebecca entered. Private and feminine—so like her dear daughter—this bedroom had belonged to Katie for over twenty-two years. Her belongings seemed to draw Rebecca, compelling her to go about the room, her fingertips trailing across the dresser doilies, the headboard, the scattered bed pillows.

Why did Katie have to be so willful in spirit? Why couldn't she be more yielding, more submissive . . . more *Amish?*

Rebecca winced, thinking of the events of the day—the church members' meeting and the pronouncement of the Meinding by Bishop John—and went to sit on the straight-backed chair near Katie's bed. Life with her dear girl wasn't supposed to turn out this way. Things had been much better, she told herself, before Daniel Fisher had come into Katie's life.

Rebecca turned and stared out the window, remembering. Daniel's mother had told her—in strictest confidence—years back that he'd gotten himself invited to a Bible study somewhere outside the Hollow. Nancy Fisher had been mighty concerned for her son at the time and had decided not to tell a soul—not even Annie, her youngest daughter, anything about it.

Rebecca had agreed. It was wiser not to talk it around, and she'd kept her word, not even telling Katie. It was the one thing about Daniel that she'd never shared with her daughter. And now . . . now with this great burden hovering over her loved ones, Rebecca wondered if Daniel had somehow played a part in all of this, influencing Katie to think for herself, maybe. . . .

The more she pondered, though, the more she began to question her suspicions. Hadn't Katie gone ahead and followed the Lord in baptism into the church just eighteen months after Daniel's drowning? Didn't that prove he'd had no evil influence on her, after all?

Rebecca stood up again and breathed in the lovely lilac fragrance permeating the room. Katie's room had always had a breezy freshness about it. Her daughter enjoyed drying lilac clumps and mixing them with various herbs and spices, placing the homemade potpourri into netting purchased at the General Store. She often concealed the sachet squares inside her dresser drawers.

Without thinking, Rebecca opened the top drawer of Katie's dresser and leaned over to sniff the sweet scent. "Oh, Katie, what I wouldn't give to make your troubles disappear," she said aloud. Then, reaching inside, she tried to locate one of the little sachets. Instead, her fingers closed over the satin baby gown.

She began to cry. Softly, at first. Then, holding the little dress to her bosom, she wept great, sorrowful tears.

And then she heard it—the delicate, almost timid strains of a guitar. Who was playing? And where?

She went to the hallway and pressed her ear against the wall. It was a solid foundational wall, shared by both the Dawdi Haus and her own home. As she listened, holding her breath, the sounds became more clear. Katie's voice—mellow and sweet—singing the saddest melody she'd ever heard.

So the girl had disobeyed yet again. Katie had not destroyed the guitar as the bishop would surely have ordered her to do at the private confession.

It was difficult to make out the words, but the mournful tune caught Rebecca's attention, suiting her own mood. Good thing Samuel and the boys were outside now, tending to milking chores. Best *they* not hear the guitar music or the singing coming from next door.

Reluctant to forsake the haunting music, she went back to Katie's room, returned the baby dress to the gaping drawer, and headed downstairs to make supper.

❈   ❈   ❈

In the painful hours that followed, not only did Katie's entire family nix any conversation with her, they also refused to accept written notes from her. Katie had come up with the idea of writing when she found herself wanting more information about Mary Stoltzfus, who had taken ill— best Katie could tell. During supper preparation, she had overheard her parents talking about her friend.

"Rachel said she's got some awful pain in her head," Rebecca told Samuel as he was washing up. "Ain't contagious, though. Sounds like something's up with Chicken Joe quitting her."

"Well, why don't you go over and offer some of your gut chicken corn soup tomorrow?" he suggested.

Katie dashed across the kitchen, eager to communicate with them. She scribbled a note on a piece of paper—*How long has Mary been ill?*—and held it up for her mother to read.

Both Samuel and Rebecca turned their backs. Katie, not about to give up, ran around in front of them, pointing to the words on the paper and holding out a pencil for them to write a reply.

Samuel shook his head, refusing to respond. Rebecca's eyes grew sad and moist, but she, too, remained silent.

Katie wrote once more: *Why didn't anyone tell me? Mary's my dearest friend!*

She pushed the paper under Rebecca's nose.

Silence.

"Well, I'll not be staying around here when my friend is in need," she announced. "I'll go where I'm wanted!" It was then that she decided to see for herself how Mary was doing, even though it was already near dusk. Surely her best friend would be glad to see her. Surely she would.

Desperate for someone to talk to, she grabbed her shawl and left the house with Molasses and the family carriage, startled at the emotions the shunning had begun to rouse in her. Angrily, she urged the old horse on.

Along the way, she passed several buggies. Instead of the usual cheerful hellos from other Amish folk, Katie's greetings were met with downcast eyes.

When another buggy approached her on the left, she could see that it was Elam and Annie, probably going visiting. Eager to greet them, even from a distance, she called out to them, "Hullo! S'good to see ya!"

They responded with the same blank stares as all the others. Tears sprang to Katie's eyes, and approximately a mile from the sandstone house, she turned the carriage around and headed home.

Heartsick and lonely, she suffered through her first meal—five feet or so away from the family table, stuck off in the corner of the kitchen by herself. She overheard the chatter of beloved voices and the friendly clink of silverware on plates, yet was not included in the conversation. Sadly, she decided that she might as well be five thousand miles away.

Later in the evening a choking heaviness settled in, and she put her dowry money—the eighteen-hundred-dollar gift from her parents—in an envelope and shoved it under their bedroom door. The money did not belong to such a sinful, rebellious soul, and she penned a note on the outside of the envelope to tell them so.

No "good-nights" were exchanged, and Katie went off to her cold, dark bedroom, undressing there while her family shared in evening prayers downstairs in the warmth of the kitchen. With a lump in her throat, she climbed into bed without offering her usual silent prayer.

CHAPTER NINETEEN

❖   ❖   ❖

One by one, the empty days dragged by, each more dismal than the last, now that winter had come early, shrouding the barren land with bleakness.

Four days had passed since Katie's first attempt to visit Mary. She longed for her friend's bright smile, the joyful countenance. Was Mary improving? No one seemed to know. At least, if they did, they weren't saying. Even Benjamin had clammed up, though he'd had plenty of chances to steal a moment away from either Eli's or Samuel's watchful gaze to speak to her privately. And Katie knew why. Benjamin, Eli—all of them—were afraid of getting caught, of being shunned themselves.

She could take it no longer. Twenty-four hours seemed like an eternity. So many eternities without Mary—lonely, friendless days. Katie sighed, wishing she and her friend had not exchanged cross words on the mule road last Thursday. It was time to make amends.

Rachel Stoltzfus met Katie at her kitchen door. But seeing who was there, she proceeded to shake her head and back away, putting both hands out in front of her.

"I've come to see Mary," pleaded Katie, wrapped up in her warmest shawl. "Is she feeling any better?"

The door was completely closed—not slammed in her face, but soundly shut—by the time the last word left her lips.

Cut to the heart, Katie turned to go. Suddenly she knew the meaning of the word *alone*. Knew it more powerfully than she'd ever known anything. She shot the word into the crisp, cold air as she coaxed Molasses out of the lane. "Alone. I'm all alone." The sound of it throbbed in her head.

In the past—when Dan died—she had experienced what it meant to be separated from someone she loved. But she'd been surrounded then by caring friends and relatives to help her over the worst days. And, on the whole, her life had never been a lonely one. There was always something to do and someone to do it with in Hickory Hollow. Some work frolic—a rug braiding or a quilting; weddings and Singings; games such as "The Needle's Eye" and "Fox and Geese," and in the wintertime, ice-skating marathons on Dat's pond under a vast, black canopy of sky, studded with a thousand stars shining down on them all.

No, she had never been truly alone in her life. But she was beginning to understand what it meant. Worse, she knew *what* she was missing—a whole community of People, lost to a bishop's decree. She couldn't help but wonder if the probationary shunning hadn't been a retaliation of sorts—John Beiler getting back at her for not marrying him!

Maybe John thinks he can win me back this way. Make me repent—then marry him on top of it. She forced a laugh that ended in a fit of coughing.

It was then she decided to turn around and go back to Mary's house. She halted Molasses on the dirt drive next to Mary's bedroom window and tied him to a tree.

"I'll throw stones," she told her horse. "That'll bring her running."

Katie went to the dried-up flower bed near the tree, avoiding the rise in the earth where tree roots had pushed up random hard lumps. Reaching down, she gathered a few small pebbles and tossed them gently, hoping not to attract Rachel's or Abe Stoltzfus's attention. She waited a moment, then tried again, aiming for the second-story window. To her great relief, Mary came to see what the commotion was about.

"I miss you, Mary," Katie called lightly, hands cupped around her mouth. "I want to talk to you." She gestured for her friend to raise the window, but Mary didn't seem to get the idea. She just stood there, looking down with a forlorn expression on her face.

"Are you all right?" Katie mouthed.

Mary didn't say a word, nor did she use sign language to make herself understood. But what happened next was more eloquent and heart wrenching than anything she could have said. She simply placed her hand on the window and held it there—as if to make contact through the cold glass— then slid it down and inched away until she was out of sight.

It would do no good to plead with her to stay, Katie knew. So she turned and trudged back toward the carriage. She climbed in with a sigh of resignation, then made a circular swing around the side yard before driving Molasses out onto Hickory Lane.

There was no song in her now, no desire to hum. She was an outcast among the People. What would Daniel think of her if he knew? Would he be ashamed?

She craned her neck to look up at the sky, wondering if the dead had any idea what was happening down here on earth.

"I best be making some plans," she announced aloud. It probably wouldn't take much to get her old housecleaning job back. But if she was going to make it on her own, she would eventually have to learn to drive a car, most likely. Maybe even go to school somewhere. One thing was certain, though, she had made up her mind that she would not confess after the six weeks were up. As difficult as it was, she might as well admit that she was as good as shunned for life.

A quarter of a mile ahead, she spied David and Mattie's place. Impulsively, she pulled into the main drive, then parked her buggy directly behind Ella Mae's Dawdi Haus. If there was anyone left on the face of the earth who would speak to her, it would be the Wise Woman.

Hesitantly, Katie approached the door and knocked.

"It's open" came the reply.

Katie stepped through the door and into the warm kitchen. "It's me, Ella Mae. Katie," she called, feeling something like a leper—as though she should sound a warning. "I might not be welcome. . . ."

The Wise Woman appeared, carrying her needlework. "Nonsense, lamb. *Kumm yuscht rei un hock dich anne*—come right in and sit down. Warm yourself by the fire. It's right nippy out there, ain't?"

At the sound of another human voice—especially Ella Mae's thin, quavery one—Katie all but hugged her. "Oh my, it's so wonderful-gut to see you! No one else will talk to me."

"Jah." Ella Mae nodded thoughtfully. "And it just don't seem right, insulting a body the way they are."

"Don't you believe in the Meinding?" Katie pulled her braid over her left shoulder, wondering if Ella Mae had noticed that she wasn't wearing her kapp.

The Wise Woman only waved her hand in the air—the way Rebecca often did when she didn't want to discuss something. So Katie sat at the table and let the matter drop.

She watched, comforted by the familiar ritual of Ella Mae making tea—putting a kettle on to boil, getting out the teacups, pinching off two sprigs of mint. . . . "I hear Mary Stoltzfus is under the weather."

"Jah, but she'll live, I 'spect."

"It's all because of Chicken Joe and Sarah Beiler, ain't?" Katie said, careful how she phrased the question since Sarah was closely related to Ella Mae.

"Love plays cruel tricks on its victims now and again."

Katie wondered if the bishop felt she'd played a cruel trick on him. "John'll find someone else someday, won't he?" she asked, hoping to justify herself. "Someone much better suited for him."

Ella Mae shook her head. "Don't be downin' yourself now. You're as fine a woman as any, with or without your kapp."

They laughed together, the old woman coming around to inspect Katie's irreverent braid. It was a shining moment they shared, a moment of triumph.

"My goodness me, it's nice to have somebody come for tea," Ella Mae said, heading over to fold up her counted cross-stitch linen. She placed it on the arm of the sofa behind her before joining Katie at the table. "You're like me, I'm a-thinkin'. Not many folk drop by to visit anymore—and the nights get long and lonesome."

"Maybe it's the weather . . . the cold and all."

"No, no, no. I know better."

"Why, then? Why don't they come?"

"Well, I'm thinkin' the church leaders got wind of my string of visitors—the ones who look to me for a bit of advice, ya know."

"That's too bad, really. I would have thought they'd know you're doing people a big favor, the way you listen to all of us talk out our sorrows and such."

"Ach, it's just that Preacher Yoder wants the People to look to *him*, I do believe. Maybe he figures I'm *Dummkopp*—touched in the head, ya know." She patted her kapp and began to laugh that warm, wonderful chuckle that started deep inside and rumbled out, on good days, when her voice was stronger.

It was pure heaven to hear her go on so. Sitting there in Ella Mae's toasty kitchen, Katie felt her spirits lift. She was

happy for herself, of course. Glad, too, to be company for
the poor old soul who had welcomed her—shunning or no.

"I 'spose word got out that young Levi and I had a cup
of hot cocoa together down at the General Store one morning a few weeks back," Ella Mae put in.

"Why would *that* matter?" Katie was truly astonished.
How could such a small thing cause the People to turn their
backs on an old woman?

"Ach, it's hard to say, really. But it's my guess that Levi
Beiler went home and told his Daed that old Ella Mae Zook
was saying this and that, and thus and so." She reached over
the table and patted Katie's hand. "We do need one another,
child. The People just ain't enough, I fear."

Now Katie was beginning to worry. Was her great-aunt's
mind truly failing her? She wasn't making sense. "Well, the
bishop and Preacher Yoder are only doing what they believe
is best for both of us now," Katie spoke up. "It's das Alt Gebrauch, the Old Way, the way we've always done things
here in the Hollow."

Startled at her own words, Katie realized what she had
just said. Had she spoken out of habit—defending the
People that way—or was she beginning to believe that she
deserved the temporary Ban? Was the weight of guilt beginning to press in on her? Was this how the Meinding ultimately worked to bring sinners to repentance?

Ella Mae sat up straighter, releasing Katie's hand. "No,
no, I ain't talkin' about your predicament with the church
just now. You're payin' for your sin, that's true, and you'll
probably be confessing here sooner or later. We all do. A
body can't go around forever without communing with
friends." She paused to catch her breath. "No, no, what I'm
talkin' about is far different. Something to do with eternity—where one life ends and another begins."

Katie gasped. "Oh, Ella Mae, you're not dying on me, are
you?"

"We're all dying in one way or t'other." She got up to take the teakettle off the stove and pour the boiling hot water into two cups. Next came the sprigs of mint leaves. "You're young, and you may be thinkin' you have all the time in the world. But I hope ya don't go wasting your allotted time—any of it."

"Don't go worrying about me," Katie reassured her, still confused. What *was* the old woman trying to say?

Then, out of the blue, the Wise Woman spoke, her words reaching deep into the private corners of Katie's soul, where no one else had ever dared to go. "I was born Amish, and I'll die the same. The Plain life is the only life I'll ever know. But you, Katie, you have a chance to see what's out there, what's on the other side of things."

"You mean . . . the modern world?"

"It's what you're looking for, ain't?"

The question struck Katie like a blast of cold air. Was it? Was she searching for the boundary line, the proverbial fence around the People? Hoping someday to break through, to find her true self? "Why are ya saying all this?"

"Because you seem out of place somehow," Ella Mae said in a raspy whisper. "Always have."

Katie felt a tingle of discovery. "I've been coming over here since I was little, telling you my troubles, trying to be a gut Plain girl—and here lately, an even better grown woman, worthy of the bishop's . . . trust. I tried . . . but I failed. . . ." Her voice trailed away.

"You're a thinker," said Ella Mae, shaking her head. "Thinkin' and submittin' to the Old Ways don't mix."

Katie caressed her braid. "You're probably right." She stared off into space, remembering that Dan Fisher had said the same thing once.

Ella Mae placed a cup of mint tea in front of her visitor, struggling with her own conscience. Should she tell Katie what she and young Levi had seen a week ago? The black limousine and the worldly woman . . . with hair the color of Katie's own? And the letter the lady was so eager to hand over?

She watched the poor girl hold the cup to her lips and sip her tea. When she set the cup in its saucer, she began to pour out her troubles in a steady stream—like the mint brew in the old teakettle.

"It wonders me about the strange thing Mam told me before my wedding day," Katie began. "And I'm more puzzled by it now than ever."

Ella Mae sipped, then sighed. "Ach, was it about that little dress you brought over to show me?"

Katie nodded. "That dress has changed everything. It's turned my whole life upside down. The family's, too."

Ella Mae appeared not to notice Katie's distress. "I believe I know what your mamma may've told ya, Katie. I wouldn't sit here and lie to ya, pretending I didn't."

Katie was elated. At last, someone else—someone she could trust—knew the secret! Of all the People she could have chosen to speak with about it . . .

Ella Mae continued. "I saw her, Katie. I saw your birth mother, clear as day."

Katie nearly choked on her tea. "My birth mother? Where? In Hickory Hollow?"

Ella Mae nodded thoughtfully.

"I can't believe it! Why was she here?"

"She's a-lookin' for ya, Katie. Isn't that what your mamma told ya?"

Katie fought back tears. "No, no, you must be mistaken somehow. Mamma never told me any such a thing."

"Himmel," Ella Mae whispered.

"Mamma told me that my real name was Katherine Mayfield—that I was given as an infant to her and Dat to raise after their fourth baby was stillborn. But she never said anything—" Her breath caught on a sob.

Ella Mae shook her head woefully. "Ach, I've spoken out of turn, I'm afeared. Forgive an old woman for heapin' more pain on your head, child." She set her cup down and removed her glasses to wipe her eyes. The startling truth, although she had suspected as much, tore at her heart.

"When did you see her . . . my real mother?"

"There was a letter over a week ago," Ella Mae began, telling Katie how the fancy lady had approached her carriage at the General Store. "She pleaded with me to help her find a woman named Rebecca. Told her there were lotsa Rebeccas in the Hollow, but she seemed in an awful big hurry to get her fancy letter into the right hands."

Without warning, Katie leaped out of her chair.

Following the direction of her gaze, Ella Mae peered into the shadows across the room. "Ach, Mattie, is that *you* standin' over there?" she muttered.

Her daughter stepped into the lantern light, revealing herself without a word, while Katie steadied herself, leaning hard on the back of the chair.

"What in the world?" Ella Mae spun around, nearly knocking over her cup of tea. "Land a-mighty, don'tcha ever knock, woman?" she scolded.

"I heard voices," Mattie said, refusing to look at Katie. "And, Mam, you know better than to be talking to a shunned person . . . and sharing your table, too!" She marched toward them. "Katie best be leaving or I'll have to report this to Preacher."

"What'll he do?" Ella Mae scoffed. "Meide a feeble old soul like me?"

"Mam! You best be reverent when ya speak of the shunning."

Ella Mae turned to see Katie sitting forward in her chair, reaching for the tea. The cup trembled in her hand. *What wretched thing has happened here?* she wondered. She ached clear to the bottom of her soul, for being the reason Mattie had overheard Katie's family secret. *We should've been more careful.* That busybody had heard every bit of their intimate conversation. Now *that* was a worry.

"How long ya been hidin' over there?" Ella Mae confronted her daughter.

"Just came in."

But the Wise Woman knew. So did Katie. And by nightfall, so did most everyone else in Hickory Hollow—including Bishop John.

CHAPTER TWENTY

❖   ❖   ❖

"Katie Lapp's adopted, and her real mamma's out lookin' for her. Now what do ya make of *that*?" Nancy Beiler asked her big brother as they swept out the barn.

"How do *you* know such a thing?"

"Heard it today at recess."

Hickory John stopped for a moment and leaned on his push broom, eyeing his sister doubtfully. "Are ya sure 'bout this?"

Nancy grinned. "Came near straight from the horse's mouth."

"Whose?"

"One of our cousins."

"A girl?" he teased.

"Jah, our second cousin, Sally Mae." She sneezed in the wake of the dust they'd stirred up. "The way I see it, if it came from one of Aunt Mattie's grandchildren, it's gotta be true. Because Aunt Mattie was the one who overheard *her* mamma tell about meetin' Katie's birth mamma face to face."

"Well, we all know how Aunt Mattie is, don't we?" Hickory John laughed. "Can't always go by whatcha hear."

Out of the haze of dust and straw, Levi stepped forward,

much to the surprise of Nancy and her brother. "Didja just say Katie's *real* mamma's lookin' for her? Is that what I heard ya say?"

"You were eavesdropping, Levi Beiler!" Nancy scolded. "That's a *greislich* thing for the bishop's son to do! Now go in and get washed up for supper."

Levi marched himself off to the house, mumbling about getting caught. "Guess maybe Daed might start payin' attention to me from now on . . . 'specially when I tell him about red-haired strangers comin' to our front door!" she heard him say.

❖   ❖   ❖

Katie waited until her father and brothers left the house for a barn raising near White Horse before deciding to speak to her mother. Rebecca had not been feeling well—an upset stomach, or so Katie thought.

Rebecca remained silent, leaning her arm against the table and sighing audibly.

"I'll bring some tea up later," Katie offered, hoping to hear *something* out of her mother. But there was not another sound.

How long would it take before Mam would start talking when there was no one around to overhear? She hadn't purposely set out to trick her mother, but Katie was desperate for answers. Answers to the questions that Ella Mae had brought to her attention only yesterday.

Mute as a fence post, Rebecca seemed bent on forcing herself through the household chores. She did allow Katie to assist with the baking—bread and six dozen each of molasses cookies and apple muffins—to take to a quilting frolic planned for tomorrow. But along about ten-thirty, her mother collapsed into Dat's big rocking chair.

Katie finished wiping off the counters and washed her hands. Then, stepping around to the small table that was hers alone, she paused and observed her mother. "It's all over Hickory Hollow about my birth mother trying to find me," she said. "Mattie got it all started, the nosy thing."

Rebecca's head seemed to bob in agreement, but Katie couldn't be sure that it wasn't caused by the motion of the rocker. "I never would've wanted to spread your secret around like this, Mamma," she went on. "You know I'm telling the truth, too, because I had Preacher Yoder promise not to tell anyone." She watched and waited, hoping Rebecca would say something—*anything.*

No comment came.

"Ella Mae said there was a letter. Do you know anything about that?"

The tiniest squeak passed Mam's lips. Was that a reply?

Katie went over and knelt down, resting her head on her mother's knees. "I'd give anything to know, Mam," she said softly.

Rebecca's hand found its way to her daughter's slender back. She began to rub in soothing, circular motions—the way she always had when Katie was a little girl.

Cautiously, the words began to slip out. "I did a wretched thing with the letter," she admitted. "I threw it in the stove—out of fear, mostly—but it got burned up all the same."

"You burned it?" Katie lifted her head and the back rub ceased, but only for a moment. "Why did you burn it?"

"Just listen," Rebecca whispered. And Katie, apparently basking in the sound of her mother's voice, did as she was told. Rebecca put her hand on Katie's head and could feel her daughter relaxing against her lap again.

"I was so awful worried and upset that day," she went on, her voice breaking occasionally. "I thought the woman—

your natural mother—was gonna come and take you away from us. But looking back on all that's happened, I wish I'd kept her letter so you could be readin' it for yourself right now."

"Why does she want to find me, do you think?" Katie asked, not lifting her head this time.

"The doctor's told her . . . she's dying." Rebecca's hand paused momentarily before continuing its healing journey.

After a heart-stopping silence, Katie looked up. Rebecca could see the tears brimming in the girl's eyes.

"What's her name?"

"It's . . . Laura. Laura Mayfield-Bennett. She must've kept her maiden name—and added it onto her married name. I've heard they do such things out in the modern world."

Katie whispered the peculiar name into the air. "Laura Mayfield-Bennett."

"Wait here." Rebecca got up and found a pencil and a scrap of paper in a kitchen drawer. "I'll spell it out for you the way I remember it."

Katie studied the name on the paper—the strange English name. The letters squinted up at her, telling her—in some disconnected way—important things about herself. Things she did not fully understand.

"Did she . . . did Laura write her address down in the letter?"

"Honest, I don't remember now." Her mamma's glistening eyes were proof she was telling the truth. "She lives somewhere in New York, I think."

"New York City?" Katie gasped. "Ach, I hope not!"

"No, no, it's somewhere else in the state."

"Well, I'll just have to get me a map, I suppose," Katie said. "A map of New York State, since I've never been outside Lancaster County."

"So . . . will you be tryin' to find her, then?" Mam's voice now sounded thin and pathetic—almost childlike as she sat back down in the rocker.

Even though Katie was momentarily distracted by the compassion she felt for her mother, a startling surge of resolve followed, surprising her with its power. "I have to look for her, Mamma, you know I do. I can't just forget about her now." She rose and took Rebecca's hands in hers, gently pulling her up and out of the rocking chair. "I don't mean to hurt you with all this. You do understand . . . don't ya?"

Her mother couldn't speak for the tears, and Katie hurried on before she weakened. "I can't stay here much longer anyway, not with the shunning and all. I thought about going next door to the Dawdi Haus, but it's no use. I can't see confessing now . . . or later. It's time I think about leaving."

"Aw, girl, no!" Then, more softly—"Where will you go?"

Katie took a deep breath. "Lydia Miller has a room for rent. I saw the sign yesterday on my way home from Ella Mae's."

Her mamma shook her head and fumbled for a handkerchief. "You're not going to leave Hickory Hollow, are you?"

"Laura Mayfield-Bennett doesn't live anywhere near Lancaster, now does she?" Katie hugged her weeping mother. "Oh, Mamma, I'm so happy you finally talked to me today. So very happy."

"It must not happen again," Rebecca declared, giving way to a coughing fit before clearing her throat. "I can . . . not speak to you again . . . not until you repent."

"I know, Mamma," Katie replied. "You're a good Amishwoman, and I understand."

When Rebecca's desperate hacking subsided, the two women clung to each other as though it was to be the last embrace of their lives.

❖   ❖   ❖

Mattie was thrilled when Elam Lapp called her to deliver Annie's first baby, a full six weeks before the due date.

About time I catch a Lapp baby again! she thought as she rode back with Elam to the young couple's farmhouse. Silly how she'd carried on over not being asked to assist with Katie Lapp's birth. But now she knew the truth and felt quite ashamed of herself for making such a mountain out of a smidgen of a molehill.

Still, it was hard to believe that Samuel and Rebecca had been able to keep such a secret. But when she tried to draw Elam out about it, it was obvious from his intense frown and pursed lips that he had more important things on his mind—like becoming a father in the next few hours.

When the horse pulled the carriage into the lane, Elam jumped out and dashed into the house ahead of her, leaving Mattie to attend to the unhitching of the horse. "These new papas," she clucked. "I do declare!"

By the time Annie's contractions were less than two minutes apart, word had spread to several Amish farmhouses, including Rebecca Lapp's—thanks to Lydia Miller's telephone and her fancy car.

Katie could hear the cries of the newest little Lapp as she helped her mother out of the carriage. "Sounds like a hefty set of lungs to me. Must be a boy." She smiled at her mother even though by this time, she didn't expect a reply.

Rebecca said nothing, lips tight.

They hurried up the front porch steps, meeting Elam as he burst through the door to greet them. "Mam, Wilkom!" he said, without so much as a glance in Katie's direction. "You have yourself a fine, healthy grandson!"

He ushered them into the downstairs bedroom, where

Annie lay, perspiring and exhausted, holding the tiny bundle.

"He's mighty pretty," Katie whispered as her sister-in-law handed the baby to Elam.

"Mamma, I want ya to meet my first son . . . Daniel Lapp." Elam held the infant up for Rebecca and the others to see. "The name's for Annie's brother, ya know."

The reference to Dan pierced Katie's heart. But she was drawn to her new nephew like a bee to honeysuckle. "May I hold him?"

Elam ignored her request, placing the baby in Rebecca's arms instead. "He may be a bit premature, but he's a fine, sturdy boy, ain't?"

"Jah, he's strong, all right." Rebecca began to coo in Pennsylvania Dutch. "Won't Dawdi Samuel and your uncles be surprised when they get home?"

Mattie, now standing next to Rebecca, began to stroke Daniel's soft cheek. "I think it's time for me to be speakin' to ya about something, Rebecca," the woman said, looking her cousin full in the face.

Not wanting to stand there and witness the busybody trying to patch things up with her mother—not after the way Mattie had spread the word all over the Hollow about the adoption and all—Katie slipped out of the room, unnoticed. She wondered about Annie's early delivery. What had made her sister-in-law go into labor so early? Had she counted wrong . . . or what?

Katie walked into the front room, stopping to examine the pretty pieces displayed in the corner cupboard. Seeing the fancy china reminded her of the gay wedding plans she and Bishop John had made. She'd let him down terribly. All the People, really. Now Elam had taken it upon himself to go a step further and punish her by not allowing her to hold his son. Whoever heard of such a thing? Not letting your own sister hold your baby? That wasn't part of the shunning!

Out of the silence, she heard her name spoken and tiptoed back toward the bedroom, within earshot. It was Mattie, saying something about Katie's horrible behavior at the wedding. "I think it's this whole shameful thing with Katie that upset Annie so awful much."

Elam had a few choice comments of his own. "I think *die Meinding* upset Annie much more than any of us thought," he agreed. "Started up her labor too soon, probably. A sensitive one, she is."

Katie backed away silently and hurried to the front door. *They're blaming me!* She was shaking—whether with fear or rage, she wasn't quite sure. *Who knows—I might've killed the poor little thing!*

She refused to cry, but took in a deep breath and ran to the carriage to hitch up ol' Molasses.

Daniel . . . they named my nephew Daniel. How could they?

For a moment she gave in to her sobs, reliving the pain of losing her beloved. Didn't they understand? No one could ever take his place!

She slapped the reins and the horse trotted away. Her haughty big brother would just have to take time away from his precious new baby and drive their mother home later on.

Meanwhile, now was as good a time as any to stop in and chat with Lydia Miller about the room she had for rent.

CHAPTER TWENTY-ONE

A spill of late autumn sunshine—like molten gold—poured into a glass-walled sun-room overlooking acres of rolling lawn and lavish gardens, now frosted with snow. Well-manicured walkways lined the area directly south of the old English-style mansion, shaded in summer by a canopy of regal trees.

From this vantage point, Laura Mayfield-Bennett could see the waterfall splashing into a lily pond two stories below. Floating lily pads shimmered silver-green in the morning light.

Laura reached for her sunglasses just as her maid came into the sun-drenched room, green with ferns and ivy and spreading ficus trees.

Rosie adjusted the chaise lounge to accommodate her mistress. "If it's sunshine you want, Mrs. Bennett, then it's sunshine you get," she remarked cheerfully.

"This is delightful. Thank you for coming up again, Rosie." Laura wiggled her toes inside her velvet house slippers, enjoying the warmth of the sun's rays on her feet and lower legs.

"Will there be anything else, ma'am?"

"Thank you, but no."

Laura sighed heavily, hearing the rapidly fading foot-steps on the marble stairs. Below her, on the circular drive-way, one of the chauffeurs pulled up, waiting for her hus-band. She watched as Dylan Bennett folded his lanky frame into the backseat.

The car sped away—down the long, tree-lined lane—leaving Laura alone with her thoughts. "Well, Lord, it's just the two of us again," she began to pray, her eyes open to take in the sweeping view. "I come to you today, grateful for life"—she paused to look up through the skylight—"and for the sky so clear and open, wearing its pale blue gown. I thank you for all that you have provided, especially for your Son, Jesus Christ.

"Please touch each of my loved ones with your tender care this day, especially Katherine, wherever she may be. And, dear Lord, although I fail to understand why her Amish family has not contacted me, I give Katherine to you, knowing that you do all things well."

Drawing a deep yet faltering breath, she continued. "Perhaps it is not in your will that my daughter see me this way. But if it is . . . please allow her to contact me while I'm alert enough to know it's my darling girl who's come to me. Grant this, I pray before . . . before you call me home. In Christ's name, amen."

What a compassionate gesture if her heavenly Father should grant her last wish, her dying wish. But to fully trust in her Lord and Savior, Laura had learned through the years that she must relinquish selfish desires and wishes.

She reached for a glass of water on the marble-topped table and sipped slowly, retracing in her mind the recent journey she had taken to Pennsylvania—to Hickory Hol-low—and the encounter with the elderly Amishwoman sit-ting in a carriage in front of a general store. The woman had seemed highly reluctant to share information, Laura re-called—had seemed almost offended to be approached. But her acceptance of the letter was tacit agreement, Laura sincerely hoped, that the woman would assist her in delivering it to the proper Rebecca—the one and only Rebecca who would understand the urgency.

Of course, she couldn't be certain that the letter had been passed around in the Plain community at all. And time was against her now. It was out of the question to think of making another such trip, a five-hour drive from the Finger Lakes region of New York to the farmlands of Lancaster County. She was not up to it—not in her present condition—and worsening by the day. Her physician would never hear of it, even if she were stubborn enough to attempt it.

So there she sat on the top of a hill, within the noble estate of her childhood, passed on to her when her mother, Charlotte Mayfield, had died twelve years before. Breathing in the tranquility, Laura longed to recapture the atmosphere of the Amish community. Something had drawn her to the Pennsylvania Dutch country—something more than her mother's fondness for the area. She had never forgotten her introduction to Lancaster County, nor the events surrounding the day of Katherine's birth. . . .

Her mother had coaxed her to take a trip by car that June day. At seventeen and in the latter stages of pregnancy, Laura had been struggling with frequent panic attacks and, in general, needed a change of scene—away from the questions of high school friends who could not understand why she was being tutored at home.

Young and petite as she was, she'd undergone an ultrasound—at her doctor's insistence—to determine her ability to deliver naturally. In the process, they had discovered that the baby in her womb was most likely a girl. So, to occupy Laura's time, her mother had suggested a sewing project— a satin baby gown.

For weeks, though, she'd been lonely and sick with grief

over the loss of her first real boyfriend, unable to control her tears most of the time. A deep depression had left her restless, and she slept fitfully, if at all. When she closed her eyes at night, she could think only of her humiliating condition and her anger and guilt in having given up her innocence to a boy who'd never truly loved her.

Fearing her daughter was on the verge of an emotional collapse, Charlotte Mayfield had consulted a therapist, who'd recommended the short trip to Pennsylvania, despite the advanced stage of the pregnancy.

In their chauffeur-driven car, they had followed the Susquehanna River south to Harrisburg, turning east to Lancaster.

Soon, there were no more residential districts, no machine shops, factories, or shopping centers. The landscape had opened up, revealing the wide blue skies, fringed with trees—as if seen through a camera lens. The fields were patchwork perfect, like the handmade quilts made by the Amish who lived here. Under a benign sun, farmers were busy working the land, using the simple tools of centuries past. It was a scene straight out of a picture book.

Miraculously, Laura began to unwind. Perhaps it was the way the ribbon of road dipped and curved past fertile fields on every hand. Or the nostalgic sight of horse-drawn carriages. Or the gentle creaking of a covered bridge, flanked by groves of willows—their long fronds stirring in a lazy breeze.

Whatever it was, her mother noticed a change in Laura's mood and asked the driver to slow the car so they could watch a group of barefoot Amish girls picking strawberries. The girls laughed as they worked, making a game of the backbreaking task.

Laura abandoned the handwork she'd brought along— the satin baby gown—to watch. There was something about these strangely ordinary people. Something that tugged at

her heart. Was it their innocent ways? The peaceful surroundings?

Months earlier, she had gone back and forth about giving
up the baby for adoption—one day deciding it was best for
the precious life within her, and the next, certain she could
never part with the baby she'd carried all these months.

Observing the simple delight of these young women,
gathering ripe fruit on a dirt road in the heart of the Amish
country, Laura had known what she must do. She'd heard
her own heart-voice speaking to her, that faithful, confident
voice she knew she could trust. She would give her baby up
for adoption.

When the contractions came unexpectedly, the driver
had sped away to the hospital. There, Laura had given birth
to the baby daughter she'd promptly named Katherine.
After holding her, with Charlotte hovering near, she'd relin-
quished the bundle to the nurse who insisted she get some
rest.

It was then, while dozing in and out, that she'd overheard one of the nurses speak to the attending physician
outside her door. "The young Amish couple down the hall
just lost their baby. Stillborn . . . full term—a perfect baby
girl."

She'd heard the doctor's hurried footsteps, and later, the
sober whisperings of other nurses. The loss wrenched
Laura's heart, and she'd wondered what it would be like to
grow up Amish—a question she had voiced to her mother
earlier in the day.

Here she was, unmarried, and with no father or no real
home to offer her baby. Yet this couple—who had just lost
their own child—could give Katherine everything good and
simple and honest. It was an easy decision.

When she told her mother, her voice was surprisingly
calm. "I know what I want to do about Katherine. . . ."

A gust of wind shook the bare trees, and, instinctively, Laura wrapped her frail arms about herself, shivering in the November sunshine that had suddenly lost the power to warm her. She should call for Rosie to bring a wrap.

She longed to be able to move about without constant help, wondering if her days of complete mobility were behind her. But she decided to put off ringing for Rosie again. She would sit here a little longer.

A foreboding sense of loneliness overshadowed the brightness of the day, and she recalled the thought that had insinuated itself into her consciousness so many times during the years. *What if Katherine, my precious child, never lived to adulthood? What if something has happened to her?*

Shaking off the dreadful idea, Laura directed her thoughts to her most recent trip to Lancaster, destined to be her last, she was certain. The memory of her time there, although disappointing in its findings, served to lighten her mood—at least for the moment.

She recalled the darling young boy of eight or nine—all shining eyes and golden hair and a spattering of freckles on his nose—who had come to the farmhouse door. In answer to her question, he had pointed out the way back to the main road, giving excellent directions for one so young.

The children . . . They kept popping up, groups of them, in their quaint, black felt hats and winter bonnets, crowded into the back of a market wagon or walking along the road to school. Mostly blond-headed children, she recalled, although there were older ones with darker hair. She had specifically looked for a lone redhead among them; had even driven past an Amish school yard during recess, searching for an auburn-haired girl, before sadly remembering that her baby was a grown woman now, not a child at play.

Where had the years flown? Lost years. Years she could never regain. Years filled with emptiness and anguish. Yet, at the time—as a distraught teenager—she'd done what she'd believed was the best thing for little Katherine. The best thing . . .

Laura lifted her sunglasses and brushed away the tears. *Katherine, my dear girl. How I long to know you.*

She leaned back on the chaise, allowing the sun to bathe her face with light and heat, and wondered how many other women had felt such pangs after relinquishing a baby—pangs as real as the birth itself.

"If I had known what I know now," she said aloud, "I would never, *never* have given you away." She spoke into the air, daydreaming in the stillness of the morning, hoping that the Lord's angels might carry the words from a mother's broken heart directly south—to the place where Katherine might be living. If she was indeed alive. . . .

CHAPTER TWENTY-TWO

Everyone in Hickory Hollow was preparing to attend the wedding on Tuesday. There would be nearly three hundred guests at this wedding; Mattie herself had seen to *that*. She'd made a long guest list for her granddaughter—had even offered to have the wedding at her house.

She was stocking up on white sugar at the General Store on Saturday morning when Rachel Stoltzfus and Rebecca Lapp came in together. Mattie waited until Rebecca was out of earshot before she wandered over to chat with Rachel. "It'll be a mighty fine wedding—my granddaughter's and the King boy's."

"Jah, right fine."

"Hickory John and Levi Beiler are gonna be two of the Hostlers. And I think Bishop John agreed to be one of the ministers."

"That's nice." Rachel headed for the aisle filled with shelves of sewing notions, her back turned to Mattie.

"You'll be comin', won't ya?" Mattie inquired.

"Maybe . . . if Mary's feeling better."

Mattie nodded. "Oh my, I forgot to ask. How is your girl these days?"

"Well, I don't think it's serious what she's got." Rachel pushed on, eager to avoid any more questions. The truth was, Mary had taken to her bed ever since Chicken Joe had asked Sarah Beiler to go to Singing with him. It was the worry about never getting married that had given her daughter a bad case of dysentery. That—and Katie Lapp's shunning.

Just then Rebecca turned the corner and Rachel hushed up. No sense in Rebecca finding them buzzing like bees.

"Well, hullo, Mattie," Rebecca greeted her.

"Mornin', Rebecca."

Seeing the two women together like this—Rebecca and Mattie Beiler—it was clear to Rachel that their old feud had cooled down. Things were actually quite different between them, and she supposed it had something to do with the news of a stillborn baby and an unwed mother so long ago. It seemed that Rebecca's secret had mellowed Mattie remarkably, even though she, and she alone, had broadcast that particular juicy bit of gossip.

Relieved to see Rebecca—knowing her presence would put an end to Mattie's wedding jabber—Rachel offered to hold her friend's basket while she checked off her list. It would do Rebecca Lapp no good to get an earful. Not with her still reeling from her own daughter's recent disgrace.

Just as she suspected, though, Mattie wasn't about to mind her own business but trailed after them in the store, trying her best to draw them into conversation about her granddaughter's wedding.

Several times she mentioned Katie, wondering how the "dear girl" was doing. "Is she any closer to confessin', do ya think?"

That did it. Rachel stepped up and looked Mattie squarely in the eye. "Just be in prayer for Katie, will ya?"

"That I certainly will do." Mattie smiled a little sheepishly and darted to the counter to pay for her items.

It was safe now for Rachel and Rebecca to go their separate ways again—Rachel, heading for the fresh coffee
grounds; Rebecca, to the piece goods counter.

Mattie was just leaving the store when Bishop John
strolled in with his son Jacob. Seeing the two pass each other
at the door, Rachel feared the nosy one might decide to stick
around. But much to her relief, the woman kept going,
straight for her carriage.

Bishop John removed his hat and approached Rachel
with a pastoral smile. "We missed having your Mary at
church last Sunday."

"She's been having quite a bout lately."

"Sorry to hear of it." John rumpled his young son's hair.

Jacob grinned, looking up at Rachel. "Mary cooks gut,
jah?"

Rachel nodded. "That she does. And I hope she'll be feelin' well enough to go to the next wedding in the Hollow—
come Tuesday." Thinking of what she'd just said, Rachel
could have bitten her tongue. Poor Bishop John, what must
he be feeling, having to stand up and deliver a wedding sermon right on the heels of his own sad wedding day!

"So it's not Mary who's gettin' married?" Jacob asked,
his eyes shining.

"No. Not Mary." Rachel chuckled at the eager look in the
child's eyes. "I'm thinkin' you're a tad young for my Mary.
But I'll tell her you asked about her."

Jacob scratched his head and glanced up at his father,
then hurried off toward the candy counter.

The bishop wiped his forehead. "Well now, it seems they
start payin' attention to the girls mighty early these days,
don't they?"

Rachel laughed again, said her good-byes, and went to
find Rebecca. But she had the oddest feeling that young
Jacob had had another reason for asking about Mary. Could
it be . . . that if Katie Lapp wasn't going to be his new Mam,

he was hoping it'd be Mary? Hmmm. Best not to say any-thing about *that* speculation. And if she did, Rebecca Lapp would be the *last* person she'd tell.

❖   ❖   ❖

Katie waited until she was absolutely sure Abe and Rachel Stoltzfus were sound asleep before she entered the front door of their house. She had left Molasses and the carriage out on the road, the horse tied to a tree nearby, so as not to cause any commotion. *It has to be this way*, she decided. *This way or no way at all.*

The next to the top stair creaked, and Katie froze in place for a second, then crept down the hall to Mary's bedroom.

There was a small gasp of surprise from Mary when Katie appeared in the doorway, lit for a moment by the pale moon, and she hurried in and closed the door softly behind her.

"Shh, don't be afraid. It's only me. I have a flashlight right here, so don't bother with a lantern." She stood at the foot of the bed, feeling awkward for having intruded on her friend's privacy this way. "I know you shouldn't be talking to me, but I couldn't leave without seeing you one last time."

Mary sat up suddenly and reached for Katie's arm, then fumbled for the flashlight. She took it from her and shone the light on herself, shaking her head. Her eyes were huge in her white face.

"If you talk to me tonight—right now—I won't ever tell a soul. Ya won't have to worry about the Meinding, Mary. You can trust me on that, I promise."

Mary stared back at her, eyes ever widening. "Don't go,

Katie," she pleaded softly. "I won't ever forgive you if ya leave here."

"How can I stay? I'll be shunned forever, don't you see? As good as dead. And my family won't be allowed to take communion if I stay on without confessing."

In the uncomfortable silence that followed, Katie twisted her long braid.

"You'll *never* confess, is that whatcha mean?"

Katie sighed. "Never."

"Then where will ya go?"

"To Mamma's Mennonite cousins down the lane—Peter and Lydia Miller." She handed Mary a slip of paper. "This is my new address, at least for the time being. When I save enough money, I'll be heading to New York."

"No, Katie, please don't!"

"I have to find . . . my real mother," Katie explained. "She's dying, and I might never see her alive if I don't hurry."

There was a long silence before Mary whispered, "I heard a rumor—people saying you were adopted—but I didn't want to believe it. Now you're saying you have to search for another Mam?" Mary wrinkled her nose. "Oh, Katie, I wish ya could just stay here where ya belong."

Katie took her friend's hand and squeezed it between both of hers. "I don't belong here. I never did, really."

"Ach, Katie, you're wrong, you're so wrong about that."

"And you're right?" She chuckled softly. "You've always been right about me, Mary. Always. Until now. But it doesn't change the way I love ya and always will."

"I'll probably up and die if you go away," Mary insisted.

Katie smiled at her friend's theatrics. "You're not going to die. I promise you that."

"But look at me now. I'm sick, ain't?"

"You're young and strong. I'm sure you'll pull through. Besides, I'll be off finding my true family, so don't go worrying about me. I'll be just fine." Katie sighed. "And before long some gut fellow'll come along, and you'll be married and having all the babies you ever wanted."

The stillness prevailed. Then Mary spoke again. "You'll never forget me, will ya?"

"How could I?" Katie's eyes had grown accustomed to the dim room, and she didn't miss the quiver in Mary's lower lip. "You're like my own sister." They hugged fiercely; the flashlight flickered and nearly went out.

"When will ya go?" Mary whispered.

"Next Tuesday, while everybody's down at the Zooks' house . . . for the wedding." Katie stood to leave.

"Will I ever see you again?"

"Someday, Mary. Someday I'll come again." Katie backed out of the room, memorizing the plump silhouette sitting with her blankets and quilt wrapped around her. Then she tiptoed down the stairs and slipped quietly out of the Stoltzfus house.

Hard as it was, she did not look back to see if Mary, who knew her heart better than all others, had left her warm bed to peer through the window and whisper one last good-bye.

❖   ❖   ❖

Annie was nursing baby Daniel when a horse and buggy passed the house along about midnight. She rose from her rocking chair to burp the little one and was standing in front of the window in the living room, watching the moon rise, when she spotted the lone figure in the carriage.

It was impossible to see who was hurrying down the lane at such a late hour. But when she looked more closely, she recognized the horse from his slight limp. It was ol' Molasses, the Lapps' driving horse.

The next morning at breakfast, she mentioned to Elam what she'd seen. "Your sister was out all hours last night. At least, I'm pretty sure it was Katie I saw."

Elam poured himself a second cup of coffee. "You'd think she'd be trying to settle down and behave herself—with the shunning and all. But not pigheaded Katie." He sipped his coffee, making a slurping sound. "I guess I should'a known all these years the girl wasn't my blood kin."

What a horrible thing to say! Annie thought, but kept it to herself.

Meanwhile, Daniel began to howl in his cradle near the woodstove. Annie got up quickly. "There, there, little one," she crooned, kissing his fuzzy head as she picked him up. She sat down at the table again and began nursing him. "Do you think we might've done wrong by not letting Katie hold her new nephew?"

"The girl's shunned, for pity's sake!" Elam spouted. "I don't want her holding our baby when she's in rebellion to the church. The harder the shunnin', the sooner she'll be repentin'."

"Maybe," Annie said, "but you just said she was pigheaded."

"She's stubborn, all right. Who knows how long she'll hold out?"

"What if she doesn't repent? Then what?"

Elam shook his head, evidently disgusted at her question. "Well, that would be a mighty awful mistake."

Katie won't make that mistake, Annie fervently hoped. And for a moment, she thought of her deceased brother, wishing Daniel were alive to see her firstborn son and to help Katie—bless her dear, stubborn soul—find her way through the shunning.

❖   ❖   ❖

Tuesday came, and before Samuel, Rebecca, and the

boys left for the Zook-King wedding, Katie turned to speak to them from her isolated table in the corner of the kitchen. "I'll be packed and gone by the time you get home," she said as they finished eating breakfast.

No one turned to acknowledge her remark. But Katie knew they were listening, and she continued. "You already have the Millers' address—Peter and Lydia. I'll be renting a spare room from them if anyone needs to contact me by mail." Her brothers were staring at her, mouths agape.

"I know you aren't allowed to speak a word to me because of the Meinding," she went on, "and I understand all that. But if you *could* say something, if you could speak to me and tell me good-bye—*The Lord be with ya, Katie*—well, I know you'd mean it . . . you'd mean it with all your hearts."

She turned away so they wouldn't see her sudden tears and began to clear off her little table. The tears dripped into the rinse water as she stood over the sink, realizing it was to be the last time she would wash dishes for her family. She was truly leaving, and the process of bidding farewell was more painful than she'd ever imagined it would be.

When the rest of the family had finished, she offered to clean up the kitchen so they could be on their way. Of course, no one said anything. And minutes later, after Katie had assumed she was alone, she was surprised to see her mother, scurrying back into the kitchen as if she'd forgotten something.

"Here, Katie," she said, all out of breath. "I want ya to have this." She pushed an envelope into her daughter's wet hand.

When Katie looked down, she knew instantly that it was the dowry money. "Ach, no, Mamma, I can't take this. It wouldn't be right."

"Nonsense. You'll be needin' to buy some different clothes if you're going up to New York to find your . . . your first Mam. Now, take it and don't breathe a word to anyone, promise?"

Before Katie could refuse again or thank her mother, Rebecca had spun around and rushed toward the back door.

"Mamma . . . wait!" Katie ran to her, flung her arms wide, catching her mother in a warm embrace. "I love ya, Mam. Honest I do. And . . . no matter what you may think, I'll always be missing you."

Rebecca nodded, tears filling her eyes. "You can't stay on here, Katie . . . I know that."

"Oh, thank you," she whispered as her mother turned to go. "Thank you for loving me so."

❖ ❖ ❖

Katie was determined to leave her bedroom tidy—the kitchen, too. So a good portion of the morning was spent mopping, washing up, and dusting. When she was packed to her satisfaction—leaving several old dresses and capes hanging on their wooden pegs—she located the satin infant gown in her dresser drawer and carried it to the window. There she inspected it carefully, lovingly, once more.

With her fingers she lightly traced the tiny stitches spelling out *Katherine Mayfield*, and in the sunlight, she noticed a tiny spot on the dress. A closer look—and she decided that Mam must have come into the room, found the little dress, and wept. The spot looked, for all the world, like a teardrop.

Waves of emotion washed over her, carrying her along on an undulating tide—sadness . . . joy; confidence . . . uncertainty. Was she doing the right thing? Mary had drilled the question into her so often during their growing-up years. But now? Was leaving Hickory Hollow "the right thing"?

Hours later, with suitcase packed, guitar case in hand, and the contents of her cedar chest stored away neatly in attic boxes, Katie went out to the barn. Her pony seemed restless as she stood beside him. "I wish I could take you with me, Satin Boy, really I do. But you'll be much happier here with the other animals."

She set the guitar down and went to get his brush. She talked to him as she brushed his mane with long, sweeping strokes. Then she let her tears fall unchecked as she began to hum one of her favorite songs. "Maybe someday I'll come back for you, boy, and take you home to live with me—wherever home ends up to be."

She hand-fed him some hay and patted his nose. "Don't grow up too fast, and don't look so sad. It's not such a bad thing, really. Eli and Benjamin will take good care of you . . . Dat, too." Speaking her brothers' names and her father's familiar nickname aloud brought a lump that seemed to stick in her throat. She knew she should walk away without looking back—the way she had at Mary's. Maybe then she wouldn't break down completely.

She took a deep breath and kissed the white marking below Satin Boy's right eye. Then, picking up her guitar case, she hurried straight to the door and out into the barnyard.

❖   ❖   ❖

The house seemed much too quiet to Rebecca when she stepped into her kitchen after the wedding. And while the men prepared the cows for milking, she headed upstairs to Katie's room, hoping she'd find a final note from her. Some keepsake to read over and over again.

Katie's room looked the same as always. The only items missing were a few dresses; she hadn't taken many of them. All the old choring clothes still hung on their wooden pegs, along with the organdy head coverings.

Searching the top of the dresser, Rebecca saw that the

hand mirror was gone, along with Katie's brush and comb. The lilac sachets were also missing from the drawers.

Lydia's spare room will soon smell wonderful-gut, I'm thinkin'. The notion brought a pain to her chest, and she put her hand to her heart and held it there as she made her way down the hall to the bedroom she shared with Samuel.

There on the bed, she spied the little satin dress lying on her pillow. *Oh, Katie, you did leave me something. You left the little dress.*

Her heart swelled with love for her daughter, her precious but unyielding Katie. She leaned down and picked up the small garment, lifting it to her face and noticing, as she did, the faint scent of lilac.

❖   ❖   ❖

Lydia Miller slowed the car as she approached the shady cemetery. "I'll be glad to take you all the way," she offered. "No need for you to walk so far."

Katie shook her head. "Thanks, but it's not that far from here, really. And I need the exercise." She got out of the car on the passenger's side and walked up the slight incline, the sloping area that led to Dan Fisher's wooden grave marking.

What do ya see when ya look into your future? he'd asked her years ago.

"Not this," she muttered to herself. "Never this."

Dan had gone to heaven, she could only hope. And soon she, too, would be leaving Hickory Hollow for good. *Things just never seem to work out the way you plan,* she thought.

Katie approached the flat area reserved for Dan's body. The spot lay cold and empty now as she stared down at the dry, dead grass. "I'm going away," she whispered. "Can't stay Amish. But maybe you already know about that." She glanced up at the blustery, gray clouds high overhead. "You see, I'm fancy inside—and soon will be on the outside, too. And the music—our music . . . well, I'll be able to sing and play as much as I want to from now on."

She didn't cry on this visit, but bent down and knelt on the spot where Dan's body would've been buried if they'd ever found it. "I'll take good care of your guitar for you," she said, leaning her head close to the ground. "I promise you that."

CHAPTER TWENTY-THREE

Katie rode into town with Lydia the next morning to make a deposit in her checking account, then accompanied Lydia to market. Because of her mother's generous gift, Katie had decided to postpone her housekeeping jobs in hopes of finding some good leads on her birth mother's whereabouts.

"Before I do anything, there's one more place I must go," Katie told Lydia. "Will it be too much bother?"

"You say the word." Lydia was smiling. "Happy to help out a relative in a pinch."

Katie nodded. Her situation was more desperate than a "pinch," but she said nothing and kept watching for the turn-off to Mattie's place.

The fancy blue car stopped in the barnyard behind the main house, and Katie got out. This time to bid farewell to the Wise Woman.

When Ella Mae appeared at the window, there was no cheerful greeting, no welcoming smile. Only a glassy blank stare.

Katie's heart sank. The Meinding and its practices had caught up with Ella Mae, too. Either that or the old woman had gone daft for sure.

A shadowy motion alerted her to the real reason for the

vacant look in the faded hazel eyes. Behind her stood Mattie Beiler, shaking her head solemnly.

"I just came to say good-bye," Katie called loudly enough to be heard through the door. "I'm leaving Hickory Hollow." She turned and pointed toward the car. "That's my Mam's cousin, Lydia Miller. You probably remember her. . . ." Her voice trailed off when she looked back at the window and saw that Mattie was still standing there, glaring at her through the windowpane.

But it was the single tear tracking a path down the wrinkled lines of Ella Mae's face that broke Katie's heart. Reassured her, too. She was not alone in the world, after all.

"I'll miss ya forever," Katie blurted, choking back the blinding tears.

The Wise Woman blinked slowly, deliberately, then smiled the faintest smile, creating the familiar dimples. One of the family traits Katie had always loved.

One last, long look, and Katie turned and walked toward the waiting car.

◈　◈　◈

Samuel pulled up his rocking chair near the cookstove, removed his socks and wiggled his toes, warming them as he waited for the noon meal. Rebecca felt the emptiness anew without Katie to help with the table setting, and she glanced over at her husband, who seemed to be settling easily into his daily routine.

Wonder how's he managing, really? she thought, turning her gaze to Samuel several times before announcing that dinner was ready.

The spot that had always been Katie's at the big table seemed exceptionally bare in the light of day, even in spite of the fact that she had not sat there for the past ten days—

since the shunning began. Still, Rebecca could not get used to it. She never would.

Casting a quick look over her shoulder, she fully expected to see the small table in the corner and was disturbed that she had not remembered seeing Samuel remove it—sometime last evening, maybe. Had she been so caught up in her own despair that she'd blocked it out of her mind?

"When did ya put away Katie's table?" she asked Samuel, who was busy forking up the beef stew.

"Didn't do anything with it," he answered, stretching his neck to have a look at the vacant space.

Rebecca pondered the situation while she cut the meat on her plate. Was she losing her mind?

Then the answer came to her, and she knew precisely what had happened. Katie herself had taken on the chore of folding up the table and putting it away in the cellar. A loving gesture for sure—one that Katie knew might soften the blow for her mother.

Rebecca started to tell Samuel what she was thinking, but her husband stopped her abruptly. "From this day on, there is not to be one word spoken about Katie in this house. We will not be speaking her name—not ever again!"

Startled and hurt, Rebecca jerked her head down. Her hands flew up over her eyes, hiding the quick tears. It was then that she felt Samuel's warm hand on her arm. His hand remained there long after she'd regained her composure. And because of it, she felt comforted.

❖ ❖ ❖

Annie was tending to baby Daniel on a frigid January morning when there was a knock at the front door. She tucked the baby into his cradle in the warm kitchen and hurried to the front room to open the door.

A round-faced postman was standing on the porch. "I have a letter here for Annie Lapp," he said, reading the name off the envelope marked Priority Mail.

"*I'm* Annie Lapp," she said hesitantly, wondering who on earth would pay so much money for a piece of mail—and why they felt they needed to send it so fast.

"Here you are, ma'am." He handed her the envelope. "Have a good day."

She closed the door against the biting wind and sat down in the living room, turning her attention to the large, cardboard envelope. A small arrow pointed to a perforated strip, and when she pulled on it, she was surprised at how easily it opened.

Before reaching inside, she turned the envelope over and searched for a return address, but there was none. "That's odd," she said aloud.

The idea that it might be a belated New Year's greeting from Katie excited her, and quickly she pulled out the smaller envelope inside, hoping she was right. Dropping the outer covering, Annie read her name on the front of the small envelope. This didn't look like Katie's handwriting, but then again, she could be wrong; after all, she hadn't had reason to see her sister-in-law's handwriting all that often. But this . . . this writing seemed strangely familiar. Where had she seen it before?

She opened the envelope and pulled out a letter written on lined paper, much like the paper she'd learned to write on at the one-room Amish school, many years ago. Curious, she began to read:

My dear Annie,

For several years now, I have wanted to contact you secretly. I trust this letter will not startle you unduly. If you are not sitting down, maybe you should be, because, you see, I, your brother Daniel, am alive.

Annie leaped out of her chair, trembling, still holding the letter. "Ach, how can this be?" She paced frantically, going to stand in front of the window, staring out but seeing nothing, then sat down again to read the next line.

Indeed, there was an accident at sea, but I did not drown on my nineteenth birthday, as you may have believed all these years.

She rushed into the kitchen, past the cradle holding her sleeping son, and out the kitchen door to find her husband. "Elam! Come quick!"

When she did not find him in the barn, she hurried to the milk house. "Elam, where are you?"

She felt her heart thumping hard and her breath coming in short, panicky gasps. When her husband was nowhere to be found, she stood there in the barnyard, shivering from the cold and her inner confusion, reading the letter from her long-deceased brother.

Now, however, I wish to come to Hickory Hollow for a visit. I must do the Christian thing and make amends, starting with Father, because it is he who I have most sorely wronged.

If it is not too presumptuous, I will contact you again by mail in a few days, and later, if you agree, I want to speak with you—face-to-face—about approaching our father with this news.

And Katie Lapp. I am wondering how she is, and hoping that she has not already married, although I cannot imagine that she has waited for a dead man all these years.

If I am to be allowed to come to the Hollow, it is Katie I want to see first of all. . . .

Annie's head was swimming with her brother's brief explanation. So much had been left unsaid. Still, her heart was breaking—for Katie. Poor, dear girl. Even if someone wanted to risk being shunned to tell her about this unexpected turn of events—even so, Katie had already left for New York.

She shook her head mournfully as she walked toward the house. Feelings of anticipation—the possibility of a reunion with her darling brother—stirred within.

When her little one began to squirm and fuss, she picked him up and walked around the kitchen. Thoughtfully, she began to tell him the story of a handsome uncle who had been dead and now was alive, and a stubborn aunt who was as good as dead because of the shunning—and how they had loved each other.

She put her lips to the top of his sweet head and kissed the warm, pulsing soft spot. Such a frightening thing to ponder—this sad love story—its end so unlike its simple beginning.

"Some things just ain't very simple, really," she heard herself saying. "Some things just ain't."

She turned toward the kitchen window, facing west. And holding baby Daniel close, she looked out over the wide stretch of pastureland that bordered the woods. The sun had slipped below the horizon, leaving long, trailing tendrils of red in the sky—like a woman's hair floating out over the trees, free and unrestrained.

EPILOGUE

❖ ❖ ❖

How swiftly my life has changed, though I 'spect things in the Hollow plod along, same as always. Tongues are forever wagging these days, but all I *really* know is hearsay.

Talk is cheap, but rumor has it that Mam has stopped her storytelling. My heart is awful pained over what she must surely be going through. Still, I don't know how I could've stayed on, not with the Meinding and all. I'd have become a yoke around my family's neck. Eventually, the People would've ousted me anyway. Bidding a sorrowful farewell was my only hope.

They say Mary Stoltzfus's uncle—her father's youngest brother—is interested in moving out to Indiana somewhere. Most likely to look for available farmland. I only hope my leaving hasn't stirred up unrest among the People.

One thing is for sure and for certain. I am free now. No more Ordnung hanging over my head. No more bishop telling me how to dress, how to pin up my bun, how *not* to sing or hum.

But freedom's come with a terrible high price tag—leaving my family and turning my back on the only life I've ever known. Honestly, sometimes I have to reassure myself, and

281

it's at those times that I stop and pray: O *God, help me to be of good courage.*

Still, I remember the shunning, and if the truth be known, I realize it's a grievous blessing—a springboard to freedom. Freedom to experience what the dear Wise Woman could only begin to imagine. Freedom to search, and hopefully, find my roots.

Yet more than any of that, I've been cut loose to discover who I truly am . . . who I was meant to be. And for the part of me that is Katherine Mayfield, it is a wonderful-good thing.

ACKNOWLEDGMENTS

It is a myth that writers work alone. In the matter of this particular book, I wish to thank the following people:

The Lancaster County Historical Society, The Mennonite Information Center, The Lancaster Public Library, and The People's Place; Fay Landis, John and Ada Reba Bachman, Kathy Torley, and Dorothy Brosey.

During the course of my research, as well as my growing-up years in Lancaster County, I have been blessed with Amish friends and contacts, most of whom choose to remain anonymous. A heart-felt *Denki!* for your warm hospitality and many kindnesses.

Deepest gratitude to Anne Severance, my editor and friend, who graced these pages with her expertise and enthusiasm.

Special thanks to Carol Johnson and Barbara Lilland, who believed in this story from its inception, and to the entire BHP editorial and marketing staff.

For ongoing encouragement, I am grateful to Judy Angle, Barbara Birch, Bob and Carole Billingsley, Bob and Aleta Hirschberg, and Herb and Jane Jones.

I forever appreciate my husband's keen interest in my work, and his willingness to talk out plot angles and ideas with me. Thank you, Dave . . . for always being there.

For readers captivated by the charm of the Old Order Amish comes SUMMERHILL SECRETS by Beverly Lewis, an engaging, contemporary series for young teens. Set in Lancaster County, Pennsylvania, these action-packed stories feature fourteen-year-old Merry Hanson and her Amish girlfriend, Rachel Zook. (*Whispers Down the Lane* is a C. S. Lewis Noteworthy List Book, 1995.)

Whispers Down the Lane
Secret in the Willows
Catch a Falling Star
Night of the Fireflies
A Cry in the Dark
House of Secrets
Echoes in the Wind

BEVERLY LEWIS

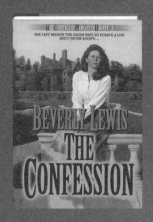

THE HERITAGE
of LANCASTER COUNTY
TRILOGY

3-IN-1 EDITION INCLUDING
The Shunning, The Confession and *The Reckoning*

BEVERLY LEWIS
THE
CONFESSION

BETHANY HOUSE PUBLISHERS
MINNEAPOLIS, MINNESOTA 55438

Scripture quotation on page 215 is from the HOLY BIBLE, NEW INTERNATIONAL VERSION®. Copyright © 1973, 1978, 1984 by International Bible Society. Used by permission of Zondervan Publishing House. All rights reserved. The "NIV" and "New International Version" trademarks are registered in the United States Patent and Trademark Office by International Bible Society. Use of either trademark requires the permission of International Bible Society.

Cover by Dan Thornberg,
Bethany House Publishers staff artist.

Published by Bethany House Publishers
A Ministry of Bethany Fellowship, Inc.
11300 Hampshire Avenue South
Minneapolis, Minnesota 55438

Printed in the United States of America.

ISBN   0-7394-3554-X

DEDICATION

To Judy Angle
Thanks for keeping the secret
and
for blessing the idea with prayer,
shaping it with wings.
With gratitude and love.

ABOUT THE AUTHOR

❖ ❖ ❖

BEVERLY LEWIS is a former schoolteacher and the author of over forty books. She is a member of The National League of American Pen Women, the Pikes Peak branch, and the Society of Children's Book Writers and Illustrators. Her books are among the C.S. Lewis Noteworthy List Books. Bev and her husband have three teenagers and make their home in Colorado.

Author's Note

❖   ❖   ❖

In writing the following pages, my heart was captured by Katie's emotional pain and her desperate search for truth. Her story now continues, just days after she abandons the Amish community and moves in with Mennonite relatives. And weeks *before* Daniel Fisher's shocking letter ever arrives in Hickory Hollow. . . .

Part I

One can never consent to creep when one feels
an impulse to soar.

Helen Keller

PROLOGUE: KATHERINE

I remember everything about my first glimpse of Cousin Lydia's kitchen. It was modern as the day is long and all aglow with electricity.

Being a curious three-year-old, I'd set out to reach the light switch, making determined grunts as I stood on tiptoe, stretching myself up . . . up while peeking around the wide doorjamb to see if the grown-ups were watching.

At last, my little fingers touched the magic. Off . . . and on, and off and on again, I made the long white ceiling lights buzz and flicker, splashing fluorescent gleams onto the floor and the wallpaper. I must've played that way for a good five minutes or more.

It was *Dat* who told me to stop. "Ya mustn't be playin' with the lights, Katie. Ya might burn 'um out," he said softly but sternly. Then he scooped me up in his long arms and carried me to the front room with the rest of my Plain relatives.

Nearly twenty years later, I had to smile at my renewed interest in the light switches found in every room of Peter and Lydia Miller's Mennonite farmhouse. Especially the shiny gold one in the boarding room I now called home.

Being raised Old Order Amish meant I'd never lived

around such fancy things, and for all good reason: the *Ordnung*, an unspoken list of church rules and regulations that had put a damper on my every word, deed, and, ofttimes, my thoughts, too.

I, sadly enough, had gone and broken those laws, several of them—hadn't kept my confession promise to Bishop John, refusing to destroy a forbidden guitar. In return for my wickedness, I was to be shunned all the days of my life.

All my life . . .

If, and only if, I was willing to go to the bishop and repent—bend my knees in earnest contrition, pleading with God and the church membership for mercy—only then could a sinner such as I ever be brought back into the fold of the People.

So Katie Lapp, the secretly "adopted" daughter of Amish parents, was as good as dead. Shunning practices were carried out that way in Hickory Hollow—the way they'd been seen to for three hundred years.

But what of Katherine Mayfield—my real name and the real me? Well, I couldn't imagine *Katherine* thinking twice about a kneeling confession for what I'd done. Not for love nor money. There was too much at stake.

Still, the steady ache in my heart persisted, and sometimes on the clearest of days, from high atop the second-floor landing window, I managed to make out the snowy outline of a distant roof and double chimneys—the old farmhouse where I was raised.

True, Samuel and Rebecca Lapp's sandstone house was just one buggy mile away, up Hickory Lane a bit, though it might've been a good hundred miles on dark December days like today. 'Cause standing here, staring my past in the face, it seemed my whole world might fade to a deep, dark purple if I let it. Stubborn as I was, though, I refused to give in to the searing pain of rejection. And betrayal. Wouldn't let the memories of the shunning drape a dark cloud over my future. In a peculiar sort of way, that was my salvation—that, and my Mennonite relatives.

If it hadn't been for Peter and Lydia, I might've succumbed to despair. But they had a way of treating me like I was really and truly one of the family. Clear from my first day here.

My eyes had begun to open up in more ways than one. The way they talked to God, for instance. Why, it was downright astonishing at times. Oh, I'd heard them say blessings over the meals off and on through the years, but family devotions and the prayers that followed were brand-new to me. Ever so joyful.

And what singing! Three- and four-part harmonies filled the house every evening after supper. My guitar had found a temporary home, and so had my broken heart.

Answering to "Katherine" instead of "Katie" took some getting used to, for sure and for certain. There was no easy way to change something as comfortable as your own first name just because one day you up and decided you were someone new. Still, I was determined to try.

Sometimes Lydia had to call me two and three times to catch my attention. I suppose it wasn't so much the sound of "Katherine" that threw me off—it was latching on to what the name stood for that was the biggest struggle.

For truth, I belonged to someone who'd never known the Ordnung and its confining practices, someone who understood all about the busy modern world I'd missed out on. My birth mother, Laura Mayfield-Bennett—*she* was my true kin. And if I could trust what I'd been told, the woman was dying of some *greislich*, dreadful disease. I needed to act quickly, but the fear in my heart was powerful-strong. At first, it held me fast, even kept me from learning to drive a car or from trying out the telephone hanging high on the wall in Lydia's kitchen.

But there *was* something I didn't hesitate on. Something

no amount of fear could keep me from doing. Cousin Lydia drove me to town and dropped me off at the prettiest beauty shop I'd ever seen. 'Course, I'd never darkened the door of one before—just looked from a distance . . . and wished. Didn't have an appointment, but they took me right in and cut and styled my hair just the same.

Glory be! What freedom I felt when the scissors started snippin' away at my long, uneven locks that'd never been cut my whole life long.

Well, the weight of the world fell right off me, in a heap of auburn hair all over the floor. I shook my head and the air swooshed through it, clear to my scalp, and I asked myself why on earth I'd waited so long for something so awful nice.

The answer was bound up in rules and expectations same as my waist-length locks—tied up in a knot under a veiled covering all these years. But there was no need for me to be carrying around a headful of long, too-thick hair anymore. I was free to do whatever I pleased with it . . . *and* my face. Clothes, too. A wonderful-good feeling.

Staring in the mirror, I saw Katherine Mayfield's painted lips smiling back at me. When she whispered, "How do you do?" I heard the refined sound of her "English" voice in my ears. Still, it would take some practice to get it right every time.

I reached up and ran my fingers through my shoulder-length hair; honestly, feeling it so bouncy and free gave me the shivers. The new cut gave me something else, too. A curtain of soft curls!

"You have beautiful natural waves, Katherine," the beautician said with a big smile.

What a day! The curls, so long hidden, had finally made their appearance. I was more than grateful and told her so.

As for Lydia's telephone, I realized I couldn't be waitin' to use it anymore. Couldn't let the fear hold me down, so I got real brave. Five days after coming to live in this fancy house—filled with electricity, microwave ovens, forced air heat . . . and the tallest, prettiest Christmas tree I'd ever seen—I picked up the Lancaster phone directory and made myself read all about how to dial up a long-distance operator.

Then closing the pages, I thought about the sin I was about to commit. Would I never stop straying from the path of righteousness? Seemed to me I'd sinned so awful much, though, what would one more transgression hurt?

A sense of urgency swept over me. My natural mother was dying . . . she wanted to see me. *I* wanted to see her, to know the woman named Laura, wherever she was.

Enough of this pondering over my faults and misdeeds. It was high time to take the first step toward finding my roots. A giant step, to be sure.

I reached for the telephone. . . .

CHAPTER ONE

❖   ❖   ❖

It was dark and bitter cold when Laura returned from the attorney's office. She was weary and sighed audibly, bearing the weight of this most recent appointment.

Theodore Williams, her longtime chauffeur, peered at her over the leathered front seat of the limousine. "Mrs. Bennett, are you all right?"

"A bit tired," she replied. "Please don't be concerned."

"Very well" came the deep yet gentle voice.

She allowed herself to lean hard against the backseat, waiting for Theodore as he made his way around to the trunk. Oh, how she longed for the days of mobility, freedom to come and go as she pleased. Could it have been only one month ago she'd braved the cold and the distance, hiring her driver to take her to a remote Amish community in Pennsylvania? She hadn't felt up to such a trip even then, but at least she had been able to get around while there, without much help.

Regretfully, the mid-November jaunt had turned up not a single lead. Her daughter—her only child—had not materialized, even though Theodore had so willingly backtracked to various spots in and around Hickory Hollow before driving home the next day, back to the place of her

17

childhood in the Finger Lakes region of New York.

Yet, in spite of the futile search, she had held stubbornly to one small hope—that an Amishwoman sitting in a carriage in front of a general store might have followed through with Laura's request. She had entreated the elderly woman to deliver her personal letter to one of the many Rebeccas living in the community—specifically, to the *only* Rebecca who would understand the desperate, handwritten plea. The woman whose adopted daughter was to celebrate her twenty-third birthday next summer, June fifth. . . .

The familiar sounds of Laura's empty wheelchair, its thin tires making contact with the cold pavement, brought her from her reverie. She began to straighten herself a bit, sliding forward in the seat as best she could, despite her frail and weakened condition.

In an instant, her chauffeur, dressed in a tailored black suit and overcoat, opened the car door. She lingered a moment, struggling to button the top of her coat against the frigid air as Theodore stood in readiness behind the wheelchair. "Rosie! Miss Judah!" he called toward the house. "Mrs. Bennett has returned."

In the space of a few seconds, the housemaid arrived, followed by Laura's live-in nurse. The two women gently assisted the mistress of the house, easing her out of the black car and settling her into the wheelchair.

Theodore paused judiciously, then—"Shall we go?"

Laura gave a slight nod and was cautiously wheeled over the wide, circular drive—freshly plowed from a recent snowstorm—and into the Tudor-style mansion.

A magnificent Christmas tree stood sentinel in the corner of the expansive entryway, adorned with white doves and lambs to represent divine peace and the Lamb of God respectively. There were lovely cream-colored roses, ivory stars, clumps of dried baby's breath and hydrangeas, and hundreds of twinkling white lights.

Laura breathed in the pine scent, relishing the rich holiday fragrance. *Will I live to see another Christmas Day?* she wondered, glancing away from the enormous tree.

She fought back tears. *Will I live to see my Katherine face-to-face?*

Faithful Theodore guided her chair down shimmering marble halls to the wide French doors in the south wing of the Bennett estate, at which point the venerable gentleman stepped aside, relinquishing the job to Natalie Judah, the nurse. "Do have a good evening, Mrs. Bennett," he said in a near whisper.

"Oh, I will, and you really mustn't worry." Then, motioning for him to lean closer, she said, "Remember . . . not a word to anyone. Are we agreed?"

"As you wish." Before straightening to his full height, Theodore pulled a long envelope from his vest pocket. "Shall I tend to this matter on your behalf?"

Laura had only to nod.

"Consider it done, Mrs. Bennett. Good evening." And he was gone.

Once settled in the commodious suite of rooms, Laura allowed Nurse Judah to assist in removing the wrap she'd donned for her errand. That done, she extended her arm as Natalie checked her pulse with a gentle touch. Frowning, the young RN—dressed all in white, including hose and shoes—then smiled the faintest of smiles and patted Laura's arm. "You've had a strenuous afternoon," she remarked, turning to speak to Rosie. "I think it would be best to serve supper here . . . in Mrs. Bennett's private quarters."

Rosie bit her lip momentarily, then made an obvious attempt to conceal her concern and came near the wheelchair, resting her hand lightly on Laura's shoulder. "I'll see to it."

Laura watched as her nurse set about preparing to administer the regular evening injection of morphine. Reticent and edgy, she stared at the needle. "If you don't mind, couldn't it wait . . . perhaps for just a while?" she asked, not certain why she'd made such a request.

"Oh? Are you experiencing some kind of discomfort? Nausea? Pain?"

The truth was, there had been no ill effects of her afternoon outing. "I'd just like to rest a bit . . . it's been a tiring day," she replied.

"We must be more careful from now on," Natalie reprimanded softly. "You mustn't overdo, Mrs. Bennett."

Laura understood perfectly, for her most recent attacks had come on with excessive fatigue and emotional stress, so much so she had made the decision to move her rooms to the main floor, primarily out of concern for her husband.

A man of disciplined work hours, many of which were spent in his upstairs office suite, Dylan Bennett was easily distracted, and what with her needing constant medical attention, and with Nurse Judah and Rosie coming and going at all hours, she had relocated. More convenient for all concerned. Indeed, *essential* for other reasons unknown to her husband of nine years.

As a relatively new believer—Laura had become a Christian three years prior—she maintained her heavenly Father was in control of her very life and that of her long-lost child's. More recently, she had begun to pray in earnest for God's will as to hers and Katherine's reunion—a reunion her husband might not welcome. A solitary afternoon would suffice for such a visit, but she knew in the depths of her being it must be soon . . . very soon, before the crippling disease advanced to claim her life.

The prayers and devotional time she enjoyed with other Christian women—Rosie Taylor, her personal housemaid, in particular—had become a thorny problem, presenting something of a nuisance for Dylan. Her husband, who did not share her newfound faith, had discouraged her from having Bible studies and prayer groups on the premises. Had he put his foot down and absolutely denied her this social and spiritual outlet, she would have obeyed, out of respect. She could only pray that Dylan would never resort to such a harsh measure.

During one such discourse, Laura had to gently remind him that the estate, in fact, was legally hers—her childhood home—having been left to her upon the death of her widowed mother, Charlotte Mayfield, twelve years earlier. The comment was not well received by Dylan, causing more of a rift between them.

Even so, Laura would occasionally invite a church friend or two for an intimate gathering, trusting that someday in God's perfect time, Dylan might join her in the study of the Scriptures. More important, that he would come to find peace with the Savior for himself.

It had not occurred to her, however, that by making arrangements to alter her will, she might be adding fuel to the already stormy debate. In fact, not until Mr. Cranston, her attorney and private counsel, had mentioned it today had she even considered the matter to be an issue. Her ultimate decision was not borne of a vindictive agenda; she was merely following the footsteps of her sensible and loving mother. That was the extent of it.

But she must be discreet. And, for now, Dylan was not to be the wiser.

❂   ❂   ❂

Natalie Judah went in search of her patient's warmest slippers, moving quickly past the lovely dressing room area, complete with jacuzzi bath and vanity, toward the large walk-in closet. On the way, she grappled with her growing emotional attachment to the kind yet determined woman she had been assigned to nurse through a prolonged and difficult illness.

Laura Bennett. A woman with so little life left in her.

Nothing in Natalie's medical training had prepared her for the intense empathy she had come to experience with her first in-home patient, a woman much too young to be dying. In fact, Natalie had found it practically impossible to maintain, as she'd been taught, a semblance of "professional detachment" in the face of Laura Bennett's single-minded goal—obsession, even. So with all the nursing skills at her command, Natalie had determined to do her best to keep Mrs. Bennett alive to realize her fondest dream—to meet the daughter she'd given away at birth, the infant who would by now be a young woman.

Sadly, all this presented a real dilemma. The very objective that drove the poor woman had the capacity to further weaken her, both physically and mentally.

At times, her patient's diagnosis tore at Natalie's heart, for malignant multiple sclerosis was an explosively progressive disease. She did not have to be forewarned as to how the final stages would play out.

❖ ❖ ❖

Laura gazed with interest at the live miniature twin Christmas trees perched on the cherry sofa table across the room on the very edge of her favorite Tibetan damask rug. Red velvet bows and long strands of wooden beads garnished the matching trees, resplendent even without tinsel or lights. She thought of all the Christmases she had missed with her daughter, the never-ending preparations, the gala events surrounding the season . . . hers, completely devoid of the laughter of children.

Had Katherine as a youngster fallen in love with the splendor, the music of Christ's birthday? Laura sighed as her thoughts flew backward in time. What sorts of things did Amish folk do to celebrate? she wondered. Had Katherine come to know the truest significance of the blessed season? Laura could only assume so, for surely the Amish knew and loved the Bible as she did.

Letting her mind wander, she considered the Plain community she'd secretly visited last month while searching for signs of Katherine. What *was* the chance of an Amish family giving up one of their own kin—by blood or otherwise—to spend time with a stranger, and all in response to a desperate plea?

She thought back to the crucial letter, and if she had been able to stand and walk to her writing desk, she would have done so, for in the narrowest drawer lay a copy of her message to Rebecca, the adoptive mother of her child. Still, she knew it by heart—every word of it.

The baby girl I gave to you has been living in my heart all these years. I must speak the truth and say I am sorry I ever gave her away. Now, more than ever, because, you see, I am dying.

Once again, her eyes drifted to the identical Christmas trees. Their bows and beads dazzled her, and she knew why, as a girl, her favorite colors had been red and green. She stared deep into the dense branches, daydreaming of other holidays . . . the breezy, casual days of girlhood, years before her precious baby daughter was ever conceived.

Tears sprang to her eyes. Then, without warning, the colors began to blur. Laura felt the hideous muscular jerking, starting on her left side. Frightened and experiencing intense pain, she placed both hands on her thigh, praying silently for the tremors to cease.

When they did not, she removed her hands slowly from her upper leg, hoping to conceal her true condition from the brunette nurse who had just come into the room, carrying fluffy blue slippers. Laura squeezed her fingers together, locking them into a folded position, and pressed them hard against her lap.

Natalie was not to be fooled, however. "Mrs. Bennett, I really must give you a shot now . . . *before* your supper comes." The soft-spoken woman stooped to remove Laura's shoes, replacing them with her favorite house slippers. Nurse Judah rose and offered a reassuring smile, giving Laura the courage to accept the intimidating injection.

Then, before the drug was ever administered—while the nurse prepared the syringe—the dreadful dizziness began. During the past several days, light-headedness had frequently accompanied the frenzied trembling. It was at such moments she would lose control and cry out, fighting off her pain with the best antidote she knew. "Oh, Lord Jesus, please . . . please help me," she would pray, whimpering.

Nurse Judah swabbed the vein gently. The moist cotton ball made a chilling, unwelcome path along the crease of Laura's arm.

"Can you make a fist, Mrs. Bennett?"

It was all she could do to cooperate at first, but slowly Laura willed her body to relax, and as the medication entered her bloodstream, the morphine began to work its miracle.

After the uncontrollable quaking had ceased, a cloud of exhaustion gathered over her. In the midst of this heaviness, Laura thought of her long-lost girl and feared her own time was short.

❖   ❖   ❖

Theodore Williams made his way out of the house to the limousine still parked in front of the grand entrance. Getting into the car, he thought of Mrs. Bennett's insistence on being driven downtown today. She'd certainly not looked well;

anyone could see that. But she seemed determined, at all costs, to discuss her last will and testament with Mr. Cranston.

Theodore's suspicions could not be quelled—the ailing woman must have it in her mind that she wasn't long for this earth, for it was the urgency in Rosie Taylor's voice, when she'd phoned at noon on behalf of the mistress, that had alerted him.

"Mrs. Bennett will not be satisfied till you agree to take her," the maid had said, stating quite clearly that no one else would do. "She insists on having *you* . . . and keep quiet about it, too." It was the latter remark that worried him greatly.

A more kindhearted lady Theodore had never met, and because Mrs. Bennett was not one to engage in manipulation or deceit, he was moved to help her as he had on at least one previous occasion. The memory served him still—that dreadful day when it was discovered her husband, shrewd man that he was, had been careless with the dear lady's accounts.

It was then that the mistress had taken Theodore into her confidence, a rather rare and ponderous position for an old Britisher solely in her employ. But he'd pulled it off—and quite successfully, too—arranging to drive her to an independent law firm, one completely divorced from Dylan Bennett's own accounts and financial dealings. To this day, and as far as Theodore knew, the man had not the faintest knowledge of any of it. None whatever.

Prudence dictated that Theodore would continue to keep this tidbit as quiet as the present afternoon's journey, when—he had a most ominous feeling—Mrs. Bennett had gone and altered her will.

He parked the black limo beside the white one, then opened his overcoat, reaching into his suitcoat pocket, where he pulled out the long linen envelope, unsealed. He would not investigate its contents, to be sure, and since it was too late to secure it in Mrs. Bennett's safe deposit box tonight, he locked up the envelope in the glove compartment of the car and headed for the gatehouse.

I'll take care of it tomorrow, he told himself. *Yes, indeed. First thing tomorrow.*

CHAPTER TWO

◆　　◆　　◆

Lydia Miller turned off Hickory Lane and onto the dirt driveway adjacent to the farmhouse. She parked her car in the detached garage bordering the converted barn, where her husband and two of their oldest sons had, years ago, set up a woodworking shop on the main level. She saw that the lights were still on in the office area. Noticing, too, the abundance of light streaming from nearly all the windows on this side of the house—upstairs included—she chuckled, making her way across the snowy barnyard, arms heavy with two sacks of groceries.

Katie Lapp's certainly having herself a heyday, she thought. The electric bill was sure to reflect it.

Approaching the house, Lydia wondered what it might've been like to grow up Amish with few, if any, comforts of a modern home. The mere thought of gas lamps, battery-operated water pumps, and horses and buggies made her grateful for the decision her elderly parents had made long ago—choosing a conservative Mennonite fellowship over the Amish church.

When Katie opened the back door, Lydia almost forgot to address her by the new name but caught herself in time. "How was your afternoon . . . Katherine?"

A smile as bright as a rainbow crossed the young woman's face. "I used the telephone today for the first time. *Ach*, it ain't so awful hard, I guess."

Lydia shrugged her shoulders. "It'll be old hat soon enough."

"*Jah*, I hope so."

Setting her groceries on the table, Lydia turned to the sink and began washing her hands. Then, with Katie's help, she put away three discounted boxes of dishwashing detergent and an array of other housecleaning supplies. "So . . . who'd you call, if it's any of my business?"

"I talked to a lady operator in Rochester, New York . . . I—"

Glancing over at Katie, Lydia hurried to set her at ease. No need for the dear backward girl to divulge the entire phone conversation. "That's all right, really 'tis. You don't have to tell me more."

"Oh, but I *want* to!" Katie closed the refrigerator door and rushed to Lydia's side. "I can't believe what I did today! Honest, I can't."

Studying the young woman next to her, Lydia sensed the yearning. "So, tell me, what did you do?" she asked softly, wondering if her cousin's daughter had already attempted to locate the ailing birth mother.

Katie pulled out a kitchen chair and sat down, touching her long auburn locks, flowing free in wavy curls. Her brown eyes sparkled, and Lydia noticed a trace of eye makeup. "There are forty-eight people with the last name of Bennett."

"Forty-eight? Ei yi yi, such a lot of long-distance calls."

"From what Mamma remembered, Laura lives somewhere near Rochester, I think. A city that sounds something like 'Canada.' "

"Well, have you looked on the map yet?"

"Just the one in the phone book, ya know, to get the

right area code." Katie beamed, looking right proud of herself—proud in a good way, no doubt—being able to spout off modern things like area codes and such.

"How on earth will you know if you've located the right person?"

Katie nodded. "Could be awful tricky, I 'spect. But I have some *gut* . . . uh, *good* . . . ideas."

Lydia sighed, feeling somewhat relieved. "Then you haven't made any personal calls there yet?"

"Not just yet." The hesitancy in the girl's voice was evident. "I wanted to ask your permission first . . . let you know I'm willing to pay for all the long-distance calls I might hafta make."

"Then we should get busy." Lydia located a book of maps from the shelf under her corner cupboard. "Here, let's have a look-see. Maybe we can find a city in New York that sounds like 'Canada.' "

They put their heads together, leaning over the map on the kitchen table—Lydia's, primly supporting her Mennonite cap; Katie's uncovered hair shining, tousled curls springing free, at odds with her upbringing.

After searching and not finding anything, Lydia checked the index for cities in New York. Her pointer finger slid down the page as she calculated each entry. "Here's one," she said. "I wonder, could this be it?" She pointed to *Canandaigua*. "Sounds a bit like 'Canada' to me. And the population is rather small, so there shouldn't be as many Bennetts to call."

Katie laughed. "Ach, you rhymed just then."

"I did at that."

The two women chuckled merrily and set about preparing supper. Katie peeled potatoes while Lydia warmed up leftover ham and buttered green beans in the microwave oven.

"Have you thought of praying about your search?"

29

ventured Lydia. "It would be a wise thing to ask our heavenly Father for His guidance. Don't you think so?"

Katie kept peeling potato skins without looking up. "I don't know how to pray thataway. Didn't learn, really. Never thought it was the right sort of thing to be doing, neither."

"Well, I believe I know just the person to teach you," Lydia replied, an excited feeling welling up in her. "Just the one."

Looking up, Katie broke into a shy smile. "Ach, really?"

"I wouldn't fool you about something like that." Lydia turned and went to gaze out the large bay window, framed in hanging ferns. "My husband has taught many a soul to pray, Katie."

"*Katherine*," Katie reminded her.

Lydia was silent. For a moment, she came close to apologizing but let it go this time. She had considered the arrival of Rebecca Lapp's only daughter as somewhat of a mixed blessing. The poor thing was really groping her way these days, insisting on a fancy name like "Katherine Mayfield." Peculiar, it was. This, and the fact that hers and Peter's home—dedicated to the Lord's work years ago—and their close proximity to the Amish community, made it rather convenient for the young woman to run from her past and rent a room outside her church district.

Lydia wondered if she was doing the right thing by the shunned girl. And what of Samuel and Rebecca Lapp . . . and their sons? What must *they* be feeling?

The situation perplexed her, and she had the oddest sensation overall. While pondering earlier, she'd wondered why Katie had reacted so harshly to her parents keeping her adoption a secret. Was this what had caused the young woman to deny her own identity? Or was it the shunning—the heartrending way she'd been treated by the People—that had changed everything so?

Lydia shook her head, bewildered. She couldn't get over the young woman's worldly clothing. She'd lost no time in buying a fancy red wool skirt and that shiny satin blouse with swirls of red, blue, and gold flowers, of all things. She figured Katie must've surely shaved her legs, too, because she was wearing the sheerest of hosiery lately. And such a hairdo! All wavy, and oh, so much shorter than any Plain woman—Amish or Mennonite—would ever dare to think of wearing.

Katie's shoulder-length hair bothered Lydia to no end— the girl was constantly fingering it and tossing it about. The usual head covering was missing. Of course, now, what with all of Katie's bright-colored clothes, the veiled cap would look completely out of place.

She sighed and turned from the window, touching the back of her own cap, Mennonite in styling. Surely there was a devout Plain woman—called Katie—hidden away somewhere inside the newly modern girl.

Surely there was.

❖ ❖ ❖

Katherine's room was high in the house, situated under the eaves, and neat as a pin. The smell of lilac had already begun to permeate the room because of the many handmade sachets she'd brought with her from home.

There was a down-filled comforter all decked out with sunny yellow tulips, and a white-and-yellow striped bedskirt that fancied up the four-poster bed. The place was mighty large, yet different from anything she'd ever seen in an Amish household. And the maple furniture, *every* piece—thanks to Cousin Peter's woodworking skill— matched the other: a triple dresser with wide, moveable mirrors; a tall chest of drawers with bright, colorful doilies; and two square lamp tables.

No dark green window blinds, cold hardwood floors, or mountains of Amish quilts. Also noticeably absent was any sign of a cedar chest, where a single woman could store hand-stitched items, awaiting her wedding day.

Katherine brushed aside the annoying thought. She'd gone and run out on her own wedding, leaving a disgusted widower-groom behind. A man who'd turned out to be the sternest bishop Hickory Hollow had ever known—Bishop John Beiler, the imposer of *die Meinding*—the shunning.

Ach! The very thought of it stung her to the core. But she was Katherine now. Body, soul, and spirit.

She stared at the foot of the bed where a hope chest might've been. 'Twasn't so important to have such a thing in a room for rent. Still, she couldn't help recalling the many lovely items she'd made during the years in preparation for her wedded future. All of it, every last hand-sewn piece, she'd packed away in the Lapps' attic. Just thinking of it, she had to laugh—a choked sound—for it was the dusty attic of her childhood home, where everything had begun to crumble and change.

Crossing the room, she went to sit in the upholstered chair near a beautifully draped window. She lifted her tired feet to the hassock and let out a weary sigh. Above her, the ceiling light shone brightly, and she decided as she relaxed that this room was her haven against the world. The world of her People who had pierced her very soul.

Shunned . . . for all time. . . . Once again, she was stricken with the paralyzing thought.

Purposely, she stared at the gold light switch across the room, and Cousin Lydia's words flickered through her mind. *Ask our heavenly Father for guidance*, the Mennonite woman had said.

But Katie—Katherine—had no idea how to do such a thing. Her strict Amish roots went too deep in her, maybe. Still, she mustn't accept that as a reason *not* to pray Cousin

Lydia's way. Besides, she wanted to break all ties with her past, so praying as if you were talking to God . . . now, that would be one way to go about it.

She got up and knelt beside the chair. "Dear Father in heaven, there's a Mennonite downstairs who says I should talk to thee . . . er, you, about findin' my real mother. I do hope thou, uh, *you* won't be minding too much. . . ."

She stopped. Such a strange way to speak to the Almighty. She resorted to beseeching Him in German, as she was accustomed. "*O Herr Gott, himmlischer Vater,*" she began.

It was difficult—no, downright bossy—to ask anything personal of the Lord God, heavenly Father, especially since she was in bald-faced disobedience to His commandments. So she didn't make a request at all but recited a prayer from *Christenpflicht,* the standard Amish prayer book, instead of a spontaneous one.

After the prayer was done, she felt as though she'd broken faith with the new person she was attempting to become—Katherine Mayfield.

Before getting off her knees, she spied the beloved guitar lying under the double bed. Retrieving it, she sat on the hassock, exhilaration replacing her sadness as she strummed the once-forbidden strings.

The lively songs she sang were old ones, some she'd made up as a little child. Another was a slower tune, one she and her first love, Daniel Fisher—who'd drowned in a sailing accident five years before—had written together during the last week of his life.

Dan, she truly hoped, would be pleased up there in Glory if he knew what her plans were for tomorrow. He was a spirited fella, Daniel Fisher. Never gave up trying till he got what he wanted. Especially when it came to religion and the Bible.

She remembered him being mighty stubborn for a young

Amishman—liked to ramrod his ideas through to those who didn't see eye to eye with him.

Katherine sang on.

Don't prejudge the dead, she could hear the conscientious voice of Rebecca Lapp, her Amish mamma. Herr Gott was the final Judge when all was said and all was done. The Almighty One was sovereign. Come Judgment Day, *He* would decide what would become of her dear *Beau*'s eternal soul.

Louder she sang, defying the thought of Daniel ever being anywhere but in Blessed Paradise. Never before and never again had someone understood or loved her more. And tomorrow, if Dan was looking down on her, she'd make him grin . . . chuckle, maybe.

She planned on using Cousin Lydia's telephone to dial up that long-distance operator in Canandaigua. She would not give up till she got hold of a woman named Laura Mayfield-Bennett. Laura, who would understand perfectly. Laura, who would recite the day of her daughter's birth and say at last, "Welcome home, Katherine."

What a fine, wonderful-good day that would be.

CHAPTER THREE

◈　◈　◈

Katherine waited for the house to clear out a bit before heading to the hall phone the next morning. She'd written and rewritten the directory assistance number for long distance on a scratch pad from the kitchen, anticipating the moment.

But when she walked up the stairs and approached the telephone, she could only stare at it. There were so many things to be thinking about. If she picked up that phone . . .

Hmm. It just might be best not to know anything about her natural mother, really. Might be best to leave well enough alone.

Her dear friend Mary Stoltzfus would say, "Stick to doin' the right thing, Katie." Well, if she was to do the right thing, would she be standing here in this Mennonite house this very minute?

She shrugged off the crippling thought. Her heart, fractured and feeble, insisted on knowing the truth.

But when she got up the courage to dial the number, the electronic answering service came on the line. Katherine waited, insisting on speaking with a real "live" operator.

"What city?" the woman asked.

"Canandaigua."

"One moment, please."

Katherine waited, her breath coming in shallow spurts.

"What listing?" was the reply.

"I need a number for someone with the last name of *Bennett*."

"Spell it, please."

"B-e-n-n-e-t-t."

"Thank you, one moment." The operator's voice sounded stiff, and Katherine wondered if that was how all of them talked. But she wasn't about to give up. She wouldn't let one uppity operator discourage her.

"There are fifteen Bennetts listed. Is there a *first* name?" the operator asked.

"Please try Laura Mayfield-Bennett. It might be under that name."

Almost instantly, the woman said, "I'm sorry, there's no such listing."

"Oh . . ."

"Would you like to try another?" came the wooden voice.

"No, thank you, but could you give me the phone numbers for those fifteen Bennetts?"

"I am authorized to give only one listing per call."

Only one? Katherine's heart sank. "But it's an emergency. Someone's dying . . . someone . . . uh, it's my real mother, she's dying . . . and I hafta find her."

"I'm very sorry, miss. You may continue to call back, however, if you wish to try all the numbers for that listing."

Katherine resigned herself to the way things must be done. After all, hadn't she always followed the most rigid rules in dress, in word, and in deed since toddlerhood? Why not go along with one more?

The operator gave her the first name—*Arthur O. Bennett*—and the number.

"Thank you," Katherine said and hung up.

Then, fingers trembling, she began to dial, remembering to include the area code.

Such a life these moderns have, she thought. On the other hand, *she* was still getting used to the simplest of conveniences.

Last evening, before retiring, she'd discussed her plans with Lydia and Peter, asking permission to use their telephone again. They had agreed to let her reimburse them for the long-distance calls when the monthly bill arrived. It would take quite a bit of her money, but Katherine thought it cheaper than hiring a private detective. Letting her call long distance like this was one of the nicest things anyone had done for her lately.

She heard the phone on the other end ringing in her ear. Once . . . twice . . . a third ring.

Then—"Hello?" a strange voice said.

"Ah . . . I . . . could I speak to Laura Mayfield-Bennett, please?" Her knees were shaking along with her voice.

"Well, I think you may have the wrong number," the voice replied.

"Oh, sorry." Quickly, she hung up.

Not to be discouraged, Katherine picked up a pencil and drew a single neat line through the name. "I'll just try the next one," she said, as though saying the words out loud might give her a bit more confidence.

But she hesitated, staring at the telephone. She thought of Cousin Lydia's kind suggestion of asking the Lord for guidance. Maybe she oughta get up the nerve to do it. Or ask Cousin Peter before she tried.

When she finally redialed the Canandaigua operator, someone new was on the line, and she had to go through the whole rigmarole again.

This time the name given was a *Clifford M. Bennett*. She dialed the new number. The phone rang and rang—ten times at least—before she halted it by hanging up. So she made a tiny question mark beside that name and repeated the process.

Next . . . *Dylan D. Bennett*.

Quickly, she cleared her throat and took a deep breath, trying to look on the bright side of things. Using the phone like this was a very good thing for her to be doing, she thought. Good practice.

But she wasn't prepared to have someone answer, not immediately on the first ring. "The Bennett estate," a confident female voice answered. "How may I direct your call?"

Suddenly, Katherine felt ill at ease. Her mouth went dry, and she was caught completely off guard, hearing a woman answer the phone this way. She almost wondered if she'd gotten hold of her natural mother by sheer luck!

"Is Laura Mayfield-Bennett at home, please?" she managed.

"I'm sorry, Mrs. Bennett is not available at the moment. May *I* help you?"

Katherine felt her heart racing and sat down quickly. *Oh my, now what?* she wondered. This woman talking to her on the other end of the line . . . this woman holding the telephone receiver up there in New York somewhere . . . she was saying, in so many words, that Laura Mayfield-Bennett—her mother, her real mother—lived there.

The Bennett estate. . . .

"Miss? Is there someone else you wish to speak to?"

"Oh, I'm sorry," Katherine said, rallying. "Yes, there sure is. Could I . . . I mean, would it be all right if I talked to . . . her husband?" She glanced at the name and number on her scratch pad. "Mr. Dylan Bennett?"

"Let me see if he's available." A short pause, then—"May I ask who's calling?"

"Oh . . . just tell him that Katherine Mayfield, his wife's daughter, is on the line. And . . . thank you. I thank you very much, I really do!"

The next voice she heard was mighty professional. The way it sounded took her aback—near frightened the wits out of her. And when she began to explain who she was and why she'd called, she forgot all her well-rehearsed "English" speech, and some of the words tumbled out in Dutch.

"I beg your pardon?" the man said. "*Who* did you say you were?"

"I'm Katherine, jah, Katherine Mayfield. I ain't for certain, but I think you might be married to my *mam*."

There was silence. Long and nerve-jangling.

"Hullo?" she said. "Could ya please tell her I called—uh, tell Laura, that is? It's ever so important."

"I'm sorry, miss. I do believe you must have the wrong number." The voice sounded oh so much different now. Cold and awful stiff. It reminded her of Bishop John's voice when last he'd spoken to her, informing her of the consequences of the shunning.

"But I don't have the wrong number . . . do I? I mean, someone just told me—someone right before you got on the line—said that Laura, your wife, wasn't taking calls. Does that mean she's getting worse . . . because if she is, I wouldn't wanna disturb her. Not for anything."

"Excuse me . . . was someone here expecting your call?" he demanded.

"Ach, I wouldn't be surprised. Laura . . . uh, my mother has been looking for me. Came to Hickory Hollow just last month, as a matter of fact."

"I see" came the terse reply. "Is there a number where she may reach you?"

"Oh yes . . . yes, there is." Katherine studied the Millers' number printed out just above her on the telephone. Because she had not memorized it, she recited slowly.

That done, she instructed him to have Laura ask for either Katherine or . . . Katie Lapp when she called back. "Because the people I'm staying with sometimes forget my new name, and I'd really hate to miss—"

"Katherine . . . or . . . Miss Katie Lapp," the man interrupted, repeating the names slowly as if writing down the information. "Very well, I'll see that my wife gets your message."

"Thank you"—and here she glanced at her list—"thank you, Mr. Dylan Bennett."

"Good-bye," he said curtly and hung up.

"God be with you," she whispered, still holding the phone, warm in her grip.

What kind of man had her real mother gotten herself hitched up with?

Katherine shivered, recalling Dylan Bennett's voice in her ear. *Such a stern-sounding man*, she thought. Panic seized her, and so as to disconnect herself completely from him, she promptly hung up the phone.

❖ ❖ ❖

Rebecca Lapp had asked the Lord God all too often to bring her Katie back to her. But she knew without a shadow of a doubt it would have to be the heavenly Father's own doing—His and His alone. And there'd have to be a startling change in the wayward girl for her to repent on bended knee.

Ach! Such a willful soul her Katie had become. But neither her daughter's past nor her present had kept Rebecca from dropping to her knees many a time throughout the day—always, though, when Samuel and the boys were out milking or away from the house.

She understood full well that Katie's return to Hickory Hollow would have to be the providence of God, because just last week, Samuel had made a fiery announcement. He'd said no one in the Lapp household must ever utter Katie's name. *"We will not be speaking of her again—not ever again!"*

His decree had come out of personal grief, she understood, and, jah, righteous indignation. Rebecca did not feel unkindly toward her husband for it, yet his words hadn't discouraged her from *thinking* of Katie. Which she caught herself doing ever so often these days. My, oh my, had it been nearly one week now already . . . since Katie had gone to stay at Lydia Miller's house?

Rebecca refolded the kitchen towel and went to sit in the front room. Katie was on her mind a lot, it seemed. And she missed her. Missed her like a cripple might pine for an amputated arm or leg.

Himmel, life had changed so terrible much, she thought. Reaching for her hand sewing, Rebecca wondered if she oughtn't to stop by and visit her Mennonite cousin. A quick visit wouldn't hurt none, especially this close to Christmas. And maybe, just maybe, she'd catch a glimpse of her dear girl at the same time. That is, if Katie hadn't already up and gone to New York.

Rebecca teetered a bit on her hickory rocker before resuming the embroidery work. No, she couldn't do it. Samuel—the bishop, too—would disapprove. Besides, it might be too soon to visit thataway. She must wait out die Meinding, hoping and praying that the harshness of the shunning might bring Katie back to the church and to God.

Yet if the truth be known, she herself was suffering from a wicked sin—jealousy. And not just a twinge of it, neither. Ach, she'd had a greislich time of it, trying ever so hard to turn her thoughts away from Katie and her stubborn desire to search for the "English" woman named Laura Mayfield-Bennett. Such a fancy, modern lady she must be.

Rebecca's mind raced near out of control at the possibility of her precious girl taking up with the likes of a worldly woman. Sometimes she thought her mind might be slipping, and she tried desperately to hide her ongoing obsession with Katie's satin baby gown

But if she could just touch it, hold it and stroke its gentle folds, then and only then could the past catch up with the present and things go on as always—before Katie got herself shunned and left the Amish community.

Here lately, the haunting cries of an infant had caused her to get up and rush down the hall to Katie's old room. Some nights she sat beside the empty bed long into the wee hours, holding the baby dress next to her bosom. She'd even quit praying in German and told the Lord God heavenly Father that she wished He'd never created her. That she herself had never been born.

Jah, it might've been better thataway. . . .

◈　◈　◈

Immediately following breakfast, Theodore hurried to the limo garage behind the estate. He opened the door and, much to his displeasure, discovered the black car was gone, apparently in use. This agitated him considerably, and he walked back and forth on the snow-packed walk, thinking what to do.

Mrs. Bennett was counting on him. He must not let the mistress down, especially not out of pure carelessness—putting that important document in a locked glove compartment. He should have retrieved it at the earliest opportunity and put it elsewhere for safekeeping, as he'd promised.

Back inside, he hung his overcoat and hat in the large utility room near the kitchen. Several housegirls were cleaning counters and sweeping the floor as he came scuffling inside, still wearing his boots.

Garrett Smith, his nephew and head steward, stood in the pantry doorway, consulting in hushed tones with Fulton Taylor, the impeccable butler—Rosie's husband.

But it was Selig, the assistant cook, brewing a fresh pot of coffee, who caught Theodore's attention. "Looks like you could be usin' a strong cup of coffee, my man. Here, try this. It's plenty hot—and black."

Theodore accepted the steaming mug gratefully and seated himself next to the bay window. *Such a thoughtless deed I've done*, he fumed, kicking himself mentally. What if the junior chauffeur needed something from the glove compartment? Why hadn't he taken the unsealed envelope along with him to his room last night?

"Two cubes?" Selig asked, waiting with sugar prongs poised.

Theodore nodded. "The usual, thank you." Lost in his thoughts, he stirred, then sipped the dark, sweet brew.

Moments later, Selig came back to the table, pulled out a chair, and settled into it. "Have you heard? We are to be hiring more help."

"Oh?"

"The master mentioned it to Fulton at breakfast, just before Mr. Bennett left for town."

Theodore shifted nervously. So it was Master Bennett who had been in need of the black limousine first thing. Feeling rather dazed, Theodore asked, "Why more help?"

"It seems Mr. Bennett wishes Rosie to assist Mrs. Bennett exclusively. The mistress, poor thing, seems to be failing rather quickly, and I . . . well, I do believe, if I may be so bold to say it, that the master is quite uneasy these days."

Not knowing how to respond, Theodore said nothing. Dylan Bennett, he suspected, was far more concerned with his wife's money and the status of the estate, should the saint of a woman expire, than with the state of her health. He'd known the man much too long to be fooled by any such benevolent charade.

No . . . something else was in the hatching; he could almost guarantee. As for Rosie having been appointed to tend to Mrs. Bennett, he mused over the apparently thoughtful gesture for a moment and decided that naming Rosie as Mrs. Bennett's personal maid was, quite possibly, the kindest thing her husband had done for her in months. Nay, years. There might be hope for him yet.

Nevertheless, things didn't set well. Why hadn't Dylan Bennett allowed his wife the benefit of Rosie's ministrations when the mistress had first requested her?

None of it made sense, and he glanced at the clock, eager for his employer's return.

Eager? One of the few times, to be sure! Theodore chuckled, unashamed.

Midmorning, Mr. Bennett returned at last.

Theodore waited the appropriate length of time before rushing back outdoors, hauling up the garage door, and inspecting the contents of the black limo's glove compartment.

Reaching inside, he located the important document, then turned it over to determine if it had been tampered with. Difficult to say, especially since the flap had never been sealed, the papers slipped snugly into the body of the envelope instead.

Nevertheless, he could feel his pulse slowing to normal and he sighed, resting more easily. What were the chances of someone searching the glove box? No one but Mrs. Bennett, her attorney, and himself even knew of the existence of the envelope.

But . . . he would be more careful from now on, he promised himself. For Mrs. Bennett's sake, if for no other.

CHAPTER FOUR

❖　　❖　　❖

Dylan Bennett lit up an expensive cigar and puffed for a moment before closing the double doors to his professional suite at the estate. Turning, he walked the width of his expansive office and stood in front of the floor-to-ceiling windows, looking out over acres of rolling lawn, newly draped in a foot of snow, and enormous frost-covered evergreens to the north. A genuine old-fashioned blizzard had presented itself during the night, creating a picturesque winterscape.

He pulled up his swivel chair and sat down, rehearsing the events of the morning. The agency contact had been satisfactory, promising to facilitate what he had in mind, thanks to a resourceful colleague.

Laura's condition was definitely on his side. In actuality—before his very eyes, it seemed—his wife's health had begun to decline. Most rapidly in the past three weeks. Just today, he'd discovered—entirely by accident—exactly what it was Laura had planned at her demise.

He grimaced at the irony of the situation, for the latest version of his wife's bequest was now quite clear. She had named her long-lost daughter the sole heir to her fortune.

Good thing—for him—that the daughter had not turned up. Not unless he took into account the backwoods female who had had the gall to call him, claiming to *be* that daughter. She'd probably gotten wind of Laura's terminal disease—through one source or another—and fabricated the whole thing. Still, where did that leave *him*?

He need not question his fate; he would be forced to scramble for a new residence if that Katherine person ever did appear on the scene. Not that he couldn't afford to settle into something comfortable and elegant, but this place . . . this was home, and he was just stubborn enough not to relish giving it up. No, after nearly ten exasperating years, the Bennett estate belonged as much to him as to his wife, he felt.

He took a long, deep draw on the cigar. *I will not be dethroned,* he decided and began to jot down the specific plot he planned to set in motion.

He was glad he'd taped the phone call from that country bumpkin—the Amish girl from somewhere in Pennsylvania, or so she'd said. Such a brassy creature, calling him here in search of Laura.

What was it—something about his being married to her mother? That Laura had been searching for her? If such a thing were true, and this Katherine or Katie Lapp—as she had so ably prompted him—*had* received word from Laura. . . . Well, time was of the essence. He must act quickly.

Finished with the cigar, he let it continue to smoke on the crystal ashtray, creating a gray haze about him. Then, leaning back, he watched the wispy tendrils curl and climb toward the high, molded ceiling. How like his own gradual ascent to fame and fortune, he recalled with satisfaction. . . .

Laura Mayfield had been so naive when first they met twelve years ago. At twenty-six, she was virtually an innocent, to the point of exuding a refreshing coyness. He remembered this because on occasion she would blush, and

47

over the slightest innuendo. This trait had taken him completely by surprise, perhaps because the girl—having grown up in opulence—seemed reticent to socialize and mingle with high society. She despised crowds—disorganized ones, that is. But the congestion of students in a classroom, for example, was an entirely different story. Stimulating, she'd say.

By sheer accident, Dylan had made her acquaintance at the University of Rochester, during the spring semester. She was taking a class in English literature—for the fun of it—and he a refresher course in economics.

As it turned out, his encounter with Laura had been a lucky break for him, which is not to say there was no attraction between them. He was smitten with her petite figure, her lush auburn hair—and her money. She, after an initial reservation or two, seemed convinced she had found her one and only true love, the man destined by heaven to marry her and cherish her for the rest of their days.

To that end, they pursued their fascination with each other, talking for hours at a time. While Dylan would have much preferred to demonstrate his passion, Laura was a stickler about keeping things on the up and up. Insisted on a "pure and honorable relationship."

Being the gentleman—and the pauper—he was, he'd determined to bide his time. Conquest would be all the sweeter for the waiting.

It was during one of their discourses on soul-fed intimacy that he came to learn of Laura's desire for children. "I want as many babies as we can clothe, educate, and adore," she said with the brightest grin on her guileless face.

"Children?" He'd nearly choked.

"Why, yes. Isn't it a grand thought?"

Anything *but*! Children were a nuisance—a liability in his book. Nothing could be more distasteful than the thought of noisy, little diapered mopheads skittering around underfoot.

No . . . children had never been a part of his agenda. Not even as an addendum. And although it seemed entirely possible that voicing his opposition might very well terminate his comfortable relationship with the beautiful and wealthy Laura Mayfield, he cringed at the thought of satisfying her desire for motherhood. Cleverly, he tempered his response, cloaking his true sentiments, never revealing his plans to have a vasectomy—before the wedding.

It was months later that Laura made herself completely vulnerable to him, confessing her mortal sin. She described —in a rain of anguished tears—how, during her junior year in high school, she had become intimate with her first boyfriend. The outcome was an unwanted pregnancy, a baby girl born out of wedlock. "I gave away my precious baby," she whispered as they sat in his parked car. "I gave Katherine to an Amish couple."

He was floored. "Why *Amish?*"

"It's a long story. One you must hear someday . . . when I'm ready to tell it . . . all of it."

He thought it over. So this was the reason for Laura's obsession with children. He remained silent, saying nothing to arouse her suspicions.

When she began to cry again, he stroked her hand, taking great pains to capitalize on this opportunity. He moved away from the steering wheel and put his arm around her. Sorrowfully, she leaned her head on his waiting shoulder.

Then ever so slowly, he traced the outline of her regal chin and with breathless anticipation, leaned close enough to smell her lovely scent. "I'm so sorry, my darling," he whispered seductively. "What can I do to make you happy?"

Laura, her guard down, smiled through her tears, permitting his touch to soothe her, much to his delight. She allowed him to tilt her face and brush his lips against her delicate cheek. He felt her body relax as he made his goal the crook of her mouth. And he moved cautiously, enticingly, toward her lips, relishing the blissful sighs she made with his each caress.

At last a tiny gasp escaped her, and she turned to him, fully responding with the suppressed desire of one long-deprived. Their lips met, and Dylan's hands cupped her face.

One kiss led to another . . . and another, and he quite happily viewed the situation as a breakthrough. Perhaps now things had the potential of steaming up a bit as they prepared for their marriage.

Laura, however, did not allow him to kiss her again until their wedding night—an interminable wait. The event took place one month after Laura's ailing mother passed away, over two long years after they had first met at Rochester. And with eyes wide and focused on his bride's rich legacy, Dylan moved his meager possessions into the grand estate that was soon to bear his name.

And why not? Laura's notion—renaming the old Mayfield mansion as part of her wedding gift to him—was an ingenious one, and Dylan made no attempt to convince her otherwise. Since he was not interested in producing sons and daughters to carry on his name, what an excellent way to secure his future.

Thus, the magnificent manor had become the Bennett estate, and the master of the house managed his accounts—and those of his wife's—with a passion equal to his desire to dominate the pretty, red-haired Laura.

Two years later, however, when she had not abandoned her maiden name but had insisted on keeping it hyphenated, their romance began to wane. Laura had surprised him, emerging as a much stronger and more dynamic personality than he'd ever supposed. She'd begun to volunteer frequently at one of the elementary schools in town.

Around the time of their fifth wedding anniversary,

when Laura had still not conceived a child, she succumbed to deep depression. Playing it safe, Dylan did not enlighten her as to the reason, letting her think she was barren. Soon after, she ceased her work with children, began to withdraw from life in general, and one day, although she kept her accounts in her own name, willingly signed over all financial records and ledgers to Dylan for safekeeping.

Evoking the past always exhilarated Dylan. Today was no exception. He had triumphed, in a sense, or at least he'd thought so. Had met his financial objectives in less than ten years. Yet now it seemed to appear his wife may have, in actuality, outwitted him in the final round.

He felt as if he'd been whipped. Spying his gym bag in the corner where he'd dropped it yesterday, he wondered if a brisk swim at the club might not do him good—just the thing to boost his spirits.

Thinking again of his scheme—his ticket to this estate and the Mayfield fortune—he put out his cigar and rang for the butler.

Fulton Taylor was quick to respond, waiting in the doorway of Dylan's office suite. "You rang, sir?"

"I did." Dylan leaned back all the way in his swivel chair, inhaling thoughtfully before speaking. "About the matter of hiring an additional housemaid."

"Sir?"

"Since you are to be in charge of interviewing applicants, I intend to trust your judgment implicitly." He studied the tall young man with the dark hair and determined jawline. Dylan's trust was well placed; the fellow had an uncanny ability to size up a person. "I suggest you get on with the business of hiring someone immediately." He swept a glance at the calendar.

Fulton nodded, presenting an air of self-reliance. "Will there be anything else, sir?"

Dylan waved his hand as if to brush the issue from his mind. There were other matters to attend to—more urgent details to finalize and finesse. He dismissed the butler.

Then, turning his chair at an angle, he unlocked the file drawer to his left and reached for a folder marked "Katie Lapp."

CHAPTER FIVE

◈ ◈ ◈

Mary 'n Katie. *For always*, they'd agreed once.

How well Mary Stoltzfus remembered. She'd made the promise to her best friend, and 'twasn't anything she or anybody else could do now about breaking it. Katie was shunned, and from the looks of it, she'd gone away for good.

And it was no wonder! Bishop John had made it quite clear the sinner was not to be spoken to—not even by her own family! The severest shunning in many years, the worst Mary had known since her earliest years of school. Unheard of for Lancaster County.

The community as a whole had begun to rally, but only at a snail's pace. If the rest of the folk felt the way she did about Katie's leaving, she suspected it could take as long as months or even years to heal over the gaping wounds—long as nobody picked at the scabs.

Mary opened the smallest drawer of her dresser, the only sizeable piece of furniture in the room besides her bed. By lantern light, she located the handwritten address of Katie's Mennonite relatives, Peter and Lydia Miller, the place where her friend had said she'd be staying when she'd come to say good-bye.

"S'pose I could write her," she whispered into the dimly

lit bedroom, wondering what she would tell her dearest friend. Would she say she'd spent most of the week in bed, sick at heart and of body over Katie's leaving? Would she tell her how lonely it was in the community without her pea-in-a-pod best buddy?

The more she dawdled over what to write, or *if* to write, the more prickly she felt. "Probably not a gut idea," she muttered to herself, got into bed, and sat there in the darkness, knees drawn up to her chest. Contact with a shunned person could result in *that* person being shunned, too. The very notion was enough to give a body a case of hives!

An icy finger of fear tickled her spine, and she pulled the covers around her. Before undoing her hair knot, Mary rubbed her bare feet against the icy cold sheets, creating enough friction to warm them a bit. Then, loosening her hair and letting it fall over her back and shoulders, she slid under several of her mamma's heaviest quilts.

She said her silent prayers, thinking about Katie bein' just down the lane, probably cozy as a bear in hibernation, sleeping in her Mennonite cousin's modern house. Central heating and all. . . .

Sometime in the night, with only a sliver of moonbeams to light the room, Mary awakened. For some reason her thoughts turned from Katie's predicament to Chicken Joe and that sweet talk of his . . . how many Singings ago? After that, he'd up and quit her for pretty little Sarah Beiler.

Puh! They'd probably be hitchin' up come next November during wedding season.

The thought of such a thing near broke Mary's heart, but because she was one who wanted to do the right thing by a person, she'd never confronted the fella. Just let things be. Still, it seemed she might never meet someone to love her. Someone who wanted to marry a right plump wife who could cook, bake, and keep house to beat the band.

She rolled over and stared across the room at her "for

gut" Sunday dress and thought of another fella—a grown
man, really—who might be feeling just as sad and empty
inside as she was this very minute. Someone who deserved
far better than to be left standing alone, without his bride,
on his weddin' day. Standing there in front of all the People
. . . without Katie.

Bishop John had come to mind too many times to count
these past couple'a weeks. Mary was ashamed to admit it to
herself, but she liked the widower. Liked him too much for
her own good, maybe, and if truth be told, had secretly admired him for several years now.

Still, she didn't know how she'd go about handling five
children, ages four to eleven, that is if she ever *did* manage
to catch John Beiler's eye. Probably wasn't something she
should go on worrying over, neither. Probably was no chance
in Paradise of the forty-year-old widower pickin' her for his
Liebschdi. Not her bein' Katie's best friend and all.

The way she saw it, if the Lord God heavenly Father
wanted her to get married, well, He'd just have to send
along the right man. Because, here before long, she'd be
turning twenty-one—awful old to be lookin' to get married,
'specially in Hickory Hollow. Jah, she'd best keep her
dreams about ending up with handsome Bishop John to herself. Nobody'd ever need to know about *that*.

Not even Ella Mae Zook suspected. Hickory Hollow's
Wise Woman would not approve, most certainly. And if she
ever *did* come to know about it, Ella Mae would be sure to
suggest that Mary put the bishop out of her mind straightaway.

Himmel . . . no sense entertaining idle thoughts over
something that would never happen, most likely.

She sighed, making an effort to cease her ponderings. If
she'd known how to pray her private wishes and dreams to
God, she would've. Right then and there. Just like Katie's
Mennonite relatives talked so boldly in *their* prayers.

She wondered if Katie might not be doing some of that same kind of praying this very night. Down Hickory Lane, one buggy mile away. . . .

Come morning, Mary awakened with a vexed feeling. She'd dreamed about her friend all night, nearly. What did it mean? That she should go ahead and write a letter to Katie?

After her bread making and baking chores were done, Mary slipped away to her bedroom, where she located her favorite stationery and a fine-tip pen in her dresser drawer. She sat on a cane chair near her bed, glanced out the window, and daydreamed for a bit.

The tall, deep window was the same one where she'd pressed her fingertips on that sad, sad day just last month when Katie had come to see why she'd not attended Sunday preaching. Not being allowed to speak to her friend, the loving, yet agonizing gesture was all Mary knew to do, hoping against hope that Katie would see with her own eyes how very helpless she felt.

In a wink, thinking back to the dreadful scene, she went all tense, almost as if she wasn't able to get enough air to keep herself breathing.

"Oh, Katie, stubborn girl," she murmured. "Why'd ya do it? Why'd ya go and get yourself shunned?"

She stared at the crooked old tree outside. And then . . . obedience to church rules went out the window as she picked up her pen and began to write.

Wednesday, December 17

Dearest Katie,
I've thought a hundred times or more of an excuse to write you, dear friend. I guess I thought maybe it would be all right if I just sent a Christmas card and short note.

It'd probably be best, though, if you didn't say anything about it to anyone.

These days without you have been downright hard on me, Katie—not being able to see you anymore. It's all I can do to keep myself from sneaking off down the lane for a visit. But you know my heart, don't you? You know I miss you and wish there could be a way for you to come back to us someday.

This whole idea of dropping a line to you may not be the right thing. I can't be sure. Well, anyways, Merry Christmas!

> *Good-bye for now.*
> *Your truest friend—*
> *for always,*
> *Mary Stoltzfus*

P.S. Please forgive me for not using your "new" name— Katherine. For some reason or other, I just can't seem to think of you with a fancy name like that. You'll always be Katie to me.

Mary put down her pen and reread the words, glancing over her shoulder. Quickly, she addressed the envelope, copying the Millers' address, then licked the seal, pressed it shut, and ran outside to slide it into the large metal mailbox. She'd timed her letter just right, it seemed, for here came the mail carrier down the long, snowy lane.

Mary smiled to herself, knowing full well she'd be reprimanded for this deed if caught. But how could that happen with the mail getting picked up right this minute?

"Good mornin', miss," the postman greeted her.

"Hullo," she replied, her eyes downcast.

"Have a good day, now." He took her letter and placed the Stoltzfus mail in her outstretched hand. With a flick, he pushed down the red flag and was on his way.

"*Denki*," she called. Then in a whisper—"And thank you for takin' my letter to dear Katie."

❖ ❖ ❖

Sleet fell on Hickory Hollow later in the day. It pitty-patted on the snowy birdbath behind the screened-in back porch of the Millers' house and on the windowpanes out front.

Twenty-four hours had come and gone since Katherine had braved repeated calls to the operators in northern New York. She sat in the corner window of her rented room and watched the weather worsen.

The gloom outdoors matched her mood, and she was thankful for the warm house. In spite of all she could do to ignore the dismal sky and bleak, raw day, the darkness pushed in upon her. Why hadn't her natural mother re-turned the call? she wondered. What was keeping her?

A troubling thought haunted her. What if Laura's hus-band hadn't given his wife the message? He'd seemed a bit reluctant, she remembered. And his voice had sounded so very . . . cold. *Like an icicle.*

Was that the reason she distrusted him?

Katherine decided, right then and there, she'd best be talking things over with Peter and Lydia just as soon as they returned.

Meanwhile, she went downstairs to the kitchen and set a pot of broth on to simmer, adding potatoes, carrots, celery, and other vegetables and seasonings. Next, she gathered the ingredients to make whoopie pies—one of her favorite Amish desserts. Wouldn't Lydia be surprised?

More than anything, Katherine wanted to help out. She missed working alongside her mamma, but she knew she daresn't dwell on that subject much or else she'd be of no use to anyone. Memories of her life with Samuel and Re-becca Lapp brought certain tears all too often. Dear, dear Mamma and Dat—how she missed them!

If it hadn't been for Lydia and Peter, she figured by now

she might've gone *wiedich*—mad! What with missing her family and her dearest friend, she felt disabled at times, like someone with a crippling disease. Especially when she thought about getting on a bus and heading for that strange-sounding city—Canandaigua.

Oh, she could see herself storming the door of the Bennett estate—but only in her mind. When it came to actually going there, knowing she would be seeing her birth mother face-to-face, well, *that* was the part that scared her, but good.

Still, something deep inside, something probably connected hard and fast to Laura Mayfield-Bennett, pushed her onward, giving her the pluck to do what she knew she must do.

So in the middle of salting and peppering the stew, Katherine decided she would allow one more day, and at the most two, for a long-distance call to come in. If she heard nothing back from Laura after that time, she'd consider using some of her former dowry money to take a bus and head north.

After a whole day and a half, Katherine had not received a single telephone call. "What do ya think I should do?" she asked Cousin Peter at breakfast.

"Well, if 'twas me, I'd probably head right on up there," he spouted off.

Lydia patted his hand, smiling. "But Katie . . . er, Katherine's *not* you, honey. She's a sensible young lady."

"I honestly don't know how sensible I am anymore," Katherine remarked. "Sometimes I wonder if I oughtn't to just call up that number again, ya know?"

Lydia nodded, looking a bit worried. "I certainly hope your Laura hasn't . . ." Her voice trailed off.

"I've been thinking the same thing," Katherine admitted. "If she's dying, like Mamma said she was . . . well, there's no tellin' how long she has to live." She rose and dished up seconds for herself and her relatives. "Seems to me I oughta think about getting up some courage. I'd hate to miss seein' her alive. Really I would."

Katherine paused, glancing out the window for a moment. "I guess I'm thinkin' that if someone as powerful-close to you as your own birth mother dies before you can ever make peace with her, well . . . *fer die Katz*. It's no good. No good at all."

Lydia sighed. "Far be it from me to disagree." She adjusted her glasses. "So are you saying you might be leaving us?"

Before Katherine could answer, Peter spoke up. "Don't you think somebody—a relative or someone—oughta ride along with you, if you go?" His blue eyes were wide with near-parental concern. "Seein' as how the rest of your family—" He stopped short of uttering the dismal word.

Still, Katherine knew exactly what the tall, blond man was about to say. He was right, of course. She was a shunned woman with no moral support whatsoever. Except for Mary's Christmas card and that sweet but awkward note, Katherine had heard nothing from the Amish community.

She wasn't surprised. This was the way shunnings were. The transgressor went into a tailspin, fretting over his or her loss of family—and the ability to buy and sell from anyone in the community, too. Lots of times, the frustration alone was effective enough to bring a sinner back.

Katherine noticed Lydia's head covering was slightly askew. "There's no rush, really," said Lydia. "You could stay here over Christmas . . . and be thinkin' about what to do after that."

"There *is* a rush, ya know," Katherine reminded her, settling down at the table with her second plate of scrambled eggs. "But thanks for your kindness."

"I'll drive you into town whenever," Peter volunteered. "You just say the word."

"Monday." The word spilled out almost before Katherine realized what she was doing. "I'll call tonight and see about bus fare."

"At least, you'll have Sunday with us," Lydia said, smiling.

Katherine was genuinely glad for that. The Millers' church meeting and Sunday school was like no other. What singing! And, oh, how the people got up and testified. It was like going to heaven before you died.

When Peter offered to help purchase her ticket, she declined. "I still owe you money for all the telephone calls." She paused, looking at one, then the other of her relatives-turned-friends seated across the table. "I owe you both so much," she whispered. "Denki for everything."

"You know you're always welcome here," Lydia said, and Katherine saw that the corners of her eyes glistened.

"I know that, and it means ever so much." She stared at the black coffee in Lydia's cup and struggled to control her own tears. The Millers' kindness and that of her Amish friend—the secret card and note from Mary—were almost more than she could bear.

Quietly, she excused herself and left the table.

❖   ❖   ❖

While her baby slept in his cradle nearby, Annie Lapp thumbed through a pile of Christmas cards. The one from her husband's parents stood out as the loveliest of them all, but when she opened to the greeting, she realized how very odd the signatures looked to her. Ach, there wasn't one thing wrong with the way Rebecca Lapp had signed hers and Samuel's names, and the boys—Eli and Benjamin.

It was Katie's name that was so obviously missing, and

that fact alone made Annie remember the events of her sister-in-law's excommunication from the church and the shunning, too—all over again.

She arranged the cards on a string she'd put up across one side of the front room and couldn't help thinking of her dear brother, Daniel. Another Christmas without him.

She sighed. If he just hadn't gotten himself drowned . . . maybe, just maybe, Katie would still be here in Hickory Hollow where she belonged. Instead, word had it Katie was living with Mennonites down the lane, paying rent to them, of all things. *Lydia and Peter Miller. Jah, gut folk. Just ain't Amish*, she thought with a sad shake of her head.

She got up and went to the kitchen, stoking the woodstove, wishing that none of the bad things had ever happened, starting with Dan's death and ending with Katie's shunning—every bit as divisive.

CHAPTER SIX

◈   ◈   ◈

On Sunday, while sitting on a cushioned pew between Lydia and Lydia's daughter-in-law, Edna Miller, Katherine was glad to experience another taste of morning worship at the Hickory Hollow Mennonite meetinghouse.

She sat quietly, reverently, as she had been taught as a child, paying close attention to the still-unfamiliar church trappings about her. All worldly, indeed, her People would say. Running a hand across the soft cushion beneath her, she thought what a stark difference—a nice change, really— from the hard wooden benches she'd been accustomed to while growing up. In front of the church, on a raised plat- form, stood a simple, lone pulpit, centered in the middle. She had known even prior to last Sunday—her first time as a visitor—that the preacher would stand behind the pulpit when he gave his sermon. She'd learned this tidbit of infor- mation from Dan years ago when he'd described the inside of several Mennonite churches. This, after having slipped away to an occasional non-Amish meeting himself.

"Oh, such a joyful time," he'd said about the forbidden services. "The people sing and testify. It's so wonderful-gut, Katie, really 'tis."

Of course, Dan had never gone on to say, "You should

really go and find out for yourself," or "I'll take you along with me sometime." None of that sort of talk. Dan had been careful that way, not willing to risk getting his sweetheart in trouble just because *he* was restless in their cloistered society. Or so she figured.

Still, she thought of Dan as she sat there, the light spilling in through the tall windows on both sides of the church like a divine floodlight. Katherine remembered her darling with an ache in her heart, wondering if they might've ended up Mennonite one day. If he'd lived long enough to marry her, that is.

When the song leader stood up before the people, he tooted softly into his pitch pipe, and the congregation began to sing out spontaneously in a rich four-part harmony.

Under Katherine's satiny sleeves, goose pimples popped out on her arms. Once again, all heaven came down, pouring right in through the lovely, bright windows. A foretaste of Glory filled the place, accompanied by the rapturous sounds of the a cappella choir.

Two rows up and just to the left of the center aisle, four young women sat shoulder to shoulder, wearing matching white organdy head coverings. The teenage quartet unknowingly captured her attention, and although Katherine didn't recognize more than a couple of the hymns, she could see that the girls, who seemed to be sisters, certainly sang with sincerity and total abandon. Hardly even glanced at their hymnbooks, they knew the song so well.

Sharing the hymnal with Lydia's daughter-in-law, Katherine was once again captivated by the musical notation and noticed something else while turning to find the next hymn. The book included gospel songs, too.

"We only sing those songs on Sunday nights or at midweek prayer meeting," Edna explained in a discreet whisper.

Nodding as if she understood, Katherine stared at the key signature of the song they were singing, "Glad Day." She wondered why it was all right with God for Mennonites to write down their music but not Amish. Least not Hickory Hollow Amish folk.

She also wondered why some women in the church wore veiled coverings and others didn't. Why some women dressed in long print dresses with plain-looking white or navy blue sweaters and others looked like tourists and other English folk.

None of it made sense.

She tried to sing along, conscious of the sound of Cousin Lydia's hearty alto voice and Edna's wavering soprano. Each time they came to the refrain, the words *this is the crowning day* stuck in her throat. She'd been taught all her life that no one could truly know the assurance of salvation while alive. You only *hoped* that the Lord God heavenly Father would welcome you into His eternal kingdom on Judgment Day. But to say with all faith you were saved—or to sing words to that effect—was nothing short of boastful.

Pride. The deadliest of sins.

As if to dispute her thoughts, the Mennonite sisters, all four of them, sang the words about going to heaven and what a glad day that would be. It seemed to Katherine they lifted their voices with complete confidence in what they were singing. And she wondered what made the Ordnung so much more important—in Amish eyes—than the Bible itself.

As a child it had all seemed acceptable and right—those regular teachings of the bishop and other preachers. Katherine's best friends were her first and second cousins and classmates at the one-room Amish school—girls and boys in her own church district. Girls like Mary Stoltzfus, who knew her nearly inside out. They dressed alike, wore their hair the same, spoke the same two languages—English and Pennsylvania Dutch—and thought pretty much alike, too.

None of them, except some of the carpenters and

furniture-makers in the community, ever had to associate with outsiders, and they'd been taught that Mennonites, Brethren, and other Christian groups around them were living in sin. If you weren't Amish, chances were good that when you died, you'd be thrown into Outer Darkness or cast into the Lake of Fire. Both, probably. So who'd want to be friends with wicked folk like that?

The Ordnung ruled—shunning or no. And even on this bright and shining day—the blessed Lord's Day before Katherine planned to step into her future, her fancy *English* future—the Old Order reached out to discourage and dismay her.

◈　◈　◈

"Tell me one of your stories, Rebecca," Annie Lapp said as she and her mother-in-law sat together in Annie's kitchen.

Rebecca's knitting needles made a soft, rhythmic *clickity-click* pattern in the silence, but she did not speak.

"It's been ever so long since I heard one of your stories," she pleaded.

Still Rebecca declined, shaking her head.

"Storytellin's a gut thing," Annie insisted. "For the teller and for the listener, ya know."

Sighing audibly, Rebecca folded her hands, staring at her knitting. "Jah, I reckon." Yet she made no attempt to start up one of her stories.

Something was terribly wrong with Katie's mam; Annie could see that. The pain in Rebecca's eyes, the bend of her back, ach, how she'd aged. And in such a short time. Annie supposed it had to do with Katie, but she dared not mention the wayward woman's name.

Elam, Annie's husband, had taken a firm stand against anyone referring to his shunned sister about the house—or anywhere else, for that matter. He'd gotten the idea from his father. Both men had decided that neither the immediate family nor the extended family must ever mention her again. Which turned out to be a whole lot of folk, so interconnected were they, what with all the marrying and intermarrying amongst themselves.

Fact was, it had gotten so, here lately, that nobody was talking about Katie Lapp anymore. Truth be told, Annie felt like the People were trying to put the agony—of losing one of their own to the devil—clear behind them. Not out of anger or hatred, no. They were simply trying to go on with the life God would have them lead in Hickory Hollow.

With or without Katie.

"What if I tell *you* a story this time?" she spoke up.

"Gut, des gut," Rebecca replied.

Annie rocked her newborn bundle in her arms, telling her mother-in-law the story she'd never shared before. Not even with Elam.

"It's about a dream I keep having," she began. "I don't understand it and probably you won't, neither."

Rebecca's eyes brightened. "Go on."

"Well, it always starts out on a bitter cold day. Right out of the fog, here comes my dead brother walking up to the house. Marches up the front porch steps and knocks on the door. His frame looks the same, but his face . . . and his eyes . . . well, Dan Fisher looks like he's been gone for a gut long time." She stopped to wrap another blanket around baby Daniel. "It's like he's come back from the dead."

"We all know *that'll* never happen," mumbled Rebecca.

"Still, it bothers me no end havin' that dream keep on a-comin'."

Rebecca looked hollow eyed again. "How often?"

"Couple'a times a week, I 'speck."

"It's just wishful thinkin' is all."

The women fell silent, each with her own thoughts, al-

67

though Annie wondered whether or not Rebecca's mind might not be clouded up in something other than reality.

"Lord knows if thinkin' could make dreams come true"— the older woman spoke up suddenly, startling Annie with the force of her words—"I'd have my girl back home by now."

Annie gasped outright. She'd never heard Rebecca talk in such an irreverent way. They'd been taught all their lives that speakin' out the Lord's name for any reason but for His honor and glory was downright sinful. And here was Rebecca, sitting in her kitchen, spouting off a near curse. "Mam? Perhaps we oughta be readin' the Scriptures out loud," she suggested quickly.

"I'll not be staying." Rebecca rose. "I best be heading home."

"Wait . . . don't leave just yet."

"It's for the best."

"But we were just starting to visit, and I—"

"What is it, Annie?" demanded Rebecca, turning to stare sharply at her. "You afraid?"

"Afraid of what?"

"That I think you've gone daft over your dead brother?"

Annie got up to put her sleeping little one in his cradle. " 'Course I'm not insane, if that's what you mean."

Rebecca kept walking toward the back door. "There's a fine line betwixt sanity and mental, I'm sorry to say."

The words were strained and ragged around the edges. Rebecca's voice sounded a bit *needlich*. To be so cross was not like Katie's mamma. Not at all.

"Are you all right?" she asked, worried.

"Never better." Rebecca's eerie chuckle was tinged with hysteria—a mixture of wailing and laughter—the high pitch of it enough to raise the hair on the back of Annie's neck.

"Why, of course you've been better, Rebecca. Much, much better." With that, she hurried to the door to help the poor woman with her coat, wishing Christmas wasn't so near.

Something about the Lord's birthday made one want to rejoice—or despair. It was clear her mother-in-law needed some counseling help, and mighty quick, at that. A talk with the Wise Woman might do the trick.

Second thought, maybe *she* would drive the carriage over to see Ella Mae one of these days—tell her about the recurring dream. She wondered what the Wise Woman would make of it.

CHAPTER SEVEN

❖　　❖　　❖

With Christmas only two days away, the Bennett estate was aflutter with activity. Freshly cut greens decorated wide doorways and narrow landing windows. The tangy aroma of pine pleased Laura, and she asked Rosie to wheel her out into the grand hallway.

At one end stood an enormous, fragrant tree, and at the other, parted glass doors led to the dining room, resplendent in bowed greenery and brass candelabra.

Scanning the entrance to the dining room and beyond, she felt as though she were seeing it for the first time. Or, perhaps more accurately, *attempting* to see it, reluctant to admit to herself—let alone to another human being—that her vision was becoming more and more hazy.

Less than a week ago, her eyes had been clear, and except for some occasional smarting behind the sockets, she wouldn't have thought her eyesight to be failing. She wasn't as certain today, however, and contemplated speaking to Nurse Judah about it.

"Is everything all right?" asked Rosie.

No need to alarm her dearest and best maid, and she *was* doing better as far as her leg spasms were concerned.

"I would say this is one of the better days for me . . . in weeks."

Rosie grinned, heaving a huge sigh. "Bless your heart," she said with obvious delight. "I prayed this might be a wonderful Christmas for you, ma'am."

Selig, along with the head steward, rushed past Laura's snug spot in the wheelchair, and she heard their chatter as it faded with their footsteps.

"You won't catch a draft out here, will you?" Rosie asked, glancing down the hall toward the entrance of the house.

"It would be next to impossible—the way you have me bundled up." She smiled at the round-faced woman, her brown eyes dark with concern. "You do take such good care of me, Rosie."

"And what a joy it is" came the meek reply.

Laura felt a soft pat on her arm and wondered if now was a good time to mention the phone call she'd made earlier. "What if I told you I'm thinking of hiring a private investigator?"

"Why, Mrs. Bennett, whatever for?"

"Regarding my daughter, Katherine. You do recall, I trust?"

At that, Rosie came around to stand in front of the wheelchair. "Yes . . . I've heard you speak of her, but why—" She broke off, frowning slightly.

Laura paused. "I had hoped it wouldn't come to this. You see, I have reason to believe that Katherine was never legally adopted."

Rosie gasped. "How could that be?"

"In all these years, I have not received a letter of intent from the couple . . . not that there had to be one for the baby—my daughter—to be raised and loved and—"

"Oh . . . but, Mrs. Bennett, it's nearly Christmas," Rosie interjected. "Perhaps you could wait until after the holidays.

Won't you give it a bit more time?"

"*What* time? I haven't any, have I?" She touched her hands to her knees. "I've lost nearly all balance and strength in my limbs . . . how long must I wait?"

"Three more days?" Rosie implored. "Christmas is upon us."

"Christmas, indeed!" a male voice was heard.

Laura turned to see her husband strolling toward them. "Hello, Dylan," she greeted him.

He was looking fit as usual, dressed in one of his favorite casual tweed sports jackets. But it was the mischievous look in his gray eyes that gave him a boyish appeal. " 'Morning, ladies."

She did little, however, to encourage his outward display of affection—not raising her cheek to his reckless kiss.

He stepped back, his shoes clicking in precision, and folded his arms. "I have a Christmas surprise for you, Laura," he said with a quizzical half smile. "The holidays are a few days off, I realize, but I think you'll understand when you see my present."

She didn't know how to respond, partly because Dylan seemed absolutely overjoyed with the prospect of presenting his early gift.

"Can you be dressed—in your finest—for, say, afternoon tea?"

"Today?"

"This very day." Her husband seemed near to bursting.

Rosie nodded. "I'll see to it that Mrs. Bennett wears her holiday best."

"Good. Take care of it, then." Dylan turned to go, then backtracked and leaned over to kiss Laura's forehead.

"My goodness, the master is jovial today, isn't he?" Rosie said as she wheeled Laura back into her private suite.

"Yes . . . he is. Quite a long time . . . since I've seen him *that* happy." In the excitement of the moment, Laura felt a moment's hesitation. What was the urgency behind the gift? she wondered.

Giving it no further thought, she shrugged the singular feeling away. Perhaps her murky vision had annoyed her unduly.

Perhaps there was nothing to question at all.

❖   ❖   ❖

Natalie Judah arrived a little before the usual afternoon tea, completely out of breath. "The streets are terribly slick," she explained her late arrival. "The weather seems to be getting worse by the minute. And all those last-minute shoppers aren't helping matters a bit." She removed her coat and hung it in the small closet in the sitting area of the cozy room.

"It's a good thing you don't have to go back out tonight, then," Rosie commented, fussing with Laura's hair.

"What a relief!" Natalie sat across the room, watching as Rosie brushed up the thick red mass and secured it with shiny golden combs high on each side.

Mrs. Bennett looked over at her, smiling broadly. "It's such a blessing having you tend to me twenty-four hours a day."

A blessing? Natalie had never thought of nursing in that light. This was her job, and she was more than adequately paid for her services. But there was more—that wrenching compassion for her dying patient. Maybe that's what Laura Bennett was feeling.

"What's the occasion?" she asked, observing Laura's upswept hairdo.

"My husband has a surprise."

"Oh?"

Rosie nodded. "Something that evidently can't wait for

Christmas Eve." A hint of sarcasm edged her voice.

Natalie ignored the comment, glancing toward the hallway door. "Will Mr. Bennett present the gift here?"

"In this very room," explained Rosie. "And I do hope whatever it is, it won't take too long." She covered Laura's legs with an afghan.

Natalie wondered about Rosie's comment. "Are you feeling worse today, Mrs. Bennett?"

"Not really worse, just . . ."

In an instant, the nurse was on her feet and at Laura's side. "What is it?" She noted the sudden pleading in the sick woman's eyes. And Rosie, who seemed to understand the unspoken gesture, excused herself immediately.

When they were alone, Laura's voice grew soft. "I've been experiencing some discomfort . . . pain behind my eyes."

Natalie approached her patient. "Let's have a look," she said, gently lifting Laura's left eyelid. She examined the eye, hoping for a sign of inflammation or something else. *Anything* but another symptom of the disease's deadly progress.

She found nothing. Stepping back slightly, she studied the woman's pale face, then—"Has this pain come on just recently?"

"I'd say in the past three days or so." Mrs. Bennett went on to describe the annoying sensation of fuzziness as well.

Not a good sign, thought Natalie. It distressed her, hearing such bad news this close to Christmas—most likely Laura Bennett's last.

Rosie, feeling maternal toward her charge, who was in actuality eight years older, had returned to stand inches behind the wheelchair. Her fingertips were poised on the handle grips as the master of the house made his entrance into

Laura's private sitting room. He carried with him a large bouquet of red roses.

Nothing new, she thought. Mr. Bennett often gave his wife flowers for known and unknown reasons. Today, however, it seemed indicative of something—perhaps only a prelude—of what was to come.

"My darling." He spoke in tender tones, coming to kneel before his wife and take her delicate white hands in his. "I don't want to startle you . . ." His voice trailed off, but his gaze was unwavering. "Someone is here to meet you," he continued, "someone you've been longing to see."

Rosie stiffened, glancing across the room at Nurse Natalie, who was staring in shocked expectation. What *was* the man up to?

"Laura, my dear, I believe I may have found your daughter—your Katherine." Mr. Bennett turned and glanced toward the doorway. "She's waiting just outside the door."

A little gasp escaped Mrs. Bennett's lips, and Rosie struggled to subdue her own concern. She sincerely hoped this revelation would not set her mistress back in any way—but then, it wasn't her place to speak up.

Master Dylan paused, perhaps allowing his wife a moment to weigh his words. "Are you ready to meet your only offspring?" he asked. "She goes by the name of Katie Lapp now."

"Katie?" came Laura's faltering voice.

Rosie shot a desperate glance at Nurse Judah, who stood quickly and came to her patient's side, leaning gently on the right arm of the wheelchair. "This is quite unexpected, sir," she remarked, slanting her patient's husband a sideways glance. Then, to Laura—"How do you feel about this, Mrs. Bennett?"

Without warning, the chair began to shake. But it was

not from a tremor brought on by the disease. Laura Bennett was crying, soundless sobs.

Rosie felt a peculiar urge to shield the woman but restrained herself, allowing the moment to unfold. After all, who was she to step in and keep the mistress from laying eyes on her daughter, at long last?

It was nearly Christmas, for goodness' sake. Miracles were *supposed* to happen at Christmastime.

Laura dabbed a tissue at her eyes repeatedly. Then after a time, she nodded—said almost pitifully, "Bring my dear one to me."

Rosie braced herself, planting her eyes on the wide doorway, and gazed at the empty spot. She felt as if she were waiting for the heroine of a play to make a grand entrance. . . .

She was pleasantly surprised when a young Amishwoman, dressed in Old Order garb and head covering tiptoed into the room, accompanied by Master Dylan himself. The slender girl, who couldn't have been a day over twenty, had eyes for Mrs. Bennett entirely. Her oval face burst into a spontaneous yet coy smile. "Hello, Mother," she said.

The master was quick to speak, even before Laura could respond to her daughter's first words of greeting. "Darling, I'd like you to meet Katie."

In spite of her husband's attempt to offer a formal introduction, Laura's gaze never once veered from the Amish girl. "Oh, Katherine, is it you? Is it really you?"

Rosie surrendered her hold on the wheelchair and stepped aside, surveying closely the glint of—what *was* that strange look in Dylan Bennett's eyes? Certainly not glee . . . or was it?

"Oh, do come closer, my dear," Laura said, fighting back tears that only served to cloud her vision further. "I want to have a good look at you. You won't mind, will you?"

The Amish girl came near, and Nurse Judah promptly pulled up a chair for her to sit, facing Laura.

"Denki," came the reticent reply.

Laura noticed Katie's polite nod toward the nurse. Her heart fairly skipped a beat as she gazed happily at the young woman before her.

Katherine, her beautiful daughter, was here at last! Here . . . in this very house!

The young woman spoke again. "Ach, but I want to look at *you*, Mam."

The Plain, simple words seemed to hang in the air. Yet Laura fell silent as fluctuating emotions overwhelmed her. Elation, bittersweet joy. . . .

The two of them—surrounded by Dylan, Rosie, and the nurse—observed each other curiously.

Laura soon found her voice. "Katherine, my precious girl. Oh, I've waited so long, so very long for this day."

Her daughter nodded, smiling sweetly.

Laura's eyes filled with tears, and she brushed them away quickly, fearing she might look up and find that her dear one had vanished. "The Lord has surely answered my prayers," she whispered, reaching for the dainty hand. "How happy I am you've come, Katherine."

"Please, you must call me Katie. It suits me just fine."

So, thought Laura, her birth daughter's Amish parents—the Lapps—had modified the name she'd chosen. Renamed her Katie. Indeed, there was something simple yet charming about it. The short, fanciful name *did* suit her.

"Then, Katie you are," she answered, surprised how the charming nickname rolled off her tongue. It was perfectly right—an acceptable substitute, being a derivative of Katherine, after all.

The notion that she had provided this name warmed her

heart, made her feel more closely connected to this stranger somehow. Gave her a link to the past. A past the two had never shared. Lost . . . lost days. Gone forever.

Still, they had *this* moment. She must cling to that. They—she and this adorable girl named Katie—had *now*. And with all the love she'd carried in vain for her daughter these many years, she decided they would indeed enjoy this time that was every bit as much a *divine* gift as it was Dylan's.

Scarcely able to keep from staring at her child, Laura was struck by Katie's lovely face—the creamy white complexion, picture perfect. And the quiet smile. Everything about her charmed Laura. Yet if there was any disappointment at all, it might've been in the color of Katie's hair.

Laura had always fantasized that her flesh and blood would surely share her own fiery red locks. Still, strawberry blond was most becoming and enhanced the girl's light brown brows and lashes beautifully.

If only she could really *see* this vision of love before her, marred only by the inability to focus her eyes and truly savor her daughter's appearance. "Oh my, there are so many, many things I want to tell you," Laura heard herself saying. "Things that a mother and her long-absent daughter might share."

Behind her, she was aware of Rosie's sniffling, and Laura was quite sure there were tears in her husband's eyes as well. A swell of gratitude to him took her breath for the moment. She must ask him how he'd managed to locate Katherine— and so close to Christmas. But that could wait. "We must take our afternoon tea together," she told the girl. "Just the two of us."

At that, Dylan spoke up, emerging from the corner of the room. "Tea is on the way."

"Wonderful." Laura kept her chin up, looking directly at him, though he appeared as a blur to her fuzzy vision.

Nurse Judah checked Laura's pulse before excusing herself. Rosie seemed more reluctant to leave and leaned over to whisper, "Are you certain I won't be needed?"

"Thank you, but no," Laura said, though a hammer in her heart tripped at an unceasing pace. The pain of the years, the excruciating loss . . . all of it came sweeping through the room, overpowering her. The weight of worry, the haunting memories nearly engulfed her as she sat helplessly in her wheelchair, and for one dreamlike instant, she had to glance around to secure the moment—to reorient herself as to what had just taken place.

It was then she noticed that Dylan had moved to a chair only a few feet from Katie. Why had he remained in spite of her request for seclusion?

She avoided his gaze and turned her attention to the primly dressed Katie, wearing the same shade of blue and the black apron she'd observed on several Amishwomen while in Lancaster County last month. In fact, if memory served her correctly, the color was the same hue that Rebecca, her baby's adopted mother, had worn the day they met in the corridor of Lancaster General Hospital nearly twenty-three years ago.

"Katie, will you consider staying over for the holidays?" she asked, smiling at the prospect.

Before her daughter could respond, Dylan cut in, addressing Katie. "Mrs. Bennett, er, your *mother* and I would love to have you celebrate Christmas with us." He turned, delivering an adoring gesture toward Laura as if the two of them were, in all reality, the happiest couple in the world.

"More than anything, I want you to stay," Laura said, her throat growing increasingly dry as she sat motionless, for all practical purposes, paralyzed. The disturbing, yet not unwelcome tension of the situation—the powerful sense of seeing yet not truly seeing her daughter—left her reeling, breathless.

Dylan seemed eager to dissipate the heaviness in the room. "If you wish, I can have the butler show you to one of our upstairs guest rooms."

"By all means," Laura added. "We'll make you quite comfortable here, Katie."

At that, the Amish girl lit up. "We'll get better acquainted, maybe? Jah?"

"Oh, I do hope so." Deep within her, Laura offered a silent thanksgiving to the Lord for bringing her precious Katie to her . . . right on time.

On time.

So was afternoon tea. Rosie served it, along with pastry delicacies fit for a newly reunited royal family.

Although a thousand questions flooded Laura's mind as they sipped tea and buttered their tarts, she refrained from voicing a single one, uncomfortable with the idea of quizzing her travel-weary daughter so soon upon her arrival. Along with that, despite her appreciation for his gift to her, she was feeling somewhat put out with Dylan, who was clearly becoming an intrusion.

If he were genuinely interested in learning of Katie's prior whereabouts and her past, why was it he continued to veer the conversation away from the very things Laura longed to discover about Katie Lapp? All of it puzzled her, and she felt a panicky sensation come over her, triggering a violent attack of leg tremors.

She cried out, grimacing in pain.

Immediately, Dylan stood to his feet, staring sharply. She was certain he was repulsed, could read it in his eyes in spite of her blurred vision.

When she heard Katie gasp, Laura tried desperately to speak, to smooth over what must be a horrifying moment for the others. But her voice was also shaky.

Nurse Judah took charge. "I'll see to Mrs. Bennett," she said, steering the wheelchair out of the room.

Not now, Laura fretted as she was sped away to her bedroom. When they were out of sight, she clutched at her left leg. *Please, Lord Jesus, not now!*

CHAPTER EIGHT

The housemaids and servants seemed to know without being told. An undercurrent of conversation could be heard throughout the Bennett mansion as hired staff flew about making additional last-minute plans.

"It seems Master Bennett has located his wife's daughter. They're getting acquainted in Mrs. Bennett's suite at this moment," Selig was overheard telling the head steward.

"By all means, create an additional place setting," Garrett replied, directing traffic by the mere lift of his brow.

"Anyone laid eyes on the mistress's daughter?" the butler asked.

One of the cooks admonished him with a wave of a spatula. "Talk to your wife. Rosie can tell you what the girl looks like, I'll bet."

"The girl?" Garrett said, holding a round tray in midair. A curious smile played across his lips. "How old *is* she?"

"No one seems to know her exact age," Selig offered from his post beside the cutting board. "But my bet is she strongly resembles Mrs. Bennett."

"One would certainly hope so," said Theodore, who had stepped into the kitchen from the utility room, where he had been observing the banter, rather amused at the playful

speculation going on about him. At his appearance, the pa-
laver did not cease; rather, it continued, and little by little,
small groups of workers could be heard whispering as they
rolled out pies, gathered necessary condiments for the after-
dinner coffee, or dispersed clean linens and accessories to
the guest room.

Searching out his nephew in particular, he spoke up.
"May I have a word with you?" He bobbed his head toward
the hallway.

Garrett, preoccupied with the precise arrangement of
hors d'oeuvres on a brass tray, continued working. "Can it
wait a moment?"

"I'd rather it not."

His nephew peered up at him, looking rather startled.
"Why . . . Uncle, what is it?"

"Drop everything and come . . . now," Theodore com-
manded, and although he hadn't recalled speaking so sternly
to his only living relative, the truth was, he had need of
Garrett.

If only for the sake of extreme curiosity.

Fortunately, Garrett did not take his uncle literally about
dropping *everything,* for the enormous platter was splen-
didly arrayed with before-dinner delicacies—tantalizing in
appearance, and at this point in the planning, quite nearly
finished.

Summoning Selig to take over, Garrett hurriedly wiped
his hands on a towel and followed his uncle into the hallway.
"What could be more important than the hors d'oeuvres?"
he asked when they were alone in a corner of the south corridor, far enough removed from the kitchen for privacy and
close enough to the butler's pantry door in case an escape
was necessary.

"The hors d'oeuvres can wait." Theodore leaned forward, glancing about to check for eavesdroppers. "Now,
what's all this fuss about a reunion with Mrs. Bennett and

her daughter? I've caught nothing but snippets all morning."

A wrinkled frown hovered on the steward's brow. "It seems the mistress's daughter has turned up out of nowhere. Straightaway . . . out of the blue."

"Hmm, quite intriguing, I must say."

"Supposedly, Mrs. Bennett is meeting with the young Amishwoman in her private quarters as we speak." Garrett glanced at his watch. "I mustn't delay now, Uncle," he said, "if tea is to be served on time."

"Very well." Theodore scanned the maze of banisters and landings overhead. Wouldn't do to get caught dawdling in the hallway. Then resting his gaze on his nephew, he dismissed the handsome chap with a wave. "We'll discuss it later . . . *after* tea."

Which was to say that Garrett would surely pay strict attention while attending to tea in Mrs. Bennett's suite, after which he would doubtless report to his uncle.

Returning to his own quarters, he mused over the happenings of the past few days. The missus had looked so pale and wan that day he'd driven her to visit the family lawyer. Surely such a reunion—with the daughter she'd lost— would only serve to sap the little strength she had left.

Had the young lady gotten wind of the fortune she was heir to? Doubtless, she had not, with the will so newly altered. Nor, Theodore felt sure, had Master Dylan. What with his comings and goings—of a dubious nature, to be sure—he'd scarcely stepped foot into the mistress's bedroom of late, not even to inquire after her health. Strange fellow, that.

Still, it wasn't likely that Laura Bennett would have discussed her private concerns with her husband.

Well, whatever happened with Mrs. Bennett and her daughter was entirely their business. Still, if it was any consolation, the day was young. Plenty of time for snatches of information from Rosie and, of course, Garrett himself.

Such revelations might quell his fears for the mistress, or so he hoped.

❖ ❖ ❖

From the bus station across town, Katherine gazed out over the parking lot to the highway. It looked like a sea of automobiles, with not a buggy in sight. A green-and-white restaurant sign blinked off and on, reminding her that she hadn't eaten in hours. But she wouldn't reward herself with a steaming hot meal until her chore was done—locating the proper address for the Bennett estate.

Why wouldn't telephone operators give out addresses? It was the oddest thing and made no good sense, because it seemed to her that if someone could get ahold of a phone number, they should also be entitled to the accompanying address. Unless, of course, there was another reason for the phone company's strict policy.

She opened the medium-sized telephone directory dangling from a chain in a corner of the bus station. Scanning the listing for Bennetts, she spotted the name: *Bennett, Dylan D.* Elated, she jotted down the address on a pad of paper and marched up to one of the ticket counters.

The silver-haired man was eager to help. "*Everyone* knows the Bennett mansion," he told her. "In fact, any cab driver in town can take you there . . . blindfolded."

"Well, that's mighty good news. Thank you." She immediately thought about calling a cab. But the idea of heading out to meet her natural mother, stomach growling and with a dizzy head, was much too discouraging.

The bus trip from Lancaster had been a long, tiresome one. An impulsive peek at the cosmetic case in her handbag told her she ought to freshen up before scurrying across the road for a late lunch.

So she headed to the public rest room and splashed

water on her face, then combed her hair, still marveling at the way it played in soft waves over her shoulders. No more middle part, with her crowning glory all done up in an ugly bun and hidden away under a devotional *kapp*.

But that was then, and this was now. Best to put out of her mind the Old Ways and plan her course of action for the whole new life awaiting her.

The restaurant was abuzz with talk, and even after the cheerful waitress served up Katherine's plate of meatloaf, mashed potatoes and gravy, and corn, she stood around, eager to chat. About the town mayor. About the problems her husband was having at his new job. About everything and nothing at all.

When she paused for breath, and Katherine mentioned that she was planning a visit to the Bennett mansion later today, the waitress perked up her ears. "Really? You're going out to see the Bennetts?"

"Well, actually it's *Mrs.* Bennett I want to see." She realized she'd lowered her voice and was actually whispering. "I heard she's been awful sick. Is it true?"

"That's what's going around about the poor thing. She's failing fast . . . advanced MS, I've heard."

Katherine felt her heart constrict. Ach! She must hurry, must get herself emotionally ready to meet her mother. Before it was too late.

Seemingly encouraged by Katherine's comment, the waitress continued. "Here lately, there's been talk that the Bennetts are taking applications for some more hired help." The friendly server snapped her chewing gum and bent over the table to swipe at a spot of water.

Katherine noticed, too, the woman's made-up eyes and bright red lipstick and wondered if her own lashes might be in need of a touch-up. Wearing cosmetics was a new, almost frightening, experience, only because she was still learning how to apply it correctly and in the most becoming manner, but she loved every little aspect of it. Occasionally, she even went to bed without removing her face rouge and powder, for no reason other than she'd been deprived of indulging in it her entire life. That and jewelry . . . and having a beautician cut and style her auburn hair. Oh, glory!

She'd kept these secret desires hidden away all through her childhood and teen years—the longing for such things as fine jewelry, beautiful hairdos, and lovely clothing. Such *worldly* things, the Amish would say.

Glancing down at her smart silk blouse and wool skirt, Katherine smiled to herself. She'd decided days ago she had much catching up to do. And here she was . . . on the verge of stepping into Laura Bennett's elegant modern world.

Still daydreaming, she touched the thin gold chain at her throat, thrilling at its icy coolness beneath her fingertips. What would Rebecca Lapp, her adoptive mother, say if she could see her now, dressed this way? For a moment she felt a stab of conscience, a prickle of remorse over leaving the dear Amishwoman who had loved Katie . . . Katherine . . . as her own.

Then she shrugged the troublesome thought aside. No need worrying about what the People thought. Not anymore. The Plain life was behind her, all but forgotten, or so she wished. A path strewn with pain . . . truly all that was left of her past. Hadn't all of them—Mamma and Dat and the boys—accepted the harsh shunning without so much as a question, turned their backs as if she no longer existed? They'd *let* her go—as much as sent her away. . . .

"The Bennetts seem to need help out there at their place," the waitress was saying. "You interested?"

Reining in her attention to the conversation at hand, Katherine replied, "What sort of a job would it be?"

"Far as I know, a housemaid's position."

"A maid?" Katherine wasn't sure why she was interested

in hearing someone carry on so about the Bennetts, but she was. If truth be told, she felt more comfortable sitting here in this restaurant, while a mere stranger rattled on about Katherine's natural mother and the estate where she lived, than with the unsettling thought of actually heading out there and meeting Laura Bennett face-to-face.

The late afternoon sun shone boldly on her back as one customer after another left the dinerlike atmosphere. She found herself caught up in conversation with her new waitress friend and ordered some pie with ice cream for dessert, unaware of the sun's steady descent toward the fading horizon.

The cab driver knew exactly where to take her when she was ready.

In the distance, the sky had already begun to turn a rosy hue in the silent moments before dusk. Katherine was mighty pleased with herself for having stumbled onto the too-talkative waitress, who seemed privy to far more information about Dylan and Laura Bennett than she'd first let on.

Thinking she'd been downright lucky—fortunate without trying, really—Katherine congratulated herself on getting an earful, the lowdown, on the Bennetts from an outsider's viewpoint. And all this without ever having to reveal that she was related to Mrs. Bennett.

She slid down a bit in the seat behind the driver, craning her head around so she could see out the back window. Then, looking up through the glass, she spotted one star after another making its evening appearance.

How many stars had she and Daniel Fisher counted in the sky over Hickory Hollow one long-ago evening? Two hundred or more, she remembered. But with the recollection came grievous pain, and she sat up, reaching for the handle on the guitar case, determined never to let anything happen to the instrument that had brought Daniel so much joy. Forbidden, true, yet he'd kept it hidden away from the eyes of the bishop and his own father and mother, unlike her own blundering attempts to conceal her rebellion. How he'd managed all the years before his nineteenth birthday, Katherine didn't know. Yet he had, and because of the circumstances surrounding her shunning, she would never *never* part with the glorious stringed instrument. It belonged to her—now and forever.

Daniel hadn't intended to flaunt his disobedience while they were courting—she was mighty sure of that. He had just done his best to follow the music in his heart. Nothing else seemed to matter much, not even the Ordnung, or what the church members set down as rules for living.

That's just the way Dan Fisher was, all right. Stubborn and bright, all stirred up together into one fascinating, spirited human being. And on top of everything else, what a wonderful-good song maker he was!

She glanced back up at the Big Dipper, thinking that her one true love would be mighty pleased with her quest to find Laura Bennett. Pleased enough to want to write a new song, maybe, if he were alive.

Well, she'd be singing her own song about it soon enough. That was for sure and for certain.

❖   ❖   ❖

The butler thought it a grand idea to make small talk with Mrs. Bennett's newly found daughter as they ascended the staircase to the Tiffany Room, the finest guest room in the house. After all, here was the mistress's beloved child, in the flesh, come home for Christmas; no sense being stodgy about it. The girl ought to feel genuinely welcomed and accepted by *all* the members of the staff.

"Is this your first visit to Canandaigua?" he asked the

young Amishwoman with the lovely strawberry blond hair.

"Yes, it is."

"Well, I hope you'll enjoy your stay." Fulton carried her luggage into the room and set the pieces down near the large closet. "Help yourself to everything and anything. One of the maids will be up in a few minutes to check on your needs."

"Denki."

"That's Dutch, isn't it?" he asked, to make polite conversation.

"Jah, for 'thank you.'"

"Ah . . . so it is." He noted the newness of the suitcases, curious that they seemed entirely out of place with the rest of her Plain appearance. Without any further comment, he excused himself and left the room.

It was the soft appearance of the woman's hands that caused Dylan's alarm. "Amishwomen use their hands for everything from chopping wood to scrubbing floors, or so I'm told. We must do something about *these*—roughen them up a bit," he suggested, still studying them. "Everything else is going so well, I'd hate for your hands to be our undoing."

Alyson Cairns flirted playfully. "My boyfriend won't be very happy if he finds out about the older man in my life."

Dylan stepped back, surveying her Amish getup. "Your young man will have you back in good time."

Her sparkling eyes, devoid of the slightest hint of makeup, tantalized him. "So . . . when did you rush up here and hide away in the closet?" she asked.

"Never mind that."

"Lucky for you your fussy butler didn't decide to put away my suitcases." She eyed the closet door, slightly ajar. "Now, exactly when is my signature supposed to appear on the dotted line? I can't stay around here forever, you know.

It's Christmas, for heaven's sake!"

"Heaven, indeed." Dylan perched himself on a chair, scrutinizing the actress standing before him. "We have a deal . . . it wouldn't do for you to become too hasty."

"Or greedy?" Her grin was discerning.

He ignored the implication. "You're taking orders from me until every last detail is accomplished." He leaned back, bracing his hands behind his head.

"And after your wife kicks the bucket, then what?"

"You'll get your cut, don't worry," he said, pondering yesterday's brief conversation with Laura's physician. The doctor had appeared highly concerned. And, yes, he'd assured Dylan that everything possible was being done to make her comfortable as the illness ran its deadly course. "Everything *humanly* possible," the doctor had reiterated. "There's always the hope of divine intervention, certainly, which is precisely what we must believe for if your wife is to survive the holidays."

Just the information he needed. Laura was not long for this world. Most likely wouldn't last past New Year's. Without question, her soul would fly straight to heaven, on angel wings. The woman was a saint. No need to concern himself over the spiritual side of things—if it turned out he was wrong and there really *was* a God. That is, unless He *did* intervene, and Laura didn't depart this life on schedule. . . .

He watched as the young woman knelt to open her suitcase. "I need a break from these Amish duds, Mr. Bennett." She eyed him meaningfully. "But I *don't* need an audience . . . if you know what I mean."

Alyson was surprised when he left with only a mild protest. She'd expected worse.

And now that he was out of the room, she wished she hadn't been in such a hurry to get rid of him. She'd needed more time to get acquainted with the traditions of the Old

Order Amish. The initial coaching session had been nearly overwhelming. All those rules and regulations! How did people put up with it? She was to dress, speak, and behave as a young Plain woman, yet she'd had only a "crash course" in the little time since the contact with the talent agent hired by Mr. Bennett.

Still, the money—or the promise of it—was incentive enough. Not to mention the challenge of the role. She'd give the performance of her life, Plain or not!

CHAPTER NINE

❖　❖　❖

Katherine paid the cab driver and turned around, facing the stately mansion. Its stone exterior was embroidered with sections of thick ivy, multitudes of vines, dried up in the dead of winter, ascending lifeless, yet aligned, to meet the moonbeams.

From her spot on the pavement, she took in the massive outline—adorned with numerous chimneys—now ominous and dark against a moonlit sky.

Lingering there, she felt as if her eyes and her very soul were being drawn to the place. Years of forbidden cravings culminated in one sweep of the eye. "Himmel! What a place!" she whispered.

She could scarcely wait to explore its elegance. First, though, she must get inside. To pass over its threshold . . . what glory!

Clutching her suitcase in one hand and the guitar case in the other, Katherine made her way across the circular driveway, guided by lantern-shaped lights near the entrance. In a moment of near panic, she hesitated at the portal. *What am I doing here?* she wondered. *How will I ever fit in with these rich folk?*

In that instant, her life seemed to pass before her—from

earliest recollections as a young girl growing up Amish on a dairy farm in a remote area of Lancaster County, to the present and her chic, modern look.

I do hope Laura Bennett will approve of me, Katherine thought, still uncertain. More than anything, she didn't want to come across as a country hick—had practiced long and hard to overcome any such traits of speech and manner, in fact.

Squaring her shoulders, she gave her hair a light toss. A dog howled in the distance, sending a shiver down her spine. She reached for the brass knocker and held her breath at the sound of footsteps.

The door opened, and a tall man, looking for all the world like something out of a store catalogue, stood straight and still, eyeing her curiously. "Good evening," he said, bending stiffly as if he were afraid he might break.

"Hullo," she replied. "I wonder if I might be able to see Mrs. Bennett."

The man stared at her, yet it was not a rude, cold stare. More of an inquisitive look, really. "Whom may I say is calling?"

She was about to speak up, to tell him, without boasting, that she had traveled many miles to see her mother for the first time, her natural mother—Laura Mayfield-Bennett. But her thoughts, yes, even the breath she'd drawn ever so deeply, giving her the pluck to go through with it—all of that—was halted when a round-faced woman wearing a short white apron and a big smile appeared beside him at the door.

"Fulton, show the girl in . . . bring her in out of the cold. She's come about the job, of course . . . and must think she's going to get it, too, for she's brought along all her worldly possessions, it seems."

Whether she was mumbling to herself or to the man she'd called Fulton, Katherine couldn't be sure. But she took note of the glance directed at her guitar case and clung to it all the more. But from the way the perky little woman addressed the towering fellow, still standing in the doorway—just the way she worked him over with her eyes—led Katherine to believe they were husband and wife.

The maid, who, by now, had introduced herself as Rosie Taylor, bustled her into the house, helping her with her suitcase and guitar, then promptly handed them over to Fulton.

Katherine had to chuckle silently at the way things had worked out just now. Here she was, inside her mother's house, without ever having said who she was or on what business she had come.

For a fleeting moment she thought perhaps the situation had been providential—something she had been taught to believe in from her earliest years as a little Plain girl.

No time for reminiscing, though; Rosie and Fulton whisked her off to the kitchen, where a chair was pulled out for her beside a long table. A single-page application lay in front of her, but only after she'd removed her coat and gloves did Katherine reach into her purse to locate her ballpoint pen.

"May we have a look at your referral?" Rosie began when she and Fulton were both seated opposite Katherine.

"I don't have anything like that with me." Katherine was beginning to feel uneasy. Maybe her thoughts of Providence had come too soon.

"Aren't you the woman sent over by the agency?" Fulton asked at once.

"Agency?"

"We *always* hire from the employment agency," Rosie explained. "They screen each of our applicants beforehand."

"Oh . . ." Katherine looked over at her tattered suitcase and the guitar case propped up against the butler's pantry. *Now what?* she wondered. Should she tell them she had no desire to be a maid anyway—that her one and only hope was to meet her birth mother?

"We must stick by our policy, you understand," Fulton was saying. "You'll have to go downtown and be interviewed."

"Well, I really hadn't planned to . . ." She paused, measuring her words. Was now a good time to reveal her identity?

Fulton cocked his head, and Katherine felt as if the man were studying her. "We're all quite busy at the moment—unexpected company, and at this time of year." He sighed. "It would be best for you to contact the agency," he repeated as he stood to his feet. "Now, if you'll excuse me, I'll see you out."

"Oh . . . sir, can't you *please* let my . . . that is, Mrs. Bennett . . . know I'm here? Won't you do that?" She felt as if she were begging.

"Under no circumstances must the mistress be disturbed. This is a very special occasion," Fulton went on to explain. "Mrs. Bennett has just received her only child—a daughter she'd given up as an infant. They're dining together at the moment."

"Her . . . *daughter*?" Katherine's words caught in her throat.

"Yes, indeed," Rosie spoke up briskly. "And the timing couldn't have been better, with Christmas just around the corner."

The timing is dreadful, Katherine thought, standing and reaching for her coat. Had she gotten the wrong phone number clear back at the Millers' place? Was this some bad-awful mistake?

"You look pale," commented Fulton. "Are you feeling quite well?"

"Fine . . . I'm fine," she said, biting her dishonest tongue. *How can this be?* she wondered, thinking back to

Rebecca's conversation with her at the farmhouse. The Wise Woman, too, had spoken of Laura Mayfield-Bennett . . . hadn't she? Katherine's thoughts lingered on Ella Mae who had certainly seen the handwritten name on the fancy envelope. Hadn't she also vouched for the fact that the wealthy Mrs. Bennett had been out searching for her daughter in and around the Lancaster area?

Rosie excused herself and hurried out of the room. Fulton, whom Katherine had decided must be the butler or someone important, seemed mighty restless, as if he were needed elsewhere in the house. Anywhere but here, apparently. After all, she had been a waste of his time—an applicant without the proper referrals.

"I'll find my way out," she offered, feeling disheartened by the way things were turning out. "But I'll be needing a cab."

"Oh yes, certainly." He located a telephone book, then apologized for any inconvenience, and sped down the hallway.

While she was preparing to use the phone, two young men flew past her into the kitchen. "We could use a bit of help," the older man said, opening one of the several refrigerators and motioning to her. "I'm Selig, assistant cook. And you are?"

"Katherine," she said quickly, purposely leaving off her last name.

He shook her hand but seemed preoccupied. "A pleasure . . . Katherine. Good to have you aboard."

She was opening her mouth to explain, but when he insisted she take off her coat and lend a hand by slicing and warming a tray of bread, Katherine did as she was told.

"Wonderful," Selig said. "You've come in the nick of time."

"But—"

"We're obviously a bit shorthanded due to the holidays,"

the younger man explained while placing crystal goblets on a wide slate counter nearby. He stopped briefly to extend his hand. "Garrett Smith, head steward . . . at your service."

"Hullo," she replied. They'd mistaken her for the new housemaid, for sure and for certain!

Grinning, Garrett resumed his work. "I suppose you've heard—the daughter of the house has come home for the holidays."

His words pierced her soul. How many times must she hear this miserable news? What if she were to barge right into the mistress's cozy supper . . . to lay eyes on Laura May-field-Bennett for herself? What about that?

These were reckless thoughts, for sure. But how was she supposed to feel, for goodness' sake—hearing that someone had taken her place?

Determined to keep her helpless, angry feelings in check, Katherine followed instructions, cutting the loaf of bread on a large cutting block with an electric knife. After that, she placed the ample slices in the warming oven. Good thing she'd had opportunity to use such modern contraptions while cooking in Lydia Miller's kitchen. She tried not to think of the hours of time she might've saved had she grown up with electricity, for bread making had forever been a daily chore in the Lapp home.

When there was a lull between Selig's and Garrett's prattle, Katherine spoke up. "The mistress's daughter . . . uh, have either of you seen her?"

"Ah . . . she's pretty enough, I suppose," offered Selig. "Plain, really, though I presume that's the Amish way."

"She's *Amish*?"

"Quite," Garrett replied, going about the business of pouring beverages in the ornate gold-trimmed goblets.

"So . . . she dresses Plain, then?" Katherine ventured, her heart in her throat.

"Totally," Selig said with a grin on his face. "Somewhat

of an eccentric style, I must admit. Especially with that formal little head covering of hers."

The mere mention of the cap took Katherine back to the days leading up to the shunning. The final battles—whether or not to wear her covering in her adoptive father's house—had been such a sore spot. As it turned out, he had required her to wear it, against her wishes, really, during one of those last days at home.

At Garrett's chuckle, Katherine's thoughts flew to the job at hand. "Mrs. Bennett's daughter could use a sound dose of makeup, if you ask me."

Katherine felt her cheeks warm with his brief, yet ardent scrutiny.

"I do believe *you* could teach Katie a thing or two," he observed.

Katherine froze, nearly dropped the platter of warmed bread. "Did you say 'Katie'?"

Glancing up, the head steward nodded. "Interesting name, isn't it? Her last name's Lapp."

"Sounds Dutch to me," Selig offered before dashing off just as several housemaids darted past with trays of dishes, probably the main course plates and silverware.

"What do *you* think?" Garrett asked. "Does the daughter's adopted name sound Dutch to you?"

Her mind whirled. Should she tell this young man why she'd come? Tell him that her given name—her former name—was also Lapp? That she'd abandoned the name Katie because of her need to be Katherine . . . wholly Laura Bennett's daughter?

Ach! How had things got so *ghuddelt*—tangled—so quickly? And how was it that Laura Bennett's daughter should have the same adoptive name as Katherine's own?

"Well, what do you say? Dutch or not?" Garrett persisted.

"It's Swiss, most likely . . . one of the more common

names for Pennsylvania Amish," she blurted.

Raising his thick eyebrows, Garrett appeared amused. "And how do *you* know about Amish names?"

"Oh, if you listen good, you pick things up." She'd almost said "gut" and was mighty glad she hadn't. The last thing the head steward should know was that there were, in all truth, *two* women claiming the name of Katie Lapp, under the Bennetts' regal roof.

Part II

It is not the criminal things which are hardest to confess,
but the ridiculous and shameful.

Jean-Jacques Rousseau

CHAPTER TEN

❖　❖　❖

Most of the lights were on inside the New Jersey bungalow when Daniel Fisher arrived home. Even the matching floor lamps on either side of the sofa remained lit.

Looking around as he stepped into his plant-filled vestibule, he wondered if *every* light in the place had been left on. *Wonderful,* he thought. The new cleaning woman had followed his instructions to a tee.

Whether working late on blueprints at home or arriving there after-hours from his drafting office, Dan insisted on being surrounded by light. Too many years of coming home to a dark farmhouse, maybe.

It wasn't only that he required light for his detailed renderings. No, it was much more than that. He'd discovered something extremely reassuring about rooms being lit up from early evening on. Because it was at night, when the sun toppled over the horizon, that he missed Pennsylvania—*home*—most. Missed his parents and brothers, and Annie his only sister, and most of all . . . Katie Lapp. His sweetheart girl would be worried sick if she knew he was living out in the modern English world, far away from Amish society. But she, along with his family and friends, believed he was dead. Drowned at sea.

103

They deserved the truth. He'd decided this on more than one occasion through the years, yet had never been able to come up with a plan. At least one that would not cause severe complications as a result of his "resurrection from the dead."

To mark the Christmas season, he'd begun to grow a beard. Though facial hair was indicative of a married Amishman, he felt it might ease his way back into Hickory Hollow when the time came. Stubble now, but the sure promise of a full beard as bushy as his father's, all in preparation for a possible meeting with the man he'd wronged.

He emptied his pockets of loose change and his keys, then reaching for the hall switch, he marveled once again at the ability to disseminate light at will. With the mere flick of a finger!

For five satisfying years, he had enjoyed such benefits yet hadn't consciously taken modern technology for granted. Nor did he wish to, though at times he agonized over the guilt of it. The deeply ingrained taboos, church rules, and regulations. . . .

He had not been raised with electricity or fast cars. His father's father and three generations of men—great-grandfathers before him—had lived their lives according to the Old Ways, *das Alt Gebrauch.*

Yet his emotions often became jumbled when he thought of his father . . . the prospects Jacob Fisher had had for him. In an Amish household, the youngest son was expected to take over the family farm at the appropriate age. Daniel had chosen another path for his life.

Surprisingly, in spite of all that had transpired between them—the passionate arguments over doctrine and such— he did not foster bad feelings toward his strict father. He had forgiven Jacob Fisher years ago.

Now the time was ripe to offer his father the same opportunity. And to speak the truth of what had happened on that fateful day in Atlantic City.

Dan glanced around his comfortable rental home, sparkling with holiday lights and trim. Too many Decembers had come and gone since his "accident." Home fires burned brightest at Christmas. As for Katie, she was still to him the dearest girl in all the world.

His thoughts flew back to their first Sunday night Singing together. Back when Katie had just turned sixteen. . . .

The sky was filled with a thousand stars that early June evening. As if someone had sprinkled out a silo full of them all over the heavens. Daniel, eighteen, was hoping—without letting on to anybody—that Katie Lapp just might be coming to Singing. Her first ever. And if she did, she'd be riding over with Benjamin, her eighteen-year-old brother, in his open buggy, the way all the older teen girls in Hickory Hollow showed up for such things.

He remembered the *Neilicht*—new moon—shining its crescent-shaped light down on the barn, 'cause he kept peering out through the loose, rickety boards every chance he could, looking for her. Looking and waiting . . . wishing there'd been a big yellow full moon high in the sky to spotlight beautiful red-haired Katie.

Ach, the Mennonites had yard lights—made perfect sense to him. 'Cept he was Amish and none of that kind of thinking was bound to do a body good. Electricity was wicked, in any way, shape, or form.

Ach, Katie, he thought. *Where are ya? What's takin' your brother so long?*

When would Ben ever figure out how to gallop that young driving horse of his? Puh, he'd best be taking some lessons, and from somebody who knew how to get a pretty girl to Singing on time.

Pacing back and forth, trying to pretend nothing special was on his mind—least not one certain girl—he picked up a long piece of straw, stuck it in his mouth, and sauntered over to yak at Chicken Joe. Now, here was a boy who never seemed to have a speck of trouble finding a girl to talk to or take home after Singings.

"What's got ya frettin'?" Chicken Joe asked.

"Didn't say nothin' was."

"Mighty restless you are."

"Not any more than anyone else around here." He glanced over his shoulder at the young men milling around, probably fifty or more of them. All wearing wide-brimmed straw hats, which they never took off, not even in warm weather.

Chicken Joe grinned, showing his upper gums. "She'll be comin' soon. You know she will."

Daniel bristled at the comment. Chicken Joe had no right to say anything like that. To pop out with something so bold. The fellow was brazen and even worse, a flirt. Biggest one around.

For himself, Dan had decided long back, about the time he was turning fourteen, that he wouldn't so much as wink at a girl lest he liked her enough to kiss her. 'Course, he wouldn't go doing any such a thing for a long time from now. Still, he knew exactly how he planned on treating Samuel Lapp's daughter. Treat her right fine, like the vivacious beauty she was.

Standing next to a hay baler, he and Chicken Joe talked up a storm for the time being. They'd worn their "for good" clothes, all spiffed up with tan suspenders, white shirts, and black trousers. Only one reason for it—two, really. First off, 'twas their Old Order custom. That, and dressing nice made the girls look twice.

A group of boys scuffled around in the haymow overhead, stirring up dust. Dan figured they'd had a drink or two before coming. Bishop John would frown mighty hard if he got wind of it, because Hickory Hollow's bishop was stricter than most, no getting around it.

When Katie did finally arrive, he stood back, waiting a bit impatiently for the Singing to get underway. Then, sitting on a hay bale in the farthest corner of the barn, he watched Benjamin's sister without ever being noticed. Watched her good, as discreetly as possible, of course.

A group of young married couples sat in one section of the barn. They got the songs going, starting out with one of Dan's least favorite, a slow hymn from the *Lieder Sammlungen*, a small songbook for such an occasion. Thing was, the hymn lasted a good eleven minutes, and he hoped it would be the only one like that. Jah, he liked attending Singings, and not just to see all the pretty girls in his church district and SummerHill's; he enjoyed the music. More than most. Raising his voice in unison with a hundred other Amish young people was good enough reason to come any day, to his way of thinking.

Still, Katie was the main reason tonight. Sitting over there under the hayloft with the other unmarried girls, smack-dab next to one of her cousins, why, Katie looked almost angel-like. 'Course, he'd never so much as laid eyes on a heavenly creature, but that didn't mean she didn't look like one all the same, wearing her good purple dress, same color as the whole row of girls with her.

On second thought, maybe it was the color of her hair that made Katie special. He hadn't quite figured out just exactly what attracted him to her, really. It was simple to see that her hair was as close to the rust red of a robin's breast as hair could be, even though he'd overheard her telling Elam, her oldest brother, that it was *not* red, it was *auburn*. And she'd been mighty firm about it, too. The girl had a powerful-strong personality, he'd noticed. But that didn't stop him from liking her. Maybe even made him fancy her more.

Daniel chewed on his straw and grinned to himself. Any

girl spunky enough to voice an opinion about her own hair color, now, that was the type of girl he'd want to invite for a ride in his new rig. Reason being, there'd be plenty to talk about with a young woman like Katie Lapp.

And talk they did. That warm summer night, with honeysuckle wafting through the air, that night of Katie's first Singing, he took her home. Many more buggy rides were to follow. Occasionally, another boy might beat him to it, talking to Katie first, asking her to ride home. But it didn't take long, maybe two months or so, for him to latch on to her. 'Cause once he took notice of her head bobbing to the rhythm of the songs, her brown eyes bright with the melodies, from then on, he knew she was the one he wanted for his girl. And someday, his wife.

Music made her smile, same as him. Which was saying a lot, 'cause when Katie smiled, the whole world lit right up. Like a hundred and one fireflies. And oh, so much more.

❖   ❖   ❖

Feeling right at home in the kitchen, Katherine accomplished a great deal while the butler and his sidekick were absent. The trappings of a place like this spurred her creative abilities and, with no coaxing from anyone, her hands had found plenty to do. She'd put together several pies—a coconut custard pie, for one—and had them tucked away in the oven when Fulton Taylor reappeared.

"Goodness me, are you still here?"

She hoped he wouldn't force her out; she'd been right good help, if she did say so herself—especially with whatever strange things were going on in the Bennetts' lavish dining room. "Mrs. Bennett's daughter . . . uh, Katie, I believe . . . well, I just wondered if she might be wanting a taste of a real Amish dessert. Something she might be accustomed to back home, you know," she explained her secret conniving.

"Amish, indeed." The butler's smile didn't quite manage to reach his eyes. "What recipe did you follow?"

Katherine tapped her temple. "Oh, one I seemed to have remembered from childhood." Now, why had she gone and said a thing like that? Next he'd be asking where she'd grown up, where she'd come from.

But the butler surprised her by saying instead, "What an excellent idea!" His eyes softened as he spoke. "How very kind of you."

"Thank you," she said, meaning it. Hopefully, he had seen how proficient she was, how completely at ease she was in the kitchen. Now maybe he'd agree to hire her.

Rosie swept into the room just then, wearing an equally astonished expression on her face as she sniffed the air. "What *is* that glorious aroma?" Switching on the oven light, she peered through the glass door. "Quite amazing . . . the pies look and smell absolutely scrumptious."

Fulton spoke up. "And authentically Amish."

Katherine thought there was a smidgen of satisfaction in the butler's voice. She held her breath, hoping against hope that she might be allowed to stay on, might be hired as the housemaid they seemed to need so desperately.

Neither one of them inquired as to how she had come upon the pie recipes. However, they *did* say they were willing to accept the extraordinary desserts as a token substitute for the "proper" agency referral.

Grinning, Rosie opened a drawer nearby and handed her a frilly apron, headpiece, and hair netting. "You'll wear these at all times . . . while on duty, of course. It works best to wind your hair up in a knot under the netting." Then explaining that her husband, Fulton Taylor, was the final authority on employees, Rosie suggested she fill out an application "first thing in the morning, when things have settled down a bit."

"Thank you," Katherine said. "I'll try not to disappoint you."

"Now"—Rosie glanced over her shoulder—"while your pies are baking, I'll show you to your room."

Katherine thought about the song she was sure Daniel would want to be writing about now. Up in the heavenlies . . . Clutching her suitcase and guitar, she followed Rosie Taylor to the long, beautiful staircase.

❖   ❖   ❖

Daniel pulled out a piece of linen stationery from his desk drawer and pondered what he might say. Annie would be shocked to receive a letter from her dead brother, no doubt. He feared the poor girl would collapse.

He would state clearly that she keep the letter confidential, not show it to Dat or Mamma. There was much to be arranged before they should be told their son was alive.

Tuesday, December 23

Dearest Annie,
  For several years now, I have wanted to write a letter to you.

He reread the first line and decided it didn't suit him. Shouldn't he warn his sister to sit down? Tell her that what she was about to read might startle her?

Annie had always been a sensitive sort of girl, so perhaps it was a mistake to approach her this way. The wheels began to turn, and he realized he ought to determine, at least, if she was still living at home. Whether or not she was married. He would have to investigate. Surely someone would know the status of his only sister.

And while he was at it, he might as well inquire about
Katie Lapp. Darling Katie . . . the girl he'd loved so long . . .
now a woman.

Rethinking the notion, he realized anew that he couldn't
bear to have word of Katie. Was it possible she had remained
single all these years?

Better off not knowing, he decided.

With a vengeance, he crumpled the beginnings of his letter and pitched it in the wastebasket next to the desk.

❂   ❂   ❂

As rooms go, the one directly above the kitchen was snug
and cozy—elegant, too. A timid flame burned in the white-
tiled fireplace behind an ornate Victorian fire screen.

"You may hear a bit of kitchen noise occasionally," Rosie
commented, "but not much more than you'll be making
down there yourself. Which is to say, the live-in staff are up
and about early, at the crack of dawn, so to speak."

Katherine nodded. "I don't mind early rising. I'm used
to it." She realized she'd done it again—opened herself up
for questioning. But good-natured Rosie only smiled back.

Katherine was informed of her duties and told that the
schedule for the day of Christmas Eve and the rest of the
week would be set in the morning. "Fulton will slip the
docket under your door before you're up and about. He'll
also give you final word on employment here—after he re-
views your application."

"Thank you again for giving me this chance to prove myself." Katherine wanted to embrace the dear woman, whose
hair had begun to gray at the temples. Embrace her and tell
her how very grateful she was. But she kept her composure,
as well as a respectable distance.

It was then that Rosie's eyes caught hers, and for a moment the two women were silent. Awkward seconds passed

before Rosie whispered, "I do believe you're a godsend, Katherine."

"I'll try to be useful."

Rosie continued to probe deeply with her clear brown eyes. "I'm counting on it." And then she was gone.

Relieved beyond words, Katherine stood at the foot of the black iron bed, observing layers of homespun linens and colorful quilts neatly placed over the sheets and bedskirt. Several handmade damask-napkin pillows were scattered over large, plump shams. She ran her fingers over the gilding highlights on the footboard.

"I'm a princess in a castle!" She spun about, hugging her arms to herself.

Aware of a delicate scent in the room, she instinctively went to the refinished antique pine dresser. Opening the top drawer, she spied two sachets of potpourri—one in each of the front corners.

"It's lavender!" She held one of the tiny cloth bags against her face, letting it linger there, recalling the very first sachet she'd made as a girl, for her own dresser drawer back home.

Then spurred on by the discovery, she opened each of the four drawers in the old dresser, removing two sachets at a time. Carefully, she spread the tiny potpourri pillows across the wide bed, remembering that as a girl, she had often lined up her faceless Amish dolls this way, humming or singing as she played.

Scurrying across the room to the highboy on the opposite wall, she found, to her heart's delight, seven additional drawers' worth of the dainty, lovely things. Caught up in the thrill, she scattered them on the dresser top, one by one—touching, smelling, examining each little treasure. They were all different in color yet similar in fragrance, and she decided after a closer inspection that the hands which had lovingly created her satin infant gown nearly twenty-three years ago surely had sewn these sachets.

Taking a backward step, she felt for the edge of the bed and sat down—Katherine Mayfield, the brand-new maid in the Bennetts' wonderful-good mansion. Caressing one of the little lavender cushions, she allowed herself to recline fully and stare at the ceiling, at the decorative molding high above her head. How far she'd come for this moment. And how far she had yet to go. . . .

Finding the sachets—a beautiful link between herself and her natural mother—helped ease her apprehensions somewhat. Had she stumbled onto something, something better than ever? If, of course, the mistress of the house *was* her true mamma. . . .

Ach, she had scarcely anything to go on, nothing tangible, really. Even the sweet-smelling little pillows weren't proof enough; lots of folk used such pretty things to freshen up their closets and drawers.

Pressing the miniature bag to her face, she wondered if she had in all actuality come to the right place. She continued to wonder, stewing over past events as she lay there, eyes boring a hole in the brass chandelier centered in the ceiling.

One thing she knew to be true. Only one. Laura Mayfield-Bennett had once come to Hickory Hollow looking for a young woman named Katherine. Yet how many Amish communities were there in Pennsylvania? Hundreds? Maybe more?

How had Laura known *where* to look in Lancaster County? She hadn't, of course.

Jumping to conclusions, Katherine allowed a bothersome thought to make a home in her head. *What if* I'm *the impostor? What if everything up till this moment has been nothing more than a dream?*

Urgency swept her inside out, and she longed to find out who the mistress of the house was, really. She must know,

too, once and for all, if *she* or the woman named Katie Lapp
belonged to Laura Bennett.

Nothing . . . *nothing* must keep her from finding the
truth.

CHAPTER ELEVEN

❖　❖　❖

Katherine hoped her guitar playing wouldn't disturb anyone. She'd waited till the first hint of light had pierced the darkness, had gone into the private bath, drawn the tub water, and closed the door. Sitting on a petite boudoir chair beside the fanciest dressing table she'd ever seen, she strummed softly.

The tune she created was not joyful, not the kind of melody she'd imagined herself humming in these early-morning moments spent within the walls of the Bennett estate. The morning of Christmas Eve!

A melancholy refrain poured forth, capturing the emotions of this her first daybreak in the beautiful house. She entertained the same old nagging doubts, asking herself the question: Could there be someone else named Katie Lapp— another Amish girl about her age? But even as she pondered it, she hoped . . . and as Cousin Lydia would say, she *prayed* it wasn't true.

Laura had gone to Pennsylvania, had given a letter to the Wise Woman, Ella Mae Zook, who, in turn, had passed it along to Katherine's Amish mamma. Rebecca had been the one to tell her of Laura's terminal illness, that Mrs. Bennett was eager—before she died—to see her flesh-and-blood daughter face-to-face.

The notion occurred to Katherine that she must inquire as to Laura's health. Why hadn't she thought of it before? But, of course, what with all the commotion last night—being mistaken almost immediately for an applicant sent from an employment agency—there hadn't been a minute to ask.

Besides, Fulton and Rosie had seemed in a dither at the time, tending to their own personal duties and trying to determine, no doubt, why a woman carrying a guitar and a suitcase had appeared on their doorstep without going through the proper channels.

Should she just assume Laura was her natural mother? Should she also suppose that another young woman was posing as Katherine while calling herself Katie?

And why would someone go to the bother of dressing Plain, playing a role that belonged to another? Who would want to be Katie, an Amishwoman, when *Katherine Mayfield* was the name sewn into Laura's infant daughter's dress?

Baffled, she put away the guitar, eager to bathe and dress for the day. Eager for some straight answers.

❖ ❖ ❖

Laura dozed, satisfied that the daughter she had so longed to see again was alive. Not only alive but right here under her roof, consenting to remain through Christmas.

In the haze between sleep and wakefulness, the slightest twinge of disappointment pricked her. She recognized the struggle between her mind and her heart. The dream—what it would be like to finally meet her dear girl, imagining how she would look, what they would say to each other—all of it—had been altered in a single day.

She felt somewhat let down but assumed this experience was normal. After all, hadn't they enjoyed a delightful supper hour together? And the surprise dessert—something the newly hired help had created for the occasion. How delicious it had been!

The taste of the Amish dish still lingered in her memory as did the look of pleasure on Katie's face when the pie was served. Laura would never forget this evening with her beloved daughter, who was so quaintly dressed in her adorable Amish attire.

Yet it was the oddest thing—the young woman's Pennsylvania Dutch accent. If Laura was not mistaken, it sounded far different from the dialect of the Plain folk she'd met in Lancaster last month.

Something else troubled her, something she wished she could grasp more fully—the fact that Katie and she were far from bonding, even after having spent hours together. They simply had not clicked upon first meeting, as she had always believed they would.

She forced away the vague, elusive inclination, praying that her instincts were off. Perhaps the heavy medication was at fault. Yes. That was probably all there was to it.

Laura lay quite still, listening. Was it her imagination, or was someone playing a guitar in the predawn hours? She strained to hear more clearly, thankful that her ears were functioning better than her eyes.

Faintly, she was able to make out the sounds of a human voice—a woman's voice. Was it her daughter? Was *Katie* singing?

But, no, the sound was coming from the other wing of the house. The room over the kitchen. The domestic quarters upstairs. . . .

The haunting music surrounded her subconscious memory with distant recollections of a mother's soprano voice, clear and true.

How she missed the shrewd yet compassionate lady. And how wise she had been. Charlotte Mayfield had repeatedly warned her about Dylan Bennett, cautioned her while they were dating. "Your father, bless his soul, will turn over in his grave if you end up with that man," she'd said.

But young Laura, caught up in the romance, had argued repeatedly for his sweet, endearing ways. "Dylan is so handsome . . . so wonderful. He won't hurt me, Mother, not the way Katherine's father did. Dylan's a gentleman."

So she'd waited until her mother died, marrying Dylan Bennett against the woman's wishes. As for Laura's father, he'd adored her; she'd always known that. Had her parents lived to see this day, they would have thrown a lavish feast. Would have invited as many guests as the mansion could accommodate.

Instead, Laura felt isolated, alone with her joy. She experienced a pulsing void, wishing her parents were here to dote on Katie, to open arms wide to their only grandchild.

Dylan's hovering annoyed her. Why had he allowed her so little time alone with Katie? Perhaps that was the very reason she and her precious child had not been able to connect, neither emotionally nor spiritually.

At any other time, she wouldn't have reacted so negatively to Dylan's constant attention, but time was running out! Too, they were no longer the dearest of friends . . . or lovers. Hadn't been in years. Not in any sense of the word. Yet Dylan was pretending they were a couple. A loving husband and wife, welcoming home a cherished child.

She considered the strange situation. Why would he behave in such a way? Was it because he had been instrumental in locating Katie? Because he felt responsible for the reunion going well?

Feeling convicted, she prayed for a sweeter spirit. What if her husband was softening toward her? Attempting to make amends for his past misdeeds in these last days of her life?

Love can change a person, she'd told her mother one night when Charlotte had begun criticizing her fiancé. But the very things that had concerned her mother during the courtship had grown into insurmountable marital problems. Dylan had *not* changed for the better. On the contrary, he had become even more controlling.

Now, as she lay in her gleaming brass bed, the trappings of wealth and loveliness about her, she remembered Dylan's countenance as he observed her with Katie yesterday. Was it genuine compassion she had seen in his eyes? Or something else?

Anger welled up. This was the same man who'd tricked her into thinking she was barren, purposely denying her the children she'd always longed for. Repeatedly swindled her out of money, misrepresenting her separate accounts, forging her name on legal documents.

In spite of her husband's wicked ways, she had never considered turning him in to the authorities, or divorcing him, although the latter had crossed her mind on occasion.

"Love him to Jesus," Rosie had once said in a fervent prayer. Yes, she'd offered herself up for Dylan, had travailed in prayer on behalf of his salvation. Yet how difficult it was to extend unconditional love and acceptance to a man who'd so wronged her. To a man whose very life seemed driven by domination and deceit.

Had she not known the love of the heavenly Father, the grace of His Son, she wondered how she might've responded to Dylan all these years.

In sickness and in health. . . .

She had made her marriage vow to only one man. She intended to keep it.

Thankfully, the legal problems had been solved by her recent visit to Mr. Cranston's office. After much prayer, she felt justified in changing her will. Not out of revenge or hatred—it was simply expedient that she do so. This way she could die peacefully, knowing the estate would remain in the family.

Breathing deeply, she allowed the guitar music to soothe her as it came trickling down through ceiling vents, carrying her back to dreamland.

❖   ❖   ❖

Finished with her bath, Katherine brushed her hair, gazing into the large vanity mirror on the dressing table. She must wind her hair back up into a bun; it was required. Ach, the irony of having to look so plain again, having to wrap a netting around her beautiful curls while living in this fancy place. She touched her hair lovingly before proceeding with the bun and maid's cap.

She smiled cautiously for the gilded mirror, wondering what might be taking place back in Hickory Hollow today, what with Christmas Eve just hours away.

Were Dat, Eli, and Benjamin out gathering up fresh branches and pinecones for the house? Would Mam be decorating the wide windowsills in the front room with the greenery? And the work frolics . . . were the women congregating first at one house then another for hours of cookie baking?

She sighed, knowing this kind of contemplation could only cause her pain. Still, she couldn't resist the memory of Mary Stoltzfus. How was *she* getting along?

Katherine worried that her friend might think it rude

for her to have ignored the thoughtful Christmas greeting. But she knew better. Of all people, Mary most assuredly would understand. After all, there was a powerful-good reason for not sending a letter back to Hickory Hollow. The fear of causing trouble for Mary, on account of the shunning.

Forcing her thoughts back to the usual cheery atmosphere of a Lapp family Christmas, Katherine recalled playful, happy chatter, the brisk ice-skating parties on the pond out behind the house, and the *Grischkindlin* exchange with Samuel and Rebecca Lapp. Other folks brought gifts, too.

Her mind whirled and in that split second, a crush of emotions sent her spirits spiraling downward. But not for long. Wasn't she right where she wanted to be? Wasn't she glad to be finding out who Katherine Mayfield really was? Who she might've become had she grown up here in this elegant world?

No, nothing in Hickory Hollow could call her back now, nothing at all. The People had rejected and betrayed her. Her *own* family, the only family she'd known.

"Today I'm going to meet my real mamma," she whispered to the oval mirror, hoping it would be so.

Turning sideways, she surveyed her fancy apron and maid's cap. Done up under the netting, her beautiful new hairdo didn't show at all. Not a bit. Sighing, she hurried to make her bed and straighten up the room.

Just as she was preparing to head downstairs, the schedule for the domestic staff sailed under her door as Rosie had promised. Katherine gave the page a once-over and determined that the entire staff was obviously shorthanded over the next ten days, during the holidays. What luck! Or was it that heaven was truly smiling on her?

When it came time to serve either tea or the main meals of the day, she would offer her assistance in hopes of discovering the absolute truth about Laura Bennett's health.

❖ ❖ ❖

Breakfast was over at the Samuel Lapp home. Rebecca quietly cleared the dishes, rinsed, washed, and dried them, and listened in on her husband's conversation with Eli and Benjamin.

"What Jake Stoltzfus does is his business," Samuel told his sons.

"But what about gut land? Soon there ain't gonna be enough to go around here in Hickory Hollow," Benjamin pointed out.

Eli snorted. "What are you worried for? You'll never have to be thinkin' about such things as that."

Rebecca turned sharply to peer at her son's face. Eli, jealous? What an ugly thing it was, she fretted to herself. She was about to reprimand her twenty-six-year-old son but hadn't the chance, for Samuel spoke up first.

"Both you boys'll be getting married, probably, come next November. You'll be needing a place to farm with your wives and later to raise your families."

Eli and Ben were silent. Rebecca wasn't surprised, for it was their custom to keep all engagements secret till the second Sunday after fall communion, when the bishop announced those couples who planned to be married. The special event was called the "publishing" of couples. For her sons, the time was a good nine months off. Still, she knew why it was that Samuel was pushing them for answers.

"I'd hate to think of you headin' off to Indiana just 'cause Jake's thinkin' of going," Samuel continued.

Why were they talking like this? she wondered. Benjamin needn't worry about not having enough land to farm.

The youngest son usually ended up with his father's main house and the acres surrounding it. And Eli . . . surely Eli wouldn't wanna up and leave.

"Can't go divvying up the land, Dat." Eli shook his head. "Ben's gonna need every inch of your forty-five acres to keep things going here for you and Mam."

Rebecca noticed Samuel's concerned look. Her husband didn't say what she was sure he was thinking. That they'd be moving over to the *Dawdi Haus* come next fall, so Ben and his bride could settle in here at the main house. Time to be thinking about slowing down some, anyways. Especially since the strangest things had started going on with her here lately.

Samuel knew all about it. He'd caught her playing with the satin baby gown more than once—touching it and talking to it like a precious little infant was a-lying in her arms.

Made her go nearly berserk at times, teetering back and forth between thinking that the little dress—hidden away for her eyes only—was a soothing balm for her soul and, other times, wondering if it hadn't come straight from the pits of hell.

She dried her hands and left the room to go find it. Growing more and more dear to her every day that passed.

Her Katie . . . gone. Darling baby daughter of her life . . . shunned. Living out somewhere in the modern world, looking for someone else to call Mamma.

Well, it was more than she could bear. Missing Katie and longing for her company, her sweet voice, seeing her grow up Amish and then losing her near overnight to a complete stranger had been too awful much.

Once in the bedroom, Rebecca located the tiny satin garment. Inside her pillowcase. She'd been keeping it hidden there, away from Samuel's eyes.

She headed for her daughter's old room just down the

hall, where nothing ever changed. Things stayed exactly the same in Katie's bedroom. Her scant possessions, like her abandoned head coverings and choring clothes, comforted Rebecca. They reached out to her in her deep grief. She hadn't told Samuel just yet, but sometimes, when she held Katie's baby dress close, she could hear the real cries of an infant. . . .

How long she sat there, she didn't know, but when Benjamin hollered up to her, saying a group of women had just arrived to bake Christmas cookies, she near leaped out of the chair.

"Himmel," she muttered, rushing down the hallway to hers and Samuel's bedroom. There, overcome with frustration, she stuffed the little dress back into the pillowcase. How could she have forgotten about the holiday work frolic? Wiped the planned event clear out of her mind.

The womenfolk would wonder about it, all right. Call her *ferhoodled*, most likely.

She shuddered to think what Samuel might say. How on earth would she convince him *this* time that she was just fine?

Jah, fine and dandy she was . . . everything was wonderful-gut. No big thing.

Her face would wear the biggest smile she could muster. Her eyes would sparkle as she greeted her kinfolk and friends.

Still, there was no getting around it. She'd forgotten, but good.

❖ ❖ ❖

Nurse Judah calculated the morphine dosage and prepared the syringe, uneasy about this powerful narcotic to control Mrs. Bennett's pain. It was bad enough that the dear lady must endure the baclofen drug pump, implanted into the skin of her abdomen, dispersing a muscle relaxant directly into her system.

"How are you feeling this morning, ma'am?" she asked, helping Laura sit up in bed.

Her patient did not reply at first, so she waited, allowing Laura ample time to put on her dressing gown, with Rosie's help. "Oh, I'd give almost anything to be rid of this blurred vision," Mrs. Bennett said softly. "It's terribly annoying. . . ." She paused. "I disliked causing such a scene yesterday."

"Please don't be upset," Natalie assured her. "Your daughter is aware of your condition. I'm sure she understands."

Laura nodded. "It's just that I wouldn't want to frighten her away."

Natalie's heart went out to the frail lady. Mrs. Bennett's long-absent daughter had returned just in time for Christmas, and now the poor woman was scarcely able to see the girl, let alone deal with the horribly painful spasms and ever-weakening muscles.

Disappointment was evident in Laura's pale, distressed face. The flare-up had brought the initial visit with her daughter to an abrupt end.

Later, when the shot had taken effect, Natalie and Rosie helped bathe and dress the mistress of the house. Mrs. Bennett's fine motor coordination was rapidly deteriorating, and once again, Natalie could see the tenacious grip malignant MS held over its victims.

"Katie will be down for brunch," Laura mentioned, her eyes brightening a bit. "At least we'll have Christmas Eve together."

Natalie frowned. What was Mrs. Bennett thinking? She couldn't give in to her illness . . . not yet.

Vague as her perception was—Natalie couldn't actually put her finger on it—something wasn't quite right about yesterday's reunion. It just didn't add up.

For one thing, Dylan Bennett had hovered about; the man bothered her to no end. And Rosie had pointed out something else—Katie Lapp's hands.

One would presume that an Amishwoman's hands would be callused from gardening and washing dishes and doing laundry. Katie Lapp's hands, on the contrary, looked like a model's. Anything but the hands of a hardworking Plain woman.

"After today," she heard Laura say, "I don't care what happens. The hospital is certainly an option; I won't put up a fuss. But . . . today . . . I want this day with Katie, alone."

Rosie's eyes widened. "But you're going to have a wonderful holiday. I know you are."

Putting on a smile, Natalie agreed. "Wait'll you see what Selig and the others are planning for Christmas dinner."

"More . . . more of that coconut custard pie, I hope," said Mrs. Bennett.

Natalie smiled. Laura wasn't thinking in terms of dying, not with an appetite for dessert!

She made note of the morphine dosage on the medical chart and replaced it on the top shelf of the linen closet. She could only hope that the narcotic wouldn't begin to suppress respiration. But she was well aware of the vicious cycle, once it started.

"Where *did* Selig get that wonderful pie recipe?" Laura asked from her wheelchair.

The woman had turned to face Rosie now, Natalie observed, and from where she stood, it appeared that Mrs. Bennett was fairly comfortable. For the present, no sign of pain or spasms.

"The new housemaid could tell you," Rosie said. "*She's* the one who made it."

"Oh? A new m-maid? What her n-name?" Laura stumbled over the words.

"Katherine," said Rosie.

A pained expression crossed Laura's face and for a moment, Natalie thought the woman might cry. Rosie must've noticed it, too, for she diverted the subject quickly, calling attention to several small gifts under the twin trees in the sitting area.

But it was Natalie who kept thinking about Mrs. Bennett's apathetic attitude. She'd said she wouldn't make a fuss about going to the hospital. Seemed so out of character, too dispassionate for the mistress—yet a common psychological symptom of her disease.

This troubled Natalie greatly. The woman had just met her daughter—the only child she'd ever borne. And now she seemed ready to give up her fight? Was the illness taking over?

❖   ❖   ❖

After brunch, when the dishes and leftovers were cleared away, Katherine sat down at the table to fill out the required application form. Birth date, place of birth, social security number. Simple enough. Quickly, she wrote the information, secretly hoping someone—perhaps Laura Bennett herself—might have a look at it.

When it came to her signature, she paused and glanced at the top of the page, suddenly realizing she had written only "Katherine." No last name. No middle initial.

It would be dishonest to make up a name. Yet she could not risk losing her job or the chance to determine if Laura Bennett was truly her mamma. So she jotted down "Marshfield," middle initial "L"—for Lapp.

127

That done, she was promptly assigned to clean the Tiffany Room—to remake the guest bed, tidy up the bathroom, and lay out fresh linens.

When she knocked on the door, the woman who called herself Katie Lapp was absent from the room. Most likely downstairs with Mrs. Bennett, having a chat—and enjoying a cup of coffee or tea. Katherine would ask if she might help remove the tea service later.

For the present, she was tickled pink to have Katie's room all to herself. It would give her a chance to look around.

CHAPTER TWELVE

❖　❖　❖

Pausing to catch her breath, Mary Stoltzfus leaned against
the windowsill in the Lapps' front room, watching a fall of
heavy, wet snowflakes shower down from a thick gray sky.

How much more of this? she thought, for it had been
snowing now, days on end. The weather affected her mood,
though she wouldn't have complained about it for the
world. The land was in need of moisture for the crops, come
spring. The Good Lord knew all about that.

She moved away from the window, thinking of Katie.
How *was* she? Was she wishing she could write and answer
Mary's letter?

Knowing in her bones that Katie had likely struggled
over this very thing, Mary knew it wasn't prudent for her
friend to be corresponding with her in any way—not even
by postcard. Not because she didn't *want* to—but because
she'd be fearin' for what might happen to Mary if she *did*!

Thinking that way lifted Mary's spirits a little. But not
enough to join the crowd of women in the kitchen. She and
her mother and grandmother—along with a number of others in the community—had come to bake Christmas cookies
here at the Lapp house. For Mary, it was one of the first

times back at Katie's former home since the shunning decree.

She heard the chatter and laughter in the kitchen, and glancing back, decided there were so many of them, nobody'd even notice she was missing, probably.

She wondered if Katie might not be feeling the selfsame way today. Maybe even remembering long-ago Christmases spent in Hickory Hollow, speculating about what the People might be doing; whether or not they were thinking of her. After all, there were so many of them in the church district—a good two hundred and fifty-some folk. What did one lost sheep matter?

Did Katie ever think of Bishop John? Did she ever wonder if *he* missed her?

Well, if it had been up to her to respond outright to such a peculiar question, Mary would've had to say that the man did appear to be a bit downtrodden. Not completely defeated, mind you. But that sad look in his eyes, and the way he carried it around on his face everywhere he went, that's what gave his feelings away.

More than anything, she longed to ease the pain in those lovely gray eyes, erase the burden in his soul. John Beiler needed someone. So did his five little ones.

Ach, the thought of jumping into a ready-made family, large as it was, near scared her to death. But the power of love could change all that, she knew.

If only the bishop had an inkling how often she thought of him. If only he had the same feelings. . . .

The bishop was a man chosen to lead the People. What sort of woman would allow sentimental notions over a man of God? Especially a man still getting over being spurned on his wedding day.

Yet romantic whims cluttered her head all the same—spinning round and only halting when she made a conscious effort to make them stop.

❖   ❖   ❖

He deliberately bumped his feet together as he came into the kitchen, muttering to himself.

"What's-a-matter with Jacob?" his big sister asked.

The Beiler children gawked from their places around the long table, where they sat making Christmas cards for each other.

"Looks to me like he's got trouble walkin'," said eight-year-old Levi, the bishop's next-to-oldest son. "Didja lop off your toenails too short?" he asked his little brother, chuckling.

"Don't be making fun," warned Hickory John, the oldest. Then to Jacob, "Are ya hurt?"

Jacob glanced at Levi out of the corner of his eye. He wasn't no baby, but—"Jah, I am . . . I'm hurt clean down to my big toe."

Nancy motioned for him to come sit beside her on the wooden bench. "Let's have a peek at them wounded piggies."

Susie, age six and two years older'n him, started giggling.

"Keep your mind on your work," Nancy reminded her.

Jacob was awful glad for a big sister like Nancy. Maybe because she reminded him of his mamma. 'Course, he really didn't know, since he was too young to remember her when she died.

He felt his foot relax as Nancy unlaced his heavy shoes and pulled the left one off first. "Which hurts the most?"

He shook his head. "They *both* hurt, and now I can't walk much. And my heart's beating hard down there." He pointed at his bare foot.

Levi and Susie snickered, covering their mouths.

"S'not nice," Nancy reprimanded. "Think how you'd feel if someone made fun of *your* toenails!"

The children, Hickory John included, howled in a fit of

laughter, and they might've kept it up if their father hadn't spoken up just then.

"It's awful nice to hear my family makin' ready on Christmas Eve," he called to them from the utility room.

Jacob heard *Daed's* work boots drop to the floor, one at a time. "I chopped off my toes nearly," he hollered out to his father. "And Levi's tormentin' me."

"Tattletales go to hell," whispered Levi.

Nancy grabbed hold of his ears, covering them. But it was too late. He'd heard the wicked word. Levi had just said the word that meant the Bad Place—where the devil lived. T'wasn't no gettin' around it this time. Levi'd have to have his mouth washed out with soap. Served him right, too. He was always spouting off things that got him in trouble with Daed.

Just yesterday, Levi had gotten his behind swatted for saying the same word about Katie Lapp. That she would burn in that brimstone-hot place for getting shunned. For leaving Hickory Hollow.

'Course, Jacob had no idea what being shunned was all about. But since he'd never had a chance to say good-bye to the pretty redhead who liked to hum a lot—that happy-go-lucky lady who was gonna be his new mamma—since she'd just up and disappeared, well, he figured maybe Katie had gone down there where Levi said. After all, she'd run away on her wedding day, hadn't she? What kinda silly woman would do such a terrible, awful thing?

Most of 'em, Hickory John said, *wanted* to get married. Couldn't hardly wait to. Like that Mary Stoltzfus. He'd never heard *her* humming, but he thought she might be a nice wife for somebody. Thing was, she was plump as a dumplin'—a wonderful-gut sign, seemed to him. Besides that, Nancy and Hickory John were whispering something about Mary first thing this morning, before Daed called the family to prayer. Nancy said she heard Mary's cousin say that Katie's best friend was thinking of dropping by with some angel gingerbread and sour cream chocolate cookies. Comin' over here to bring treats for Christmas!

Well, if that be true, Jacob decided he'd be real nice to the round-faced girl. She might be feeling just as bad as he was about their Katie having to go down and live with the devil, probably.

❖ ❖ ❖

Dylan spent the morning going over several end-of-year financial records. When he was satisfied with his progress, he made an impromptu call to Laura's doctor, informing the man of Nurse Judah's suggestion that hospital arrangements be made should the need arise.

The conversation was brief. It was quickly decided that a private room would be available and waiting.

Around midmorning, Dylan was somewhat startled to receive an unexpected visitor. Rosie Taylor. "Do come in." He motioned her into his office.

"Are we quite alone?" She closed the door.

Dylan nodded. "What's on your mind?"

"Christmas Eve dinner, I suppose. I'm wondering how we might make it more comfortable for Mrs. Bennett." She paused for a moment, looking rather chagrined.

"Go on."

"Your wife has asked that she and Katie be allowed to dine alone . . . in her private suite, that is."

He picked up a pencil and twirled it between his fingers, suppressing the urge to chuckle. So the two of them were getting along famously, it appeared. "Not a problem," he replied. "Is Katie with Mrs. Bennett now?"

"She is."

"Very well. You'll see to it, then?"

"Consider it done." Then, before leaving, she posed an

interesting question. "Where is it you'll be taking *your* dinner, sir?"

He hadn't thought of it, really. But eating alone in the enormous dining room, elegant as it was, seemed out of the question. Not on Christmas Eve. This night was a time for family, for sharing one another's company, wasn't it?

If his wife chose to exclude him . . . well, he might just make other plans. He stood up and addressed the matter at hand. "If Mrs. Bennett prefers to dine *without* her husband . . . fine. I'll have the meal brought up to me."

"Here, in the office?"

"On second thought, perhaps I'll go *out* for dinner," he said, offering Rosie his most congenial smile.

He was almost certain this tidbit of information would throw Laura for a loop. Rosie would rush downstairs and report what he'd said about dining out . . . alone. And Laura would feel terribly guilty, excluding him this way; after all, her Christian conscience would not permit her to ignore a man who'd gone out of his way to bring a beloved daughter home for Christmas.

She'd come around. Most certainly, his wife would insist on inviting him to join their intimate soiree. Of this, he was soundly certain.

◈　◈　◈

She knelt on the floor, pondering whether to open the suitcase. Did she dare snoop? The thought poked at Katherine's conscience. 'Twas not the right thing to be doing—intruding on someone's personal privacy this way. And it was the last thing she would've done . . . under any other circumstance.

But knowing what she'd just discovered about Laura's illness—that the mistress was truly dying—how could she resist?

It was Garrett who'd told her. While they were in the kitchen earlier this morning. "Very ill," he'd replied to her question about Laura Bennett's health. "Nurse Judah has made preliminary plans at the hospital. It's that serious."

"You mean . . ."

"She's dying, yes. Mrs. Bennett, sad to say, may not see the light of New Year's Day."

The steward had been ever so kind to tell her, she thought. Gently he'd broken the news, as if shielding her, their newest staff member, from the grave situation.

And now here, before her, lay the Amish girl's suitcase. It seemed almost providential somehow. Carefully, she opened the lid.

One glance, and she discovered the most immodest clothing she'd ever seen. Yet the skimpy garments couldn't really be classified as clothing, could they? The red sheer top and scant underpants were the farthest thing from any nightwear *she'd* ever worn. Still, she held the silky things, unable to put them down, her eyes searching the suitcase for more evidence.

When she spotted additional non-Amish attire, she felt decidedly uneasy. Nervously, she rearranged the items just as she'd found them, then closed the suitcase and went about cleaning the room.

She'd heard of Amish teenagers purchasing fancy underwear, sometimes even English clothes to wear when they were in town on weekends. That type of thing happened usually only during the *Rumspringa*—"running around" years—when strict Amish parents seemed to look the other way, letting their young people have a taste of the modern world.

But this woman, *this* Katie Lapp, was long past all that. Of course, Katherine would know for sure if she caught a glimpse of the woman, or if she could see for herself if Katie wore a cap. If so, that would mean the young woman had indeed been baptized into the Amish church and had no business hiding such fancy, wicked things!

Katherine was soon back downstairs, offering to help clear off the mistress's dishes. "The guest room is finished," she told Rosie, "and I have a little extra time now."

"Very well, but take care not to interrupt Mrs. Bennett's conversation with her daughter."

"I'll be quiet." *Quiet as a field mouse*, she thought. And her heart leaped up as she scurried down the hallway toward the suite, following Rosie's directions.

Oh, to see my birth Mam face-to-face! she thought. *What a wonderful-good Christmas present that would be.*

But someone's voice intruded on her thoughts. Someone calling, "Excuse me!"

She turned to see Fulton, the butler, running down the steps. "Yes, sir?"

"Are you busy at the moment?" Whatever he needed seemed terribly urgent.

"I . . . I s'pose I'm not." She said it reluctantly, right away hoping the words hadn't come across as grouchy.

"Good. Then come with me."

Katherine obeyed, casting aside her dearest wish in response to Fulton's request. She followed him to the kitchen, her mind whirling.

So close, she thought. *Ach, so very close!*

❖   ❖   ❖

Dan prayed silently as he sent a fax to the Lancaster County Court House. Although he'd decided to check the public record as to requests for marriage licenses over the past five and a half years, his conscience pricked him like nettles.

Within the hour he had the information he needed. The only thing lacking was the street address where his sister Annie now lived with her husband, Samuel Lapp's eldest son, Elam—a fellow he'd run buggy races with years ago. They'd attended farm auctions, often playing vigorous games of corner ball with other Amish teens. And there were those too-serious games of baseball during recess at the one-room schoolhouse.

So . . . Elam Lapp had ended up with his sister. He shouldn't have been surprised, really. Katie's big brother had always taken a shine to Annie. From the earliest days, he'd watched them play together at picnics and barn raisings—and, later, make eyes at each other at the Singings.

Turning off the computer, he dismissed glowing memories of Christmas in Lancaster County.

And of Katie.

❧ ❧ ❧

By lunchtime, the women had made thirty dozen cookies. Rebecca apologized over and over for having other things on her mind. For completely drawing a blank about the morning's plans.

"It's understandable," said Ella Mae Zook. "You've been through a painful time, Rebecca."

"We *all* have," Mary Stoltzfus remarked. "Losing someone you love is the hardest thing in the world."

Annie Lapp nodded solemnly, buttoning her wrap.

Rebecca followed her daughter-in-law to the back door. "Must ya go already?"

"Jah, Elam's baby-sittin' little Daniel, and he'll be more than ready for me to take over, for sure." She clucked, her eyes twinkling. "You know how awkward Elam is with infants."

Rebecca nodded. She'd seen her son trying to burp the new baby. "We'll look forward to seein' ya tomorrow noon, for Christmas dinner, then."

"I'll bring the pies." Annie leaned over to kiss Rebecca good-bye. "Anything else?"

"Got everything pretty near under control, denki."

"Gut, then. Merry Christmas, Mam." Annie turned to go.

Glancing out the kitchen window, Rebecca watched as Annie and the other women made their way to the parked carriages. Thankfully, Samuel and Eli were busy with the womenfolk's driving horses, bringing them back one at a time from the barn where the animals had been watered and fed.

Rebecca turned to face the Wise Woman at last. "Painful's not the only thing about this situation with my wayward daughter," she said, waving her hand distractedly. "I've near lost my mind over my shunned girl."

Ella Mae came and wrapped her arms around her, and for one of the first times since Katie had fled Hickory Hollow, Rebecca felt free to pour out her woes, sobbing as she did.

When she was through, she blew her nose and sniffled a bit. The elderly aunt just sat quietly, as if waiting for Rebecca to pull herself together. "There's been lots better Christmases than this," Rebecca blurted.

"And there'll be lots worse, probably."

"Can't see how that could be," she mumbled into her hankie.

"None of us do, really, I 'speck. It's mighty hard trying to see anywheres past our noses when it comes to problems, but 'this too shall pass.' Remember that, Rebecca. Ain't nothin' put on ya more than you can bear. The Good Lord said so."

She nodded in agreement but scarcely believed a word of it. Aunt Ella Mae had never gone through suffering as miserable as having a daughter shunned. Never.

"I've thought of going over to Lydia's for a visit, since

it's Christmas and all," she found herself saying.

"Wouldn't recommend it, Rebecca. Doubt the bishop would, neither."

Rebecca was going to be honest even though it could turn around and get her shunned if she wasn't careful. "No, but I can't help thinkin' I'd sure like to see my girl one more time, at least. Not talk to her—just gaze on her."

"I know you would, and I'd go with you if ya thought it might look better . . . less suspicious," Ella Mae offered.

"You'd *do* that? You'd come with me?"

"Ain't got too many years left on this here earth. S'posin' I can take a risk . . . if *you* can."

Rebecca allowed the old woman to hug her once again.

So it was settled. She'd hitch up Ol' Molasses this very afternoon and drive on down the lane to see Lydia Miller . . . and whoever else was home.

CHAPTER THIRTEEN

❖ ❖ ❖

Katherine felt awkward about eavesdropping on the kitchen conversation, but she rolled out the pie dough, listening anyway.

"Mrs. Bennett has requested a portrait be made of herself and her daughter," Garrett remarked to Rosie. "A special Christmas and welcome-home gift all wrapped up in one. A splendid idea, don't you think?"

"Well, that all depends. The mistress may not be up to posing for it today. She's had to rest . . . had to postpone her visit with Katie, even."

"Is that so?" Garrett seemed surprised. "Then what of the portrait?"

"Couldn't say. All I know is she's retired for the afternoon and is skipping tea in hopes of feeling a little stronger tonight."

"Poor thing," the steward muttered. "And we had all hoped that seeing her daughter again would be just what she needed to turn the corner."

"What she *needs*," declared Rosie, "is a miracle!"

So do I, thought Katherine, her chest tightening. Oh, she just had to see her real mamma before something dreadful happened.

What if she dies tonight? What if I never get the chance to tell her who I am? She resisted the horrid thought and those that followed. How frustrating, how painful, to miss out on getting to know Laura Bennett, the woman she was sure was her mother.

Waiting until talk of the oil painting had diminished some, Katherine inquired about her application form. "Has Fulton decided anything permanent about me yet?"

Rosie smiled. "He's upstairs just now. But you should be getting your formal acceptance any moment, I would think."

"I'd be most grateful," she murmured and resumed her work, filling the pie. As she did, her thoughts took wings, and she saw in her mind's eye a little girl, pulling a chair across the kitchen floor to the countertop. The youngster crawled up on the chair and stood tall as she could, watching her mamma make pies. With great interest she remained there until Rebecca asked if she wanted to help pinch the crust down around the edges. Of course she wanted to. And she had. She'd done a right fine job of it, too, her Amish mamma had said.

Katherine stared up at a row of gleaming copper pots hanging from the massive hood over the gas range. What was Rebecca doing today? Was she entertaining the womenfolk . . . making pies?

She wished she'd quit thinking about Hickory Hollow so much. *This* was her home now. This beautiful, fancy place.

❖   ❖   ❖

Fulton Taylor, a man of few words, rang the bell, summoning his wife. Rosie arrived swiftly, somewhat out of breath, he noticed.

When they were alone, he showed her Katherine's application. "What do you make of it?"

Rosie took the sheet from him and followed his pointed finger as he read the name out loud. "Katherine Marshfield. Seems a bit odd, don't you think?"

"Hmm, Marshfield. It does seem rather strange."

"Who *is* this new maid we've brought into the house . . . so close to Christmas?"

Rosie shook her head. "I don't know, Fulton. But there's something peculiar about her. That is, something about her that reminds me of someone."

"You may be right." He nodded thoughtfully. "Though who it could be escapes me. . . ."

Rosie jumped in. "Just this morning, Nurse Judah mentioned how unusual it was that the new maid's last name so nearly resembles the mistress's maiden name—*Mayfield*."

"The name is one thing . . . but the birth date . . . quite another."

"What do you mean?" Rosie peered at the application, getting her nose down close to the paper. "Dear me, I need my reading glasses. Can't see much of anything without them."

He rattled off Katherine Marshfield's date of birth. Then—"What do you remember of Mrs. Bennett's journal? Didn't you record some entries for her a while back?"

"Only when she was feeling her worst. On three separate occasions, I believe."

"And wasn't there a place in the journal for important dates?" he asked, feeling edgy now. "I rather remember your mentioning it."

"Yes . . . why, yes! June fifth is a most important date in Mrs. Bennett's book. I noticed it in all three entries. Her baby daughter was born that day."

His wife's face flushed with color, and he watched as she rushed to the desk drawer. Still holding the application, he waited for her to locate her bifocals.

Rosie hurried back to his side to study the page. Her

forehead creased with deep lines as she read. "It looks like
. . . can it be? Katherine Marshfield's birthday is the same as
Katie Lapp's!"

They were silent, staring at one another, mouths agape.

It was Rosie who spoke first. "The Amishwoman doesn't
look the least bit like Mrs. Bennett—not at all. The thought
struck me straightaway."

"Both are redheads," he observed.

"But nothing close to the same color."

He went to sit on their double bed, saying no more.

Rosie hovered near. "Something smells rotten to me. I
intend to investigate. Are you in?"

"It may be best to wait," he suggested calmly. "Let things
play themselves out . . . without interference from us."

Rosie squinted at the application once again, shaking her
head before removing her glasses. "Why not push for
answers? Today . . . before the artist comes to paint the
Christmas portrait."

He folded the application in half and placed it inside his
white butler's jacket. "Keep your eyes and ears open, Rosie.
But say nothing at all, do you hear?"

His wife grinned back at him. "Yes, sir." She saluted him
comically.

"Very well, then." And he was off like a drum major to
oversee supper preparations.

❖   ❖   ❖

Lydia Miller was quite astonished to find Rebecca Lapp
and the woman's great-aunt standing on her back steps.
"Welcome," she said, opening the door wide.

"Merry Christmas, Lydia!" they called out in unison.

"And a Merry Christmas to you," she replied, showing
them in.

Once their wraps were off and they'd gotten themselves

143

settled in her living room, Lydia offered her visitors something warm to drink. "Hot chocolate, maybe?"

"Tea for me, please," said Ella Mae.

"Hot cocoa would be nice," replied Rebecca.

Scurrying off to the kitchen, Lydia wondered what was on their minds. Goodness' sake, it was Christmas Eve, or at least would be in a matter of hours. And the cold . . . the ladies had braved the harshest winds and dropping temperatures to make this trip.

"It's been such a long time since we've come," Rebecca commented when Lydia was back from the kitchen.

Lydia sat down in an overstuffed chair. "What's kept you away?" She felt suddenly awkward. Shouldn't have said it that way, probably.

She noticed Rebecca's sidelong glance at Ella Mae and realized that Katie's mamma must've caught the message. "Oh, I didn't mean to say anything hurtful, not at all," Lydia spoke up quickly.

"You're an awful kind woman to take my girl in like this." The words seemed to stumble out of Rebecca's mouth. "I couldn't have hoped for a better place . . . not if I'd planned it myself."

Lydia couldn't be sure, but she thought the woman's lips trembled. "Peter and I . . . we were happy to do it. Glad to help Katie out . . . anytime."

She could've said more, much more. Could've asked why they'd shunned the young woman so harshly, not allowing the People to speak to her. But she kept her lips shut. This was none of her business. What the Amish did in the Hollow was not her concern.

Now Rebecca seemed to be fidgeting, looking about the room with anxious eyes. Was she searching for Katie? Was this the reason for the visit?

Lydia's heart ached with the desperate situation at hand. Should she say anything? she wondered. Should she break the disappointing news to her poor, dear cousin that Katie was already off to New York?

When the water was hot enough, she excused herself and went to the kitchen. What would the Lord have her do or say to Rebecca?

It was very nearly a prayer, her thought was. More than anything, she wanted to lift the dejected woman's spirits. Set her heart free of worry, free of care. If the Amish allowed part-singing, now would be a good time to burst forth with hymns of praise, thanking the Creator God for His tender mercies over the lives of His children. She thought of such a hymn and hummed it silently.

Soon the hot drinks were ready. She found her favorite hand-painted serving tray—so nice and sturdy it was—and placed three cups on it. "A little something to warm you," she said, heading back into the living room.

She served them, yet prayed without speaking, asking the Lord for wisdom and guidance while her Amish relatives sipped hot cocoa and tea here in her house. Here, without their dear Katie near. On a quiet Christmas Eve afternoon.

Rebecca felt the heat seep through her ceramic mug—not plastic as were her cups at home. Was Katie also enjoying the fine and fancy things here at Cousin Lydia's?

Gazing around the room, she realized that her wayward daughter had for sure and for certain gotten a taste of the English lifestyle. She noticed the wall-to-wall carpeting, the comfortable sofa and chairs, even an overstuffed footrest, of all things! And there was the electric lighting, with a right fancy glass lamp next to her on a round wooden table—something Peter had made with his own hands, probably.

Framed family photographs and paintings decorated the walls, and, ach, those worldly floral drapes at the windows. . . .

'Twasn't the first time she'd laid eyes on Lydia's frills and

things. Shameful, these Mennonites . . . branches off the
original Swiss Anabaptist faith. Too bad they hadn't followed Jacob Ammann's teaching back in the late 1600s and
"stayed in Jesus." Too bad they'd gone and let electricity and
cars corrupt their lives.

Nevertheless, her Katie had run to this Mennonite home.
She'd come here and rented a room, told her mamma all
about it before ever leaving the Amish farmhouse. Yet being
the obedient woman she was, Rebecca had heeded the stern
shunning decree given by Bishop John—harshest one she'd
known in all these parts. Only other place she'd heard of not
being allowed to talk to a shunned party was somewhere out
in Ohio.

"I suppose you want to know how Katie, er . . . Katherine is doing," Lydia said out of the blue.

Because she had been ordered by Samuel not to speak
their daughter's name, Rebecca thought most carefully how
she should answer. Oh, how desperately she wanted to talk
about her daughter. To know how she was doing here. She
felt as if something were filling her up, wanting to spill out
of her, something starving deep within. "It would be awful
nice to know, jah," she answered. "Is she well?"

"To tell the truth, Katherine's had the hardest time dealing with her pain, but having the guitar did help her out
quite a bit, I think," Lydia remarked. "Singing is good for
the soul."

"Oh" was all Rebecca could say. Sounded like an insult
to her, and she hoped Lydia wasn't going to dicker over doc-
trinal differences. Now wasn't the time.

Lydia continued. "Katie's gone, left yesterday—headed
up north to find her natural mother, but you probably figured that was gonna happen sooner or later."

"Jah, I did." She looked down, shaking slightly, and welcomed Ella Mae's gnarled hand on hers. The warm and
tender touch reassured her, let her know that someone

146

cared. Someone wise and old loved her in spite of the actions of her headstrong daughter.

"I believe your Katie will be all right," offered Lydia, coming over to stand beside her. "Peter and I have been praying. So are many others. God cares for His own."

Rebecca nodded. She wouldn't let on to a Mennonite that the Lord God heavenly Father was listening in on *her* prayers more than He'd ever have time for Lydia's. Reason being, the Millers and their church friends and relatives had left the faith of their fathers. How on earth did they expect God almighty to hear and answer prayers from the lips of unrepentant souls?

"Well, I hope ya have a nice Christmas with your family." She forced a smile for her cousin.

What she really wondered was how Katie would manage, off in some strange place for the holidays. 'Course, she said nothing of the kind, didn't even ask to be reminded of the exact city the girl was headed to. Wasn't any of Lydia's business how or what she was thinking concerning her daughter most nearly every hour of the day . . . and night.

"Will Elam and Annie be having Christmas dinner at your place?" she heard Lydia ask.

"Jah, they'll be spending all day tomorrow with us— baby Daniel, too." She turned to the Wise Woman, just then realizing that Ella Mae had said not a word the entire visit.

The old woman let out a gargled sigh and smiled. "Better hope for clear weather so's everyone can get to where they wanna go."

Rebecca noticed the snow was still coming down awful heavy, and she placed her mug and spoon on the coffee table in front of her. "Looks to me like we'd best be headin' on home."

"Do keep in touch," Lydia said. "And don't wait so long between visits."

Rebecca helped Ella Mae up out of the cushiony seat.

The elderly woman stood tall, not without several squeaky grunts, however. Then waiting for her aunt to stand in one place for a moment, regaining her equilibrium, no doubt, she offered her arm. The last thing she wanted was for Ella Mae to fall and break another hip. Not at her advanced age. Not on Christmas Eve.

"Are you ready?" she asked the Wise Woman.

Lifting a finger, Ella Mae paused a moment before speaking. A strange film came over her eyes. "The Lord blesses those who bless Him—and you, Lydia Miller, have taken a young one into your care." Then she quoted from the Scriptures in her husky little voice. " 'Inasmuch as ye have done it unto one of the least of these my brethren, ye have done it unto me.' "

The verse pricked Rebecca's heart. Like sharp stones stuck inside an old work shoe, they stung her.

CHAPTER FOURTEEN

❖   ❖   ❖

It was Rosie who first noticed the backs of Katie Lapp's hands. She had just wheeled Mrs. Bennett into the sitting room, where appetizers were soon to be served. Surprised that Katie had not so much as turned to acknowledge her mother's arrival, she went over to where the woman was standing before one of the tiny Christmas trees. "Your mother's feeling some better since she rested."

Katie did not respond. Holding one of the lavishly wrapped presents, she seemed lost in thought.

As Rosie rescued one of the delicate tree decorations dangling from a low-lying branch, she got a closer look at the young woman's hands. *Odd*, she thought. They appeared to be terribly rough and raw, where just this morning they had been white and smooth as silk. One of them was bleeding slightly—on the middle knuckle.

"Miss Lapp?" said Rosie.

"Oh, uh . . . I'm sorry. Must've been daydreaming." Katie seemed startled. "Did you say something?"

"Well, I noticed the cut on your hand and thought to offer you some salve. Nurse Judah must surely have some around here."

"Oh, it's nothing," Katie said, her face showing more

awareness now. "Rough hands come from doing chores all day long. You can imagine."

Rosie didn't believe her, not for one second. Nary a flaw had she seen on the woman's hands earlier.

"Don't the Amish have *any* modern conveniences?" she asked.

Katie smiled, showing perfectly straight white teeth. Almost too white, too perfect. "Nothing to write home about."

"Excuse me?" Rosie said, glancing at Mrs. Bennett who seemed content enough to sit where she could admire her daughter. Thankfully, the mistress was too far away to catch their whispered conversation.

"I'd rather not talk about my life with the Amish," Katie said abruptly.

The response took Rosie aback. Lowering her voice again she went on. "Are things going well for you in the Amish community?"

"Good as can be expected" came the reply. "But I'm here to spend time with my mother. At least for now."

Rosie nodded. "Yes . . . yes. Your mother." She turned and paused to glimpse the lovely, frail lady in the wheelchair situated near the mahogany mantel.

Almost unconsciously, she began to compare the two women—the set of their eyes and the color of their hair—as Katie made her way across the room to Mrs. Bennett. Without being conspicuous, Rosie studied the young woman who still seemed rather muddled. Or was it something else . . . reluctance to join them, perhaps?

The more she observed, the more she wondered if it was possible Mrs. Bennett's daughter resembled her natural father instead of the mistress.

She dismissed the idea as ridiculous. Anyone could see that Katie Lapp was not the mistress's daughter. Had not a single physical trait in common. Saddest of all, Mrs. Bennett

150

might never see the truth for herself. Not the way her eyes seemed to be failing a little more each day. Nor the way she'd freely consented to hospital admittance . . . whenever the time came.

The young Amishwoman had not a speck of Laura Bennett in her! Not her gentle spirit, her sweet ways . . . not a bit of it.

Rosie wanted to announce a prayer meeting on the spot, wanted to call down the heavens. Poor Mrs. Bennett would need the Good Lord's help for the days ahead—not only to come to grips with her dying but to deal with something far worse. The fact that an impostor, in the form of a quaint Amish girl, was living right here in her own house!

But who was to reveal the deceit, get to the bottom of things? My, oh my, how would the bitter truth affect the dear missus herself?

❖   ❖   ❖

Dylan noticed her immediately upon entering the parlor area of Laura's suite. She very nearly blended in with the Christmas trees on either side of her. Would have, too, had she not been wearing that frumpy black apron over her long green dress. *Amish green* the seamstress had aptly described the fabric wrapped around the long bolt at the fabric shop.

He noticed, too, her slumped stance . . . the droopy face. Was she missing Christmas with her boyfriend?

He wanted her to stand erect, to behave as if she were enjoying herself. Excellent posture and a pleasant facial expression went a long way toward playing a convincing role. She was being paid well enough!

"It's nearly Christmas Eve, isn't it?" he announced, fingering the lapels of his suit coat. The question was rhetorical—mindless small talk—primarily for Laura's benefit.

Perhaps she would feel a stab of guilt for not including him at her party and relent.

He was well aware of her lovely attire. She was dressed to the nines for an evening of exquisite dining and intimate conversation with "Katie," the clever actress otherwise known as Alyson Cairns. Had Laura had a change of heart about wanting him seated at her table?

The actress strutted over and sat down across the sofa from him, casting occasional shy glances around the festive room. Those innocent expressions seemed only to emerge when either Rosie or Laura spoke to her, he noticed. The sensual parting of her full lips and those smoldering eyes— they were for him. Embarrassing, though it was.

What was going through her mind? he wondered. Certainly not the task at hand—portraying herself as an innocent Amishwoman . . . Laura's daughter. He frowned, hoping she was not discouraged with her role.

Had it not been for the fact that the hired model was wearing the homespun getup he'd acquired from the best seamstresses in town, she might've been any young college student.

For a moment, he recalled Laura in her prime—before the disease had left her gaunt and hollow eyed, a shadow of the vibrant beauty she'd been.

Several times he caught "Katie" looking back at him as he attempted a lively conversation with Laura, juggling the frequent asides with Rosie and now Nurse Judah, who had come in from the hallway to join the group.

It struck him that Laura seemed fidgety. Had she been adequately medicated? This was not a good time to risk a lighter dose, what with those horrid tremors and contractures erupting seemingly out of nowhere. Perhaps he should have a word with Natalie.

He was about to motion the nurse to join him in the hall when Rosie spoke up. "We'll be having the appetizers served here in a few minutes, sir." She eyed Dylan with dark, probing eyes, growing even darker as she stared pointedly.

So that's how they're going to play this, he thought, pulling his gaze away from Rosie and purposely concentrating on Laura.

He waited.

But her eyes remained fixed on her lap, more precisely, her hands. Yet he continued to regard her. Would she speak up—invite him at the last minute? Now was her chance if ever there was to be one. She could show her true colors, display her undying devotion to the man who'd brought her Amish daughter home to her.

The waiting turned awkward; an annoyingly empty space of time ensued, one devoid of a response.

So be it. She'd dug her grave . . . let her lie in it. This he thought without remorse.

"Do have a wonderful evening, all of you." His words slipped out, smooth and measured. He dared not look at "Katie" now. Neither Katie nor Laura.

His wife desired an evening alone with her daughter, and he presumed to know the reason. For questioning, no doubt. For gaining an understanding of Amish life and its peculiar customs. For catching up on all she'd missed through the years.

He almost sneered as he contemplated it. Thankfully, he'd already anticipated the cozy scene between mother and daughter. And Katie Lapp—model and actress—had been well rehearsed for just such a quiet evening alone with Laura. He had been over this business—what to say . . . how to respond—a million and one times with her.

Tonight was the night. With or without him at the table, his wife's supposed daughter was on the verge of pulling the entire woolen cloak over the eyes of the soon-to-be-deceased mistress of the Bennett estate. Conning her way into Laura's good graces, she would inherit Katherine's birthright, which would, in due time, be transferred to Dylan's own hefty accounts.

He could scarcely wait for a report of the evening. A play-by-play would be most entertaining, indeed. He stood and excused himself. Then, planting a guileless grin on his face, he went around the wheelchair, leaned over, and gave Laura a tender kiss on her cheek.

Not exactly a victory kiss, he thought. Oh, but very close. *That* kiss would be forthcoming.

"Good night, my darling," he crooned. "Have a marvelous evening . . . both of you."

"Thank you" was all she said. Her manners were intact, obviously. Yet he knew without a doubt that she was most eager to get on with becoming better acquainted with Katie. Was ready for him to be gone, on his way.

Irritated, he rushed up to his office and rang for a chauffeur. He'd misjudged the final outcome of the evening entirely. Thought he had Laura figured out better than this. "Fulton," he thundered into the intercom, "have Theodore bring a car around to the front."

"Theodore's busy presently, sir."

"Oh?"

"I believe he's en route with Mrs. Bennett's commissioned artist—a Mr. Justin Wirth."

"Yes, yes, I know of him." He was now feeling annoyed at Fulton, of all things. One delay after another.

Justin Wirth, indeed. His sickly wife was certainly cunning when she wanted to be.

"Shall I page Rochester for you, sir?" asked Fulton.

"Rochester will do." The new driver was rather young. Not his first choice on any given day.

Intent on getting out for the evening, Dylan was rather looking forward to a fine dinner and a few drinks. Heaven knows he needed a diversion.

Looking out over the grounds, he watched the snow as

it fell. Heavier now and falling fast. Would it never let up? Just as well. There'd be no arguing with Alyson over staying on for Christmas if she was snowed in. Boyfriend or no.

Laura's "heir" would have no recourse but to fulfill her contractual agreement. In short, play the part to the finish.

❂   ❂   ❂

Besides wanting to figure out a way to get herself into Laura's private suite, Katherine was eager to lay eyes on Katie Lapp. She knew, from recent experience, that she wouldn't sleep a wink tonight if she didn't get herself some answers. At least a sensible explanation to set her mind at ease.

Therefore, she must determine if the Katie woman strolling the corridors of this house wore the Amish devotional cap. Finding out for sure had become an obsession as she spent her day working in the kitchen, assisting in dining room preparations for the feast, and, in general, filling in wherever Garrett or Fulton needed help.

An unexpected turn of events came early in the evening when Selig asked for help shaping and rolling the hors d'oeuvres. "I'll need someone to take this platter to Mrs. Bennett's sitting room shortly." He looked right at her. "Katherine?"

When she realized he was addressing her, she replied, "Me? You want *me* to take the appetizers to the mistress?"

Selig nodded. "They're hors d'oeuvres, Katherine."

"Yes . . . I know." Out of the corner of her eye, she noticed one of the housemaids coming out of the pantry. Rosie Taylor. The woman wore a most suspicious smile on her face and tossed a conniving glance at Selig as she bustled into the kitchen.

Putting two and two together, Katherine felt just as she had the first time the wind had caught hold of her covering, making it stand straight out behind her little-girl head. Tendrils of loose hair had tickled her face that day. She was *schtruwwlich*, for sure and for certain. But never mind her unkempt hair; she had experienced total exhilaration.

She felt the selfsame way now. Her Christmas Eve wish might be coming true after all. Katherine Mayfield, fancy English girl at heart, was about to lay eyes on her one true mamma.

Glory be!

CHAPTER FIFTEEN

❖ ❖ ❖

The smell of fresh pine was heavy in the air as she carried the silver tray down the marble hall. Her heart pounded so hard she thought it might lift the ruffle right off her maid's pinafore apron.

Ach, she hoped her hair was in place, lipstick on straight. How many times had she imagined this moment? Too many to count.

And the dream last night, that unrelenting nightmare. . . . She must've dreamed it half a dozen times.

Always, she was on the wrong side of an enormous door. That door, how it towered above her. Yet she could hear the sound of Laura's voice behind it, inviting her, nay, *pleading* for Katherine to come inside.

The door represented a blockade, as honest-to-goodness real as any she'd suffered in life. Yet the vision had persisted, its message one of despair. She had been kept from her real mamma by a door—a door of secrecy, a door of deceit.

She shivered, thinking of the lengths her Amish parents had taken to hide the satin baby gown . . . to keep the secret hidden all the years of her life.

Now . . . *now* she stood before a pair of wide French doors. Glass, with lovely rounded transoms overhead. Just inside, four women sat around a roaring fire, two of them with their backs to her, talking softly. A nurse, a maid—Rosie—a young Amishwoman, apparently, and a patient in a wheelchair . . .

A sob caught in her throat. The woman in the wheelchair—was it Laura Bennett? How could it be that she looked so young and so very ill at the same time?

It was Laura's hair that captured her attention. Caught it and pulled her gaze so intensely she found herself longing to touch it. What of the texture? Richly auburn in color, yet was it thick—so heavy at times the tresses weighed heavily on her scalp?

The woman's profile seized her as well. She couldn't take her eyes off the fine nose, the delicate chin line.

So many similarities. . . . Why hadn't anyone noticed?

Katherine tried desperately to control the joyful tears that threatened to spoil her view of the gathering. It was all she could do to keep the floodgate in check. But she knew if she gave in to one little drop, there'd be more tears than a body could count.

Taking a deep breath and refusing to cry, she gradually regained her composure. She did it partly by turning her scrutiny away from the mistress and concentrating hard on the youngest woman of the group—the one wearing the Amish dress and unusual cap—the strangest getup she'd ever seen. Was this the woman who called herself Katie Lapp?

She wanted to step in closer, see if the clothes might be similar to the ones worn by other church districts in Lancaster. Then she remembered she was supposed to be serving appetizers, not gawking at strangers, for pity's sake!

Overcome with rapture at seeing Laura even from this distance—the gladness all mixed up with apprehension—she was stopped suddenly by a slight commotion. The Amishwoman had gotten up out of her chair and was hurrying over in Katherine's direction. The young woman looked frantic, as if, for all the world, she needed some air.

Pushing past her at the threshold, Katie Lapp nearly knocked the tray out of Katherine's hands. "Excuse me" came the muttered words.

Katherine peered over her shoulder, wondering what was going on. Had someone said something to upset her? "Are you all right?" Katherine asked, turning to inquire.

"Just feeling a bit . . . uh . . . oh, I don't know. It's getting too hot in there—so close to the fire."

Strange, she thought, *no one else is complaining.* In fact, when Katherine glanced back at the cozy threesome remaining—Laura Bennett snugly wrapped in an afghan—there was no evidence to suggest any of the other women were suffering from the heat.

"Are you *sure* you're too warm?" she pressed.

The woman seemed to force a smile. "Maybe more lonely than anything."

"Lonely?"

"You know, homesick. For my family. We Amish are very close-knit."

Katherine was caught off guard. She understood that feeling, all right. The woman looked so absolutely miserable. "Is there something I can do for you?"

"No, there's nothing anyone can do. But it would be wonderful to get my hands on a phone somewhere." Her eyes lit up as she spoke. "That would be real nice."

Katherine's ears perked up. The Amish didn't use phones for the sake of carrying on a conversation or visiting. They got in their carriages and went off to see their friends and relatives. The bishops liked it that way—kept church members more closely connected.

She was about to explain but caught herself. Shouldn't be letting on what she knew about Plain life. Wouldn't be right smart.

"There are plenty of telephones in the house," Katherine found herself saying instead.

"Oh, I know. It's just that . . ." Obviously frustrated, Katie flung her arms wide, bumping the tray. Quickly, the women righted it.

"Here, let me take this for you," the young woman offered, "since I ought to get back in there anyway."

"Oh no, it's my job." While still holding the tray, Katherine got a closer look at the woman's dress. It *buttoned* down the front, of all things. Lancaster Amish used hooks and eyes, sometimes straight pins, but never, ever *buttons*!

Then, somewhere between supposing and knowing, she got a bright idea. Squinting out at the thick snow flurries, she said, *"Des is bidder kalt haus."*

Katie looked at her with a wary expression in her eyes. "What did you say?"

"I'm sorry, I thought you spoke Dutch," Katherine replied, her heart in her throat.

Katie mustered up a feeble "I used to."

"Well, then?" Katherine realized she was in way over her head, as Dat would always say.

For the longest time, Katie stared at her. "My family hasn't spoken Dutch in years," she scoffed. "We ain't Old Order anymore."

"Oh? What *are* you, then?" Katherine insisted, thinking she'd rather be asking, *"Who* are you?"

Without warning, the young woman lunged for the appetizer tray, and without a backward glance, marched into the sitting room.

Katherine stood there aghast—angry, too—unable to comprehend what had just taken place. But one thing she understood, for sure and for certain. This Katie Lapp was no more Amish than the man in the moon!

❂   ❂   ❂

Theodore didn't ever remember a time when the roads had been this treacherous. At every intersection he applied a pumping motion to the brakes to avoid slipping and sliding. Thankfully, the streets were abandoned, as even those shoppers who had procrastinated till the eleventh hour had finally made their purchases. A few huddled here and there, waiting in shop windows for the bus or a taxi.

Clocking his speed, he noticed the limousine was inching along at about nine miles per hour. Maybe less.

"We're going almost as slow as a horse and buggy," he said, chuckling to the passenger in the backseat. "Appropriate, I suppose, as we've been entertaining an Amishwoman at the estate."

Theodore glanced into the rearview mirror at the young man.

Justin Wirth was nodding. "So I hear." He paused a moment, then—"I was surprised, and saddened, to hear of Mrs. Bennett's failing health. She seemed quite well a few months back."

"It's terribly unfortunate, and I'd be the first to say that the kindhearted mistress doesn't deserve such a debilitating illness."

"Seems to me that finding her daughter might serve to raise her spirits."

"One would think so."

"How good of Mr. Bennett to locate the girl," Mr. Wirth remarked.

Theodore gripped the steering wheel. "Mr. Bennett, you say? *He* was the one to locate the Amishwoman?"

"Didn't you know?" came the reply. "Why, when Mrs. Bennett phoned me, she seemed quite pleased."

"Indeed?" He felt as if he might not be able to pry his hands free from the wheel.

So Dylan Bennett had been responsible for finding Katie Lapp. Of course—it made sense. *Perfect* sense. He pondered the situation. The man was worse than devious. *Worse.*

Why hadn't he put two and two together?

◈ ◈ ◈

Natalie wheeled her patient into the bedroom to administer the evening shot. Supper would be served in a few minutes, and she was encouraged by the way Mrs. Bennett seemed to be feeling tonight. Rather a surprise after her exhausting morning.

"Mr. Wirth is an absolute wonder," the mistress remarked. "Braving the weather on a night like this . . . and coming out on such short notice—Christmas Eve on top of it."

It was obvious Laura was pleased. The color had risen in her face, and Natalie noticed a renewed sparkle in the brown eyes.

"You're very lucky, I'd say," she replied. "The mother-daughter portrait will be a lovely gift for Miss Katie."

Mrs. Bennett turned abruptly. "You don't think she will mind, do you?"

"Having her portrait made? Why should she mind? She'll love it."

Mrs. Bennett smiled. "Good."

"Your daughter seems to be having a wonderful time."

"Well . . . it's taken longer for the two of us to warm up to each other than I'd ever anticipated. Perhaps because we have so many years of catching up to do."

Natalie was careful to guide the needle, inserting it into the bulging vein. Mrs. Bennett winced, and Natalie regretted for the hundredth time having to inflict yet more pain on the gentle woman. A soul who never complained, unlike many MS patients who often became irritable and hard to handle.

"Your pain's nearly over," she said softly.

"I know," said the mistress, blinking. "Yes, I know."

The words and the inflection in the weak voice took Natalie by surprise, and without further delay, she unlocked the wheelchair. "We have a party to attend," she said, willing the lump from her throat.

"And a portrait to sit for," Mrs. Bennett added, more brightly. "A portrait with my own dear Katie."

Things seemed to be working out between the mother and daughter, after all. Surprisingly, Katie's interest in Laura had taken a sudden turn, almost to the point that Natalie wondered what had been said or done to liven things up between them.

Oddly enough, she felt she could accurately pinpoint the moment when everything had begun to change. Katie had come in from the hall, carrying the appetizer tray. She'd served her mother first, then glancing over her shoulder, seemed to be looking at someone.

Turning, Natalie had noticed the new maid, apparently too shy to enter the mistress's private quarters. For a moment, the young woman had gazed longingly from beyond the glass doors. And when their eyes met, Katherine had scurried away.

❖ ❖ ❖

Rosie observed the artist briefly as he set up his easel and canvas in the sitting room, off in the corner, to be sure; nevertheless, his paints and brushes and things were already scattered across the drop cloth beneath.

What an interesting turn of events, she thought. *A mother-daughter portrait sitting on Christmas Eve.*

Wouldn't Mr. Bennett be surprised when he returned? The man was accustomed to having his way about managing the affairs of the estate—not giving in to what he would surely consider a whim of his dying wife. Rosie sincerely hoped Mrs. Bennett's decision to hire the artist would not cause more conflict than merriment for the holidays.

She shoved the gloomy thought aside and went about her duties, assisting in serving the mistress and the woman called Katie Lapp.

The table was tastefully furnished in every respect. Small in comparison to the immense formal one in the dining room, yet charming, enhanced by the mistress's favorite nineteenth-century floral dishes featuring a poinsettia and holly motif over a tablecloth of ecru lace.

The servants had had to scramble to put together this impromptu supper setting, but nary a complaint from Selig or Garrett about the change in plans, Rosie noticed. The mistress was a jewel of a lady, she was. They all loved her unreservedly and would never leave her—not as long as she drew breath. But she'd not think of that—not now.

Without purposely eavesdropping, Rosie caught snatches of conversation as Garrett held and served abundant food platters and matching service dishes for the mistress and her guest. Rosie would assist Mrs. Bennett by feeding her.

"What was it like growing up without electricity?" Mrs. Bennett asked her daughter.

"Ach, not so bad" came the reply. "We made do with oil lamps and lanterns."

Mrs. Bennett leaned forward. "Did you ever entertain secret thoughts, ask yourself how it would be to plug in a radio or television? Or to operate a computer or cook on an electric range in your own home?"

"Not that I remember. But I did always think it would be *wonderful* to live in a mansion like this."

Rosie chuckled quietly. The unlikely twosome were getting along famously . . . *now*. Still, she noticed how vague Katie's answers seemed—responses most anyone could give at the drop of a hat.

In the midst of this congenial conversation, she puzzled over the new maid—Katherine, who seemed to know all about making coconut custard pie, Amish style. Katherine, with hair the identical color of Laura's.

Perplexed, Rosie left for the butler's pantry. She must speak with Fulton as soon as possible.

CHAPTER SIXTEEN

◆ ◆ ◆

The longer Laura posed for the artist, the better she liked what was evolving on canvas. Justin had already begun to create a warm holiday setting, sketching Laura first and leaving a blank space for Katie. "For later," he told her when she casually inquired.

Did he think she might die before he finished? A reasonable assumption, to be sure. The more she thought of it, while sitting as still as the medication would allow, the more she was fairly certain that *was* the reason Justin concentrated so carefully on her outline alone.

Feeling perkier than she had all day, Laura listened closely as Katie spoke of her life, growing up on an Amish farm. "We were always up by four-thirty every morning, even Sundays. After all, someone had to milk the cows."

Laura found herself laughing along with the woman. She'd turned out to be so very talkative and charming. Laura couldn't quite fathom the difference between the original shy, almost sullen Katie, and this vivacious creature seated across the table from her.

"Tell me about your church services. What sort of music do you sing? Or is there music at all?"

Setting down her fork, Katie smiled. "We don't have instrumental music at church. Someone leads out in a song from the hymnbook, and the rest of us join in."

Laura nodded, trying hard to imagine only a cappella singing for the worship. "Do you sing in English?"

Katie shook her head. "Never."

Impulsively, she asked, "Will you say something in Dutch for me?"

The girl turned pale. "Oh, I mustn't speak it to outsiders. The bishop wouldn't approve."

"The bishop?"

"He makes all our rules—what we can and can't do around non-Amish folk."

Laura reached out to touch her elbow. "Well, I'm not just *any* English person, am I?"

Smiling, Katie agreed that she was not. "But it's best I don't break the rules."

Laura folded her hands in her lap, eager for more information about doctrine and religious beliefs. She was met, however, with obvious resistance each time she quizzed her daughter. Katie was clearly uncomfortable. "Very well. Let me tell you something of my own beliefs—my faith in Jesus Christ, my Savior and Lord."

Katie was polite enough to listen, although Laura suspected along about dessert time that her girl was truly bored with the Scripture references and favorite Bible passages she had been quoting. It was evidenced by the way Katie began to fidget and lose eye contact with her, something Laura had so enjoyed earlier in the evening.

"There is only one reason I wish to bring up spiritual matters," she found herself explaining. "I lived my life without Christ for thirty-six long years. Are you familiar with the hymn 'Amazing Grace'? Well, God's love is all that and so much more, and only because I love you, Katie, do I share my personal experience." She took in a deep breath, and praying a silent prayer for guidance, she forged ahead with her personal testimonial.

When she finished, Katie spoke up. "I've never heard such a thing. God's Son coming to earth to die . . . for me?"

"The first time I heard it told, I, too, could scarcely take it in."

The younger woman looked pensive. "But I don't see how I could just throw away my Amish belief," came the tentative reply. "My parents . . . my *adoptive* parents would be so hurt. And my brothers and sisters . . ."

Laura felt weak suddenly. "I don't expect you to believe the way I do just because we've found each other. Please understand that."

Nodding, Katie spoke in a near whisper. "You don't know how hard it's been to leave my family and friends to come here . . . even for this short time."

"I understand, and I appreciate it very much." She sighed, turning the conversation toward Katie's adoptive family. "How many brothers and sisters do you have?"

"Five sisters and four brothers. Most of them are grown and gone."

"So . . . your parents had children before . . . before the stillbirth?" Laura recalled the first moment of meeting. How devastated and forlorn the Amish couple had looked, there in the corridor of Lancaster General Hospital. The day was as fresh on her mind as if it had happened yesterday.

Katie's expression changed; she seemed stunned for a moment.

"Perhaps I shouldn't have mentioned—"

"No, no, it was just such a painful time for my parents," the girl said with little emotion. "I first heard about it when I was ten."

"I see." She wondered if Katie had also been informed of the money hidden away in the folds of the baby blanket. The money and the note—showing how much Laura, as an unwed teenage mother, had cared and loved her newborn baby. She hesitated to bring it up, lest the adoptive parents had seen fit to keep that part a secret. Perfectly acceptable, of course. Sometimes undisclosed family secrets were better left alone.

Still, she wondered when the right moment might present itself to speak about the future. The moment she would inform her daughter of her rightful inheritance.

Glancing away, Katie remarked, "Look, how pretty!"

Laura turned slightly in her chair to see Justin adding a hearty Christmas tree branch on the canvas background. "Mr. Wirth is an excellent artist—the best—wouldn't you agree? That's why I hired him to paint this portrait."

"How long before it's to be finished?" asked Katie.

"The artist will stay on here through Christmas week. And when the project is complete, the portrait is my gift to you."

Katie's eyes lit up. "For *me?*"

"That and so much more." Was now the time to tell her?

A burst of gladness swept across Katie's face. "You're the most generous woman I've ever known . . . Mother." Without warning, the girl stood up and planted a kiss on Laura's cheek.

"You've been in my heart these many years," she said, choking back the tears. "When we are completely alone, you'll hear what I have planned for you."

Laura continued to observe her daughter throughout the course of the evening. How her face shone . . . and what radiant love in her eyes!

Indeed, the girl seemed almost giddy with delight.

❖   ❖   ❖

Rosie managed to track down Fulton and bend his ear with her concerns about the supper conversation she'd overheard between Mrs. Bennett and Katie.

"I scarcely recognize that Amishwoman anymore," she said when they'd stepped out on the screened-in porch for a quick chat. "She's changed entirely."

Her husband listened, though seemed restless to get back to work. Then, lowering his tone, he said, "I've been noticing *Katherine* much more than Katie, and I think you and I were on to something before. The new maid has obvious physical traits, if you grasp my meaning."

Glancing about nervously, Rosie agreed. "I have an idea," she whispered. "Do you think we should allow Katherine to help serve dessert tomorrow? Mrs. Bennett's annual birthday cake for Christ?"

Fulton pondered for a moment. "It's worth considering."

"Well, shall we plan on it, then?" she asked, happy with the idea that a tradition started by Mrs. Bennett three years back might, in fact, be the perfect moment to usher in the new maid—at least get Katherine *inside* the private quarters. A marvelous opportunity for the two women to behold each other . . . at last. Perhaps then she and Fulton would be able to confirm their growing suspicions.

Fulton rubbed his chin. "By all means, instruct Katherine not to converse with either the mistress or Katie, except as needed for courtesy's sake. Then we'll see what happens."

Like a schoolgirl on the trail of a mystery, Rosie put her hand to her throat. "Oh, I do hope this works out. Nothing would please me more."

Flushed with anticipation of the daring scheme, she hurried inside.

❖ ❖ ❖

While the mistress and Katie dined in quiet splendor down the hall, the servant staff and Nurse Judah gathered at the long kitchen table—an antique—bearing intricate carvings along its sides, and far removed from Mrs. Bennett's intimate suite.

It was to be a quick supper. Enjoyable, though.

Katherine hadn't remembered seeing all the domestic help in one room before, least not all at the same time. Wasn't as if she were being presented formally to them, but it came mighty close.

Several, including Nurse Judah and Garrett Smith, shook her hand, welcoming her to the "busy Bennett place," as Garrett put it. And she wasn't absolutely sure, but it almost seemed that he'd slanted her a quick wink.

She noticed the older gentleman—Theodore Williams— who moved about the kitchen in ceaseless silence, and after one rapid assessment, she pegged him as the most interesting person in the room.

Appearing rather subdued, the chauffeur located a vacant chair near the bay window overlooking the east gardens, now buried in snow. It was already too dark to investigate just how deeply the ground might be covered.

With an air of reluctance, Mr. Williams sat down. He turned his head to face the window and remained in that position for a time. She watched him for what seemed a solid minute or more, before the man sighed audibly and tendered a faint smile when their eyes met.

What's bothering him? she wondered. Something was, 'twas plain to see. Ach, the weight of the world seemed to rest on the man's slight frame.

Years ago, her Amish girlfriend, Mary, had told her you could tell things about a person's face—whether or not they were telling the truth—when they talked. But this man wasn't saying a single word. She didn't know why on earth it was so important for her to know if he could be trusted. No reason, really, she decided, and went about the pleasant chore of buttering her baby peas, carrots, and baked potato.

The roast pork was so tender, she cut off bite-sized portions with only her fork, paying close attention as Natalie Judah, the sweet-faced nurse, explained what was taking place in Mrs. Bennett's quarters. "Katie and her mother seem to have broken through the first icy layer . . . and I'm not sure what has made the difference."

Panicky feelings surfaced, yet Katherine dared not speak up. Not now. She'd just have to wait and listen. Yet sin stirred within her soul—the sin of jealousy. She did not want an impostor "breaking the ice" with *her* mother, and she didn't want to be sitting here enduring a report about it, either!

Still, she found herself helpless to listen as Natalie continued. "I was beginning to wonder if they would ever click—those two—after their shaky start yesterday."

Katherine caught a curious exchange of glances between Rosie and her husband. What was that peculiar look that passed across the butler's face?

Discreetly, she stole additional glimpses at the husband-wife duo sitting up the table from her. She was not disturbed by the frequency of what seemed to be secretive looks shared. Oh, she'd seen her Amish parents do the same thing, and often. People connected by love often passed silent intimacies with their eyes.

She knew it to be true, for she and her darling Dan had experienced something quite similar in their teen years. Especially during house church, while sitting on those hard wooden benches for three hours on a Sunday morning. A rather bittersweet circumstance for a girl who could scarcely sit still, yet a girl in love. The sweet part was that the men sat segregated from the women, which made it possible for Dan's doting blue eyes to dance for her, offering love messages only sweethearts cherish. . . .

Attempting to rid her mind of past lovely things, she tore her bread in half before buttering it. She savored the first bite, thinking how nice and even she'd cut the loaf tonight, with the aid of electricity, of course.

Natalie was talking again, and Katherine found herself hanging on every word, occasionally peering down the table at Mr. Williams. Why wasn't *he* entering into the conversation about the mistress and the Amishwoman?

Naturally, if someone wanted to be rude, they might be asking *her* the same question. But it had been drilled into her—her whole life—to "fade into the woodwork," so to speak, when elders gathered at the table or any other time. And with a quick look round at her new friends and colleagues, it was clear she was the youngest person present. Not only that, but she was a woman.

Rebecca had taught her total submission to a man's authority—under God, of course. Sitting here, enjoying Christmas Eve supper in the house of her natural mother, Katherine supposed—even though she was a woman grown and out on her own—that she was still attempting to throw off deeply ingrained practices. Customs so much a part of her, she could not shake them off at will or on a mere whim, either one.

Had she not been a paid employee, she might've had the nerve to speak up and enter the conversation. Especially when it came to the part about Katie's leaving the room so suddenly this evening. "And lo and behold, if Mrs. Bennett's daughter didn't turn around in the hallway and return with a tray of hors d'oeuvres," said Natalie. "I couldn't believe it!"

"Well, of all things." Theodore broke his silence, looking up, then wiping his face with his folded napkin.

Katherine sat spellbound. Oh, she wanted to explain the situation. Tell them—all of them—that Katie Lapp, or whoever she was, had pulled the tray out of Katherine's own hands and flounced back into the mistress's room with it. That the young woman hadn't understood a stitch of Pennsylvania Dutch, not even a simple comment about the weather being bitter cold.

She wanted to tell them she thought Katie Lapp was an impostor, wanted to holler it out into the frigid New York air.

Tonight, though, the cat had her tongue, no getting around it. So she sat there, enduring perpetual speculation about this and that and thus and so till she thought she might burst.

It was moments later she realized Mr. Williams had spoken, as much as to agree with Natalie Judah that the Amishwoman *had* done something completely out of order. Katherine worried that what might follow could be a reprimand, and rightly so. Would the old man turn and speak to her next?

She was fairly sure he didn't know it was she who'd been assigned the tray of hors d'oeuvres. Relieved, she reached for her glass of ice water and sipped slowly, letting the coolness soothe her throat as it trickled down.

Due to the snippets of information she'd overheard in the past twenty-four hours, she had come to understand that Mr. Williams was the mistress's favorite chauffeur. Rosie had even hinted that the gentleman was also Mrs. Bennett's confidant. This knowledge intrigued her, for the man had grandfatherly qualities. Some of them even reminded her of Dawdi David, her mamma's father, long deceased.

Pondering this, she wondered: *What secret things does Mr. Williams know about Laura Mayfield-Bennett?* Had Katherine been more confident of her place in the household, she might've taken him aside and pumped him full of questions.

When dessert was served, she focused her attention on the couple with the ongoing parade of darting glances. Jah, Rosie and Fulton Taylor seemed to know something they weren't letting on to anyone. Might be, *they* were just the folk to help her.

❖   ❖   ❖

Laura realized, much later, that Dylan had not returned home from his supper outing. Strange that Katie had been the one to mention it.

"Dylan's in good hands," she reassured her daughter. "We hire only the best of help, drivers included."

That seemed to suffice, and they went on talking about casual, carefree things—becoming more and more comfortable with each other.

Rosie hurried in from the hall and began to clear away the holiday dishes. "You've had a long day," she warned, cocking her head in that concerned way she had.

"Long but happy."

"But tomorrow will be another full day—exchanging gifts and dining."

Smiling at her daughter, Laura replied, "I wish to soak up every minute I have left with my girl."

Then, not wanting to put a damper on things, she did not bring up the matter of her husband's delay. Never said a word, even though her personal maid appeared altogether eager to engage in small talk. Especially with Laura's daughter. So eager was she that Rosie slipped once and referred to Katie as Katherine.

Laura promptly reminded her of the woman's nickname. "She wants to be called by her Amish name."

"Yes, I'd just forgotten." Rosie blushed. "Please, do forgive me, Katie."

The young woman nodded agreeably. "That's all right. I've been called many things in my life."

Except Laura Bennett's daughter, thought Laura, grateful for this day. And for the love.

The hour was late when Natalie came to check on her. "You seem to have enjoyed yourself," the nurse said, preparing to take her back to the dressing area.

Smiling at her daughter, Laura reached for Katie's hand. "I'd say one of the best days of my life."

Katie smiled sweetly. "For me, too."

She felt her throat constrict with emotion. "We'll have another lovely time tomorrow. The best Christmas ever."

"I'm counting the hours," Katie said, standing to leave.

The women hugged briefly, then Laura watched, with failing eyes, her dear one depart for the Tiffany Room upstairs.

Tomorrow's the day, she decided. *I'll tell Katie about my family—her grandparents—and all that is to be hers . . . on Christmas Day.*

Chapter Seventeen

Dylan Bennett, sitting in the plush armchair of a hotel lobby, gazed about him at the crowd of stranded travelers mobbing the area, arranging for a room. Just his luck—lousy timing to boot!

Not to worry, he told himself. His aspiring New York actress could handle herself quite nicely, with or without him at the estate. He smiled, commending himself on a choice pick. The girl could go far—maybe even Hollywood, after this stint.

Now, if he could just obtain a luxury suite—the kind he'd first requested. Because of crowded conditions, the place was packed, the best rooms taken. He might've easily succumbed to the offering of a simple room for himself and Rochester, the bumbling idiot who'd driven them into a snowbank. But given the circumstances, he'd rather lounge . . . and fume in the elegantly furnished sitting area. In the meantime, he would consider his options: either wait out the storm, or hire a tow truck to pull the Mercedes out of the ditch. Anything to keep from sharing cramped quarters with Rochester.

Fact: Apparently, no end was in sight for the ferocious Christmas Eve blizzard, howling lionlike as it dumped a record-breaking blanket of snow on the city. No hope of obtaining even the most primitive of tow trucks at this hour. Had he not just heard from the bellhop that roads east of Canandaigua were impassable—County Road 10 having been blocked off moments earlier by highway patrol—he might have seriously entertained the notion of summoning Theodore, his senior chauffeur, to retrieve them.

Alas, he was stuck . . . trapped only a few miles from home. And to top it off, the phones in the entire place were tied up. All of them. He could kick himself for leaving his cell phone back home. So here he sat, a man of means . . . displaced, unsettled, and waiting, waiting for some loser to get off the phone.

Glancing across the atrium, he noticed Rochester lingering near the phone booths. Present assignment: to signal Dylan when a telephone was available. Just reward for the young, inept chauffeur. The lad had much to learn, he decided.

He checked his watch. Nearly midnight. Was his wife resting now, happy as a lark? Had she enjoyed a satisfactory evening, become comfortable enough with Katie to reveal the generous plan for her daughter's future?

Knowing how Laura adored Christmas—her religious beliefs being what they were—he suspected that if things had gone well, tomorrow might be the day he'd been waiting for. Waiting was the name of the game—in business and in matters of life—and legacies.

Annoyed that he might have to spend the holiday marooned, he reached for *The Wall Street Journal*. Rochester would just have to call to him when the next phone was available. In the meantime, before he dialed up the estate, before he disguised his voice to address whomever answered, and before he spoke with drowsy Miss Katie Lapp, impressive impostor, he'd have a look at a few stock prices, just to pass the time.

❖   ❖   ❖

The clock on the mantel chimed twelve times, wakening Dan Fisher out of a deep sleep. He'd drifted off at his desk, and although the angle of his head in relationship to his neck was creating an annoying crick, he stayed put for a few more minutes.

In spite of this being the night before Christmas, he'd spent the entire evening composing a letter to his sister. Had he not been thoroughly exhausted afterward, he might've headed upstairs to bed. But emotionally spent, he'd fallen asleep with his head resting heavily on his hands.

Slipping back into a half dream state, the images before him were as real as the day the sailing accident happened. And always the same. . . .

He found himself face down, regaining consciousness on a sand reef, having been swept up by the ocean below. How he'd gotten there, he did not know, but he knew one thing sure: he was alive when he should have drowned!

Swimming to shore had been excruciating . . . he thought his arms might give out after more than an hour in the swirling waves. Attempting to make headway toward shore, yet not seeing, not knowing where he was in the midst of the vicious storm, at one point he thought of allowing the ocean's fury to roll over him, bury him at sea. He contemplated merely breathing in the deadly salt water, receiving the ocean into his bursting lungs . . . succumbing . . . relinquishing the will to live, to stop the pain, the horrid wrenching in his chest.

But he had survived. By God's almighty hand, he was alive!

The half-hour chime jarred him to life again thirty minutes later. This time he picked himself up, left the study lamp lit, and ambled toward the stairs.

He looked back at the letter.

The letter.

The startling message would change everything, would rearrange his family's very existence—maybe even alter the lives of the People.

Shatter yesterday, awaken truth.

With the fracturing of years would eventually come the Ban and Meinding—excommunication and ultimate shunning.

His.

By returning to confess to his father his grave deception concerning his accident, yet at the same time refusing to return to the Amish community—by doing that, he would be setting himself up for high jeopardy. Exposing himself to an Amish bishop's decree. This by the mere mailing of a letter.

The envelope, contents inserted, lay diagonal on the desk, unsigned, and as of yet, undated. Still, he was certain of one thing: *This* message must be the one mailed to Annie. None of the previous rough drafts were acceptable to him. Yet he wondered how his sister would take the news, worried that quite possibly, after reading and discovering he was alive after all, she might faint . . . or worse, fail to believe the honest words he'd written.

He hoped rather she might study the handwriting. Look past the words, the English-sounding phrases learned from his years out in the world, find her "deceased" brother buried between the lines. The one who'd long loved her, missed her, wished things had turned out far differently for all concerned.

Falling into bed, he knew what to do about the timing of the letter. It was imperative Annie receive it when she might be most likely to fully concentrate on his request— to consider meeting him face-to-face. He must not procrastinate further. Each day counted, in God's eyes and in his own. Too much time had passed and there was much to set right. Yet he was reluctant to disrupt his sister's Christmas, would not intrude upon it for the world.

For him, the most difficult part—composing the letter—was finished. He would wait and send it immediately after New Year's Day.

Settled about his decision, he slept, conjuring up joy-filled dreams of his former sweetheart girl and the bittersweet Hickory Hollow days of yore.

❖   ❖   ❖

Along about one-thirty, Katherine awakened with a start. Somewhere in the house, a telephone jangled. At last, it stopped, and she sat upright, uncertain of her precise whereabouts for a moment.

Commotion outside her bedroom door followed shortly, and she crept out of bed to lean her head against the door.

"Miss Katie," someone was whispering. "Can you come downstairs? You're wanted on the telephone."

Curious, Katherine opened the door a crack. She saw the phony Amishwoman emerge from her room at the end of the hall, far removed from the servants' quarters.

"Who's calling at *this* hour?" the impostor said sleepily.

There was more whispering, and, although Katherine wasn't totally certain, she thought it was the butler who was delivering the message. When the man turned, she saw Theodore Williams' face instead. The old gentleman lumbered down the hall to the long, grand staircase.

What on earth is going on? she thought. It was the middle of the night, for pity's sake!

Closing her door a bit more, allowing for only the slightest of a crack, she waited for the senior chauffeur's footsteps to fade before opening the door wider again. Just in time to see the strawberry blonde, in a flurry of flaming red slippers, hurry down the hallway, turn, and dash down the stairs.

Katherine closed her door and rushed over to the dressing room where a walk-in closet swallowed up the few items of clothing she'd brought from Lydia's. There she donned a blue terry cloth bathrobe and slip-on house shoes.

Directly, she passed through the dimly lit hallway and made her way down the stairs. Not to appear nosy, and to avoid being noticed, she sat halfway down the steps, near the landing, listening. But the house was silent as the moon.

She held her breath in hopes of lessening the noise of her own breathing. Then, getting up, she tiptoed farther down the steps, straining to hear.

In the distance, coming from the library, perhaps?—she heard the faintest of sounds. Someone's voice.

Grateful for Garrett's guided tour that first day—pointing out the mansion's corridors and general layout—she knew enough to enter the opposite side of the enormous library room, there being two separate entrances. She slipped in without being noticed, glad for the dark hue of her blue robe.

Bookshelves, housing hundreds of volumes, loomed tall above her, like windmills, their vanes breathless in the darkness.

She listened as the impostor spoke. "You expect *me* to pull this off by myself?" came her peppery words. "I'm only here because you hired me."

Hired?

Katherine was aware of her own heartbeat. Not only did she feel it pumping inside her chest, she felt the pulsing . . . no, the *throbbing* . . . in her ears.

"Yes . . . yes, I can handle Christmas dinner, but I'd feel better about things if you were here . . . at least in the house."

The pause was much longer than before, as though the

person on the other end had much to say.

Who's calling this late? Katherine wondered.

Then the revealing words pierced her through—words that made the hairs on the back of her neck prickle. "But I can almost feel it—I'm *that* close. Tonight your wife told me, in so many words, she has some big news. Probably about the money."

Your wife? Who was Katie Lapp talking to?

Suddenly, Katherine knew. The fake Katie was on the phone with Mr. Bennett! But . . . what did she mean about "the money"?

Her heart pounded wildly, though she refused to stand by, privy to a possibly wicked, greislich scheme. An innocent, dying woman's money must surely be at stake. Letting herself out, Katherine waited in the darkest corner of the hallway for the woman to finish her loathsome chat.

No wonder, she thought. No wonder Dylan Bennett had had such a chilling effect on her when first she'd called here.

Her mind spun in all sorts of directions. Such connivings and finaglings! Something, something must be done to set the record straight. She must move in where angels fear to tread. Yet what could she say or do to prove she was truly Laura's daughter—and Katie was not?

She had no proof. Or did she?

She remembered the little lilac sachets she'd brought from Hickory Hollow—so like the ones she'd found in the bureau drawers here. Would they be enough to persuade the mistress?

How she wished she could sit down with the Wise Woman. Ella Mae would gladly help her decipher the situation, if only Katherine had not been shunned.

She couldn't leave New York and return to Pennsylvania. No, she must stay put, stay here in her mother's house. Protect Laura Bennett's money, estate, or whatever it was, from falling into the wrong hands. Do something to bring a black-hearted soon-to-be-transgression to a screeching halt.

Do something. . . .

Just ahead, in the darkened hallway, a figure emerged from a curtained entryway. She wondered who on earth was lurking in the corridor. When the shadow evolved into a man—a man with a determined stride—she was reminded of the senior chauffeur, Theodore Williams.

What was the old gentleman doing? Snooping?

She stood glued to the spot, unable to think of what she might do to get his attention without alerting the imposter. Well, by the looks of things, she wasn't the *only* one who'd just overheard a most suspicious telephone conversation.

Katherine waited until the hallway was completely clear before heading back toward the stairs. As she was about to reach for the banister railing, she stopped and thought of her ailing mother, the dear, unsuspecting woman. What lay in store for her?

Turning, she made her way toward the south wing, in the direction of Laura's suite of rooms.

Wide awake, with no hope of falling back to sleep, at least not tonight, she tiptoed down another long passageway. Her destination was the tall French doors. As she crept through the darkness, she thought of the artist's portrait and knew she must see the canvas for herself.

At once, Katherine realized she was standing on the spot where she'd first encountered Katie Lapp, the "Amishwoman" who hadn't understood even a few simple words of Dutch. The woman who was concocting something evil with Laura's *husband*, of all things!

Silently, Katherine moved through the open glass doors and into the formal sitting area. A lovely dinner table, displaying two crocheted place mats, was situated off to the side near a fireplace, embers dying fast.

To her right, she spied an easel where a large canvas, now

draped, had been erected. Wondering if this was the commissioned work Rosie and Garrett had spoken of yesterday, she stole over to it, careful not to bump into several brushes drying on the floor.

With a steady hand, she pulled back the sheet and peered at the unfinished painting. Stepping aside, she allowed the window's snowy reflection to cast a silver glow over the canvas.

She caught her breath as she studied the art. Off to the right side of center, Laura's outline was evident. What seemed odd was the hollow space directly in the middle. Was this to be the spot for Laura's daughter? If so, why hadn't the artist sketched in at least *something* there?

Katherine tilted her head, wondering what it would be like to pose for a portrait. To be painted alongside her natural mother. Her rightful place!

Anger rose up in her. Ach, she must devise a way for Mr. Wirth to paint the *correct* person in the designated location on the canvas: Laura Bennett's true daughter—Katherine herself. Otherwise the portrait would be a lie. As deceitful as the man named Dylan D. Bennett, she recalled from the phone book in Lydia Miller's kitchen.

Thinking about Mr. Bennett's name, she wondered if the middle initial might not stand for Devil. She couldn't imagine what sort of man would plan to hurt his own bride in such a way, a desperately ill wife at that. A wicked, wicked man, for sure. Not in the sense he would dish out harsh treatment according to a religious ruling, as Bishop John had done, not *that* sort of man. But a sneaky, conniving person. For sure and for certain.

Shivering with emotion, she redraped the canvas, remembering she had been accused of being that way herself—more conniving than any of the People in all of Hickory Hollow.

But not anymore. She was different through and through

because of who she was—Katherine Mayfield, the upstanding daughter of a kindhearted woman. She figured that because of Laura Bennett's close connection with the Almighty, she, too, was somehow linked to righteousness. Hadn't this been the real problem all along—trying to measure up to the Ordnung without knowing who she really was?

She thought of her Amish mamma, how gentle and honest Rebecca had always seemed. Yet how sadly mistaken Katherine had been, discovering that the woman she thought of as her angel-mother had in all truth been a liar, had kept from her supposed daughter a secret so painful it gouged out an instant wedge between them.

Jah, Rebecca Lapp had been a wonderful-gut storyteller, all right, in *every* sense of the word. The secret of Katherine's so-called "adoption" had been so devastating, it jolted her right out of the place she'd called home.

Now she lived *here*, safely under her birth mother's roof, and she resolved to do everything in her power to halt this treacherous scheme. That horrible thing Dylan D. Bennett was cooking up with the impostor Katie, even at this very moment!

She left the large parlor room silently and hurried back upstairs to her own quarters. Then before going to bed, she gathered up the potpourri sachets from each of the drawers and placed them on her pillow. The smell of lavender sweetened the dreary wee hours and soothed her soul.

CHAPTER EIGHTEEN

Theodore slept fitfully that night, tossing about, even punching his pillow off the bed at one point. His dreams were anything but good ones; nightmares best described the visions of villainy he experienced.

Upon arising, he thought nothing of traipsing across the hall to the room where Fulton and Rosie Taylor made their marital love nest. Lightly, yet firmly, he knocked on their door.

The sleepy-eyed butler came promptly. "Theodore? Is everything all right?"

"Not on your life. I have to speak with you . . . immediately."

Fulton put his hand on the doorknob, pulling the door closed behind him. Wearing his white nightshirt and nothing on his feet, he stepped into the hallway. "What *is* it, Williams?"

"How quickly can you dress?"

Fulton nodded as though he understood the urgency. "Give me three minutes."

Satisfied his friend had taken him seriously, Theodore added, "I'll wait for you in my room, and don't bother to knock." He sighed. "What I have to tell you must be kept in strictest confidence."

❖   ❖   ❖

"I could use your help presenting the Christmas cake during dinner at noon," Rosie told Katherine. "You'll light the candles. Of course, you'll be careful not to utter a word either to the mistress or her daughter—attend only to your duties. Do you understand?"

Katherine cringed at hearing the phony Amishwoman being referred to as Laura's daughter. Still, she couldn't believe her luck—being asked to look after dessert in the grand dining room. "I'm to light the candles . . . on the cake?"

"Yes, Mrs. Bennett has been enjoying this tradition for several Christmases now; in fact, she's the one responsible for it in the first place." Rosie went on to explain that the cake was to be in commemoration of Christ's birth. "A birthday cake, so to speak."

"Oh" was all Katherine could say. Such a thing was strange to her—not having been given birthday cakes as a child growing up. Still, Lydia Miller had made them for her sons, and sometimes Katherine, along with the rest of her Amish family, would be included in the Mennonite frolic, enjoying a piece of cake—ice cream, too—with candles representing the appropriate year of celebration. So it wasn't as if she were completely in the dark about it.

Smiling, she realized again her natural mother seemed to possess a childlike heart and a flair for fancy things. *Just like me.*

After all, birthday cakes were for children—English children—weren't they? She was delighted Rosie had asked her to serve Laura Bennett on this special day.

She went about her routine work, grateful she had not been appointed the task of cleaning the Tiffany Room, where the dreadful impostor was staying. Surprisingly, Rosie had assigned the room to herself today, in spite of the fact that Rosie Taylor was clearly the mistress's personal maid.

❂   ❂   ❂

Before Laura's breakfast was served in bed, she received a telephone call. The estate operator answered, patching Dylan through. "Merry Christmas, darling," she heard him say.

"And to you," she replied happily.

"You may have heard I wasn't able to make it home last night."

She nodded silently. Many nights her husband's whereabouts were suspect. Nothing new.

Yet she listened as he continued. "Rochester and I have been holed up downtown—snowbound—waiting for the roads to open. Minutes from home but stuck all the same."

"You're *stranded?*" Instantly, she felt sorry for him. It was Christmas, after all. "You stayed in a hotel, I trust."

"Yes, and I'm awaiting a tow at the moment. Should be home in time for the holiday dinner, though. At least, that's our intention."

"Well . . . I do . . . I do hope you'll make it all right." In spite of her faltering speech, she thought of telling him how lovely her evening visit with Katie had been, but she thought better of it.

"How are you feeling today, Laura?"

He sounded genuinely concerned, and she found her heart lifting, daring to hope her Christmas miracle might include some kind of reconciliation between the two of them. "I think I may be improving. It's most extraordinary what's happening . . . it's the discovery of Katie, I believe. Getting acquainted with my daughter is putting me over the top, giving me a new lease on life. And I have *you* to thank for it, Dylan."

She sighed, pulling the bed comforter close. Tears welled up unexpectedly. "I do so appreciate what you've done for me . . . about locating Katie, I mean."

Anticipating a reply, she waited. Strangely enough, the line seemed to have gone dead. "Dylan . . . are you there?"

"Ah yes . . . yes," he sputtered. "Glad to hear of your improving health. I'll be home very soon." And without saying good-bye, he hung up, giving the impression of being terribly rushed as their conversation came to a close.

Rushing home to *her?* She sighed again, choosing to dwell on Dylan's timely present. A true and glorious Christmas gift.

❖   ❖   ❖

"Please, tell us a story, Mam," Elam pleaded. "Just a short one'll do." He sat next to his wife, Annie, leaning elbows on his parents' kitchen table. His younger brothers, Eli and Benjamin, were finishing up their desserts, helping themselves to seconds and thirds of ice cream. They'd had the noon meal early, at their usual time, in spite of Christmas.

"Ach, my stories are for the womenfolk," Rebecca replied, waving her hand the way she always did.

"No, no," Annie chimed in. "Not necessarily true. You've told many a story right here round this table, Mam."

His mother looked downright haggard and pale, far different from the rosy-cheeked woman he knew. Her hazel eyes had always been clear and alert; today they seemed cloudy and, jah, sad.

If only his sister hadn't gone and gotten herself shunned, none of this would be happening with Mamma. *Katie's fault*, he thought as angry thoughts crowded his mind.

Benjamin spoke up. "Tell us about the time the horses ran off with ya. Now, that's a gut one."

The rest of the family, even Samuel, joined in the chorus, attempting to get Rebecca to loosen up her tongue. Too long since any of them had heard her go on and on with one of her stories. Much too long.

Elam was worried. From everything Annie had told him, he wondered if his mother might not be losing her mind. Still, he had to try to get her talkin' 'bout the past . . . *any* part of her life she deemed worthy to recite.

" 'There was once a girl named Rebecca,' " began Elam, prompting her. " 'She was out in the potato field, doin' the plowing for her Pop when—' "

"Elam, now stop right there! You daresn't trick me into storytellin' thataway."

His face stung with the rebuke. "Sorry, Mamma. I just thought—"

"Don't be getting yourself into trouble by thinkin'. Do ya hear?"

"It's all right, Rebecca," his father spoke up. "Our son meant no harm."

"Dat's right. Honest, I didn't, Mamma."

"My storytellin' days are behind me," declared Rebecca. "And nobody, not you, not any of the family, can make me start again."

Elam was silent, hoping she might go on to explain herself, to tell the family gathered here what was so awful troubling to keep her from sharing the stories she'd always held dear. But his mother clammed up right then and there, and that was the end of the discussion.

Eli and Ben got to talking about Jake Stoltzfus, Mary's uncle, who'd headed out to Indiana somewheres already, even before the holidays. While they gabbed, Elam daydreamed, watching Annie snuggle their baby son close.

Out of the blue, Mamma leaped clean out of her seat,

ranting on about hearing a baby crying. Annie shot him a concerned glance, and he caught the bewildered looks of the others, too. It was as if their mother had gone daft before their very eyes.

"Baby Daniel's sound asleep," Annie said softly, reassuring her.

"No, it ain't my grandson I heard," replied Rebecca. She cocked her head, listening as she stood in the middle of the kitchen floor. "There . . . don'tcha hear that?"

Elam shook his head. "Why not sit down and rest a bit, Mamma. No one's crying."

By now Samuel had gotten up and gone over to wrap his long arms around the glassy-eyed woman. "Come on, now, Becky, let's have ourselves a little chat."

"No, no . . . no," came the frightening reply. "There's a baby upstairs a-cryin'. I hear her, Samuel. I do!" She was pushing her husband away now, the glazed look spreading across her tear-streaked face. "My little daughter needs me, don'tcha see? Ach, my baby needs me so."

Elam fought back his own tears, hot vexing ones. Just look what Katie had done to their precious mamma. Look what she'd done to *all* of them.

CHAPTER NINETEEN

❖ ❖ ❖

As far as Fulton was concerned, Theodore's plan was splendid. They'd simply wait for the master of the house to return. If he was marooned somewhere in town, as his phone call to his wife had indicated, Master Dylan would be fidgeting about now, anxious to get home to oversee his underhanded plot. And, no doubt, to enjoy the lavish Christmas feast.

Meanwhile, Rosie had decided to do some plotting of her own, astute woman that she was. In the last-minute preparations, she might inadvertently question the woman who called herself Katie Lapp.

"Do be careful, my love," Fulton said in the privacy of their quarters. "I'll not have anyone scolding or picking a fight with my sweet pea."

"Oh, now, you mustn't worry. Miss Katie Lapp, whomever she is, has nothing to say to me!" And she was off down the hall to tend to her duties.

When he encountered the artist coming down for breakfast, Fulton greeted the man with generous praise. "I hope you won't mind, but I had myself a peek," he admitted. "Last evening."

Justin Wirth smiled, his blue eyes shining. "It's not always possible to keep a project under wraps, I've found."

"Especially at Christmas?"

"The most fickle of seasons, unfortunately." The young man was as cordial as he was comely.

"Do keep up the good work," Fulton said with a knowing wink, excusing himself. He was eager to assume his tasks today—the Lord's birthday. To assist God almighty with some "housecleaning"—well, just a bit. To help right the wrongs of this manor, he and his good wife, Rosie.

❖ ❖ ❖

Mary Stoltzfus thought it would be nice to deliver her home-baked sweets *before* the bishop's family had their Christmas dinner. She'd heard through the grapevine that the meal was set for twelve-thirty sharp. Later than many of the holiday meals served up at dairy farmers' homes in the Hollow.

Somehow, she would plan to make an honest excuse to run an unexpected errand, tell her parents and grandmother she'd be back in a jiffy. 'Course, they'd all know what she was up to, but that wouldn't do no harm, really. Most everyone in Hickory Hollow felt mighty sorry for John Beiler and his five motherless children. Woe be it unto her not to help spread Christmas cheer to the only widowed bishop around these parts.

So, trying not to think much about her best friend and all that Katie had gone through to keep from marrying the good Bishop, Mary selected several dozen each of angel gingerbread and sour cream chocolate cookies, packed them carefully, and took them in her father's carriage to the bishop's.

Little Jacob answered the front door. "Hullo," he said, letting her in, eyes wide. "Merry Christmas to ya."

"Same to you, Jacob." She stood there in the front room,

feeling mighty awkward now that she was here. Still holding her basket of sweets, she smiled down at the beautiful boy with wheat-colored hair and the bluest eyes she'd ever seen.

"Didja bake somethin' for me?"

"Jah, for you and your brothers and sisters."

"*Daed* too?"

She nodded.

" 'Cause my father needs some gut home cookin', ya know. He needs to find us a mamma awful bad."

"Oh?" The youngster's words surprised her.

"Jah, 'cause after Katie went down to you-know-where, we just kept on waitin' round for the Lord God to send us someone else. So far, we ain't seen no one pretty as your girlfriend."

"Jacob!" The bishop came rushing in the room to snatch up his young son and carry him back into the kitchen.

She heard bits and pieces of the reprimand but was glad to know the little fella wasn't in too terrible much trouble, bein' only four and all.

In a short time, she was handing over her basket of goods to Bishop John, saying, "Merry Christmas to all of you."

"It was gut of you to pay us a visit, Mary. Thank you kindly." The bishop's voice sounded softer, more compassionate than at any Sunday Preachin' service. Soft as a breeze in summer. She wished ever so much she might stay and linger in its tenderness.

❖   ❖   ❖

"Ousting Katie Lapp is the least of our worries," Theodore whispered to Rosie in the hallway. "What'll we tell Mrs. Bennett?"

"Well, I'd hate to add to her misery, poor soul," she said, brushing back a strand of graying hair. "But, according to the nurse, the mistress seems to be improving . . . ever since she

195

and the young woman started getting on so well. Even *I* can see the progress she's made. So you have a point. Running the impostor off may not be such a wise move at the moment."

Theodore mulled it over, stepping back to lean on the banister railing. "We may not have long to work out the details—that is, if you plan to confront the Amishwoman this morning. Do you?"

"That's just it—she's not Amish," Rosie informed him on a triumphant note. "She's an actress or model from New York City. Can you imagine?"

Theodore scratched his head. "You took some liberties with the master's files, I do believe."

Rosie nodded sheepishly. "Fulton and I happened upon a random file marked 'Katie Lapp'—and . . . well, we couldn't resist a peek."

"Unscrupulous rogue," he whispered.

Turning to go, Rosie called over her shoulder. "Better wait to decide until after I have a chat with Natalie. She'll know what best to do for the mistress."

Heart sinking, Theodore walked down the hall and into the kitchen. They'd had their chance while Dylan was out. Could've sent the Amishwoman packing right after breakfast. A delay could cause unnecessary tension among the domestic staff for the holiday. In fact, he was most certain it would.

Already this morning, word had spread through the ranks that Mr. Bennett and Rochester had gotten themselves stranded in town somewhere—the best limousine thrust into a snowbank.

He stifled a laugh, thanking his lucky stars. It might've been *him* stuck overnight with that snake, Dylan Bennett.

Time was of the essence. He scurried to his post.

❖ ❖ ❖

It seemed providential, almost. Katherine had gone outside to shake rugs from the butler's pantry when she'd happened upon Theodore Williams. He was whistling as he worked, shoveling the snow off the back steps and walkway.

When he noticed her, she was surprised that he stopped what he was doing to speak. "A fine Christmas morning, isn't it?"

"Yes, and a good thing to see that the worst of the storm is over." She shook one of the smaller rugs a bit longer than necessary, wondering if the old gentleman would return to his work.

She was pleasantly surprised when he struck up a real conversation. "It's high time we got better acquainted, you and I. Yes"—and here he seemed to mutter to himself. Then he came out with it. "I do believe I owe you an apology, Katherine."

"Whatever for?"

He offered her that faint yet grandfatherly smile. "For not properly welcoming you to the Bennett estate."

"Thank you." How truly good of him, although she could see no reason for him going out of his way to say such a thing. For a moment, she thought again of her Dawdi David. Mr. Williams' words rang out as soundly and confidently as those of her Amish mamma's father.

The gentleman struggled to pull up his coat sleeve with a gloved hand, studying his watch. "I best keep shoveling. It'll be dinnertime before we know it. Season's greetings to you," he said, as though dismissing her.

"Merry Christmas, Mr. Williams."

He chuckled. "Please, call me Theodore."

She said nothing in response, only smiled back at the man. The pitch of his voice, the way he looked at her—all of it—unnerved her more than she cared to admit.

❂   ❂   ❂

Dan Fisher thought it terrific to have been invited to dinner at the home of the boss and wife. Owen and Eve Hess were his dearest friends in all of Jersey. No finer Mennonites around. He felt blessed of the Lord to have been privileged to work alongside such genuinely devout and caring people.

Sharing office space in Owen's firm had been a godsend from the start. Not many established architects would've given a farm-boy-turned-draftsman a job fresh out of college. Yes, Owen had been kind to him all these years, assisting Dan in establishing an ever-growing clientele. Yet as generous a man as Owen was, Dan had never spoken of his Amish background. Or of the sailing accident that had triggered the ripple effect in his life.

Thinking he ought to ask ahead for some time off after the New Year, he'd volunteered to work overtime during the holidays. And the good man had agreed. "You haven't missed a day since you came to work for me," Owen had pointed out.

So everything was in order to return to Hickory Hollow for a visit. Only one problem could he foresee: telling Owen how to get in touch with him while there. He'd rehearsed various ways of revealing where he was going. To visit old friends . . . to see his only sister . . .

What could he say without divulging his past? He didn't know exactly how to handle the situation. Perhaps it was time to reconsider the long-kept secret. Not that he was ashamed of his heritage, not in the least.

But things *were* complicated, did not appear on the surface as they truly were. Nothing about that day five years ago could be described in black or white; nothing about his impromptu decision was simple. . . .

The storm had come out of nowhere, else he would've stayed ashore—never even rented the sailboat. Mercilessly, the squall had tipped the boat, tossing him overboard. From that point on, everything had become muddled up in his mind.

The very reason for going to Atlantic City had been to give himself opportunity to think. To contemplate his future with the Hickory Hollow church. And even though it was a relatively common thing for a baptized Amish boy to hire a Mennonite van driver to take him to the ocean on a birthday spree, he'd felt somewhat awkward going it alone that day.

Thankfully, the driver had known of him from his birth, being Peter Miller's brother-in-law, a God-fearing Mennonite who lived only a few miles from Hickory Hollow. And oh, how they'd talked—practically the whole way to the shore. Mostly about religion, especially in regard to Dan's points of contention with the Amish church.

It wasn't unheard of for professional drivers to take Amish folk here and there in their fancy cars or vans. For a price, of course. And Dan had paid dearly, but not so much in terms of the cents-per-mile quote to his final destination. *His* payment had come in costly denominations of love lost: relationships with dear ones, family and extended family— church members he'd known and loved all his life. Paid for with a single report from the Coast Guard.

Gone . . . his former life. Gone, his future with Katie.

Pinning a gold clasp to his tie, Dan wondered what Samuel Lapp's only daughter would think of him now if she could see him dressed this way. "Fancy like the English," Katie would say. A sobering thought, to be sure.

Would he never stop thinking of the girl he'd left behind? All these years, the one thing that had kept him going was the hope that his sweetheart girl must have surely found happiness with another man. A good fellow in the Amish church who embraced the same faith as her forefathers.

Yet thoughts of Katie—sweet, headstrong girl that she

was—married to someone else tore at his soul. He was caught in the middle, with no way out.

Outside, the noonday sun made ribbons of gold on the deep, deep snow, and as Dan left his home, most of the house lights shone out from the windows, upstairs and down. Giving no thought to the huge electric bill sure to follow, he drove his fine car through icy streets, his heart as heavy as the new-fallen snow.

CHAPTER TWENTY

❖   ❖   ❖

Tall tapers were flickering on the dining room table when Dan arrived at the Hess home. In spite of the snowy brightness outside, Owen's wife had set a festive table, complete with candlelight.

He and his boss settled into comfortable chairs in the living room, visiting, doing their best to avoid "shop talk" while Eve worked in the kitchen. "It's good you're taking some time off here soon," Owen commented.

"I'm looking forward to it. Hope to visit relatives in Pennsylvania."

"Oh . . . whereabouts?"

"The Lancaster area. Ever hear of a place called Hickory Hollow?" A lump constricted in his stomach. Even speaking the name of his birthplace brought on a mixture of emotions—both stress and bliss.

"Can't say I've ever heard of it, really. Must be a little hamlet somewhere off in the hills."

"That's right." He paused.

"What relatives do you have living there?" came the curious reply.

"Actually, my entire family lives there. My parents and

brothers—all married. And Annie, my sister, she's a married woman now, I hear."

"Well, you should've asked off for her wedding," Owen said, smiling. "I'm an understanding man."

Dan leaned forward, feeling the tension knotting in his neck. "It's been over five years since I've seen any of them." The realization brought renewed sorrow. "It's time for a visit."

"I should say so." Wearing a serious expression, Owen folded his arms across his chest. "I think you've been working too many long hours here lately."

Dan sighed and plunged in. "I suppose . . . well, there's a reason why I work so much." And he began to unravel bits and pieces of his secret past.

When his chronicle was through, he sat back and let out a deep breath. He'd purposely left out a few sacred details. Couldn't bring himself to verbalize everything—the wounds still so raw. Couldn't just blurt out the reason why he'd let the People—Katie, too—think he'd died in the sailing accident.

Owen sat up, folded his hands, and expressed a desire to pray. "Let's ask the Lord to go before you, to open the doors for you to speak to your father. We'll pray that God will soften the hearts of your people . . . your family."

Owen had not mentioned a word about Katie. But then, Dan's friend wasn't the type of man to risk embarrassing anyone. Not in the least.

❖   ❖   ❖

"Do I have time to make a phone call?" the impostor asked as she and Katherine passed in the hall, a few feet from the library. The woman looked well rested, Katherine thought, after having been up all hours the night before.

She shrugged. "Dinner will be served any minute now, but go ahead."

"Then you'll cover for me?" The woman sounded much too demanding, but before Katherine could reply, Katie Lapp scurried off into the enormous room filled with many, many books and one telephone.

Not interested in listening to another disgusting conversation, Katherine stayed put, waiting outside as the young woman placed her call.

Fortunately, the phone chat didn't last more than a few minutes. Katie rushed out of the library, her eyes bright. "I haven't missed anything, have I?"

"Not a thing."

"That's good, because I was dying to talk to my boyfriend. He's really put out with me that I'm not home for Christmas."

Katherine decided to take a chance. "Oh? Where is home?"

"Pennsylvania."

"Really? I'm from there, too."

The smile faded instantly. "Small world," mumbled the woman, and Katherine thought she heard a groan.

"So it is." Unconsciously, she reached up to adjust her cap. A mere habit, a reflex born of the Plain years. Instead, her hand found the ruffled maid's cap, the fancy thing that marked her new life.

◈   ◈   ◈

It had been harder to deal with his wife than Samuel Lapp would ever have thought possible. Rebecca was pretty near hysterical.

"I *said* I was sorry about the baby crying and bothering everyone's dinner. I *knew* I shouldn't have let her sleep all by herself upstairs," she sobbed in the front room.

Samuel had no idea what to do or say to get his wife calmed down. She'd caused such a scene at the table, and Annie, dear girl, was left to clean the kitchen alone.

Elam, Eli, and Benjamin, much to his relief, had vacated the house. But now here *he* was, with a dilemma on his hands: how to help Rebecca get ahold of herself.

He took both her hands in his. "There's no baby upstairs, Becky, honest there ain't. There's only one baby in the house right now; it's little Daniel, and lookee here"—he guided his sniffling wife over to the doorway, and they peered through to the kitchen—"he's sound asleep over there in the cradle Elam made."

His wife's eyes were dark, unusually so, and the look in them was alarming. He thought about riding over to see the bishop after a bit, have a quick, quiet talk. On second thought, he didn't want to disrupt John Beiler's Christmas with his family. Didn't want to let on anything was wrong in front of the children, neither.

Rebecca was crying more softly now. "I want my baby girl back. Can't live another day without my Katie girl."

He took the sobbing woman in his arms, held her close. There was no rebuking her now. She'd spoken their shunned daughter's name, not out of willful disobedience. Rebecca was clearly out of her mind.

"I'll see what I can do," he said, groping for something to ease her pain. "We'll keep on a-praying for her soul."

It had been the only approach to take. The weeping ceased and his wife pulled away. A smile broke across the tear-streaked face. "Ach, you *will* help bring her home, won'tcha, Samuel? You gonna help me get our baby girl back?"

He leaned down and kissed her wet face. "I miss her, too, Becky . . . I do." And he brushed away his dear wife's tears gently with his thumbs, wondering if and when she'd ever be right again.

❖ ❖ ❖

Dylan let himself in the front door, catching the aroma of roast duck. "Splendid," he whispered, ignoring the fact that Fulton was not at his post.

He kept his overcoat and scarf on until after arriving in his upstairs office, where he removed both, draping them over the leather couch. How good to be home again, he thought and wondered when he ought to seek out his Amish impersonator.

Quickly, he located his files—his secret copy of Laura's last will and testament. He was pleased. Everything was in order, where it belonged.

A loud knock came at his door, and he jumped, startled. "Who's there?" he called.

"Fulton, sir."

"One moment." Dylan gathered up the papers and stuffed them back into the file drawer. Then moving around to his desk, he sat down, folding his hands in front of him. "Come in."

The door opened and in walked the butler. "Christmas dinner will be served in ten minutes, sir."

"In the dining room?"

Fulton nodded slowly, then paused for a moment. "Mrs. Bennett and her daughter plan to join you there as well."

"Ah . . . good." He'd guessed the three of them might share this special meal. "Together at last," he quipped.

"Indeed." Fulton stood there, waiting to be excused, his eyes set in a cold, unforgiving stare. "Will that be all, sir?"

"One more thing. How are the mother and daughter getting along, would you say?"

"Famously" came a stony reply.

"I see. And what of Mrs. Bennett's health?"

"Sir?"

"Is it safe to assume the mistress will be comfortably sedated for the meal?"

"Nurse Judah is better prepared to answer that question, sir."

He rubbed his chin, waiting, yes, taunting the tall man. "I see, but what is *your* assessment of the mistress's overall demeanor?"

Obviously annoyed, Fulton shrugged. "I'd say she's quite delighted, sir. Happy to be celebrating the Good Lord's birthday."

Dylan cringed. Why must the man bring the Lord into it?

"But what of her illness? Is she improving?" he pressed further.

An eye-opening smile played across the butler's face. "With God's help, I pray Mrs. Bennett might outlive us all."

Suppressing a curse, Dylan excused the butler immediately.

❖　❖　❖

Katherine held the box of matches in her hand, gazing down the hallway for a long moment. Mr. Bennett was home; she could hear his deep voice, mingled with Katie Lapp's and Rosie's, who was most likely feeding the mistress her dinner.

Apprehension gripped her, threatening her resolve.

This is what you've been waiting for. Now is your moment.

But she wasn't ready to seize it. Couldn't get her confidence back, for one thing. She thought of the sachet link between herself and the mistress, the color and thickness of their hair . . . everything and anything to encourage herself. Boost her spirits.

But it was the painting, and her rightful place in it, that made her blood pressure rise. She would move heaven and earth to see that the phony Katie never, *never* showed up in that mother-daughter portrait!

When Selig burst through the kitchen's double doors carrying a two-layer cake perched high on an elegant silver cake stand, she was ready and eager to follow him down the hall and into the luxurious dining room.

Inside, Rosie was seated to Laura's left, feeding her a spoonful at a time. The sight of it pained Katherine greatly, and she had to look away. Yet doing so forced her to view either Mr. Bennett or Katie Lapp. Neither a worthy subject.

With a flourish, Selig set the elaborately decorated cake in the center of the long table, between two candelabra—directly across from the masquerader. Mr. Bennett and Laura sat at either end, and Katherine was surprised to hear both of them join in when Rosie started up the "Birthday Song."

That was her cue to light the candles. She took several steps toward the table, and leaning over opposite the impostor, she struck the first match, willing her hands not to tremble. Not to cause the slightest mishap in the lighting.

❖ ❖ ❖

Dan pulled his gaze away from the candle flame positioned in front of his dinner plate on the Hess table. How he longed to see his sweetheart again. If only for one glimpse.

When he visited Annie, he would plead with his sister to tell him of Katie's marriage. This, only after they discussed thoroughly a plan to approach their father for Dan's confession.

Yet he wondered, when the time came to hear the truth, could he take it like a man? Could he bear the pain?

If only he could arrange to observe Katie discreetly from afar. Across the barnyard, perhaps? As she hung out the week's wash on the front porch clothesline, maybe. She'd never have to know. . . .

"Can I get either of you some more coffee?" Eve asked as she snuffed out the candles and turned up the dimmer switch.

"Not for me, thanks." Dan watched the spiral of smoke as it curled toward the modest chandelier overhead. "Everything was delicious, Eve. Thank you for sharing your Christmas dinner. I really appreciate it."

"Oh, anytime." She smiled at him and turned to go into the kitchen.

"We mean that, you know." Owen wiped his mouth with the napkin. "Now, about the young woman you mentioned earlier. How will Miss Katie take the news of your being alive?"

Dan wished his friend hadn't mentioned it. "It's hard to say, really, but I don't plan to be around when the People find out about my confession. Katie included."

"So you'll leave Hickory Hollow without seeing her?"

He felt very nearly ill. Never before had he allowed himself to consider how he might handle things.

"She's better off hearing it from Annie. My sister's her oldest brother's wife."

"Ah . . . so you're nearly related, then," offered Owen.

Dan hadn't thought of that. Hadn't wanted to. There'd been enough of a love-bond between them without having to look the present facts squarely in the face. He didn't need his and Katie's past tied to an extended-family relationship in order to reconnect them.

Anyway, it was cruel to anticipate such a reunion. He wouldn't taunt himself, wouldn't entertain the hope of having Katie back. No, Elam's little sister was long married. He was almost sure of it.

CHAPTER TWENTY-ONE

❖   ❖   ❖

As it turned out, Laura hadn't gotten around to telling her daughter about her grandparents—the original owners of the estate. She'd planned to inform Katie of the will earlier this morning. This she felt to be a wise move, since who could tell what Dylan might do to get his hands on the young woman's inheritance after Laura's death?

A violent contracture of her ankle and lower leg had occurred after breakfast, and much to her dismay, Nurse Judah had had to notify the doctor. He, in turn, had ordered an hour of physical therapy. Excruciating as it was, the procedure had limbered up her muscles, easing some of the cramping, as well. But she'd completely missed out on her time with Katie.

Now as she sat in her beautiful dining room, she wondered when the appropriate time might present itself. Between bites of lemon cake, she tried to draw Katie out, to get her to share more of her life in Amish country.

"Perhaps she'd rather not talk about it in front of everyone, dear," Dylan piped up.

From the corner of the room, she noticed the blurred shape of Justin Wirth turn and face this way, curiously. "Oh, but I find the Plain lifestyle fascinating," the artist remarked.

Laura had nearly forgotten the man was even in the room, he worked so effortlessly, so silently. "Yes," she said softly, the word sticking in her throat. She was having much more difficulty swallowing. More so each day that passed.

"Where is it you come from?" Justin asked Katie.

"Lancaster, Pennsylvania. About five hours south of here."

"Nice place," he remarked.

Laura made another attempt at communicating. "Yes . . . it was beautiful even . . . even when I visited many . . . years ago." She was not about to reveal the truth of her most *recent* journey to Pennsylvania Dutch country. Besides, it was an effort to get the words out today. Sheer frustration had come with this untimely speech impediment where, always before, her enunciation had been precise. She was mortified.

Most upsetting of all was the humiliation of having to be fed in front of her husband and daughter. Still, she would not give up hope. Not until after she'd spoken with Katie in private. Then, and only then, would she allow the disease to run its terrible course.

❖ ❖ ❖

Here lately, Benjamin Lapp had been spending more time with the family pony, his shunned sister's pony, really. Funniest thing, he couldn't get the animal to come when called. Didn't seem to know his name—Tobias. But it was, after all, the name Katie had given him, long before she'd up and gone ferhoodled, disobeying the bishop over a guitar and some ridiculous tunes she'd made up.

Truth was, he couldn't get Tobias to eat much, either. The beautiful animal had turned downright dumb. Ben had told his father and Eli about it, but he guessed they'd decided to pay him no mind, 'cause nobody but Ben seemed to care a hoot about coaxin' the poor thing to eat or drink.

Today he'd decided to try something new. Something sweet, straight from the dinner table. A sugar cookie, with extra sugar sprinkled on top.

He held the treat under Tobias's nose, letting him have a whiff, then crumpled it into the feed trough below. "There now, have yourself some dessert mixed with hay." He stroked the pony's mane. "Katie ain't here to spoil ya rotten, but I am. Now, please, won'tcha eat?"

He heard the scrape of work boots behind him. Turning, he saw his father's scowling face, and the angry words spewed forth. "Benjamin, didn't I tell ya weeks ago not to be mentioning your sister's name in my house? That goes for the barn, too. Your sister's under the shunning, have ya so soon forgotten?"

"No, sir."

"Well, then, what do ya mean by talking to this pony about that . . . that . . ." His father slumped down, bent his knee to the dirt floor.

"Dat? What's-a-matter?" He ran to his father.

Weeping, Samuel leaned his elbow on one knee and smothered his face into his big callused hand. "Your mamma's going crazy, Ben . . . and I can't just stand by and watch . . . watch her. . . . She's not herself no more."

"Aw, Pop, it'll be all right," he managed to say. "The bishop did the right thing, shunning my sister . . . didn't he?"

Shaking his head, Samuel moaned like he was in terrible pain, then he blurted out a whole slew of words in German, hurling profanities into the bitter cold air.

Tobias seemingly understood and began to whinny over and over, shaking his head again and again. But Ben couldn't bring himself to weep along with his father or to have a temper fit with stubborn Tobias. Still, his innards sure felt tore up, but good.

211

❖ ❖ ❖

When it was time, Katherine returned to the dining room with Garrett to clear away the dainty dessert dishes. She took Laura's plate and fork, handed to her by Rosie, and stopped in her tracks when she glanced over at the easel. Mr. Wirth was beginning to sketch some Amish clothing, the impostor's, probably.

She wanted to rush over and set him straight, tell him that not even the fake daughter's clothing represented any of the Lancaster orders. Truth be told, *nothing* about the woman was honest or decent.

Just when she thought she might disregard Rosie's request and actually speak to the artist while assisting at the table—just at that moment the fork slipped off the plate in her hand, and embarrassed, she bent down to retrieve it. When she did so, her maid's cap fell off and Katherine's hair cascaded over her shoulders.

Justin Wirth turned and looked at her, acknowledging her with a nod, staring at her hair. Their eyes locked for a long, long moment; he released her at last by turning to study his own painting, then glancing over at Katie, who was chattering away to Laura.

"Katherine," prompted Rosie, "you may take the dishes to the kitchen, please."

"Yes, ma'am," she replied, holding her hair back from her face with one hand. She escaped into the kitchen to repair the bun and replace her cap, then hurried back to the dining room.

When she returned for the crystal goblets, she knew she dare not look in the artist's direction. Those scrutinizing blue eyes . . . ach, how they haunted her. Disturbed her no end, for they reminded her of Daniel's.

"How do the Amish celebrate Christmas?" Mr. Bennett spoke up.

Startled for a moment, thinking it was *she* the man was speaking to, Katherine opened her mouth to reply. Thankfully, she caught herself in time to remember she was no longer Amish. In time to overhear a pathetic, inaccurate account of Plain folk running around with handsaws, cutting down trees, dragging them out of the forest to their homes to be decorated with quilted homemade ornaments. She almost laughed at the ridiculous spiel. And something about the way it all tumbled out, something about the way the impostor's lies seemed to roll off her tongue, told Katherine the whole thing had been very well rehearsed.

"Excuse me, but that's not the way it is," Katherine blurted out. "Amish people don't celebrate Christmas with decorated trees."

Rosie and Garrett gawked at her, but she couldn't stop. Had to explain things the way they truly were.

"How would *you* know?" the false Katie accused.

"I know" was all Katherine said, turning her full gaze on the woman in her Amish costume.

Mr. Bennett stood up suddenly. "Who *is* this woman?" he demanded.

Katherine cringed. Himmel! She'd spoken out of turn, should never have given in to her emotions. Now she was done for.

Rosie made an attempt to gloss things over. "This is our new maid, sir. Fulton signed her on two days ago."

"Does the woman have a name?" he bellowed.

She spoke up quickly. "Katherine, sir."

His face flushed bright red. "Yes, well, may I see you outside?" He gave a nod toward the hallway.

"Excuse me," she said, especially for Laura's and Rosie's sake. But she kept her eyes on the floor when it came to Katie Lapp, sitting so smug in all her glory. Puh!

"So . . . it's Katherine, is it?" He purposely lowered his

voice, hoping for a chilling effect.

"At your service, Mr. Bennett." She curtsied.

"What is the requirement for servants' communication at the table?" he drilled her, captivated by her stubborn yet refreshing naiveté.

" 'Speak only when spoken to in regards to table or food needs,' " Katherine recited.

"Very well. You broke the rules of the house, and what?—during your first days of employment? Not a good beginning."

Would she break down? Cry for him? he wondered.

"I'm sorry, sir. I'll try harder next time" came the meek little voice. Much like a child would address her parent.

He had to suppress a laugh, lest he be heard in the dining room. Initiating their movement down the hall, he led her farther away from the gathering. "We'll certainly see about that, won't we?"

"No, sir . . . I mean, yes, sir," the young woman stammered.

She couldn't be much older than his New York model. Still, he looked her over, up and down, surprised that she was still casting an innocent gaze back at him when his eyes fell on her face once more.

This woman . . . what was it about her? So very different from the brazen, even seductive Alyson Cairns he'd brought here to deceive his dying wife.

"I shouldn't have said anything about the Amish, sir."

It would seem she was begging . . . pleading with him not to reprimand her further. Remarkable!

He added, "You will be placed on a probation of sorts."

"Probation?"

It was clear the woman had no clue of the word's meaning, and he chuckled. "Where've you been all your life?"

"Hickory Hollow, sir."

"I see." He wouldn't let her unsophisticated demeanor

rub him the wrong way. Yet what was it—that look about her?

"Hickory Hollow's an Amish community, sir," she continued. "I know about the Amish ways because I grew up in the Old Order."

He felt his eyes narrow into judgmental slits. "What did you say your name was?"

"Katherine, sir . . . from Hickory Hollow, Pennsylvania. I called you up on the phone not too long ago. Don't you remember?"

And he'd thought she was merely a misinformed yokel! How could he have miscalculated so?

"Pack your bags this instant," he hissed, glancing over his shoulder.

"I'm your wife's true daughter" came the amazing reply. "You mustn't force me to leave, Mr. Dylan D. Bennett. I've come such a long way!"

"What's your proof?"

"I have her hair." Katherine ripped off her maid's cap, auburn curls once again tumbling about her face, then turned her profile toward him. "And her chin. See?"

"You have nothing, you conniving little tramp!" He restrained her when she tried to push past him. "I'll have you arrested," he threatened. "You'll *never* set foot in this house again!"

Struggling, he clamped his hand over her delicate mouth and forced her to the stairs.

The commotion in the hallway disturbed Laura. She kept looking to Rosie for some explanation. "Dylan seemed terribly upset just now."

But the maid could only shrug her shoulders. "Something's got Mr. Bennett riled is all I know."

Even Justin had abandoned his brush to peer out the doorway. Such a bellowing. And for what?

Laura supposed it had to be something out of the ordinary to ruffle Dylan's feathers so. Possibly the new maid's outrageous comment. How did *she* know about Amish celebrations?

With the stress and the worrisome questions, came another attack. This time the pain shot through her face, accompanied by tremors in her throat. When she tried to speak, to cry out, only the most guttural sounds emerged.

Natalie was summoned, and before she could be excused, Laura found herself being whisked out of the dining room.

Christmas Day . . . oh, her heart went out to her daughter left sitting there alone at the table.

She prayed silently that the Lord might allow something beneficial to come of the exodus. Perhaps *now* Justin could focus on Katie, on painting her into the mother-daughter portrait.

❖   ❖   ❖

It was late afternoon by the time Katherine checked into a roadside motel, having arrived by taxi. She stopped crying long enough to pay the lobby clerk for two day's rent. What she would do after that, she didn't know. Acquiring a job should be ever so easy, though, for a former Amishwoman who could cook, keep house, care for children. . . .

But landing a job was the last thing on her mind.

She dried her tears and set about the chore of unpacking her bag, then put her guitar away last of all. Sitting at the desk in the small, musty room, she clenched her fists against the thought of having been thrown out of the estate . . . threatened, too, by that vicious man, Laura's husband! She thought too, of her brief stay at the Bennett mansion, regretting having no time or opportunity to say her good-byes to the servants. For in such a short time, they'd become friends.

She thought of Rosie and Fulton, how they'd taken her under their collective wing, so to speak. And Mr. Williams—she did believe the old gentleman was just beginning to warm up to her.

Everyone had been so kind. Everyone except the master of the house. *He* had acted like the devil himself, and she wasn't all that sure that he wasn't.

After her unpacking was done, she realized the pot-pourri sachets had been left behind in the corners of the bureau drawers. All of them, even her own lilac ones.

The thought of having abandoned her own handmade creations caused her to try all over again. But in the sadness—the pitying of herself—came the surprising answer to Mr. Bennett's accusation.

What's your proof? he'd roared at her.

Suddenly, she knew . . . realized fully what she needed for evidence, as sure as she was Laura Bennett's daughter, she knew. Now . . . how would she go about getting it? Who did she know in Hickory Hollow with a telephone?

Lydia Miller, of course! For the first time in several hours, Katherine smiled. Smiled so hard that half a dimple popped out on one cheek; she spied it in the wide mirror over the dresser.

There *was* proof. The kind of proof Mr. Bennett could never dispute. The rotten-to-the-core man would drop his teeth. For sure and for certain.

Now . . . how to get her hands on the satin baby gown?

Part III

The Lord is my light and my salvation—
whom shall I fear?

Psalms 27:1

CHAPTER TWENTY-TWO

Lydia Miller went about the living room, gathering up crumpled wrapping paper amidst toys and games—Christmas presents to her young grandchildren. She was truly surprised when Edna summoned her from the kitchen wall phone. "I think it's long distance," her daughter-in-law said, covering the receiver. "Sounds like it might be Katherine."

"Katie Lapp?"

Edna nodded, and Lydia swept loose strands of hair into her covering before taking the phone. "Hello?"

"Cousin Lydia . . . it's me, Katherine, calling all the way from New York."

"Well, Merry Christmas to you. How nice to hear your voice."

There was a slight pause. "Lydia, uh, I was wondering . . . well, I need your help."

"Are you all right?"

"I'm fine, really I am. But I wonder if you could drive over to my mamma's house. I need you to talk to her. To-day."

Lydia wondered what could be so important on a busy Christmas afternoon. But as the sketchy details began to unfold, she felt the weight of responsibility begin to settle on her shoulders. Still, she wasn't at all unwilling to do Katherine's bidding. "I'll see what I can do," she promised.

"Remember to ask Mamma gently. You'll do that, won't you, Cousin Lydia?"

"Of course I will." She sighed, wondering if she oughtn't to mention that Katie's mother and Ella Mae Zook had dropped by for a visit.

Stepping out in faith, hoping what she was about to say might help things, not hinder, Lydia told Katherine about the unexpected visit.

"Mamma . . . and the Wise Woman, really? They came to see you?"

"I know . . . I was surprised, too."

"Well, how's Mam doing?"

Lydia stared at the lights on the tree. "I'd say she must be awful preoccupied. She's suffered a terrible loss."

"True," came a tentative reply.

There was an awkward pause.

"So . . . you want me to get your old baby dress from her, then?"

"That's right. Only please tell my mother you want to *borrow* it. See what she says about that."

"I won't lie, Katherine. You know better than to ask me to." She wondered if the world had begun to rub off on her cousin's daughter.

"It wouldn't be a lie," Katherine insisted. "She'll have it back . . . in all good time."

Lydia sat down on the wooden stool near the wall while the caller continued. "Once you have it, I'll need you to mail it . . . by overnight mail, please. To me." And she gave the address of the motel.

"Aren't you staying at your natural mother's place?"

"Not now. It's a very long story, and I hope to share it with you someday, but . . . well, I'm paying for long distance."

"I understand, but I hate to think of you being at a motel somewhere, especially on Christmas Day. Bless your heart. Why, Rebecca would be worried sick if she knew."

"Oh, but she *mustn't*! Please don't tell Mamma that part. I'm fine here, Cousin Lydia, really I am. But getting the baby dress will solve everything. So if you'll save the receipt for the mailing, I'll pay you back. Please . . . this is ever so important to me."

Lydia could hear the longing in the young woman's voice. "I'll try, Katherine. But I'm telling you it may not be easy. Word has it your mother's not well."

"Mamma isn't?"

"Well, she's not herself, to say the least."

"Ach, no!"

"It's been a real blow, losin' her daughter both to a bishop's decree and then to a fancy, worldly woman."

"Oh, but you're wrong. My natural mother is anything *but* worldly. She's a good, honest woman. And I think she's about to be hoodwinked, possibly out of a lot of money. Maybe even her entire fortune."

Alarmed, Lydia promised to do her best to get the baby gown mailed up to New York. Fast as she could.

Nothing about the visit to the Lapp home was easy. To start with, Samuel almost didn't let her in—"because Rebecca's lyin' down just now," he apologized.

"Oh, I can come back later," she said.

At that, he seemed to open the door a bit wider even as he stood there making excuses for Rebecca who "ain't in any shape to be comin' downstairs for company."

Unconsciously, Lydia fixed her eyes on his tan suspenders, the sound of Katie's pleading over the phone echoing in her mind. The poor displaced girl was counting on her. And it was odd, but something inside her—a surprisingly powerful resolve—wouldn't let Lydia back off this first attempt at seeing Rebecca Lapp. Not without trying harder, at least.

"Maybe I could run up and see her. That way she wouldn't have to get dressed and all . . . unless she's sleeping."

Samuel shook his head. "No, no, she ain't asleep, but she's been through a horrible, awful time today." A long pause. "'Tis our first Christmas without . . . without the girl. You can imagine. . . ."

But, no, she *couldn't* imagine. Her children were all grown and gone, true, but to have one of them leave the community because of some age-old ridiculous shunning practice! No . . . never.

She noticed the man's sunken eyes. One look at his forlorn countenance and Lydia could readily see the aftermath of grief. He, too, was suffering great loss.

"I'm so sorry . . . wish Peter and I could've helped Katie out more." She'd struggled off and on with guilt, having opened her home to Samuel and Rebecca's runaway daughter.

"You did all ya could," Samuel replied, and with that, he motioned her inside, took her coat, and led her upstairs.

When Lydia first laid eyes on her cousin, she felt near like crying herself. Rebecca was all doubled up on the bed, as though she was experiencing tremendous pain. She lay on her side, clutching a rose-colored baby dress in both hands.

The part that evoked tears was seeing the Amishwoman's lips move as if she were talking to the little dress; yet not a sound escaped her lips. Only Samuel's hard, frightened breathing could be heard in the room.

Lydia searched her pocketbook for a tissue. What had gone wrong? she wondered. How had her cousin slipped from yesterday's semidetached behavior to *this*? Had the severe shunning of her daughter pushed the woman over the edge?

Lydia could easily see there'd be no approaching Rebecca about giving up the beloved gown. Not today. Not with her clinging to it as if it were a lifeline to Katie, somehow.

Even if she went ahead and asked for it the way Katherine had suggested—to *borrow* it for a while—even then she knew the plea would be refused or misunderstood. No, borrowing the only threadlike connection to Katie—a symbol that might well be preserving the confused woman's sanity—well, it was out of the question completely.

How long she stood there, Lydia didn't know exactly. But when she turned to whisper to Samuel—that she'd best be going—Rebecca stirred a bit.

Startled, she hurried to the distraught woman's bedside. "Rebecca . . . it's your cousin Lydia. Is there something I can do for you?"

Rebecca's eyes were empty, dazed, and she began to moan—long, low-pitched groans, as if in travail.

The glassy-eyed look took Lydia by surprise—she was that shook up. "You don't have to speak, Cousin, but maybe a nod of the head?" She hated to inquire this way, as if she were talking to someone other than her own blood kin. Someone completely unrelated. "Are you in pain?" She had to know.

It was then that Katie's mamma placed her hand on her breast and tried to sit up.

"Are you in *physical* pain, Rebecca?"

Her cousin stared back blankly.

"Can you hear me?" she tried again.

Unexpectedly, there came a nod. "I must get up . . . must take care of Katie. Don't *you* hear my baby crying?"

So baffling was such a question, Lydia knew she couldn't bring herself to follow through on Katherine's request. Perhaps someone else, someone *closer* to the Amish community, might be able to pry the baby dress away from the fingers of a brokenhearted mother.

Who would be willing to help Katie? Who in Hickory Hollow could Lydia turn to?

❖ ❖ ❖

Mary couldn't stop thinking about her encounter with the bishop. How mellow and strangely subdued his voice had been. Honestly, she'd never heard him sound thataway. Not at Preachin', for sure not at barn raisin's or nowhere else, neither.

She wondered, had he softened his voice for her? To let her know that the same man who'd shunned Mary's dearest friend in all the world had another side to him? A kind and gentle aspect to his soul?

Pondering this, she helped her mother prepare fruit salad and leftover main dishes from the noon meal. She dared not discuss her thoughts with Mam or Mammi Ruth, though she'd thought of nothing else since arriving home from the visit with John Beiler.

Oh, she hoped her sour cream chocolate cookies had absolutely melted in his mouth—his and the children's. One good way to a man's heart was through his stomach, her mamma had always said. Jokingly, of course. But she'd seen her mother's cooking work wonders with her Pop many a time.

She thought of the next scrumptious recipe she might offer to the bishop and his half-orphaned brood. Ach, she wouldn't be waitin' long, neither. Come next Sunday, she'd have another mouth-watering surprise for John Beiler.

And . . . she was gonna be listening; comparing, too, the sound of his "delivery voice" during the sermon, weighing it against the almost romantic utterances of this most glorious Christmas Day.

❖　❖　❖

She struggled to get past the haze in her mind. Fuzzy . . . woolly. *Everything* about Rebecca's thoughts felt that way— like peering through gray cellophane paper.

Fighting off a precarious feeling that if she let herself relax—even while lying in her own bed—if she gave in to the pulling, the all-consuming murkiness, it might swallow her up. Might devour her entirely, and she'd never be right again.

Something in her consciousness told her there was someone standing in the room. Someone besides Samuel. But she couldn't begin to guess who.

Then, intruding on her attempts to think . . . *think* . . . the crying returned. The insistent wail of a newborn baby. *Her* baby.

Frantic feelings pulled at her, deeper . . . deeper into the wailing. Into a tunnel, the corridor long and narrow. The desperate wail of a helpless child—her heart-child who could not receive nourishment.

Crying echoed in her ears, reverberating through the white, sterile passageway. Rebecca closed her eyes, trying to block out the heart-wrenching sound. As she did, the tunnel gave way to people—two women. One, a teenage girl carrying a sleeping baby, the other, the girl's mother.

"I want you to have my baby," said the girl with red hair.

Eagerly, Rebecca's arms went out to receive the beautiful infant. Her arms felt the slight weight of the tiny one, and she offered a warm bottle. But the rosebud lips would not suck.

More crying . . .

What would she do if she could never quiet the infant,

never be the kind of mother her baby truly needed?

But when she opened her eyes, longing to see the darling bundle, oh, yearning to gaze on her child, she looked—and Katie was gone.

Sitting up in bed, Rebecca listened, listened with all her might, but heard nothing. She hobbled down the hallway to another bedroom. Ach, the house was still. Dead still.

Sighing, she sat on Katie's bed, holding the satin baby gown. When she'd kissed it, she laid it back in its hiding place.

It was then she realized the infant's crying had stopped.

❖   ❖   ❖

Mary was caught off guard after supper when a big, beautiful car pulled up in the driveway. "Who's this?" she said to her mother.

They gawked out the window as a woman hurried to the back door. "Looks an awful lot like Rebecca's Mennonite cousin," whispered Rachel.

"Jah, I see whatcha mean."

When the knock came, Mary rushed to the door, welcoming their neighbor inside.

"Can't be staying long," Lydia said, keeping her coat on as Mary pulled up a chair. "I'll get right to the point."

Mary listened carefully as the woman described a phone call. One from Katie. "She called this afternoon, Katie did, needing a baby dress that her mamma's kept around all these years, I suppose. It's made of satin . . . pink, and has the name *Katherine Mayfield* embroidered on the back facing."

Completely in the dark as to what Lydia Miller wanted with either her or her mamma, Mary kept still and paid close attention.

"It seems Rebecca's mighty taken to the dress. I don't

know how to describe it, really, other than to say, she's cling-ing to her daughter's baby clothing for dear life, like it's all she has left of the girl."

"What's Katie need the dress for?" Mary asked, wishing more than ever she could help her friend.

"She really didn't say in so many words," Lydia an-swered, "but I think it has something to do with her natural mother in New York. Anyhow, she needs it mailed up there as soon as possible."

An overwhelming feeling welled in Mary's heart, and she found herself volunteering out of the blue. "I'll go and get the dress for Katie."

Lydia's face brightened instantly. "You will? You'll go over to the Lapps' and talk to Rebecca?"

"I know she's hurtin' awful," she told the woman. "*All* of us are worried sick about her mental state. But I have an idea about the dress."

"Oh, I'm so glad I came over," Lydia said, putting her hand to her throat. "I almost didn't come, almost had to call Katie back and tell her the bad news."

"First thing tomorrow, I'll pay Katie's mamma a visit." She couldn't put her finger on it, couldn't have explained it to anybody if she'd wanted to, but for some unknown rea-son, Mary could hardly wait.

CHAPTER TWENTY-THREE

The morning after Christmas, Laura discovered that her speech had become more distinct again, nearly back to normal. She had even felt confident enough to ask Rosie to invite her daughter downstairs to share a late brunch.

"Are you sure?" Rosie pressed her.

"I *must* see Katie today. It's very important."

"Very well." And Rosie was off.

While waiting for the two of them to return, Laura rehearsed the inheritance information she was about to impart. First, though, there were questions, things she'd reflected on year after year while separated from her baby girl. Oh, she realized such inquiries might have no merit for her daughter. Yet they burned within her, and because life was winding down swiftly, she wanted today—this very morning—to be the moment she finally opened her heart completely. She must hear Katie's answers, give the girl ample opportunity to fill in the missing pieces, the lost heart-knowledge of the years.

After they enjoyed a light breakfast of fresh fruit and tea, Laura and her daughter were alone at last.

"For years, I've wondered about certain things," she began. "About your babyhood and growing up."

"That's understandable," Katie replied, smiling. "What would you like to know, Mother?"

Laura stared at the fire snapping in the fireplace across from them, thinking she must tread lightly, perhaps. "Well, I've always wondered how you were told about your adoption . . . what your family might have told you . . . about me."

Katie nodded, pulling on one sleeve. "I've always known I was adopted. It was something my parents spoke of freely."

"Oh, then you *were* legally adopted at some point?"

"I was adopted right away, as far as I know. As an infant."

"And the birth certificate—was one issued, naming your parents as legal guardians?" Her heart thumped hard.

"They always told me it was as if I was born to them. But, no, they never said who my real mother was, maybe because they didn't know for sure."

"So even though I was never contacted, and no attempts made to locate me," Laura pressed on, praying her voice would hold out, "you're saying that in all legal respects, you are *their* child?"

Katie was silent. She shook her head suddenly, stood up, and went to the window. "I don't know, Mother. I believe I did see some legal documents when I was very young, but I don't remember them exactly. Maybe I never was adopted. Maybe I'm still your daughter . . . legally, I mean."

"But if you aren't absolutely sure . . . ." She paused, desperately worried that her wonderful surprise might well be on the verge of disintegrating.

"I don't think it's a problem," Katie was saying. "Because whatever you have in mind . . . about . . . well, about when you pass away, I'm sure things can be worked out."

Laura stared at the young woman, silhouetted in the window. What was she saying? Did she have some inkling of the revised will? And if so, how could that be?

Theodore had been the last person to see a copy of her

last will and testament. She fully trusted her friend and chauffeur. There was no questioning *his* integrity.

A flood of inquiries came to mind, but she first wanted to look into her daughter's face. Still, the strain on Laura's eyes—having to squint into the light from the window—was giving her a headache. "Come sit closer to me, Katie. My eyesight is failing fast."

Her daughter came quickly. "I'm sorry, Mother. I hope you don't think I'm rude or forgetful. It's just been such a long time since—"

"I know, dear. I know." She sighed. "Now, you must forgive me for prying, but ever since you arrived here, I've wondered about something else. You see, I recently gave a letter to an elderly Amishwoman in Hickory Hollow while I was there . . . searching for you."

"Oh?"

"I've wondered if you had opportunity to read it, and if, perhaps, my letter was the reason you were found and brought here by my husband."

"A letter? Well . . . no, I don't think so. Anyway, everything happened so very quickly."

"*What* happened, exactly, Katie? How was it you came to Canandaigua to be my Christmas gift?"

Katie blew her breath out with force but did not speak for the longest time.

"It's very important to me. I must know how you located me," Laura insisted.

Katie stood up again, this time heading for the fireplace, her back to Laura. "I wasn't found . . . not the way you might've supposed."

Waiting eagerly for more, Laura forced herself erect, instead of leaning against the back of the wheelchair. "Was there a private investigator involved? Did my husband hire someone to search for you?"

"Oh, you could say there was some hiring going on, all

right. But no, not a private eye."

Bewildered, Laura felt her gaze boring into Katie, trying desperately—through distorted vision—to read her expression. What was the girl endeavoring to say?

Laura felt as though her breath wouldn't accommodate her need for it. Struggling as she inhaled, she thought of calling her nurse.

When she was nearly certain the conversation was at a standstill, Katie suddenly turned around to face her. Her daughter seemed tentative—Laura could hear her breathing erratically. "No one discovered me in Hickory Hollow, or wherever it is you think I'm from, Mrs. Bennett." Removing her prim head covering, Katie shook out the strawberry blond hair with the mere loosening of two pins. "I'm *not* your daughter, Mrs. Bennett. But please know that it wasn't my idea to deceive you!"

The truth stabbed Laura's heart.

"I am so very, very sorry I ever consented to come here," the woman said before fleeing the room.

With the emotional pain came shortness of breath and the worst bout of tremors Laura had suffered in weeks.

❖   ❖   ❖

There were always a great many folk visiting in Hickory Hollow during the Christmas holidays, and today was no exception. Mary hurried her horse along the snow-packed lane, meeting up with a whole caravan of carriages heading in the opposite direction. She figured Rebecca Lapp wouldn't be all that surprised to have extra company, probably. Still, she hoped her visit might help her shunned friend . . . someway, somehow.

A blast of warmth from the Lapp kitchen met her as Samuel welcomed her inside. A glance into the next room let her know that Rebecca was up and about.

Gut, she thought. With Katie's mamma up and dressed, well, she wondered if her chat might not go over lots better than if Rebecca were lying flat on her back in bed.

As it turned out, she was wrong. Awful wrong. "Whoever heard of takin' clothes away from a helpless baby?" came the first heated refusal.

"But Katie needs the dress," Mary said softly. "She wanted me to ask you for it. I'll give the baby dress to your daughter."

"I have no daughter!"

Mary shuddered, almost wishing she'd never come.

"My daughter died in a hospital over twenty-two years ago. Stillborn. Dead . . ."

"I'm sorry, Rebecca. Truly I am." She got up out of the chair, then turning, faced her friend's precious mother and spoke the real truth. "But Katie Lapp ain't dead. She's shunned."

"The bishop killed her. John Beiler did it . . . he's the one to blame for my Katie leaving. *He* is."

Mary left the room, heading back to the kitchen. She passed Samuel on the way. "I think she might need a talk with the Wise Woman."

"Jah, couldn't hurt nothin'," Samuel said, stroking his long beard. "Bishop John can't help her now."

"I'll see if Ella Mae won't come over after bit. I'll bring her myself."

"Denki, Mary. We'll be waitin'."

Five minutes with Rebecca had left her shaken to the core. Five minutes. . . . She felt sorry for Samuel. He had to live with Rebecca twenty-four hours a day. Poor, dear man.

The way the storytellin' woman talked just now, you'd think she'd given up on the Lord God Almighty. Almost made Mary herself wanna quit believin'.

❖　❖　❖

234

When Rosie asked to see Justin's progress on the portrait, he declined. "From now on, the mistress of the house and everyone else must wait for the unveiling," he told her. "Something to look forward to in the New Year." The man grinned, obviously quite pleased.

She left the artist alone with his canvas and hurried back to the kitchen, wondering who should inform him of the most recent events. It was certainly not *her* place. Laura would have to break the news about the impostor's unexpected departure. Laura . . . or Mr. Bennett himself.

Meanwhile, she hoped the time spent painting such a fine portrait hadn't been for naught. After all, wouldn't it be lovely to have a likeness of their kind and loving mistress—the woman who'd brought the Christian faith to this house? Brought the love of the heavenly Father to both Rosie and her husband?

She could visualize the portrait hanging in the library or drawing room. And if Mr. Wirth was the sort of highly creative master she supposed him to be, it might take very little to refine the oil painting, placing the focus on Mrs. Bennett alone.

When morning duties were attended to, she brooded over the woman called Katie Lapp. The actress had exited rather abruptly—similar to Katherine's leaving, with one glaring difference. Mr. Bennett himself had driven one of the limousines, taking the woman to the airport. *Good riddance!* Rosie thought.

Had she been forced to, however, she would have had to confess she was more than a mite discouraged that *Katherine* was gone. She and Fulton had both felt they might be on to something with the responsible, demure maid. And what a cook! Why, she could bake the finest of Amish pies. They'd even toyed with the notion that *she* might be the mistress's true daughter.

But given the opportunity, things between the former

maid and Laura Bennett had never clicked. Besides, if it were true, wouldn't Katherine have spoken up? Declared her identity?

Then why *had* Katherine left? Was it plausible the excuse Mr. Bennett had given? That there had been a death in the family and she'd had to return home quickly?

Whoever had expired so unexpectedly, she did not know. But she *did* wish there had been time for a fond farewell.

As for the so-called Katie Lapp . . . what a revolting situation! Begone with the charlatan!

But the dear mistress was in such a bad way over it, suffering one contracture after another. The stress of the day, unraveling the self-confessed fabricator, had taken its grave toll. Fearing for Laura's life and the future of the manor, Rosie went to her knees in prayer.

◈　◈　◈

Her face, though blurred in the mirror, looked gray and waxen, her lips pale. She struggled to inhale, the anxiety of the morning clawing at her with each breath.

Natalie had tried to persuade her to go to the hospital. "You'll be much more comfortable there."

But she had vowed not to leave "until Dylan returns, because I must speak to him one last time."

"Then it is necessary that you lie down, Mrs. Bennett," Natalie urged. "I'll prop you up with pillows."

She refused the nurse's suggestion and continued to inspect herself as best she could. Looking down, she studied the skin beneath her fingernails—dusky. Her hands—clammy and cold.

Natalie began to move the wheelchair nearer the bed, away from the dresser mirror. "I want you to rest now, Mrs. Bennett. It's very important."

"Nothing's important now. Nothing, except seeing my husband again."

The nurse began to treat her as if she were a child, putting her to bed against her will. How she resented it and fought back, slapping at the youthful hands.

Then, unexpectedly, there were more of them surrounding her, people subduing her. And she cried out, using up so much air she nearly passed out.

Despite all her efforts to resist, the horrid nurse gave her another injection . . . no, there were so many others pushing on her now. Forcing her limp and sore body against the bed. Weighing her down, down. . . .

Then, within seconds, came the peace. The lull after a storm.

Later, she thanked Natalie, apologizing for her irrational behavior.

"You don't have to excuse yourself, Mrs. Bennett. I understand that your flare-ups cause you great distress."

She was silent for a moment, then spoke in a whisper. "In the end . . . will I lose control completely?"

Nurse Judah pursed her lips. "You mustn't think that way. Do concentrate on living, Mrs. Bennett. We . . . I want you to survive this episode."

Laura was comforted by Natalie's hand on her perspiring forehead. The affectionate touch made the crises of the day somewhat more tolerable, indeed.

CHAPTER TWENTY-FOUR

The next day, Katherine sat alone in her motel room, trying to work the TV remote. "What's keeping Lydia?" she said aloud. "Mamma wouldn't hold on to that baby dress if she knew I needed it. I *know* she wouldn't."

Giving up on the television, it being a tool of the devil anyway, she picked up the newspaper to read the "Help Wanted" section. Though her eyes scanned the ads, her mind was still fixed on her last moments at the Bennett estate.

What a fierce man—Dylan Bennett! She felt horribly frightened for her birth mother, a considerate and sweet lady having to live out the remaining days of her life with such a person.

When she thought of the wonderful-good oil painting, there was rage. The *other* Katie was going to wind up next to Laura Bennett! The thought infuriated her, and she wished more than anything that she'd shouted out her identity to her mother. Instead of that wicked Mr. Bennett.

Even now, sitting in this pocket-sized motel room, cigarette smoke slowly seeping through the cracks, she wanted to do something to change things, with or without the little satin gown. But she'd never get past that monster, Dylan

Bennett. She knew better than to try. Might wind up in jail
. . . or worse.

She'd wait for the package from Lydia Miller, wherever
it was. With the baby gown—sewn by Laura herself—with
that kind of proof in hand, she could walk right over the evil
man. And no one and nothing could stop her!

◈　◈　◈

After lunch, Natalie called the doctor, informing him of
Mrs. Bennett's persistent flare-ups, as well as her labored
breathing.

He, too, recommended admission to the hospital. But
her patient seemed completely confused, insisting that she
must wait until her husband returned from the airport. That
Dylan had important business in town—arranging a romantic cruise for the two of them.

Natalie wondered how long before she herself would
have to make the call—decide *for* the sick woman that she
be taken by ambulance to the hospital. Surely no more than
a few hours at the most.

Mrs. Bennett continued to ramble incoherently, and on
occasion even behaved with uncharacteristic irritability toward her caregivers. Yet Natalie offered nothing but kindness in return, nurturing her dying patient.

The instant the choking occurred, Natalie spun into action. Laura had been sipping cold juice through a straw
when she began to cough and gasp for air. In seconds, her
pale complexion had turned bluish.

Natalie knew all too well the dangers present, and as
soon as the coughing subsided somewhat, she listened to
Laura's lungs with a stethoscope and heard crackling. A definite sign of aspiration pneumonia—a deadly complication
she had been expecting.

By late afternoon, Laura had developed a temperature.

Alarmed, Natalie knew the woman needed supportive IV therapy, and because she was having such difficulty swallowing, a feeding tube would also be necessary.

Natalie decided not to say a word to Mrs. Bennett. Instead, she took Rosie aside. "I'm going to need your help, as well as Garrett's and Selig's, when the ambulance arrives."

"Ah, I hate for Mrs. Bennett to leave us this way," the maid said in the tiniest voice. "I'd hoped it wouldn't come to this."

"So had I." Intent on maintaining her medical professionalism, Natalie did her best to hold back the tears.

"How long before. . . ?" Rosie shook her head, unable to finish.

"Hours, maybe a few days . . . if she's lucky."

Rosie blew her nose. "She's ready to go, our Laura is. She knows where she's headed after this life."

"I don't claim to share Mrs. Bennett's beliefs," said Natalie. "But if there is a heaven, it will be a better place when she gets there."

"This *house* has been a better place because of her," Rosie remarked, eyes glistening. "As for heaven—it's always been glorious because *Jesus* is there."

Natalie kept quiet. The maid could say what she wanted to about eternity. But as far as Natalie was concerned, the simple fact was she would miss her patient, and yes, she honestly hoped there *was* a heaven, for the sake of a fine Christian lady named Laura.

❖ ❖ ❖

The sound of a siren rang in her ears, and before she could protest, she felt her body being lifted up and onto a wheeled cot.

She sensed they were taking her away—to a place where she did not want to go. These cruel people in white. These people who could breathe freely at will. Without worry that the next breath could be their last. For though she pulled hard, she found no air.

Where was Dylan? Why hadn't he returned with their plane tickets? Their plans would be useless now. All their future hopes and dreams—Dylan's and hers—dashed to pieces. . . .

⬥   ⬥   ⬥

Mary hitched up her father's best horse and drove the carriage over to visit Ella Mae. But it was Mattie, her daughter, who came to the door of the Dawdi Haus, the small addition for aging relatives, connected to the main house.

"Oh, hullo. I guess I was expectin' to see your mother," she said, stepping back from the door.

"She's sick in bed with the winter flu."

Mary's heart sank. She thought about going upstairs to speak to Ella Mae but figured there was no use risking her own health, not if the Wise Woman wasn't able to help her out today anyway.

"Well, I'm sorry to hear she's sick. But can ya tell her I stopped by?"

Mattie smiled. "Seems my mam's second only to the bishop around here. Sure, I'll tell her."

Mary turned to go, hoping Ella Mae's illness wouldn't keep her down for too long. 'Cause she knew if Katie's great-aunt couldn't help her out—and soon—there'd be nobody else.

Nobody knew how to patch things up between people or give advice like the Wise Woman. You'd've thought she was hooked up with the Lord God Himself.

Seemed odd, really. When it came right down to it, Ella Mae Zook never actually preached if you went to see her about a problem. No, sometimes—*most* of the time—she'd

241

quietly quote a psalm or a proverb from the Bible. Or she'd just sit and listen to what you had to say. Didn't even tell you what you should or shouldn't do. But when you walked away from her little house, you'd most always feel like you knew the answer. Felt better for having gone to see her.

Thinking about all that, Mary realized the Wise Woman was a lot like herself—wanting to do what was right, yet not ever wanting to step on folks' toes. And something else she'd learned from visiting Ella Mae—holding grudges weren't gut for nobody. Made your heart fill up with blackness, crowding out the spaces for love.

"But some of us just ain't never content with what the Almighty sends our way, t'ain't so?" the Wise Woman had told her days before Katie was supposed to marry the bishop but didn't.

Mary had agreed. Some of the People—folks like herself—were always wishing for more than their lot. 'Specially when it came to wanting a husband and a good, loving marriage.

Still, she wouldn't give up on the bishop. Wouldn't give up on a man who'd filled up quite a few of those heart spaces inside her, in spite of her friend Katie's harsh shunning. In spite of all that.

She hurried home and told her mamma how sick Ella Mae was, hoping the old woman would shake off the flu bug in record time. Hmm. Maybe she could help the illness run its course a little sooner.

What *would* the Wise Woman think if she showed up tomorrow with a batch of freshly stewed prunes?

CHAPTER TWENTY-FIVE

More than a week had passed with no word from Hickory Hollow. Katherine stewed and fretted, in a constant state of panic, wondering what to do next. She had found a part-time waitressing job at a fifties-style diner nearby and, in the early morning hours, created one frenzied or melancholy tune after another on her guitar. All in a sad minor key, notating each one, just the way Dan had shown her. This, she believed might keep her sane.

After dark, she'd hire a taxi and have the cabbie drive slowly past the Bennett estate, her eyes fixed on two large windows—the bedroom she knew to be Laura's. Her thinking was that if light poured out from the windows, chances were her mother was still alive.

In addition to the nightly treks, she would dial up the Bennett mansion, disguising her voice, trying her best to get some word of her mother's condition. But the estate operator never put her through to Rosie or Natalie. In fact, this voice was different from the one she'd heard when calling for the first time over two weeks ago.

There was so little time. Might be too late already.

Honestly, she'd just assumed that with Lydia Miller in charge of things at home—her being such a responsible woman—she would have managed to locate the tiny satin dress by now.

Katherine had no idea what was holding up the process, but she couldn't sit by and wait any longer.

Lydia answered on the first ring and seemed relieved to hear Katherine's voice on the other end of the line. "I thought of calling you, more times than not," her cousin explained.

"Oh? Is there a problem?"

"I'm really sorry, but I've had no luck. And that's not to say that I—*we*—haven't tried." And she went on to tell how Mary Stoltzfus had gone to see Rebecca, too. "Your mamma's mighty attached to that baby dress. No one, not even Samuel, has been able to talk her into loaning it to you."

"Not Dat, either?" She could hardly believe it. "So my father must know that I called you, then."

"Yes. And he's not the only one. Several others know now." And Katherine listened as Lydia spelled out the latest holdup. "It's Ella Mae, your great-aunt . . . she's been sick with the flu for days."

Feeling as though the whole idea was a lost cause, Katherine sighed into the phone. "Well, guess I should've been praying about all this before now."

The voice on the other end was silent for a moment. "Peter and I are praying, Katie. We're praying for *you*."

Katherine almost corrected her, wanted to remind her that she wasn't Katie anymore, but she let it go. "Well, since you're talking to God about me, here's something else you can tell Him. It's about Laura Bennett—my natural mother. She's awful sick, you know. And I can't be sure, but I wouldn't be surprised if she's in the middle of some evil scheme. Can't go into it, but there were some terrible, dreadful things going on while I was there."

"And you're not with her now?"

"No. But the minute Ella Mae's well again and gets my old baby gown, soon as that happens, I'll be on my way back to Laura. Then I'll prove I'm Katherine Mayfield—I'll march right in past her horrid husband and see her again. Oh, I want to know her, Lydia. Want to spend time talking with her before she dies."

"Well, then, I'll send the dress the minute I receive it," promised her cousin.

Katherine wanted to believe Lydia, because all she had now was hope. Hope . . . and the bold English prayers of her mamma's Mennonite cousin. Without any of that, she might've felt truly alone.

⊗   ⊗   ⊗

Dan hurried into the church where Owen and Eve met him in the foyer. "Slow down, you're not late," teased Eve.

He checked his watch. "Just wanted to get a good seat for the concert."

The three of them settled into a pew near the middle of the sanctuary. The evening's presentation was to feature both vocal and instrumental music.

During the first number—a female soloist accompanied by gentle guitar chords—he thought of Katie. This music, this harmonious music, filled him with joy . . . sadness, too. And he wrestled with troublesome doubts as he sat in the Mennonite church, knowing beyond all question how right his sweetheart girl had been for him, yet—even then—not wanting to influence her against the Old Ways. Still, thinking back, he *knew* he'd let things slip out. Things that haunted him to this day.

He wished he could apologize to Katie, confess to her, along with his father. But he would never do anything to threaten her present . . . or her future, by bringing up his past misdeeds. No sense in piling another mistake on top of all the others.

The jubilant hymn being performed spurred him on, giving him courage for the task ahead. His sister would've received his letter by now, he figured. And tomorrow he'd write the follow-up letter, asking Annie to round up some Amish clothing in preparation for his visit to Father.

How he longed to share his newfound joy—his Christian witness—with his father; his mother, too. Yet he suspected that Jacob Fisher, terrified by the consequences, would be obligated to report him to the bishop once Dan made it known that he'd been saved and had joined the Mennonites. The irony of it—and the renewed heartache his confession surely would cause—all of it, had discouraged him from making amends.

Now hearing the music—especially the guitar background—spoke peace to his soul. Tomorrow he'd follow through with his plan to mail a second letter to Annie. That way, at least he wouldn't be accused of dampening Hickory Hollow's holiday spirit. For that, he was thankful.

Come what may, his sister—his entire family—was soon to see him. Alive and well . . . face-to-face.

❖   ❖   ❖

"Rebecca, someone's here to see you," Samuel called, leading Mary and Ella Mae into the front room.

Hoping that *this* visit might turn things around, Mary followed the Wise Woman through the kitchen.

"Well, hullo there, Rebecca," said Ella Mae, touching the woman's hand. "I've missed ya."

Rebecca began nodding her head in a most curious way, and Mary felt a sting in her stomach, observing Katie's mamma. So unlike the cheerful Rebecca Lapp she'd always known. Unlike anyone she'd ever known in Hickory Hollow.

"I hoped you'd be showing off that little baby dress ya made for Katie," the Wise Woman began, her voice crackling like always. "Thought maybe we could try it on your baby today."

Mary nearly dropped her teeth. What on earth was Ella Mae saying? Is *that* how Rebecca was thinking these days?

"Can't find it no more," said the daft woman. "Been a-lookin' and can't seem to find it."

"I'll help ya. Honest, I will," said Ella Mae, reaching for Rebecca's hand and leading her around the house. They looked like two young children playing a game of hide-'n-go-seek.

So while Ella Mae began to shape a story, one she might be telling to a group of women the way Rebecca often had, Mary sat and talked to Benjamin.

"Didja ever hear of an animal refusing his own name?" Ben asked her.

"You talkin' about Satin Boy?"

"We call him Tobias now."

"Oh . . . well, maybe that's why he doesn't come," she said. "Ya know how . . . well . . . could be that's the reason he's not respondin' to ya. Try calling him by the name *she* gave him."

Ben shook his head, chuckling softly. "Himmel, what trouble that girl's caused . . . even the animals don't know which end's up."

She let him finish jabbering on about the pony. Then when he was quiet for a bit, she spoke up. "I was wonderin' what ya might think of something, Ben."

"Think of what?" His thick blond hair lay flat against an oily scalp, showing the ring mark where his winter hat had sat on his head.

"I've been thinking about talking to the bishop."

"What for?"

"Oh, I just a wanna ask him some questions . . . about

the shunning. Do ya think he'd shun me, too, for talking to him about it?"

Ben laughed. "Doubt it. 'Cause everyone's a-thinkin' you may be his next wife, Mary."

She gulped hard and tried to cover it up by coughing, leaning off to the side of her chair. "The bishop . . . and me? Married?"

"And why not?" he said. "Don'tcha think it's a gut match?"

Secretly, she was elated. But, of course, she'd be keepin' those kinds of thoughts to herself. Deep inside, where no one could guess how she felt about Bishop John Beiler. Or so she'd thought.

When Ella Mae came downstairs, she came alone. "Rebecca's havin' herself a nap." She pointed toward the ceiling. " 'Speck we best be goin'."

Mary hopped up and went to get their coats. "Didja get it?" she whispered, helping the Wise Woman into her wrap.

"Is the bishop *standhaft* . . . unyielding?" replied Ella Mae, wearing a crooked smile. Then out from the old woman's basket came something shiny and pink.

"Is that *it*? Is that the baby dress . . . uh . . . *her* real mamma made for her?" Mary couldn't bring herself to speak Katie's name right out loud, but she could think it!

Ella Mae looked Mary straight in the eye. "Never you forget it, honey girl. The *real* mamma's right upstairs."

Even though she tried repeatedly on the ride home, Mary never could pull it out of the Wise Woman how she'd got ahold of the baby garment. Jah, she tried asking many different ways, even though she felt it wasn't the right thing to do at all—trying to trick someone into telling you something against their will.

By the time they arrived at Peter and Lydia Miller's house, though, she didn't much care anymore *how* Katie's infant gown had ended up in Ella Mae's basket of sewing and stitchery. The main thing was, this being Saturday, Katie'd have it by Monday morning.

"Before noon, guaranteed," Lydia informed her after she'd run up the front porch steps and delivered the dress.

"Hope this makes her happy," Mary remarked, not meaning it sarcastically, though it might've sounded that way.

"Oh, she'll be mighty happy, all right," said Lydia, grinning broader than Mary'd ever seen her.

Then the smile faded and Lydia folded her hands as if in prayer. "You must ask the Lord to protect your friend. She's off by herself in a motel room somewhere. But . . . something tells me . . . that's not her biggest worry. . . ."

Of course, Mary had to know what on earth Lydia meant by that, and the two women whispered their confidential chatter until Mary had to rush off and get the Wise Woman home to a warm fire and some piping hot coffee.

CHAPTER TWENTY-SIX

❖   ❖   ❖

On Monday, January fifth—before noon—Katherine received a UPS delivery. Heart pounding, she studied the package the man had brought her, recognizing Lydia's handwriting immediately.

Tearing open the parcel, she found the rose-colored baby gown wrapped in tissue paper. "Oh," she whispered, and hugged the tiny garment to her cheek, remembering with absolute clarity the first time she'd ever laid eyes on the shimmering fabric.

She sat in silence, struggling not to cry lest she stain the little dress. Then, remembering that, before ever leaving Hickory Hollow, she'd once found a single mark on the garment. Believing it to be her mamma's teardrop—she searched for it. Finding it, she wept.

After a time, she called a cab. Staring at the name embroidered on the facing, she ran her fingers across it, feeling the stitching, still intact after these many years. Rewrapping the dress, she bundled up and waited for her ride—the short ride back to her mother's estate. As she waited she prayed, in German, that the Lord God heavenly Father might keep Laura Bennett alive, at least for a few more hours. That He'd protect her from the wrath of Dylan Bennett, as well.

Katherine asked the cab driver to drop her off around the east side of the estate, closest to the servants' entrance. That way she could slip past anyone who might try to detain—or arrest—her, so strong was her need to see her mother, to reveal the truth to the person it mattered to most.

Bold with determination, Katherine crept through the outside doorway, checking to see if anyone was near, then hiding in the first room she came to—a spacious storage closet. Inside, she paused, listening, straining to hear the slightest sound. Perhaps Garrett or Selig. Anyone.

When it seemed the corridor was clear of servants, at least, she opened the door, moved quietly into the hallway, and tiptoed down past the grand staircase, toward the south wing—her mother's quarters.

Once again, she stood to the side of the tall French doors, peering around them to see into the sitting room. Odd, she thought. No one was there. Not even Natalie Judah, the live-in nurse.

Suddenly frantic with worry, she rushed past the love seat and comfortable chairs arranged near the fireplace, past the cherry sofa where tiny matching Christmas trees had brought gaiety to the room.

She was standing in her mother's private bedroom now, her heart in her throat. There the bed had been stripped bare of all coverings and sheets.

"Rosie?" she called. "Nurse Judah?"

There was no answer, so she called the louder.

Still no reply. Even Mr. Bennett's presence might've been welcomed at this moment. Yet there was no one.

Seized with a choking terror, Katherine dropped to her knees beside the empty bed and began to cry out to God in English, abandoning her familiar German rote prayers, praying for the first time the way Peter Miller had taught her to.

"Oh, dear Lord Jesus, please, please don't let my mother be dead. Please . . ."

She heard the scuffle of feet and turned to see Theodore Williams coming into the sitting room.

"Katherine?" he called to her.

"Oh, Mr. Williams, where's my mother?"

The old gentleman's face went ashen and he muttered something under his breath.

"My mother . . . Laura . . . is she dead?"

Afraid, so afraid, of his response, she looked down at the UPS mailer—knowing what wondrous thing she'd hidden there—and she cried. She cried so hard that Mr. Williams came over and offered her his own handkerchief.

❖   ❖   ❖

Samuel had his hands full taking care of his wife. Sitting next to her, talking softly to her, watching her writhe in their bed, he figured he must've been out of his mind to let Ella Mae come and take the one and only thing Rebecca had cherished so.

Now his dear spouse could speak of nothing but Katie's baby garment. Yet she had it no longer. Without the fancy dress to hold, to stroke, to whisper to, her world seemed to have fallen near apart.

He didn't know what on earth to do about it, 'cept summon the bishop. Maybe if John Beiler could see what his pompous ruling had done to Rebecca, maybe then he'd see the error of his standhaft ways. The unbending ways of the Old Order.

The minute he began to reflect on these defiant thoughts, though, he was filled with remorse. Still, he wondered if it might not do the community some good knowin' what the shunning had done to the wife of Samuel Lapp.

❂ ❂ ❂

He'd see to it personally. Katherine—*Miss* Katherine, it was now—would be driven safely to the hospital. "Mrs. Bennett's life hangs by a thread," Theodore told her as they headed for the limousine. "The doctors don't give her much longer."

The young woman wiped her tears and, of all things, insisted on riding in the front seat opposite him. The next thing he knew, she was showing him an exquisite baby gown.

"This is the dress I wore on the day Laura gave me away," she said. "See the name embroidered in the back?"

He glanced over to consider what looked like tiny stitches forming the name *Katherine Mayfield*.

"It appears that our missus was most creative, even as a teenager," he commented. Then he broke the news delicately to the young woman. "Not long after you left, your mother discovered the truth about that woman parading around as Amish. Katie Lapp, or whoever she was, has left town . . . and so has Mr. Bennett."

Katherine frowned. "He has? When?"

"Days ago, and no one has heard from him since."

"I wonder why," Katherine said. "Wouldn't he want to stay around . . . until . . . ." She choked back tears.

Poor girl. How could he tell her? Drawing a deep breath, he began. "There is strong evidence to indicate that the man was . . . in cahoots with one of his partners, as well as the New York model-turned-actress. Evidently, they'd planned to swindle your mother out of the estate . . . and possibly more."

"How awful evil." Katherine tucked the baby dress back into the tissue paper.

"Yes, and we're still trying to piece things together.

Thankfully, the estate will not fall into the wrong hands upon Mrs. Bennett's death."

"What do you mean?"

He realized he'd already said more than was prudent. "I believe it is Mrs. Bennett's place to discuss her affairs . . . at the proper time."

And that was all he would say.

❖   ❖   ❖

Because she was Laura Bennett's only living relative and had merely to say so to the head nurse—without even showing her the baby dress, none of that—Katherine was told she could see her mother for fifteen minutes at a time, every hour on the hour.

The initial visit was most painful. Katherine tiptoed into the private hospital room, holding her breath as she saw before her a woman wired up with tubes going every which way. Clear oxygen tubes in her nose and intravenous therapy connected to the veins in her arms, one of the nurses was kind enough to explain.

Katherine clutched the UPS parcel and willed herself not to faint. Truth be told, the sight frightened her no end, made her weak, as if she might need to sit down.

And she did. Sat there on a chair beside the bed and stared at the woman who'd given birth to her nearly twenty-three years before.

At one point, Laura's eyelids fluttered, and Katherine stood up slowly. But she stepped back a bit, hoping her mother might be able to focus her eyes on her, for the nurse had explained that Laura's vision was severely impaired.

"Mother? It's Katherine, and no, you aren't dreaming. I really am here."

Laura's eyes closed quickly, and Katherine couldn't

blame her for that—so viciously had her dear mother been duped.

She crept over to the side of the bed. Standing there, patiently waiting for Laura to give her a second chance, she pulled out the satin baby gown.

When her mother did not respond after a time, Katherine reached down and placed the little dress under Laura's right hand, her fingertips resting lightly on the folds of the garment.

"This is the dress you made for your baby girl," she whispered. "My Amish mamma—Rebecca Lapp—saved it all these years. There's some lovely embroidery stitched in the back facing. Do you remember sewing my name there?"

She stopped talking and waited. What she saw broke her heart—and began to heal it—all at the same time.

Big tears rolled down either side of the pallid face. "Katherine," she heard her mother whisper. "Oh, Katherine. You're here at last."

She didn't want to hurt the dear lady or disturb any of the numerous tubes going in and out of her body. Oh, but she wanted to be near her. Hug her—not hard—just embrace a part of her.

Two thin hands came together, slowly grasping the satin baby gown. It was then that Katherine leaned over and kissed the hand nearest her, letting the tears flow freely.

"I've missed you all my life," she managed to say. "I've never been truly Amish, not through and through." Then, so as not to tire her mother unduly, she picked the choicest portions of her life to talk about. Things like her cravings for beautiful music and fine, fancy clothing, jewelry, and different types of hairstyles. She told about the letter Laura had written to Rebecca, Katherine's adoptive mother, and how it had gotten burned up before she'd ever laid eyes on it. About living in Hickory Hollow, always wondering what she might be missing out in the world.

Sometime before the nurse came in to let her know fifteen minutes was up, sometime right before then, Katherine told her mother about the boy with blueberry eyes. Her one and only true love, Daniel Fisher.

"What . . . a wonderful boy," her mother said. "I wish he were . . . still here."

"All of us—all the People—were sorry, too. It was the most dreadful time of our lives." She said it without holding back her love feelings for Dan, so free she felt with this woman. *This* mother. And hoping her first mamma might forgive her. Someday.

CHAPTER TWENTY-SEVEN

Two days later, Laura was still alive and wearing thick glasses so she could see Katherine more clearly. The new lenses had given her spirits a tremendous boost. Furthermore, she'd felt a quickening in her, a most unusual feeling. She was convinced she was getting better. And she told her daughter so . . . the nurses, too.

She'd felt something similar upon first meeting that vile impostor of a woman, and she'd heard that such occurrences had a tendency to induce a kind of remission sometimes. She could only hope *this* one might last, though, that she might beat this disease, once and for all.

But she was bright enough to know she mustn't put her trust in physical improvements alone, not when it was her emotional health that had seen the biggest lift. Her daughter had come home. The girl had moved heaven and earth, as she'd put it, to search for Laura. And what things she longed to share with her. Fifteen minutes here and there during the course of a day simply wasn't enough.

When Natalie Judah—who was no longer responsible for her care—came for a quick visit, Laura implored her to get the hospital visiting rule lifted.

"I'd love to do that for you, Mrs. Bennett, but I believe

it would be futile to try," the nurse said.

"Please, see if someone will listen to you," Katherine pleaded. Then when Natalie had left to do whatever she could, Laura's daughter told her something her friend Mary Stoltzfus had always said, growing up in Hickory Hollow. "Ya never get if ya don't ask."

When Laura asked her to repeat it in Dutch, Katherine laughed and obliged her, putting on the thickest German accent she'd ever heard. But she loved it, every minute spent with her adorable Katherine.

Not long after, Natalie returned, sporting a broad smile. "I guess I should've pleaded your case before this. The hospital has consented to give you unlimited time together— the two of you. That is, if Mrs. Bennett agrees to rest periodically."

Because of the new glasses, Laura noticed happily that Katherine appeared as delighted as she.

❖   ❖   ❖

The drive to Lancaster seemed much longer than Dan had remembered, even without a horse and buggy. It may have only *seemed* long because of the many boyhood landmarks along the way, especially once he made the turn off Highway 340.

The closer he came to Hickory Lane, the more he found himself slowing down to savor the rolling hills, the tall, tall trees, the way the sun played on blanketed white fields. Even in the dead of winter, this part of Pennsylvania was rich with beauty. And the memories . . . how they beat a path to his brain.

Fighting off the impulse to drive past the Lapps' red sandstone house—see for himself if Katie still lived there— he turned onto a narrow road, leading to Weaver's Creek. It was here that he and Katie had written a love song together while sitting on a boulder. They'd watched the creek ripple past them that day, and he'd tried to tell her of his doubtings, his questionings about the Amish church. He had tried, but the only thing he could even begin to say, really, was that no matter what happened, no matter if he got himself shunned, he'd still always love his Katie.

Of course, if his recollections were true, about the only thing he *did* do that day, at least when it came to declaring his love, was kiss her. Again and again. Till she had to wriggle free from his arms and take him on a walk toward the bridge and the creek below.

There, perched on a boulder in the middle of the stream, he had pulled out some folded staff paper and a pencil from his pocket and shown Katie how to notate music for the first time.

The music. . . . How he'd always longed to share it as a gift to his People, to his precious Katie, so full of melodies and lovely lyrics herself.

Yet the Ordnung forbade it.

Over the years, prayer and fasting had brought him to his knees in holy communion with his Lord and Savior. But it was the music and spiritual worship within the church walls, like a balm of Gilead, that had soothed his splintered soul.

He wondered how Katie had ever survived without it, for he questioned whether anyone might've come along to fill his disobedient shoes in that regard. Who else would've offered her the same sort of bonding—the love of music they'd shared so intensely? Still, it was sin, according to the Amish church. And for her sake, he rather hoped she hadn't pursued that particular interest, especially if she wanted to remain in good standing with the People of Hickory Hollow.

Checking his watch, he realized the appointed hour was upon him. For in his second letter to Annie, he'd asked her to meet him near the old one-room schoolhouse, knowing

259

it would be vacated well before four in the afternoon. It was the perfect place for him to change into Amish clothing, too, and he hoped she wouldn't disappoint him in this.

Annie was right on time, and he waited in his car for a bit before getting out, allowing her to pull the carriage into the school lane.

Spying each other at almost the same instant, they literally ran into each other's arms, laughing and crying. "Daniel!" sobbed his sister. "I can't believe it's really you." And she pulled back to look him over. "You're so tall, ach, you're a grown man, ain'tcha?"

He picked her up then and twirled her around. "I've missed you, Annie!" he shouted into the frosty air.

Holding hands, they ran together toward the Amish school, letting themselves inside. "I didn't know what on earth to think when I got your first letter," Annie began. "I thought it was some kind of horrid joke at first. But then, before long, I knew it was you." Her voice grew softer. "By reading it over and over again, I *knew*."

She was full of questions, so many it made his head spin. But what she wanted to know more than anything was the truth of what had happened in Atlantic City five years ago.

He pulled in a deep breath, then began, praying she'd understand, could forgive him. "I ran away on my birthday, angry at Dat," he explained. "It started out to be an innocent outing—a sailing expedition, all by myself."

"Just you, alone?"

Dan took it more slowly, gave her a moment to digest his news. "I needed time to think . . . to think where my life was headed. So much of what I knew about religion and God had been passed down to me from our parents—their parents before them. I know you may have trouble with this, but I needed something in *writing*, something I could read for myself. For another thing, I wanted to be sure I was saved, so . . . I was secretly studying, even memorizing parts of the Bible."

"You were?" The light left her eyes.

"I wanted to spare you, Annie. Wanted to protect you and the rest of the family from thinking I was sinning." He didn't go on to tell her that he'd had the same reason for shielding Katie Lapp, as well.

Continuing with his story, he recalled the unexpected storm. "A severe one . . . I was knocked overboard. Almost drowned swimming to shore."

Dan told the truth, all of it. In the end, there had been ample opportunity to explore a faith to stand on—not one built on tradition or man-made rules. Now for him, he told Annie, the Ordnung had long since been replaced by the Word of God. Many long hours of personal Bible study and fellowship with other Christians had convinced him, had served to boost his confidence and faith in the Almighty.

"Ach, I don't know what to say," Annie spoke in a near whisper.

"I don't expect you to understand, Annie, or forgive me—neither one, for that matter." He shrugged sadly. "I was a foolish nineteen-year-old boy, terribly immature. But I've come home to repent."

"Well, you'll be needin' these if you're to meet with Dat." She held out a bag of clothing. "And don't forget this." She handed him a black felt winter hat.

"Thank you, Annie. I appreciate your help."

"Ach, my husband has plenty of hats, ya know." Then she told him about her marriage to Elam Lapp.

The Lapp name touched a nerve. For the life of him, Dan couldn't bear to hear Annie spill things about Samuel's daughter . . . Katie. Who *she'd* married, where she lived . . . things like that.

The huge lump in his throat made it difficult to speak.

He cleared his throat. "I hope to see you again before I leave."

"Leave?" Her eyes widened. "But you just got here."

"I'm Mennonite now," he told her.

"Then why'dja come back?"

"To confess my wrongdoings, to come clean before the Lord and Dat. I had a spirit of rebellion in me back in my younger days. Our father needs to hear that I am truly sorry."

Annie appeared stunned, as though she couldn't believe her ears. "But don't you know that if ya leave, you'll be shunned?"

"I've come to face it like a man . . . at last."

She burst into tears. "Oh, we've got the harshest bishop ever!"

"Who?"

"John Beiler, remember?"

"But he's *always* been hard on the People."

Annie shook her head. "I never thought much about it, till here lately." She began to cry again. "Oh, I wish ya didn't have to go through the Meinding, Dan."

He reached for her, wrapping loving arms about his sister. She sobbed bitterly, and when he thought she might never quit, she looked up at him through wet lashes. "Don'tcha see? It'll be like losin' ya twice. Like you're dead *again*. Oh, Daniel, can't ya stay? Can't ya come help Elam work the farm for a bit . . . live with us? Just don't leave again. Please, don't."

Her pleas tore at his heart.

"We have a baby son," Annie said suddenly, as if telling him might make him change his mind. "We named him Daniel . . . after *you*."

Drawing a deep breath, he touched his sister's chin, realizing, as he stood near the desk where he'd learned his ABC's, that if he didn't change into Elam Lapp's clothing soon, if he didn't drive over to his father's house, he might never be able to go through with any of this. It saddened him that much.

"If ya hafta leave again, will ya at least come say good-bye?" beseeched Annie, and she told him how to get to hers and Elam's house.

"Yes, I'll come," he said. "I won't leave this time without saying 'God be with you,' sister."

❖   ❖   ❖

It had been an awful selfish thing not to tell Daniel about Katie Lapp's shunning—that his former girlfriend was off in New York somewhere, searching for her birth mother. Annie pondered the problem while driving the horse back to the house.

If she *had* told her brother about Katie, if he knew his sweetheart no longer lived here in Hickory Hollow, well, she could almost predict how Daniel would react. And then, even if her father did talk some sense into Dan after he offered his confession, even so, she understood the drawing power of love. *Their* love—a love so sweet, so strong, that if truth be known, she'd have to say she'd envied it through the years. Oh, she hadn't committed the *sin* of envy. No, it was more like the wonder in a child's heart on Christmas morning. It was *that* kind of feeling she felt when she saw them together.

'Course, Bishop John might not think so if he knew about it, but she didn't care. Main thing was, she had high hopes of Daniel returning to the Amish church. And by keeping this one little secret from him, least for now, it was the best thing she could do. For Dan, mostly, but also for herself.

263

Chapter Twenty-Eight

Katherine was shocked when she heard the news.

"You'll . . . be the mistress of the manor, darling . . . after I'm gone," Laura Bennett gasped out.

Shaking her head, Katherine could only reply, "I'd rather be poor and have you alive, Mother. . . ."

"Nevertheless, what's mine today . . . will be yours . . . soon."

With growing horror, Katherine realized that the deadly pneumonia was squeezing the life out of her mother's lungs. There'd be no more talk of the inheritance—not now. She must hear Laura's story—how it came to be that she'd decided to give her newborn infant to an Amish couple. Still, when that moment came—later in their conversation— she'd be very, very careful how she phrased the question. The subject was much too painful—for both of them.

Meanwhile, sitting here beside the hospital bed, Katherine realized how very similar they must appear. Hair color and texture, even their noses matched . . . and the bold, determined line of their chins.

Catching her studied appraisal, her mother smiled. "I'm afraid I'm not looking . . . my best," she managed with a wry look. "My hair . . . so thin now . . . probably the medication."

Katherine took the fragile hand, like a bird's wing, it seemed. "Did the boys ever tease you about being a redhead?" she asked in a lilting tone, hoping to steer the conversation to more pleasant paths.

"Your . . . father did sometimes . . . your *birth* father."

The comment caught her off guard. She hadn't considered another man—other than Samuel Lapp—as her father. Strange, how she'd felt so instantly at home with her natural mother, with not a thought for the young man—her real father—who'd loved Laura as a teenager, then left her pregnant and brokenhearted.

There was a pause when the nurse came in to check for vital signs and see that her mother's IV and oxygen tube were in place. Immediately after that—when they were alone again—Katherine began to ask more questions. Several that had remained lodged in her recollection ever since the day she'd first spied the baby dress.

"Why did you pick satin fabric for the dress?" she wanted to know.

"Perhaps it was because . . . I've always loved the feel . . . the swish of satin."

There were other such questions—favorite foods, whether Laura had a craving for sweets. . . . Then—how it was that her mother had happened to be in Lancaster on the day of Katherine's birth.

At that, Laura's face blanched pale as death, followed by a pained expression. "Oh," her mother moaned. "Quick . . . the nurse!"

Katherine ran to the door to summon help. "My mother's in terrible pain. Please help her!"

A rush of nurses swept through the door, one politely asking her to leave the room.

Had her never-ending questions set off her mother's illness . . . caused undue stress? Katherine fretted. Why couldn't she have been content to sit beside Laura's bed, letting her mother talk only when and if she chose to.

Why must I be so bold, so curious?

Standing outside the hospital room door, she prayed that if this flare-up was to cause her mother's passing—*if* it were—that the dear Lord Jesus, Savior of the world, of Lydia Miller and Laura Mayfield-Bennett, might ease the pain and cushion the tug-of-war between life and death.

Recalling the past hours of intimate conversation, Katherine counted up her blessings. Not only had her natural mother desired to pass on a vast fortune to her only offspring, but her strong faith as well. Laura had explained her relationship with Christ Jesus—in glowing terms of love and acceptance— such things Katherine had never heard.

The idea that God's Son should come to earth and die for *her*—hardheaded and conniving as she was—made Katherine stop and think. Really think about her place in "God's kingdom," as Laura had put it.

As she waited in the hallway, hovering close to her mother's door, she recalled the sweet moments spent talking about spiritual things. It was then, while thinking back over this part of their conversation, that she began to comprehend how unimportant it was to know *who* you were—her biggest hang-up in life, it seemed—but *whose* you were.

Her natural mother had had it all—wealth, the most stylish clothing, the finest foods, even golden combs for her long auburn hair. There were mirrors galore and the best furnishings money could buy, but it hadn't been enough, Laura had told her. Laura Mayfield-Bennett needed something—Someone—greater in her life. Someone who would never run off and leave her or betray her. The Lord Jesus.

Tears sprang to Katherine's eyes, and she wondered suddenly if this was what Daniel had tried to explain to her five years ago. Could it be that Dan, too, had come to know

Laura's Lord? Really *know* Him . . . before he died?

❖   ❖   ❖

Dan knocked on the back door of his father's house. He'd probably made a mistake by not asking Annie to warn his parents. What if they couldn't handle seeing their dead son's "ghost"?

He stood far enough back so that they might see him fully, not merely his face pressed close to the storm door.

For a brief moment, he was glad that it was his mother who appeared at the door but watched in dismay as the blood drained from her cheeks.

"Jacob!" he heard her call out.

"Oh, Mamma, don't faint!" Quickly, Dan opened the door and held on to her until his father came to assist him— this stranger with the beginnings of a beard and a borrowed Amish hat. But he kept his head down, not letting Dat see his face.

"Ah, Elam," said Dan's father, "what didja do to your mother-in-law?"

By now Daniel found himself inside the utility room, helping his mother into the kitchen, where she fell into the big old hickory rocker. He wondered again why he hadn't thought to fine-tune this plan. After all these years—some of them spent in a trade school—shouldn't he have had more sense than to burst in on his loved ones this way?

He found himself sputtering out an apology. "It's not Elam, Father. It's . . . I'm your own son, Daniel."

"Who? What's that ya say?" his mother shrieked and stared, long and hard.

But Dat promptly grabbed both his wrists, squeezing them in a viselike grip. "But you're dead! We thought you died years ago . . . drowned in the ocean!"

He let his father lash out at him. Let him spend his fury.

267

"How could you go off and let us think you were dead?" the old man bellowed. "Didja know how awful hard your mamma would mourn and grieve your death, till the tears in her eyes all dried up?"

Standing in the middle of the kitchen, Dan did not budge an inch, even after his father released his arms. Then, trying to reckon with his own pain, Dan watched his father pace the floor like a distraught lion. Every now and then the gray-haired man glared back at him, his eyes red-hot with righteous indignation.

Dan was taught as a child to believe that the eyes of his father were near sacred, that they could emanate such emotions as anger, displeasure, and disapproval—yet without sinning.

Truth be known, Dan felt as though he had been transported in time, back to his late teen years, during one of the daily "preaching" sessions his father had imposed on him.

At last, Dan, still standing as if on trial, spoke up. "I've come home to confess, Father. I want to make things right between us."

His anger dissipated, Jacob pulled out a straight-backed chair and sat down near his wife. "The Lord God almighty is sovereign and just," the man said, not sternly, but with conviction. "Welcome home, son."

Then, removing his hat, Dan knelt at his father's knee, praying silently for grace and forgiveness. "I come to you, carrying the memories of my past sins," he began with folded hands. "Transgressions I committed against *you*, Father. And I'm here to ask you to forgive me."

◈ ◈ ◈

"Can you ever . . . forgive me?" Laura begged, struggling to speak. A suffocating cloud of heaviness weighted her chest. "I wish I had . . . kept . . . you as my own, Katherine. I wish. . . ."

She could not finish. The air was gone, and she could not consume enough to say more.

Lying there, hooked up to a lifeline of whirring machines, she longed to hear Katherine's answer. Waited for the words that could free her, those precious words to fill up the past emptiness, the pain-filled years alone without her child.

"Please, Mother, don't be worrying about what you did . . . about choosing Samuel and Rebecca to raise me." Her dear girl stood up unexpectedly and bent down to whisper close to her ear. "I love you. I love you in spite of all the past."

❖ ❖ ❖

"The past is under the blood of Jesus," Dan continued. "The Lord God heavenly Father has brought me home, to offer my confession, full repentance at your knee, Father," he said, using the Amish terminology they would best understand.

Here, he reached for his mother's hand. "Will you forgive me, too, Mam? Can you understand that I didn't intend to fake my death as it seemed I did?"

He didn't wait for either of their answers but went on, recounting the story of the day he'd nearly drowned while swimming to safety. He told them of the Coast Guard boat he'd seen from the reef, watched it comb the raging waters, searching for his body. He repented of his immature behavior, his teenage rebellion, his defiance against his upbringing. And he explained how he'd decided, there on the sandbar, that the easiest, most compassionate way for the People, for his family—for all those who loved him—was for them to presume him dead.

"By not revealing the truth, though, I deceived you. I allowed everyone to think I'd drowned, let them mourn for me. I was only hoping to spare you the Meinding . . . release you from having to shun me."

He paused for a moment, their eyes fixed on him. "Don't you *see*? I thought to save you . . . keep you from having to turn your backs on your son, to treat me as if I were dead. But I know now that I was wrong, Father. It was the worst thing I could've done to you."

His parents listened, their faces solemn and expressionless. Dan stood up and pulled out the wooden bench under the kitchen table. With a sigh, he sat down, facing them. The confession had made his hands clammy, his mouth dry.

Yet, before almighty God, his heart was pure. At least in *His* sight, Dan Fisher was forgiven.

❖   ❖   ❖

She held her mother's bluish hand, unconsciously breathing hard as the dear lady continuously gulped for air. Her color was ashen now, and the death pallor frightened Katherine.

"Don't die, Mother," she whimpered. "I've just found you. Please don't leave me now."

Watching her mother's struggle to breathe, she felt as if she might not survive this crisis herself. She might die along with the fancy English woman who was her real, true mother.

Ach, she'd never witnessed a person die before; didn't think she wanted to even now. Yet she would not abandon the woman who'd given her life.

"My dear Katherine . . ."

"I'm right here with you, Mother."

"Do you . . . know . . . my Jesus?" There was much gasping again, and she felt guilty that her mother had used up so much air for such a sobering question.

What could she say? She wouldn't lie. Not as Laura May-field-Bennett lay dying, preparing to meet her Maker.

"God's Son knows *me*," she managed, hoping she believed her own words. "He knows me, and He brought us together . . . just in time."

"Yes. He knows . . . you, child."

Then without warning, Laura's breathing stopped. And Katherine began to cry.

❖   ❖   ❖

"Why, then, does my dead son return home to confess these things?" Jacob Fisher asked. "What has changed?"

Dan breathed deeply, praying for courage. "So much has changed. More than you know, Dat. I'm a grown man now, able to think for myself, to understand God's precepts. I'm no longer afraid to express my beliefs and compare them with those of the People. And I can now follow the will of my heavenly Father and be the kind of son I should've been to you all those years ago."

"What are ya really tellin' us, Daniel?"

He turned to look at their bewildered faces. "I came here to confess my sins . . . but I cannot return to the Amish church. And for that, I am truly sorry."

"So now you give us no choice but to shun you," Jacob said, frowning hard. "Bishop John will hafta be told."

"My life is in God's hands." Dan stood up, knowing that if he were to stay longer, his time of confession might very well turn into a heated debate. One-sided.

"I love you, Dat . . . Mam." He leaned down to kiss his mother's face. "I wish we could see eye to eye about God's plan of salvation. It would be so good to be able to share the Good News as a family, to break the Bread of Life together."

Much to his surprise, his father accepted his handshake and did not attempt to refute his parting words.

CHAPTER TWENTY-NINE

It was an endless day, even though Katherine never once resented sharing or bearing the dying experience with Laura. She felt she'd gained something most valuable by sitting there as her mother slipped away, pain gone forever.

But she'd been mistaken about that first moment when it seemed for all the world as if Laura was no longer breathing. Several more times, before the end, her beautiful mother had slipped in and out of consciousness, her chest barely rising and falling.

Laura had made one last effort to speak, and Katherine, in retrospect, was grateful for it. "Look for . . . my . . . journal."

"You kept a diary?"

"While I carried . . . you."

Katherine had wanted to hear more, but she sat quietly, holding her mother's hand. The coolness of Laura's hand in hers let her know that heaven was near. Gradually, ever so slowly, the delicate hand had grown lifeless . . . cold.

Laura's last thoughts had been of her daughter. *While I carried you*, the whisper had come, almost inaudibly.

Long after Laura's spirit had left her body, long after, Katherine sat beside the bed. She imagined her mother greeting loved ones who'd gone before. Daniel, too, maybe. Remembering the way he was, she figured her darling would be one of the first in line to receive Laura Mayfield-Bennett, just as soon as her mother passed through those pearly gates.

❖ ❖ ❖

Dan had decided long before today that he would not interfere with his former girlfriend's life. He must protect his own emotions, as well, and by simply not inquiring, he could accomplish both. If he hadn't gone back to his sister's to say good-bye, though, he would've missed hearing about Katie.

Annie dropped the bombshell almost as soon as he arrived, after he began telling her that he needed to leave for New Jersey soon.

"Aw, must ya go?" Tears glinted in the corner of his sister's eyes. "Can't ya stay, Daniel?"

He reached for her hands. "It won't be long now before the People will be shunning me. We won't have many opportunities like this to spend together."

"Might not even be allowed to talk to each other, neither." She frowned and shook her head as if in pain. "Same way we treated . . . Katie," she whispered the name.

"Katie Lapp? *My* Katie?" His eyes searched hers, longing for answers.

"Ach, she's had the harshest Meinding put on her I've ever lived to see."

"What happened? How'd *she* get shunned?"

"It's not an easy story, really, but it all got started with a baby dress made of satin that Rebecca kept hidden in a trunk up in their attic."

Shocking as the story was, he listened to his sister's account of how his sweetheart girl had run away from her wedding, gotten herself shunned, and left Hickory Hollow to search for the natural mother she'd never known.

When Annie was finished, he found himself weeping in her arms—not due to Katie's painful shunning. No, the tears he shed were joyful . . . selfish tears.

❖   ❖   ❖

Ella Mae Zook was on the back stoop, shaking out her kitchen rug, when a right fancy English car pulled into her side of the lane. It slowed down, and she squinted, shielding her eyes from the afternoon sun.

When a young Amishman got out of the car, she had a closer look at him—strikingly handsome, he was. But she near lost her false teeth after spying the blueberry eyes.

"Well, whatdaya know?" she said to the January sky, to God, and anybody else who might be listening. Then the Wise Woman laughed right out loud.

❖   ❖   ❖

Mary wasn't seeing things; not hearing them, neither. Sunday morning, after the *Ausbund* hymns were sung, she watched Bishop John and listened to him, trying to decide whether or not his mellow voice—the one she'd heard on Christmas Day—was one of his Preachin' voices.

Then it happened. Right smack in the middle of a sermon on pride and how "one should run from it at all costs," he looked her way, resting his eyes on her longer than necessary. She wouldn't dismiss it as wishful thinking, but when his gaze strayed mostly for the rest of Preachin', she wondered how she might speak to him afterward, during the common meal.

If she *did* get a word with him, she might say that since he'd been put on this earth to save the souls of men, wouldn't he just consider thinkin' about saving Rebecca

Lapp, too? From going insane, that is?

Oh, she'd tell it to him awful gentle, sweet as can be, and if the bishop was the kind of man she figured he was, deep down inside his soul somewheres—if he truly was God's choice for the People, a man who could change his voice at will—well, he just might consider her request. Just might think twice about lifting Katie's harsh shunning. At least so they could talk to the disobedient woman. Use the voices God gave them, all different ranges and tones, for sure, to witness the love of the Lord God heavenly Father himself and maybe even bring her back to the fold.

It was just a thought. Maybe not the *right* thing to do at all. But what with the bishop sending unspoken messages with his eyes during Preachin' and all, in light of that, she could surely hope.

❖ ❖ ❖

By the time she'd climbed two long flights of stairs, the breath in her was gone. Katherine was reminded of Laura's labored breathing at the end—completely ready when the call from heaven came.

Finding the journal her mother had mentioned as she lay dying had proven to be a challenging task. Yet each day Katherine had searched the estate—even several attics— with help from Theodore and Garrett. All to no avail.

Not to be outdone, she decided to meet with the entire domestic staff. Assuming her new role of mistress of the manor had not come easy, perhaps because she was more than eager to share the size and the warmth of the upstairs rooms. Because of this, because she wanted to allocate the space to her friends—Laura's loyal servants, and now hers— she encouraged them to scatter out. They were to choose various guest suites, even Dylan Bennett's former office area—now vacant—for their own private quarters.

So it happened that while Fulton and Rosie, Theodore, and the others were resituating themselves, Justin Wirth came to call, several days after Laura's funeral. "I thought you might consider accompanying me to the unveiling of Mrs. Bennett's commissioned work." His smile was genuinely warm.

She realized, to her amazement, that she'd forgotten all about the oil painting. Someone—Rosie, maybe—had mentioned that the artist had probably salvaged the portrait, since none of them were interested in hanging it anywhere in the mansion. Not with the impostor's face beside that of their dear deceased Laura.

"How about it, then? Would you like to keep me company this Friday evening at the Fine Arts Center downtown?"

Katherine didn't know what to make of this request. It had been a good long time since a young man had asked to socialize with her publicly. She recalled one of the last Singings; she'd gone with her Beloved. But that was years ago.

It seemed rather apparent by the expectant smile on Justin Wirth's handsome face that she might have difficulty saying no. Still, she couldn't help thinking of Dan. Would she feel she was being disloyal to his memory? To their love?

Standing tall and confident, Mr. Wirth grinned down at her as the two of them stood silent in the foyer. When their eyes met, as they had in the dining room on Christmas Day—after she'd lit candles on a birthday cake for the Christ child—she felt something like butterflies flitting around in her stomach. A strange yet lovely sensation. One she'd quite forgotten.

She nodded, returning Mr. Wirth's smile, curious to see how he might have altered the portrait to display her birth mother more prominently. "I'd like to go, Mr. Wirth, I really would," she replied at last. Then realizing she'd almost slipped into her Hickory Hollow speech, she paused and modulated her voice, in a tone more befitting the mistress of the manor. "It would be a pleasure."

She felt mighty pleased with herself, learning to speak the fluid phrases of high society. She'd picked up ever so much from Laura, too, and figured that after only a few more days spent with either Theodore or Rosie, right fine British folk, she'd be speaking and pronouncing the king's English with grace, probably.

Shouldn't take long for her to pick up on doing or saying something right fancy, not when she set her mind to it. And she would, too—for the sake of her natural mother—she would follow through with being Katherine Mayfield. For sure and for certain.

The attractive man nodded. "Please, Miss Mayfield, call me Justin."

"Thank you, I will." Then noticing the genuine warmth in his blue, blue eyes, she thought of Daniel unexpectedly. Thought of him and hoped he wouldn't mind if she got all dressed up and went out on the town with this nice young artist. That is, if Dan just happened to be looking down on her from Paradise.

CHAPTER THIRTY

❖ ❖ ❖

What a beautiful satin gown, Miss Katherine!"

Katherine stood in front of the full-length mirror, making the long dress swish for Rosie. "You don't know this, but once when I snuck away to a little boutique back in Lancaster, I promised myself that someday I would wear a dress like this . . . out in public." She smiled at her reflection. "And just look, here I am!"

Rosie put the finishing touches on the sash at Katherine's waist. "I'd say you look absolutely smashing, love."

"Oh, thank you, Rosie." Then turning, she spun like a top, around and around as she had in her Amish mamma's attic months ago, the day she'd found the little satin baby dress.

Remembering, she went over to the dresser, feeling a bit dizzy but giggling near like a schoolgirl. "I wonder if Justin could paint me a picture of *this*." She held up the tiny infant gown. The garment that had caused so much heartache yet brought so much joy.

"Might be, though I rather think he prefers to work with *live* models for his inspiration." Rosie looked her over, grinning broadly. "And inspiring you certainly are tonight, Miss Katherine. Now, we'd better get you settled in the drawing room."

"Is it time already?"

Glancing at her watch, Rosie nodded. "The evening awaits you . . . Miss *Marsh*field." And they laughed together over the fancy made-up name.

But when Justin, looking right fine in his tuxedo, arrived to fetch her, there was more than admiration shining in his eyes. No, at least for the space of a heartbeat, Katherine thought she could see something *more*, something beautiful for them both. To her surprise, she felt the coldness in her spirit begin to dissolve—that powerful-strong numbness that had never quite left her since the shunning.

Arriving at the Fine Arts Center in Justin's rented limousine, Katherine was breathless with excitement. Assisted by a uniformed doorman, she stepped through a canopied entryway into a foyer, enchanted with her elegant surroundings. Under her feet, the plush pile of carpeting the color of ripe plums. Fine paintings, cleverly lit up by overhead lamps, lining the walls on either side of a long hallway. Lush green foliage and arrangements of forced blossoms—tulips, jonquils, and narcissus—their heady perfume a sure promise of spring.

Her hand tucked into the crook of Justin's arm, Katherine floated beside him toward the main gallery where the unveiling was to take place. Such a gathering it was, too. Important-looking people with important-sounding titles.

"Good evening, Mayor Bledsoe," Justin was saying in his deep, velvety voice. "May I present Miss Katherine Mayfield."

Following Justin's polished lead, she smiled and murmured, "How do you do?"

His Honor was a portly man with silvery hair and a walrus-style moustache. But he seemed pleasant enough as he shook her hand, then inclined his head toward the stunning blonde in his company. "My wife, *Mrs*. Bledsoe."

The woman, her silky hair swinging about her face, seemed young enough to be his daughter, Katherine couldn't help thinking. And when a cool gaze swept her from head to toe, then settled on her left cheek, she was flustered to the point of distraction. *What if I've put on too much blush!* she fretted. *But surely Rosie would've told me, wouldn't she?*

There was no time for further speculation, however, for Justin was introducing her to yet another couple, and Katherine found herself parroting a few well-rehearsed phrases in her new English voice. Still, with Justin never leaving her side, his hand cradling her elbow protectively, she was soon feeling much more at ease, meeting his friends—some, elected officials; others, artists-in-residence who made Canandaigua their home.

Honestly, she couldn't say she wasn't relieved when they finally made their way past the many well-wishers to the main exhibit hall for the unveiling. Immensely pleased, too, with the wonderful-good seat Justin had arranged for her in a row of plump cushioned chairs up at the very front.

As she took her seat, she noticed right away the heavily draped object resting on an easel before her. A pair of spotlights beamed down on the folds of ebony velvet.

For a moment, there was a wave of apprehension as Katherine pondered. How would she feel when the gold-tasseled cords were pulled, and the curtains parted to reveal the portrait? How would she react to the sight of her mother's face depicted on canvas? Would it bring tears to her eyes? The unveiling so soon after the funeral and burial services?

She bolstered herself by remembering that the dear lady was in Glory . . . no pain there, she was most assured. And she hadn't known Laura for all her life as most daughters know their mothers, so maybe the grieving wouldn't be as painful, she hoped. Still, Justin was known for "bringing people to life" on canvas. . . .

Just as the string ensemble ended their number, he stepped forward. Katherine held her breath, bracing herself for whatever feelings might be stirred up by the revelation of his artistic rendering.

But she was *not* braced. Not really. *Nothing* could have prepared her for the startling yet splendid oil painting. For there on the large canvas were depicted *two* women. Two auburn-haired women. Laura Mayfield-Bennett and Katherine, her real, true daughter.

She found herself breathing again, wanting to laugh and shout for joy. But she did the ladylike thing. She sat there, applauding the work, wondering how on earth the artist knew to put *her*—not the impostor—alongside her mother. Not Miss Alyson Cairns—New York actress turned Katie Lapp!

Later, while they mingled with others around the buffet table, she asked Justin about it. "Was it physical similarities between my mother and me that you noticed first?"

He chuckled at that. "Not many people have the privilege of wearing the rich colors of autumn all year long."

She knew he was referring to her hair, delighted that he hadn't called it "red."

As for her chin line and nose, "There are more important qualities than looks when it comes to relationships," he told her. "Even if I hadn't known, I would've painted you next to Laura."

"Oh? Why is that?"

His eyes shone with understanding. "Because, Katherine, you and Laura Mayfield-Bennett shared each other's hearts."

On the drive home, the present mistress of the newly named Mayfield Manor and her friend, the award-winning artist of Canandaigua, shared with each other their childhood backgrounds and interests. During the course of the ride, they discovered a variety of things they had in common, so much so that it was difficult to bring the evening to an end.

"Would you like to stop somewhere for coffee?" Justin asked.

Katherine consented to the after-hours coffee bar, delighted. She never would've guessed the two of them would find themselves so attracted to each other. Or that the evening would hold so many surprises, especially the portrait of herself and her natural mother.

It was much later, when the limo driver stopped at a red light, that she noticed a tall man crossing the street just ahead of them. Briefly, he glanced at their fancy car, and it was then she saw his face. She stared, intrigued.

This man—had she seen him before? In Lancaster . . . at market, maybe?

The more she thought of it, the more she assumed the untrimmed beard was the reason for her curiosity, probably. Maybe he was a member of one of the Old Order Mennonite groups, certainly not Amish, for he wore a handsome fur-trimmed overcoat and leather gloves.

When the light changed, she glanced back and watched the young man walk to the streetlight and pull something out of his coat pocket. It almost looked like a map, the way he unfolded it, and she remembered when she, too, had felt overwhelmingly lost . . . not in the midst of a new location, but among her own People.

She couldn't be sure, really, and it didn't matter anyway. She and Justin were on their way to have coffee and talk away the hours. Her future as Katherine Mayfield was brighter than any star that shone that night. Brighter than either the buzzing white ceiling lights in Cousin Lydia's kitchen or the crystal chandeliers in Katherine's own elegant dining room.

A verse from Ecclesiastes came to mind just then, for she'd heard the Wise Woman quote it many times. *Truly the light is sweet*, she thought.

And Katherine felt she understood. For the very first time.

283

EPILOGUE

It was long past midnight when I found myself sitting at my birth mother's dressing table with only the moonlight to keep me company. I couldn't help thinking about the mighty exciting evening I'd just had. Such a refined gentleman my new friend was, and, ach, so terribly English. Yet a sensitive sort for sure.

"Must be my artist's temperament," he'd joked as we had sipped black coffee in a cozy corner of the restaurant.

Well, whatever an "artist's temperament" was, I didn't rightly know, but there was one thing I *did* know. I liked Justin Wirth, and even though we'd spent only one evening together, I had a wonderful-good feeling that he liked me, too.

His face was before me now as I sat staring at the frosty windowpane, snowy reflections mingling with my memory of his facial features. Quite unexpectedly, I began comparing the artist to my deceased Amish boyfriend, and, next thing I knew, the two handsome faces took shape in my mind's eye, clear as day.

Justin seemed to smile back at me, and I hugged myself, thinking, *Oh, glory, such a night!* Then his image began to fade and Dan's grew ever so much stronger, blocking out Justin's cheerful expression.

To my dismay, I saw the light go out of the blueberry eyes. So awful sad Dan seemed, looking down at me now, and my heart went out to my long-expired loved one. In that moment I wondered if dear ones who'd passed on *could* see what things we do down here on earth.

Surely he would understand; surely he knew that I'd loved him, and he alone, for all these years. That I'd been ever so loyal—yes, and lonely and heartsick.

"Oh, Dan," I whispered, almost like a prayer, "please . . . can ya forgive me? Can you forgive your Katie girl?"

I surprised myself by uttering my former name—first time I'd spoken it since leaving Hickory Hollow—and I brushed back the tears. "Please, my darling, won'tcha put away your sadness and . . . and see my heart? See my *joy*?"

Silent then, I dismissed the mental picture by out-and-out willpower, hoping for a good night's sleep. And in that moment, I thought of my Amish mamma and wondered if Rebecca's beautiful eyes—those heavenly hazel eyes— might also behold me with sorrow if she knew of my English life now.

Katherine Mayfield, Mistress of Mayfield Manor.

I stood up, noticing as I headed into the bedroom that Rosie had turned down the coverings on Laura's bed—now mine. This room, where my first mother had suffered so, where she'd prayed for me, desperately hoping that I might come to her before she went home to Jesus, *all* of it belonged to me. Everything around me, everywhere I looked. And to think that my dear, prayerful mother had given this wonderful-good place to me boggled my mind!

Feelings of unworthiness sprang up, but along with that came a sense of anticipation, wrapped up in one trembling bundle. How I missed Laura; how I wished that she'd lived long enough to grow old in her beloved childhood home.

That I might've come to know her better, share her life, her dreams. I wished, too, that I could find her journal, the one she'd written while I was growing inside her . . . so long ago.

"If only Laura were still here," I said to the darkness. Oh, I was for sure and for certain she could guide me through the maze of my future, because I had no inkling what it might hold.

Still, I had always pined for such an English life as this. And a truly good part of me could hardly wait for every speck of it to unfold.

ACKNOWLEDGMENTS

Special thanks to Kathy Torley for her professional medical assistance, the Multiple Sclerosis Society of Colorado Springs, and June Heimsoth for her research help.

My appreciation to John and Julie Sullivan—delightful innkeepers of Morgan-Samuels B&B Inn of Canandaigua, New York—for allowing their beautiful, 1810 English-style mansion to be featured on the cover of this book. (Listed in *The Innkeeper's Register*, I highly recommend it.)

I wish to thank Anne Severance, my prayerful editor and friend, as well as Barbara Lilland and Carol Johnson, who offered their faithful editorial guidance throughout the writing process, along with Dave, my dear husband, encourager and friend, and "second eyes."

For readers captivated by the charm of the Old Order
Amish comes SUMMERHILL SECRETS by Beverly Lewis, an
engaging, contemporary series for young teens. Set in
Lancaster County, Pennsylvania, these action-packed stories
feature fourteen-year-old Merry Hanson and her Amish
girlfriend, Rachel Zook. (*Whispers Down the Lane* is a C. S.
Lewis Noteworthy List Book, 1995.)

Whispers Down the Lane
Secret in the Willows
Catch a Falling Star
Night of the Fireflies
A Cry in the Dark
House of Secrets
Echoes in the Wind

BEVERLY LEWIS

THE HERITAGE
of LANCASTER COUNTY
TRILOGY

3-IN-1 EDITION INCLUDING
The Shunning, The Confession and *The Reckoning*

BEVERLY LEWIS
THE
RECKONING

BETHANY HOUSE PUBLISHERS
MINNEAPOLIS, MINNESOTA 55438

Published by Bethany House Publishers
A Ministry of Bethany Fellowship International
11300 Hampshire Avenue South
Minneapolis, Minnesota 55438
www.bethanyhouse.com

Printed in the United States of America by
Bethany Press International, Minneapolis, Minnesota 55438

ISBN 0-7394-3554-X

DEDICATION

To Sandi Heisler,
childhood friend and confidante . . .
ever dear to me.

ABOUT THE AUTHOR

❖   ❖   ❖

BEVERLY LEWIS is a former schoolteacher and the author of over fifty books. She is a member of The National League of American Pen Women—the Pikes Peak branch—and the Society of Children's Book Writers and Illustrators. Her books are among the C. S. Lewis Noteworthy List Books. Bev and her husband have three teenagers and make their home in Colorado.

The truth shall make you free.

—John 8:32

The Lord will bless his people with peace.

—Psalm 29:11

PROLOGUE:
The Mistress of Mayfield Manor

Years ago, as a young Amish girl, I decided that I would age *very* gradually. Cheerfully, too. I'd become the kind of old grandmother who finds contentment in sowing simple, straight rows in her vegetable garden, whispering proverbs to her rutabagas.

After the untimely death of my first and only love, I feared I would grow old thinking only of Daniel Fisher. I would hoe my garden, weed my tomato plants, all the while missing Dan and wishing he'd never drowned on his nineteenth birthday.

Ach, I'm still a young woman, only twenty-two. My adult years stretch out before me. Yet I find myself thinking back to carefree childhood days in Hickory Hollow—giving my Plain past the once-over, so to speak. At the same time, I know that I am a shunned woman, an outcast from the People, my adoptive parents and brothers—excommunicated from those who loved and raised me. A sobering thought, true, but I have come to terms with what has been done to me and the necessity of *die Meinding*, at least from the Amish viewpoint. The pain of rejection gnaws at me each and every day. Yet in contrast, I cherish the memories

11

of my birth mother's words of love—*for me!*—spoken as she lay dying.

"I wish I had kept you for my own."

Revealing and bold, Laura's loving expression has begun to mend my broken heart. Daily I continue my search for her journal, the one she wrote before I was born.

I've begun to nestle down for the winter in my sumptuous new setting in Canandaigua, New York, truly celebrating the remarkable turn my life has taken. How very surprising it is, for often through my growing-up years, I had fantasized about the ways of *Englischers*—non-Amish folk—secretly wishing I could taste just a sip of what I might be missing. And here I am: *Mistress of Mayfield Manor*.

A right dignified name, I suppose, yet the implications of such a title have me all but befuddled at times. The sprawling estate, every square inch of the rolling grounds and magnificent old-English mansion—one hundred percent—belongs to Laura Mayfield-Bennett's flesh-and-blood daughter.

And all this has come about because of an unexpected encounter with Dylan Bennett and his smooth-talking attorney. In just a single meeting with Mr. Cranston—Laura's own attorney—the idea that any part of the estate might rightfully belong to Mr. Bennett proved indeed to be laughable. Not only could he not gain Laura's wealth through deceptive means, but he might well have lost his own resources in an ensuing court battle had he continued to contest Laura's revised last will and testament.

No, the *Schwindler* left the state and his business affairs behind, including papers found in his personal effects proving that he'd employed and encouraged an impostor, a false daughter for Laura.

So the scoundrel is gone, and Katie Lapp—the former me—has also departed. No more holding fast to the rigid rules, the restrictive dress code, the do's and don'ts of my past.

Still, if there is anything I might've done differently, it would've been to soften the blow somehow for Rebecca, my adoptive Amish mamma. I cannot stop thinking of her, missing her, wondering what Cousin Lydia *really* meant when she said "Rebecca's not herself" last time we spoke. Surely my leaving wasn't the only cause for Mamma's pain. The shunning decree—Bishop John's bitter pronounce-ment—had to have been the more grievous.

I have thought of writing her a long letter, telling her that I am safe; that little by little I am growing accustomed to the strange, modern world around me. And that I am, for the most part, happy. I fear, though, such an honest letter might stir up false hope of my return, and I would never want to put such a notion in her head. Not for the world. So when all is said and done, it's best for me to keep still, hoping that Rebecca and all the others will simply forget me. Though I am not so sure the People *can* forget.

For sure and for certain, they'll remember me as having been romantically linked to Dan Fisher. Our names will be eternally sealed in the cement of history, in the chronicles of the Amish community I once called home. The People—Bishop John, too—will long remember the stubborn auburn-haired woman they so cruelly shunned and the young man with blueberry eyes who loved her. So . . . both Dan and Katie are lost to the Old Ways. One to death, the other to life.

Truth be told, had it not been for my artist friend, Justin Wirth, and my renewed hope of marriage, I might've gone ahead and lived out my morbid plan of growing old. Old, without the pleasant laughter of grandchildren. Forever puzzling over long-ago memory pieces, wondering what might have been. . . .

CHAPTER ONE

❖ ❖ ❖

Daniel Fisher was roused from slumber by the song of morning birds. Sitting up, he imagined himself awakening in his own bed.

Upon further investigation, he realized that this room was not the upstairs bedroom of his New Jersey bungalow. Rather, it was a well-appointed suite of rooms in a Canandaigua bed-and-breakfast establishment.

He stretched and yawned, shaking himself back from his dream, a dream as vibrant as any real day. In it he had seen Katie, his sweetheart girl, gathering daisies in a wide green meadow. She wore a blue Amish dress without the apron and no devotional covering on her head. Her auburn hair fell in waves, long and lovely, over her slender shoulders.

The sun stood high in the treetops, its intense rays blinding him, momentarily blocking his vision. When the light parted, he saw her look his way, smiling slightly. Then, unheeding, she turned and skipped barefoot away into a thin gray mist.

"Katie, wait . . . *wait!*" He called to her again and again.

Dan groaned, recalling the summerlike dream. Such visions had taunted him on many a night, but this portrayal of a young, seemingly reckless Katie gripped him anew.

His eyes fell on his Bible, near him on the bedside table. Reaching for it, he eased himself off the bed, sitting on the edge as he shuffled through its pages till he found the letter to Katie—one she would never receive. A confession from his heart to hers, it was a way to spur himself on to do what he must do this very day.

My dearest Katie,

I'm writing this to you in a bed-and-breakfast here in Canandaigua. I know from the map I purchased days ago that the mansion you now live in is only a few short miles from where I sit tonight. Lately, it seems that I am likely to lose my focus on the important things if I do not put my thoughts down on paper. And though I do not expect that we will ever really be able to talk the way we used to, I'm hoping that my visit with you might turn out to be a positive, good thing for us both.

Just last week, I went to Hickory Hollow to visit with my parents—the first time in over five years. I met with my sister, too. It was from Annie that I first heard of your shunning and your subsequent leaving. There was pain in her eyes as she spoke of your yearning to find the mother who gave you birth.

If only God will allow me to see you for even a few moments and you would hear me out. Believe me when I say that I let you down, dear Katie, that I should have done something to right this wrong between us a long time ago. All these years, trying to fit in with the English world around me, I longed to know if you were all right—if you were safely settled in the Amish church—yet constantly wished for a gentle, perhaps divine, way to say that I loved you in spite of my "death." And I always prayed that you might find the truth of God's grace through His Son, Jesus Christ.

Nothing matters now but meeting you face-to-face, hoping you will not be too startled at my return from the "grave."

Please forgive me for not making things known to you sooner. For running away from my religious disputes with my father and the People. For letting you think I'd drowned on that boat so many years ago. Please . . .

Sighing, he held the letter in his hands, glancing over at a pastoral scene in a gilded antique frame across the room. "You may never believe that what I did, I did for us," he whispered. "For our love . . ."

He slipped the handwritten letter back into the leather Bible, closing it thoughtfully. *The matter is in God's hands*, he decided and stood to walk the few steps to the washbasin, leaning hard against its porcelain surface.

Staring into the mirror over the sink, he ran his fingers through a scraggly beard. Though in no way a vain man, he turned sideways, surveying his profile. Which should it be—with the beard or without?

He opened his shaving kit and pulled out his electric razor and a small pair of scissors he kept there. Leaning closer to the mirror, he picked up the scissors and thoughtfully opened and closed the blades a few times while he studied his face. The absence of a beard would clearly indicate his singleness—in the eyes of the Amish community, at least. Yet he'd come to realize that facial hair tended to make him look older—even, perhaps, wiser. *Believable* was the thought that came to mind as he stood there, scissors ready.

How will *Katie react to seeing me alive?* he wondered. He tried but couldn't begin to imagine the personal impact his appearance on her doorstep might make. She would be shocked, at best.

Never mind the beard, would she be happy to see him after so long a time, after thinking he was dead and gone? More than that, would she understand? Would she forgive him upon hearing his story—the truth, at last?

He vacillated between trimming the beard and shaving the whole thing completely off. In the end it remained, neatly clipped and quite bold, marking the outline of his jaw. He dressed in his finest clothes: a dark business suit and his favorite maroon-and-blue striped tie. Stomach rumbling, he proceeded out the door and down carpeted steps to enjoy breakfast with the other B&B guests.

"A good Saturday morning to you, Mr. Fisher," the lady of the house greeted him. "How do you take your coffee?"

"Black, thank you."

She led him through a sitting room where tufted antique chairs and cherrywood lamp tables were scattered about on a large area rug. An inviting fire crackled in the fireplace, warming the room and the intimate breakfast nook just beyond.

Through the expanse of windows, he glimpsed patches of a January sky, sapphire and bright off to the southeast, with brooding clouds gathering in the north. Wide-trunked beech trees stood ancient and stark against the snow-covered terrain. A shaft of sunlight teased the tip of a squirrel's tail as it scampered across the yard.

"Looks like we're in for an afternoon storm," said one of the guests, a stout, bejeweled woman, as Daniel took his seat at the table.

Her husband craned his neck to peer out the window. "Certainly does."

The guests introduced themselves all around, a total of six seated at the round, candlelit table. Daniel was politely curious and inquired about their homes and destinations. Two women—mother and teenaged daughter—had come up from Jersey for the weekend; another guest hailed from Kansas; and the only married couple present was from Florida, on their way up the coast to Maine on vacation.

Daniel spent most of his breakfast time chatting with the mother and daughter who were seated next to him. They were in town visiting an elderly uncle who lived in a nursing home a few blocks away.

"Nursing home? There are some folks who don't ever need such places for their elderly." The comment slipped out before he realized what he'd said.

The girl, about fifteen, looked startled. "Are you talking about Amish people?"

He did not wish to reveal his ties to the Plain community but felt the need to explain. "*Both* the Amish and Mennonites often look after their aging relatives."

She studied him curiously. "You seem, uh . . . you must be . . . Plain yourself."

So the girl had guessed it, in spite of his tailored suit and colorful tie. Perhaps it was because of the lingering Pennsylvania Dutch accent, beard, and the absence of a mustache. "Well, not anymore," he replied.

She seemed rather excited about this admission. "Is it true that the Amish never buy medical insurance?"

"We . . . uh, *they* don't need insurance. Their people grow old at home, surrounded by the extended family." He explained how it was commonplace for families to build on additions to their houses, making space for aging parents and grandparents.

"One *big* happy family?" She laughed good-naturedly.

"You could say that."

Her mother spoke up. "Did you ever ride in a horse-drawn buggy?"

He chuckled. "Always."

"Why not cars?" asked the man from Kansas.

"We could ride in them, just as long as someone else did the driving—someone English."

"English?" the girl's mother said.

"Amish refer to outsiders that way. You're either Amish or English."

A frown appeared on the girl's face. "What's so terrible about owning a car?"

He sighed, remembering the *Ordnung* and its grip on his former life. "Cars offer too much freedom . . . makes it too easy to abandon one's important family life."

The topic drew the rest of the folk like a magnet. "What was it *really* like growing up without cars or electricity?" asked one.

Dan was taken aback by their eagerness, their curiosity, having nearly forgotten the many years of answering similar questions from tourists who flocked to Pennsylvania, their cameras poised for sneak shots of the "horse-and-buggy people."

"Well, my *Dat* used to say 'Yer never gonna miss whatcha never had,' so I guess that's how it was."

They chuckled at the dialect. "Do you speak Dutch?" the teenager asked.

"*Jah*, but not so much anymore. That part of my life is all but over for me now." He paused, reaching for his napkin and wiping his mouth. "I've come to know a better way. Some of the People back home tend to disagree with me, though I know a good many Plain folk who've experienced God's gift of salvation through grace, same as I have."

The girl's eyes lit up with recognition. "Mom and I are Christians, too." She turned to nod at her mother.

Dan smiled, continuing the conversation and enjoying the opportunity to share and witness at the same table. Later, when asked again about his childhood, he replied, "Unless you've grown up Amish, it's hard to explain. The life, in general, is quite simple, yet mighty hard all the same, and there's often a price to be paid."

The girl was about to speak, but the man from Kansas said, "We have Amish and Mennonite settlements scattered in different parts of our state. What's confusing to me is the way they dress—they all look a little bit different."

Dan agreed. "Like Heinz—fifty-seven varieties, right?" That got them laughing, though he hadn't intended to poke fun.

"What about shunning?" the girl asked. "Do Amish actually kick their people out of church for disobeying rules?"

Dan felt a twinge. Though he hadn't actually suffered the sting of excommunication directly, he figured Bishop John Beiler and the Hickory Hollow membership had most likely started his initial six weeks of shunning probation. "Some groups still ban unrepentant members, but there are large church districts in Ohio, for instance, that have split away from the stricter groups, because they couldn't see eye to eye on shunning practices."

She shook her head. "A heartless thing, seems to me."

"Cruel, in many cases, but its legitimate origins are found in the New Testament, nevertheless." He paused, choosing his words carefully. "I'd have to say, though, that too often folks are shunned for mighty petty transgressions." At their urging he mentioned one instance: a man's hat brim—just one quarter inch too wide. " 'Worldly,' the bishop called it. And because the fellow was too stubborn to confess and buy another hat, he was cast out of the church and the community, severely shunned." That brought a few muffled snickers and even more ardent discussion. Dan, however, was especially grateful that no one pressed him for answers as to why he'd left Hickory Hollow.

Moments later the hostess came in to clear the table, an unspoken cue for her guests to wind things up. Dan observed the hasty brushing off of crumbs and the removal of water glasses and took the hint.

"Very nice chatting with you," he said to the group.

The girl followed her mother out of the room but stopped to say, "Have a nice day!"

"Thank you, and God bless you, young lady."

A nice day, indeed! Come rain or come shine, he was off to see his Katie girl!

He headed upstairs to wash his face and brush his teeth once again. Eager for the day, this first encounter after years of separation, he knelt at the desk chair and prayed for divine guidance. "Assist me, Father, as I speak the words of truth . . . surprising as they will sound to Katie's tender ears. I pray that she may receive me with an understanding heart, that I might be a witness of your saving grace and love." He hesitated for a moment. "And if it be your will, I ask that in due time, I may woo her back to the love we once knew. In Christ's name. Amen."

He left by way of the front walk, glancing upward through bare tree branches. The sky had grown dark, now an ominous charcoal gray. The air was brittle and cold, sharp against the throat. He was glad for his fur-trimmed overcoat and leather gloves as he walked briskly to his rental car, city map in hand.

❖ ❖ ❖

Katherine scoured each of the closets on the main level of the mansion, looking for her mother's journal. One after another, she discovered well-organized linen closets—tidy stacks of velvety monogrammed towels, satin bed sheets, and plush blankets—and now *this* closet not far from her own suite of rooms.

She removed folded sheets from the bottom, then moved on to the next shelf, inspecting each piece of linen, including doilies and crocheted dresser runners on the middle shelf and the one above, stacked clear to the ceiling. There were numerous seasonal items—damask tablecloths and napkins in every hue imaginable, matching napkin rings, and floral table accessories.

When she had completed her rummaging, Katherine

closed the door and headed upstairs to the spacious sun-room. Her ailing birth mother had spent many hours soaking up warm, healing rays in this room, praying for a reprieve from her pain.

With a sigh, she settled on the chaise lounge nearest the south exposure. *Where did Laura keep her diary?* she wondered. *Where?*

Katherine thought of Lydia Miller, her Mennonite relative, who—right this instant—would doubtless be encouraging her to seek divine assistance in this frustrating matter; that is, if Lydia lived close enough to be aware of the problem. The woman prayed about everything, no matter how incidental.

In like fashion, Laura Mayfield had often prayed, beseeching the Lord in conversational tones. Rosie Taylor—her birth mother's longtime personal maid and now Katherine's—had recounted the prayers she and Laura had shared during the weeks before Laura's passing.

"Your dear mother prayed in earnest for you," Rosie told her one evening as they sat by the fire in the library.

"That I'd be found?"

"Indeed, yes. She prayed faithfully that you would come to her before the MS made her mind hazy or confused. With all of her heart, she wanted to get to know you before she died. But in spite of her pain, in spite of her longing to see her daughter again, she was deeply grateful for life. Each new day was another opportunity to rejoice in her Savior."

Her Savior. Rosie had mentioned the name with such reverence and joy. It was obvious to Katherine that the devoted housemaid and her husband—Fulton, the butler—had found salvation, same as Laura.

So Katherine had been surrounded by prayer. "All these years," she whispered, leaning back with her head against the soft chaise pillow. She wondered if it had been Laura's prayers that ultimately had brought her here to Mayfield

Manor. If so, what of Rebecca Lapp's? Surely *she*, too, was pleading with the Lord God heavenly Father for her adopted daughter's return. How, then, could *both* women's requests be heard and answered?

She didn't rightly know but pondered the question. Her eyes took in the lush green ferns and other plants in matching terra-cotta pottery, and she tried to relax in the luxurious room, far removed from the hustle and bustle of modern-day life. It provided all the conveniences she'd always longed for.

Suddenly thirsty, she noticed the pitcher of ice water and several clean glasses facedown on a tray next to her. Pouring herself a glassful of water, she began to hum softly. The song was one of the many she had made up over the years. Forbidden, according to the Ordnung of the People.

Crossing her legs in front of her on the chaise, she sang her song, taking occasional sips. Something about the clear, cool taste of the water or the way the ice cubes clinked against the sides brought to mind an Ascension Day picnic she had attended with her parents and brothers when she was only eight years old. . . .

It was at Uncle Moses Lapp's farmhouse situated on a broad bend of Weaver's Creek, several miles from Hickory Hollow, that the sun beat down hard on little Katie's back as she stood on the front porch step, gulping down a tall glass of ice-cold lemonade.

"You'll have yourself a headache if ya drink too fast," Mamma called from the shadows, rocking and fanning herself to beat the band.

"Ach, Mamma, it's so awful hot," she complained, holding out her glass. "Please, mayn't I have more?"

Mam obliged cheerfully, getting up and going inside to bring out the entire pitcher. "Here's just for my little girl." She poured the sweetened lemonade into Katie's glass.

"Ach, young Katie's spoilt, I'd say," whispered *Mammi* Essie. "Ain't so?"

The other women—her mamma's married sisters, Nancy Yoder and Naomi Zook; feisty Cousin Mattie Beiler, the midwife; and three aunts, including Ella Mae, the Wise Woman—*all* of them, just kept a-rockin' and a-fannin', the strings from their prayer veils floating forward and back, forward and back. Katie couldn't rightly tell if the womenfolk were agreeing with her mamma's mother or trying to ignore Essie, the way they were known to on occasion.

Never mind them, she decided and poured herself a third glass and guzzled it right down in front of them. Satisfied, she went to sit *under* the porch in a sort of nesting spot where the shade was cool and damp, the breeze sweet, *and* the listening-in right fine. Happy to have chosen this private place away from the critical eye of Mammi Essie, she folded her long dress tightly around her legs so no *es Mickevieh*—pest of flies—might go a-soaring up her skirt. She sighed, pushing stray wisps of hair back into the braids that wound around her sweaty head.

She stared out across the yard and over to the barn. On past the newly plowed corn and potato fields to the ridge of trees in the distance. The landscape was as familiar to her as the seams that ran up and down the inside of her long dress and apron. This land was her home, her world.

Above her, the gossips and storytellers of the homeland took turns talking in their native tongue. The rolling *thump-a-thump* of hickory rockers overhead lulled her for a time, and she was comforted by the sounds of the familiar.

Leaning back on her hands, the dirt dug into her palms, making prickly indentations. Uncaring, she whispered to herself, feeling terribly pleased about it, "I'm spoilt because Mamma loves me."

At that moment, nothing else much mattered.

Katherine stretched her arms up behind her head as she lay on the chaise, wondering what *Grossmutter* Essie would think of her now. Would she say Rebecca's spoiled daughter was much too pampered, living like a princess in a New York mansion far from home? What would she think of the gourmet cooks and sumptuous meals, the staff of servants . . . the housemaids? And the rayon trousers, silk blouses, and angora sweaters Katherine now loved to wear?

She took another long drink from her glass. What Essie King, or anybody else, might think about her now was irrelevant. This was the fancy sort of English life she'd longed for as long as she could remember.

The sun had disappeared, devoured by a slate gray bank of clouds that seemed to spread its vastness from the horizon directly toward her. She felt the cold of the glass begin to seep into her, making her feel chilly, and without a second thought, she got up and turned on the space heater fixed in the wall. Returning to the chaise, she felt gleeful at having flicked a switch, producing warmth at will.

Music filtered through the intercom on the far wall, and she silently congratulated herself on recognizing the composer—Johann Sebastian Bach—who, had he been Amish, would have fit right in, what with the twenty children he helped produce. But then again, the prolific side of Bach's *musical* creativity would have posed a problem for the People. A source of contention, they might have decided.

Thinking on this, she tried to hum along a passage here and there, not in defiance of her past—no need—but merely enjoying the moment.

When she was fully rested, she got up, turned off the wall heater and headed downstairs to her private quarters. There she began to play her guitar, thinking of Mary Stoltzfus.

Mary.

Such a beautiful, perfect name for a woman. One who

had always tried to do the right thing before God. To think that Mary had secretly written her a note back before Christmas was right surprising, to say the least. Yet Katherine couldn't blame her friend for doing such a disobedient thing. Cords of sisterly love were mighty strong between the two.

Had it not been for the fact that Katherine was adopted, the intermarrying and crisscrossed bloodlines deep in the Hollow might've made them cousins, if not a mite closer.

What are you doing today, Mary? wondered Katherine. *Do you have any idea just how much I miss you?*

CHAPTER TWO

❖   ❖   ❖

What if somethin' could be done to lift the Ban off Katie just a bit?" Mary Stoltzfus asked her mother. "It's much too harsh, seems to me, not bein' able to communicate with her and all." She didn't mention anything about not being able to write letters to her friend, of course. Still, she would've liked to be able to do so, without going behind the bishop's back about it, the way she'd up and done once already.

Her mother turned from the woodstove, where she was steaming carrots. "If we ease up on Katie Lapp, where will that put Daniel Fisher?"

"Jah, 'tis a knotty problem, I 'spect." Mary thought of her best friend; missed her more than words could tell. Yet she was anxious, today more than any other, to hear Mam's feeling on the matter. Mostly because she was supposed to spend the afternoon with Katie's former *Beau*—the man her wayward girlfriend had stood up on their wedding day back in November.

John Beiler had invited Mary to accompany him on a ride into town. Just where they were headed, she did not know. But, to her thinking, it wasn't so much the place the horse and carriage would be taking them as the fact that they were going *anywhere* together that was a godsend.

"Daniel's gonna be under the Ban in a bit . . . soon as the six-week probation's up," Rachel was saying. "Unless he hightails it back here and offers a kneeling confession. Not so likely, I 'spect, what with him having five years to think on his sinful ways."

"Prob'ly so."

"No prob'lys about it," retorted her mother. "Word has it, that boy's as rebellious as ever. Believin' he's saved and all. Why, it'sa out-n'-out manifestation of pride . . . nothin' less."

Mary sighed. "Dan's not a boy anymore, Mamma. He's a grown man with ideas and opinions. Can't go blamin' him for wanting to follow his heart." She'd almost said his *Bible* but knew that sort of talk would get her in more than just hot water. No, for a girl who'd grown up with a consuming desire to do the right thing, this was a startling notion. She would voice it to no one. Not to Mamma, and never to the bishop.

Bishop John Beiler was the divine answer to her prayers, widower or no. She had more sense than to risk losing her chance to be courted and married, not with her twenty-first birthday fast approaching. Besides, she'd fallen in love with John's ruddy-faced grin, his twinkling gray-blue eyes, and all five of his children. Even Levi, that eight-year-old rascal of a boy.

Thing was, she was worried sick what Katie might think if she ever got wind of Bishop John's growing interest in her. Would she just assume that Mary thought the widower was fair game, having been spurned as he was?

Mary shuddered to think what it might do to their friendship if Katie ever did return to Hickory Hollow to make amends. *What then?* she wondered. Surely, Katie—who had adamantly insisted on being called Katherine Mayfield before she ran off in search of her *real* mother—surely she'd overlook her best friend's relationship with John

Beiler. If she understood anything about forgiveness and love, she would.

Besides, now that Dan Fisher was out searching for Katie, who knew what still might happen between the two? Mary brushed away the romantic notion with a sigh. Ach, what she would give to be a little mouse in the same room as the unfortunate lovers, when and *if* they found each other again.

Mary went about setting the table, even though the men wouldn't be coming in for lunch just yet. Dat and her married brothers had gone over to the Gordonville Print Shop to see about picking up some curriculum for the Amish school. They'd planned to return around noon—another *gut* hour or so away.

"Do ya think I oughta bring it up with Bishop John?" Mary ventured.

"About Katie's Meinding?" Rachel looked up from the stove, a curious expression on her face. "*Puh*, ya must be jokin', daughter. Besides, it would do no good spoilin' your chances—"

"Mamma, please . . ." Mary felt her pulse race. The afternoon's buggy ride was a secret and must be kept so. John Beiler had promised to pull his carriage off to the side of the road and wait for her.

Just past the wooden bridge, near the clump of fir trees, he'd told her two days ago when she'd bumped into him quite by accident at Preacher Yoder's General Store.

Her mother went back to stirring the carrots. "Don'tcha worry none. I won't breathe a word. Wouldn't do any gut for somethin' to leak out 'bout you and the bishop."

Mary agreed, and her face grew warm with the romantic thoughts tumbling through her head.

❖ ❖ ❖

Rebecca Lapp was so weak in the legs, she wished off and on all morning that she were a fattened sow left to lie in the sun, wallowing in the muddy grief of her life. But she headed down to the cold cellar beneath the house, where hundreds of quarts of vegetables and other foodstuffs were stored for the winter.

Standing there in the dark, damp place, she momentarily forgot what vegetable she'd had in mind for the noon meal. "Oh, what'sa matter with me?" she mumbled, fighting back tears. "Will I never stop thinking of my Katie?"

Locating her flashlight in the pantry cupboard, Rebecca allowed her eyes to roam over the cellar, coming to rest on the handcrafted pine cupboard in the corner—a constant reminder of the weeks before Katie's shunning and the ultimate hiding place for the satin baby gown.

Ach, how she longed for the soft, perty thing. Missed it so. If she could just hold it next to her heart again. Hold her daughter, too. If she could only be near the girl, her precious Katie . . .

How long had it been since she'd heard the forbidden guitar music creeping through the walls of the *Dawdi Haus* next door? How long since she'd kissed Katie's tear-streaked face?

Shivering, she turned back to the task at hand and chose some green beans and corn from the orderly pantry shelves. Samuel, Eli, and Benjamin would be mighty hungry, wondering why a hot, hearty meal wasn't awaiting them, hard-working men that they were.

She turned and trudged upstairs, one foot in front of the other, till at last she stood at the top, winded and tired. Leaning against the door momentarily, she sighed and caught her breath a bit before letting herself into the warm, savory kitchen. Oh, she wished for a day when she might search out and find the entrance to a place of wholeness in her mind. How far off was such a day? How long before she'd start adjusting to life without her little girl?

Sadly, she pried open the canning lids and dumped *both* the corn and the beans into a large pot, completely by accident, before realizing what she'd done.

❖ ❖ ❖

Ella Mae Zook sat at her daughter Mattie's kitchen table, surrounded by quilting squares stacked in groups of nine. She was making ready to teach Sally Beiler, one of her younger great-granddaughters, the arrangement of a "Ninepatch"—the simplest quilting pattern. "You'll catch on in no time," she promised. "Watch me once."

The girl paid close attention, and when it was her turn to try, the Wise Woman jumbled up all the squares again, handing them over to Sally. Carefully, the youngster positioned the fabric on the long wooden table so that one dark square lay next to a lighter square, in the familiar tic-tac-toe pattern.

Across the room, Mattie stood at the cookstove, seasoning a pot of creamed potato soup. Every few minutes, she came over to check on Sally's progress.

Without ever glancing up, Sally asked, "It wonders me . . . when do ya think Bishop John and Mary Stoltzfus'll end up tying the knot?"

Ella Mae harrumphed, feeling the need to set the conversation on course. "No need to be speculatin' on such things. If it's God's will, they'll get together in all good time. Won't matter just when, I should say."

"*If* they do," Mattie added. "You know the poor man is probably still heartsick over Katie Lapp, what with the way she jilted him . . . on their wedding day, no less. Why, if it was me, I'd be laying low on the subject of marriage, I 'spect."

"Well, it ain't you, so just let it be," Ella Mae advised.

"The man needs a good mother for his children, and he's smart enough to make up his own mind. Mary, well . . . bless her heart, John Beiler's the man of her dreams."

"Ach, ya mean it?" Sally spoke up, blushing slightly. "You think she's been dreaming 'bout the bishop?"

Mattie shook her head, muttering as she walked back to the simmering potato soup. But Ella Mae kept on, attempting to smooth things over, without divulging any secrets. "You know, sometimes it just seems that one person fits right fine with another. Belongin' is what it's all about, I do believe."

Right then, the old woman thought of Daniel, wondering how the dear boy was doing. He'd come to visit here lately, knocked hard on the door of her side of the house— come straight back from the dead—inquiring as to Katie's whereabouts. Ella Mae had filled him in as best she could. 'Course, she didn't have much hope of his ever finding the shunned girl, not as awful crowded as New York was. But true love sometimes wins out over great odds, she thought. Lord willin', that would be the case.

Sally silently worked at her grid of nine patches while Ella Mae observed, still struggling with unsettled feelings over the whole notion of Daniel's being alive and all. Where had he been all that time? And how was it that Bishop John had up and slapped the Ban on him, almost the minute the People found out Daniel had not drowned in that sailing mishap years ago?

Oh, and they'd faulted him for "finding salvation, full and free," Dan had told her as he sat sipping tea in her little kitchen. A body could see he was telling the truth, too. His face purely shown with a radiance, and when he asked to see her Bible, she gave it to him gladly, listening with eagerness as he read one verse after another.

One passage stirred her very soul. "He that believeth on the Son of God hath the witness in himself . . . and this is the record, that God hath given to us eternal life, and this life is in his Son."

The promise of salvation right there in the Scriptures! It was ever so clear. Daniel *knew* he was saved.

By the time he'd said his good-byes, she was altogether convinced that Dan was telling the truth about his finding eternal life in Jesus Christ. *Himmel!* The more she thought about this Meinding business, the less it made any sense.

❖   ❖   ❖

Daniel parked the rental car out some distance from the entrance to the Mayfield mansion. The circular drive was configured in such a way as to allow for several parking spots along the side before the grand bend led up to the paved walkway, now dusted with a layer of snow.

Refolding the map, he placed it on the seat next to him and stared through the windshield at the fine English-style country estate. To think that his Katie had come *here* to find her birth mother! What a grand and beautiful place it was. The startling information was still in the process of seeping through to his brain, thanks to his sister Annie and beloved old Ella Mae. It gave him no insight, however, into the girl he'd once known and loved. Her parents were and always would be Samuel and Rebecca Lapp, the kind and generous folk who'd raised Katie as their own. What could have happened to make their adopted daughter want to abandon them and go on such a search?

The answers, he knew, were bound up inside the rambling, vine-covered dwelling. Inside Katie's heart, as well. If only he might unlock those secret rooms and find his sweetheart girl waiting there.

Yet the Wise Woman had warned him, "She's not the girl you grew up with. Katie's suffered great pain; is more headstrong than I've ever seen her. If you find her, best go gentle on her . . . let her take her time tellin' you her side of things."

Oh, he'd gladly give Katie all the time in the world. Beginning right now.

Prayerfully, he opened the car door and walked the long drive. Up past lantern-shaped lights that lined the walkway on either side, to the portal. "Dear God in heaven, help me. Help *Katie* and me," he whispered, running his fingers through his beard, still wondering if he'd made the right decision by keeping it intact.

Without further delay, he reached for the brass door knocker.

CHAPTER THREE

❖ ❖ ❖

Katherine sat with her back to the blazing fire. She had spent the morning playing her guitar and singing freely, allowing her voice to fill the sitting room, one of the several comfortable places to relax in her private suite. She had kept the arrangement of furnishings the same as when Laura was alive: overstuffed chairs and a cherry sofa table placed so as to accentuate the Tibetan area rug, a favorite of her birth mother.

Flitting from one song to another, Katherine let her mind roam back to Pennsylvania, settling on the letter Mary had written in mid-December. She had read it so many times now, she had it nearly memorized.

It's all I can do to keep myself from sneaking off down the lane for a visit. . . .

She knew just what her friend must've been feeling as Mary penned those words. They *both* had missed out on friendship by losing touch with each other.

Katherine curled her toes inside her house shoes, despising the bishop—that wretched man who might've become her husband if she hadn't had the gumption to walk out on their wedding service. She stopped singing, stopped strumming her guitar. John Beiler had cut her off from her loved ones, *her* People. A typical shunning was one thing, but declaring that none of them could speak to her or she to them! The memory stung like a hundred angry wasps.

Getting up, she strolled to the windows, still carrying her guitar as she looked out at the snow-covered lawn and formal gardens. Hundreds of barren trees—beech, fir, and maple—stood at graceful attention over the rolling acres as far as the eye could see.

A light snow had begun to fall. The enormous flakes seemed to suspend themselves momentarily, high in the air, as if holding their breath before consenting to drift to earth. The overcast sky and the mood of the day reminded her of midwinter days in the Hollow, when snow-encrusted country roads were sliced deep by narrow carriage wheels and trampled over by one trotting horse after another.

Then and there, she decided to make contact with Mary. She wouldn't put her friend in jeopardy by writing the letter herself. No, she had a better idea. Rosie, her trusted maid, might be the ideal person to take dictation.

Katherine turned slightly, ready to put her guitar away and call for Rosie Taylor with her plan, when her eyes fell on a bright blue sedan parked off to the side of the circular driveway. Looking more closely, she noticed a single set of footprints, their indentation breaking through to the pavement beneath.

It was then she heard the muffled sound of the door knocker, followed by Fulton's hurried steps. She knelt to place the guitar in its case, a flicker of a memory surfacing as she did. Tired of his share of run-ins with his father, Dan had insisted on giving the beloved instrument to her years ago. "Will you hide it for me?" he'd asked, smiling down on her that sunshiny day.

How could she have refused? " 'Course I will."

"You'll take good care of it, won't you, Katie girl?"

And care for it, she did. Marched right off to the barn

and hid it away from eyes that would misunderstand her need—*their need*—to create the prohibited music.

She might've lingered, taking pleasure in the endearing scene from years gone by, had it not been for the sound of her loyal butler, his voice rising to an ever higher pitch. Goodness' sake, the man sounded ruffled. Who on earth could be at the door?

She went to the window but saw nothing out of the ordinary. *Must be a traveling salesman,* she assumed, seeing only the back of a man's overcoat. *Fulton will get rid of him.*

How secluded and safe she felt. Sighing, she wondered what it might've been like having servants to wait on you hand and foot your whole life, people responsible for making your existence as sweet as cherry pie. Had Laura kept her infant daughter, she, Katherine, would have experienced such a life. This estate was the home of Laura's parents long before her birth mother had ever conceived and borne her first and only child.

Dismissing the clamor, Katherine went to sit at the petite writing table across the room and searched for her prettiest stationery.

Daniel stepped back, away from the door. "Are you saying . . . that Katie Lapp no longer lives here?" His breathing was coming fast.

"Lest I repeat myself, young man—she is gone like so much rubbish," the butler said, his nostrils flaring like an irritated horse. "The no-good woman left on her own accord weeks ago, though I rather regretted not having thrown her out myself."

Daniel shook his head, pained by the man's words. "Is it possible that we're talking about the same woman? You see, it's *Katie* I wish to see—the Amish girl from Lancaster County. We grew up together, we were sweethearts. . . ." Daniel made an attempt to demonstrate just how tall Katie might be, then mentioned the color of her hair, physical traits—all to no avail.

"Sounds as if the woman's got you fooled, too."

"But I was *told* she'd come here."

"Come she did . . . caused absolute mayhem, too." The butler's face grew red. "Over the holidays, no less."

Dan grimaced at the stranger's disparaging remarks. How could this be? Where *was* his precious Katie?

Quickly, he had the presence of mind to inquire, "Do you have any idea where she might've gone? The slightest tip—anything—would be appreciated."

"I would expect she returned to New York City, from whence she came."

"Who in the world does she know there?" he said, more to himself than to the distinguished-looking gentleman before him.

"Contacts at a talent agency, I was told." The tall man reached for the door handle. "I don't mean to be rude, but the woman was a phony, through and through. Now, if you'll excuse me. . . ."

"Uh, I'm very sorry to have bothered you." His hopes were dashed. "Thank you for the information."

"Good day," said the butler.

Turning, Daniel made his way across the wide snow-dusted driveway to the car. He thought of the Wise Woman, her words of warning. *Katie's not the girl you grew up with.*

Well, certainly, she would've changed some since their teen years—their blissful courting days. Given the circumstances of the imposed shunning, she may have seemed somewhat rebellious in her coming here, but understandably so.

Despite what he thought he knew about his former girlfriend, this encounter with a stranger—a butler—at the door of Katie's birth mother's estate troubled him greatly. And the information offered made no sense. None whatever.

The noise from the front door disturbed Katherine. She'd gone to stand just outside the wide French doors leading from her suite to the main hallway. She listened, though no matter how hard she strained to hear, it was impossible to make out the nature of the exchange taking place on her doorstep.

Unexpectedly, two housemaids rounded the corner, nearly bumping into her. Stepping back, she decided against eavesdropping and closed the glass doors behind her.

Preoccupied with her plan to have Rosie write a cordial letter to Mary, she slid open the narrow drawer in the center of the desk. There she found several plain white pages, just right for taking a few notes, making something of a rough draft.

Picking up a pen from the drawer, she began to write an example for Rosie:

Saturday, January 17

Dear Mary,
You do not know me. However, I know something of you.

Stopping to read, to see how the English words looked on the page, Katherine wondered if they sounded affected. Stilted.

"I'll ask Rosie," she said aloud. Mrs. Taylor would know. After all, she was of British descent. In fact, her writing style might seem even more formal than the forced, sophisticated way Katherine was attempting to word her initial thoughts.

She sighed, not sure if she should begin by owning up to the fact that the ultimate writer—Rosie—knew only of Mary through Katherine. That the Amish girls had been dear friends all their lives, but because of the physical separation caused by the Ban and the many miles between them, they'd lost touch with each other.

She wrote several more first lines before crumpling those pages, too, into the wastebasket. Clearly, she needed help. Going to the wall, she pulled a velvet rope, the bell that would summon her favorite housemaid.

Rosie arrived quickly, appearing rather puzzled about Katherine's idea once the explanation was offered. "Here, I'll give you an idea of what I mean." She showed Rosie a newly written single-line greeting.

Wide-eyed, the maid read the beginnings of a letter. Sliding her reading glasses down off her nose, she shook her head. "Won't it seem rather peculiar for your friend to receive a letter from a perfect stranger?"

"Maybe, at first." Katherine hurried to her writing desk. "But it's the best way, I think. Wouldn't want Mary getting in trouble. The bishop would never hear of it . . . her receiving mail from me. Never . . . *never*."

"Well, if you say so." Rosie, looking a bit stumped, sat down and picked up a pen.

"This might seem a bit awkward, but I think we—you and I—will make a great team," Katherine said. "You see, I really miss talking to my friend. We grew up sharing everything."

Rosie, wearing her prim white apron and maid's cap, nodded. An understanding smile played across her lips. "I fear you've been through too much for one so young."

"I've brought a lot of it on myself." Katherine pulled up a chair next to the desk, staring into Rosie's kind face.

Leaning back in her chair, Rosie sighed, laying the pen on the table in front of her. "Why don't we begin by *you* telling *me* about your girlfriend. I would like to know more about Mary." She chuckled. "After all, she and I are soon to become pen pals, right?"

Katherine had to laugh. Then she and Rosie spent the rest of the afternoon talking about her fondest memories of Hickory Hollow and her bosom buddy. She was careful, however, not to speak a word about either Bishop John or her long-deceased love, Daniel.

When they finished their letter-writing collaboration, Rosie addressed the envelope to Mary Stoltzfus in her own hand, and the two headed down the long hallway to the kitchen.

At Rosie's insistence, Katherine joined the staff—Selig, the assistant cook, and the other domestic help, including Garrett Smith, head steward and nephew of the grandfatherly chauffeur, Theodore Williams—for lunch. The tasty meal consisted of a fruit and nut salad, tuna casserole, homemade rolls, and a warm mug of cocoa.

This was not the first such occasion. After several days of eating alone in the grand dining room—not much fun at all—Katherine had decided she much preferred the company of her new friends. After all, she'd grown accustomed to sharing meals with family and friends after house church meetings and quilting frolics. Breaking bread and fellowship went hand in hand with community living.

Selig hadn't forgotten Katherine's weakness for sweets, she soon discovered. The noontime dessert was a delicious, moist German chocolate cake. While enjoying a slice, she thought of Mary once again. Her friend's birthday would be coming up in a couple of months. Lifting a forkful, Katherine stared at her plate—Mary's all-time favorite cake. She knew it sure as the day, desperately missing her friend and hoping the unusual letter might not offend or cause trouble.

"Will you drive me to town this afternoon?" she asked Theodore, who was sitting in his usual spot next to the spacious kitchen window.

"Just state the time, Miss Katherine."

"Theodore's got cabin fever, I suspect, what with the weather being so dreary," Fulton spoke up, glancing down the table at the older gentleman.

"I wouldn't be surprised if we got snowed in," Rosie

observed, at which they all turned their heads toward the window.

"I see what you mean," Katherine said, peering at the overcast sky. "So we'd better plan to leave right after lunch."

"Very well, miss," Theodore replied.

She shook her head. "I wish you'd call me Katherine—just plain Katherine. I wouldn't mind it one bit if you never addressed me as 'miss' again."

"Consider it done," Theodore replied with a grin.

"Better mark it down," Fulton teased, and Rosie elbowed him playfully.

They continued to eat amidst chatter and laughter.

Garrett, at one point, leaned up against the table, looking now at Fulton. "Excuse me, but what was all that racket this morning?"

The butler adjusted his glasses. "Quite odd, I must say. The fellow showed up at the door asking for Katie Lapp. Of all the gall."

"Did you tell him we sent her packing?" Katherine said, glad of it.

"Absolutely, but the man seemed intent on tracking her down. He persisted with an inquiry as to her destination upon leaving here."

"Did he say who he was?" Rosie asked, no longer smiling.

Fulton was thoughtful, frowning as he placed his dessert fork next to a few chocolate crumbs on his plate. "The fellow never stated his name. But he assured me that Katie and he went a long way back . . . to Pennsylvania Amish country, no less."

That brought a volley of laughter from them all, including Katherine, who couldn't help but wonder if the poor fellow had been duped by the impostor, or if he was in fact an actor himself, seeking unlawful employment as the fake Katie Lapp had. "You got rid of him, then?"

Fulton nodded. "And if I'm not mistaken, the young man seemed quite upset by the end of our conversation."

Katherine didn't feel one bit sorry for whoever had come to call this morning. In truth, she hoped she'd never have to see hide nor hair of that woman . . . that obnoxious "Katie"!

❖ ❖ ❖

A brisk breeze blew as Mary hurried down Hickory Lane, careful not to stumble on icy patches of snow along the roadside. The sky was a vast cloak of gray hanging in heavy folds overhead, nearly close enough to touch. Two crows flew across the road, their black wings flapping hard against the impending sky.

The Hollow seemed deserted this afternoon. Maybe *everyone* had gone to Gordonville to shop—plenty of stores to buy such things as fabric and sewing supplies. On Saturdays, Amish folk often hired Mennonite van drivers to take them places, shopping, and such. Folks liked to get out and about, even in the middle of winter, especially if the roads were fairly clear of snow. And they were this afternoon, although the darkening clouds held the threat of a winter storm. Best to get out before the weather turned nasty.

Not a quarter of a mile away, the bishop's enclosed gray carriage was parked off to the side, by the grove of trees, just as he'd promised.

"Glory be," Mary whispered as she quickened her pace, willing her heart to resume its normal pace, but to no avail.

Several yards away, as she approached the buggy, she slowed to a proper walk, not wanting to give the bishop the notion that she was too eager.

John surprised her by jumping out of the carriage. "*Wie geht's*, Mary?"

"*Hullo*, John."

They fell silent straightaway, Mary keeping her head down, wondering what to say next.

He coughed a little. "Trouble gettin' out today?"

She knew he was asking if anybody might be privy to their planned rendezvous. "Dat has no idea." Careful not to mention Mamma's womanly intuition, she changed the subject. "A *wunderbaar schee* day, jah?"

"Nice, it is, though a bit nippy and gray." He offered his gloved hand, helping her into the carriage, then hurried around to the other side to get in.

More than anything she wanted this—her first time alone with John—to go real smooth. Without a hitch in conversation, deed, and thought. The lovely moments must pass perfectly. Yet her heart thumped hard against her woolen shawl.

The bishop flapped the reins, and the horse moved out onto the road, into plain view. They rode for miles and miles without saying a word, the sleek bay mare steaming in the cold, clip-clopping along at a comfortable trot.

At last John broke the silence, speaking of his eldest son, young Hickory John. "The boy's leanin' hard toward learning a trade instead of farming. Said it just this mornin' . . . wants to be a blacksmith like his old *Daed*.'"

"Ach, but you ain't old," she said cautiously, lest he think she was debating him. "Really, you ain't."

He turned to her and gave her a broad smile. "S'right kind of ya, Mary."

"Well, it's not just *my* opinion." Her voice felt fragile, as if it might give out on her.

"*Your* opinion matters more than ya know."

She was thankful to be sitting down just now, for she felt the strength drain clean out of her legs—downright weak-kneed as always whenever she was around this man of God. "The smithy's a good callin' for a boy, I'd say," she managed.

"Jah, I tend to agree."

She was aware of the wind against her bonnet as they neared the town of Bird-in-Hand. It was ever so much like riding through a dream, floating through a familiar yet somewhat hazy world. She found herself holding her breath, lest the ride come to an end and she awaken.

John halted the horse, bringing the carriage to a smooth stop, then excused himself to run into the bank. Watching a man of his years scamper across a parking lot like a colt was a sight to see, to be sure. She thought she might laugh out loud. Oh, joy! Was John feeling the first stirrings of love for her? Did he feel half as giddy as she?

The horse puffed out plumes of warm air from bulging nostrils as Mary waited. Then lickety-split John was back, pushing a bank receipt into his coat pocket. Mary was amused by his rushing to and fro. Whatever the reason, she dared not surmise . . . or question. She must be careful lest she jump to conclusions.

"Do ya care for some ice cream?" he asked, almost shyly.

"Sounds gut." She couldn't imagine anything colder on such a chilly day, though, and had to keep her face muscles in check so as not to let a chuckle loose.

Up the road a bit, they pulled into a roadside stand. John drove the carriage right up to the order-out window. "Would ya like a chocolate sundae?" He smiled as he asked.

"Jah, with plenty whipped cream and nuts, please." She was awful surprised that he seemed to know her taste in desserts.

He turned to the window and ordered the chocolate sundae for her and a banana split for himself.

The return trip to Hickory Hollow was pleasant enough, but terribly cold by now—what with the ice cream settling in her stomach, frosty and sweet, and a sizable case of nerves—sitting next to the bishop thisaway. Her teeth began to chatter uncontrollably.

"Feelin' a bit chilly, are ya?" Before she could answer, he

reached back and pulled up another heavy lap robe from the backseat, letting go of the reins in order to place it gently over her legs.

"*D-denk-ki*," she stuttered, ashamed of herself for not being able to conceal it, yet glad for another layer of warmth.

"I best be gettin' you home."

It was the last thing on earth she wanted to hear. She'd much rather freeze to death than have the ride come to an abrupt end. Still, in spite of her disappointment, she nodded submissively. She thought for sure he'd let her out somewhere away from the house, the way they'd arranged the meeting in the first place. But when nothing was said, even when they passed the familiar shoulder and the grove of trees, her pulse quickened. It looked as though he was really going to drive all the way into the barnyard before letting her out.

Mary folded her mittened hands as the horse made the turn into her father's long lane. Her heart felt ever so soft toward the widower. And when he turned to bid her goodbye, his eyes were filled with tenderness toward her as well.

"I'll be seein' ya, Mary, at the meeting tomorrow," he said, tipping his black felt hat like a real gentleman.

"Jah" was what came out. Oh, but she wanted to say so awful much more to the kind and gentle widower. Things such as were not becoming to a quiet, submissive young Amishwoman on the verge of being passed over for marriage. She was smarter than to say anything except, "Denki for the ride . . . and the ice cream."

"I hope we might ride again." His eyes brightened as he said, "God be with ya, Mary Stoltzfus."

"And with you." By now, she couldn't even whisper his name at the end. But it was strong in her mind all the same. *John Beiler . . .*

Despite dark clouds and the lack of sunshine, she believed this to be the most beautiful day the good Lord had likely ever made.

Mary's legs held her up just long enough to push open the back door and rush into the utility room off the kitchen, collapsing on the old cane chair. Giggling under her breath—trying for all the world to keep from bursting out—she struggled to remove her shawl and outer bonnet.

Certain that the family would be waiting by the kitchen stove, she took several deep breaths to calm her flutterings. And when her composure was restored, she marched into her mamma's scrumptious, warm kitchen.

Much to her surprise, nobody was around. "Gut," she said to herself, going to the sink and running water over her cold hands to warm them gradually. In many ways, she was delighted to have the house all to herself. With no one to dampen her spirits by probing too much, she could day-dream to her heart's content, reliving every single second of the afternoon's ride.

Strangely enough, her tryst with the bishop had been truly a secret one in every way. Perhaps by Divine Provi-dence.

CHAPTER FOUR

◈ ◈ ◈

After lunch the phone rang at Mayfield Manor. Katherine unconsciously heard the ringing but ignored it, her ears unaccustomed to the newfangled device. She checked the address on the envelope once more. Seeing the words *Hickory Hollow Lane*, a tiny burst of air flew past her lips. *How odd—kariyos*, she thought, Pennsylvania Dutch invading her thought freely.

Many weeks had come and gone since she'd spoken much of the Old German dialect. It would be impossible to forget her first-ever language, she figured, yet with no other Amish around, she wondered if her native tongue would lie dormant in her brain. Not that she was worried about it. No, she was more concerned these days with learning how to put words and phrases together in a more sophisticated manner. Especially now that she was seeing the likes of Justin Wirth and wanted—for his sake, if for no other—to become a refined English lady.

One of the young maids came to her French doors, standing between them, giving a quick curtsy. "Miss Katherine, a Mister Wirth is on the line . . . for you."

"I'll take it in here, thank you." She hurried to the phone, surprised that he was calling her so soon. My goodness, she'd

51

just seen him last night! "Hello?"

"Katherine, how are you today?"

"Fine, thank you. How are *you*?"

"Never better." His voice held a hint of intrigue. "I wonder if you might join me for dinner Sunday evening. I know of an elegant, quiet place not far from Canandaigua. An old castle."

She could hardly believe he was asking her *again*. "It sounds lovely."

"Shall I come for you about five-thirty?" he asked politely.

"Five-thirty is fine with me." She felt so terribly unsure of herself. "Good-bye" came out a mite too quickly she feared, yet Justin's farewell sounded altogether pleasant . . . almost sweet. The sound of his lilting voice rang in her memory as she set about gathering her coat and a stamp for Mary's letter.

❖   ❖   ❖

When Theodore pulled the car up for her, he was wearing a mischievous grin. "Your wish is my command," he said as he opened the back door.

"The post office, please."

"Right away, miss." He closed the door and walked around to the driver's side.

All the way downtown they talked—chatted, really. At one point she asked, "Why are *you* so happy today?"

"Can't a chauffeur be jolly now and again?"

"Why, of course!"

He glanced over his shoulder. "I must say, it's quite delightful seeing *you* so chipper, Miss Katherine."

She wondered about his comment. "Do you think I should be more sober . . . in mourning for Laura?"

"Oh my, no. I didn't mean that at all."

She didn't dare mention Justin and their dinner plans. Theodore, being the older gentleman he was, might not think it proper for such gaiety so soon after Laura's funeral. Sighing, she settled back for the short ride to town. The limousine was pure luxury and the drive as smooth as vanilla pudding.

"Warm enough for you, Miss Katherine?" asked Theodore at a red light.

Pointing her finger, she wagged it at him. "I'm plenty warm, but remember, don't call me 'miss' again, or I'll . . ." She paused. "Let's see, how could I possibly threaten you?"

He chuckled, tilting his head and glancing through the windshield at the falling snow. "Well now, you could taunt me with a norther on top of this white stuff. In fact, that just might be what's in store for us. Take a look at that sky."

She did as he said, surprised that the snow was descending on them at such a fast rate—a cloudburst of flakes. "Suppose we *do* get snowbound like Rosie said?"

"What of it?"

"Well, are there plenty of candles in the mansion?"

"Always."

"And the pantry. Is it well stocked?"

"That's been taken care of," he assured her.

"What about firewood? Anyone thought of chopping a pile just in case the electricity goes off?"

He shrugged his shoulders. "If I remember correctly, more than two cords of wood were delivered back in early fall."

She couldn't help chuckling. "Just might be you fancy folk could take a lesson or two from an Amish girl. A *former* Amish girl, that is."

Theodore seemed to ignore her mistake. "Well, you may be right about that." He turned the car into the post office parking lot. "Here we are, Katherine . . . without the 'miss.' "

"Thank you, Theodore, minus the 'sir.' "

He grinned, tipping his chauffeur's hat. "Let's keep it that way, shall we?"

She agreed, handing the letter to him to be mailed, mighty glad that she could stay snug and warm inside the beautiful car. She thought of her brothers—Elam, Eli, and Benjamin. Wouldn't they be flabbergasted to see her riding in such a fancy automobile? Why, she even wondered if such a vehicle might not tempt one of them to have a ride. Or worse.

"Probably not Elam, though," she whispered to herself, thinking better of it. Her married brother was much too straight-laced to think of straying from the Ordnung. His young wife, too. Puh, there'd be no getting either Elam or Annie and their new baby inside a car like this.

She watched for Theodore's return, thinking that if she ever did go back for a visit to Hickory Hollow, it would be to see her mamma—shunning or no—and she'd take Theodore along to drive her around. Oh, she wouldn't be flaunting her new station in life, nothing like that. But she'd show the People, especially that bishop of theirs, that no matter how badly they'd treated her, they could never squelch her adventuresome spirit.

◈ ◈ ◈

Back in his room at the B&B, Dan Fisher dialed the long-distance number, using his calling card. The receptionist for the New Jersey drafting office answered.

"Hello? May I speak to Owen Hess, please?" he asked.

The secretary patched him through without hesitation.

"Dan, good to hear from you" came the familiar voice. "How's everything up north?"

He smiled, relieved that he hadn't told his boss the specific nature of his trip. "Nothing more to be done here," he said. "I'll catch a flight the minute I check out."

"Glad you called, Dan. God bless you."

Owen's comment rang in his ears as they hung up. *"God bless you."* He needed to hear such words, especially on a day like today. Thankful that he had placed his faith and trust fully in the Lord Jesus years ago, he packed his personal belongings, scanning the suite for any stray items. Setting his suitcase by the door, he went to make one more phone call before checking out. He would have to arrange for a change in flight schedules before driving to the airport.

After making the call, he headed downstairs with his luggage. This was to have been an ecstatic moment in his life, a glorious reunion day with his sweetheart girl. He was leaving town without ever having seen Katie's sweet face—enduring the butler's horrendous slurs instead.

The owner's wife looked surprised to see him. "Oh, Mr. Fisher, you're leaving us so soon?"

"Yes, well, I hope this won't be an inconvenience for you. My stay has been shortened considerably, but I appreciate your kind hospitality and will offer to pay for an additional night if it means that I might return in good standing—if ever the need may arise, that is." He had no idea why he'd said such a thing. There would be no returning to this place. His Katie girl was gone—flown the coop.

The woman dismissed his offer with a nod of her head. "You mustn't pay a cent more than is due. But be sure to sign our guest book before you leave."

With that, Dan paid for a night's lodging, said his farewells, and rolled his luggage outside to the rental car, his heart as heavy as the snow clouds.

As he pulled out, he noticed the young girl and her mother making the turn into the parking area. They smiled and waved back, setting his mind on course for a replay of the morning's events, beginning with breakfast and the curiosity over his Amish background.

Once his luggage was checked in at the airport, Dan was free to sit and rest a bit. Emotionally exhausted, he found himself wishing he'd never made the trip. Not the way things had turned out for him—the closed doors, the overwhelming disappointment, the not knowing where Katie had gone in New York City, or why.

What's left to do? he wondered. It made no sense to pursue her, searching hundreds of talent agencies. The idea that she might be interested in such a lifestyle—that sort of vocation—had him truly perplexed.

Dear Lord, be with Katie, wherever she may be, he prayed silently. Then, to keep from dwelling on the most worrisome aspects of the butler's comments—that Katie was a phony and had caused such mayhem—Dan went to purchase a paper at the newsstand.

Forcing his attention to the minuscule newspaper in his hand, he studied the front page. Anything to keep his thoughts from wandering back to the disheartening encounter.

It was on the society page that he spotted a curious caption. *Young Amish Woman, Sole Heir of Local Estate*. Reading further, he began to mumble the words as he searched the page. "Katie," he said suddenly. "Katie is Katherine Mayfield!"

Slamming the paper shut, he rushed back to the flight counter and made arrangements to have his luggage retained. Without delay, he ran all the way to the front of the airport terminal, hailed a cab, and sped away to Mayfield Manor.

❖ ❖ ❖

After the brief stop at the post office, Katherine found herself daydreaming about her Sunday plans. An elegant dinner for two, Justin had said. A castle setting . . .

Such events required anything but Plain clothing: rather, fanciful, shimmering dresses of satin and lace or embroidered velvet. And an array of accessories. Rosie had been willing to assist her on a recent shopping expedition, offering her opinion of Katherine's purchases at a local department store.

Since her first real date in over five years, Katherine had pondered her attraction to the artist. Yesterday she'd indulged herself a bit, curling up by the fire at the coziest end of the library to think about the possibility of a future with the likable young man.

A short time had passed since their first meeting—Christmas Day. The handsome blue-eyed artist had come to the mansion, commissioned by Laura as a portrait painter. He was much more than good-looking. He was sensitive and kind—an honest man. She admired such wonderful-good qualities in a person. Perhaps because the same characteristics had been so evident in her dear Daniel. Dan . . . who'd shared her love for music and the guitar, who'd put up with her headstrong, impulsive ways, yet loved her still. If he hadn't drowned, she was sure they would be married by now. With several children, no doubt. As sure as the sun. Sure as the moon, too.

Dan Fisher, forever adored by the People. Forever missed by his Katie girl, the woman who'd mourned his passing far longer than need be. Longer, because she believed the two of them had really and truly belonged together, had found utter joy in discovering each other's heart.

Now there was someone else. Someone who was alive. Two social events in two days. Ach, Rebecca Lapp would say such a fella had courtship on his mind. Snuggling against the backseat, Katherine grinned, hugging herself.

"Looks like you may have some company," Theodore said, his voice startling her out of her reverie. He nodded his head at a taxicab parked in front of the main entrance.

Katherine could see just the back of a tall blond man wearing a dark overcoat as he stood at the doorway. She also noticed Fulton, his arms crossed at his chest as if annoyed. "I wonder if it's the same fellow who was here earlier looking for that horrible woman, that actress who—"

"Allow me to spare you a run-in with such a man," Theodore said, pulling the limousine around the side of the house. He turned, looking over his shoulder, his eyes kindly searching hers. "You won't mind going in through the east doorway, will you?"

Nodding, she gave her consent. "It's not like I haven't used this entrance before." She remembered the unnerving time when she'd slipped into the mansion, sight unseen, hoping to find her birth mother still alive.

"Very well, miss . . . uh, excuse me, *Katherine*. I'll let you out here." He parked the limo and got out, hurrying around the car to open her door for her. The snow was piling up quickly and because of it, the chauffeur accompanied her, his hand supporting her elbow, right up to the entrance.

"Thank you, Theodore. You're so very kind." She offered him a warm smile and quickly entered the house, stomping the snow off her feet before heading into the main hallway, still wearing her coat and hat.

Approaching the grand staircase, she heard voices—the measured, low tones of men arguing but doing it politely. Curious, she peered down the long hallway and saw Fulton standing like a sentry in the doorway, a human barrier. If she wasn't mistaken, he was doing most of the talking, quizzing the stranger with many questions.

She stopped to listen. Studying what she could see of the caller and making note of his overcoat, she was fairly certain it was the same man she had seen earlier that morning. Inching closer, she focused on his thick hair—just visible over Fulton's head. It was striking, like a thousand dandelions in summer. Something about its golden color reminded her of someone back in Pennsylvania. A schoolmate? One of her cousins? She couldn't be sure, probably because she had so many relatives, distant and otherwise.

Beyond the two men, the snow was falling fast and heavy. Like someone had cut open a feather pillow and was shaking it hard, creating an intermittent curtain of white.

She heard her name and a sharp response from her butler. "I cannot allow you to see the mistress if you refuse to state who you are or the nature of your visit," came the curt reply.

By now Katherine had crept close enough to make out the stranger's words. "Miss Mayfield is a dear friend of mine."

"I'd be surprised at that," Fulton shot back. "You said the same thing about Katie Lapp earlier today."

"But . . . I plead with you, let me speak with Katherine. Let her decide for herself."

Katherine fell against the wall, stunned by an impossible thought. The soft-spoken voice seemed as familiar to her as her own. Yet it could not be.

Fulton began to push the door closed. "I'm sorry, sir. Once again, I'll have to ask you to leave."

"Wait!" Katherine called, taking a step forward. "Please . . . won't you let the man in, just for a moment?"

Fulton's eyebrows arched in a pinnacle of astonishment. "Miss? Are you quite certain of this?"

"He says he knows me . . . and it's all right," she assured him, barely breathing. "I'll meet with the gentleman in the parlor."

The butler was blinking his eyes rapid fire, but nonetheless he opened the door wider and showed the man inside.

Katherine stepped back and turned toward the hallway mirror, not looking at the young man as Fulton showed him into the formal sitting room. Rosie hastened down the hall to her, offering to take Katherine's coat and hat. "Oh, thank you, Rosie. I nearly forgot." Her mouth felt terribly dry, her lips stiff.

Turning back toward the mirror, she stared in it, straightening her sweater and fluffing her hair with trembling fingers, but seeing little. Stepping back, she took a deep breath and entered the parlor with a forced smile.

Fulton and the stranger remained standing as Katherine made her way across the room, past polished tables and numerous Victorian-style chairs and a cherrywood love seat upholstered in powder blue velvet.

"Sir," the butler said, turning to the stranger briefly, "may I present Miss Katherine Mayfield."

The man stepped forward to reach past Fulton, his hand extended. "Hello, Miss Mayfield."

Reluctantly, she accepted his hand, her mind reeling as she stared into his rich blue eyes. "And you are?" She waited, hardly daring to hear the reply.

"An old friend" was all he said.

Katherine nodded to Fulton. "Thank you. That will be all," she said, relieved to have remembered the proper words, the ones Rosie and the others had taught her. In that at least she found comfort.

"Please, be seated," she said, motioning stiffly toward the love seat. She clung to the security of the formalities, feeling as though she were in the middle of a terrible, confusing dream.

"Thank you . . . but I don't mean to take up much of your time." He seemed reticent to sit, awkward now that he was finally alone with her. He remained standing for a moment, then perching on the edge of the love seat, he examined her face. It was as if he might possibly be mistaken about every really knowing her at all.

His voice dropped to a whisper. "I've been waiting for a long time to see you again, Katie." He studied her, a flicker of a frown crossing his brow again and again. "Perhaps it is too late," he added.

"Oh?" She, too, was staring at his face, his eyes, still unable to comprehend what she thought she was seeing.

"Perhaps you should sit down," she heard him say. Trembling, she lowered herself into a chair. The sensation was akin to floating through a muddled dream. A most outlandish dream.

Himmel, what was happening to her mind? Was she losing her sanity? This man reminded her of Daniel . . . but it *couldn't* be!

"I hesitate to go on," he said softly, gently, his words falling like raindrops on a rose petal. "I don't want to frighten you. I know you believe that I died five years ago."

She caught her breath, searching his face. "I don't understand. Who *are* you?"

He paused, his face intent on hers. "I'm Daniel . . . from Hickory Hollow."

A pain stabbed her. "Daniel? But Daniel Fisher drowned at sea." Her eyes searched his. She struggled to breathe, a hundred memories whirling in her mind. "I . . . I . . . ." Her voice caught on a sob. "I don't know what to say."

"Please don't say anything, Katie. Let me explain."

She could hear him no longer, could feel the wrenching, black disbelief, the confusion. Looking away, a knot in her stomach twisted and churned.

Even so, her gaze was drawn back to his bearded face, his modern haircut. Most everything about him reminded her of Daniel. The blueberry eyes, the golden hair, the gentle voice. Especially the voice.

She held her breath for a moment, then spoke, barely able to utter the words. "How . . . can you be . . . alive?"

He paused, inhaling deeply, his eyes finding hers. "I never drowned, Katie. I made a terrible mistake."

She choked back tears, refusing to let them take over.

She found the courage to speak. "A mistake? You let me *think* you died?"

He bowed his head. "I don't blame you for being upset."

She clenched her fists in her lap. "How do I know you're really Daniel?"

Wincing, he looked up at her as if to recall times and dates . . . grasping for something, anything. It was then that a lightness came into his eyes. "Do you remember the day we sat on the boulder—*our* boulder—there in the middle of Weaver's Creek? I taught you to write music that day."

She folded her arms across the front of her, as if protecting herself from the reality of this unbelievable moment.

"I gave you my guitar. You hid it in your father's barn . . . in the hayloft."

Shaking uncontrollably, she glanced away, wishing she might hold herself together against the incredible truth, the torturing pain of remembered love, the mounting hurt and anger of having been deceived.

"Oh, Katie, I've missed you terribly . . . all these years."

She drew in a sharp breath. "I'm *Katherine* now. Katherine Mayfield."

He sighed, nodding his head slowly. "Annie told me about your adoption, that you'd left Hickory Hollow after the bishop imposed your shunning—that you'd gone in search of your birth mother. But it was old Ella Mae who was brave enough to tell me where to look for you."

She turned her face toward him. "So . . . you've been back to see the People?"

"Only to speak with my father and mother . . . and Annie." He stopped, as if there was much more to his story than he dared offer.

Her eyes found his, her heart breaking anew. "The Daniel I knew said he loved me. *He* said, 'No matter what happens . . .'" Her eyes filled with angry tears. "*That* Daniel would never have tricked me this way."

"That's why I came here. To ask your forgiveness." He stood up, rushing to her side. "I can explain everything."

"What's to tell?" she said, her voice rising without restraint. "You fooled me, Daniel . . . you broke my heart. I never thought I could live life without you. You let me grieve until I was so sick the People worried that I might never be well, and here you are—coming to me this way?"

He knelt before her. "I wish I could turn the clock back, Katie, truly I do. I should've taken you away with me."

She shook her head. "The past is done. *Should have*'s never solved anything."

His eyes glistened, but he was silent.

"I'm not the girl you once loved." She stood up abruptly, the pain of their past, the burning anger consuming her. "I wish you'd never come here."

He was on his feet. "Katie . . . I—"

"No more. Please, I can't talk about this." Her hands flew to her face, hiding her tears, muting her sobs.

She felt his hand on her shoulder. "Oh, Katie, I'm so very sorry."

"Please . . . will you go?" she whispered, stepping away. And with all the energy she could muster, she called for her butler. The click of Fulton's shoes on the floor brought her some relief. Fulton would handle things now. *He* would take care of her.

Daniel looked back at her once more as the butler stood in the wide doorway. "I never meant for this visit to cause you pain, Katie. God be with you."

Silently, helplessly, their eyes met and held.

Fulton wasted no time in leading the man to the door, and Katherine turned and fled to her suite.

CHAPTER FIVE

❖　❖　❖

Daniel's return from the "dead" was all Hickory Hollow could think about, and all Mattie Beiler could talk about following dinner, when dusk lingered about the old farmhouse deep in the Hollow. She'd gone so far as to say that the young man was "of the devil"—him and his deceitful ways—running off to New Jersey somewheres to rub shoulders with them Englischers.

Glancing at her mother, the elderly Ella Mae, Mattie spoke up again. "Goodness knows Dan Fisher broke his mamma's heart . . . letting her think he was dead and gone."

"Ach, don'tcha be judgin' him so," Ella Mae chided, looking up from her knitting with a stern gaze. "The poor fella knows what it means to suffer."

"Poor fella, my left foot!" Mattie scoffed, scooting her chair closer to the woodstove in the kitchen. "He brought his pain on himself, don'tcha know?" She bit her tongue, waiting for her Mam to strike out in defense of the likable lad. Rocking hard against the hand-hewn rocker, she gripped the thick-eyed needle and her handiwork, mumbling in disgust.

Her mother remained still, yet Mattie kept looking over at her, hoping the Wise Woman might size things up from

65

her own perspective and add a little spice to the conversation.

Seconds passed, empty and unfulfilling. Mattie itched, nay *longed* to stoke the fires of discussion. Fidgeting, she could scarcely sit by and watch a perfectly good evening go to waste.

Finally, unable to withstand the silence any longer, Mattie huffed, "Seems to me, Daniel's folks been put through the wringer. And Bishop John's got every right to slap die Meinding on him—same as he did on Katie and anybody else who disobeys around here."

Ella Mae's knitting needles kept flying, clicking softly in a soothing, rhythmic pattern. Keeping mum, she never once looked up. The needle's song, gentle though it was, annoyed Mattie almost worse than if her Mam had stopped knitting altogether and lashed out about Daniel. About *anything.* Ella Mae was doing about as much talking tonight as a deaf mute, and Mattie figured she knew why. The old woman supposed she had a corner on things when it came to Daniel. Jacob Fisher's downright rebellious son had shown up clean out of nowhere to confess his past faults. "Word has it that Dan's not plannin' to stick around these parts. And he won't be making amends with the People or the church. He's got other things on his wicked mind—things like leaving Hickory Hollow all over again and going right back into the world to make money. He's a fancy draftsman now, you know—drawing up them blueprints for modern folk. Puh, if he had his head on straight, he'd know he could use the talents the Good Lord gave him right here in the Hollow. No need rushin' off to take a tainted paycheck from *sindhaft* men. No need a-tall!"

"Mattie, you're workin' yourself up over nothin'," her mother said at last, staring her down like she was so much bear bait.

"Well, what's a body to think?" she muttered, moving

her chair away from the fire a bit. "That boy's confession wasn't worth the air he breathes. And not staying around for the membership meeting, not bowing his knee in holy contrition—" She flapped her hand in the air. "Instead, he had to go and say he was saved—found grace in the sight of the Lord. Such pride! He'll rue the day, for sure and for certain."

The Wise Woman looked mighty disgusted, even though everything said just now had been honest-to-goodness truth. Mattie knew it was, 'cause she'd talked things over with a good half of the older female population in the Hollow. The consensus was that Dan and Katie probably *did* belong together in more ways than one, and if somebody didn't do something to bolster the Old Ways, and soon, they'd be losing even more young people to the world and the devil before long.

❖ ❖ ❖

Benjamin Lapp hauled several buckets of fresh well water from the pump, helping his older brother get the farm animals settled down for a bitter, cold night.

The young men exchanged a few heated remarks till Ben could stand it no longer. "I got eyes in my head, ain't I?" he shot back. "Mamma's gettin' worse, seems to me. Can't keep her mind on much of anything these days."

Eli pitched some hay for the mules. "Ya can't expect Mam to be gettin' over our sister's shortcomings all that quick."

"But what about Pop? He's strugglin', too."

Eli snorted. "*En wiedicher Hund*—a mad dog, he is."

Shaking his head, Ben walked toward the milk house. "It's all her fault, every bit," he muttered, stewing over the way things were around the house these days. Not a contented place no more. His Mam seemed upset and awful nervous most of the time, getting the jitters when a body'd least expect—leaning hard on Pop, of all things. The bishop had even come calling a time or two. But all for naught, so far as he could tell.

There was only one person who could calm Mamma down, and he'd witnessed it on several occasions. Most folk had quit referring to Ella Mae Beiler as the Wise Woman, what with the bishop putting the clamps on her lately. But from what he'd heard, the kindly woman had had herself a private chat with Dan Fisher, the boy who'd loved his sister way back when. The fella'd gotten himself shunned, too—comin' back here and strutting around, talkin' about finding forgiveness for his sins and all.

Why, he oughta have better sense than to be telling the People such things. Didn't he know what the Good Book said: "The fruit of righteousness is sown in peace of them that make peace"?

Ben spit a piece of straw out of his mouth and stood looking out the dirt-streaked window of the milk house, trying to think what it was he'd heard one of Bishop John's boys say the other Sunday after preaching service. Something about there oughta be a law about folk going around spreading such prideful talk. "We oughta put a stop to 'em when they boast that way."

Ben knew better than to flaunt any attempt at being holy. *Saved*, the Mennonites called it. He was raised up to be a right-gut Amishman, knew enough not to toot his horn about being washed and righteous. "Self-praise stinks," Dat had always said. From the time Ben was a little boy at his father's knee, he'd heard words like that; filled with goodness and truth, they were.

He turned to go to the house. The night was damp and cold, pushing its sting deep into his bones. High in the sky, stars peeped in and out of a wispy veil. Across the wide, open field to his right, the moon had risen, wearing a silken halo all around. "S'gonna snow to beat the band," he said to himself.

"Who're ya talkin' to?" his brother called, running across the barnyard to catch up.

"*Yuscht* myself."

They fell silent for a moment, walking toward the house. Then—"You miss her, don'tcha?" Eli said.

Ben pulled his coat collar up around his neck, holding it there with both hands.

"Well, don't you?"

"S'nobody's business if I do or don't."

Eli burst out laughing. "I could've sworn you'd say that!"

"We don't swear, brother. You oughta be ashamed." He wanted to slap Eli—him making a mockery of honest feelings and all. He really wanted to take his brother down on the miserably cold ground and pound him a good one. And he just might've, if it hadn't been for Mam poking her head out the back door, ringing her little bell like there was no tomorrow.

"Time for evening prayers," Eli spouted off, second cousin to a sneer.

"And a gut thing . . . for *your* sake."

Eli forced his breath out hard, and Ben saw it spiral up over his brother's worn-out work hat, toward a black sky. "Guess, if truth be told, all of us could benefit by a bit of prayin'. Lest we . . ." He paused. "Lest *all* of us end up shunned like Daniel Fisher and our sister."

Surprised at the forthright comment, especially coming from one so glib, Ben said nothing, and they hurried up the back steps and into the sandstone house.

❖　❖　❖

All five of the bishop's children knelt at the long bench in the kitchen, the warmest room in the big house. John

Beiler prayed a short prayer, thanking God for His many blessings and for leading and guiding them in His will and providence. Then he offered up to the Almighty the reins to his life and his family.

"*Gut Nacht*, Daed," said Hickory John, the oldest, when the prayer was through. The younger children—Susie, six, and Jacob, four—came to give their father a hug before following big sister Nancy, carrying a lantern, to the stairs.

"Sleep gut and fast," he called to them, hearing their feet pitter-pat up to the second floor and being comforted by the pleasant sound.

Ah, such a day it had been. Nippy . . . almost brittle cold with a dampness that chilled a body clean through. The brightest spot in the day had been his afternoon ride with Mary Stoltzfus. A right sweet girl, she was. And mighty happy to be invited to accompany him, it seemed. She hadn't succeeded in hiding the blush on her round cheeks or the hesitancy in her voice when she spoke to him. Still, Mary's qualities outshone her best friend by a country mile. He could kick himself for ever giving Katie Lapp a second glance. 'Course he hadn't known then what he knew now.

Tired from the day's work, he turned off the gas lamp and made his way to the stairs. It was no bother to climb them in the dark. He was accustomed to the slant of each one, the creaks on the third and the fifth, and the wood railing, rubbed smooth by so many hands, young and old alike.

He thought of his dear deceased wife. Miriam would chuckle to see him now, a middle-aged man trying to court but a *Maedel*—a twenty-year-old maiden. And he, with a houseful of children between the ages of twelve and four. Jah, she'd laugh, prob'ly.

Sighing, he sat on the bed, staring out at the darkness. For weeks now, Mary had been watching him hard during preaching services, especially on those Sundays when he was responsible for the Scripture readings.

Wondering just when his heart might begin to beat a little faster at the sight of her—the way it used to with Katie Lapp—he'd decided to take Mary along with him to the bank. As it turned out, not only was their time together surprisingly comfortable, he found that he really did enjoy having Mary sit beside him in the carriage . . . sharing sweets, too. Maybe, when all was said and done, it didn't matter so awful much if your heart was stirred up like a giddy schoolboy. Deep friendship was good enough to start things out—and the best thing about growing old together. Nobody would ever dispute that. After all, a man of his stature in the community needed a fine young woman to bear him more offspring and to help him raise the children he'd fathered with Miriam.

And Mary had the patience for such a task. Slipping into bed, he said his silent prayers and afterward decided that he wouldn't make *this* courtship a long and drawn-out matter. He'd go ahead and make Mary right happy by revealing his intentions in the next couple of weeks or so.

❖   ❖   ❖

Katherine propped herself up in her bed with as many plush pillows as she could gather. She'd brought with her a stack of books from the library just down the hallway, thanks to Rosie, who had shown great concern, even though Katherine had made every attempt to disguise her puffy eyes and splotchy face. She had even requested that the evening meal be brought to her in the privacy of her own sitting room.

It was Rosie who had assisted her in finding some of the old classics that Laura had enjoyed reading and rereading over the years. The nicest part of discovering the books was that some of them had Laura's childish handwriting in the front pages. This discovery delighted Katherine, and for all good reason.

In her present distraught state, she needed a reprieve, a moment of escape. Try as she might, the trauma lingered long after Fulton had shown Daniel to the door. She'd returned to her quarters weeping, and nothing Rosie or any of the other maids could do would console her. When asked about the stranger, she only shook her head and wept all the more.

Rosie sat with her now on a chair near Katherine's bed. "Perhaps if I read to you, the sound of my voice will lull you to sleep."

She turned to her maid, still suffering from having cried so hard and long. "Rosie, you're very kind, but why are you treating me this way . . . like a child?"

"You've had a trying day. No need to fret about it." Rosie got up to smooth the coverlet on the bed. "Not a thing wrong with pampering the mistress, now is there? One can certainly see you need someone to cheer you."

Nodding, Katherine searched through her pile of books, not wanting to discuss the tearful encounter. No one needed to know the story behind what had happened today in the parlor. Or anything else regarding Dan Fisher, for that matter. "This book looks interesting," she said, examining a well-worn edition. "*A Girl of the Limberlost*." She handed it to Rosie.

"Oh my, yes. This was one of Laura's very favorites." Rosie opened the book to the first chapter. "Shall I begin?"

Katherine nodded, sighing deeply.

"Chapter one is titled, 'Wherein Elnora Goes to High School and Learns Many Lessons Not Found in Her Books.' "

"Such a long title for a chapter," Katherine said, getting cozy in her mountain of pillows. Listening intently, she wondered about the many life lessons she, too, had learned. *Most* of them difficult . . . not found in books.

Although the story began with Elnora arguing with her mother over her desire to attend high school, of all things, Katherine was not able to relate one iota. Amish schools provided for only eight grades; then came graduation. The boys went home to help their fathers farm or to learn carpentry skills; girls became their mothers' right hands in tending to younger siblings and keeping house, vegetable gardens, and canning and preserving food.

The sound of Rosie's voice, though she read with considerable expression and interest, served to make Katherine quite sleepy. She already understood from past experience—the weeks and months following Dan's supposed drowning—that continuous weeping brought with it great fatigue and an overwhelming sense of helplessness.

"I should've taken you away with me. . . ." His tender words followed her into the oblivion of sleep.

❖　❖　❖

She moaned and turned in her bed, realizing with a start that Rosie was nowhere about. The room was dark now, and a slice of muted light shone through the windows high above the headboard, casting dim shadows on the comforter near her feet.

"Daniel, was it really you?" she whispered against her pillow as tears involuntarily slid from her eyes. "Are you *really* alive?"

Falling again into tormented sleep, she dreamed she was a little girl, growing up Amish in Lancaster County, Pennsylvania.

CHAPTER SIX

❖ ❖ ❖

Smoke thickened the skies over New Jersey. Dan smelled its pungent tang as he hurried down the steps to his car parked at the curb. During his commute to church, this being the Lord's Day, he mistakenly pushed the fresh-air button on the dash instead of the heater, and the noxious odor filled the car.

He was tempted to go back home, to be reclusive, yet he knew he must not forsake the assembling of believers, regardless of his state of mind. The precious little sleep he'd had last night was fitful at best, squandered with snatches of troublesome dreams.

Stopping at a series of red lights, he felt hemmed in by the heavy weekend traffic. And the dismal gray sky. All of it reminded him of his brief visit to Canandaigua and the bleakness he'd felt upon driving to the airport for the second time. Desperately weary, he had fallen asleep during the flight to Newark, awakening to the hard impact of tires on the runway, the force of the landing thrusting him back against his seat.

"Daniel would never have tricked me. . . ."

Shifting gears, he kept his eyes on the lane in front of him, moving in and out of traffic only when necessary. How good it would be to see his Mennonite friends again, to sing praises to God, to hear the message by the Lord's anointed. Owen Hess and his wife, Eve, would be eager to see him, no doubt. But they would not inquire beyond courtesy as to Dan's trip to Canandaigua; thankfully, he could count on that.

If this had been Monday and he were headed for the office, his somber mood may have affected his work, distracting him beyond his ability to pull his thoughts away from Katie. Even with business typically slow this time of year, he'd have had to force himself to concentrate. He knew that. Yet ceaseless memories flooded his mind every waking minute. The past five years had been filled up with similar thoughts. In reality, nothing had changed.

"I wish you'd never come here. . . ."

He turned into the paved driveway that led to a parking lot behind the church building. Switching off the ignition, he pulled hard on the hand brake, then checked his watch. A few minutes to spare.

"Dear Lord," he prayed, "I ask for your strength today. Help me release Katie—Katherine, as she now calls herself—to your safekeeping and care. Yet help me win her to you. Open doors so that I may witness to her of your love and saving grace. I'm ready to do your will, no matter the cost. In Jesus' name. Amen."

Opening his eyes, he gazed through the windshield at the sun doing its best to pierce the gray pall of smoke and clouds. He scanned a stand of trees situated between crowded buildings, their spartan limbs like three- and four-pronged pitchforks thrust against the misery of the pollution-stained sky.

In spite of his prayer, Dan was smitten with gloom and might as well have worn mourning clothes to announce it to the world.

As he looked on, several other vehicles pulled in and

parked on either side. It was time to get out of the car and head into the white-columned Colonial-style church. Friends waved cheerful greetings, and though Dan might've given in to the urge to simply back out of the lot and drive home, he pressed on, eager to find solace in worship and the preaching of the Word. And especially today, he needed the fellowship of brothers and sisters in Christ.

❖ ❖ ❖

Katherine felt sorry about having to decline Rosie's thoughtful invitation to attend church services with her and her husband.

"Perhaps some other time," Rosie said with a smile. "Do take care of yourself, Katherine."

She hoped Rosie would understand. It wasn't that she had no interest in going to the church where Laura had been a member; there was so much more to it. Katherine felt terribly tired, emotionally exhausted from a night of tossing about in bed crying, even though she willed the tears to stop. Her world had tilted nearly off its axis yesterday. Everything . . . *everything* had changed. Even her dinner plans with Justin Wirth were now in question. And there was the letter to Mary, mailed just hours before Daniel's appearance.

Oh, if she'd only known, she might not have dictated the letter to Rosie at all, might not have started up such a preposterous correspondence. Her desire to reach out to her Amish girlfriend might've been hampered, truly, by her knowledge that Dan was alive.

She sighed deeply, deciding to spend the morning in her bedroom, taking her breakfast there. She preferred to stay put—alone, still wearing her nightgown and robe.

The weather played a role in her lethargy, she was nearly sure, and she sat near the window, watching the snow pile up, hoping her butler and maid had arrived at church safely.

After she'd eaten her breakfast of scrambled eggs, bacon, toast, and juice, she slipped back under the covers, desiring a reprieve from troubled thoughts. Trying her best to relax, she began to sing softly in German, an old song from her childhood. "What a friend we have in Jesus, all our sins and griefs to bear. . . ."

Griefs to bear.

The words filled up the hollow places in her heart, and she wondered about Laura's love for Jesus amidst the perplexing reality of her own life. It was hard to imagine the Son of God understanding her grief, leaning over the balconies of heaven to be intimately involved in one person's life. The idea seemed worldly, even heretical.

Turning on her side, she drew her knees up and wrapped her hands around her stomach, trying to get warm enough . . . secure enough to sleep again.

Several hours later, close to dinnertime, Justin Wirth phoned. Leoma, one of the several elder housemaids, came to the French doors leading to the secluded sitting room where Katherine was lounging. "Mister Wirth is on the line for you, Miss Katherine."

"Thank you," she said, reaching for the telephone on the small table next to her.

Justin's voice sounded edgy. "Hello, Katherine. I hope my calling this late won't upset your plans for the day, but the roads are becoming treacherous, according to news reports. I don't think it would be wise to risk taking you out on a night like this. I'm afraid the castle will have to wait."

Katherine was secretly relieved. She hadn't felt she could pull off such an event anyway—not the way she was suffering. "I understand."

"Would it be all right if I called again in a few days?" he asked. "Maybe then we can plan for another time."

"Yes . . . when the storm is past."

He paused. "Well, I trust this snow will end quickly."

They said good-bye without chatting further. She hoped she hadn't been too abrupt or aloof. Thinking back, she wondered if she might've mentioned something about looking forward to seeing him again. Something kind and gracious like that.

But she hadn't felt at all kindly toward him. Hadn't felt much of anything, really. Truth be told, she wished she were as young as her dreams last night. If so, she'd crawl right up in Dat's lap and let him rock her to her heart's content in his great big hickory rocker. And when she grew tired of it, she'd munch on one of Mamma's whoopie pies till she was that close to a stomachache. That's just what she'd do if she weren't all grown up and . . . English.

❂ ❂ ❂

After the morning worship service, Dan was invited to have dinner at a restaurant with Owen and Eve Hess. "Our treat," Owen said, wearing a broad grin. "We haven't seen much of you lately."

Politely, Dan asked for a rain check. "I'd like very much to eat with you, but—well, it won't suit this time. I hope you'll understand."

Eve linked her arm in her husband's, casting a curious gaze on Dan. "Are you feeling all right?" she asked as they moved down the church aisle toward the foyer.

"A bit under the weather, I suppose," he replied, not wanting to go into how he really felt.

"Very well, then, I'll see you tomorrow at the office." Owen gave a broad smile and turned to go.

It had begun to sleet during Sunday school, and as Dan made his way out of the church, he noticed that the parking lot had glazed over. Gingerly, he headed for his car and started it, letting the engine warm up while he scraped the ice off his windows.

Back in the car, he waited his turn, while church traffic snarled in the lot, tires spinning and vehicles lurching forward. Well, he was in no hurry. He reached over on the seat and picked up his Bible, thumbing through it till he found the letter he'd written to Katie the night before he visited Mayfield Manor. Holding it, he stared at the words, not seeing them but recalling Katie's demeanor, her modern dress . . . the changes her appearance had taken in the more than five years since he'd last seen her. Still as attractive as ever— same fiery hair, same bright brown eyes—yet her speech patterns, her choice of words, had thrown him somewhat as he sat in the well-furnished parlor. The lack of Amish attire, the absence of the head covering especially, and the stylish haircut had mystified him. Yet he assumed that she, too, must surely be grappling with the same unfamiliar images as she stared back at him.

In all the years he'd known her, Katie had never worn makeup. Never sought after or *needed* beauty aids. He wondered what had led her away from her Plain upbringing. The way she carried herself—her posture—spoke of a finishing school somewhere. But when would she have attended such a place? And why?

He was curious about her birth mother, the woman Katie had set out to find. Had Katie discovered and embraced qualities in her biological mother—traits she'd never known in Rebecca Lapp?

Dan turned on the windshield wipers. The snow was falling more heavily now, and inadvertently, he glanced in his rearview mirror and noticed a lady driver motioning for him to back out. He waved his thanks, chuckling softly to himself.

Ruth Stine. A sweet young lady, one that several of his single friends had mentioned on occasion. Owen and Eve, as well. He knew better than to think that any of them might arrange for a get-together with Ruth without his consent. Yet at the same time, he had never told those same friends of his sweetheart girl, now the mistress of an impressive estate. Though Owen had heard the story of Dan's long-ago love—at least some of it—he had no idea that Dan had met face-to-face with Katherine as recently as yesterday.

It would not do to try to explain things. Not since his encounter with the modern Katie had blown up in his face. And, really, what could he expect? Impulsive and headstrong, Katie had often exerted herself in a rather forceful way. Even during their courting years, she'd fired questions at him. Why was he going off to a Bible study, of all things? Why did he have so many friends outside the Amish church?

He was quite certain she'd suspected him of associating with Mennonites during those years. He hadn't gone out of his way to keep that part of his social life from her. And if it had seemed so, it was only out of concern for her, not wanting to stir up religious doubts in Katie, not wanting her to think that the Amish life might not have been right. . . .

The drive home was less stressful; traffic was sparse due to the snowstorm and icy roads. He thought of what he might cook for lunch, remembering the savory aroma and the mouth-watering taste of oven-fried chicken. Such a "plain-good" recipe! He'd copied it onto an index card years ago while living alone for the first time. The secret was in the amount of butter used. Planning this tasty treat occupied his mind as he turned cautiously onto the side street—*his* street—too narrow and deserted to be either plowed or sanded, even in a ferocious storm.

He parked the car by the curb and ducked his head against the stiff wind. Inside the house, Dan removed his coat and scarf, flinging it over the coatrack in the small entryway. Hurrying to the refrigerator, he opened the freezer, took out a package of frozen chicken and stuck it in the microwave, setting the control to automatic defrost. He went to the kitchen window and stood there, watching the snow—thick as goose down—fall through the gray fog. Thoughts of Katie filled his mind, his heart. He wondered now if perhaps she was right. Maybe he *should* have left well enough alone. Had he erred in locating her—going to the mansion unannounced, disturbing her life in such a manner?

Unable to think of much else, he felt the need to pray for her, pray that she might encounter someone—*something*—to lead her to faith in the Lord Jesus.

Turning back to the chore at hand, he gathered the ingredients to prepare the chicken—flour, salt, poultry seasoning, pepper, and butter—something to do to keep his hands busy. A man ought to allow himself a big meal in the middle of the day, if only to fortify himself against the pain of love lost . . . love wasted and betrayed.

CHAPTER SEVEN

In Hickory Hollow the Amishwomen all looked alike, Katherine recalled while snowed in for the second day in a row. She sat snug by the fire in the enormous library, reading *A Girl of the Limberlost*, captivated by the similarities between herself and Elnora Comstock, a girl who caught moths to pay for her schooling. Elnora, a young woman growing up in Indiana during the 1860s, lived by the Golden Rule, loved nature, and longed to be loved by her mother.

Sighing, Katherine could almost feel the drab brown dress around her own ankles as she read the excruciating account of Elnora's first day of high school, entering the auditorium to taunts and jeers. She knew just how this dear girl from "the olden days" had felt. Katherine, too, had experienced the selfsame thing, usually while running errands in town at Central Market or at Roots, another gathering place where Amish farmers and other merchants sold their wares.

People, especially tourists, liked to gawk. She keenly remembered her feelings of resentment at being the object of ridicule, even if she never said anything about it. *All* the Plain women attracted attention—the way they pulled their hair into tight buns at the back of their heads, the severe clothing, the devotional head coverings. Looking the same as every other woman in Hickory Hollow had made her feel empty. Yet, at the age of thirteen, while her best friend had begun to fill out, growing rounder by the day, Katherine was still slender and underdeveloped. At times, she'd scrutinized Mary and the other girls in her grade at school, thankful for the differences between their bodies and hers. Even the shapes and sizes of their shadows at recess offered her reason to rejoice, for it was only in the dim reflections that she could sometimes see her own individuality.

❖   ❖   ❖

"Right nippy out, jah?" Mary's mother came in, carrying more wood for the cookstove.

Monday being washday, Mary had nearly froze her fingers hanging the wash out front on the porch. "Don't think I ever remember a January this cold," she said, going over to the stove to help push pieces of wood into the fire below.

"Guess we come to that conclusion every winter. It near bruises the bones, I daresay," Rachel said, heading for the sink to wash her hands.

Mary set to work, making ready for bread baking and whatnot. "Come next Sunday, we'll have a houseful of folk," she remarked, thinking ahead to their turn for Preaching services. Bishop John would come with his five motherless children and stand in the front room of this very house, opening the Scriptures and reading aloud whole chapters at a time.

"Having church here doesn't come around for us all too much anymore," Rachel added. "The district's gotten so big, it's near burst its seams."

Mary laughed. "The seams are runnin' from Weaver's Creek all the way out to the highway."

"Jah, one of these days Preacher Yoder's gonna be callin'

for some of us to divide up, I 'spect. Make a new district of families."

Mary was surprised to hear it. "Ya mean it? We're *that* many Amish?"

Her mamma nodded, going to the pantry for some flour and sugar. "Ministers' council will be coming up here before long. Decisions will be made then."

Mary kept her thoughts to herself. In all truth, she was more than happy to hear of it. She could only hope that somehow or other, the People might be allowed to speak to Katie, if ever the shunned girl returned to Hickory Hollow. But if not . . . and if the Samuel Lapps were among the families chosen to move to another church district, well then maybe whoever became Preacher for that group—by the drawing of lots—might confer with the new bishop about the matter. 'Course, she had plans to speak to Bishop John about that very thing herself . . . someday. Even so, women were expected to keep their noses out of church affairs. And on top of that, she didn't want to take any chances with the budding romance. Nothing—well, hardly anything—was worth losing the interest of John Beiler.

◈   ◈   ◈

Katherine marked her spot in the book she was reading and placed it on the tea table in front of her chair. She walked the length of the library to the tall window and looked out. Snow was falling nearly slantwise and so thick with its steady motion that she felt momentarily dizzy. Leaning a knee against the low windowsill, she fixed in her mind the setting, taking in the expanse of meadow, the ridgeline of trees far to the east—the most beautiful place on earth. How all of this had come to belong to her, really and truly, she could scarcely comprehend. Yet it was so.

Here she was, settled in and quite snowbound, surrounded by shelves of intriguing books, flickering candles, and a roaring fire. At once, she realized that aside from the lovely furnishings, rugs, drapes, and wall hangings, she might well have been standing at the front room window in Samuel Lapp's home in Hickory Hollow, enjoying the afternoon without the luxury of electricity or indoor heating.

"What do you see when you look into your future?"

Daniel had asked her the question when they were yet young, back one summer while the two of them ran barefoot down a dusty lane, chasing after a stray pony in the squelching heat. Dog days, they'd always called the hottest weeks of July and August.

He'd asked the same question the following winter while they played outside during school recess. 'Course, she had no idea what he was really trying to say, and she went about patting the snow into a hard round ball.

She remembered the day as if it were yesterday—the way the snow had come down hard all around them, piling up steadily and erasing the footsteps that led away from the one-room schoolhouse in less time than it took to have recess. The first real blizzard of her life!

She recalled the heavy old boots she'd worn, the giant snowman she and Daniel had begun to make together. Still, they'd had so much help from their cousins and Plain friends that before they knew it, the snowman stood tall and finished, looking quite cheerful with eyes made of olives from somebody's sack lunch. The turned-up mouth was designed with broken bits of carrot sticks, as she recalled, and the black felt hat . . . young Daniel's.

He'd stepped back to survey the fat creature, laughing right out into the frosty air, laughing harder than she'd ever heard him. The sound rose from his belly, deep in the pit of him, and his face had turned peach red when she'd started chasing after him, yelling at him to please let her catch him.

And he had. He'd turned himself around without warning and stopped in the snow.

She'd plowed into him . . . hard, landing against his strong chest, but only because the snow was so deep and so slick she couldn't really help it at all.

Smiling now, she could see his eyes—blue as berries and all twinkly—like he was mighty glad she couldn't stop, glad she'd crunched into him like that, and probably glad she'd found herself all flustered up about it, too.

She moved back from the library window, wishing to let such childish memories fade, hoping that recollections from the past might not continue to confuse her, creating havoc with her recent decision to send Daniel away.

Garrett Smith came into the library just then, placing a round silver tray on the low table near the fireplace, a stately presentation. "Tea is served," he said, bowing. "Selig made your favorite cookies."

She knew without looking. "Please tell Selig thank you for me."

Garrett stood waiting for her dismissal as she strolled to the area where four matching wing chairs were situated around a wide oval table in the center of an expansive rug. "I was wondering," she began. "Could you . . . would you be willing to play a game with me?"

His eyes grew wide, followed by a peculiar grin. "Miss?"

"Checkers," she said. "Will you play a game of checkers with me?"

He nodded, bowing again. "At your service, Miss Katherine."

She shook her head, tiring of the proper conversational tone. "I won't call you 'sir,' if you'll promise not to call me 'miss.' How about that?"

He nodded, his cheeks turning red in the firelight.

"And furthermore, let's disband with such formal talk. It's starting to make my brain hurt . . . really 'tis."

"As you wish," he said, forgetting.

"Try saying 'gut idea.'" She watched him closely, his face not about to crack. "And make sure it sounds like 'goot' . . . jah?"

He shifted his weight from one foot to the other. Then nodding, he agreed. "Very well."

"Very *goot*," she prompted him.

"Goot" came the echo. And with that, the young steward poured a cup of tea, letting a few drops of milk drip into the china cup. "Sugar?"

"Always."

A game table was brought out, set up, and placed in front of the fire, so the blaze might light the checkerboard.

"You take the first move," she said as they sat opposite each other.

"As you wish."

"No . . . no." She wagged her finger at him, playfully.

"Ah, yes. Very gut."

She leaned forward, her eyes intent on him. "This is going to be a right-gut game. Ain't so?"

"Jah, right-*goot*," he said, surprising her.

❖   ❖   ❖

Katherine beat Garrett at checkers—three rounds worth—then called for Rosie. "Are there any lanterns around?"

"In the outbuildings, perhaps," Rosie replied. "Would you like one for your room?"

She rose and went to the fireplace. "Seems to me we could all gather here in the library for supper tonight. But it might be a bit dark without a lantern or two."

"Or at least a few candles," Rosie suggested. "Power lines are down all over the county. There may not be electricity yet tonight."

Katherine waved her hand. "I think we can adjust." She turned her back toward the fire. "It might be right fun, really."

Rosie cocked her head. "Perhaps you can teach us to enjoy it."

She knew the maid was referring to Katherine's childhood days—the absence of modern conveniences. "Oh, here's a thought. After supper, let's tell stories around the table."

Rosie chuckled and went to find someone to look for a lantern.

"Denki," she called after her friend and housemaid. Then, to herself Katherine whispered, hoping to make the words ring true, "A wonderful-gut night this will be."

She would try to enjoy herself while having supper in the library and sharing stories with her new friends around a crackling fire. Though, try as she might, it would be impossible to numb the sting of knowing that Daniel was alive . . . that he had been all along.

CHAPTER EIGHT

❖　❖　❖

The postman got his little white truck stuck in a snowdrift, smack-dab in front of the Stoltzfus mailbox. Mary's father ran out to help push as she observed the situation from her bedroom window.

The day had dawned bright, with the hope of much sunshine, but scudding clouds soon rolled over the Hollow, bringing with them heavy snow.

Mary had to laugh, watching her father huffing and pushing while the mailman revved up the engine of the tiny truck, spinning his tires to beat the band. Now, if he were Amish, the man could've hitched up a horse to a sleigh and gone about his duties, delivering the mail without any worry, just the way Dat used to take her and her older brothers to school back years ago on the worst days of winter. 'Course, there was no tellin' them Englischers how to carry the mail around to folks. She shook her head, thinking that there was nothing like right fancy tires for getting a body stuck in snow. Guaranteed.

She sat down at the window, entertaining thoughts of her next visit with John Beiler. When would he invite her to go with him somewhere again? Maybe he'd see her after church and speak to her about another ride in his family

Kutsch. Or maybe sooner. She could hope, because being around the bishop seemed so awful right . . . like the Divine Providence he often preached on. Spending time with John Beiler was just the way she'd always supposed it might be—back before he was ever really free to dream of. Back when he was engaged to marry Katie Lapp.

"Mail's here!" Abe Stoltzfus called up the steps to her. "There's a letter for ya, Mary."

For me? Hurrying to the steps, she ran down all the way. "Who's it from?"

"Hard to say. Looks like a New York postmark." His eyes squinted almost shut as he studied the return address. "Know anybody by the name of Taylor? Mrs. Rosie Taylor's the name."

She shook her head. "Never heard of such a person." But she was eager to read it anyway and headed for the kitchen, where she found a sharp knife and sliced the envelope open.

Sitting by the woodstove in her father's rocking chair, she began to read:

Saturday, January 17

Dear Mary,

   Although I have never met you, I am told that you are a kind and devoted friend, and that you will understand fully the nature of this letter.

   It has come to my attention that there is a young woman whom you know, but with whom you may no longer have contact. I am thinking of Katherine Mayfield, formerly Katie Lapp. I must confess to you that I do not understand such things as Amish shunnings, nor do I wish to pry. The reason I write today is for the sake of your friend Katherine, who does not want to cause trouble for you. Rather, she would like you to know that she misses you greatly and has not forgotten the many kindnesses you have shown her in the past. She is also concerned about Rebecca Lapp, the woman who raised her, and hopes that you might relay the message that Katherine loves and misses her mother as well.

She would not think of writing to you directly, though she would be pleased if such a thing were permitted. Katherine is not certain as to this way of corresponding—whether or not your bishop would allow such a way of "speaking" to her dear friend.

> *On behalf of Katherine Mayfield*
> *(formerly Katie Lapp),*
> *Mrs. Rosie Taylor*

Mary folded the letter and slipped it back into the envelope, hoping Dat would not come into the kitchen just now and see that she was breathing hard, fingers trembling. Pressing the letter to her heart, she held it there, desiring with all her might that she could reply to the sender, to the thoughtful woman, Rosie Taylor, who'd written this message with both Katie and Mary in mind. What a wonderful-*gut* lady she must be.

Leaning back in the rocker, Mary was thankful that dear Katie had met someone so kind, even though Rosie must surely be English, for sure and for certain. Mary might've spent the entire afternoon stewing over Katie, missing her terribly, wishing she'd never left Hickory Hollow, but there was work to be done. So she got busy with her mother and Mammi Ruth—her father's Mam—patching Dat's work trousers.

They sat around the kitchen table telling stories and enjoying each other's company. After a bit, Mary took to darning socks, thinking how she'd like to be doing the same thing for Bishop John someday—for his children, too. She felt that it wouldn't take much time at all before she would be feeling true compassion for the whole family.

"Abe mentioned a letter postmarked somewhere in New York," Mammi Ruth said, glancing up over her needlework.

Mary was silent for a moment. Wasn't sure what to say to her grandmother about it.

Rachel, however, didn't wait for Mary to speak up. "Isn't that where Samuel Lapp's daughter headed to? Seems to me Rebecca said it was."

Mary wouldn't go hiding the truth from her loved ones. Still, she wanted to keep the letter just for her own eyes, precious as it was. "The postmark was Canandaigua, a city up in New York somewheres," she managed.

"Jah, and who do ya know up there?" Mammi Ruth shot back.

Why the woman had to be so pointed, Mary didn't know. But she wished she might've kept the letter a secret, at least for a day or so. Then, if she *had* to say anything, it would be her idea alone.

"Mary?" Now Mamma was inquiring, and not about to let up on her, it seemed.

"Someone by the name of Rosie Taylor wrote to me," she replied with a sigh.

"Rosie?" Mammi Ruth stuck her needle in a spool of white thread and scratched her head through the prayer covering. "I don't know any Rosies in New York, do you, Rachel?"

Mary wondered if she should just go ahead and spill the beans on Katie . . . on herself, too. For if the People found out that Samuel's shunned daughter was using a stranger, an Englischer no less, to convey a message to one of the membership, well, there was no telling what an uproar might come of it.

Both women were looking over at her now, having abandoned their mending, just staring across the table.

"Ach, I don't know of any Rosies livin' up there, neither," she finally said.

"Well then . . ." Mammi Ruth picked up her needle and the loose knee patch, resuming her work.

"Jah, well . . ." Mamma did the same.

Mary sighed softly so as not to stir things up again. She was truly relieved that the matter had been dropped and quite abruptly at that.

❖   ❖   ❖

"You just have a bad case of cabin fever, that's all," Rosie said. "Which is quite easily remedied."

Katherine wasn't so sure. "Have you looked out the window lately? There's still plenty of snow everywhere. I don't know if it would be safe to go out just yet."

Rosie shook her head. "Street crews are out in full force. Have been all morning."

"So you think Theodore might be able to get around on the road all right?"

Rosie continued to dust and straighten up the sitting room adjacent to Katherine's bedroom. "I've never known a better chauffeur than Theodore Williams. You were very fortunate to have him stay on."

Katherine was curious. "What do you mean? Was he thinking of retiring?"

"Well, when Laura became so ill, he'd toyed with the possibility of ending his duties here—if and when she passed away."

"Really?"

Rosie nodded. "Yes, he'd thought of quitting, leaving the work to Rochester, the junior chauffeur, but you know what happened to *him*."

Circling the large room, Katherine wished she were the one cleaning up the place. It still seemed odd to have paid help working around her, always straightening things up, things *she'd* made messy. "I guess I don't miss Rochester much," she admitted. "But then again, I hardly knew him."

"The young man needed lessons in etiquette, among other things," Rosie said, lifting a vase to polish the sofa table. "It wouldn't surprise me if he changed vocations after Master Bennett dismissed him."

"Oh . . . why's that?"

"He just didn't seem to fit in around here. In my opinion, Rochester wasn't cut out to chauffeur high-society people."

Katherine felt suddenly self-conscious. "You mean fancy people like Dylan and Laura Bennett?"

Rosie stopped dusting. "Oh, dear me, no . . . I didn't mean what you must be thinking. *You're* one of them, too. A refined young lady. I see it in the way you enjoy fine things."

Rosie was overstating her case, it was clear to see. "But I was raised Plain . . . Amish," said Katherine. "I'm really not one of the elite, so to speak."

"Oh, but you *are*," Rosie insisted. "And you'll be surprised at how very quickly your backward ways . . . thoughts, too, probably, will begin to drop away. It's only a matter of time. You'll see."

Just now, the way her housemaid was going on about things, Katherine wasn't sure at all how she ought to view herself: English or just not quite.

Rosie began to explain further. "Look at the way your artist friend has taken to you. Certainly, Justin Wirth has noticed your aristocratic roots shining through—your *mother's* genteel background, of course."

Shivering at this awkward revelation, Katherine dismissed Rosie's comment, hoping that the interest Justin had shown her had more to do with Katherine herself than her fancy biological roots. Politely, she excused herself and went in search of Theodore Williams.

She found him outdoors, sweeping the back steps free of snow, the heavy shoveling already done. "Good afternoon," she called to him as she stood on the wide side porch.

Tipping his hat, he grinned. "What a nice change from such a storm." He paused to look up.

She followed his gaze, breathing in the crisp air and watching clouds skitter across a still-hazy sky. In the distance, the ridge was a gray-blue smear on the horizon.

"Is it safe out on the roads yet?" she asked hesitantly.

He nodded. "Where is it you'd like to go?"

She hadn't told a soul of her plans, but she was eager to find out about doing some volunteer work. "What about the hospice downtown . . . where Nurse Judah sometimes works?" she asked.

"Oh, the Canandaigua Hospice?"

"Yes, that's where I'd like to go." She said it with all confidence, hoping to see again the cheerful nurse who had personally tended to Laura during the most critical phase of her illness.

Theodore leaned on the broom. "When would you like to leave?"

She checked her watch, still unaccustomed to wearing jewelry, and—of all things—a right fancy jeweled timepiece. "Is one hour from now too soon?"

"Absolutely not. I'll bring the car around the front entrance promptly at three o'clock."

"Thank you, Theodore. I'll be ready." She turned to go inside, nearly bumping into Rosie, who was waiting just outside the kitchen, near the butler's pantry.

"May I have a word with you?" Rosie asked, her face drawn, eyes anxious.

"What is it?"

"I'm afraid I may have offended you, Katherine. I may have spoken out of turn—talking about your . . . past, that is."

"Please, don't think a thing of it." Katherine understood what the maid was attempting to make right between them. She had wondered, upon further reflection, if Rosie might not come to this conclusion regarding her comments made in the sitting room earlier. "You've done nothing but good for me since I came here. You owe me no apology."

Rosie's face broke into a smile. "It's a pleasure to serve you, Miss—"

"Just *Katherine*."

Rosie's eyes met hers. "That's what I like about you. You're so easy to be around . . . no airs. None of the elitist manner of thinking."

She agreed. "Let's keep it that way, jah?"

Rosie had to chuckle. "Very well."

Without further discussion, Katherine excused herself once again and hurried past the main kitchen by way of the narrow hallway, then to the main corridor of the house and to her suite.

❖   ❖   ❖

Downtown, the streets were well plowed and adequately sanded, according to Theodore, who sat squarely in the driver's seat while Katherine occupied the back, off to the right side.

She watched several people, wearing heavy coats, hats or scarves, boots, and either mittens or gloves. Peering out from behind the tinted limousine window, she contemplated each of the folk, some waiting at stoplights to cross the street.

In those faces she saw purpose. Some were headed to

make deposits of money at the bank, no doubt, others, to visit the post office. Still others were out for a bit of fresh air after having been cooped up for two solid days. Store lights twinkled in shop windows, and she thought of the Englischers having to suffer without electricity indefinitely. Why, their world would surely crumble over such a hardship. Yet, if truth be told, she'd enjoyed the lack of electrical lights, an excuse to use firewood for heating and cooking at Mayfield Manor. And just now, thinking about it, she wondered how the staff might feel if, on occasion, they outened the lights and used candles and lanterns in the mansion. Something to consider. . . .

❖ ❖ ❖

Natalie Judah's face lit up when Katherine first spotted her. "Well, hello again."

She smiled at the nurse. "It's good to see you."

"You're looking well," Natalie said, extending her hand.

"Thank you." Katherine glanced around the common room. Its walls were bordered with lush and leafy greenery, and at one end an aviary was filled with many colorful birds flying about. Such a tranquil setting for a terminally ill patient. "I can feel the peace in this room," she said.

Natalie, dressed in a soft blue sweater and cream-colored trousers, looked so natural and relaxed that it dawned on Katherine she'd never seen Laura's nurse in street clothes. Nurse Judah must've noticed Katherine glancing at her nonprofessional attire. "The charge nurse and all the staff wear casual clothing here at the hospice," she explained. "One of the ways we can connect more closely with our patients."

"How many are there?"

"We have a twelve-bed unit here presently but could

care for ten more if we had the space." Natalie went on to say that the hospice was highly regarded in the community. "We've been here for many years and have literally outgrown the building."

Katherine paid close attention, concerned that she not miss a single word of the nurse's comments. "Do you have a music program?" she asked, thinking of her guitar.

"We have a traveling unit that can be rolled from room to room, and once a week we have a flutist and harpist duo who come to entertain. It's quite therapeutic, even for the staff," said Natalie, smiling. "So, yes, we do encourage volunteers who are musically inclined. Would you like to have a tour?"

"I'd love one, thanks."

Although she didn't ask to see any of the private rooms, where hospital beds and personal belongings were located, Katherine did enjoy touring the dining area. Long family-style tables encouraged conversation and fellowship for those who were able. Most of all, she was taken with the enormous aquarium filled with numerous colorful fish.

She decided toward the end of the tour that a hospice such as this was a lovely, peaceful place to spend one's final days on earth.

Farther down the hall, Katherine was surprised to see a young boy, gaunt and pale, sitting in a wheelchair. He couldn't have been more than eight or nine, and something about him reminded her of Levi Beiler, Bishop John's son in Hickory Hollow. Her heart went out to the child . . . to all the patients, and she was glad to offer her time and her services.

At the end of the quick tour, she asked if she could discuss the process involved in becoming a volunteer. "I'm very interested."

"Sure. Come with me." Nurse Judah led her to a small

room where several nurses' aides sat, having coffee. "Would you care for something to drink?"

"Water's fine."

Natalie let the water run before holding a clean glass under the spigot. "How have you been, Katherine . . . since Laura's death?"

"As well as you might expect. It's never easy losing a family member, even though my birth mother was someone I hardly knew." She remembered her manners. "How have *you* been?"

"Oh, busy as usual. I meet myself coming and going these days." Natalie handed her the glass of water, then motioned toward a vacant table in the center of the room.

Katherine sat down and took a sip, knowing how it felt to be that busy . . . to fall into bed at night, completely exhausted from the day's activities. She'd grown up that way, getting up nearly as tired as she'd gone to bed. But those days were far behind her now.

"I was hoping I might be able to help out with your younger patients," she offered.

Natalie seemed pleased. "Client volunteers are always welcome. We do offer a concentrated two-week training program, and an interview is required along with an application."

"I'll be glad to do whatever is required."

Natalie poured herself a cup of coffee. "We're shorthanded at the present time, so I can set you up with the screening right away."

"Thank you. It means an awful lot to me." Katherine felt out of control suddenly, an unexpected lump forming in her throat.

"Are you all right?" Natalie's gaze narrowed, and she reached over to cover Katherine's hand with her own.

"I'm looking forward to getting out around people again," Katherine admitted. "The mansion, as big as it is, is quite confining at times. I don't know how to explain it, really."

Natalie seemed to understand. "Yes . . . I imagine it would be, by contrast."

"I'm also thinking of starting a quilting class. I want to set up frames in the manor library. Know of anyone who might be interested?"

Natalie's eyes grew big. "Are you serious? You're going to teach traditional Amish quilting patterns?"

"Beginning with the popular Ninepatch and working our way up to one of my favorites—the Country Songbird," she replied, growing more excited about the idea as she watched Natalie's face.

"Count me in. When do we start?"

"Right away. As soon as I can round up a frame or somebody to build me one."

Natalie blew on her coffee. "I know of several Amish settlements in and around Canandaigua. Someone from our fund-raising committee might know who does that sort of thing."

"Really?"

"Oh, absolutely. One of the reasons is that we have specially handmade quilts—some are Amish-made, I believe—displayed on the wall in each patient's room."

She'd never thought of doing such a thing with a quilt, though she could see why English folk might choose to. "What a nice way to decorate."

"Oh, it certainly is. Quilts are warm and cheery; often tell a story. We even have a few with the creators' names sewn right on the individual squares . . . really lovely."

They talked more about Katherine's idea to offer a class for beginning quilters at Mayfield Manor. Natalie's response was so surprisingly positive, Katherine felt spurred to act quickly. Along with her volunteer work at the hospice, the quilting class would help crowd out nagging thoughts of

Dan. Such a wonderful-good plan it was.

On the return trip, Theodore slowed the limousine to a stop in front of the post office, waiting for a red light. Spying people rushing in and out to mail their letters and packages, Katherine's thoughts wandered back to the letter she and Rosie had concocted for Mary, and wondered whether or not it had been delivered to the Hickory Hollow address.

She could only hope that her friend might receive it with all the love that was intended, and that it might not pose a problem for one so dear.

CHAPTER NINE

❖　　❖　　❖

Mary's bedroom—with only a bed, a small table next to it, an upright cane chair, and a narrow dresser with a medium-sized mirror attached—was nearly bare. She wasn't bothered by the room's simple furnishings. Rather, she liked the openness, preferred the expanse of the hardwood floor to fancy rugs and coverings.

She wrapped herself in a quilt and sat on the edge of her small bed, *kischblich*—silly—with delight. Tomorrow, *here*, in this house, she would come face-to-face with John Beiler again. Oh, she could hardly stand the thought of wasting the night by sleeping through it, not with the moon coming in through the window like a spotlight on her soul!

The quilt dragged behind her as she went to the window and stared out at the barnyard and on past the tobacco shed and beyond, where the land lay open in wide, sweeping patches. Snow lay heavy on the ground and in the distance, against the evening sky, two bright stars grinned down at her.

It was cold in the room, yet she shivered with joy, remembering the obnoxious way her muscles had tensed up on the ride back from the bank with Bishop John last Saturday afternoon, already one week ago. Seemed like just yesterday, and she held her breath in anticipation of the People coming for preaching tomorrow. More than that, she hoped to hear for certain that the bishop was actually going over to Schaefferstown, to attend the funeral of an old preacher friend. She'd overheard such talk at the General Store two days ago when young Levi Beiler, while chatting with Preacher Yoder, had said that his father was off to a funeral come Monday.

Her ears perked up right good as she crouched down behind a row of sacked sugar, eavesdropping on Levi and the preacher.

"I s'pose your pop'll be needin' someone to watch over you younguns while he's gone," said Preacher Yoder.

Levi nodded absentmindedly, reaching over to lift the glass lid off the peppermint sticks. "Daed's got someone in mind for us, all right."

Mary's heart leaped up at the boy's words. Who was the bishop thinking of asking? Did John have her in mind to stay with his brood?

She turned from the window and scurried across the floor, removing the quilt she'd wrapped herself in and placing it on top of the pile of quilts that draped over the single bed. Then, because the floor was ice-cold, she slipped under the sheets to say her prayers. The Good Lord would surely understand. This night, this moonbeam-filled night, she would pray under the warmth of her mamma's and Mammi Ruth's quilts, thanking the Lord God heavenly Father for His watchcare over her life. And . . . over John's.

Around midnight, Mary was still lying awake, wide-eyed in the scant light of a fading moon. She had devised various ways lately to occupy her mind when she suffered from insomnia. One way was to think of the days when she and Katie were little girls. Her favorite memory, among many, was the summer night they'd sneaked away from a picnic at the Lapps' place. Making sure no one noticed, she and Katie had run down the mule road that led to the cornfield, past the clearing, and toward the deep, wide pond with its cloistered island.

Under a fingernail of a moon, they'd rowed out on the slow water in the old boat, whispering and giggling to each other. When they reached the middle, Katie decided they wouldn't row all the way to the island but should stop and just drift along, lying back, staring up at hundreds of light points in the silvery sky.

Neither of them spoke for a time, then Katie sneezed, and the sound echoed across the water like ripples. Mary got the giggles all over again. And they sat up and faced each other, best friends, listening to the peaceful night sounds of talk and laughter carrying across the water, coming from the Lapps' farmhouse nearly a half mile away.

"Wish someday we could marry each other's brothers so we'd be sisters," Katie said softly.

"It don't matter really. We're already closer than that, jah?"

"Sisters in our hearts," Katie whispered, her eyes shining back at Mary.

"Right ya be," she agreed.

Mary closed her eyes, thinking of her dear sister-friend, and when she did, tears squeezed through her eyelids onto the old feather pillow.

Right ya be. . . .

Quickly, she thought of another way to fall asleep. She would say her Amish rote prayers over and over—several times in German, three times in English. If that didn't make her tired enough, she'd think of everything that had happened to her from the day she could actually remember things, which, she supposed, was around age four or so till the present time.

Try as she might, it seemed the years got all jumbled up in the routine of Amish life . . . over and again the same things. Getting up, making breakfast, choring inside and out, putting up quarts of food, helping other women can *their* harvested produce, sewing, mending, cleaning, baking, cooking, going to church every other Sunday, visiting, and going to bed. Not till Katie ditched Bishop John and got herself shunned had Mary ever noticed any departure from the rituals of her life. Not that there needed to be anything much more interesting than daily living, not really. But it *was* a noticeable thing—Katie leaving the bishop behind on their wedding day like she did. If nothing else, the sad yet surprising tale gave the women something to wag their tongues about. But it gave Mary much more than that. In her grief for Katie, she'd found hope.

So right then and there, in the darkness of her silent room, she decided she must *not* tell the bishop or anyone else about the letter from Rosie Taylor, who lived somewhere up in New York.

❖   ❖   ❖

Sometimes Samuel Lapp would read out loud to Rebecca on a Sunday evening when the house was quiet and they'd all had their share of seconds at dessert. She especially liked hearing him read from the many columns in *Die Botschaft*, a weekly newspaper for Old Order Amish and Mennonite communities.

"Listen here to this," her husband said with a chortle. "This 'un comes from Kutztown . . . seems there was an awful big commotion over at Luke Hoover's pigsty the other night. Sounded like one of his pigs was in serious trouble, a-howlin' and complainin' over in the hog house. And then if Clarence Leid's fussy old rooster didn't start a-crowin' and offerin' his sympathy to the noisy pig. 'Course the duet didn't last too much longer as the rooster seemed to out-howl the sow. And that was that."

Rebecca sat quietly rocking while her husband had to put down the paper and remove his glasses. He was laughing so hard his eyes were moist, but she tried not to gawk. Part of her had listened, taking in his words as he read the true anecdote. And she'd heard enough to offer a slight smile at the amusing story, nodding occasionally when he glanced over at her as he read.

Yet her heart seemed like a big chunk of ice, hard and cold. And the more she wished it would melt and leave her soft the way she used to be, the harder it felt.

When he'd composed himself, Samuel glanced over in her direction. "Now, what do ya think of that?"

"Well . . ." She pushed a little smile onto her face. "If you're tryin' to get me to laugh, ach, there's just not much that strikes me funny these days." She could've gone on to say what the reason was, but she figured he ought to know by now.

Samuel nodded, picked up the paper, and read to himself all the rest of the evening. She didn't blame him for it, not one little bit. The man had had his own share of sorrow over their daughter's rebellion and ultimate shunning. When she'd upped and left town, Rebecca knew he had suffered terribly, but here lately she just assumed he was handling his loss pretty well, in a manner of speaking. There were the upsetting occasions when he'd raise his voice to her or their sons, getting angry over hardly anything at all, far as she could tell. The look on Eli's and Benjamin's faces would tell her that they, too, knew something was still bothering Samuel awful much. Probably as much as it bothered all of them.

She leaned her head back on the rocking chair and sighed. And far off in the distance she heard a hoot owl calling for its mate from the trees beyond the creek.

❖ ❖ ❖

Her new grandbaby, Daniel Fisher—named for his uncle Daniel, who everyone thought was dead but had turned up alive—was howling like that sow her husband had read about the night before when Rebecca Lapp entered the kitchen door of her oldest son's house bright and early Monday morning.

Annie, her daughter-in-law, greeted her, waving her into the kitchen. "Baby's got the colic, I daresay." Reaching into the cradle, Annie lifted the bundle up into her arms.

Rebecca took off her wraps as the little one continued to wail. "Has a tummyache, all right." She went over and rubbed his tiny back in circular motions. "This'll sometimes help relieve the gas. Try that." And she stepped back, letting Annie take over the gentle patting.

Meanwhile, she went into the front room, where two large quilting frames were set up and ready for the womenfolk who would be arriving later, after breakfast. "Mary Stoltzfus won't be comin' over today," she said, going back to the kitchen.

"Jah, I heard. Seems she's been asked to stay all day with John Beiler's children." Annie's face blossomed into a big smile. "Suppose the bishop's taken a liking to her?"

Rebecca sat down at the long table, a frown appearing as she sighed audibly. "Your guess is as good as mine, but you know the sayin' same as I do: 'One who wastes time wastes life itself.' Wouldn't expect John to want to remain a widower much longer."

Annie shook her head, still rubbing the baby's back. "He's not gettin' any younger."

"No, none of us are that."

Daniel stopped crying and made sweet little sucking sounds. "Guess now he might be gettin' hungry," said Annie, preparing to nurse the baby.

"I'll do your dishes for ya." And Rebecca went to the sink and drew the rinse water.

"Denki, Mam." Annie sighed. "It's mighty hard keeping everything clean around here with a little one . . . and another one already on the way."

"You ain't tellin' me anything I don't know already." Rebecca clearly remembered what it was like having three children right in a row—all of them clamoring for attention while the housework and chores piled up. But not for one minute had she regretted birthing three fine sons and, later, embracing the infant Katie as her own. No, given the chance, she'd do it all again. Only one thing would be different if she could change things. She would have destroyed the satin infant gown that had stirred up such commotion with Katie, leading her away from the People—up to that English woman in New York. As much as she'd loved the perty rose-colored dress, she knew, for sure and for certain, the fancy little thing was the reason why her secret—her and Samuel's—ended up having to be told. Now the baby gown was gone, tricked out of her own hands by Ella Mae Zook. No wonder folks called her the Wise Woman. She wasn't just wise, she was shrewd. And more than ever, Rebecca suspected her of being in cahoots with Katie. Why else had she entertained the shunned Daniel Fisher in her Dawdi Haus several weeks ago? Why else had she told him where to go and look for Katie?

Once the womenfolk started coming for the quilting frolic, the tormenting questions subsided, and she set to sewing her straight, tiny stitches on a brand-new quilt to be given to one of Annie's cousins as a birthday gift. For the first time in a long, long time, she came ever so close to volunteering a story. "I'll try to tell one today," she said hesitantly. "It may not happen. I just don't know yet. . . ."

Annie and the others burst into applause, grinning and cheering her on like nobody's business. She felt her cheeks flush with embarrassment, but when she opened her mouth to recite the opening lines of an old favorite, she knew she wasn't quite ready. Someday she would spin her tales again, 'cause this was a gut and right thing. Something she'd yearned for—honest-to-goodness missed—but just couldn't bring herself to do. Not just yet.

❖　❖　❖

Mary met the bishop's four older children at the back door as they came in from school. Jacob, the youngest, held her hand as they stood there, propping the storm door open. "How was school today?" she asked as they filed in, one by one.

Nancy and Hickory John launched into a long description of what they'd studied. But the minute Susie stepped into the utility room, she started bawling her eyes out.

"What'sa matter?" Mary asked, brushing stray hairs from the girl's forehead.

Susie hitched up her skirt tail and pointed to her skinned knee. "Oooow! I hurt . . . myself . . . awful bad!" she wailed.

Mary knelt on the floor, eye level with the six-year-old. "Let's see how *awful* bad it is."

"I . . . I falled down and skinned my knee." Susie leaned down and showed her the wound, crying all the while.

A quick look and Mary saw that a scab had begun to form already.

"It hurts!" Susie fussed some more.

Levi rolled his eyes and pursed his lips, as though he knew something about the injury but wasn't saying. He pulled his boots off and lined them up next to Hickory John's.

It was Nancy who offered the telling explanation about her sister's accident. "She fell outside during recess this morning. And she never told the teacher about it . . . so *now* she's cryin'."

Mary gathered the tiny girl in her arms. "Aw, you held

in the pain all this time? Well, come on in and have some hot chocolate. That'll help better'n *anything*."

Nodding, her lower lip protruding, Susie took Mary's hand and went without further complaint to the table, scooted onto the bench, and waited with glistening eyes for her cocoa.

Several hours later, with Nancy offering to help, Mary set a fine table and served up a delicious batch of chicken and dumplings.

"You should come on over more often," Nancy said, grinning at her across the table. "Daed likes gut cookin'."

"Sure does!" little Jacob said. "And me too!"

Susie, her knee scrape forgotten, nodded her head up and down. "We need a mamma . . . real bad."

Mary grinned, growing more attached to the Beiler children with each minute that passed.

Hickory John spoke up. "When's Daed due back?"

"Sometime tonight," she told him.

Nancy smiled and ducked her head. "Best save some dumplin's for him," she said softly into her plate.

"Gut idea," Levi agreed, though he never once looked up at Mary.

Sitting there with the children scattered around the table, their hands busy with dinner, their faces bright with hope, she knew for sure and for certain that this home was where she belonged—what her heart was longing for.

Sighing, she decided yet anew that she would not answer the warm and honest letter from the stranger named Rosie, who'd written her in Katie's stead. There was only one way she would ever consider doing such a thing. Bishop John would have to remove the ban on talking to Katie of his own accord, without any mention of it from Mary.

CHAPTER TEN

❖ ❖ ❖

The search for Laura's journal continued all week long. Even after Katherine tired of rummaging through the two large attics, Selig and Garrett continued, with Fulton's and Rosie's help.

"I suppose it'll turn up if the Good Lord wants me to find it," she said at last.

Rosie encouraged her not to worry. "I'm sure it's around here somewhere."

All at once Katherine was struck with concern. "Could it be . . . do you think Dylan knew about Laura's diary and took it with him when he moved his things out?"

Rosie turned quickly to look at her husband. "What do you think of that, Fulton? Is it possible?"

The butler stood tall and, shaking his head, assured Katherine and Rosie that could not be the case. "Certainly not. What use would he have for it?"

"None, unless he thought it might lead him to secret accounts or such things," Rosie added with a groan. "But, of course, that would have been long before Laura had any accounts of her own."

"You're right." Fulton sat in a tufted Victorian chair near the butler's pantry just outside the kitchen. He scratched his head, glancing up at the staircase nearby. "I don't believe Dylan Bennett had any idea the young Laura's diary even existed."

Rosie placed her hand on his shoulder. "She must have packed it away safely with other treasures from her youth."

"Should I call Mr. Cranston?" Katherine spoke up. "Would *he* know anything about it?"

"I doubt it. The diary is over twenty-two years old. I'd have to say there's little chance an attorney would be privy to it."

While Fulton was talking, Katherine had the feeling, once again, that Lydia Miller would wholeheartedly suggest going to prayer over the lost journal. "God cares about every detail of your life, Katie," she'd told her on several occasions.

Still, Katherine continued to look in every closet, search every nook and cranny of the old mansion, not bothering God with such a mundane thing as the lost diary of a teenage mother-to-be, even though that mother had been her very own.

◈ ◈ ◈

Four cars were parked in the circular drive in front of Mayfield Manor ten days later: Natalie Judah's and the vehicles belonging to three other women who'd responded happily to the quilting class ad in the Canandaigua newspaper. Katherine was overjoyed with such interest in her free class. In fact, she stood where Fulton usually positioned himself, personally greeting each lady at the front door.

She had all of them gather in the drawing room to get better acquainted before asking Garrett to bring in some hot tea and pastries.

"So good to see all of you here," Katherine said, standing near the fireplace and leaning against the mantelpiece. She introduced herself first, then Leoma, Natalie Judah, Missy

Braun, Elizabeth May, and Rosie's sister, Ada. "All future quilters," she said of them.

They smiled, nodding. The ladies exchanged pleasantries, and Katherine discovered that Ada and Elizabeth had taken a quilting class together years ago but hadn't run into each other since. "We probably need a refresher course," Ada spoke up, casting a smile at Elizabeth. "But since Katherine used to be Amish, well, maybe we'll actually remember better this time."

Used to be Amish.

The phrase took Katherine quite by surprise. Probably because she'd never heard herself referred to in that way before. At any rate, she stood there, preparing to teach the fundamentals of quilting, when a fleeting memory surfaced and she recalled a month of school days. At just sixteen, she had served as substitute for the regular Amish teacher. Once again she was an instructor, only tonight the topic for discussion did not involve the three R's.

The evening proved to be a lively one, and even though some of these women had come to her as strangers, Katherine felt, midway through this first quilting session, that she really liked these fancy English ladies and hoped there might come lasting friendships out of their time together.

❖　❖　❖

The remaining weekdays were spent attending the training sessions at the hospice. Natalie Judah was always jovial and kind, grateful for Katherine's interest in the hospice. Glad that her birth mother had had the opportunity to know the nurse before Laura's passing, Katherine derived great strength from Natalie. After only a few days, she was also becoming a dear friend.

When Katherine had finished up her two weeks of training and sailed through her exit interview, she was delighted.

Her schedule was set for Mondays and Wednesdays, two hours each day.

"I'd like you to read to Willy," said Natalie on Katherine's first official day as a volunteer.

She followed a nurse's aide to the common area, eager to interact with one of the patients. Willy turned out to be the blond boy she'd seen on the day she'd inquired about volunteering. He was a beautiful eight-year-old, diagnosed with a malignant brain tumor. Willy's eyes, blue as they were, filled her with compassion, for she could see the agony of cancer imprinted there.

She sat with him in the sun-filled gathering area, getting acquainted. "What's your middle name?" he asked her after they'd exchanged first and last names.

"I was never given a middle name," she told him.

His eyes widened. "Really . . . no middle name?"

"Is a middle name very important?"

"Well . . . maybe." He broke into a smile. "I've got *two* middle names."

"You do? Well, I think that's very nice. What are they . . . if you don't mind telling me?"

He seemed more than happy to tell her. "My name is William James Lee Norton. I have my dad's name, my grandpa's name, and my uncle's name."

She couldn't help smiling. She had her birth mother's *choice* of a name, but that was the extent of it. "I like all of your names, Willy," she commented, wondering why she was so drawn to the youngster.

Later, after they'd discussed favorite colors and foods, and the best kinds of smells, books, and animals, he asked out of the blue, "Are you married?"

She had to chuckle. "Not yet, but I hope to be someday."

"Then will you have lots of children?" His face was full of questions as they sat side by side on the wicker settee.

"If the Good Lord sees fit, I suppose I will."

"It's one of your wishes, right?" He reached for a small ball with his foot, his legs limp as wilted celery.

"A wish?" she said. "Well, I guess I never thought of having children as being a wish."

Willy asked if she'd help him sit on the floor so they could roll the ball back and forth. Carefully, she lifted him down and got him propped up on the floor with several pillows. Then she sat on the floor opposite the bright but fragile boy and pushed the ball gently, glad she'd worn woolen trousers instead of a skirt.

"My father says that God gives His people the desires of their hearts," young Willy continued, "if they're linked up with Him."

Linked up with God?

Katherine had never heard such talk. Especially coming from one so young . . . one so desperately ill.

On Wednesday, Willy talked even more openly, and Katherine remembered hearing or reading—or maybe it was Dan who'd told her this years ago; she couldn't recall which—that "a little child shall lead them." Honestly, she didn't feel as though she needed to be led anywhere, so she didn't quite know from where such a recollection had sprung. Or why.

As far as she was concerned, she was right where she wanted to be, enjoying every minute of her high-society English life, partly due to Justin Wirth and his many contacts and friends.

Katherine turned her attention back to Willy, and when he'd tired of their checkers game, she slowly wheeled him over to have a close look at the aquarium. Several large blue and green fish caught their interest, and one very fat brown snail, too, which they quickly agreed to name Fred.

When it came time to say good-bye, Katherine was reluctant to leave the boy. With all of her heart, she wished

119

she could do something significant to make Willy's cancer go away—and never return.

On the ride home, she forced her thoughts away from Willy, daydreaming of Justin, yet careful to conceal her smile from Theodore's view.

Just last Friday she had dined with him at Belhurst Castle, a turreted, red Medina stone structure located in Geneva, less than a thirty minutes' drive from Mayfield Manor. It was the romantic setting he had promised her before the crippling snowstorm.

The cordial waiter had chosen a table for two, situated near a window in the banquet hall overlooking the shores of Seneca Lake. The breathtaking vista and sweeping expanse of snow-covered lawns gave Katherine the notion that she *was* a princess, dining in a real castle.

Justin, dressed impeccably in a double-breasted navy blazer and tan slacks, was very attentive—more so than ever—leaning toward her at one point as they sat across from each other at the candlelit table. "They say an Italian opera singer once lived here. Have you heard the story?"

She shook her head, but her gaze was riveted on the handsome face, the azure eyes, as he told the haunting tale.

"A Spanish don and his ladylove lived here long, long ago." His voice was softer now. "The couple ran away from home . . . an ill-fated romance, some say."

"And they built this castle?" She felt as if she might be the runaway ladylove, especially tonight, so far removed from the cloistered life of the Amish. "They came here to hide?"

"Yes, amidst secret tunnels and buried treasure, they hid here . . . from their own people."

She looked about her at the flagstone floor, the stone walls, the high windows, wondering about Justin's simple story. "Is it really true?"

He smiled, offering her a mischievous wink, and her

pulse quickened. "No one knows for sure," he said.

When the waiter came back to take their order, Justin was the perfect gentleman, ordering the salmon dinner she chose from the menu. She felt helpless to slow her heart to its normal pace, sitting there, her eyes fixed on his face, his hands—the well-bred, attractive man whose words flowed like warm honey, whose gestures were artistic, as enchanting as this mysterious place.

He had reached for her hand and held it all the way back to Mayfield Manor as they rode in the moonlight. Later, upon their arrival, he got out and opened the door of the limousine, asking the driver to stay put as he walked her to the door. "The castle was the perfect setting for our first dinner out together," he remarked as they made their way to the double doors of her mansion.

"Yes." She could hardly speak past a whisper.

Turning to face her, he took both her hands in his. "I hope one day we'll return."

"To the castle?"

"As runaway lovers," he said, smiling down at her in the light of the rustic lamppost.

Surprised, she didn't know what he meant exactly, but she liked the sound of his voice in the stillness. So quiet, she felt as if the earth held its breath.

Then he kissed the back of each of her hands. "I'll call tomorrow," he said, smiling down at her.

"Good night," she said, turning toward the door lest he reach for her, sweeping her into his arms unexpectedly. Oh, as much as she might've welcomed it, she was hesitant. Something held her back, though she was not sure what.

"Until tomorrow," he said. "Good night, dear Katherine."

She smiled to herself, hearing his footsteps on the pavement. Turning for a parting glance, Princess Katherine leaned against the heavy door that led inside to her very own castle, her heart filled with longing for the next glimpse of her artist prince.

Not until she turned off the lamp beside her bed did she even once think of Dan. And because of that, she assumed she was moving away from the initial shock—pushing her pain far away from her, pushing away the realization that out there in the world somewhere her dear first love was alive and well.

In her silent rote prayers, as she had always learned to pray at bedtime, she thought of young Willy, wondering if his wish might come true . . . if *he* was to have his heart's desire. She tried to pray for the poor, sick boy but felt every bit at odds with it, the same as she'd felt about praying in that way back at Lydia Miller's when she'd first tried.

Once asleep, she dreamed of Justin. He was planning a picnic in the snow . . . for her and Willy. Mixed-up and hazy, the wintry, pastoral dream was filled with spicy ferns growing ankle-deep out of a dense snow crust, ending with Daniel Fisher arriving just as they were putting the food away, packing up, ready to go home.

Gasping for breath, she woke with a start and sat up in her bed. "He's still . . . in my dreams," she whispered, hand at her throat.

Fully awake, she climbed out of bed, slipped into her bathrobe and house shoes, and made her way through the bedroom to the sitting room. There she stopped and stared at the dying embers in the fireplace, then headed out into the hallway, her steps guided by low-burning wall lamps.

A late-night snack might help her forget the peculiar dream. Oh, she longed for one long night without thoughts of Daniel intruding on her sleep. And one pleasant day without the memory of his eyes probing hers, his words burning into her soul.

"I don't mean to take up much of your time," he had said in her parlor. The scene had replayed itself a thousand times

122

in her mind. He wasn't only taking up her time, he was disrupting her life.

"I've been waiting a long time to see you again. . . ."

She sat at the table where her domestic help always ate their meals, except for the one snowbound night in the library. Clapping her hands over her ears, she longed to stop his voice. More than anything.

Little Willy had said something about God giving His children the longings of their hearts. Well, now was a good time for the Good Lord to start, she decided. Because if God didn't stop the memories, heal her immense pain, how was she ever to focus her romantic attentions on the dashing, very *honest* Justin Wirth?

She folded her hands in front of her. "Please, dear God, will you make the past die? Make *my* past go away," she said softly into the darkness of the kitchen.

Then, weeping, she nearly forgot where she was. In the dim light, the enormous kitchen almost looked like her mamma's, and for a brief, intangible moment, she was sitting on the wooden bench next to the trestle table, wishing Rebecca might come and find her out of bed in the middle of the night and make her some warm, soothing cocoa.

CHAPTER ELEVEN

❖ ❖ ❖

Mary had promised herself that she would try to not think about the bishop so much. 'Course, it was next to impossible to keep that promise really. Every waking minute he was on her mind. She could only hope that he was pleased with the way she'd looked after his children.

She arose at four-thirty, eager to help with breakfast, and even volunteered to assist her father with milking chores.

"No . . . no, you stay in where it's warm," he said, hurrying out the back door into the predawn blackness.

"Are ya sure?" she called after him, experiencing such a surge of energy she could hardly contain herself.

Abe turned around, staring at her from the bottom of the snowy steps, a frown pinching his brow. "Goodness' sakes, Mary, ya haven't helped with milkin' for several years now."

"Well . . . just thought I'd offer." She knew her words must sound awful peculiar; still she waited, wondering if he'd change his mind.

Her father shrugged, turned, and shook his head as if to say he wasn't about to try to figure out his youngest off-spring, which didn't discourage her one little bit. She rushed back into the kitchen to help stir up some milk and flour and eggs, making ready for homemade waffles.

Even as she stirred the mixture, John Beiler was a big part of her day, of her thoughts, and she felt like a young girl again, getting ready for the Christmas Eve program at school . . . or something just as exciting. She hailed him from past days, recalling the fun, the laughter . . . jah, the love that was beginning to flower between them.

And there was to be yet another get-together. The evening she had prepared to leave the bishop's house, after John had arrived home from Schaefferstown, he'd invited her on a sleigh ride. "For just the two of us," he whispered as she stood in the privacy of the utility room, pulling on her mittens.

"Where will we meet then?" she'd managed to ask.

His eyes sparkled as he smiled down at her. "Can ya take your Dat's horse and carriage over to the bridge at Weaver's Creek?"

"Jah . . . I think so."

"We'll leave the buggy there. The horse will be all right tied up to the fence post." He paused for a moment, his eyes searching hers so much that she felt she might blush right there in front of him. "Meet me after nightfall . . . about six-thirty."

She smiled, imagining the sleigh ride, bundled up in her warmest coat and winter bonnet, maybe even snuggling a bit under the furry lap robe.

"What're *you* smilin' about?" her mamma said, staring over at her from across the kitchen.

Mary straightened, turning away, so her mother and grandmother wouldn't see the heat rising into her face. "Oh, was I smiling just now?"

Mammi Ruth cackled, going about the chore of setting the table. "She must be thinkin' on her new Beau."

Not to reply would mean acknowledgment. So Mary spoke softly, keeping her face to the wall as she stirred the flour and baking soda into the bowl with swift, hard strokes. "What new Beau?"

Now both women were hooting with uncontrollable laughter. Mary had to smile herself. She couldn't help it; the corners of her mouth turned up at will. But she was able to hide the jubilant grin from the women most dear to her. She did it merely by facing away, fixing her eyes on the waffle batter.

❖   ❖   ❖

She accepted John's extended hand, allowing him to pull her up into the box-shaped sleigh filled with sweet-smelling straw and more lap robes than she could count.

"Nice to see ya, Mary."

"And you too."

He helped spread the fur-lined blankets over her legs before taking the reins in both hands. "Ready?" he said.

"Jah."

The tinkle of bells echoed in the night as the moon peeked through trees, casting silvery shadows on the ground. Mary heard the swishing, crisp sound of the runners cut through hardened snow, and the icy earth glistened under ten thousand stars.

She laughed right along with John as the horse seemed to fly over acres and acres of snow-laden fields, pulling them through space, away from their work and toil, away from those whose eyes might pry, those suspecting that love just might reside in the chill of the wind on this night.

John leaned his head back at one point, sniffing the cold air. "Smell that?"

She did the same, breathing in deeply. "Ach, it's skunk."

They had to laugh again, pinching their noses shut. After the smell had dissipated, they rode on in silence. Mary, content enough just to be sitting next to John this way, squeezed her mittened hands under the heavy blanket on her lap.

It seemed as if eternity might pass before John spoke again. Oh, how she longed for it, to hear his voice so very close to her ears. *So close.* . . .

When John let go of the reins with one hand and reached behind her, putting his arm around her, she felt as if she might cry, so in love with this man she was.

"A right-gut night for a sleigh ride." He turned to face her. "Ain't so?"

Her eyes met his. "Jah, right fine," she whispered.

Then John moved closer, pressing his forehead gently against hers. The motion tilted her winter bonnet back a bit, but she didn't mind, didn't even bother to put up her hand to steady it.

"I'm a bit old to think of goin' for steady, ya know," he said, his breath warm against her face.

She knew. "If ya say so."

He sat up straight just then. "Well, what would ya think of marryin' your bishop in the dead of winter?" His voice was strong and confident, taking her by surprise.

Her heart beat wildly. "Marryin'?"

"I want you for my own . . . for my wife, Mary Stoltzfus." His eyes were wells of affection.

"Oh . . . I . . ." Her throat felt like cotton. "I—"

Gazing intently on her face, he reached up and traced her hairline with his fingertips. She held her breath, and his bare hand cupped her trembling chin. "It must come as a surprise to ya, Mary. I'm sorry if I—"

"I'm . . . I'm as happy as can be," she said softly, so as not to break the spell, her eyes searching his.

Then slowly his lips found hers in a tender kiss. He backed away, looking deep into her eyes yet again. "Oh, Mary, I want to make ya happy. Honest I do. . . ."

Before she could answer, his lips met hers again—a lingering kiss to seal their unspoken commitment.

Mary wasn't sure how long they snuggled that way. For all she knew, the horse might've lost his way for the lack of direction on the part of the driver, yet Mary cared not how many sweet kisses her beloved showered upon her that night, his strong arms enfolding her in his loving embrace. Nor could she think clearly of anything but of her longing to be near him, for ever and always.

❖   ❖   ❖

It was well past eight o'clock when they turned back toward Weaver's Creek, to her parked carriage and the poor abandoned horse. "Sugar might be too cold to be trottin'," she said, glancing up at the moon.

"We were gone longer than I thought," John said, getting out of the sleigh and throwing one of the lighter blankets over Sugar's back. "That oughta help. Just let him go at his own pace. And . . . if ya don't mind, I'll follow you out to your lane."

"Denki. That's kind of you." She wished John would come and give her a parting kiss before they went their separate ways. But she knew it was best that they not show affection right there on the road. Too many courting couples out on a night like this. Too many eyes . . .

He helped her into the cold buggy, then went to the fence and untied her father's horse. "Why don't ya use one of my blankets? Already warmed up."

"Gut idea." She had to smile as he jumped up into her carriage unexpectedly, wrapping her up in the furry thing, treating her as tenderly as a child.

"This'll keep ya warm till you're home." He turned, looked both ways up and down the road, then sat beside her. "I'll be missin' ya, Mary. I will." He took her in his arms and gave her a long good-bye kiss. Her head was swimming, though she did not pull away first. "Good night, Mary, dear."

"God be with you," she said, completely out of breath.

Grinning, he backed out of the buggy and stood there in the snow, waving. "Meet me here again?"

"When?"

"Tomorrow, maybe?"

She nodded, wishing the night might never end or, better yet, would depart on swift wings of day until Sunday evening could come.

❖ ❖ ❖

Katherine had been completely surprised by the letter in the late afternoon mail. Because of her scheduled plans to have the quilting class meet again that evening, she purposely waited until the ladies left for home, before ever sitting down with the envelope postmarked Newark, New Jersey.

Sighing, she leaned against the plump antique chair just a few feet from her bed. She might've guessed Daniel would pursue her, especially after the way she'd dismissed him. Though, thinking back on it now, she wished he had done so years ago, long before she'd discovered that her Amish upbringing had been a fakery. That she was truly English.

Unsure of herself, she held the envelope in her hand, studying the handwriting. She'd know it anywhere. The old feelings stirred within her, and she hardly knew what to do.

Slipping a finger under the loose part of the flap, she opened the envelope, her breath coming more quickly now. *Dare I do this?* she wondered.

She hesitated, eyes scanning the return address. So this was his residence, the place where he'd hid from her all these years? In Newark, New Jersey—not far from Lancaster County. She almost laid it down or threw it away, still uneasy about holding the envelope in her hands.

Was she giving Dan a second chance, another opportunity to hurt her, by reading his letter? She laid the envelope on her lap, staring at the formally draped window across the room.

Was it the right thing to do? A soft chuckle escaped her lips. *The right thing.* The very words that had always defined Mary's position in life. Her friend would probably say to go ahead and open the letter, find out what Daniel wanted to put in writing. Mary, it seemed, was still advising her in spirit, though they were miles apart. Friends for life, in spite of the shunning. Connected in spite of all that had transpired.

Her dearest friend would say to read it. So she did. With shaking hands, she unfolded the letter.

Thursday, March 7

Dear Katie,

Nearly two months have passed since I saw you in Canandaigua. At the time, I worried that I might upset you unduly, and as it turned out, that was the case. You were not only upset, you were clearly pained at my visit, and for this, I am truly sorry.

No amount of asking on my part can make it possible for you to forgive me, though I could only pray that it would be so. You see, I have never stopped loving you, and hard as I try to think of you as Katherine Mayfield, it is difficult for me to remember you as anyone other than the dear Amish girl I first fell in love with that day many years ago—when we were but children. Perhaps I never told you about the first time I saw you standing there by the old buck stove in the schoolhouse. Your hair was not yet in the traditional bun, but pulled back with braids wrapped around your little head. You must have been no more than seven, but I can't be sure. If I'd had any sense I would have recorded the day, the year, the moment. I never told you of the feeling I had that day, but it has never let go of me since that time. To think that all those years from my nineteenth birthday until now have been wasted, literally a great waste of our love. And now, here we are, once again separated.

I take all the blame for this, Katie, as I tried to tell you when we met briefly, and you may not accept it now as you did not then. How can I tell you? What I did was wrong. I should have returned to my father that very day, made things right with him, turned from my rebellion, and then, after much prayer and counsel, left the Amish church. Instead, things turned out much differently for me—for everyone. Someday I hope you'll allow me to tell you the whole story, everything that happened.

In the meantime, I have found a love I've never known . . . this I find in the Lord Jesus. And if nothing ever comes of my love for you on this earth, it will not be for naught. You see, Katie, I pray that you may find this same joy and peace that I have. It is not bound up in the rules and requirements of a church. My happiness is in knowing my sins are washed away, my name written in the Lamb's Book of Life. You can have this peace, this assurance of salvation that we were taught to believe was wrong, even prideful. The truth is, God's Word clearly states the way to redemption—through faith in Jesus, the Savior. If you ever yearn to know more, read the book of John in the New Testament. You'll find there what your heart searches for.

I don't mean to sound like a preacher, but I cannot keep this peace to myself. Truly, it passes all understanding. It is this Good News that compels me to witness of Jesus' love for you.

Yours always,
Daniel Fisher

P.S. Do you ever play the guitar I gave you?

Had she known the contents of the letter, she might never have opened it. Slipping the letter back inside the envelope, she tried to push his written words out of her mind. The man was clearly insane . . . declaring his love to her in a letter like this.

And telling her what to believe about God, of all things!

She wondered where such boldness had come from, for she had not remembered him being quite this way as a youth, well . . . maybe he *had* been more brash than most, now that she thought of it.

There was no need to belabor this. She went to her bureau drawer and placed the letter inside, beneath the satin baby gown still wrapped in tissue paper.

◈　◈　◈

Justin called as he had promised, inviting her to tomorrow evening's symphony concert, followed by a reception in honor of a retiring violinist. She agreed to go, thinking that another evening spent with her dashing boyfriend might lay all her troubles to rest.

Had she been a praying woman, she might've mentioned this in a prayer to the Almighty. But she was far too suspicious of such praying—to plead for mercy or help from the Creator of the heavens and the earth. Besides, how could she really know if God was as intimately involved in her life and in her plans as both Lydia Miller and Daniel Fisher seemed to think? She considered this concept, so foreign to her way of thinking and to her Amish background, and recalled Laura's glowing deathbed description of her love for God's Son, even going so far as to ask Katherine if she, too, knew Jesus.

At the time, Katherine had been moved to tears, but now she was able to think more rationally about the matter and wondered if her heart had been so touched then because she was attending the death of her birth mother. Surely, that's all there was to it.

CHAPTER TWELVE

❖ ❖ ❖

Every other Sunday was always spent visiting in Hickory Hollow, and Mary could hardly wait to take an afternoon drive to see Rebecca Lapp. It seemed—if she could believe the hearsay—that Katie's mamma was slowly inching out of her depression over the shunning and whatnot all.

Mattie Beiler had been heard telling Preacher Zook's wife at the General Store that Rebecca nearly launched off on one of her stories back last Monday at Annie Lapp's quilting frolic. In fact, she'd come *that* close to actually starting one of her old familiar yarns.

Praise be! Mary thought it right-gut news, but she just had to see for herself. So she hitched up Sugar and hopped in the carriage.

"*Hott rum!*" she called to the horse, flapping the reins lightly. He turned to the right and hurried down Hickory Lane.

Rebecca did seem mighty glad to see her. Mary could tell by the way the woman greeted her with an enthusiastic, "Wie geht's, Mary? Gut to see ya."

She went inside, letting Rebecca assist with hanging up her coat, scarf, and outer bonnet. "Denki," she said, following the older woman into the warm kitchen, where cherry

135

pie and vanilla ice cream were already spread out on the table, almost as if she had been expected.

"Sit down and have something to eat," Rebecca invited.

Mary glanced around, surprised to see that Samuel wasn't sitting in his usual spot—the hickory rocker near the woodstove. "Isn't your husband at home?"

"He's out checking on Tobias, our pony. The poor thing's got a stiff leg or some such ailment. Samuel and the boys are having a look-see."

Mary remembered the pony. Satin Boy was the name Katie had given Tobias, right out of the blue, around the time she started obsessing on fancy things—out and out disobeying the Ordnung. At least that was the way Mary remembered it.

"It's awful nice of you to come," Rebecca was saying. "Since our daughter left, I don't see too terrible much of you, ya know."

Mary nodded. "I'll hafta remedy that, I 'spect. It's a shame we don't talk more." She was working up to telling the woman about Katie's letter—that her shunned daughter had inquired of her. But Mary felt she ought to wait till she knew, for sure and for certain, that it was the right time to bring up the subject. And that Rebecca would keep it quiet.

"Care for a piece of pie?" asked Rebecca, positioning the knife over the crust.

"Jah, looks delicious."

Rebecca dished up a hearty serving of the homemade dessert, piling a big scoop of ice cream on top, after getting the nod from Mary.

The two women enjoyed the sweet pastry together, smacking their lips in the quiet of the kitchen, a room filled with the smells of yesterday's baking. Mary wondered how terribly much Rebecca must miss her daughter's help around the house, especially in the kitchen, preparing food, baking bread and things.

"I . . . uh, don't really know how to go about sayin' this, Rebecca, but . . ." She paused a moment, noticing instant concern creep into the woman's hazel eyes. "No, no," she assured her, "it's nothing bad I have to tell you, not at all. I received an unexpected letter from a stranger in New York . . . someone who knows your daughter, is all. Anyways, the woman—her name was Rosie Taylor—wanted me to tell you that Katie, er, you know—Katherine—was worried about you, is thinkin' of ya. Guess she heard from Lydia Miller that you weren't feelin' all that gut for a spell there."

Rebecca put both hands in her lap and blinked several times in a row, creating an awkward silence. At last she spoke. "You say my daughter sent a letter written by someone else . . . to you?"

"Jah, but she was awful careful about it—didn't want to cause trouble here in the Hollow. So I guess I'm thinkin' we should keep this under our hats, ya know . . . not mention it to anyone."

Rebecca smiled slightly. "Probably a gut idea."

They finished eating their pie, stealing glances back and forth. Finally, Mary got up the nerve to say something else. Something just as important as letting Rebecca know that Katie was thinking of her, missing her. Something she'd *thought* of discussing with the bishop but had only mentioned to her own mamma. No one else.

"I was wonderin'," she began again. "I thought maybe there might be a way to correspond with my dear friend up there in New York if . . . well, if I might speak to Bishop John about the possibility of being allowed to talk to her, or just maybe even write to her . . . lift the talking part of the shunning. That way the People might be able to have some influence on the poor shunned girl."

Rebecca's face brightened. "How do ya plan to go about such a thing?"

"Well, I don't rightly know, but I'm hopin' something—

some powerful-gut idea might come to me when . . ." She almost let it slip that she was going to be seeing the bishop privately or some such revealing comment. "*Whenever* it is that I might have a chance to speak to the bishop about it." It was a feeble attempt to cover her tracks. Watching the expression in Rebecca's eyes, she was pretty sure that Katie's mamma didn't suspect much of anything from the slip of Mary's tongue.

Sighing softly, Rebecca gathered up the plastic dessert plates and rinsed them off. "You and the bishop seein' each other some?" she said from the sink.

Mary's heart leaped up at the question. So Rebecca Lapp was smarter than she thought. "Oh, ya know . . . after Preachin' services and all." That sort of answer might not satisfy, but it was the best she could do without lying.

Turning now, Rebecca looked her square in the face, the dishwater dripping down off her wrists. "Then . . . are ya sayin' that you think ya might be able to get my shunned daughter to see the light and return and confess on bended knee?"

"I can only pray so."

"But if she did do all that—come back to the bishop and the People and repented her sins—she wouldn't have the opportunity to enjoy the blessing of marryin' Bishop John, after all. That is, if he'd even have her back."

Mary felt like a fool. Why *had* she bothered to bring the topic up? She wished she'd never said a word about it.

Rebecca continued. "You must be thinkin' that by speaking the words of the Ordnung to my girl, it could bring her back, only to have her suffer the pain of singleness all the rest of her days. Or maybe you're hopin' she and Daniel will find each other out there in the world and return together." She crossed the kitchen to come to the table, a fierce look on her plump face. "Well, if that's what you're a-thinkin', Mary Stoltzfus, let me tell you right now, that's no way to treat a best friend . . . takin' her prospects for a husband right out from under her nose."

"I . . . uh, I don't think you understand, Rebecca," she said, trying her best to talk sense to the woman.

"No, *no*. You listen to me! You know what you're doin', Mary, and I don't like it one bit. It's not becoming to Amish ways, neither." Rebecca's face was flushed pink, her eyes moist with angry tears, welling up and threatening to spill. "If you ask me, I think you must've been waitin' all along for the bishop. You waited till my girl left town to make your move."

Mary was horrified, shocked. She could scarcely breathe now; her heart pounded hard beneath the bodice of her dress and apron. "That's not true. Honest it ain't." She might've tried to explain further, but she heard the sound of the men coming in the back door, the clump of their boots on the utility room floor, the banter between them.

"You best be goin' now," Rebecca said sternly, turning her back to tend to the dishes in the sink.

Mary rose and left quickly. She never said a word of thanks for the pie, not a word of greeting to Samuel or his sons. And she didn't speak softly to Sugar as she hitched him up to Dat's carriage. It was all she could do to get herself inside the buggy and covered up for the cold ride home.

Then, seeing the heavy lap robe John had loaned her the night before, she gritted her teeth and found the reins, shaking more from the stinging words than from the chilling breeze.

❖   ❖   ❖

Katherine marveled at the concert hall—the lovely seating, the large stage framed with enormous velvet curtains. She hadn't recalled ever being inside such a fascinating place but didn't let on to Justin, who was dressed in a tuxedo for the evening event.

Glad that Rosie had helped her choose the perfect dress for the occasion, Katherine settled back in the cushioned seat, reveling in the dissonant, yet pleasant sound of the string section tuning to the first violinist's instrument. *Wonderful-gut*, she thought, ready for a night of music.

Justin glanced at her, offering a gentleman's smile. Once more she understood her attraction to this man, her charming date. He was more than attentive, always thinking of her, it seemed. Always willing to offer her an interesting time. Yet she wondered how he might feel if he knew that she felt awkward in his high-society circles, that she was still trying to acclimate herself to the newness of her life.

Rosie's words had come to her on several occasions since the maid had uttered them frivolously, then had apologized speedily. *Justin Wirth has noticed your aristocratic roots. . . .*

Sitting here next to him, she wondered just what role her inherited wealth had played in influencing Justin. Would he have been attracted to her had she been just an ordinary Plain girl?

Then she recalled how their eyes had met on Christmas Day, how he had known, almost by instinct, that she was Laura's daughter. He was a good man, through and through, she told herself.

Before the lights were lowered and the orchestra director took the podium and raised his baton, she read the program and notes carefully, thrilled that there was a piece by J. S. Bach. His music soothed her wholly, and she contemplated her state in life—*this* present time of her life—content to be wearing the satiny dress, delicate shoes, and glittering jewelry at her throat and on her wrist.

Sighing, she folded her hands over the program, wondering what lovely things the night might reveal. She didn't have to wait long. As the lights went down, Justin reached for her hand and caressed it during the first piece. Try as she might, the music got lost in her head somewhere; she could scarcely hear it for the beating of her heart.

❖   ❖   ❖

John was waiting at the appointed spot in the road when Mary reined in Sugar, pulling the horse and carriage over to the shoulder. Instead of anticipating the secret rendezvous, she was dreading it. After thinking through Rebecca's harsh comments, she felt at odds with herself and with her and John's budding relationship. Truth be told, she'd just as soon have stayed home tonight, sitting under the gas lamp in the kitchen, cozy by the fire, reading.

But she was here as she'd said she would be, and by the looks of John's cheerful countenance, he was delighted that she was.

"I thought the day would never end," he said, helping her down out of the carriage. "I've missed ya so."

She nodded, keeping her chin up, so to speak, putting on a happy face for the bishop, who was kind enough to help get her settled in the straw-laden sleigh and wrapped up with the same furry lap robes as the night before.

The moon was the slightest bit rounder tonight, and John made note of it to her. "Such a shame the children aren't out enjoin' the evening with us."

"How're they doin'?" she asked, glad for this topic instead of romance.

"Ah, gut . . . right fine, they are. Eager for their old Daed to find 'em a mamma, I 'spect."

She grimaced at his words. Was that all she was to him— someone to take care of his young?

Unable to think clearly, she felt herself stiffen, relieved that John hadn't felt at ease enough with her to slip his arm around her just yet.

The silence between them was deafening, and she wished now she'd never gone to see Rebecca Lapp. What *was* she thinking? The woman was completely daft; at least it seemed so. For as much as the womenfolk had said she was improving, Mary knew better. She knew now firsthand that Katie's mamma had not totally recovered from the loss of her daughter. No, she was clearly suffering from deep grief—and worse. *Senseless* and *absurd* were the words that came to mind regarding Rebecca's harsh comments to her.

Shadows from the moon played tag with the horse-drawn sleigh as it sped over fields and down the glen, deep into the Hollow, past the rickety covered bridge at Weaver's Creek, where several open buggies—courting buggies the Englischers like to call them—were parked off the side of the road to accommodate smooching. Past ten or more farmhouses, all Old Order Amish, and she knew they were because not a single electrical wire ran from the road to the house.

"You're awful quiet," John remarked. "Somethin' bothering ya?"

She had no idea what to tell him. "Best to be silent if there's nothin' to say."

John pulled on the reins, halting the horse. He turned to her, wearing a concerned frown. "Mary . . . darling, what is it?"

Hearing her name coupled with the endearing term caused her to feel renewed compassion for him. She kept her eyes on her lap as she began. "If my shunned girlfriend returned . . . what would happen to . . . you and me?"

He sighed. "Are ya wonderin' if I'm still in love with her?"

"Well, I'd hardly think so, not after last night." She was thinking of his kisses, his declarations of love. "It's just that, well . . . folks talk, ya know. And maybe they're wonderin' if she *did* return and repent anytime soon, whether or not you'd rather have *her* for your wife."

"Nonsense," he exclaimed. "The woman's as disobedient as any I've known, and I have a strong feelin' she'll always be struggling with it, even if she does return and make things right."

It wasn't exactly what Mary wanted to hear. She'd longed to hear that John loved *her* . . . not Katie. But he hadn't said that, not in so many words. It made her wonder if his choice in a wife had more to do with devotion to God and the church than it did with love.

"What if there was something we could do? What if *I*, her best friend, could do that something to bring her back to the fold?"

She felt him reach under the blankets and find her mittened hands, taking one of them in his own and bringing it out into the air. He held it against his heart. "Are ya askin' for special treatment for Samuel Lapp's daughter?"

Now was her chance; it might be her only one. Yet she didn't want to tie her acceptance of his marriage proposal to her request for leniency on Katie's behalf. 'Twas a ticklish situation, and she had to be mighty careful what she said. "I'm thinking of a way to admonish her . . . instruct her, ya know."

"It was a harsh thing I did, not allowing the People to speak to her." He fell silent and let her hand go.

Quickly, she put it back under the lap robe, thankful that there was no real breeze to speak of tonight. "What if some of us could write her, speak to her in love about her rebellion?"

He wrapped his arms around her. "If this is what you wish, Mary, I will allow it."

She relaxed in his arms. "I want it more than almost anything."

"Then let it be so," he said. "I will lift the speech ban . . . because your heart is pure. And mine was filled with anger, wrongly so." His confession surprised her.

"Oh, thank you . . . John. Thank you ever so much!"

They embraced, and she felt as if her worries were far behind her as he leaned down to kiss her cheek, then her lips. "I do love ya, Mary," he whispered.

"And I love *you.*"

With one arm around her, the other holding the reins, John drove through the night, her head on his strong shoulder. Ach, she was more than happy and could hardly wait to write and tell Katie the good news.

As for Rebecca, well . . . Katie's Mam would just have to wait and hear about this wonderful-gut turn of events at the membership meeting after Preachin' come Sunday. Jah, that was the best way.

CHAPTER THIRTEEN

❖ ❖ ❖

The hospice was especially quiet on Monday morning. Katherine had gone early, taking her guitar along, hoping to play soft music to entertain the patients as they ate their breakfast in the family-style eating area.

First, as was the procedure each time she came, she was given the update on all the inpatients. Two patients had passed away since her last visit, sadly enough. Willy, however, had remained the same.

When she asked permission to play, Natalie was thrilled with the idea. "Feel free to bring your guitar anytime you come, Katherine. Music is good therapy for the patients."

One of the nurse's aides took her back to the dining room and introduced her to the patients. "This is Katherine Mayfield, and she would like to play some breakfast music for you."

Some of the patients clapped, but most of them just smiled up at her. For a moment, she wondered if maybe *this* was the reason she had come to Canandaigua. Maybe this, in God's providence, had been the real purpose for her search so far from home.

Willy's eyes lit up when he saw her, and she played

several old tunes from Hickory Hollow days, then got brave and actually sang along.

The boy's face beamed with approval and afterward he asked about the songs. "How'd you learn to play like that?"

"Oh, I had a little help, I guess you could say."

"From your daddy, maybe?"

She chuckled. "No, my father didn't help me play music."

"Then who?"

"A good friend of mine."

A broad smile broke out on his face. "Your boyfriend, right?"

He had her, but she wouldn't admit it.

"What's his name?" Willy probed.

This conversation was going too far, too fast. But, looking into his curious eyes, she decided it wouldn't hurt to share a bit with the boy. "Dan. That was his nickname."

"What happened to your Dan? Did he help other people learn to play, too, besides you?"

She hadn't ever thought of that, really—had never wondered about it, come to think of it. "I don't know, but maybe he did. Dan was like that . . . always enjoyed being around lots of people, eating and talking, and sometimes just being quiet with a good friend."

"I think you must've loved him," Willy said softly.

She was startled by the comment. But she wouldn't deceive this wonderful boy, this adorable child who was dying a little bit every day before her very eyes. "Yes, I loved Dan very much."

"Then why didn't you marry him?"

"He went away . . . for a long, long time."

"Too long?" He stared at her, waiting for an answer.

"Maybe so." It was surprising that she'd allowed herself to be pulled into such a conversation. But there was something innocent and sweet—trustworthy, too—about Willy.

And each time she had come to visit, to cheer him with her presence, she was aware that *he* had encouraged *her*. Yet, sadly enough, his determined spirit, his will to live, seemed to be fading. She could see the light slowly going out of his eyes.

Today, though, while she played the guitar, she'd noticed a flicker of vitality in him. She hoped her eyes weren't playing tricks merely because she longed to see him improve, growing stronger instead of weaker. Natalie had suggested in passing that music possesses a healing power. She wondered if Dan had ever heard such a thing. Thinking about it now, she was startled that her former love had come to mind at all.

She remembered Dan's postscript at the end of the unexpected letter. He was still thinking of the guitar, it seemed, inquiring of it, pondering the past firm connection between them. Was their mutual love of music still weaving their lives together, like an ancient tapestry loom?

She glanced at her watch. "It's almost time for me to leave," she told Willy.

"Aw, do you have to go?"

"My ride is probably here." She didn't want to mention that she was a lady of means, that she had a private chauffeur who took her anywhere she pleased. None of that was important to her friendship with the boy. Or to any of the other precious patients in this secluded retreat, where they came to spend their last months, weeks, and days being nurtured and loved, even by volunteers who had more than just time to give.

"Before you go, can I hold your guitar?" Willy asked, trying to scoot forward on his chair.

"Sure." She positioned it carefully on his lap, steadying the instrument in his hands. "Would you like to pluck a string?"

He nodded his head up and down. "Wait'll I tell my

147

brother . . . Josh will be so jealous."

Katherine put the pick in his right hand, pressed his thumb over it, and guided his hand to the middle string. The string hummed softly. "You have a nice touch, Willy James Lee," she said, grinning at him.

His face was filled with surprise and delight. "You remembered?"

"Of course I did. How could I forget such wonderful-gut names?"

"You think they're wonderful . . . really?"

She looked at him, his hair catching the light as it swirled in ringlets at the nape of his neck. And his sweet countenance. "*You're* wonderful, Willy," she replied.

He reached for her hand and clutched it. "I think *you* are . . . just plain Katherine."

They burst into laughter, although Willy had no idea why it was that she was so tickled at his comment.

Later she read to him from the Bible at his request and afterward recounted several of the many old tales from Rebecca's storytelling repertoire.

As she was preparing to leave he asked, "Do you think I could learn to play the way you do?"

"I don't see why not. I'll do my very best to teach you, all right?" Her heart was warmed by his reaction, and once again she saw the faint sparkle of energy in his eyes.

"Why are you so nice to me?" he surprised her by asking.

"Well, I'd like to think I'm nice to just about everyone."

"Everyone? Even Dan?" he asked without blinking.

She waved her hand at him. "I was *always* nice to Dan . . . yes."

On this day especially, it was difficult to say good-bye, and she wondered if this was what it might've been like having a little brother. An English brother with two middle names. . . .

❖   ❖   ❖

On the ride home, Katherine had a yearning for Theodore to drive her to the outskirts of town. "To see the landscape," she said, hoping to stumble upon Mr. Esler's farmhouse. She'd hired the Amishman to construct the quilt frame, and the day he delivered the pieces and put it together, he'd mentioned that his wife sold homemade preserves.

"Do you think we might be able to find the Eslers' place?" she asked Theodore.

"I'll certainly do my best." He pulled over, stopped the car, and took a map out of the glove box. "Where is it these folks live?"

She told him as best she could, from having heard Mr. Esler describe the rural location. Theodore pinpointed the spot on his map and folded it so the specific section was visible. Then, sitting tall and proper in his black overcoat and hat, he signaled for the left turn and pulled away from the shoulder and onto the highway.

They rode past several miles of sweeping fields, covered with snow, and she thought of the many times Samuel or her oldest brother, Elam, had taken her and Rebecca on sleigh rides down across the glen and up over the high meadows of Hickory Hollow. And there were several times, too, when she and Mary had taken the pony, Tobias—before she'd changed his name to Satin Boy—out on a snowy day, going from farm to farm, loading up the pung sleigh with schoolchildren.

She squeaked a chuckle in the back of her throat, realizing that they had never once missed school for bad weather while growing up in Lancaster County. Public schools often had to close due to drifted roads, but never Amish schools. Outsiders might scoff at the Old Ways, wondering why Plain folk didn't seem to care about "catching up" with modern technology, but when it came right down to it, the horse-drawn sleighs came out way ahead of the snowplows and the street crews during the worst of winters.

Katherine had to smile at her memories. Sentimental, perhaps, though she cared not to admit it to anyone who knew her here in New York. Not when she had every possible convenience at her disposal. Fancy and modern.

When they arrived at the Amish farmhouse, she instructed Theodore to pull in to the barnyard. The layout of house, barn, and sheds seemed all too familiar, and for a moment she wondered if these folk might be related to some of her own Plain relatives.

"I won't be long." She reached for the door handle before Theodore could jump out of the driver's seat and come around to assist her.

"Katherine, please, let me help," Theodore argued.

"No . . . no, I'm perfectly fine." But she thanked him, nevertheless.

A sign that read "Tourists Are Welcome" invited her to ring the bell at the back door, connected to a screened-in porch just off the kitchen area, similar to the long utility room she was accustomed to in Hickory Hollow.

The plump woman who came to the door and greeted her reminded her of the old Wise Woman, only about forty years or so younger and maybe the same number of pounds heavier. She was rosy-cheeked and smiling, wearing a long blue dress and a black pinafore-style apron over it. The veiled head covering was only a slight bit different—a few less pleats sewn in—but otherwise, the woman might've been part of Katherine's former church district in the Hollow.

"I'd like to buy some jellies," she said politely, trying not to gawk, for she was keenly aware of how it felt to be stared at, up one side and down the other.

"*Kumm mit*," the woman said, sporting a cheery smile and inviting Katherine inside.

The kitchen was large with a checkered pattern on the linoleum floor, a black woodstove in the corner, and a trestle table surrounded by long wooden benches. The room was very much like the one she'd grown up in—baking, cooking, and canning with Rebecca and, oftentimes, with many other women from the community. A scenic calendar hanging from a door that surely led to a cold cellar caught her eye. She felt a rush of overwhelming feelings. Mixed emotions, true. Yet a surprisingly strong tug that she could not deny.

"Do you make strawberry rhubarb jam?" One of her favorites. "And apple butter, too?"

"Jah, I have plenty of those on hand. How many jars do you want?"

She had to stop and think. "Oh, I'd say three of each. That'll be enough for now."

The portly woman scurried over to a corner cupboard there in the kitchen and opened it to reveal fifty or more jars of preserves. She counted them out, placing them in a sturdy brown produce bag, similar to the ones Rebecca gave to summer tourists who purchased her delicious fruit preserves and jellies.

"Thank you ever so much," Katherine said, taking a fifty-dollar bill out of her wallet.

"Oh, goodness me. Don't ya wanna write me a check instead?"

"No . . . is cash all right?" she asked, fearful of offending with her show of wealth.

The woman grinned. "Ach, you'd be awful surprised how many folk ask to pay with check. Never seem to have much cash, them locals."

She remembered, all right. "Well, have a nice day." Then, before she left—"Go ahead and keep the change."

"Oh my, no . . . wouldn't think of it."

"Well, just remember all those customers' checks that never cleared the bank," Katherine said, observing the sudden odd expression on the woman's face.

"How would *you* know about such as that?"

Katherine touched the woman's elbow. "Please . . . just save it for a rainy day." And with that, she left.

The drive home wasn't half as exciting, although she told Theodore all about the Amishwoman and her reaction to getting the extra money for her jellies.

"Sounds as if some folk take advantage of the gentle people," he said, referring to the Amish.

"Sadly, they do."

"It's troubling, to say the least. Why aren't people more considerate of each other?"

Her feelings exactly. But she was no longer thinking of the many cheap tourists roaming about. Her thoughts were on the most considerate person she had ever known. Mary Stoltzfus.

She longed to hear from Mary, though if she'd had better sense, she might've guessed that her friend wouldn't risk her good standing in the community to write a reply to a letter written by a stranger. Maybe Katherine herself should've written directly. But, no, if that had been the right thing to do, she would have done it in the first place.

Still, she was more than anxious to have some word from Mary . . . or anyone else back home, for that matter.

CHAPTER FOURTEEN

❖   ❖   ❖

Katherine's quilting class met again on Wednesday evening. She was excited to see the women picking up speed with the placement of pieces and working with the tic-tac-toe shading pattern in general.

"It's like following a recipe," Natalie Judah remarked, looking pert in her kelly green pants outfit. "So I guess anyone can learn to quilt, right?"

Rosie and Leoma exchanged glances, shrugging. "Speak for yourself," Rosie said, laughing.

The other women studied the copies of Katherine's sketches of what the finished Ninepatch should look like.

Later she showed them the beautiful Country Songbird pattern. "I love to make this one," she said, pointing out the striking redbird appliqués interspersed with flowing vines and graceful green leaves throughout.

"It looks very difficult," Ada remarked. "Can we really learn to make it, too?"

"If we work together as well as we have been, I don't see why not," Katherine replied.

"A challenge, to be sure," said Leoma.

The women were nodding in agreement.

"How much would a quilt like that sell for?" Elizabeth

asked, sitting across the frame from Katherine.

"Oh, probably over a thousand dollars for a queen size, at a store catering to tourists. If you knew where to go—to a private Amish residence, for instance—you'd only pay about five hundred dollars."

They talked about what to do with the Ninepatch quilt the seven of them were already in the process of making. "*If* we ever finish it," Natalie said with a grin.

"Maybe we could sell it to raise money for the hospice," Katherine suggested.

Missy, Elizabeth, and Natalie immediately decided that was a good idea. Leoma, Rosie, and Ada didn't seem to mind either way. "We're just thrilled to have the opportunity to learn firsthand from someone who knows what she's doing," Ada said, acknowledging Katherine.

"Yes, thanks for being Amish," Missy teased, offering a smile.

Katherine didn't quite know how to respond. Truth be told, if Missy, or any of the other women gathered here, had the slightest idea what she'd experienced for having been an unyielding Plain woman, maybe they wouldn't be so quick to jump to conclusions. But, of course, they couldn't possibly know. They had no way of understanding the rigid, nearly unattainable, expectations placed on one growing up in a cloistered society. So she said nothing.

"What made you leave your people?" asked Elizabeth.

Katherine noticed Natalie's concerned look but took the question in stride. "I wanted to find my birth mother, Laura Mayfield-Bennett. My search brought me here to Canandaigua and this mansion."

Several of the ladies looked surprised. "So you were adopted by the Amish?" asked Elizabeth.

"Yes, as an infant, but I wasn't told until just last year." She was beginning to feel uncomfortable about exposing her past.

"Oh . . . I know just how you must feel," Ada offered. "One of my cousins recently found out she was adopted. She's in her late forties."

"Why would parents keep something like that from their child?" Missy asked, frowning as she looked across the frame at Ada.

Ada shook her head. "In the case of my cousin, she never felt connected to her family. I guess, from what she says, she always sensed that she didn't really belong."

Didn't belong . . .

Katherine wondered if her quilting class was turning into the type of therapy sessions she'd recently read about in the newspaper. Was this how English folk aired their pent-up emotions?

Natalie, being the professional she was, must've picked up on Katherine's mood. Because before you could say *Geilssch wanz*—horsetail—she had steered the conversation away from adoption to the nasty weather and news of another storm front heading their way.

In more ways than one, Katherine was mighty glad the nurse had joined the group.

❖   ❖   ❖

When Daniel arrived home after putting in another long day at work, it was coming on toward twilight, and the city lights were beginning to twinkle up and down his street.

Sorting through the mail, he scrutinized each return address and the handwriting as well, hoping for a reply from Katie. But, as had been the case each day, nothing had come from Canandaigua. If he'd been honest with himself, he might've realized that Katherine Mayfield was not about to write a letter back to him. He was simply not going to hear a word from the woman he'd once called his sweetheart girl.

His boss, Owen Hess, and his wife must have observed

his pensive mood the last few times they were together. Owen had gone so far as to invite him to their home for dinner, talking of including Ruth Stine, *if* Dan would agree to a semi-blind date.

Ruth was a year younger than Dan. A devoted Christian, she believed in waiting for God's choice in a mate. She had literally given up on the idea of dating, and Dan couldn't blame her for that. The social scene in some of the churches tended to lean more toward worldly, selfish motives. The Mennonite way taught that a woman, no matter her age, was to abide under the protection of her father's roof—physically live in the house of her parents—until such time as God brought along a life mate of His choosing.

Ruth was trusting the Lord for His will in the matter, and Dan was aware of it. Not only was she devout in her faith, she was a beautiful woman of humility and grace.

"Thanks for thinking of me," he'd told Owen.

"Pray about coming, why don't you?" his boss replied.

Dan had prayed, though not in regard to developing a friendship with Ruth. He'd fasted and prayed for Katie. And because his affections were still very strong for her, he felt it unwise to accept Owen's kind invitation.

As far as he knew, Katie had never come to faith in Jesus as Savior and Lord. He'd inquired of the Wise Woman about Katie's beliefs, but Ella Mae seemed hesitant to say for sure, one way or the other. The assurance of salvation issue was a touchy one. He knew this to be true, because he'd been brought up to believe that such doctrine was a disruption to the community. "It is a manifestation of conceit, not humility," his father had said when first they'd discussed it years back.

Dan had tried repeatedly to show his father the passages of Scripture stating the truth of the gospel, that Christ had come to bring salvation . . . eternal life. But Dan's words had fallen on deaf ears.

Tired and hungry, he wandered out to the kitchen and warmed up some leftovers. He would not permit his mind to dwell on the fact that Katie apparently had not felt inclined to reply to his letter. He'd waited five long years to approach her. She was entitled to take her time about responding.

❖   ❖   ❖

Snow was falling gently as the People made their way to the Preaching service over at David and Mattie Beiler's house on Sunday. Mary sat in the back of the enclosed carriage with Mammi Ruth, while Dat and Mam sat in front.

The thought crossed her mind that she could easily spill the beans and let them in on what they were going to hear from the bishop about Katie Lapp, when the adults met for a membership meeting after Preachin'. But she held her tongue and did the right thing—kept all of it to herself.

She was overjoyed that John had been mindful of her request, and she figured he loved her an awful lot because of it.

The membership meeting didn't last very long, especially once the People realized how adamant John was. Mary, too, could see it all so clearly—the look on his face, the sound of his voice, the hushed awe surrounding the moment.

It was his apology that came as a surprise.

"I stand before you today to ask your forgiveness for the hasty and indignant way I dealt with Katie Lapp's shunning. It was an unjust thing I did, and I pray that none of you will follow my example in this," he said, standing before the membership.

Mary felt her burden lift as she sat on the hard bench next to her mother. She listened attentively as Bishop John explained that the shunning itself was to be kept in force.

"As stated in the Scripture, we will not keep company with such a sinner, no, not eat with such a one." Still, he was lifting the worst part.

Rebecca's face radiated pure joy, and Mary couldn't help but notice how the dear woman sat just a bit taller than before. Glory be! They could communicate with Katie!

Mary wondered if Katie's mamma would ever forgive her for agreeing to marry the bishop. Whatever time it took, whatever words were required, she'd see to it that there were no hard feelings festering between them.

If Katie ever *did* come back and repent, Mary knew she would wholeheartedly welcome her friend—without reservation, encouraging Rebecca to think wonderful-gut thoughts about the possibility of Katie getting married, no matter what age she might be at the time. 'Course, there was always Daniel, that is if he'd been able to locate her. But Mary wasn't about to hold her breath for *two* shunned young people finding the courage to confess. Usually, the way it worked, only one might be willing—at least, that's how it had been in a good many cases over the years.

As Mary sat there, she noticed that Samuel Lapp's eyes were moist, and his cheeks twitched with emotion. She was careful not to stare, even though a large group of men sat on the opposite side of the house, and it was next to impossible *not* to observe his facial expressions.

The first thing Mary wanted to do after the common meal and the visiting and after they all left for home was to write Katie a letter. She felt like a young girl again, just thinking about being allowed to correspond freely with her bosom buddy. Sure, she'd offer words of spiritual assistance, but she'd be sharing other things, too. Plenty of things.

❖   ❖   ❖

Sunday, March 15

My dearest friend,

I have the most wonderful news for you. The bishop has lifted the Ban a little. The People are allowed to communicate with you! I'm mighty happy about it, because I've wondered how to let you know that I got your letter (the one Mrs. Rosie Taylor was so kind to write me). Thank you, Katie. It meant ever so much to me for you to be so cautious that way.

Rebecca and I had a nice chat last Sunday afternoon— one week ago today it was—and her eyes lit up when she heard that you'd asked about her. Of course, you wouldn't have any way of knowing what your poor mamma's been through since you left. Even Bishop John went to see her to try to help her, so depressed she was. But now, honestly, I think I see a change coming. I wouldn't be a bit surprised if Rebecca wrote to you sometime soon.

We all believe that in time you'll see the error of your ways and rejoin your Amish family here in Hickory Hollow. Until then, I remain your faithful friend,

Mary Stoltzfus

She took time to read what she'd written, second-guessing herself about not having told a speck of news regarding her romance with Bishop John. The more she pondered the letter, the more she supposed *that* news was not the best thing to be writing just yet. She could only hope that Rebecca wouldn't go and let the cat out of the bag.

As for informing Katie that Dan was alive, well, she'd thought long and hard about trying to explain the mighty strange story in a letter—as confusing as it would sound to Katie—but she chose not to. Chances were, Dan had already located his beloved by now.

❖   ❖   ❖

Mattie Beiler had made some hot tea, the mint kind her mother always loved. "Here now, this oughta get ya warmed up," she said, setting the cup and saucer in front of Ella Mae.

"Jah, somethin' oughta." The old woman leaned over the table to sip her tea, but her hands were shaking. "Goodness' sakes, what'sa matter with me?"

Mattie took the teacup from her and set it down on the table. "Here, let me help ya, Mam." Then taking a good hard look at her, Mattie asked, "Have ya been feelin' poorly all day, Mam?"

"Ever since after Preachin,' I guess."

"That long? During the meal, too?"

"Jah."

She wasn't surprised that not a single complaint had come from Ella Mae. The woman was a stoic when it came to physical ailments, of which there were very few for her advanced age.

Ella Mae began to shake her head back and forth, her eyes blinking fast. "Aw, probably nothin' to worry about much." More sipping, then she tried to add some honey to the hot liquid, but when it came to stirring the tea, the spoon jiggled about in her gnarled hand.

Mattie sat down at the table, noting that her Mam didn't seem quite as alert as usual. "Would ya like to lie down a bit?"

Ella Mae looked at her, eyes smooth and shiny—almost glassy. "M-maybe s-so," she mumbled, her words coming thick.

"Mamma?" She leaned over next to the white-haired woman, touching her hand. It felt damp to the touch and Ella Mae's breathing seemed irregular, as if she had to pant for breath.

"O-oh" came an uncontrolled sound, deep and frightening. And Ella Mae slumped over, her body falling forward on the tabletop.

Mattie ran to the back door. "Something's wrong with Mamma! Come quick!" she called to David, who was busy outside, folding up long benches from the Preaching service and putting them back in the bench wagon with several other men.

Her husband hurried inside, going over to lift Ella Mae out of her chair. "Don'tcha worry none, Mam," she heard him saying as he carried the Wise Woman out of the kitchen to the Dawdi Haus adjoining theirs.

Mattie followed close behind, fretting that her mamma was going to die of a stroke. Right here in the house where, not but a few hours before, they'd had a right-gut Preachin'. Where their bishop had come clean with the most startling personal confession she'd ever heard; all that business of lifting part of the Ban from Katie Lapp and whatnot all.

Ella Mae continued making that horrifying low-pitched groan. It came right out of the depth of her being. A painful, treacherous sound.

Mattie had seen enough of this sort of thing to know what was happening. Too many elderly aunts and uncles had ended up this way. And now *her* mamma.

The thought crossed her mind to ride for a telephone— to one of her Mennonite neighbors. Such times as this, a phone would come in mighty handy. But her mother had repeatedly expressed her desire that when the time came, she did not want to be sent to some English hospital, wired up to contraptions to keep her heart beating against its will. "I'd rather die in my own bed," she'd always said.

Because of that, Mattie dismissed the notion of using anybody's telephone at all.

"Be gentle," she advised her husband and pulled back the bed quilts and other handmade coverings.

Leaning down, David lowered Ella Mae into her bed. Mattie couldn't help thinking, with a chilling shudder, that it was much like the lowering of a coffin. When she'd covered her mother carefully, tucking her in almost as if she were a child, Mattie slid a chair over next to the bed and sat there, holding her breath as the left side of Ella Mae's facial muscles began to weaken and sag.

Mattie appreciated her husband's comforting hand on her shoulder as he stood behind her, watching . . . waiting.

CHAPTER FIFTEEN

❖ ❖ ❖

The weather was cold and gray for a full week, and Katherine was glad to have another social event to look forward to at the end of it. She had read and reread the letter from Mary more times than she could count, for it brought a great sense of relief.

Shortly after Mary's letter had arrived, she marveled to receive one from Rebecca as well, though her mamma's letter seemed less spirited, more of a means to admonish and instruct than to convey compassion. And there had been news of Ella Mae, who'd had a bad stroke. Katherine wondered how the dear woman was doing. Surely the womenfolk would assist her in her recovery. They were known to be able to bring a body near back from the grave.

There'd been no mention of Dan's visit to Hickory Hollow, though, which made her wonder. Still, she cherished the letter with all her heart.

Katherine sensed a mysterious stirring in the air, though she couldn't quite put her finger on it. She had not known of a bishop—not anywhere in Lancaster County—backing away from his initial declaration of shunning. Never—*niemols!*

She couldn't help but wonder what was happening in

the Hollow. Was Bishop John floundering as a leader? If so, wouldn't Mary have said something?

To clear her head, Katherine bundled up and headed outside to walk the grounds, though some patches were too deep with snow to explore.

She went around to the south side of the mansion, where Rosie had told her there was a little lily pond surrounding a small fountain. "You'll enjoy sitting out there with a good book come summer."

She smiled at the thought of warmer weather, thinking that the expansive lawns might be just the place to bring Willy for a picnic. That is, if she could get permission from the hospice. On second thought, Mayfield Manor would be a perfect picnic spot for any number of terminally ill young children. She could hardly wait to discuss the idea with Natalie.

◈　◈　◈

Justin was indeed charming as he sat at the end of the elegant table that evening. It was the occasion of his cousin's birthday, and the evening was complete with a roving string trio, and later, dancing. Never having attempted to dance ballroom style, Katherine declined Justin's cousin's invitation as politely as she knew how, which may or may not have been a slap in the face to the guest of honor. She couldn't tell for sure by the way Justin continued to make conversation with several others at the table, never so much as raising an eyebrow.

Observing his interaction with others, she was learning a great deal about her handsome Beau. She hadn't known it before, but just this night she discovered that he was fluent in two other languages besides English. Not to let that tidbit of information get the best of her, she boosted her morale with the fact that *she* was fluent in two. Thankfully, Justin wasn't the type of person to reveal the secret Plain past of his date. He carried on, smiling often and throwing her an occasional wink.

Clearly, she felt like a fish floundering on a beach somewhere, what with the blue-smoke, high-society atmosphere. Especially tonight. Even the chandelier over her head far surpassed the exquisite one in the dining room at Mayfield Manor. She was dressed appropriately for the occasion, so the feeling she suppressed had nothing at all to do with the way she'd arranged her hair in a lovely updo, secured with one of Laura's diamond-studded combs, or the gown she'd chosen with matching heels and bag. No, it had more to do with the awkward way she felt while in such grand and fancy surroundings, her own mansion not included.

She wondered if she was trying too hard to fit in with Justin's friends and his extended family. So far, he had not mentioned taking her to meet his parents, though she almost expected it, in lieu of his recent comments about their "future together."

She honestly felt as if he might be getting close to a proposal of marriage, and the thought of it made her tingle with expectancy. Perhaps, in time, he would present her with a beautiful ring, too, just as everything else she'd ever really dreamed of had seemed to wend its way to the doorstep of her life.

❖　❖　❖

The drive over to Ella Mae's took less than five minutes, and Lydia Miller was thankful for a warm car on such a cold day. Peter, her good-natured husband, had consented to drop her off for a visit with the ailing Wise Woman on his way to town. "Do you think she'll even know you?" he asked as they turned into the lane leading to David and Mattie Beiler's big farmhouse.

165

"If it's as bad a stroke as some are saying, maybe not. But that won't scare me away," she answered truthfully. "I can still pray for her whether she knows me or not."

Peter nodded, then got out and went around to help her out. "You won't be able to phone me when you're ready to leave, but maybe you can visit with Mattie for a while, and then I'll be by to pick you up." He glanced at his watch. "Say, in about an hour from now?"

"Suits me fine," she said as he leaned down to peck her cheek.

"I'll be in prayer for you, dear. And for your friend."

She waved. "See you soon."

At the door, Lydia was greeted and made to feel at home by Mattie and several other Amishwomen who were close relatives of the David Beiler family, but none that Lydia herself had ever met.

Mattie, talking softly, led her through the front room to the door that connected the main house with the smaller addition. "I s'pose you should know that she can't speak at all," Mattie cautioned as they went into the main floor bedroom. "But Mam loves havin' visitors, so don't let that hinder ya one bit."

Glad she could be of some help, whether spreading cheer or just sitting by Ella Mae's bedside, Lydia prayed silently that she might be a blessing to the woman.

"I'll give ya some time alone with her," Mattie said, closing the door behind her as she left.

The room was serene and dim, and Lydia felt she ought to tiptoe, which she did, but then stopped and stood at the foot of the bed, looking down on her friend's thin frame there under several layers of cozy quilts. "Hullo, Ella Mae," she said softly. "I heard you could use some company, and, well . . . I'm right here."

The Wise Woman's cheeks were sunken and drooped, her eyes glum, yet she blinked as if to say, "Glad ya came."

Lydia pushed the chair closer to the bed so that it was right up next to the mattress, where she could comfortably reach out and hold the paralyzed hand, stroke the limp arm. "I've been thinking and praying for you every day since I heard," she said.

Leaning forward, she put her face up close to the wrinkled one. "The Lord's presence is here, Ella Mae, right here in this room."

Minutes passed. Lydia remained silent, squeezing the fragile hand in hers. Ella Mae's loving hands had helped many a person with domestic chores over the years: sowing seeds in charity gardens, harvesting, canning and preserving, quilting, mending—even churning butter on occasion. They'd touched many a little one's head, gently blessing her children, grandchildren, and great-grandchildren with her generosity and love. And her hands had helped weather the storms of life, soothing the brow of her dying husband and years before that, of Essie, her twin sister.

Now it was Ella Mae's time to be touched with tenderness. Lydia was content to reach past the stiff immobility, past the deadened limbs, and communicate God's love.

As she held the misshapen hands, the bluish veins bulging up past the surface of crinkled skin, she prayed aloud, "Dear Lord Jesus, thank you for Ella Mae's life, that she has lived it for you—helping others, offering her life as a sacrifice to those who have come, searching for truth. I pray a special blessing over this your child. It if be your will, bring her out of this condition. Allow her to regain the use of her hands and limbs, her voice and her mind. I pray this in Jesus' name. Amen."

As she stood to leave, she was aware of Mattie's presence. "Oh, I didn't hear you come in," she whispered.

"Your prayer was awful perty," Mattie replied. "Thank you, Lydia. You're a . . . kind woman."

She nodded, feeling a bit uneasy. No one had ever complimented her on a prayer. "I . . . I hope Ella Mae—*both* of you know that the Lord understands what you're going through."

Mattie's eyes were bright with tears, yet she didn't make an attempt to hide them, and when she blinked, they spilled over and coursed down her face. "We don't often hear that kinda thing about the Good Lord. It would be awful nice to know that what you say is true about almighty God bein' interested in each and every person's life. I'd give just about anything to know for sure and for certain. . . ." Her voice trailed off.

Lydia went to Mattie and reached for her hands, holding them in both of hers. "Oh, but you *can* know. You can!"

Nodding her head, Mattie's lip quivered, unable to speak.

Lydia glanced over her shoulder at the sleeping Ella Mae. "Your mamma knows. She's filled up to the brim with the love of the Lord, Mattie. That's why people are drawn to her. God's given her a great gift of wisdom."

"Jah," Mattie said, brushing the tears away. "I remember the day things changed for the better for Mamma. It happened weeks before my father died of a heart attack. She'd met up with some churchgoing folk in town somewheres. Never really said who they were or what had kept her so long, but I saw by the shine on her face that somethin' was different. Not long after, that same kind of joy showed up on Dat's face . . . and 'twasn't but a few weeks later, and he up and died."

Lydia paid close attention to this story, though she'd suspected as much for years.

Mattie sighed, adjusting her apron. "Thinking back on it, I suppose Mamma felt she had no choice but to live out the rest of her life in the Amish church."

"Well, I can understand that."

"She probably should've turned English on us and fol-

lowed her heart to the Mennonites," said Mattie with a
dainty smile. "I 'spect the thing that kept her was the
Meinding. Our bishop's mighty hard on the People, ya
know. Doesn't bat an eye 'bout puttin' the Ban on someone
who shows signs of arrogance—which is what John Beiler
would've said about Mamma if ever he'd known."

Lydia couldn't help but think that the Wise Woman had
made a difficult choice, yet prudent—following the Lord by
serving the People right in her own community.

When the time came for Lydia to say good-bye, it was
like leaving behind a thirsty woman in a desert. Mattie's
heart had been softened by Ella Mae's stroke.

"Come by for pie and coffee," Lydia offered. "Come anytime at all."

"Denki . . . I just might do that."

Lydia prayed that she would.

CHAPTER SIXTEEN

❖ ❖ ❖

Katherine was more than eager to attend church with Rosie and Fulton Taylor. The Lord's Day morning had started out quite early, with her trying to read another one of the old classics she'd found in the manor library. Yet she turned the pages without reading it. Such a peculiar feeling she had, like she was marking time, waiting for something to happen, perhaps something unforeseen. Though she was not impatient about whatever that something might be, she felt a lurking sense of excitement residing in the back of her head, though she had no way to comprehend it. Not one iota.

Were the letters from Mary and Rebecca the reason for her aloofness, her disinterest in the book she held in her hands? Odd as it seemed, she felt she was stepping toward a new phase of her life, not knowing where it might leave Katherine Mayfield's hopes and dreams.

She shrugged off her brooding feelings and went to find Rosie to say that she would like to go to church today.

Not two hours later, she entered the doors of the beautiful sanctuary, recalling that the last time she'd come here, she was saying a final good-bye to a mother she'd barely known.

Having never visited any church except the Mennonite

meetinghouse in Hickory Hollow, she was in awe of the windows—cut up in little parts of colorful glass and put back together like a quilt—the massive pipe organ, and the sloping aisle that created a carpeted path through the many cherrywood pews. Surely she had noticed such beauty on the day of the funeral, yet she vaguely remembered.

"Himmel," she whispered to herself, following Rosie and Fulton to their pew. She sat next to Rosie, with Fulton closest to the aisle, and sang along with a few of the hymns, though she didn't know many of them. As she tried to follow the notes on the staff, she thought again of Dan, who had first taught her to read music.

The music presentation by the choir, followed by an organ solo, set her spirits soaring. She could hardly wait to try out the melodies on her guitar.

But it was the sermon that touched her most. The pastor's delivery and style was so foreign to her, so entirely different from what she'd grown up with in the Amish church. Yet she was captivated by the message on the love of God . . . a *personal* heavenly Father who adored and cared for His children. This message about a God who was involved in her life—she'd kept hearing it, from Dan and then little Willy and now the minister. Could it really be true?

She thought of Lydia Miller, too, knowing that her cousin would approve of such a sermon. The more Katherine listened, the more the minister explained, the less heretical the idea seemed to her. What *was* strange was hearing Scripture passages she'd never known existed.

Quickly, she scribbled down the references on the bulletin she'd received from one of the ushers. She had to read them for herself, wanted to hold Laura's Bible in her hands, to search out some of these verses she'd never heard read by any of the preachers in Hickory Hollow.

Well, now she would. Hearing the minister expound on the verses was shaping something life-giving inside her, a craving in her heart for truth—something she'd experienced as a child on several occasions but had had no idea what to do about it.

She was ever so glad she'd come and could hardly wait to tell Justin. Maybe *he* could bring her next week. Yes, that's exactly what she'd do. She'd invite him and they would come together.

◈　◈　◈

The minute she arrived back at the mansion, she rushed off to the south wing. There, in the stillness of her suite, she wrote two short letters—one to Mary, the other to Rebecca. She described what she'd encountered at church, not hesitating in the least. The bishop would probably slap the no-communicating part of the shunning back on her when he found out, but she *had* to share it.

Dinner was served in the dining room at her request, and she spent much of the time discussing the church service with Garrett, Theodore, Leoma, and all the others. She noticed Rosie and Fulton nodding in agreement, but they seemed a bit surprised when she came up with the idea to bake up "a batch of goodies to take to the children at the hospice."

Garrett was all for it. "What's your pleasure, Katherine?"

She paused to recall her favorite sweet treat as a child. "Mississippi Mud."

"I beg your pardon?"

Several of the maids were chuckling.

"It's the perfect thing for children—rich and gooey, just right. They'll love it!"

Garrett appeared to be flustered. "I don't believe I know of a recipe for . . . uh, this mud treat you mention."

"Mississippi Mud," she said again. "I'll write out the

recipe for you. I have it memorized."

"Very well," he said, concentrating on the prime rib steak on his plate.

"In fact, I'll help make it," Katherine offered. She didn't go on to say that this gesture of kindness was only the beginning of her plan to share her wealth with the people of Canandaigua.

❖ ❖ ❖

Rosie waited until her husband's hands were free of clean table linens before sneaking over to give him a hug. "I'm so excited, Fulton!"

"Over me?" He grinned, bussing her cheek.

She poked him playfully, wriggling away. "You know what I'm talking about, now don't you?"

"Yes, I believe I do. And isn't it remarkable what a single church service can do for a person?"

"I daresay it's been a long time coming for our young mistress." She followed him out of the dining room and down the long main hall. It was her assumption that if a person mulled and puzzled over something as important as everlasting life long enough, and was open to God's leading, he or she would ultimately find it. Katherine, in Rosie's opinion, had been searching for truth all her young life. "I suspect the prayers of certain key people, not only Laura's, have played a part in what may be happening."

He gave her an approving wink. "Once again, I believe you are right, my dear." And he hurried into the kitchen.

❖ ❖ ❖

Promptly after the noon meal, Katherine headed to the library—down the main hall, past the grand staircase, and to the left. She located a section where numerous Bibles were shelved. She had no idea which one had been Laura's personal Bible, or even if she had had a favorite. So Katherine chose a large leather-bound King James Version and carried it off to her room.

Finding her notes scrawled on the church bulletin, she began to look up the minister's sermon text. *Behold, what manner of love the Father hath bestowed upon us, that we should be called the sons of God. . . .*

She read the verse a second time, letting the words sink into her heart. Tears clouded her vision as she contemplated what this very Scripture might've meant to her as a child. Oh, to have heard this verse at the knee of Dat or Mam— such words that had endured thousands of years since the Bible was written. *The test of time,* Preacher Yoder might've said, if only he'd known.

To think that the minister who said this phrase had been anointed by the almighty God himself! Reading the passage again and again, she began to know, without a shadow of a doubt, that if she had read the complete Bible while growing up—perhaps even owned a Bible—her whole life might've turned out much differently.

Quickly, she went to the dresser drawer where she kept the handmade baby dress and found Dan's letter, scanning it again for the sentence that had pricked her heart when the letter had first arrived. *I have found a love I've never known . . . this I find in the Lord Jesus.*

She wondered if this discovery had something to do with the restless anticipation she'd experienced earlier today. She thought of Laura's sunny disposition. In spite of the woman's debilitating disease and constant pain, her mother's day-to-day dealings with the servants and the domestic help were exemplary of godly love. And she had prayed for Katherine's salvation, of all things! Rosie had talked of it on several occasions. Laura, though she was dying, had spent her morning hours talking to the Lord . . . here, in this room.

She read again each of the Scriptures, this time out loud, and as she did, God's Word sprang to life in her, and she began to weep.

CHAPTER SEVENTEEN

❖　　❖　　❖

Before the mixing of the muddy Mississippi confection ever began on Monday morning, Katherine placed a phone call to Natalie Judah. She told her of the plan to surprise the children, and without the slightest hesitation, Natalie sanctioned the idea.

"I'll make the delivery sometime this afternoon," Katherine promised.

"What a thoughtful gesture," said Natalie. "I'll alert the other nurses so they're aware of your coming."

"I almost forgot to ask—will this cause a dietary problem for any of the children?"

"Better bring along the recipe."

Katherine agreed, grinning to herself. She'd mentioned the name of the treat, and Natalie, misunderstanding, had asked her to repeat it. But Katherine made it clear that the dessert recipe was an old Amish delicacy. "It's been in my adoptive family for hundreds of years," she explained.

This comment seemed to spark the nurse's interest even further.

"I'll make copies for anyone who wants one," she volunteered.

Overjoyed, Natalie thanked her. "Say . . . maybe we

could have an Amish emphasis this year at our annual bazaar. It's coming up on May first."

"Maybe sell our class quilts?"

Natalie laughed about that. "We'll have to hustle in order to finish the Country Songbird pattern."

"If we work fast, we can do it." After hanging up the telephone, Katherine scurried off to help Garrett and Selig make the mouth-watering recipe.

It was while they were making the syrup, while the brown sugar and butter were boiling, that the rich and sweet aroma transported her back to Rebecca's kitchen when Katie was just six years old. . . .

A stiff wind blew flakes of snow mixed with sleet, making tapping sounds on the windowpanes and the storm doors. The sun, hiding behind the heavy layers of snow clouds, refused to shine. Still, Mary and her mother and grandmother had come to help make four double batches of the tasty dish she loved better 'n most anything.

Katie and Mamma washed their hands at the sink, then tossed the hand towel back and forth merrily before starting to melt and brown the butter.

"Won't Dat and the boys be excited?" Mamma said.

Katie giggled. "Jah, and they'll prob'ly finish off the whole dish before we can ever get seconds," she said, standing on a chair to reach the top of the counter.

She held a long rolling pin in her little hands and was making ready to help squash the graham crackers when it came time. Later, she would help her little friend Mary spread the crumbs all over the top of the gooey dessert. But the best part of all was the lip-smackin' session just around the corner—eating the delicious dish.

Mary scooted a chair over next to her. "I'm almost as tall as you," she said.

"Almost, but not quite."

They leaned close together, taking turns trying to measure each other, but they giggled so much they couldn't stand up straight long enough.

"Ach, hold still now, and I'll see where your forehead comes on me," said Katie.

Mary sucked in a deep breath and held perfectly still until Katie got the job done. "Half a head shorter," Katie announced, to which Mary blew all her air out. "And ya have bad breath, too!" she hollered, then burst into laughter again.

"Miss Katherine?" Selig said, waving a tea towel in front of her face.

"Oh . . . er, what?" A bit startled, she apologized for daydreaming. "I guess this recipe pulls me right back to my childhood."

"We had a feeling you might've gone back and decided not to return," Garrett teased her.

Selig and Katherine joined in the laughter. What a wonderful-good time they were having. She could hardly wait for the "mud" to cool.

❖　❖　❖

The children who could respond with spoken praise for her surprise treat did so.

Willy was especially expressive, his fingertips covered with graham cracker crumbs. He put up both thumbs and wiggled them in the air. "Can you teach my mommy how to make this stuff?" he asked.

"I'll see that she gets this recipe—good enough?" Katherine folded the piece of paper in half and placed it on a clean spot on the table.

They talked about his weekend, what he did on Sunday.

179

"Mommy and Daddy took turns reading my Bible to me," he told her, his eyes wide.

"I'm glad they did." She paused, remembering the church service and the Scriptures she'd looked up afterward, and how moved she was by the message of God's love.

"My brother came to visit me, too." Willy's expression was serious. "Josh looked real sad, though."

She knew he was speaking of his older brother. "I'm sure he was very happy to see you."

"Josh thinks I'm going to die, but I'm not. I'm going to get well and go home again and . . ." He stopped in midsentence.

Katherine's heart ached for the little boy. So young to be dealing with issues of life and death.

"I want to get well," he whispered, as if confiding a secret.

"We all want you to."

When it came time for him to rest, she wheeled the boy down the hall to his room. Colorful balloons floated gently in the corner near the window, and a lovely handmade quilt covered a portion of one wall. There was a recliner and a hide-a-bed for family members who wished to spend the night. Bright and cheery, Willy's room was filled with large, graceful ferns and freestanding plants.

She helped him into bed, pulling the covers up for him. "Sweet dreams, now."

"Aw, we didn't have time to play guitar today," he said suddenly, as if it were terribly important to him.

"I'll come again on Wednesday," she said. "You can learn to play another chord then."

He nodded reluctantly and reached his arms up for a hug. "Good-bye, Katherine. I'll miss you."

She leaned down and caressed his head. "I'll miss you too, Willy."

"Come back tomorrow, okay?"

"I'll see what I can do," she said, knowing that it would mean changing the schedule and having to get permission from the charge nurse. A bit complicated, but she would talk to Natalie and see what could be done.

On the drive home, she wished it were midsummer so she could take her young friend outside. They would sit in the shade of a maple tree, enjoying the fragrance of garden phlox and honeysuckle vines, feel the warm breeze, and watch the sun cast short shadows on the birdbath in the courtyard behind the hospice. As it was, she feared Willy might not live long enough to see July come at all.

Later Theodore drove her to the mall, where she found a gift shop. She wanted to purchase several cards for the sick boy, but as she was standing in front of the "Get Well" section, she noticed two Amish teens enter the store. Their dresses were similar to those worn in Lancaster County, and the connection instantly drew her to them.

"*Wie bischt?*" she said, forgetting she wasn't dressed Plain, let alone Amish, and that these girls might be frightened by a greeting from a stranger who spoke their language.

They *were* shy, lowering their heads, eyes cast down.

Katherine stepped back a bit before she made a complete fool of herself. "Uh, sorry. Have a nice day." She turned to go, the cards for Willy still in her hand.

"Didja forget to pay?" the older Amish girl called.

Katherine felt her neck and cheeks grow warm. "Oh my, yes. I certainly did. Thank you ever so much."

The girls glanced at each other, grinning. Then one spoke up, "Weren't you out at our place buying jam the other week?"

Katherine couldn't believe it. These girls looked an awful lot like Mrs. Esler. "Yes, I bought the jellies. Are you related to her?"

"We're her youngest daughters," said one shyly.

"Jah, we spotted you from the front room that day," said

the other. "We had an old quilt that was worn through, so we were puttin' some new batting in, which was why ya didn't see us. Usually we help Mamma with the jam and jelly business."

"Well, that makes sense, then."

The younger girl was eyeing her. "Do ya have any need for a good homemade quilt or two, miss?"

She smiled. "To tell you the truth, I'm working on one right now myself—along with six other women." She didn't say she was teaching a quilting class, though. "Have you ever made the Country Songbird pattern?"

Their faces brightened as if they'd just met up with an old friend. "Jah . . . we know it well. In fact, Mamma said just the other day we oughta start one of those with the birds all in blue."

She stood there, enjoying the company of these Plain girls immensely. Suddenly, she thought of the hospice bazaar. Here might be a way to finish the quilt in time for such an event.

She stuck her neck out even further and explained the craft show fund-raiser and what it would mean to the terminally ill children who were inpatients at the hospice. "If we could finish the quilt, I think it might bring quite a lot at the bazaar on May first."

The girls were still smiling. A good sign, she thought.

"How would you like to help finish the Country Songbird? I'd be happy to pay you to work with us."

They were shaking their heads, sharing sober expressions now. "We wouldn't think of takin' pay for it. But we'll hafta talk to Mam first," said the younger girl.

Katherine opened her purse and looked for a piece of paper. Quickly, she jotted down her address and phone number. "Won't you keep this handy, just in case?"

"Denki. We have a telephone . . . for the jelly business. So we can call and leave you know."

Katherine was so thrilled to have met these kindred spirits, she came close to walking out of the store again without paying for the cards. Fortunately, she caught herself. "I'll look forward to hearing from you, then."

Later, she realized that she'd fallen back into the old speech pattern—adding "then" to the end of her sentence. It was plenty obvious to her that Rosie had been right when she'd said it would take some time getting used to the way English folk speak.

Still, she hadn't remembered feeling so completely comfortable with anyone. Unless it had been the day she'd stopped in at the Eslers' home to buy rhubarb jam.

Justin would find this amusing, she was quite sure. And she would tell him—the very next time he phoned.

❖   ❖   ❖

Sitting at her writing desk, Katherine's mind was awhirl. She signed the cute card and wrote Willy's name on the envelope, wishing there was something she could do to add days and weeks to his life. Even years. But the tumor in his brain was inoperable, Natalie had said. "Our mission here is to make our patients as comfortable . . . as *contented* as possible."

If money were the obstacle to his health, Katherine could've helped cure Willy easily enough. She would have given up her inheritance in order to give the darling boy his health. With all her heart, she wished it were possible.

❖   ❖   ❖

Willy was smiling for her the next day. He held her colorful elephant card in both his hands, too close to his eyes, it seemed to Katherine.

She glanced at Nurse Judah, wondering about it.

"It's all right," Natalie whispered, nodding her head. "He can see the words best that way."

A pain stabbed in the pit of her stomach. How long before the sunshine boy would go blind from the tumor? Or worse?

She stooped to open her guitar case, but Willy began to moan and the card fell to the floor. Before she could retrieve it or offer to play a soft, sweet lullaby, Willy rang the call bell. The nurse in charge arrived in seconds, and Katherine left the room.

Hours later, upon her return home, she went immediately to the drawing room and started a fire on her own. She began to play her guitar, remembering snatches of the hymn melodies she'd heard at Rosie's church. After several unsuccessful attempts at finishing, she turned to her old songs, strumming hard as she sang.

Rosie inched her way into the room at one point, during an interval of silence between songs. "Are you feeling all right, Katherine?" she asked, a deep frown on her face.

"Well . . . no."

Rosie crept closer. "Is it the hospice child? Is Willy worse?"

Her throat closed up, the lump stinging hard against the glands in her neck. All she could do was shake her head back and forth.

"Oh, dear lady. I'm so sorry." Rosie came and put her arm around Katherine's shoulders. "May I pray with you?"

She agreed, sobbing silently into her hands. Rosie's prayer was short but it calmed her, gave her hope. "Thank you," she said much later. "Suppose I've been needing that."

"The cry or the prayer?" Rosie offered a box of tissues.

Looking up, Katherine nodded. "Jah, I 'spect I needed both."

Rosie smiled down at her. "There is still a good portion of Amish in you, I daresay."

"Puh . . . I said it that way just for fun."

"Are you positively sure?"

She brushed the tears away and moved closer to the fire-place. "I met two Amish sisters yesterday . . . at the card shop in the mall. They might come and help us finish the quilt in time for the hospice bazaar."

Rosie offered her another tissue to blow her nose. "That would be lovely, having more Amish folk around here."

"You think I'm going home someday, don't you, Rosie? Back to Hickory Hollow?" The question came clear out of the blue; she wasn't sure where.

"Well, I wouldn't be too surprised perhaps."

Katherine shook her head. "This is home to me now. I love my mother's mansion . . . and everyone in it."

"If you returned, where would that leave your Justin Wirth?" It was as if Rosie hadn't heard Katherine's comment about the beautiful estate.

"This mansion . . . *and* Mr. Wirth are absolutely wonderful," she insisted, and the thought of Justin all dressed up, sending his enticing smiles her way, made her heart flutter.

Rosie's eyes twinkled mischievously. "Has he popped the question yet?"

"Popped . . . what?"

"Has Justin asked you to spend the rest of your life with him? You know, say 'I do' in front of a preacher and a churchful of witnesses—be his Mrs. Wirth?"

She gazed at the ceiling, trying the name on in her head. "Mrs. Katherine Wirth. Hm-m, sounds pretty, don't you think?"

Rosie's eyes narrowed. "And are you ready to change your name again?"

Katherine turned and stared at the fire, purposely ignoring the pointed question. "Justin's a good man. I have a feeling he'll take me somewhere very special to dine when the question pops out."

They laughed together, Katherine reaching out to grasp Rosie's sturdy hands. She clung to her housemaid as one might hold fast to an older sister, and felt all the better for it.

CHAPTER EIGHTEEN

Rebecca was indeed surprised and happy to receive yet another letter from Katie. But she was alarmed at her daughter's comments about the worldly English church she'd attended. All that music—*Ei, yi, yi*—and the apostasy that minister had preached from his pulpit. It broke her heart anew to think that her girl was outside the fold—farther away than she'd feared.

She sat right down and started writing, never once thinking that she might oughta wait a few days before penning her thoughts.

Wednesday, March 25

Dear Katie,

I'm awful worried about you. Wish you'd be more cautious about the kind of meetings you go to with your English friends.

How's the weather there? We've had our share of cold and snow here.

Nothing much new, except that I've been going over to help Mattie exercise Ella Mae's limbs, trying to get the muscles to come to life again so she can at least feed herself. But it's a right slow process, as you probably remember from when Mammi Essie had hers back years ago.

Mary said she didn't say anything in her letter to you about Daniel Fisher. Maybe it's because he's shunned, too, only the situation's much different with him. His Pop's terrible troubled over it. That's all I better say. Mattie said that Ella Mae told her that Dan stopped in to see her before he left again for New Jersey, that he was heading up north to look for you. Have you seen him yet?

Such a story Daniel has to tell. I suppose you've heard it all by now anyways. It is sad, really, when you think of it. The poor fellow . . .

Well, news is all, so I best sign off. Never forget how much all of us love you. The People want you to do what's right under God and the church. (Bishop John stands waiting and ready to hear your confession, dear girl.)

Your Mam

She sealed the envelope and got it right out in the mail before she could change her mind about some of what she'd written.

Because she was in a hurry, she chose Daisy, who could trot no matter the weather because she was young and downright spirited. The snow stung her face and the wind whipped at her skirt as she hitched up the horse to the family carriage. She was determined to get over to Ella Mae's and help Mattie with afternoon chores as well as exercising the Wise Woman's arms and legs some.

The ride took longer than usual due to the blizzard-like conditions. She could scarcely see the outline of Daisy's head, one horse-length ahead. Heavy, thick flakes blanketed the road, drifting up in uneven piles, but she persisted, shivering beneath the furry lap robes.

Only one other buggy was parked outside when Rebecca arrived at the Beiler home. One of Mattie's married daughters maybe.

Sure enough, when she got herself inside and out of the

biting cold, Anna was boiling water for peppermint tea. "Wouldja care for some?" she asked, big brown eyes smiling.

"Jah, I'll have some, with plenty sugar."

Mattie looked up from the table where she was sitting with young Sally, choosing a pattern for a quilt. "You look like ya could use a gut hot drink about now."

She nodded. "It's awful bad out, making like it's gonna dump heavy on us."

Young Sally glanced up, smiling. "Ach, a blizzard? Yuscht what we need to have us a school vacation."

Rebecca eyed her. "Your Pop has a right fine sleigh, don't he?"

The girl nodded, looking mighty sheepish.

"Well, then, I don't 'spect there'll be any chance of school closin'—no matter how gut and hard the snow comes," Rebecca said, taking a sip of the tea.

Sally scrunched up her face and got back to her quilting work. "Jah . . . maybe."

Grinning at her, Mattie hugged her granddaughter to herself, holding her there for a moment. "This one needs extra learnin', if ya ask me."

"Maybe Sally just oughta have herself a taste of summer school come July," said Anna sternly. "Then maybe my daughter won't dawdle so during the school year."

The awkward subject was soon dropped and the conversation turned to Ella Mae. "How's she feelin' today?" Rebecca wanted to know.

"Oh, she's itchin' to talk—tries her best to make little grunting sounds, tryin' hard as anything to communicate," Mattie said. "Poor thing's havin' a time of it."

Rebecca was sorry to hear it. "Would she like some tea?"

"Well, you know as gut as I do how she feels about a hot cup of mint tea." Mattie pulled herself up off the table bench with a sigh and went to pour her mamma some.

Rebecca spoke up. "I'd be glad to take it over to her," she

said. "And while I'm at it, I'll have her doing her daily calisthenics."

Young Sally giggled, and Anna said 'twasn't funny being two months shy of eighty and having just suffered a stroke.

"Sorry, Mamma," Sally said, wearing a repentant face.

"You best be" was all Anna replied.

Something about feisty Sally made Rebecca think of Katie at that age. But she brushed the thought aside and took a tray of tea, honey, and some fresh cream across the house to the Wise Woman.

❖   ❖   ❖

Katherine did tell Justin about the Amish girls at the gift shop when he phoned her after lunch. "I wish you could've seen me there talking with them. It was the oddest thing, really."

It was hard for her to know what he was thinking or how he might look on the other end of the line, but she was happy to hear the cheerfulness in his voice. "It's intriguing, this recent connection with the Amish . . . after your church shunned you, Katherine. I'm a bit surprised that you are still drawn to Plain folk."

She understood his reservations. "I suppose it does seem strange, but I really don't have any animosity toward my People. I don't dislike them . . . not at all." She was thinking especially of Mary.

"But you can never go back, can you?" The words were confident, pointed.

She was silent. In such a short time, Justin had come to know her heart better, it seemed, than almost anyone. "That's true, I can't go back. I'm someone altogether different now."

"Well, if that's settled"—he chuckled—"why don't we plan a trip together?"

"A trip? Where?"

"Have you ever heard of Niagara Falls? It's a true wonder of nature."

"And only a short drive from here—am I right?"

He laughed again, and the warmth of it was merry in her ear. "Only about an hour away. We could leave in the morning, spend the afternoon, and dine somewhere lovely at sunset."

She wondered if this might be the location for a marriage proposal, though she supposed it might be just another opportunity to spend some time alone together. "Sounds wonderful," she heard herself saying.

He explained that he was nearing the completion of a new oil painting and that he'd need another few days—"at the most a week, though I doubt it."

"Whenever you're ready," she said, smiling to herself.

"In the meantime, let's have lunch somewhere exotic. Tomorrow?"

"Tomorrow's fine, thank you."

"I'll come by and pick you up around eleven-thirty?"

"All right."

"Good, I'll see you then." He paused. "I miss you, Katherine."

Her heart danced in her chest. "I'm looking forward to seeing you, too."

They said good-bye, and she hung up the phone, more than eager to see him again.

❖   ❖   ❖

Katherine kept her word, but when she went to visit Willy, he was scarcely aware of her being there. "Is he slipping away?" she whispered to Natalie, who was administering his afternoon shot.

"I'm afraid it's just a matter of days now," Natalie replied, gently easing the needle out of his vein.

"And he was so happy about . . ." She paused, trying to compose herself. "He was talking about going home and . . . and . . ." She simply could not go on.

Willy's mother and brother came in the room just then, and Katherine felt she should leave. Before she could do so, the petite woman with shoulder-length blond hair spoke up. "I want you to know how much our Willy has talked of you, Katherine." She smiled, glancing down at the guitar case. "He was telling his father and me just last night that he's decided he doesn't want to play a harp when he goes to heaven."

"Oh?"

"Willy wants to play *guitar*."

"For all the angels," said Josh, straight-faced.

That brought a smile to Katherine's face, and she wanted to tell them what an amazing boy Willy was. "He's a delight—a ray of sunshine in many ways," she said, keeping her comment short and to the point for fear of breaking down emotionally. Quickly, she exited, giving the little family some privacy.

Standing in the hallway just outside Willy's room, she breathed in deeply, wondering why she felt even more at a loss for words than she had when Laura lay dying. Willy was so terribly young—hadn't even had a chance to live—and now his life was ending.

She busied herself reading to several other patients, passing out cups of water in the common room, and sitting silently in the darkened room of another cancer patient. Hoping for another moment or two with Willy before she left for the day, Katherine was happy when his mother and brother came looking for her.

"We're going to the cafeteria for a snack," Willy's mother said. "Would you mind playing your guitar softly in the room until we return?"

"It's no use," Josh spoke up, his countenance glum. "Willy won't hear it anyway. He's dangling somewhere between earth and heaven."

Katherine cringed, remembering Nurse Judah's remark—that the boy might have only a few days at the longest.

When Mrs. Norton and Josh left, Katherine slipped back into Willy's room. He was lying very still in his bed, his little arm wrapped lovingly around all three of his teddy bears. Going over to stand at the side of his bed, she noticed the elephant card in his right hand.

In the quietude, she played a new song for him—a lilting, happy tune she composed as she went along. Strumming softly, she pictured a meadow with daisies and a hot sun high overhead. She and Willy were romping through the high grass, their faces flushed with the heat of summer.

"Are you married, Katherine?"

She could hear his innocent words, could see his blue, inquisitive eyes. Sweet . . . dear Willy. Dying.

She wished his cancer might go into remission, then he could be the boy who carried the ring at her and Justin's church wedding—the ring bearer, she thought it was called, though she couldn't be sure. Such a selfish thought; at least it might seem so to anyone who didn't truly know her.

"Will you have lots of children?"

She played on, changing keys as she sang the song just for him. It was a song of sheer joy, for the boy had given her much in the way of friendship, and on several occasions he'd offered her hope. Yet *she* had been the one volunteering to encourage *him*!

"God gives His people the desires of their hearts," he'd said once, startling her by adding something so profound that she could hardly comprehend it. *"If they're linked up with Him,"* he'd said.

At the time she had seen the sincerity in his eyes. Now,

thinking back to that moment, she wondered why such great faith hadn't given Willy *his* heart's desire. Could it be that the all-wise, all-knowing heavenly Father had a better plan for the child? Was *that* the reason Willy was dying?

Katherine played her guitar as beautifully as she ever had, thinking that it might very well be the last time. Her fingertips tender, she played till both Mr. and Mrs. Norton and Josh returned. Again, they thanked her for showing kindness to their son.

"I'm happy to have spent so much time with Willy," she said. "I can't begin to tell you the many things he's taught me."

His father nodded. "We're very proud of him."

When they'd said their good-byes, she excused herself and went to page Theodore, waiting outdoors where she could breathe the crisp, cold air. Her head needed a good airing out. "Dear Lord, must you take Willy now?" she prayed, reminding God of the child's youth. "He doesn't want to die. Please, could you reconsider?"

For the first time in her life, she did not feel that such a prayer was bossy or presumptuous.

CHAPTER NINETEEN

❖ ❖ ❖

Katherine took the call in the library, where she'd spent most of the morning reading.

Natalie Judah was on the line. "Hello, Katherine. I called to tell you about Willy Norton." She paused briefly. "I wanted you to know before you come in on Monday."

Katherine braced herself. "Yes?"

"The boy passed away in his sleep early this morning" came the report.

Silent, Katherine let the message seep into her consciousness. *Willy James Lee . . . gone.*

"Katherine? Are you all right?"

Immediately, her thoughts flew to Willy's parents and brother. "How's the family taking it?"

"Our spiritual-care people are with them now," Natalie assured her. "The family has a strong faith."

"Yes," she whispered. "Yes, I know."

After she had said good-bye, Katherine put in a call to Justin. She didn't feel much like having lunch with anyone today, exotic dining room or not. He answered on the first ring.

"I'm very sorry to cancel our luncheon date," she said. "But I don't believe I would be good company for you." She went on to tell him about Willy's passing.

"I'm sad to hear that, but perhaps you'll change your mind in a few hours. Why don't you page me later? You might feel like having something to eat after all."

It was generous of him to offer, she thought, extending himself that way. "Yes, well, I might, but I hope you won't be offended if I don't . . . not today."

"It's entirely your choice, Katherine. Whatever you decide, my dear."

"Thanks for understanding."

"Certainly. We'll talk later, or maybe tomorrow—as soon as you feel up to it."

When they'd hung up, she sat there in the stillness. Feeling suddenly hemmed in, the towering library shelves seemed to close in on her as she brooded. The tea table, with her books scattered on it, was near the fire, and a plate of cookies and other sweets enticed her to linger awhile.

Getting up, she wandered over to the windows, staring up at a clean sky. Only an occasional puff of a cloud, far in the distance, caught her attention. Yet she watched them drift, break into pieces, and float aimlessly across the expanse of blue.

She thought of Willy's passing in light of her Amish upbringing, and it wasn't so unnatural to think in terms of death being all wrapped up in life—merely part of the cycle we humans must celebrate. Funerals, as seen through the eye of one who'd experienced a good many of them in Hickory Hollow, were a gathering together of loved ones and friends to rejoice in the life of the deceased, no matter how short or long. No weeping and wailing over the loss of one of the People. "For every soul who goes, another will be born to take his place," Samuel Lapp used to say.

No, she would never want to wish Willy back. With the Lord's blessing—and Willy certainly seemed to have a corner on that—the boy would find his own mansion in paradise just fine.

Still, she felt overcome with grief. Another loss, one so close to the other. And she supposed—had she been given to drinking wine—that she might have been tempted to drown her sorrow. Instead, she turned to Laura's books, and for the next several hours lost herself in classic literature.

It was much later, after Justin had called to check up on her, that she felt compelled to visit her birth mother's grave. A quick call to Theodore brought the limousine promptly around to the front entrance.

There was precious little talk between herself and the chauffeur this time, even though a hint of spring in the air served to evoke frivolous chatter on the part of Theodore, the day being warm in contrast to the severe weather of past weeks.

"I certainly wouldn't think it would be much longer until spring is more than official," said Theodore, looking dapper as usual. "We're on the downside of bitter weather, if I do say so myself."

He had a pleasant pattern of speech—a kind of good-natured, yet British way of bantering—with or without the listener ever having to interact. The sound of his voice was as warm and welcome as her long-deceased Dawdi David's approach to loafing around with other Amishmen. They'd huddled together on many a springlike day, sitting out under the shade of their gnarled oak tree on a low wooden bench, chewing the fat—some of them chewing the tobacco leaf, too.

Katherine listened without comment. After a time, though, she was less aware of his soft patter and more absorbed in her own private thoughts.

The cemetery was several miles from town, situated off one of the county roads a bit. The burial place—removed from urban life, yet accessible enough for visitors, be they mourners or merely lovers of nature—was as serene as it was haunting.

Huge iron gates yawning open reminded her that it was also quite secluded and separate from the rest of Canandaigua. This, she was fairly certain, was the reason Laura's parents had purchased burial plots here years ago.

The trees seemed taller than she'd remembered. Today they created an entangled sanctuary of branches high above the gravel road that stretched, narrow and bending, around the sections of the graveyard.

She imagined the place in full summer, the orchard to the south filled with bees moiling the magic of pollination, the lovely, fragrant smells, the margin of woods to the east where tall goldenrod and ironweed would bloom tawny gold and sky blue come autumn, where starlings bickered and swallows swooped down to say hello.

Katherine, awestruck by her surroundings, had never felt so vulnerable, so breathless, in the Amish cemeteries in Lancaster County. Yet she simply could not shrug off the heaviness as she donned her snow boots and left the limousine to search for her birth mother's headstone.

Minutes later, she stood in front of Laura Mayfield-Bennett's grave and silently read the words etched on the stone. " 'But the salvation of the righteous is of the Lord: he is their strength in the time of trouble.' "

The salvation of the righteous . . .

These words, read by one of the ministers at the funeral, had been ever so dear to Laura. Reading them again, Katherine felt the vigor, the unexpected drawing power.

Dropping to her knees in the snow, she began to share her secret grief. "Oh, Mother, I never understood the things you said as you were dying. Not fully. You were such a kind and compassionate woman. Everyone who knew you says so. I only wish I might've known you longer . . . better."

She sighed. "There's a dear little boy. His name is—

was—Willy, and I came to love him in spite of his terminal disease. But now he's gone. I never, never dreamed I could care so much for a child . . . one who was not my own."

Pausing, she heard the gentle wind in the trees, the hushed reverence around her. "Willy has two middle names, Mother. Something I've never heard of, but he has them all the same. Surely Willy James Lee must be skipping down the golden streets, playing ball with the other children in paradise along about now. I was just hoping that you might be able to look out for him, dear Mother. He was such a fragile boy. Will you care for him for me?"

She couldn't quite get out *until I can come and watch over him myself.* Feelings of unworthiness kept her from voicing it, though she knew that someday she would have to reckon with her choice: either for or against the blessed faith of both young Willy and benevolent Laura. She could not continue on much longer, torn between her unyielding past and the indoctrination of her childhood and the gentle, life-giving passages of God's Word. And she was puzzled as to why it seemed that at every turn she kept stumbling into some biblical reminder of divine love.

CHAPTER TWENTY

◈   ◈   ◈

The day trip to Niagara Falls fell on the following Sunday, much to Katherine's dismay, although when she mentioned attending church, Justin promised to take her the next opportunity he had.

"The Taylors—Fulton and Rosie—go there," she told him, hoping to engage him in some conversation about his religious beliefs.

"Ah, churches . . . they're a dime a dozen around here." His comment left her cold, though she continued to pursue the topic.

"Did your parents ever teach you about God when you were small?"

"Not, perhaps, as much as yours did, though I did attend an occasional summer church camp." He smiled at her from behind the wheel of his own car. They'd decided to abandon the limousine and chauffeur, giving them more privacy for the day. Actually, it was Justin's idea, and Katherine was rather glad about it.

"Church camp? What was it like?"

He mentioned a few hair-raising scenes of boys catching toads from the creek and hiding them in the girls' quarters, but nothing of spiritual substance.

"What made it church related?" she inquired.

He reached over and took her hand. "Is everything all right today, Katherine? It seems you've talked of nothing but church and God since we left town."

She nodded. "Yes . . . I'm curious, I guess you could say."

He squeezed her hand. "Your loss of young Willy, is it?"

Tears sprang up unexpectedly. "I . . . I miss him . . . terribly," she stammered.

Justin pressed the turn signal and pulled over on the shoulder, slowing down gradually, then coming to a complete stop. "Katherine, darling." He gathered her into his arms, and she wept for the little boy who'd seemed to know her heart with such ease. "His pain is past," Justin whispered into her hair.

She snuggled next to him, her face against the smooth lapel of his overcoat. "I never thought he'd die. . . ."

"Sh-h, now, don't say more. You'll be fine, Katherine. I'll take good care of you."

When she'd regained her composure, the subject of Willy seemed to fade naturally, and she hoped her emotional state hadn't altered the course of the day.

"I want to show you my art studio sometime," he said later as they entered the Niagara Falls tourist area and headed for the lookout tower. "Would you like that?"

She smiled, glad her tears were over. "Very much."

"My painting is nearly complete now, and I'd like your opinion of it."

Hearing that he wanted to include her in his professional life—even just showing her around his work studio—was an exhilarating thought. "I'd be happy to see your work."

They found a parking spot close to the lookout on the American side, and Katherine was in awe of the movement of the vast river as it plunged over the falls. Even at this distance, the mighty surge of power was riveting.

Standing next to Justin, she felt a bit nervous at the

thunderous roar. To think that stunt men had braved tight-ropes and barrels and lived to tell about it!

"What are you thinking?" he asked, slipping his arm around her shoulders.

"This place . . . it's the most unbelievable sight I've ever seen."

"There are many wondrous and scenic spots in the world. This happens to be one of my favorites, close to home." He turned to face her. "It's only the beginning of what I want to show you, my darling."

Her heart beat wildly as he caressed her face with his hands, leaning down for their first kiss. His lips were sweet and lingered gently. Smiling into her eyes, he said, "Some-day we'll bring our children to see the majesty of these falls."

Our children . . .

She had to suppress a giggle. Justin was taking much for granted. He hadn't even asked her to marry him yet!

They strolled along the walkway, Justin's arm curved protectively around her waist. Nothing more was said about their future for the rest of the excursion. No "popping of the question," as Rosie had so humorously called it.

Katherine fell into bed late that night after enjoying another candlelight supper with fine food and music, won-dering what Justin had said or done to cause her such dis-satisfaction. Thinking back through the entire day, she knew she ought to have been on "cloud nine," as Rosie or Leoma might say. But something was troubling her, and she couldn't put her finger on it.

❖ ❖ ❖

Rachel Esler called first thing the next morning, and for a moment, Katherine wasn't sure who was on the line. "Who did you say you were?"

"Ach, I'm sorry" came the Amish reply. "Guess I must've

forgotten to tell ya that we met over at the mall at the card shop. You gave your phone number to my sister and me."

Katherine now knew exactly who was calling. "Of course I remember you, Rachel. You had me stumped there for a minute, because you sounded like one of my relatives—back in Pennsylvania."

"Jah, I see. Well," the girl continued, "I wanted to let ya know that my sisters—all three of them—and our mother would like to help you finish off your Country Songbird quilt for the hospice bazaar."

"Really? You do?"

"For sure and for certain" came the familiar reply. "We could come for two or three hours at a time but only on weekdays."

"I understand," she said. This was too good to be true!

"So when do ya plan your next frolic?" Rachel inquired.

Frolic? Katherine hadn't heard the word in ages. What a lovely sound—so charming, she nearly forgot to answer the caller's question. "Uh . . . *when?* This Wednesday evening, we'll meet again."

"Gut, then." Rachel went on to ask if there would be enough people in all to have twelve quilters.

"Let's see . . ." Katherine thought for a minute. "There's seven of us here and five of you. Perfect!"

"We'll see ya after supper on Wednesday then."

"Thank you, Rachel. Good-bye."

She spun around, twisting the phone cord about her. "This is wonderful-gut," she announced so loudly that Rosie and Leoma leaned their heads into the French doors.

"Sorry," she said, untangling the cord while the housemaids exchanged comical glances.

"Must be something about Justin Wirth," she heard Rosie say as the women turned to leave.

Katherine had herself a good chuckle—somewhat subdued, however—over that. Wouldn't the ladies be surprised to meet their new quilting comrades?

❖ ❖ ❖

The studio tour was enlightening, and Justin was quite the humble host as he showed her around the next weekend. Most remarkable of all was his oil painting of Mayfield Manor—Katherine's estate.

"Oh, it's amazing," she cooed, looking closely to inspect the detail, then stepping back to survey the grandeur. "You really captured the feel of the place."

He smiled, standing off to himself in the corner, where books on castles and bridges stood on a display shelf, facing out.

"I mean it, Justin. You're branching out, aren't you?"

His arms were folded tightly against his chest, his expression serious and subdued. "I've always been most interested in portraying people, but more lately—and I'm not exactly sure why, unless it has something to do with the splendor of your mansion—I've become fascinated by architecture and nature."

She went to him, resting both hands on his folded arms. "So *that's* why you took me to Niagara Falls. You're going to paint it, too. Am I right?"

He unwrapped his arms and pulled her close. "What do you think? Is it a good idea?" he asked, his lips pleasantly close to her face.

The smell of his breath, his musk cologne, all of it made her wish he'd say how much he loved her . . . ask her the important question. Instead, he waited for her response, gazing down into her eyes.

"I, uh, should think the water would be hard to paint, especially because it's moving so quickly," she managed to say.

Gently, he brushed the tip of her nose with his lips, gave

her a loving hug, and led her by the hand to his easel. There, he began pointing out various brush strokes that would lend themselves well to depicting the motion of the Niagara River. "So you see, it *is* possible to capture such energy and movement with paint," he said quite adamantly.

"Yes, I think I see that." It was obvious the man was fond of his work, and rightly so, for he was as talented as he was admirable. And at that moment, Katherine was altogether sure he was the dearest man in all the world.

CHAPTER TWENTY-ONE

❖ ❖ ❖

The pipe organ enthralled Katherine with a piece she'd never heard before—*The Palms*—though she wondered if Justin's presence on this day, Palm Sunday, might not have enhanced the musical experience for her.

Churchgoers thronged the chapel, joyfully looking ahead to Easter. Katherine heeded the minister's message, hoping to discuss some of the Scriptures with Justin over dinner.

The topic that seemed to be most interesting to him, however, was another trip. "To Toronto, Canada," he mentioned as they dined. "What do you say, Katherine? Will you come with me?"

He told her of his plan to sketch one of the cathedrals there. "We could have a lovely time, just the two of us."

She felt somewhat awkward about it, unsure of the travel plans. "I . . . wouldn't want to miss out on my scheduled days at the hospice or the quilting sessions," she told him.

"No, no, I don't want you to forego any of your plans." He brushed aside her unspoken concerns. "We could leave on a Friday evening, after your quilting group and return by Sunday night."

She didn't need to remind him that they weren't married; therefore, she would not feel comfortable sharing a hotel room with him. Miraculously, she didn't have to bring up the subject. He must've seen the puzzlement on her face—she didn't really know how he knew—but he winked at her and assured her that they'd acquire separate rooms.

"Could we wait to go until after Easter?" she asked, longing to attend church on that special day.

Justin's response was not as animated as she had hoped it might be, but he agreed to postpone the trip. So it was set. He made all the necessary arrangements in regard to accommodations; Katherine merely had to alert her domestic staff.

Rosie raised her eyebrows when Katherine filled her in on the details. The maid's eyebrows stayed up when Katherine explained that she'd toured Justin's art studio as well.

"Hm-m, it's starting to sound more serious between the two of you," Rosie said with a curious smile.

"I think he must love me, or he wouldn't be spending so much time taking me to dinners and nice places."

Rosie's eyes penetrated hers. "But do *you* love him?"

"I care for Justin very much, if that's what you mean."

"Does he share your interest in church?" The question was as pointed a comment as Rosie had ever made.

Katherine didn't quite know how to answer, other than to be completely honest. "I suppose not."

Rosie said no more. Katherine, however, felt she wanted to defend Justin's lack of interest in religion. After all, America was the land of the free, wasn't it? Yet something kept her from speaking up, something desperate and hidden from view.

❖ ❖ ❖

The afternoon sky was featureless, but the road that stretched ahead for miles took Dan past two covered bridges, a single one-room schoolhouse, and numerous farmhouses. He recognized the private lanes leading into his relatives' barnyards—knew them like the back of his hand. Yet coming here, uninvited, on an off-Sunday, posed definite drawbacks for a shunned member of the Amish church.

Starting out first thing after church, he had decided it was high time he laid eyes on his namesake, four-month-old Daniel Lapp. Impulsively, he'd set out for Lancaster County, not bothering to stop for lunch. Annie would be surprised, he knew, but she wouldn't turn him away, not even if Elam were home. He could count on her warming up some left-overs for him, too, though she'd not let him eat at the same table. Without question.

Her face brightened pink when she spied him at the door, then paled considerably when he bent down to kiss her cheek. "I've waited too long to see my young nephew," he said, apologizing for not letting her know ahead of time. "Hope it's not an inconvenience."

"Puh! Come on in, Dan." She quickly closed the door behind him. "Elam might not be too happy about havin' you here much—not too long, anyways—but *I'm* glad you came!"

He understood. "I'll stay only a short time," he promised, following her into the kitchen.

She set to work immediately, pulling food out of the pantry. "You must be starved, drivin' all that way."

"I'll eat whatever you give me." He glanced around at the familiar trappings of the kitchen: the corner cupboard that housed the big German Bible and other books, the typical calendar hanging on the back of the cellar door, the trestle table in the middle of the floor, the woodstove, the hickory rocker, and the dark green blinds wound up tight and high at the windows. One Amish kitchen was like any other, comforting and familiar.

Annie called to Elam in the front room. "Daniel's here for a visit."

Thinking it was nice that she hadn't said a "quick visit," Dan felt more comfortable, though he knew they wouldn't feel too kindly about him wearing out his welcome—being under the Meinding and all.

"Would you like for me to get the folding table out of the cellar?" he offered.

Annie shook her head. "You sit yourself right down at the big table, Dan. Nobody's gonna be sittin' there with ya anyhow."

She looked so young to be married and a mother already, he thought. And if he wasn't mistaken, she wore the blush of motherhood on her cheeks and in her eyes—he'd seen it enough times to know that she was probably expecting her second baby come early autumn.

"Well, Daniel, what brings you here?" Elam asked, standing in the doorway between the kitchen and the front room. His high forehead and blond hair immediately reminded Dan of Rebecca Lapp, though the lack of a smile hid the dimples so prominent on his mother's face.

"I came to meet your son . . . my nephew."

"Let's see if the baby's awake." Elam left the kitchen and headed for the stairs.

Annie smiled sweetly. "I'm sure Daniel's up." She glanced at the day clock high over the sink. "It's been an hour or more since I put him down for a nap. Such a gut baby . . ."

Soon Elam came downstairs carrying the blanketed bundle.

"Ach, hold him up," Annie said, going over and leaning on her husband's arm. "He's right big already. Jah?"

They removed the blanket, and Elam held little Daniel up in the air, the baby's feet kicking and his arms flapping about, till Annie rescued the poor thing. She reached for him and cradled him in her arms, coming around to the opposite side of the table where Dan sat in front of a plate of chunky potato salad, homemade bread spread with honey-butter and jam, and cold slices of chicken. "Here's the little fella," she said, bringing him over to Dan.

Surprised at first, he took the squirming mass of humanity and looked into the bright blue eyes. "Hello there, young man. I'm your uncle Dan Fisher."

The baby didn't fuss as Dan expected, just stared up at him and cooed. The weight of the tiny body in his arms, the little round eyes looking back at him, and the joyful gurglings—all of it stirred something in him, and he wondered what it would be like to father and raise a fine son or two or three someday.

The shape of young Daniel's mouth and chin line reminded Dan of himself. Though he hadn't ever seen himself in pictures as a youngster, for there had never been photos taken—not even snapshots—not of any of the People all those years. Still there was something terribly familiar about the baby's facial features. He felt as if he were looking into a mirror, one that reflected the past. "All the little fella needs is a beard and we could pass for twins."

Annie agreed. "I thought the same thing when he was first born. There's a strong family likeness."

"Suppose I ought to shave my beard. That would work just as well." He was laughing now, which seemed to amuse the baby, who reached up and pulled on his beard.

"Mary's about to marry herself the bishop," Annie said, pulling up one of the rocking chairs.

Elam stood close to the table, eyeing Dan—his eyes watching the baby like a hawk. "Won't be a public weddin', this one," he spoke up. "Last I heard, they were ridin' over to SummerHill come Saturday afternoon."

"The day before Easter—ain't that nice?" Annie said.

"Speakin' of Zooks, Ella Mae had a stroke here a while

back," Elam spoke up, shifting his weight from one foot to the other. "I only say that because you two were close."

Dan caught his breath. "Will she be all right?"

"She's a fighter, Ella Mae is," Annie said. "I 'spect she'll get over her paralysis in due time. She'd wanna see ya if she knew you were in town."

Dan shook his head. "I'll have to come back and see her some other time."

"Well, then, I won't say nothin' about you bein' here."

The baby started to fuss, and Annie came quickly to take him from Dan. Holding the baby in one arm, she pulled the rocker across the floor closer to the woodstove, sat down, and began to nurse him.

Dan picked up his fork and lit in to the food his sister had been so kind to set out for him. Elam made an awkward grunt and left the room. Daniel ate in silence and Annie sat quietly; the only noise in the room came from the little one making contented sucking sounds.

"I suppose you found Katie already," Annie said softly, without looking at him.

He sighed, wiping his mouth with the paper napkin. "Turned out she didn't want to be found."

Annie's eyes were on him now. "She's a right hard one to figure."

He nodded. "She's Katherine Mayfield now . . . lives in a mansion. Even has a houseful of servants looking after her." He was thinking of the dutiful butler he'd encountered at the front door.

"I can't imagine Katie livin' that way—right fancy and all."

"You wouldn't be so shocked to see her, Annie. Under all those nice clothes, there's still a girl from Hickory Hollow. You'd recognize her. I know you would."

"What's she gonna do up there all alone?" asked Annie, rocking hard.

"The Lord's up there in New York, too. Same as He is with you and Elam and little Daniel. Prayer can change things for Katie. You'll see."

"Then what about *you*?" she asked, casting a disparaging look at him. "When's God gonna answer my prayers and bring you back home?"

He knew he shouldn't start to defend his beliefs. Not now. Not here in Elam's house. His prayers for his loved ones would be more effective than anything he could say on his first visit back since the shunning.

When it came time to say good-bye, tears welled up in Annie's eyes. "Ach, I miss ya so, Daniel. Come back to the People. We could use another gut pair of hands here in the Hollow." She reminded him that their father was getting up in years, that Dat could use more help than he was already getting.

"Sure, I'd love to come home, but I can't." His soul-deep need for family—the loved ones he'd grown up with—remained ever strong, yet he resisted explaining why he could never return to the Amish church.

She clung to him, and he hugged her hard, leaning his cheek down against her devotional kapp. "I love you, Annie."

"The People are ever so anxious to hear your confession. Please . . . don't wait too long" was her soft reply.

Elam didn't wave at him when Dan turned to go to the car. He stayed inside with the baby.

It was Annie who followed him down the back walk to his car. "Won'tcha think about it, Dan?"

"I've done all I can possibly do. The Lord's in control of my life now." He said the words, though he knew she might not comprehend.

"Will ya come again?"

He nodded, waving. "Take good care of my nephew."

That brought a smile. "Good-bye, Daniel."

Getting in the car, he turned the ignition. The engine roared to life, and his last glimpse of Annie was of her closing the back door, eyes cast down as if she might cry again. Then she was gone.

CHAPTER TWENTY-TWO

◆   ◆   ◆

With Katherine's help, Selig baked up another batch of Mississippi Mud for the quilting class. Mrs. Esler and her daughters—Rachel, Ruth, Nancy, and Anna—arrived by horse and buggy about six o'clock.

Standing at the window in the drawing room, Katherine watched as Rachel Esler helped her mother out of the buggy, followed by the other girls. One unhitched the horse and tied him to the fence post in the grassy area on the far side of the driveway.

She remembered the first time she'd ever taken a harness off a horse, the feel of the warm leather in her hands. It was a heavy chore for a young girl, so Dat had helped her. Still, something about the memory made her miss Satin Boy, her first-ever pony. She sincerely hoped her mild-mannered pet was adjusting all right without her, that Benjamin was taking good care of him.

Noticing that the group of Amishwomen was now heading toward the house, Katherine moved away from the draped window and hurried across the room to the grand entryway, to be ready when the doorbell rang.

"Please, come in and make yourself at home," she said,

greeting Mrs. Esler once again, as well as the two daughters she'd met at the gift shop.

Rachel introduced her older sisters, Nancy and Anna. "They were awful excited to come and see your mansion," she added.

"And here you are," said Katherine as the butler took their wraps. "Would you like to see the place?"

Shyly, the sisters nodded their heads. "Well, come along, then." And she signaled for Fulton to assist with the tour.

The evening turned out to be one of the most joyous ones she'd spent at the mansion—much laughter and story-telling and, of course, the delicious Mississippi Mud dessert and various flavors of coffees served up by Selig and Garrett.

Mrs. Esler and her daughters were a cheerful addition to the quilting class. In fact, in many ways, the five of them helped Katherine teach the others. All in all, it was a night of hard work and fun mixed together in one delightful package of inspiration and relaxation.

"We'll come again next Wednesday," said Mrs. Esler as they prepared to leave.

"Good Friday's a fast day for us," Rachel explained.

Katherine recalled that the Amish in Hickory Hollow also observed the day as a prayerful one. "Maybe *we* won't work on the quilt Good Friday, either," she spoke up, and Rosie, Leoma, and the other non-Amish women agreed.

When she returned to her private sitting room, Katherine found herself reflecting on Mrs. Esler and her girls. Their patient, agreeable way with English folk struck her as appealing, and she truly hoped that her housemaids and the entire domestic staff felt the same about her. Before she dressed for bed, she decided that she, too, would fast and pray come Good Friday, just like her new friends.

◈   ◈   ◈

It was the bluest, clearest day of April. Each breath Mary took in was as sweet as could be, for it was her wedding day. And the day before Easter, of all things.

She and Bishop John had agreed that they'd get married in SummerHill, not but a few miles from Hickory Hollow, across the highway, up Snake Road, out past Hunsecker Mill Bridge, and on over to Preacher Zook's church district. It made right-gut sense to Mary, too. After all, John had already been through his share of wedding services, the last of which had turned into a miserable day for all concerned. No sense going to all the trouble of a full-blown wedding. Besides, it being the wrong season for a wedding in Lancaster County, this was the best way.

The children—all five of them—rode to Preacher Zook's big farmhouse with them in the enclosed buggy. The day was warmer than any she'd experienced in ages, and because of the springtime weather, Mary thought it must surely be a good sign. She could only hope that it was, for she'd waited her whole life long for this one, special day.

She turned to look over her shoulder at the bishop's children, sitting so tall and straight, going to their Daed's wedding. *I hope I can be a wonderful-gut Mamma to them*, she thought almost sadly, ever so sorry for the lonely years they'd been without Miriam, their dear mother—John's first wife.

When it came time for her to say "jah," promising to be loyal to John Beiler, to care for him in all hardship, affliction, illness, weakness, or faintheartedness, her heart opened up with great love and compassion for this man. She would show him the kind of affection that he deserved, no matter that he'd shunned her dearest and best friend. No matter that he was thought of as a rigid, *standhaft* bishop. Sure as the dawn, she desired to love him, to serve him, to be his faithful wife till the day she died.

After the short ceremony, Nancy and Susie both kissed

her cheek. Hickory John, Levi, and young Jacob shook her hand, but Jacob sneaked in a quick hug when no one was looking. "I've got me a mamma now," he said, then scampered off to play outside with Preacher Zook's children.

Mary had to smile. "And I've got me a family of my own," she whispered, watching as Jacob's little legs carried him across the barnyard.

Turning back to her handsome husband, she wondered how on earth she could break this news to Katie, especially now. She'd heard from Annie Lapp that Dan had been in town last Sunday, and from what he'd told his sister, the poor lad was heartsick over Katie—not being received too well by her and all.

Was it the right thing to share her joyous news, let Katie know that her friend had found true happiness right here in Hickory Hollow? Because it sounded, for all the world, as if there was someone awful sad and alone up there in New York.

CHAPTER TWENTY-THREE

❖ ❖ ❖

On Easter morning, Katherine arose early and hurried to the closet. She slipped into her warmest robe and house slippers, then scurried to the kitchen at the other end of the house. Gut! No one was about.

Opening the refrigerator, she took out the square plastic box the florist had delivered to her yesterday afternoon. Eager to see the lovely corsage without being observed, she decided to take it to her suite. Back in the privacy of her own room, she opened the lid and lifted the delicate arrangement of tiny pink rosebuds and a sprig of the daintiest baby's breath she'd ever seen. The fragrance was as pure as any rose her Amish mamma had ever grown in the family rose garden. Maybe all the sweeter because it came from Justin.

The card that had arrived with the corsage had thrilled her upon first reading it. *Wishing you an Easter filled with love. Yours always, Justin.* Even more thrilling was the fact that he would be sitting beside her in church!

Written in his own hand, the words now delighted her once again, and she savored the prospect of a lovely day.

❖ ❖ ❖

Outside, the air was warm and breezy, and the sky was as blue as a robin's egg, with not a hint of rain. A perfect Easter Sunday. Justin drove her to church in his own car, and she was secretly glad they could talk without being overheard by a chauffeur.

Glorious music, both choral and organ, filled the church before and after the sermon. Katherine battled thoughts of Dan upon hearing the offertory—*Hallelujah, What A Savior!*—a hymn she'd sung at some of the livelier Singings at SummerHill get-togethers during her teen years. But she couldn't allow anything or anyone to spoil her day with Justin, and she tilted her head slightly to breathe in the sweet scent of the flowers pinned to her cream-colored linen blazer. Glancing down, she smoothed her tea-length floral skirt, marveling again at the feel of the lovely fabric, so unlike the coarse and heavy homespun dresses of the past.

She daydreamed periodically during the sermon, though she wouldn't have wanted to admit it to a soul, this being a house of worship. Yet she had difficulty keeping her eyes fixed on the pulpit, so preoccupied was she in scanning the sanctuary and thinking how nice it would be to have her and Justin's wedding here. A candlelight service . . . in the fall. Yes, that's what she would like. Her vows to Justin should take place at dawn, just as the earth held its breath, awaiting the sun's rays; the emerging of little birds from their nests, the mist hugging the trees at the gossamer first light of daybreak.

She glanced at Justin to her left, wondering if he, too, might be thinking similar thoughts. He caught her eye and smiled, then reached for her hand. Katherine's heart beat a bit faster, and she hoped he would kiss her again, sometime today. Easter Sunday . . . after dinner perhaps.

❖ ❖ ❖

"Ach, I've never missed an Easter Sunday Preachin' in all my born days," Ella Mae complained, her speech still awkward.

"It's out of the question, Mamma."

"But I'm feelin' gut already."

"Sorry, Mam. You best stay home today."

She wanted to fuss some more, make a bigger bother about not getting to go to Preaching, but she knew by the determined look on Mattie's face, not to mention the frustrated sighs, that her daughter wasn't going to budge an inch.

"You've had a bad stroke, for goodness' sake," Mattie said, straightening the quilt at the bottom of the bed.

"I won't enjoy bein' alone." Her final attempt at guilt. There was no reply, though, and she figured Mattie was trying to make a point by shuffling out of the room and down the hall.

The house was mighty quiet with everybody gone over to Jake and Becky Zook's—her son and daughter-in-law's place. Ella Mae felt just awful about it, missing out on Easter the first time ever. "I oughta up and die," she said, chuckling a bit. "Would serve 'em right for leavin' me behind like this."

She didn't feel quite bad enough to die, though. With all that exercising of arms and legs her friends and relatives were insisting on doing, she was actually improving, even getting her speech back little by little. And best of all her mobility.

Scooting herself up in bed, she reached behind her and folded her pillows in half to support her back. It would do her good to read away the hours, help pass the time till David and Mattie returned. 'Course, they wouldn't be so unthinking as to stay for the common meal after the sermons. No, they'd come on home, and Mattie would fix up some cold cuts, maybe even warm up some potato soup. Jah, she'd like that just fine.

The book she chose to read was one Lydia Miller had brought over just yesterday. Lydia had always been a faithful friend, but here lately—ever since Ella Mae's stroke—the dear girl had come nearly every day, bringing flowers from an English florist or her own homemade soups or an occasional book. Goodies, too. Jah, Lydia knew what made her smile.

The book she held in her hands was far different than anything she'd ever read. It was a small book, told from an Amishwoman's viewpoint, about how she witnessed to the folk who came to her bed-and-breakfast establishment. Ella Mae had to smile when she read the prologue, describing the real-life woman. It seemed downright uncanny that something like that was going on right here in Lancaster County. Maybe because she'd thought of doing something very much like it, back years ago.

As it turned out, she'd opened her heart and her hearth to many a weary soul, eventually relinquishing the idea of an Amish B&B. Still, she found the reading interesting—oh, so true. The woman, who'd assumed a pen name, had the right idea. A wonderful-gut idea it was to pass along the love of the Lord. 'Course, she didn't suppose the woman had to contend with such a strict bishop as John Beiler. But from what she knew of marriage, she figured the bishop was long overdue for some tender, loving care. Maybe just the thing to soften him up some. She only hoped that young Mary was up to the task of keeping a husband happy and five *mun-der*—oh, so lively—children well fed. Still, if anyone could do it, she s'pected plump and perty Mary Stoltzfus was the one for the job.

Ella Mae reined in her wandering thoughts and got into the book real deep, turning one page after another, laughing here and there, imagining herself doing just what the B&B owner had done.

The pages captured and held her interest until she

drifted off—not quite knowing when it happened or if she'd read through to the end of the book. But when she awoke with a start, she found the book half covering her face, open to a page toward the back.

"Dear me," she mumbled, sitting up. "Wonder what time it could be."

She listened, hearing voices in the main house. David and Mattie were home. She wouldn't call out to them, she decided. She'd sit, silent as a snipe, and wait for the report of the Preachin' service she'd missed.

◈　◈　◈

Katherine was excited about the upcoming trip to Toronto, although she wasn't sure why. She had only the vaguest idea of what to expect from such a trip. Time to talk and share each other's goals and hopes for the future was high on her list.

"I'm thinking of painting your Songbird quilt when it's finished," Justin said as they rode along the highway, heading north. "I think it will be a unique approach to art."

She was surprised. "I never would have thought of such a thing, but it sounds interesting."

Justin turned and winked at her. "Think about it. When have you ever seen a rendering of an Amish quilt on canvas?"

It was an absolutely wonderful idea. Katherine could hardly wait for him to begin, but the quilt itself had to be completed before Justin could paint it. And there was the matter of the hospice bazaar. "How will it work—if the quilt's going to be sold in a few weeks?"

"Oh," he said, frowning. "I hadn't thought of that."

They discussed his exciting idea, thinking of various ways to approach the problem. Katherine suggested taking a photograph, but Justin didn't think he could capture the essence of the quilt from a photo. Finally, Katherine said, "Maybe you could sketch the pattern ahead of time. You could come to my quilting class and begin a pencil drawing as we work."

He nodded, grinning. "Splendid idea!"

She didn't say so, but she was thrilled at his response. Having Justin come to the mansion two or three hours on Wednesday and Friday evenings would be delightful. She was glad she'd thought of it.

❖   ❖   ❖

The first few hours in Toronto were spent locating one particular cathedral, then taking photographs of it for Justin's file. Katherine enjoyed watching him angle the poses with his expensive camera, but most of all, the trip gave her ample time with her Beau.

While there, she began composing a letter to Mary, anxious to tell her about her new love and inquiring about life in Hickory Hollow.

By the time they returned to Canandaigua, she realized how much she had enjoyed Justin's company. So much that she had not thought of Dan Fisher. Not even once.

CHAPTER TWENTY-FOUR

❖　　❖　　❖

Days and weeks sped by, and with the delicate shifting of the season to summer, Katherine began to enjoy the warmer weather, though the temperatures weren't nearly as hot as she remembered them in southeastern Pennsylvania—not for late June. Still, she had plenty of picnics out-of-doors, several with her new friends—Rachel Esler and her sisters—and two barbecues for the terminally ill patients at the hospice.

And there was a steak fry for two. She and Justin had spread out a blanket on the south lawn near the lily pond, behind the mansion, enjoying the birds and sky and laughing softly. They talked about anything that came to mind, then sat quietly, reveling in the warmth of the still air and the music of nature. To top off the day, Justin had presented her with a delicate gold locket in the shape of a heart, which she'd worn ever since.

The quilts—the Ninepatch *and* the Country Songbird—were long since completed, with the expert help of her Amish friends. Justin's painting of a colorful quilt flapping on a clothesline, as well as his version of Niagara Falls in full moonlight, left exhibitors standing wide-eyed and Katherine herself in awe of his talent.

She couldn't imagine a life more blissful. Yet she found herself thinking of Mary's letters almost daily, even discussed her concern with Justin one evening as they ate apple pie and ice cream on the screened-in, second-floor balcony high above the estate grounds.

"Mary seemed almost reluctant to mention her marriage to John," she said, recalling the letter that had come the week after Easter. "I hope she isn't worried that marrying the bishop will change our friendship."

Justin's eyes were intent on her. "Mary means a lot to you, doesn't she, darling?"

"We're as close as sisters."

"The way I see it, if the shunning didn't keep the two of you apart, neither will a new husband."

"I hope not." She described for him the bishop's severe course of action once it was clear that she was not going to confess—about not having destroyed the guitar.

"Sometimes people change," he said, his soothing voice attempting to console her.

"You don't know John Beiler."

"No, but I know what love can do, especially for an unfeeling sort of man." He continued on, telling her about one of his uncles on his mother's side. "The man was the harshest fellow you'd ever want to meet. Even young children shied away from him. Dogs cowered, cats hissed. . . ."

She thought about that. "What made him change?"

Justin smiled. "It may be hard to believe, but I think for him it had to do with finding the right woman, though I wouldn't say the perfect mate is always going to alter someone's bad behavior. In the case of my uncle, though, it did."

She pondered Justin's true-life story. Hard as she tried to imagine it, Mary's patient, loving ways would never be apt to transform the bishop of Hickory Hollow, not entirely. Yet the more she thought about Mary married to John, the more she suspected that her friend was the force behind the lifting of the talking aspect of the shunning. Surely *that* was the truth.

For the first time in many weeks, she thought of Dan. How severely had John Beiler shunned *him*?

❖ ❖ ❖

Mary didn't have time to go out and get the mail—not a minute to spare—until nearly four o'clock. By the time she wiped her hands on a towel and ran outside barefooted, it was almost time for afternoon milking. 'Course Hickory John, Nancy, and Levi were probably already out in the barn bringing in the cows. No need to be frettin' over that chore. Bishop John's children pretty much knew what to do and when to do it. Just keeping up with the mountains of laundry, the constant cleaning and cooking, and whatnot all, left Mary near breathless most days. Still, she wouldn't have gone back to being a single lady for all the world. Her life revolved around her husband and his children, and if anyone had asked, she would've declared she was the happiest woman alive!

Now with summer in full swing, she was worn to a frazzle, so hot and humid it was. Fanning herself with a hankie, she sat down to catch her breath and read a letter from her rich and fancy girlfriend.

Tuesday, June 30

Dearest Mary,

Will you be happy for me if I tell you that I think I know who I'm going to marry? His name is Justin Wirth, and he's an artist—paints beautiful oil paintings. I don't remember when I've ever been so happy, Mary. Honestly, it's strange this feeling I have about Justin. We talk for hours about most anything, even personal things these days. I'm so glad that I can share this with you freely and

*do hope that you won't worry about my future with an
Englischer.*

*I don't know how you'll be able to come for my wed-
ding, though I'd feel completely lost if you weren't here to
share my joy. Do you think John would consent to let you
ride the bus?*

*When I look at the sky, I never see a single cloud—even
when they're scattered everywhere! Oh, Mary, did you feel
this way when first you fell in love with John? Did you?*

*More than anything, I wish I might've witnessed your
vows, seeing the precious little Beiler children gathered all
about you there in Preacher Zook's front room. How sweet
that they could share the special day with both you and
the bishop. Although I have written this before, I will repeat
that I have no hard feelings about you ending up with
John. I trust he treats you with the kind of love that you
deserve, my dear friend.*

> *Forever and always,*
> *Katherine*

The porch swing creaked a long time after Mary finished
reading. Pushing her bare toes against the wooden floor, she
sat quietly, taking in the cornfield across the road while Katie's letter lay in her lap. She remembered the summer days
of her childhood, growing up with Katie Lapp—the girl
with all the adventuresome ideas. Like the time they played
hidey-seek in the cornfield, the stalks being so thick and all,
neither of them could find the other. By dinnertime, she was
gut and lost . . . and crying her eyes out.

She had to smile a little, thinking back to what Samuel
Lapp had said about Katie playing in the cornfield with her
girlfriend. "Best be careful, girls." He'd looked mighty serious, almost worried. " 'Tis a gut way to get yourselves harvested."

Of course, they'd burst out laughing at what he'd said,

and *he* had, too. But Mary never let Katie talk her into playing in the corn again.

She sighed, ignoring the flies and several mewing barn cats looking for a handout. Katie was gonna marry a right fancy artist, she said in her letter. Sure sounded like she was just gonna forget all about her Plain upbringing, keep on turning her back on redemption, and be right contented with her new English life.

Mary sighed so hard she pushed all her wind out, then all of a sudden realized that Jacob was hollering for her out back. Quickly, she returned the letter to its linen envelope and hurried down the porch steps, around the side of the house, past her pansy garden, and to the barnyard to see what on earth was ailing her stepson. Later on, when she had time to sit a spell, she would read the letter again—and decide what, if *anything*, she could do about it.

Chapter Twenty-Five

Along toward the end of July, the lima beans were coming on mighty strong—and the ripest red Early Girl tomatoes a body ever did see. A group of women sat under the elm tree at Mattie's place, *blicking*—shelling limas—and slapping at mosquitoes.

"What's anybody hear about our wayward girl?" asked Ella Mae, sitting in a chaise lounge, doing her share of work.

Mary looked over at her and shook her head gloomily. "Last she wrote—oh, several weeks back—she was planning on gettin' married."

"Married?" said Ella Mae.

"Jah."

Rebecca started hacking, another one of her coughing fits, so Rachel Stoltzfus went inside to get her a glass of water. Meanwhile, Lydia went over and sat beside Rebecca, patting her lightly on the back. "Don't you worry now, the Lord's got His hand on your girl's life," the Mennonite woman was saying, trying to soothe the distraught mother.

"But . . . but she never wrote a thing about it . . . to me," Rebecca sputtered.

All eyes were on Mary, since she seemed to be the one

with the most recent news. "She says she's in love with an artist."

"Well, what's his name, for pity's sake?" Ella Mae spoke up, wishing she didn't feel so upset and hoping it didn't show.

"Justin Wirth," Mary replied. "A nice enough Englischer, I 'spect."

"Puh!" Ella Mae didn't like the sound of it. Why, the girl had up and gone *ferhoodled*, for sure and for certain. 'Course 'twasn't the first time. She thought of Katie and the day she'd run off from her wedding to Bishop John. Such a case she was—all fiery tempered. Impulsive, too.

While the women talked about other things—topics unrelated to shunnings and disobedient offspring—Ella Mae fumed. Ach, she hated hearing that Katie was so awful confused—and she'd *have* to be to contemplate marriage to anyone but the boy she was meant for. The one and only fella who could make her heart sing.

She was feeling real tired now—not her fingers, from hulling limas, as much as her eyes, drowsy from the heat and humidity. She fought off snoozing like a stubborn child long past bedtime, forcing her mind to ponder the somber and complicated story of Dan and Katie, miles apart.

Her head felt right dizzy now, yet she tried to shake it off, wondering if it was a warning sign—that she might be close to having another stroke. *What if I died today?* she thought. *Would I hear the Lord say, "Well done, thou faithful servant"?*

She felt sick all over. Still, she kept hulling limas, not wanting to call attention to herself. She thought of the People—ach, she'd failed her loved ones and friends all these years. *All these years . . .*

Her whole life had been given over to kindly works, compassionate deeds. She'd leaned her ear to a gut many folk in the Hollow—more than she could ever begin to count. That was all well and gut, yet she knew she'd betrayed them, hadn't given them what their hearts yearned for: the Good News of Jesus Christ.

An orange and yellow butterfly flew over the heads of the women, lighting on Mary's shoulder briefly, though the bishop's young bride never noticed. But the Wise Woman did, and nature's caress—and the confidence in her heart—got her thinking about miracles and such, and what she could do to change things. If it just wasn't too late.

Lydia stayed awhile after the Amishwomen left. While the other guests retrieved their horses from the barn and hitched them back up to the buggies, Lydia helped Mattie take Ella Mae indoors and get her settled in a rocking chair in the front room—even though Ella Mae said she preferred to sit outside on the front porch. Mattie thought it was time her mother stayed inside for the evening and told Ella Mae so, and the older woman didn't seem to mind too much.

Lydia sat down, talking softly about the day with her Amish friend. "We got a good many limas done."

"Jah, we did."

"And lots of catching up, too." She meant that they'd gossiped plenty.

Ella Mae nodded, but her thoughts seemed to be off somewhere else.

"You all right?" she asked.

"Ach, Lyddie, I never wanted to hide my light under a bushel basket. Never, ever," Ella Mae blurted, her eyes filling with tears.

Lydia stopped rocking and placed her hand on Ella Mae's. "The light of Jesus has been shining out of your eyes for a good many years now. I knew you loved the Lord. Everyone who ever confided in you or sipped your tea knew it, too."

Ella Mae closed her eyes. "I shoulda told them about the

Lord outright," she whispered. "Shoulda passed it on."

"It's never too late for that."

"I'm a-countin' on it, Lyddie. Before I die, that's what I'm gonna do. Starting with Mattie . . ."

They were quiet then, both women rocking in the matching hickory chairs, while Mattie rattled some pots and pans across the house in her big kitchen.

Outside, a dog barked at the buggies making the turn onto Hickory Lane, and the late afternoon sun cast a fragile glow on Ella Mae's head.

❖ ❖ ❖

Thinking that she'd gone and spilled the beans in front of all the womenfolk out of turn, without ever thinking things through, Mary gently slapped the reins against John's best Belgian horse.

She examined the sky as the light began to fade ever so slightly, though there were several more summery hours till dusk. Crickets were just waiting their turn to chirp, owls eager for nightfall. She sensed the silent expectancy in the woods as the horse trotted along leisurely. Mary was in no hurry to return home. Not just yet. The children would be clamoring for attention, though she would give it graciously . . . jah, happily. But these moments—with just herself sitting in the buggy and the steady *clip-clopping* of the horse's hooves—provided time for some peaceful reflection after a long day of work and chatter.

She hoped the news about Katie's pending marriage to the Englischer up north wouldn't set Rebecca back to where she couldn't enjoy the summer. Poor dear. The last thing in the world she wanted was to upset Katie's mamma. Only the Good Lord himself had any idea of the depths of sorrow the woman had endured for having kept the adoption secret all these years—not to mention the reality of the Meinding.

Ach, she could kick herself for blurting the wedding news out like that. What *was* she thinking?

◈ ◈ ◈

Rebecca's brain felt divided in half as she drove her buggy toward the red sandstone house. The part of her that wanted to head on up to New York and talk Katie out of marrying into the fancy world kept tormenting her. The other part wanted to honor the Ordnung, wanted to heed it without question, wanted to be prayerful for Katie, hoping the Good Lord would answer her prayers and bring her daughter back home without a battle.

And how odd. She'd come that close to volunteering to tell one of her favorite stories, yet when all the dismal talk started up about Katie in love with some artist fella—English and all—she'd clammed right up again. It was ever so strange the way she *wanted* to be the storyteller, honest she did, yet something kept her from it. Something mighty painful.

And, too, she wondered about the haunting look in Ella Mae's eyes there toward the last of the lima shelling. Himmel, she worried herself almost sick over the disturbing gaze. Something was up. As sure as she knew her aunt, something was brewing.

CHAPTER TWENTY-SIX

❖ ❖ ❖

The minute Katherine read the letter from Hickory Hollow, she rang for Theodore, who drove her downtown to make arrangements with the hospice. "I really hesitate to ask you this, but may I change my schedule for this week?" she asked the charge nurse.

Natalie came in the office, looking glum at first, then brightening when she spotted Katherine. "You're just the person I need to talk to."

"Oh?"

"I was wondering if you could entertain the patients with your guitar tomorrow, on your regularly scheduled day."

She noticed the dark circles under Natalie's eyes. "Is everything all right? You look exhausted."

The nurse shook her head sadly. "I've had to turn three more patients away—just this week. There's simply not enough bed space."

"Where will they go?"

"That's just it. There's no other option. Many families don't want their loved ones to die in a hospital . . . or even at home, where the cares of life can weigh in so heavily. They desire the tranquil setting that we offer." She sighed.

237

"If we just had a larger facility."

"Maybe something will open up," Katherine said, offering encouragement, though she had no idea where such a place might be. Not in Canandaigua. Perhaps in Rochester. But that city was inconvenient for families and loved ones who lived here. She understood perfectly why Natalie's eyes were sorrowful.

"I wish I could help you tomorrow with the music, but I really must beg off. I've been called home," she explained. "An old friend has suffered a stroke and wants to see me again before she dies."

"Of course, I understand. Take as much time away as you need."

"I'll be glad to make up more than my share of hours when I return."

"That's kind of you," Natalie said, wishing her well.

Katherine left the hospice to purchase her bus ticket, though she wished she had the nerve to travel by plane to Pennsylvania. Something about flying brought back the Ordnung and its expectation, and for the life of her, she couldn't break the rules just now, not with her great-aunt possibly wasting away on her deathbed.

❖   ❖   ❖

"I'll be traveling to Pennsylvania tomorrow," she told Rosie upon returning to the estate.

Rosie stopped what she was doing, holding a handful of unpolished silver in midair. Fulton, who sat at the kitchen table sipping coffee with Theodore, turned and gawked as well.

"My great-aunt may not have long to live. It may be days or weeks . . . hard to say," she explained. "But I don't want to risk not seeing her ever again."

"I'm terribly sorry about your aunt," said Rosie, coming

over, the silverware still poised in her fist.

"Ella Mae's lived a full life, so there's no need to feel too bad."

"Well, is there something we can do?" asked Rosie, her eyes bright with concern.

Katherine couldn't think of anything, except that she would need a ride down to the bus station first thing in the morning, a matter she mentioned to Theodore.

"My pleasure." He got up and went to the bulletin board where the week's schedule was posted.

"Thank you so much," she said, including both Rosie and Fulton in her expression, and left to start packing.

❖ ❖ ❖

At the first glimpse of Lancaster County, Katherine experienced a surprising lump in her throat. Yet she couldn't help peering out the bus window, wishing the driver would speed up and deposit her on the familiar street so she could hail a taxi and be on her way to Ella Mae. And Hickory Hollow.

The bus approached the station, and she noticed the narrow streets of downtown Lancaster, the brick row houses with their tiny stoops and cobblestone sidewalks. There was something painfully pretty about the area, the familiarity of it. A rush of memories came back. Buzzing, hot summertime: the swish of skirt against bare ankles, the feel of scorching soil between her toes, the long, fun-filled days of raspberry picking with twenty or more cousins . . . the sweet aroma of new-mown hay.

She pressed her face closer to the window, longing to see Hickory Lane again, scarcely able to wait to get there.

Once she was on her way via taxi, out of the downtown area toward Route 340, she began to relax. Past Smoketown and Bird-in-Hand, past the pretzel factory smack-dab in the middle of a tourist center at Intercourse, and on to Cattail Road and the turnoff to Hickory Hollow.

"Know anybody out here in Amish country?" asked the cab driver.

She smiled at his inquiry. "Oh, a good many."

He glanced at her in his rearview mirror. "From everything I hear about Plain folk, they like to keep to themselves—don't take too well to 'Englischers.'"

"Most of the time, that's true." She didn't especially want to reveal her circumstances. Mentioning that she had been raised Amish and then shunned would open up a whole can of worms. She wasn't in the mood.

Another couple of miles—more familiar landmarks—and she was leaning forward, fidgeting in the backseat. "Would you mind slowing down a bit?" she said, as they came within a quarter mile of David and Mattie Beiler's place.

"Want me to turn in there?"

"Stop at the next lane, please. I'll walk the rest of the way." When the taxi stopped, she paid him and stepped out.

Looking around, she took in the perky pink and white petunias lined up in meticulous rows, the red roses climbing up the lattice, the newly painted white front porch, and the rustic yard bench under the age-old elm on the east side of the Dawdi Haus. Even the air smelled remarkably fresh and homey, though she wouldn't tarry on such thoughts.

"Hullo!" Someone was calling to her. "Is that *you*, Katie?"

She recognized the voice and turned to see Lydia Miller. Her mother's cousin came running across the lawn, arms outstretched. "I didn't expect to see *you* today. How in the world are you?"

"I'm fine, thanks," Katie replied, hugging her. "How's Ella Mae?"

Arm in arm, they headed up to the house. "Oh, she has good and bad days, though I think she'll perk up a bit when she sees the likes of you." Lydia stopped in her tracks. "How did you hear?"

"Ella Mae wrote . . . asked me to come."

"Ah yes, I suppose she did," Lydia said with a knowing look.

A swarm of bees flew over their heads, and Katherine held her breath and stood still automatically, the way Rebecca had taught her to do as a child. The sound of laughter—little ones at play somewhere out in the barn, most likely—caught her interest, and she wondered which of Ella Mae's great-grandchildren might be here.

At the door, Mattie's eyes popped wide when she spotted Katherine. "My goodness gracious, where'd *you* come from?"

"Ella Mae invited me for a visit."

"Ah, sounds like Mamma," Mattie said, shaking her head.

Katherine wondered about that. "Is it all right if I come in . . . just for a short while?"

Glancing over her shoulder and looking a bit sheepish, Mattie actually dawdled about whether or not to allow her entry.

Lydia was breathing hard, as though she was terribly embarrassed over it. "Aw, Mattie, it can't hurt none for Katie to visit," she said softly. "Last I heard, the shunning was lifted a bit."

Mattie waved her hand as if shooing a fly, her face languid. "What if Bishop John gets word?"

"Ella Mae will be expecting me," Katherine insisted. "I won't stay long. I promise."

Reluctantly, Mattie opened the front screen door. "I

don't want this gettin' out—don't need any trouble just now."

"I understand," she said.

Lydia stayed in the kitchen with two other Plain women, and Mattie offered to take Katherine through the front room to the Dawdi Haus.

Ella Mae was sitting in her rocking chair next to the front room window when Katherine entered. Looking up, the woman's face broke into a crooked smile. "Oh, Katie . . . Katie," she said, holding out her shriveled hand, her voice huskier than ever.

Katherine didn't bother to correct Ella Mae. Even though she very much wanted to be called Katherine, things were different here. "Glad to see you up and dressed," she said. "I came as soon as I received your letter."

Ella Mae nodded, offering a weak smile. "I hoped you'd come. Denki, I appreciate it . . . more than I can say."

Pulling up one of the cane chairs in the room, Katherine sat beside her aunt. "It's been the longest time since we've had a chat. When was your stroke?"

Ella Mae began to count on her deformed fingers, then gave up as if she couldn't recall. "Not too long ago. Couldn't talk or move my hands . . . hardly anything worked on me there for a gut while."

"Did you see a doctor?"

"No, no. Don't need no doctors when I've got friends."

She expected that. "You haven't changed a bit. Still have your spunk, that good sense of humor."

Ella Mae worked her head up and down. "You haven't changed neither . . . not really. Under all them fancy clothes, I think we've still got our Katie girl."

"Well, I don't know. I suppose there's a good part of me that's similar." She went on to say how nice it was to be back in Hickory Hollow. "Especially now. I felt like taking my shoes off as soon as I got out of the taxi."

"You came thataway? By taxi?"

"Did you expect me to ride up in a golden carriage?" She chuckled, feeling free and easy. "I left my fancy limousine back in New York. Best not to stir up the bishop, right?"

They had a good laugh over that. Then Ella Mae's voice softened, her eyes filling with tears. "There's something I wanna tell ya, Katie. I shoulda come out with it long before now." Her face was flushed.

Katherine reached for her hand. "Are you all right?"

The Wise Woman nodded but remained silent. Tears began to flow down her wrinkled face. "I never told you about Jesus," she whispered. "All these years I kept it to myself. Oh, I showed God's love to folk, sure, but I didn't say nothin' about the way He changed my life, forgave my sins . . . gave me joy." She paused, her eyes on Katherine. "Now I'm tellin' everybody I know. 'Course, the People think I'm *Dummkopp*—clear off my rocker."

"I never knew this about you," Katherine managed. "But I'm not surprised. There was always something special about you."

"Will ya forgive me for waitin' so long, Katie?"

An unsettled, prickly feeling came over her, something akin to the way she'd felt on that first visit to Laura's church. She felt her throat constrict, making her unable to speak. So she nodded, tears clouding her sight.

Ella Mae continued. "I just couldn't let myself die before tellin' you what I know in my heart, that I'm goin' to heaven someday. And it has nothin' whatever to do with pride or any such thing. I'm saved, Katie . . . I belong to Jesus."

The salvation of the righteous is of the Lord. . . .

The words on Laura's headstone echoed in her memory.

"It seems here lately," Katherine confessed, "everywhere I turn, I keep hearing the same thing—that the Lord Jesus loves me, that He died for *me*. . . ."

Ella Mae was still, eyes fixed on her.

"I knew there would come a day like this . . . sure as the heavens." Katherine searched her skirt pocket for a tissue. "I've felt it for months now." She paused to dry her eyes. "Oh, Ella Mae, I think you're right. God *is* calling me."

The Wise Woman closed her eyes, and tears squeezed out of the corners. Leaning her head back against the rocker, she remained that way without speaking—absolutely motionless—until Katherine thought she'd passed on to glory.

"Ella Mae?"

Weary eyes fluttered. "Praise be" came the raspy reply. "I prayed I'd live to see this day."

Katherine got down on her knees beside the rocking chair. Looking up at the Wise Woman, she pleaded with her; the ache in her heart had become unbearable. "Will you . . . help lead me to your Jesus?"

❖   ❖   ❖

After her tearful prayer, Katherine felt light as the clouds flitting across the afternoon sky. She stood in the window, marking the moment. She memorized the way the sun's rays cast a holy light on Hickory Lane, on the many-sided martin birdhouse in the front yard, on the wide, toothed leaves of the elm tree.

A warm breeze blew against her face and hair, and she knew she was a child of God. "My birth mother should be singing with the angels along about now."

Ella Mae cocked her head, thoughtfully. "I think I hear music."

Katherine leaned down and kissed her aunt, so weak and

small there in her chair. "I'll never forget this day . . . or what you did for me."

"What *Jesus* did for you," Ella Mae said, a smile bursting across her ashen face.

"Yes," said Katherine. "What *Jesus* did for me."

◈　◈　◈

She hadn't considered the idea of accommodations, though acquiring a room for a night or two would not be a problem. It was out of the question to think of staying in any of the Amish homes in the district. None of the People would risk putting up a shunned woman, especially a "saved" one.

"Will ya be visitin' Mary while you're here? And Rebecca?" Ella Mae asked as Katherine was about to leave. "They'll be heartsick if ya don't."

"I hope to see as many folk as I can." She patted the back of her aunt's hand. "I'll come again tomorrow."

"I'll be here . . . Lord willin'."

On the way out of the Dawdi Haus, Katherine waved to several of the children—young Sally Beiler and her cousins, Ben, Noah, and Jake. How they'd grown, the boys especially.

Seeing the youngsters made her think of the bishop's family, and her thoughts flew to Mary. Dare she wander down the road to the bishop's place? She could hardly contain her joy; she had to tell her best friend about this wonderful-good day. The best day of her whole life!

She followed her heart, her feet skimming the lane.

Before she knocked, Katherine peered in through the back screen door. She could see Mary scurrying here and there in the kitchen. Checking to see if John was around, she opened the door just enough for her to slip through. Then she tiptoed to the wide doorway leading from the outside utility room to the kitchen, and craning her neck around the corner, she waited till Mary might come over to the cookstove.

Just when her friend was at the right angle to spot her, Katherine cupped her hands around her mouth. "Pst!"

Mary stared, her mouth gaping.

"Kumm mit," Katherine whispered, motioning with her pointer finger.

"Katie? Is that *you*?" Mary rushed to her and embraced her in the privacy of the utility room. "Ach, girl, let me look at ya." They held on to each other's arms, twirling around.

Laughing, they hugged again. "I can't stay but a minute, Mary, but I had to let you know I'm back."

"You've come home?"

"Just to visit. Ella Mae invited me."

"Jah, she's suffered so."

She couldn't stand there discussing her aunt's stroke, not with John bound to show up soon. "Meet me at our island tomorrow morning after milking. Can you get away?"

Mary thought for a second. "John's got some horses to shoe first thing after breakfast, and the children have their outdoor chores. So, jah, I guess I can."

"Good . . . I'll see you there." She knew Mary needed no description of their childhood retreat.

"I'll be over soon as I can."

Katherine kissed her friend's plump cheek, then turned to go.

"Katie? Are ya married?"

"Not yet, why?"

Mary's eyes twinkled. "Well, ya just look so awful happy . . . that's all."

"There's a right good reason for that. I'll explain it tomorrow."

"Gut, then," Mary whispered, seeing her to the back door. "Hurry now, and God be with ya, dear friend."

"Oh, He is, Mary. He *really* is!"

CHAPTER TWENTY-SEVEN

❖ ❖ ❖

It was a morning of bright haze. Sunlight poured into the upstairs bedroom at Lydia's. Katherine had had only to show up on the Millers' doorstep the evening before and she was taken in with open arms. "No rent due here," insisted Peter, grinning when he first spotted her.

So she was back in her former room, high in the eaves, close to the sky . . . no, heaven. She'd had difficulty settling down to sleep after talking away the supper hour with Peter and Lydia, long after dishes were done. There was much she wanted to say, so much she wanted to hear from them as well. Questions to ask, prayers to be prayed, hymns to be sung. They were ever so delighted to hear of her life-changing experience.

Now as she sat quietly in bed, contemplating her day with Mary, she read the Bible on the nightstand and afterward bowed her head. "Dear Lord Jesus, help me to share your love with my friend today. May she have an open heart. Amen."

She decided to go barefoot—it had been such a long time. And instead of wearing her hair down, she wound it up in a bun to keep her neck cool, wrapping a sheer scarf around it. The rayon dress she selected from her suitcase was short-sleeved, a sage ground floral print with broom-stick skirt. Last of all, the golden heart locket from Justin.

❖   ❖   ❖

A big white duck waddled after her, following her all the way down the mule path, out past the thicket to the pond. She cast her gaze on the pink sky—surely a foretaste of heaven—and thanked the Lord for His fingerprints on all of nature.

The duck quacked behind her, and she turned to look down at him. He'd stopped a few feet away, his beak held up, just enough to appear inquisitive, not proud. His beady eyes were fixed on something in the distance.

"Are *you* thankful, too?" She had to laugh. Here she was, on the backstretch of her Amish father's land, con-versing with a duck, of all things. Who would've thought when she left New York yesterday that her eyes would be opened to God's goodness, His love, everywhere she looked?

"Better run along now," she admonished him, hurrying to the rowboat.

Not to be discouraged, the old quacker plodded to catch up. Feeling sorry for him, she snatched him up and put him in the boat with her to wait for Mary. But he must not have wanted to be confined. Jumping out, he opened his wide wings and flapped to beat the band, landing in the water.

It wasn't long before Mary came running barefoot down the dusty path. "Been waitin' long?"

She shook her head. "Get in. We've got an island to ex-plore and plenty of catching up to do."

They sat across from each other in the rowboat, just as they always had as children, laughing and talking, their voices echoing off the water as swallows trilled overhead.

Partway across the pond, Mary brought up Dan Fisher. "Word has it, he's given up on you."

"I suppose he has, and for all good reason." She explained about the visit in New York and his unexpected letter weeks later. "I never wrote back. Didn't see the need."

"Your lives have changed too much? Is that it?"

"Everything's changed, Mary. Everything."

"So you know all about what happened to him, then—why he decided to let us think he was dead after the boating accident?"

"Well, no. I never gave him a chance to. That day when he showed up out of nowhere . . . I was so upset, I really couldn't think straight." She hung her head, suddenly ashamed. "I asked him to leave, actually."

Mary's eyes were understanding and kind, as always. "I 'spect that's all you could do."

"Mamma wrote once that Dan's story was a sad one, but I never bothered to ask what she meant."

So Mary began to tell her everything, how Dan had wanted to spare his loved ones—all the People, really—from having to shun him. "And especially you. It would've torn his heart out, having to endure you turnin' your back on him. He'd rather have been dead."

She sighed. "Which he was to *us*, all those years."

"He thought he was protecting us, I s'pose."

Katherine pondered these things in silence and wondered how Justin might feel if he knew she was discussing her first love, all these miles away.

"You look like you just had your first kiss," Mary said, staring right at her.

"I guess I do." She stopped rowing. Now was a befitting time to speak up about the glorious thing that had happened at Ella Mae's yesterday. "I don't know if you'll understand what I have to tell you," she began. "Lately, I've been hearing, almost on every hand, that the Lord Jesus is close to us in everything we do."

Mary listened, still rowing toward the island.

Forging ahead, Katherine told about the New York minister's sermon and the very words she'd read for herself in Laura's Bible. She revealed, too, what things Dan had written in his long letter. "I understand now why he wanted to study the Bible . . . why he was always sneaking off to prayer meetings with the Mennonites."

Mary gave ear, though she wasn't as receptive as Katherine had hoped. Her reluctance came out of fear, no doubt.

"John wouldn't hear of this, would he?" Katherine asked finally.

Mary's deep frown gave her away. "You *know* what I believe, Katie. I'm trusting God for my salvation, and I do hope with all my heart that heaven will be my reward when I die."

She shook her head. "But we don't have to earn our way. Jesus died so that we could *know* our sins are forgiven—here and now."

Mary clammed up instantly. It seemed that enough seeds had been sown for one day.

Still, Katherine was bubbling over. "You must think I'm silly, talking about the Lord this way and not saying a word about confessing . . . returning to the Amish church."

"It's hard, not knowin' what to think." Mary's eyes were earnest.

The young women rowed all the way to the island. "I pray that you'll find this happiness, too," Katherine said, stepping out of the little boat onto dry land.

Mary nodded. "I'm as happy as I ever dreamed I'd be. John's a gut husband, and I love him."

Katherine said no more, lest she spoil things between

them. And when the air had cleared a bit, they began to relive the old days. They laughed together, carefree and childlike, as they ran among the willows, splashed each other in the pond, and tossed seeds to the ducks.

Out of breath, they sat on the grassy bank, overlooking the sparkling pond. They wiggled their bare toes, enjoying the hot sun.

Mary squinted up at the sky. "I 'spect it's about time I headed back home."

"Aren't much used to *duckmeisich*—sneaking off—are you?"

Mary smiled, then her face grew serious. "It's time to put away childish things. I'm a wife and a mother. I've had my fun." She picked up two pebbles and tossed them into the pond. "Won't ya come home for gut?"

Katherine's heart ached. "I'm sorry . . . really I am. I just don't see how."

Silently, they got in the boat and rowed away from the shore to the other side.

◈　◈　◈

Hours later, Katherine heard a knock on Lydia's front screen door and went to investigate.

There stood Rebecca. "I heard you were back," she said, her hair disheveled some, apron smudged. "I rushed right over."

Katherine opened the door and wrapped her arms around the stout woman, hugging her hard. "Oh, Mamma, I'm glad you came!"

They stood gazing into each other's eyes for a time. "I figured comin' to see ya at Lydia's was the best thing."

She knew Rebecca was referring to the Meinding, which in spite of her furtive visit with Mary was still in force. Nothing much had changed. She was an outcast of the People, compelled to meet her best friend, and now her adoptive mother, in secret.

"I wanted to see you in the worst way, Mamma—my brothers, too—but didn't want to get Dat's ire up."

Rebecca nodded, hazel eyes bright. "I figured so."

It was Katherine's idea to go upstairs to the room where she was staying. The house was peaceful and still, and the large bedroom afforded the hideaway they longed for.

Sitting opposite each other near the wide front window, both barefoot, they talked, eager to spend time together.

Katherine told her mother about her new friends, the Esler girls. "They're Amish. Funny, isn't it?"

Rebecca agreed that it was.

"I've been doing volunteer work at a hospice in Canandaigua. It's truly rewarding," she said, sharing the story of Willy and his family.

"You sound right settled at your new place." Rebecca's eyes narrowed a bit, though a slight smile presented itself.

"It's everything I've ever dreamed of—and more," she admitted.

"Home's where the heart is, ain't so?"

She had to say *yes* to that. Mamma was smart that way. "Well, sometime soon I'd like to pick up my chest of linens and things, maybe even the corner cupboard Dat made for me, if that's all right."

"Jah, that'd be just fine." Rebecca paused, her face peaked all of a sudden. "You'll be gettin' married soon, then?"

"Come fall, I'm thinking." It was enough to mention the wedding season, but she would bypass saying anything about Justin just now. "I would've written about it but didn't want to hurt you more than I already have. It's a sticky subject, I suspect."

"But ya wrote Mary 'bout it."

"Another one of my mistakes, probably."

Rebecca shook her head. "No . . . no, a body needs someone to talk to. I understand."

Ever kind and loving Rebecca. Katherine could hardly contain her feelings for the woman who'd raised her from infancy. "I miss you something awful," she confessed. "It's not so easy living far from your childhood home."

"I 'spect so," Mam replied.

The subject of her newfound joy came naturally, though Rebecca seemed mighty skeptical, hearing her daughter call herself anything but Amish. "Saved isn't for us to know," Mam argued.

Refusing to upset her mamma on this topic, she let Rebecca speak her mind, not interrupting. She could only hope and pray that in time, Mam would see the light of Jesus in her shunned daughter's eyes and want it, too.

❖　❖　❖

After lunch, Katherine felt restless—anxious to wander around Hickory Hollow. Lydia offered to drive her different places, but she wanted to be on her own. Reminisce alone.

She wished she'd brought along her guitar, for there was a spot she sorely missed. A very special place she hadn't laid eyes on for the longest time. This afternoon, with sun sizzling down on her bare head, she walked west on Hickory Lane, past Samuel Lapp's sandstone house, Bishop John's farmhouse, and the one-room schoolhouse, to Weaver's Creek.

Still barefoot, she scurried across the wobbly covered bridge, hearing the boards rumble gently under her feet. She cared not for splinters or nails, though her feet seemed mighty tender these days. On the opposite end of the bridge, she headed down the steep embankment to the creek below.

A cool breeze brushed her face as she stood there in the shade of giant trees, in awe of the site. Many an afternoon had been spent here during her teen years, though one clearly stood out above all others.

Lifting up her broomstick skirt just a bit, she waded into the cold creek, ignoring the age-old stepping stones and thrilling to the bold, splashing current. She did not hurry but took her time getting over to the huge boulder situated almost exactly in the middle of the rushing water.

"Ach, it looks smaller," she said aloud, eyeing the slab of rock. Without another thought, she climbed to the top and sat down.

Sunshine twinkled around her, making diamonds dance on the water, casting flickering shadows on the side of the bridge above. The boulder felt warm and hard beneath her hands as she sat there, breathing in the sweet air. She closed her eyes, thanking the Lord for all He had done in her life.

Three swallows flew into the spruce tree above her, and she leaned back to watch them spring from one branch to another as they chirped their secret language back and forth. She even tried to mimic their sounds, but her voice frightened them away.

"Sorry," she said, hugging her knees, wishing the sun would stand still and the earth would stop spinning long enough for her to share her delirious contentment with all the world.

Softly, she began to hum the love song she and Dan had created on this very location. The birds warbled along and the creek picked up the rhythm. In her secluded world, unseen by anyone but her Lord, Katherine began to sing the old song out loud. Feeling carefree, she sang it again, this time changing the words. She was creating a love song for the Lord Jesus, her special gift for Him.

It was as she finished the final phrase, just as she'd stood up to balance herself on tiptoes on the peak of the rock—just then—she heard whistling.

Quickly she crouched down, hoping she hadn't been noticed. Through the sun-dappled grove she saw a tall, clean-shaven man walking along the road, nearing the bridge. He could not be seen clearly, though she noticed snippets of blond hair through the trees. Had she been closer, she might've been able to make out who it was. Yet squinting and moving her head, trying to capture the full image, she concluded that the man was English, for there was no straw hat, no white shirt and suspenders. Curiously, she watched as he turned off the road and descended the steep bank of earth.

It might have been the vibrato in his whistle, the gait of his steps. Something. The way he carried himself erect perhaps. But in that moment Katherine knew him.

Her hand flew to her mouth. *Dan!*

Certain that she'd only thought his name, she was startled that he answered. "Who's there?"

She stiffened, wanting to hide. Had he been following her? But how could *that* be? No one knew she was visiting here except Rosie and Fulton and her domestic staff. Surely Dan hadn't gone back to Canandaigua, discovered she was here, and pursued her. Surely not!

As he came into the clearing at the water's edge, the light shone on his face. Their eyes met.

"Katie?"

They stared at each other awkwardly.

"What are you doing . . . here in the Hollow?" he asked.

"I should ask *you* that question." She felt suddenly defensive, not willing to give up her tranquil setting.

He held out his empty hands in surrender. "I'm out for a walk—nothing more."

She wasn't convinced. "So you *weren't* following me?"

Smiling now, he ran his fingers through his hair. "I was in the area . . . heard Ella Mae was ill."

Katherine didn't budge from her perch.

"Honestly, I had no idea you'd be here," Dan said, still standing on the edge of the creek bed. "How've you been, Katherine?"

She nodded, not certain of what to say, though it was lovely hearing him call her by her true name. Yet telling him how she *really* was—at least, at the present moment—would be a terrible mistake. She could say that she was feeling rather flustered at seeing him again, that she'd forgotten how handsome he was. Ach, she'd never admit such things.

Standing up, she said, "I'm fine, thanks, but I really have to be leaving now."

"Please . . . stay a few minutes, won't you?"

She thought it over. "Well, maybe. But not for long."

Dan stepped on the smaller rocks that dotted a path to the boulder. Before climbing, he stood at its base, frowning. Then, surveying it in much the same way as she had, he commented that the "ol' rock has shrunk some."

She had to laugh, sliding over to make room for him. "That's just what *I* thought."

Dan seemed pleased, nodding at her as he sat down with a sigh. "And I guess I'm getting older."

"Aren't we all?"

They chatted about Ella Mae for a while, then Dan grew quiet. He stared at their surroundings. "I miss it here. The Lord willing, I plan to set up my own drafting business here in Lancaster. Sometime in the fall, maybe, if things work out."

She was conscious of his nearness, listening as he discussed his hopes and dreams. "Will you be working with Mennonite contractors?" she asked later.

He turned to face her, leaning his arm on his knee. "Since I'm a shunned man, I don't expect to have any business dealings with Amish, at least not in Bishop John's district. But Mennonites, yes."

She smiled, fingering her heart-shaped locket. "So you're not coming back to confess?"

"My confession is before God, and I can honestly say that He's forgiven me."

"I know about divine forgiveness, too," she said softly.

His eyes blinked rapidly. "Are you . . . have you. . . ?"

"Yes, I've become a follower of Jesus. Ella Mae led me to pray a sinner's prayer just yesterday."

"That's wonderful, Katie!" He shook his head, obviously grateful. "I knew there was something different about you. But I thought it was just the sunlight."

They laughed about it, and Dan announced that they were now brother and sister in Christ. She heard the cheerful ring in his voice, glad she'd stayed after all.

One thing led to another, and she found herself telling him that she knew the truth of his lost years. "Mary told me why you stayed away. Honestly, I think I understand now."

His face was sober. "I prayed you'd forgive me someday, though I didn't expect it would be this soon."

"The Lord works miracles. Sometimes when we least expect them."

"That He does." He was grinning at her now.

Feeling a bit unnerved at his ardent smile, she stood up to stretch her cramped limbs. "Let's go for a walk."

He leaped to his feet. "C'mon, we'll go to the high meadow behind the school." It had been one of the favorite spots of their childhood.

She followed as he ran across the creek, marveling at the

coolness of the grass along the brook. Then up through the wide, grassy terrace for a good acre or more to open pastureland. It was almost as though the years between them had dissolved. *Almost . . .*

"Katie," he called to her, "race me to the old outhouse."

"Never," she hollered back.

"Aw, come on!"

"Not on your life!"

He chuckled, letting her catch up with him. "That's my girl."

"What did you say?"

"I . . . uh, didn't mean to say that." He shrugged, a sobering expression followed. "Come back with me, Katie. Please, come back to Lancaster." He paused, his eyes searching hers. "I have no right to say this, but I still love you. With all my heart, I do."

She was out of breath from running *and* from this strange proposal. "It's . . . it's too late. I'm seeing someone else. Someone . . ." She couldn't go on. Her heart and mind struggled with differing emotions.

"Oh, Katie . . ." He reached for her hands, holding them in both of his.

She pulled away. "You and I—we've changed so much. I have a new home and new friends. I'm fancy now, just the way I've always longed to be. You're a Mennonite . . . still Plain."

"But we're *both* Christians." He argued for all the things they loved: the outdoors, their music, Lancaster County.

"I'm sorry, Dan, really I am. If there is to be anything between us, it would have to be honest friendship."

He moved to embrace her. "For all the old times," he whispered in her ear. She patted his back in response.

She agreed to let him walk her back to Lydia's, though

their long talk turned to the weather and the landscape. Safe things.

As they approached the Millers' house, he offered his business card. "If you ever want to contact me," he said, pointing out his home address and phone number, "please, feel free."

"Friends then, jah?"

He smiled at her Dutchy remark. "The Lord bless you and your new life in Christ."

"Thanks, Dan. God bless you, too." She waved and turned to go.

"I pray you'll be very happy," he called after her.

His gracious words rang in her ears as she hurried up the porch steps.

Chapter Twenty-Eight

Theodore listened as Katherine discussed with Fulton and Rosie the differences between Amish and Mennonite practices. They had been at it for more than an hour, and his lemonade needed freshening.

Excusing himself, he headed indoors, where Selig and Garrett were preparing lunch. "How many religious perspectives do you suppose there are in the world?" he commented.

"More than one can count, I'd say," Garrett spoke up as he sharpened a butcher knife.

"But you have to hand it to Katherine," Selig offered. "She's different somehow. And she plays hymns on that guitar of hers every spare minute. Quite rousing, if I may say so."

"Even the way she looks. Why, there's a radiance to her," said Garrett. "Have you noticed?"

Theodore agreed that he had. "Life's too short not to be searching for heaven. I'm all for it."

Selig and Garrett exchanged shrugs and went back to doing what they had been doing.

He went to the pantry and opened up a new bag of white

sugar. Taking two additional teaspoons, he sweetened his glass of lemonade further.

❖　❖　❖

When her hospice work was finished for the week, Katherine decided it was time for some fall housecleaning. She offered to help Rosie tackle the library first, knowing that a thorough cleaning would involve dusting the many books shelved there. It would be too much for one person to accomplish alone.

"Good idea," Rosie said, scurrying off to get the cleaning supplies.

They were in the midst of dusting the topmost shelves, lifting handfuls of ancient-looking classics to clean them off, when Katherine stumbled upon several small leather-bound volumes hidden behind the thicker library books. "What are these?"

Rosie stopped her feather dusting and came to investigate. "My goodness, I believe you may have found Laura's writings."

"Her journals?"

Opening one of them, Rosie grinned. "The very ones. These are your mother's personal diaries."

It was all Katherine could do to continue the cleaning project. Rosie insisted that she stop what she was doing and take the books to her sitting room immediately for private scrutiny. Yet, in spite of her maid's coaxing, Katherine refused. What she'd started, she must finish.

So it was much later in the day, after both she and Rosie were fairly winded from climbing up and down the library ladders, dusting everything in sight, that she finally had a chance to sit down with the journals. Earnestly, she located the one Laura had spoken of on her deathbed—the bright blue journal with the correct year printed inside.

Her stomach contracted into a tight ball. What things would she discover? Had Laura *really* intended for her to find and read these intimate writings?

Before ever reading the first entry, she prayed, "Lord, please guide me to what you want me to know about my birth mother."

Then, getting herself situated in a comfortable chair, she opened to January, the first day of the new year—six months before she was born, the year Laura was only seventeen.

January 1

> *Today, Mother and Daddy and I took another long drive to the country in the snow. It's nice to have off another few days for the holidays before returning to high school. So far, no one outside my family but my boyfriend knows I'm going to have a baby. He's acting horribly strange about it, though.*
>
> *Mother says not to worry. She and Daddy will take good care of me . . . and the baby. (At least they aren't forcing me to go away to an unwed mothers' home like one of the senior girls had to last year.)*
>
> *I'm gaining weight, and sometimes I feel queasy first thing in the morning. Mother says all this is normal.*
>
> *I miss my shape . . . but I love the baby inside me.*

❖ ❖ ❖

Katherine read each page through March, poring over every word. She stopped at one point and took the diary outside, propping herself against the trunk of a tree.

April 1

> *I'm as large as a blimp—at least I feel like it. Daddy's worried because I want to drop out of school until the baby is born. He thinks I'll miss out scholastically and won't get*

to attend a good college after next year.

I cry a lot these days. Can't seem to get on an even keel with my emotions.

Mother dotes on me constantly. It's amazing what she goes through to make sure I'm comfortable. I hope (if I keep my baby) I might be as dear a mother as she is to me.

❖ ❖ ❖

April 7

A tutor from the school district comes three times a week. It's so much better than having to put up with the cruel comments at school. Especially from boys.

❖ ❖ ❖

Katherine looked up when Fulton came outside with a tray of lemonade and cookies.

"Thank you," she said and went back to her reading.

April 15

My doctor wanted to do an ultrasound so we'll know if I can deliver my baby naturally. There is a tiny little girl growing inside me.

Mother and I looked through a book of names tonight. My favorite—the most beautiful of all—is Katherine.

❖ ❖ ❖

May 5

I cried every day this whole week. I feel exhausted and dreadfully hopeless. Mother says I'm having panic attacks. Daddy wonders if I need psychological counseling.

I'm heartsick! My first and only boyfriend never loved me. Never! Why did I believe him?

I can't sleep at night. I can only cry for what I've lost. Little Katherine may never know that her father abandoned me when I needed him most.

Katherine allowed her tears to fall unchecked. What despair—the tremendous pain—her birth mother had gone through, to give life to her.

By the end of the May writings, she felt fatigued and filled with sadness for young Laura's plight.

Rosie peered out the upstairs window. "Oh, I do hope she's going to be all right, out there all by herself."

Fulton joined her at the window. "Miss Katherine appears to be weeping."

"Yes, and I doubt she'll feel much like dining with Justin tonight."

"Perhaps a lavish dinner with the artist may be just the thing to cheer our Katherine," her husband remarked.

Stepping away from the window, she hugged Fulton. "Well, aren't *you* the optimist?"

He stuck out his stomach, nearly popping the buttons on his butler's vest. "I'll take that as a compliment, my dear."

"Thank you, indeed." And she turned back to the window, praying that Katherine would learn the precious things that Laura had so wanted her to discover.

❖　❖　❖

June 1

I've been making an infant gown for Katherine. It's the prettiest satin fabric, all rosy and sweet.

Daddy isn't putting pressure on me to make a decision, but his eyes fill with concern every time I look his way. Mother, on the other hand, I think is hoping that I keep my baby. She's left big hints about being ready for a grandchild.

Either way, I want my little girl to be happy. I think I'm leaning toward raising her myself. But I'm not so sure about bringing another child into this mansion. Would it be the best thing for her? The servants will spoil her terribly, and she'll never know what it means to work for what she wants.

Sometimes, I secretly wish we were of moderate means . . . or even poor. The books I read about poor people make me wonder if they aren't happier.

Little Katherine kicks me hardest in the early morning. I wonder if that means anything.

❖   ❖   ❖

June 4

Mother wants to take me on a trip to Pennsylvania. She has the go-ahead from the doctor. I know what she's thinking. The trip will be a distraction for me. I don't blame her for worrying. I've been through the wringer in more ways than one.

She promises that I'll love Lancaster County. I almost feel like I've visited there before, maybe because Mother loves it so much. We'll see what I think of the Plain people she keeps describing.

Getting away from here might not be such a bad idea. I want to take Katherine's baby gown along. The hem stitching is all that's left to do. Won't my darling baby look beautiful?

❖ ❖ ❖

June 6

Yesterday I gave birth to Katherine, the most darling baby I've ever seen. But I gave her up, and my stomach felt so sick later, and my head ached for hours. The doctor gave me a sedative so I could sleep.

I don't know if it's possible for me to write everything about the day without sobbing my way through, but I must try. I never want to forget the way I felt or how I made my important decision about my baby—so I'll hurry to get it down on paper while the memories are fresh.

Our chauffeur drove around the back roads in Lancaster on such a pretty day. Even Mother said it was a perfect day to spend in Amish country.

Now I know why she wanted me to come here. It was so peaceful and charming, like pictures out of an old classic. I started to relax the minute we got off the busy highway. Little gray buggies with horses pulling them were everywhere, and farmers with straw hats—even young boys and girls—worked the fields.

When I saw the first covered bridge, I couldn't believe it. It was enchanting to me—so foreign to what I knew, yet so inviting.

The more we rode around, the more I fell in love with Amish country. Strange as it is, I even wondered (and mentioned it to Mother) what it would be like to grow up Plain. Such a different world from my own. The farmhouses and the barns with their tall silos made me want to look inside. Why was I so curious about this simple life? Why, when I had everything a wealthy family could ever offer?

I hid my tears while I watched a group of barefoot Amish girls work in the garden. They were picking strawberries and making a game of it. (Something I know nothing about.)

I think I cried because I didn't want my baby to grow up the way I had, an only child. No brothers or sisters to play with. (And, worse, little Katherine would have no father.)

Something beautiful was calling to me. I felt like I had come home—to a place I'd longed for my whole life. And if this was how I felt while carrying my baby—so close to being born—maybe there was a very special reason why Mother had brought me here.

She stopped reading, the realization of Laura's decision encompassing her thoughts, her heart.

The sky was bluer than she'd remembered seeing it since last summer, and a hint of fall was in the air. A flock of birds flew overhead, their flapping wings reminded her of the duck who'd stubbornly tagged along after her that July day as she and Mary were about to revisit their island.

Leaning her head against the tree trunk, she opened the journal again and finished reading the June entries.

My heart nearly broke when I heard Katherine's first wails. The doctor placed her in my arms and we cried together. I kissed her soft head and wondered if I'd ever love another human being as much as I loved tiny Katherine at that moment.

Minutes later, there were noises in the hallway. People rushing about. A nurse was telling one of the doctors that there'd been a stillbirth. A young Amish couple. . . .

I must have known then in my heart why we had come to Lancaster. My baby was going to grow up here. I wanted her to fill the empty arms of a broken-hearted woman. I wanted her to run barefoot in the meadow, catch fireflies, learn to make quilts, and pick strawberries in the hot sun. I wanted my dear Katherine to work and play hard, to have all the simple things I'd missed out on. Most of all, I wanted her to be loved by a complete family. And I wanted her to grow up Plain.

Gazing heavenward, Katherine wept silently. A gentle breeze blew a handful of leaves off the tree, a sure sign of fall.

After a time, she dried her eyes and rose, hurrying into the house. Justin would be arriving in only a few hours, and she suspected that the evening had been well-planned, possibly a special occasion. She'd caught him whispering to Rosie in the entryway a few nights ago when he'd escorted her home from yet another fancy outing.

Quickly she bathed and dressed, then swept her hair into an elegant twist, securing it with another one of Laura's gem-studded combs. Tonight she would tell her darling of the beautiful journal she'd found. Because Justin had been extremely fond of Laura, she knew he would appreciate, too, the cherished words.

The apple green dress she chose was the most exquisite in her wardrobe, and yet it boasted simple, clean lines—less dazzling than other gowns she owned. And it was satin. Even as a teen, her birth mother had also loved the feel and sound of satin.

Katherine stood in the drawing room, not wanting to wrinkle the tea-length dress. Waiting for the doorbell, she placed a light stole around her shoulders to ward off the evening chill.

"You look truly lovely tonight," Rosie commented, an inquisitive smile on her round face.

"Do enjoy yourself, Katherine," said Fulton, standing in readiness near the door.

She thanked them both cordially. Then merrily, yet modestly, she smiled back at herself in the wall mirror across the room. Standing there, she grasped the effect her image represented. Yes, everything young Katie Lapp had ever dreamed of had come to her, to the mistress of Mayfield Manor, in the most extraordinary fashion.

Only one desire remained yet to be fulfilled.

◈   ◈   ◈

Candlelit and elegant, the stately dining room was as intimate and lovely as any setting Katherine had ever visualized. Justin was attentive, as always, and she felt at ease sharing the revealing phrases from Laura's year as an unwed mother.

"She loved you dearly," he said, reaching across the table for her hand. "Just as I do, Katherine." His sincere smile warmed her heart.

Waiting, longing to hear his words of commitment, she spooned up a bite of the fruit-flavored sorbet.

Eyes shining, he reached into his suit coat pocket. "This is for you, Katherine." He presented her with a small square box.

With trembling fingers, she opened the lid. A brilliant diamond solitaire! "Oh, Justin, it's . . . exquisite!" She could scarcely speak for the emotion.

"May I?" He placed it gently on her finger.

Staring down in amazement, she blinked back the tears. "I . . . I don't think I've ever seen such a ring."

"You'll wear it every day for the rest of your life, my dear," he said, his eyes shining.

Something beautiful was calling me. . . .

She held her hand out in front of her, admiring the engagement ring. Ach, what a large gem. It must have cost him a fortune.

I secretly wish we were of moderate means . . . even poor.

"My goodness, you're going to spoil me," she found herself saying. "I never dreamed I'd own such a wonderful piece of jewelry."

"Every time you look at it, Katherine, I hope you'll be reminded of my love, darling."

I wanted you to run barefoot in the meadow . . . to be loved by a complete family.

They went about their dining, enjoying the next course, served up on fine china, the edge of the platter rimmed in gold. She supposed she should feel elated just now, thrilled beyond belief. Every aspect of the evening was lovely: the tantalizing setting, her handsome suitor, and the engagement ring.

But the longer she stared at the diamond, the less it suited her. Not that it wasn't the prettiest thing she'd ever imagined. Oddly enough, she was thinking of Rebecca's hand. Never had Mamma worn even the simplest wedding band. Yet lifelong vows had remained as strong as her love for Samuel Lapp and for each of her four children—the boys and Katherine, too.

Her chest felt ever so heavy. Excusing herself, she fairly ran to the ladies' room. Great sobs wracked her body, and she had to sit down at the dressing table, her head buried in her hands.

Laura's whispered words as she lay dying had made all the difference. Now Katherine understood completely.

Lest she embarrass herself, she removed several tissues from the receptacle, wiping the mascara smudges from her cheeks. She dabbed at her face and applied fresh lipstick, her thoughts racing back to the things she'd most enjoyed while living here in the Finger Lakes. Ironically, they included her Amish friends—the Esler girls and their mother—the many quilting sessions at the estate, bread baking with Garrett and Selig, and entertaining and treating the hospice patients with music and Mississippi Mud.

Yet she had desperately longed to abandon her background, wanting to experience the fancy English world. The realization bewildered her, and over and over she murmured as she repaired her face, "I was meant to be Plain."

Then, bowing her head, she began to pray. "Dear Lord Jesus, I believe you placed me in Samuel Lapp's home for a reason. You had your hand on my life, always protecting me for the day when you would reveal the truth of the gospel . . . waiting for me to come to you with open arms, to accept your love. Please forgive me for coveting the world and its extravagance. This I pray in Jesus' name. Amen."

As difficult as it would be, she had to pull herself together and return to the romantic setting. Justin would worry, and he should not be kept waiting.

CHAPTER TWENTY-NINE

❖ ❖ ❖

She set out early to accomplish a full day of errands and appointments, starting with a visit to Mr. Cranston, her attorney, as well as a stop at the bank and a visit with Mrs. Esler, Rachel, and Ruth.

By nightfall she had summoned her entire domestic staff. The meeting was held in the library—cordial for some, tearful for others. Rosie seemed resigned to the announcement, though Theodore's eyes were cast down as Katherine's plans were revealed.

The next day Theodore drove her to the hospice. "I can't say that I agree with what you wish to do, though I suspected the day might come."

She listened, feeling sympathetic toward the old gentleman. "I'll always remember you, Theodore," she said. "You've been like a grandfather to me, you know?"

That brought a smile, and in the rearview mirror, she could see it spill across his dear face.

Natalie seemed pleased to see her, especially on an unscheduled day. "What a nice surprise," she said, inviting Katherine into her office.

They exchanged pleasantries, even chatting about various patients, some who had passed away since her last visit.

"What brings you today?" the nurse asked, sitting at her desk.

"I've decided to make some major changes in my life."

"Oh?" Natalie's face was sober.

"For the longest time now, I've had an idea stirring around in the back of my head," she began, her heart pumping with the excitement. "I've taken the initial steps and have discussed the plan with my attorney, so there won't be a holdup on the legal end of things."

Natalie leaned forward, eyes intent on her.

"On behalf of this hospice, I would like to make a proposition. . . ."

❖ ❖ ❖

The bed linens and a few items of clothing were the only things left to be packed. Dan had kept at it for two days straight, accepting offers of help from Owen and Eve, though he hesitated to have them quite so involved in the moving process, since Owen was losing his business partner because of Dan's decision to relocate.

Moving back to Lancaster as a grown man—a businessman accustomed to a large clientele in the Newark area—would be risky, to be sure. But he longed for his roots, was eager to get home again. Though the Old Order relationships would be strained for many years to come, he desired to fellowship with his Amish relatives on some level, guarded as it would always be. Perhaps it was the error of his ways—the manner in which he had abandoned them for so long. In some subconscious way, returning home might partially remedy that, might atone for his five-year misdeed.

It was late in the afternoon when he paused to pour himself a tall glass of water. Thinking about what he could fix for a light supper, he stood at the living room window, staring out.

A long black limousine crept slowly down the street, coming to a stop at the curb in front of his house. He peered out curiously, the darkened windows hampering his view of the people inside. Some very important folk had taken a wrong turn and had ended up in this quiet middle-class neighborhood.

Taking a deep breath, Katherine glanced down at the business card in her hand. "I think this must be the house."

Theodore turned and nodded. "If you don't mind, I'd like to wait . . . just to be certain."

She thought it a good suggestion. Gathering her bag and her guitar, she waited for him to come around and help her out of the car. She'd learned over the months not to argue with the portly gentleman. And he was definitely that: a gentleman of the highest order.

He surprised her by giving her a courtly kiss on the cheek. "I'll miss you, Katherine," he said. "All of us at the manor will."

She threw her arms around him. "I'll miss you, too, Theodore. But we'll see each other again. I promise!"

A slender, auburn-haired woman emerged from the limousine wearing a long, flowing simple dress. Her hair fell softly over her shoulders, and she stood with the poise of a princess.

Dan gave a furtive glance, attempting to determine who this pretty young woman might be. Watching as she embraced the dignified-looking chauffeur, he was astonished when she turned to walk up the sidewalk. "Goodness' sakes, it's Katie!"

Briskly, he smoothed his hair, fumbling with his shirttail, pushing it down into his jeans, striving to look presentable amidst his packing and boxes. His Katie girl was coming to his doorstep. What could it mean?

Breathing fast, he checked the window again.

Katherine's heart was in her throat. Trembling, she reached for the doorbell, wishing she'd taken time to brush her hair.

But the door swung wide, almost before she was truly ready for the moment. There stood Dan, his eyes fixed on her, same as the day he'd come upon her at Weaver's Creek.

"Katie?"

She felt awkward, at a loss for words, quite nearly aching. "Still friends?"

His eyes searched hers and held their gaze. "The dearest friend ever." Then he stepped aside, opening the door. "Please, will you come inside?"

She could see that he was packing as she set down her guitar. "I hope I'm not interrupting. I wouldn't have come if—"

"I'm *glad* you came."

She looked into the face of the boy she had loved, a grown man with tender blue eyes, disheveled blond hair, and a tentative, heartbreaking smile. She felt the beat of her own heart. Trying to smile for him, her mouth quivered uncontrollably. "Can you . . . forgive me, Daniel?"

"Forgive *you*?" A frown lit on his brow.

"For rejecting you, for—"

"Oh, Katie." His hand reached up to caress her face. It was as if he was reaching back through the long years, through the pain-filled past—to her. "I *love* you, darling. There's nothing to forgive." And he took her in his arms.

Yielding to his strong embrace, she felt his heart pounding, fast as her own. "Take me home with you," she whispered. "Take your Katie girl home to Hickory Hollow."

The past and present faded with his kisses, and her heart sang, responding with joy.

EPILOGUE

My struggle with the Old Order prayer veiling has come to a blissful end. Reverently, I now wear the formal Mennonite covering in obedience to God and to my husband. Such a blessing and delight it is to follow my dear Lord Jesus in this simple act of faith.

Daniel took me as his bride, before God and the many witnesses—mostly Mennonites—who assembled at the Hickory Hollow meetinghouse. I had no idea until much later, after most everyone had gone home, that Mamma had been present for the wedding service, too.

I had returned to the church sanctuary to locate an extra bulletin for our wedding scrapbook. High in the balcony Rebecca stood, looking as radiant as any bride's mother should. "Stay right there," I called to her, rushing around to the stairs.

We kissed and hugged like the long-lost friends we were.

"Katie," she said, touching my white dress, "you're as perty as a picture."

"I can't believe you came, but I'm ever so glad you did!"

She smiled and her hazel eyes lit up like heaven, the way they always used to, back before my shunning. "I wouldn't have missed seein' ya joined with your Daniel . . . not for the world."

"Oh, Mamma, thank you." I held her close. "You don't know what this means to me."

She asked if Dan and I would come for dinner sometime soon. " 'Course you'll hafta sit at separate tables from us, but we'll scoot them close and throw a tablecloth over both of them."

"Yes, of course, we'll come. But, Mamma, following the Ordnung isn't what matters. Don't you see, being a follower of *Jesus* is what counts?"

Her eyes were misty now, and she gripped my hands in hers. "Keep on prayin' for us, Katie. Will ya?"

"I promise you that."

She asked about our honeymoon plans, and I said we were headed up to Canada. "But we'll be stopping off in Canandaigua on the way home. Dan and I are planning a hymn concert of two guitars at the Mayfield Hospice."

Rebecca looked puzzled, then the light dawned. "What did you *do*, Katie—give away your birth mother's estate?"

I wanted her to know. "Not to boast, Mam, but I offered Laura's mansion to the hospice, and they accepted. The Taylors—Rosie and Fulton—have decided to live there, working as full-time volunteers, and last I heard, Selig and Garrett were thinking of staying on as cooks."

"Ach, what a blessing you are." Her hands were clasped close to her heart as if she were about to pray.

"My search is over, Mamma. All the scraps and pieces of my life are a God-ordered design . . . like one of your beautiful quilts. I was looking for fancy things and found a personal relationship with the Lord Jesus. I was yearning for my roots and found a portion of heaven on earth." I patted the small white Bible I'd carried under my wedding roses. "It's all right here, Mamma. I just didn't know it."

"Jah," she said, grinning. "You're soundin' like a wise woman to me."

Thinking of Ella Mae, I said, "I believe that spot was filled years ago."

Mam's eyes brimmed with tears. "I gave my first Tellin' yesterday. The first story in a gut long time."

"And it won't be your last." I hugged her to me, then looked her full in the face. "Mamma, I'm ever so thankful the Lord chose *you* to raise me . . . to be my mother."

She smiled so sweetly I thought my heart would break anew.

❖　❖　❖

When the time came to set up housekeeping in our new home, I selected a place of honor for both the corner cupboard and the cedar chest Dat made back when Daniel was first courting me. How pretty they both look, and what a joy to have them as a reminder of God's goodness.

Yesterday, I sorted through my handmade linens and came across the blue Amish dress I'd sewn nearly a year ago. Rather than discard it, I wrapped it in tissue paper, along with the rose-colored baby gown. Together, the two articles of clothing tell a wonderful-good story, truth be known.

So, the Lord willing, I'll grow very old with Dan by my side. He'll serenade me on his guitar while I sow straight rows of tomatoes and a few rutabagas. I'll sing and play for him, too, after his long days of blueprint making. Above all, we'll share the love of Jesus in song wherever He leads us. And should the Lord bless us with children and grandchildren, they'll hear our story and probably beg for more.

ACKNOWLEDGMENTS

◈ ◈ ◈

I wish to thank the National Stroke Foundation, the National Multiple Sclerosis Society Volunteer/Internship Program, and the Hospice of the Comforter in Colorado Springs, Colorado. I am grateful also for the friendship and medical research assistance of Kathy Torley, as well as Harriet Mason, retired hospice charge nurse, who shared the joys and sorrows and her daily routine.

Without the support of my prayer partners and dear reader-friends, this book might still be in outline form. Blessings and deep appreciation to each of you!

As always, it is a delight to work with my editors, Barb Lilland, Carol Johnson, Anne Severance, and the entire BHP editorial team. Thanks to my incredible husband, Dave, for ceaseless encouragement and vital involvement in the creative process, as well as my parents and children who helped pray (and cooked!) through the tedious times of juggling writing, parenting, and life in general. Above all, I thank my Lord Jesus, who inspires me and directs my work.